Anonymous

Practice Reports in the Supreme Court and Court of Appeals of the State of New-York

Vol. XXIV

SALZWASSER
VERLAG

Anonymous

Practice Reports in the Supreme Court and Court of Appeals of the State of New-York

Vol. XXIV

Reprint of the original, first published in 1863.

1st Edition 2022 | ISBN: 978-3-37500-161-2

Verlag (Publisher): Salzwasser Verlag GmbH, Zeilweg 44, 60439 Frankfurt, Deutschland
Vertretungsberechtigt (Authorized to represent): E. Roepke, Zeilweg 44, 60439 Frankfurt, Deutschland
Druck (Print): Books on Demand GmbH, In de Tarpen 42, 22848 Norderstedt, Deutschland

PRACTICE REPORTS

IN THE

SUPREME COURT

AND

COURT OF APPEALS

OF THE

STATE OF NEW-YORK.

VOLUME XXIV.

ALBANY

1863.

CASES REPORTED.

Cases Reported.

PRACTICE REPORTS.

COURT OF APPEALS.

CHARLES F. CLAFLIN, ALBERT S. WARD and WALTER H. TAYLOR agt. THE FARMERS' AND CITIZENS' BANK OF LONG ISLAND.

A *bank check* drawn by the president of the bank in his individual name, payable to another person, and certified "good" by the drawer *as president*, renders the acceptance *void* in the hands of the drawer, irrespective of the question whether or not he has funds in the bank.

The want of authority in the president as agent, to bind the bank, appears upon the *face of the check*; of course there can be no *bona fide holder* of the check.

And it does not alter the case that a general authority to certify checks had been conferred by the bank on the president. The question is one of agency, where the president cannot act as the agent of both parties to the contract, nor as agent in regard to a contract in which he has any interest, or to which he is a party, on the opposite side to his principal.

September Term, 1862.

THIS action was commenced on the 20th day of January, 1855, by the above named plaintiffs, to recover from the above named defendants the amount of three checks or drafts drawn on the defendants' bank, and alleged to have been certified and accepted by the bank through C. W. Houghton, its president.

A copy of the summons and complaint was served on the said 20th day of January, and a copy of the defendants' answer, on the 8th day of February, in the same year. At a circuit court held in the city of New York on the 6th day of May, 1856, by Justice DAVIES, the action was referred to E. P. Cowles, Esq., to hear and determine all the issues therein—the defendants' attorney, S. L. Griffin, Esq., then being absent from said court.

On the 28th day of May, 1857, John M. Martin was substituted attorney for the defendants in the place of Mr. Griffin.

The trial before the referee was commenced on the 28th day of February, 1857, and the testimony was closed on the 28th of August, 1858. On the 26th day of November, in the same year, the referee reported that the plaintiffs were entitled to judgment against the defendants for $26,-224, with costs; and on the 20th day of December next following, judgment against the defendants was entered on his report for that amount and $907.71 costs, making in all the sum of $27,131.71.

The pleadings are as follows:

Plaintiffs complain of the defendants, and aver that the defendants are a corporation created by and under the statutes of the state of New York, and transacting business at Williamsburgh, in the county of Kings, in said state.

That at the dates of the several instruments hereinafter mentioned, one Charles W. Houghton was the president of the said bank, and as such had power and authority to accept drafts and certify checks drawn upon the said bank, and to bind the said bank thereby.

That on or about the 31st day of December, 1853, one Thomas Green drew his draft or check in the words following:

"No. . . . Williamsburgh, Dec. 31, 1853. Farmers' & Citizens' Bank of Long Island. Pay to the order of W. A. Cleaveland five thousand dollars. $5,000. Thos. Green."

["Good. C. W. Houghton, Pres."]

And then and there delivered the same to the payee thereof. That said draft or check was presented to said defendants, and that said defendants by their said president accepted the said instrument in writing; and said Charles W. Houghton, so acting as said president, then and there in writing on the face of said check or draft, certified the same in the words following: "Good. C. W. Houghton, Pres."

That said check or draft was indorsed by said payee, and so indorsed, accepted and certified was by him transferred and delivered to the plaintiffs. That the said draft or check was presented to defendants for payment, who then and there refused to pay the same, and that the same remains wholly unpaid.

And for a second cause of action the plaintiffs allege that one C. W. Houghton drew his draft or check in the words and figures following:

"No. . . . Williamsburgh, Feb. 4th, 1854. Farmers' & Citizens' Bank of Long Island. Pay to the order of W. A. Cleaveland fifty-five hundred dollars. $5,500. C. W. Houghton."

["Good. C. W. Houghton."]

That said defendants by their said president accepted the said instrument in writing, and said Charles W. Houghton acting as such president then, and in writing on the face of said check or draft, certified the same in the said filling. "Good. C. W. Houghton." That said check or draft was indorsed by said payee, and so indorsed, accepted and certified was by him transferred and delivered to the plaintiffs.

That the said draft or check was presented to defendants at their banking-house for payment, who then and there refused to pay the same, and that the same remains wholly unpaid.

And for a third cause of action plaintiffs allege that C. W. Houghton drew his certain draft or check in the words and figures following:

"No. . . . Williamsburgh, Feb. 25th, 1854. Farmers' & Citizens' Bank of Long Island. Pay to the order of W. A. Cleaveland, Esq,, ten thousand dollars. $10,000. C. W. Houghton."

["Good. C. W. Houghton, Pres."]

That said defendants by their said president accepted the said instrument in writing, and said Charles W. Houghton acting as said president then and there in writing on the face of said check or draft, certified the same in the said filling: "Good. C. W. Houghton."

That said check or draft was indorsed, accepted and certified, was by him transferred and delivered to the plaintiffs.* That the said check or draft was presented to defendants at their banking-house for payment, who then and there refused to pay the same, and that the same remains wholly unpaid.

Plaintiffs aver that said checks are wholly unpaid.

Wherefore plaintiffs demand judgment against defendants for twenty thousand and five hundred dollars, and interest from December 31st, 1853, on five thousand dollars; and from the 4th of February, 1854, on five thousand five hundred dollars; and from February 25, 1854, on ten thousand dollars, besides costs.

The defendants, by Sidney L. Griffin, their attorney, answering the complaint in the above entitled action, deny that at the dates of the several alleged instruments mentioned in said complaint, one Charles W. Houghton was the president of said bank, and as such had power and authority to accept drafts or certify checks upon said bank, or to bind the said bank thereby, as alleged in said complaint.

And said defendants also deny that the alleged check first mentioned and described in said complaint, was then and there delivered to the payee thereof, or that it was presented to said defendants, or that said defendants by their said president accepted said instrument in writing; or that said check or draft was indorsed by said payee, or was by him transferred or delivered to the plaintiffs; or that said draft or check was presented to the defendants for payment; or that the same remains unpaid, as particularly set forth in said complaint.

And said defendants also deny that said defendants, by

their alleged president, accepted the alleged instrument in writing, mentioned and set forth for a second cause of action in said complaint, or that said Charles W. Houghton, acting as such president, there and in writing certified the same as set forth in said complaint, or that said check or draft was indorsed by the payee, or was by him transferred or delivered to the plaintiffs; or that the said alleged draft or check was presented to defendants at their banking-house for payment; or that the same remains unpaid as particularly set forth in said complaint.

And said defendants also deny that said defendants, by their alleged president, accepted the alleged instrument in writing, mentioned and set forth for a third cause of action in said complaint; or that said Charles W. Houghton acting as such alleged president, then or there in writing certified the same as set forth in said complaint; or that said check or draft was indorsed by the said payee, or was by him transferred or delivered to the plaintiffs; or that said draft or check was presented to defendants at their banking-house for payment; or that the same remains unpaid as particularly set forth in said complaint.

And for further answer to said complaint said defendants say that the several drafts or checks mentioned and described in said complaint, were drawn or made; and if certified, as set forth in said complaint, were certified at the office of the Long Island Water Works Company, Nos. 45 and 46 Merchants' Exchange, in the city of New York, and not at the banking-house of defendants, without authority, and when neither said Thomas Green or said Charles W. Houghton had money or funds on deposit in said Farmers' and Citizens' Bank, to enable said bank or said defendants to pay the said drafts or checks or either of them. And that the defendants or said bank were never informed in any manner by said plaintiffs or said Cleaveland, or by any other person, that said several alleged drafts or checks were drawn or certified, as alleged in said complaint, until about the time of the commencement of this action; nor that said alleged drafts or checks were held or claimed in any manner by said plaintiffs until the service of said complaint and summons in this action on the defendants.

And for further answer to said complaint said defendants say that the amount of the alleged draft or check first mentioned and described in said complaint, was paid said Cleaveland in full by said Thomas Green, as these defendants are informed and believe, shortly after the drawing of said draft or check by said Green to said Cleaveland, to wit: before the alleged transfer and delivery of said draft or check to said plaintiffs, and at the time of said payment and oftentimes since, said Cleaveland promised to return said draft or check to said Green, but excused himself for not doing so by alleging that said check was in his box at his residence in Brooklyn.

And for further answer to said complaint said defendants say that the several amounts of the alleged drafts or checks mentioned and described in the second and third causes of action in said complaint, were severally paid said Cleaveland in full by said Charles W. Houghton, as these defendants are also informed and believe, shortly after the alleged drawing of said several drafts or checks by said Houghton, to said Cleaveland, to wit: before the alleged transfer and delivery of said drafts, checks, or either of them, to said plaintiffs, and at the several times of said payments and oftentimes since, said Cleaveland promised to return said drafts or checks to said Houghton, but excused himself for not doing so by alleging that said check or checks were in his box at Brooklyn.

And for further answer to said complaint said defendants say that each and all of the alleged drafts or checks mentioned and described in said complaint was or were transferred and delivered by said Cleaveland to said plaintiffs, if the same or either of them was or were transferred or delivered to said plaintiffs without consideration and for the accommodation of said Cleaveland, and said checks and each of them were, as the defendants are informed and believe, drawn and delivered respectively by said Green and Houghton to said Cleaveland, usuriously and in contravention of the statutes of the state of New York, against usury, and a sum greater than seven per cent. was agreed on and reserved for the money advanced respectively on said drafts or checks, to wit: one-eighth of one per cent. a day, to wit: nine thousand dollars, to wit: 45⅝ per cent. per annum, and the same was accepted and received by said Cleaveland, and he never had any other or different title to sa id drats or checks or either of them.

At a circuit court held at the city hall in the city of New York, on the sixth day of May, 1856—in open court—present, Hon. Henry E. Davies, Justice.

This cause having been called in its regular order on the calendar for trial, on motion of Burrill, Davison & Burrill, plaintiffs' attorneys, no one appearing in opposition thereto, ordered that the above action and all the issues therein be, and the same are hereby referred to E. P. Cowles, Esq., counsellor at law, of the city of New York, as sole referee, to hear and determine the same.

To the court: The undersigned referee reports as follows:

I have been attended by the counsel for the respective parties, and have heard their proofs and allegations, and the arguments of counsel, and find as matter of fact the following:

First.—That the three checks set forth in the complaint were drawn by the respective drawers thereof on the days of their several dates, and severally accepted and certified, indorsed and delivered, as therein alleged.

Second.—That the said checks at the times they were respectively drawn and delivered to the payee therein named, were so accepted and certified by C. W. Houghton, as president of the said bank; and he at the time of such acceptance and certification was the president of the defendants' bank, and as such president authorized by such bank to certify checks drawn upon said bank; such checks were so certified by said Houghton at his business office in the city of New York; but of such fact the plaintiffs when they received the same and paid the money thereupon, had no notice.

Third.—The said checks so certified were each of them on the several days they respectively bear date, delivered to the payee thereof; who upon receiving them paid to the respective drawers of them upon the same days, the full amount of the face of each check.

Fourth.—The payee of such checks, on the same day of the respective dates of them, respectively indorsed and transferred the same and each of them to the plaintiffs; and the plaintiffs when they received the said checks respectively, paid to the payee thereof the full amount of the face of each check, and that the said plaintiffs so received the said checks in good faith.

Fifth.—The plaintiffs have, ever since the said checks were severally passed to them as aforesaid, been the actual holders of them and each of them.

Sixth.—On or before the first day of December, 1854, the plaintiffs presented the said checks to the defendants at their bank for payment, and payment thereof was demanded and refused.

Seventh.—The amount of such checks with interest thereon from the 1st day of December, 1854, is as follows:

Principal, - - - - - -	$20,500
Interest to date, - - - -	5,724
	$26,224

Upon these facts I determine as matter of law, that the defendants are liable upon such checks, by reason of such certification of them by the president of such bank.

Second.—The plaintiffs are entitled to judgment for

twenty-six thousand two hundred and twenty-four dollars, ($26,224,) with costs.

All of which is respectfully submitted.

EDWARD P. COWLES, *Referee.*

The following is the opinion of the referee:

The drawers of the three several checks in question, Green and Houghton, received from the payee, Cleaveland, on the day of the dates of the checks respectively, the full amount of the face of them, and each of them. They were, therefore, valid securities in the hands of Cleaveland, the payee. Upon this point there is no dispute. If Cleaveland passed them on the days they respectively bear date, to the plaintiffs, for full value, then it is quite immaterial whether Green and Houghton subsequently paid Cleaveland or not; since, if plaintiffs, not Cleaveland, were at the time of such alleged payment, the actual holders of them, the payment to Cleaveland without the production by him of the check, would not operate to discharge the securities. Upon a careful analysis of the whole testimony, I must find, as a matter of fact, that plaintiffs became, on the days of the drawing of the several checks, the *bona fide* holders of them from Cleaveland for full value.

If the testimony of Cleaveland upon the question of plaintiffs' title to the checks is entirely discredited, even then there remains the positive testimony of the plaintiff Ward, supported in part at least by the checks given by the plaintiffs to Cleaveland on the 31st of December, 1853, and 4th of February, 1854. The circumstance which, unexplained, would tend to cast suspicion upon Ward's testimony, would be mainly the long holding of these checks by the plaintiffs without presentation to the bank. When Ward was on the stand, plaintiffs offered to prove by him the reason why plaintiffs held the papers so long without presentation. To this the defendants objected, and the referee improperly, as he now thinks, excluded the testimony so offered.

Now, while it is true that the protracted holding of these

checks by plaintiffs, without presentation, would, unexplained, be a circumstance of the grossest suspicion as respects to good faith of their title, yet it is not competent for the defendants to urge such objection, and at the same time refuse to hear the proffered explanation.

The explanation offered was ruled out on defendants' motion, and the absence of it must not now be invoked to impeach the plaintiffs' title.

If, therefore, the case depended on Ward's testimony alone, uncorroborated by Cleaveland, the finding must necessarily be in favor of plaintiffs. But it is proper to remark further, that upon the whole testimony, Cleaveland seems to be sustained by the weight of the evidence.

It is not pretended by either Green or Houghton, that they ever saw the checks in Cleaveland's hands after their respective dates; and while it is not impossible, it is yet out of the ordinary course of things for parties to pay outstanding paper without its production and cancelation.

Green certainly does not give any very satisfactory account of his alleged payment to Cleaveland; he produces neither memorandum or vouchers for it. Houghton produces no voucher for the payment of the precise amount of his two checks.

While, by the account of moneys received from and paid to Cleaveland, which he, Houghton, says is in Cleaveland's handwriting, there was a large balance due to Cleaveland, both on the 13th and 27th of February, (the days on which Houghton says his two checks in suit were paid,) over and above the payment he made on each of these occasions. In the absence of express proof of any order for the direct application of these payments to these checks, the inference of the law, from the state of the accounts as shown by such statement, would be, that those payments were on general account. It is not singular that Cleaveland should have put both of these checks, those in suit, into his account with Houghton, being, as he was, indorser upon both of them, as such liable to the holder. Again: taking into consideration the large pecuniary transactions which had taken place between Cleaveland and Houghton, the amount and varied character of the securities which Cleaveland had held at different times against Houghton, the testimony of the witnesses other than Houghton, to the conversations about securities which Houghton claimed should be surrendered to him by Cleaveland, is of little value as contradicting Cleaveland, or as tending to show that such conversations had reference to these two checks. None of these witnesses were pecuniarily interested in the discussion. None of them knew particularly the details of the business then under discussion. None of them heard all that passed between Houghton and Cleaveland. Some years have elapsed since those conversations, and there is too much indefiniteness and vagueness in this testimony to render it of any great value as impeaching Cleaveland or supporting Houghton. To these considerations must also be added the testimony of Ward, which, if credited, tends to support Cleaveland. I cannot, therefore, regard Cleaveland's integrity as having been successfully assailed.

If I am right in holding the plaintiffs to be *bona fide* holders of the checks, the only remaining question is as to the liability of the bank upon Houghton's certificate. Upon this question I can entertain no doubt.

The by-laws of the bank, in restricting the power of certifying checks to certain specified officers, of which the president was one, have thereby conferred such power upon those officers in direct terms, or in what is legally tantamount thereto.

A check is a bill of exchange.

The certificate of a check by the proper bank officer as "good," is, in all its legal effects, the same as an acceptance of the bill, and binds the bank to its payment. Whether Cleaveland, knowing that such certificate had been given at a place other than that of the bank parlor or counter, could hold the bank on the certificate of the president, it is unnecessary to discuss, for no such knowledge is brought home to the plaintiffs.

The report must be for the plaintiffs. Interest cannot be allowed further than from the date of the demand of payment. Ward supposes, although he cannot know, that his partner, Claflin, made the demand some time in June, 1854. There is no certain proof that the demand was earlier than the fall of 1854. The date of the demand being late in the fall, though not fixed with entire certainty, I shall adopt the first of December, 1854, as the date from which to charge interest, although the demand was probably in fact somewhat earlier than that. The report will therefore be as follows:

Principal of checks—1st, - - -	$5,000
" " 2d, - - - - -	5,500
" " 3d, - - -	10,000
	$20,500
Interest from Dec. 1st, 1854 to date of report,	5,724
	$26,224

EDWARD P. COWLES, *Referee.*

Dated November 26th, 1858.

From the judgment entered on the report of the referee, the defendants appealed to the general term of the supreme court, on a case containing exceptions.

WILLIAM C. NOYES and JOHN M. MARTIN, *for appel'ts.*
CHARLES O'CONOR and JOHN E. BURRILL, *for resp'ts.*

By the court, LEONARD, Justice. An agent cannot, in general, act so as to bind his principal in matters touching his agency, where he has an adverse interest in himself. (*Stone* agt. *Hays*, 5 *Denio*, 575; *Bentley* agt. *The Columbia Ins. Co.*, 17 *N. Y. R.*, 423.)

There is an exception in the application of this principle

in favor of the holders of negotiable paper acquired in good faith before due, for value, without notice of the misconduct of the agent, or the knowledge of such facts as would amount to a want of good faith in the taker of such paper.

In the case before us, the interest of Houghton is assumed to be at variance with his duty. His interest was an inducement to him to certify his own checks without funds. It was his duty not to do it. The public, however, cannot be apprised, from the face of the checks, of the existence of this conflict between interest and duty. The president of the bank may have money there on deposit as well as another man. The money being in bank, the certification of his own check would not be adverse to the duty of the president. As between the bank and its own officer, it is entirely clear that such a certification would create no liability.

The general authority to certify checks had been conferred by the bank on their president. The identity between the name of the drawer and the president of the bank who certified the check, did not necessarily inform any one, by the mere force of that fact, that the drawer had certified his own checks without funds in the bank. It was possible that he had so done. It was not probable, however; and the usual presumptions of innocence and fair dealing were against the existence of doubts about the conduct of the president of the bank.

The presumption of bad faith on the part of the plaintiffs does not necessarily arise from the manner of certification. That fact, with other circumstances, might have brought the referee or a jury to the conclusion that here was a want of good faith on the part of the plaintiffs in taking the checks; but the certification in the manner mentioned was not conclusive, as evidence, to deprive the plaintiffs of the protection afforded to *bona fide* holders of negotiable paper. (20 *How. U. S. R.*, 345; *Story on Bills*, § 194; 34 *Eng. L. & Eq.*, 131.)

The legal principles respecting the subject of agency as applicable to the certification of checks, their character and negotiability, and the protection to which *bona fide* holders thereof are entitled, are fully considered by the court of appeals in the *Farmers' & Mechanics' Bank of Kent County* agt. *The Butchers' & Drovers' Bank*, (*reported* 14 *N. Y. R.*, 634, *and* 16 *id.*, 125,) and are controlling as far as they are applicable in the case now before the court.

We agree with the referee, that the defendants cannot now urge any reasons against a recovery arising from the delay occurring before the checks were presented for payment, after having by objections at the trial prevented the explanations offered by the plaintiffs in that respect.*

The several objections taken during the progress of the trial to the admission or exclusion of evidence, &c., so far as they were urged at the argument, have been examined, but none of them are considered well taken, and do not seem to require an extended review.

Judgment is affirmed, with costs.

From this judgment the defendants brought an appeal to this court, and also asked leave of the court to review two intermediate orders of affirmance of the supreme court, which it was claimed necessarily affected the judgment.

JOHN M. MARTIN and WM. CURTIS NOYES, *for appel'ts.*
JOHN E. BURRILL and CHARLES O'CONOR, *for resp'ts.*

By the court, SELDEN, J. The only question in this case which seems to me to require serious consideration, is, whether Mr. Houghton could bind the bank by accepting

* NOTE.—It appears from the case, that after this ruling by the referee, he remarked to the counsel on both sides, that he thought upon reflection, that such ruling was erroneous; but the defendants' counsel did not withdraw his objection, nor did plaintiffs' counsel put, or offer further to put the question, and the case proceeded without any change of the referee's minutes. Now, it is a settled doctrine, that where evidence is ruled out, and the judge afterwards allows counsel an opportunity to introduce it, which he declines, error does not lie for the ruling out. (*D'Homergue* agt. *Morgan*, 3 *Whart.*, 26.)

checks or drafts drawn by himself. It is a well settled rule of the law of agency, to which I apprehend there is no exception, that no person can act as the agent of both parties to a contract, although he may himself have no interest on either side; nor can he act as agent in regard to a contract in which he has any interest, or to which he is a party, on the side opposite to his principal. In the present case, Mr. Houghton, as the drawer of the checks, was the party with whom the contract of acceptance was primarily made, and stood therefore precisely in those opposite relations which the rule referred to forbids. It is not necessary for the principal in such cases to show that the agent has acted unfairly, or that he himself has sustained any injury. The act of the agent is deemed to be unauthorized, and the contract is void.

It is conceded, in the opinion of the supreme court in this case, that as between the bank and Mr. Houghton, the certificate of acceptance of the latter would not be obligatory. But that court supposed that a subsequent *bona fide* holder could nevertheless avail himself of such certificate. The difficulty in the way of this conclusion, however, is, that the want of authority in Mr. Houghton to bind the bank appeared upon the face of the check. There could be no *bona fide* holder of such an instrument. An indorser of commercial paper may, it is true, very frequently acquire rights superior to those of the original party; but never, so far as I am aware, when he has notice of the defect. If he knows the facts which would render the paper void in the hands of the party from whom he derives title, he can not recover.

The supreme court seems to have supposed that to prevent the plaintiffs from being considered as *bona fide* holders, they must have known that the drawer had no funds in the bank to meet the check. This was clearly an error. The acceptance was void in the hands of the drawer, irrespective of the question whether he had or had not such funds. The double relation in which Mr. Houghton stood alone rendered it void, and of this the plaintiffs were apprised by the check. It could not be necessary that they should have had notice of any other fact in order to defeat their recovery, as the same facts which render commercial paper void in the hands of the original party, will equally avoid it in the hands of any subsequent holder having notice of such facts.

It is of no importance that the referee has found as a fact that the plaintiffs were *bona fide* holders. This finding is opposed by the plain law of the case, and is therefore nugatory. This reasoning applies to two only of the checks upon which the action is brought. I see no obstacle to a recovery upon the check drawn by Green.

The judgment of the supreme court should be reversed, and there should be a new trial ordered, with costs of the two appeals to be paid by the plaintiffs, the residue of the costs to abide the result of the new trial.

NEW YORK SUPERIOR COURT.

GEORGE WILLIAMS agt. JOHN O'KEEFE and another.

A *corporation ordinance* forbidding a greater rate of speed than that fixed as legal therein, for vehicles in the city of New York, is competent and proper *evidence* in an action for damages caused by being run over by a vehicle in such streets, to show that the plaintiff was free from negligence, though it furnishes no evidence of negligence in fact on the part of the defendants.

A citizen of the city of New York is presumed to know of the existence of its ordinances and their provisions, and has a right on the presumption that they will be obeyed. The law of negligence discussed by MONELL, J.

Unless proof of negligence on the part of the plaintiff is so strong that the court would set aside a verdict in his favor as against the weight of evidence, it is not proper to take that question from the jury.

General Term, October, 1862.

BOSWORTH, *Ch. J.*, MONCRIEF, ROBERTSON, BARBOUR and MONELL, *Justices*.

APPEAL from a judgment. Case was tried by a jury.

On the 23d of November, 1859, in the evening, plaintiff was passing up the Bowery. When crossing Second street the plaintiff was struck by one of the defendants' stages, (whose route lay through the Bowery and Second street.) The pole struck the plaintiff, knocked him down, broke his arm and injured his neck. The plaintiff testifies that the stage was going "furious," "pretty hard," "a hard trot," "going fast." The plaintiff offered in evidence an ordinance of the corporation, declaring it to be unlawful to drive any vehicle in streets of the city faster than six miles an hour, or faster than upon a walk in going around the corner of any street. This was objected to by the defendants. This objection was overruled, and the defendants excepted. The defendants moved to dismiss the complaint, on the ground, substantially, that the accident was occasioned by the plaintiff's negligence, or that his own negligence contributed to produce the injuries. The motion was denied, and the defendants excepted. Considerable testimony was given by the defendants, designed to contradict the plaintiff's evidence. The jury rendered a verdict in favor of the plaintiff for fifteen hundred dollars.

A motion for a new trial was denied at special term, and this appeal is as well from the order denying the motion, as from the judgment.

Geo. R. Thompson, *for the appellants.*

I. The verdict is clearly against the weight of evidence.

II. The ordinance of the city of New York against driving at a greater rate of speed than that allowed therein, was inadmissible in evidence to show neglect on the part of the defendants. An infraction of such an ordinance is, in itself, no evidence of negligence; and, besides, there was no evidence to show such an infraction. The ordinance may have been violated, and the party violating it have been still guiltless of negligence. Indeed, cases may be supposed in which it would be evidence of great neglect not to violate the ordinance. The ordinance was no evidence, and should have been excluded. (*Brown* agt. *The Buffalo & State Line R. R. Co.*, 22 *N. Y.*, 191.)

S. C. H. Bailey, *for the respondent.*

By the court, Monell, J. There was no valid objection to proving the corporation ordinance regulating the rate of speed of vehicles in the city. The objection to it was, that no infraction of it having been shown, it was immaterial. It does not appear for what purpose it was offered, and although it furnished no evidence of negligence in fact on the part of the defendants, (*Brown* agt. *The B. & S. L. R. R. Co.*, 22 *N. Y. R.*, 191,) yet it seems to me it was proper and competent evidence for another purpose, namely, as tending to prove, in connection with other testimony, that there was no negligence on the part of the plaintiff. This ordinance was one of the public laws of the city, and as such was presumed to have been known to all citizens. This knowledge was calculated to regulate, in a greater or less degree, the care which any one traveling upon the streets would exercise. The presumption is, that the ordinance would be observed; that in turning around a corner from one street into another, necessarily passing over the cross-walk, the pace of the horses would be slackened to a walk. Surely, then, a foot passenger knowing that such an ordinance existed, and believing that it would be observed, would not be called upon to exercise that care and prudence which he would exercise if there was no restriction upon the rate of travel. So that, if he had reason to believe the vehicle would hold up to a walk as it approached the side-walk, he would and might properly and with safety act very differently than if he believed the vehicle would continue on across the side-walk at a rapid rate. The evidence, in my judgment, was therefore proper as tending to relieve the plaintiff from the imputation of negligence on his part, and could well be considered by the jury in connection with other evidence for that purpose.

As I understand the law as now settled by the court of last resort in this state, *negligence* is a question of fact for the jury to determine, whether it be negligence on the part of either party. The plaintiff must be free from fault, but he need not show it affirmatively in the first instance. He must be able to satisfy the jury, from all the facts and circumstances in the case, that he has not by his own neglect contributed in any degree to the injury. (*Johnson* agt. *The Hudson River R. R. Co.*, 20 *N. Y. R.*, 65.) DENIO, J., in this case says, (*p.* 69,) after stating the general rule: "the plaintiff's case when presented to the jury, must not be defective on that point, any more than upon that of the defendant's negligence." He further says: "it is not a rule of law of universal application, that the plaintiff must prove affirmatively that his own conduct on the occasion of the injury was cautious and prudent. The *onus probandi* in this as in most other cases, depends upon the position of the affair as it stands upon the undisputed facts." And again: "the culpability of the defendant must be affirmatively proved before the case can go to the jury, but the absence of any fault upon the part of the plaintiff may be inferred from circumstances."

Accordingly, it seems to be well settled that unless the proof of negligence on the part of the plaintiff is so strong that the court would set aside a verdict in his favor as being clearly against the weight of evidence, it is not proper to take that question from the jury. Independently of this view, I cannot discover any evidence in the case, up to the time the plaintiff rested, which can properly impute any negligence to him.

The motion to dismiss the complaint was properly overruled.

The relation given by the defendants' witnesses of the accident as seen by them, if I could believe it referred to the same accident testified to by the plaintiff, would certainly excite the suspicion that the jury had not dealt fairly between the parties. But without entering upon an analysis of the testimony, it is sufficient that I believe the defendants' witnesses saw another and different accident occurring possibly on the same evening, at about the same place, and near the same hour. The plaintiff's relation of the accident and of its consequences is, that he did not leave his house for nine or ten days after he received the injury. The plaintiff's and defendants' witnesses stood confronting each other, and the jury who tried the cause were best able to determine whose was the correct version of the affair. It is enough for us that we cannot say their verdict is clearly against the weight of the evidence.

The case seems to have been fairly put to the jury. The judge charged as requested by the defendants, that there could be no recovery by the plaintiff, if the jury believed that the accident was caused by his negligence, or that his negligence in any degree contributed to the accident. The jury have found against the defendants upon all the questions, and we see no reason for disturbing their verdict.

The judgment must be affirmed.

SUPREME COURT.

SAMUEL S. ELLSWORTH agt. WILLIAM FULTON, JARVIS LIGHT and HENRY LIGHT.

Where a party has given *notice of appeal* by *service* thereof on the opposite party, but *not on the clerk*, he is not authorized to *amend* under § 327 of the Code.

Yates Special Term, March, 1862.

Before WELLES, *Justice*.

MOTION by plaintiff for leave to perfect his appeal from

an order of special term dated December 24th, 1861, granting leave to defendant, Henry Light, to issue execution on the judgment in his favor for $42.84, docketed in Yates county clerk's office May 6, 1853, and vacating the satisfaction-piece upon said judgment lately filed in said office.

The leading facts were as follows: Prior to April, 1853, the plaintiff commenced an action of ejectment against all the defendants, to recover possession of a parcel of real estate situated in Yates county. The action was tried at the circuit held in that county in April, 1853, when the plaintiff recovered against the defendants Fulton and Jarvis Light, and the defendant Henry Light had a judgment in his favor, with costs. The costs were duly adjusted at $42.84, and judgment was docketed therefor on the 6th of May of the same year. The plaintiff, some time during the latter part of the year 1861, procured from the defendant Henry Light, a satisfaction-piece upon said judgment to be duly acknowledged, and filed the same in the office of the clerk of Yates county. At the special term held for Monroe county, in December, 1861, the defendant Henry Light obtained an order upon notice for leave to issue an execution on the judgment, and that the satisfaction be vacated. The order was granted, after opposition thereto, at the special term, on the part of the plaintiff, and a copy thereof was served personally on the plaintiff on the 26th day of December aforesaid, but no notice in writing of said order has been served on his attorney at any time. Mr. Judd was the plaintiff's attorney in the action of ejectment, and the plaintiff has had no other attorney in said action at any time. At the time the motion was made upon which said order was granted, and for a long time after, he was too much out of health to attend to business, and upon learning the result of the motion, he requested another person, who was an attorney and counsellor of this court, to perfect an appeal from the order of the general term. The person so requested, undertook to perfect such appeal, and with that view served upon the attorney of record for said defendant Henry Light, a notice of such appeal, which was directed to such attorney of record, and was not directed to the clerk where the order was entered, nor served upon him. This notice was served within thirty days after the copy order was served upon the plaintiff personally, and done in good faith, and with the *bona fide* intention of perfecting such appeal; and the omission to serve the notice on the clerk was through the inadvertence only of the person who undertook to perfect the appeal.

The notice of motion made at the December special term for the order, and the notice of the order were signed "John D. Wolcott, att'y for deft. Henry Light."

Charles G. Judd, *for plaintiff.*

John D. Wolcott and J. S. Glover, *for deft. Henry Light.*

Welles, Justice. This motion is made upon the assumption that the plaintiff has given, in good faith, notice of appeal from the order, but has omitted, through mistake, to do an act necessary to perfect the appeal, under the provision of § 327 of the Code. The part of the section in question is as follows: "When a party shall give, in good faith, notice of appeal from a judgment or order, and shall omit, through mistake, to do any other act necessary to perfect the appeal, or to stay the proceedings, the court may permit an amendment on such terms as may be just."

The question is, whether the plaintiff has given notice of the appeal within this section? The same section provides how an appeal shall be made. It is simply by the service of a notice in writing on the adverse party and on the clerk with whom the judgment or order appealed from is entered—stating the appeal from the same, or some specified part thereof. Then follows the provision above quoted. The notice of appeal was served on the attorney of record of the defendant in whose favor the order was entered. The omission was in not serving the notice on the clerk.

To give notice of appeal in order to give the court jurisdiction to allow the amendment under the section, means, to make out a notice in writing and serve it upon the adverse party and on the clerk. To serve it upon either, and not on the other, is not giving notice of the appeal within the meaning of the section. This I think evident from what the omission is from which the court has power to relieve the party—which is, to omit to do any *other act* necessary, &c. Other than what? Clearly than to give notice of appeal. No other interpretation is admissible. The only construction which could aid the plaintiff would involve the following absurd reading of the section: "When a party shall give, in good faith, notice of appeal from a judgment or order, and shall omit, through mistake, to give notice of such appeal as required by this section, or to do any other act necessary," &c. The section is general, and relates to all appeals provided for by the Code in civil cases to which its provisions, in whole or in part, can be made to apply; and that part of it under which the plaintiff seeks relief, was intended to apply to such cases as an appeal from a judgment of the supreme court to the court of appeals, where the party appealing has served written notice upon all the proper persons, but has neglected by mistake to give the undertaking, or to make the deposit, as required by § 334, without which such appeal is not available for any purpose;—to a case where an undertaking is necessary to have the appeal operate as a stay of proceedings, and such an undertaking has been omitted by mistake;—where the judgment appealed from directs the assignment or delivery of documents or personal property, and the party appealing has inadvertently omitted compliance with such directions, which is required by § 336, as a condition of the appeal operating as a stay of proceedings, together with all other cases where something necessary to be done, besides giving the notice of appeal, has been omitted from the same cause, and which is necessary to perfect the appeal, or to stay the proceedings.

The foregoing views lead inevitably, I think, to a denial of the present motion. The motion is therefore denied.

SUPREME COURT.

HASBROUCK, adm'r, appellant agt. ISABELLA HASBROUCK and others, respondents.

After an executor has filed an *inventory* of property belonging to the estate, he is not precluded from showing that property *not belonging to the estate was inventoried*, and may also show that the property belonging to the estate *was of less value* than the amount at which it was inventoried.

That is, the inventory is not *conclusive* evidence against the executor, of what the assets consist of, and of their value, although it is *prima facie* evidence against him on the accounting before the surrogate.

New York General Term, November, 1862.

INGRAHAM, LEONARD and BARNARD, *Justices*.

By the court, BARNARD, Justice. Although an inventory filed by an executor is, on an accounting, *prima facie* evidence against him of what the assets consist of, and of their value, still it is not conclusive. The executor has a right to show that property not belonging to the estate was inventoried, and may also show that the property belonging to the estate was of less value than the amount at which it was inventoried.

In this case the executor has done nothing to deprive him of that right. If in his account rendered, he had charged himself with the actual cash value of the interest of the deceased in the firm of Kingon & Hasbrouck, it can not be doubted that he would have been entitled to introduce proof showing such cash value, and that the interest had been put at too high a valuation in the inventory.

It does not necessarily follow from the fact of the executor's having sold the testator's interest in the firm at a credit, that the ascertainment of either the then cash value of the interest, or of the sum which would have been produced to the estate on winding up the partnership matters in the usual manner, would be either impossible or attended with much difficulty.

The fact that the executor, doubtless under the supposition that he could turn over the securities he took on the sale, filed an inventory and an account, fixing the value of the interest of the deceased in the firm at $14.703.91, should not preclude him, when he is sought to be personally charged with that amount, from showing, if he can, the actual value of the interest if it had been sold for cash, or if the partnership had been wound up in the usual course. The executor in this case does not seem to have acted fraudulently, or with any improper motives; but, on the contrary, appears to have had the good of the estate he represented in view, in all he did, and to have been actuated with a desire to make the assets bring as much as possible.

Under such circumstances, the law does not require that the executor should pay individually to the estate more than the assets, if prudently administered, would have produced.

For these reasons the proof offered by the executor, as to the value of the interest of the deceased in the partnership was admissible, and the rejection of it improper.

Order reversed, and a new accounting directed before the surrogate, with costs of the appeal.

SUPREME COURT.

Hoe and others agt. Sanborn.

Where, in an action for the recovery of money, the plaintiff enters judgment against the defendant for the amount (over $50) which the defendant offered that plaintiff might take judgment, and the parties go to trial for the balance of the plaintiff's claim, and the verdict of the jury is for the plaintiff, but for a sum less than $50, the plaintiff is nevertheless entitled to *costs*.

Because, the *judgment roll*, (and there should be but one,) if properly made up, containing the whole history of the case, including the verdict of the jury, shows that the plaintiff recovered over $50, and an amount *greater* than the sum mentioned in the offer of judgment served by the defendant.

Saratoga Special Term, August, 1862.

Motion to correct a judgment roll. Also separate motion to strike from the entry of judgment, plaintiffs' costs, and that defendant be allowed to recover his costs by a proper entry in the roll.

U. G. Paris, *attorney for plaintiffs.*
L. H. Northup, *attorney for defendant.*

Bockes, Justice. These motions were heard together, and, on the merits, depend on the same question. They will therefore be considered as one motion.

The facts of the case are these: The plaintiffs brought their action on a promissory note for $467.88, made by the defendant, August 17, 1855, payable five months from date. The defendant answered, denying the indebtedness on the note, and alleging that the note was given on a sale of saws, as to which there was a warranty; and he averred a breach of the warranty, and damages which he claimed to have allowed to him in satisfaction or reduction of the claim. The plaintiffs replied, denying the material allegations of the answer. Thereupon the defendant served plaintiffs' attorney with a notice, offering to allow plaintiffs to take judgment against him in the action for $317.88, with interest from January 20th, 1856, and costs and notaries' fees. This notice bears date May 14, 1856, and was probably served about that time. The offer was not accepted. The cause was moved for trial at the January circuit, 1859, when, the defendant having moved to postpone the trial, an order was made and entered, that the cause go over the circuit, on condition that the defendant pay to the plaintiffs the costs of the circuit, and stipulate to allow the plaintiffs to enter judgment for the amount due by the terms of the note, less $150, and interest on that sum since the maturity of the note, without costs—the cause to proceed as to the last mentioned amount and all other matters in controversy in the action. Thereupon the defendant gave the stipulation—stipulating and agreeing that the plaintiffs might enter judgment pursuant to the provisions of the order. On this order and stipulation the plaintiffs entered a judgment, or an order in the nature of a judgment, by which, after reciting that the action was noticed for trial at the January circuit, 1859, the motion to postpone, and the order thereon, "it was ordered, adjudged and decreed, that the said plaintiffs do recover of the said defendant, Jesse K. Sanborn, the sum of three hundred and eighty-six dollars and eighteen cents, and that he have execution therefor." This order or judgment was entered January 31, 1859. The sum thus recovered was the sum specified in the defendant's offer of judgment, less the notaries' fees and costs, and was paid and satisfied by the defendant in 1859.

The cause again came on for trial at the May circuit, 1862, and was tried by jury, which rendered a verdict in favor of the plaintiffs for $10.84. For this sum, with costs of the action to the plaintiffs, in all $826.16, judgment was entered June 2d, 1862.

[Other proceedings were had in the action, which, however, are of no importance on this motion.]

The principal, if not the only, question to be determined here is, whether the plaintiffs are entitled to recover the costs of the action. It is conceded, too, that if they are not entitled to recover costs, the defendant is entitled to recover his costs of the action. The Code provides that costs shall be allowed of course to the defendant, (in actions like this,) unless the plaintiff be entitled to costs therein, (§ 305.) Are, then, the plaintiffs entitled to costs in this action?

Section 304 declares that costs shall be allowed of course to the plaintiff upon a recovery in the cases therein specified, among which is the following: "*In an action for the recovery of money, where the plaintiff shall recover fifty dollars or more.*" The plaintiffs have recovered in the action, and it is in an action for the recovery of money. Have they also recovered fifty dollars or more?

When this subject was first opened to me, it struck me that the recovery was only for the amount of the verdict, $10.84. It seemed to me that the case should be considered the same as if it had come down to the circuit for trial on all the issues, and that on trial it was found and determined that the plaintiffs were entitled to recover only $10.84 in the action. But on more deliberate consideration, and after examining the record, I am satisfied that the case stands before me in a very different aspect. The question is, how much have the plaintiffs recovered in the action? The answer is furnished by the record—the judgment roll. They recovered $350 and interest from the maturity of the note, under the order and stipulation of January 25th, 1859, and also $10.84 by the verdict of the jury. There was a judgment for $350 and interest. The stipulation was to the effect that the plaintiffs might enter judgment for that amount, and judgment was entered pursuant to it. It was a *recovery* in the action under an adjudication by the court. The record therefore shows conclusively these three facts: 1st. That the plaintiffs recovered in the action. 2d. That the action was for the recovery of money. 3d. That the plaintiffs recovered over fifty dollars. It follows, therefore, that the plaintiffs are entitled to costs pursuant to section 304.

But it is insisted that the judgment roll is improperly made up, and that when corrected, as it is claimed it should be, under one of the motions now before me, it will show a recovery of only $10.84 in plaintiffs' favor.

The Code (§ 279) requires the clerk to keep a book for the entry of judgments, to be called the "judgment book," and (§ 280) that judgments be entered therein; also (§ 281) that the clerk, unless the roll be furnished, attach together and file certain papers, which shall constitute the judgment roll. In a litigated case the roll is made up of the summons, pleadings, verdict or report, the offer of the defendant, if any, the exceptions, case, and all orders and papers in any way involving the merits and necessarily affecting the judgment, with a copy of the judgment, (*sub.* 2, § 281.) In this case the roll is made up in strict conformity with the requirements of this section, with the exception that the verdict of the jury is omitted. The important objection to the record is this: that the verdict of the jury and the judgment thereon should form part of another or distinct record from that which evidences and directs the recovery of the other sum of $350, and interest. And it is urged that the record for the recovery of the $350 and interest, was and is perfect and complete without the addition of the entry of judgment for the $10.84 and costs. The effect of the argument is, that there should be two separate and distinct records or rolls, one of which would be evidence, and direct the recovery of the $350 and interest; the other of the $10.84, in which latter case, and on that record, the defendant would be entitled to costs, for the reason that it would then appear of record that the plaintiffs recovered less than fifty dollars.

There can be, however, but one roll, which should contain or state every thing necessary to a perfect history of the action from its commencement to its conclusion, beginning with the summons and ending with the entry of final judgment. The roll becomes the evidence of the proceedings and judgment, and should disclose every step in the action in consecutive order. It is suggested that a roll can properly contain only one judgment; but it is often the case, under the present practice, that it contains several. Often judgments are interlocutory, being but a partial adjudication of the matters in difference between the parties. So, too, when the answer admits part of the plaintiff's claim, the court will order such part satisfied, which order should go into the record. It is in effect a judgment. It operates as a judgment and is enforced as a judgment. By force of the adjudication the plaintiff recovers the sum directed to be paid. I can discover no substantial ground of objection to the record. It is informal in not containing the verdict of the jury; but it seems the omission was through inadvertence, and, as the plaintiffs' attorney swears, it was agreed at the time of the re-adjustment of the costs, that the clerk might make the correction, which he promised to do. This omission was not of the substance of the motion, I apprehend.

Perhaps the recitals in the judgment, entered June 2, 1862, were not, all of them, necessary, but they do no harm, and are not, as I conceive, entirely inappropriate.

So, if we look to the record for the purpose of determining the amount recovered in the action, we find it to appear that the plaintiffs recovered over fifty dollars. The defendant cannot claim costs on the ground that he served an offer to allow the plaintiff to take judgment for the amount of the note, less $150, for the reason that they recovered in the action an amount greater than the sum specified in the order.

I have therefore arrived at the following conclusions: 1st. That the judgment roll is in substance regularly and formally made up, except the omission of the verdict. 2d. That it conclusively appears from the roll that the plaintiffs recovered over fifty dollars, and an amount greater than the sum mentioned in the offer of judgment served by the defendant.

It follows that the motions must be denied, except the clerk will be directed to affix the verdict to the roll.

The motions having been heard together, I will allow only ten dollars costs. Perhaps, too, the fact ought to be considered that the defendant succeeds in part on one motion; although, I presume, no motion would have been made, nor does it seem any way necessary, merely to correct the record by affixing the verdict of the jury. As the order will be drawn, it will be the same in effect as if no costs were allowed to either party on one motion, and ten dollars allowed to the plaintiffs on the other.

NEW YORK COMMON PLEAS.

David Klen and others agt. Catharine Gibney.

Where a *married woman* carries on the *millinery business* upon her own account, and purchases goods upon credit for such business on her own account, an action may be brought against her the same as if she were unmarried, and a judgment recovered, and the amount collected by execution out of property belonging to her in her own right. (*This agrees with the case of Barton agt. Beer*, 21 *How. Pr. R.*, 309.)

New York General Term, November, 1862.

Daly, Brady and Hilton, *Judges*.

This was an appeal from a judgment rendered by Justice Van Cott in fourth district court, in July, 1861. The appeal was argued in October, 1861. The general term rendered its decision at this term, reversing the judgment.

J. Solis Ritterband, *for plaintiffs and appellants*.

F. Byrne, *for defendant and respondent*.

By the court, DALY, F. J. The justice erred in dismissing the complaint. It was admitted that the defendant, who is a married woman, was carrying on the millinery business upon her own account when the goods were sold to her. That the premises where she carried it on were leased to her in her own name. That the goods were sold to her in November, 1860, on her own separate account. That the term of credit had expired; that the bill had not been paid, and that her husband had no connection with or control over her business.

The sale in this case was made after the passage of the act of 1860, authorizing a married woman to carry on any trade or business on her sole and separate account. (*Laws of* 1860, *p.* 157.) It was decided in *Barton* agt. *Beer*, 21 *How.*, 309,) that this power to carry on trade and business includes the right to make such contracts as are incident to do it. That, when entered into by a married woman engaged in business upon her separate and sole account, they are valid, and may be enforced against her in the same manner as if she were a *feme sole.* I most fully give my assent to the construction given in this case to the statute.

In *Lady Wilmer's case*, (1 *Roll. R.*, 400,) it is said, that if the husband is banished by act of parliament, the wife shall have her action, and shall account as if she were a *feme sole;* and in *Derry* agt. *The Duchess of Magazine*, (1 *Ld. Ray.*, 147,) it was held, that when the husband is an alien enemy, and under an absolute disability to come and live in England, the law makes the wife of such a husband chargeable as a *feme sole* upon her debts and contracts. The act of 1860 impliedly recognizes the right of the wife to enter into such contracts as the one upon which the present action is brought, by declaring that her bargains and contracts in and about the carrying on of any trade or business, shall not be binding upon her husband, nor render him, nor his property in any way liable therefor; and as a preceding section declares that she may carry on any trade or business upon her sole and separate account, it necessarily follows that she is the party to be held responsible for the contracts and bargains she makes in business. The act also declares that "she may sue or be sued in all matters having relation to her property;" and the whole taken together shows very clearly that it was the design of the legislature that, upon all contracts made by her in the course of business, she should be proceeded against the same as if she were unmarried; that an action might be brought against her, a judgment recovered, and the amount collected by execution out of property belonging to her in her own right.

The judgment must therefore be reversed.

SUPREME COURT.

PHINEHAS A. SMITH, respondent agt. NORMAN AYLESWORTH, appellant.

Where a defendant delays until the *second day of the circuit*, to file and serve an *affidavit of merits* in order to prevent an inquest, he is bound at his peril to *serve it* in such a way as, in all reasonable probability, to bring the service to the knowledge of the attorney or counsel of the plaintiff having charge of the cause at the circuit, *before the inquest is taken*.

A service made on a *clerk in the office, in the absence of the attorney*, must be regarded equivalent to a service upon the attorney personally.

Monroe General Term, September, 1862.

JOHNSON, WELLES and CAMPBELL, *Justices*.

APPEAL from an order of special term denying motion to set aside an inquest taken at the Monroe circuit, in January, 1862.

The circuit commenced on Monday the 6th of January. On that day the defendant made the usual affidavit of merits, which was filed on the following day (Tuesday) at 8½ o'clock in the forenoon, and before the opening of the court on that day. The affidavit of one of the attorneys for the defendant states, among other things, the following facts: That the cause stood No. 212 on the circuit calendar; that he, the attorney, after filing the defendant's affidavit of merits with the clerk, went directly to the office of the plaintiff's attorney, and served a copy of said affidavit of merits, indorsed with a notice of filing the original with the clerk, by leaving the same with the clerk of the plaintiff's attorney, in his office, at from ten to fifteen minutes before nine o'clock, the time for opening the court on said 7th day of January. That said clerk told him that plaintiff's attorney had gone to the court. That he, the deponent, went immediately to the court room and clerk's office, and could find plaintiff's attorney at neither place. That the court bell had not then rung, nor was there any one in the court room but a constable. That on the afternoon of the 7th January aforesaid, the plaintiff's said clerk told deponent, that on receiving said notice and affidavit of merits, he went at once to the court-house with the same, to find plaintiff's attorney, but could not find him. The deponent further states, that after returning to said court room, and not finding the plaintiff's attorney, he returned to his own office in the Arcade, and had been there some time, drawing an affidavit in a suit for Mr. Cochrane the clerk, before the bell rung for court. That when the bell did ring, he went at once to the court room, and there learned that the plaintiff's attorney had taken an inquest in the action, out of its order on the calendar, for $133.21, being the first inquest taken. That deponent then at once, and before the order of inquests was over, and before any order had been entered in the action, told the plaintiff's attorney, then in court, and in presence of the court, that an affidavit of merits had been duly filed and served before the opening of court, and asked him to open the inquest, which he declined.

The opposing affidavits fully exculpate the plaintiff's

attorney from any unfairness, and show that he acted in good faith in taking the inquest, and that at the time it was taken he had no personal knowledge that an affidavit of merits had been made or served. They do not, however, deny that such affidavit had been made and filed, and a copy served upon the clerk of the plaintiff's attorney, and in the absence from the office of the attorney, with notice that the original was filed with the clerk of the court, before the opening of the court, on the second day of the circuit. There are some circumstantial differences in the statements in the affidavits in behalf of the respective parties, but not of sufficient consequence to be stated here.

George B. Brand, *for the defendant, appellant.*
Jno. Van Voorhis, *for the plaintiff, respondent.*

By the court, Welles, Justice. The only question presented on this appeal is, whether the affidavit of merits was filed and a copy served in time to prevent the inquest. The affidavits read on the motion establish, as I think, that both were done before the opening of the court, on the second day of the circuit. The copy affidavit and notice of filing, &c., were properly served on the clerk in the office of the plaintiff's attorney, he not being in his office at the time. No unfairness or laches are attributable to any one, unless it was laches on the part of the defendant's attorney in not filing and serving the affidavit of merits as early as the first day of the circuit. The plaintiff's attorney had noticed the cause for an inquest, and without any actual knowledge, or any notice that had reached him personally, he proceeded at the proper time to take the inquest. The defendant's attorney, on the morning of the second day of the circuit, filed the affidavit, and served the copy on the clerk of the plaintiff's attorney, before the opening of the court, and went immediately in search of the attorney to inform him what had been done, but did not succeed in finding him,

The 29th standing rule of the court is as follows: "Inquests may be taken in actions out of their order on the calendar, in cases in which they were heretofore allowed, at the opening of the court on any day after the first day of the court, provided the intention to take an inquest is expressed in the notice of trial, and a sufficient affidavit of merits shall not have been filed or served."

The defendant was literally within the latter provision of the rule. At the time the inquest was taken, a sufficient affidavit of merits had been actually filed and served. Unless there is some provision of law or rule of practice requiring the copy affidavit to be served personally upon the attorney, under the 29th rule, the service upon the clerk of the plaintiff's attorney, under the circumstances detailed in the affidavits, was sufficient. (*Code*, § 409, *sub*. 1.)

It is contended by the plaintiff's counsel that the inquest was regular, and the case of *Brainard* agt. *Hanford*, (6 *Hill*, 368,) is referred to. That case was much like the present in most of its features. It was a motion to set aside an inquest taken at the New York circuit, on the alleged ground of irregularity on the part of the plaintiff. On the second day of the circuit the court was to open at half past ten o'clock in the morning. About twenty minutes before that time, the attorneys for the plaintiffs left their office in the city, for the purpose of attending the circuit, and on the opening of the court took the inquest, not having then heard of an affidavit of merits. On leaving their office they put up a written notice, in a conspicuous place on the outside of the door, stating they had gone to the city hall. Very soon afterwards, and before the inquest was taken, the agent of the defendant's attorney entered the office, the door being unlocked, and finding no person there, served a copy of the affidavit of merits, the original having been properly filed, by leaving the same in a conspicuous place on the table in the office. The defendant's attorneys resided in Kingston, and sent the affidavit to their agent in the city, to be filed and served. The court held the inquest regular, on the ground that the copy affidavit of merits was not served until the day when the inquest might be regularly taken, and the plaintiff's attorney not knowing of the service. The court put their decision on the further ground that the agent made a mistake in leaving the paper in the vacant office, or that if he left it there, he should have sought the attorneys, and informed them of the service.

The rule which I extract from this decision is, that where a defendant delays until the second day of the circuit, to file and serve an affidavit of merits, in order to prevent an inquest, he is bound at his peril to serve it in such a way as, in all reasonable probability, to bring the service to the knowledge of the attorney or counsel of the plaintiff having charge of the cause at the circuit, before the inquest is taken. In the present case, the service was made on a clerk in the office in the absence of the attorney. This, I think, should be regarded equivalent to a service upon the attorney personally. The attorneys for each party resided and kept their offices in the city of Rochester, where the circuit court was sitting, and I think it is to be presumed the clerk could have found his principal, and informed him of the service, before the inquest was taken, if he had made the effort, which he should have done. It is quite different from a service in a vacant office, as in the case cited; especially as in that case the agent was informed by the notice on the side of the door, where the plaintiff's attorneys could be found.

Upon the whole, I am of the opinion that the order should be reversed, and the inquest, with all the subsequent proceedings on the part of the plaintiff, set aside. On the question of costs, which is in the discretion of the court, I am not disposed to award any to the defendant.

He shows no sufficient reason why he did not file and serve the affidavit on or before Monday, which, if he had done, would have probably avoided the necessity of this motion and appeal.

SUPREME COURT.

Cadwell agt. Manning and others.

There is no enactment either of the Code or otherwise, changing the practice of obtaining and filing *security for costs.*

A *chamber order, ex parte,* containing a *peremptory order* to file security for costs, and in default thereof to show cause why the complaint should not be dismissed, is *irregular.*

New York Special Term, November 5th, 1862.

An order was made in this cause in July, requiring the plaintiff to file security for costs within twenty days, or show cause on the 7th day of August, 1862, why the complaint should not be dismissed.

F. G. Burnham, *for motion.*
Ira D. Warren, *opposed.*

Barnard, Justice. Prior to the Code, the established practice to be pursued when it was desired to obtain security for costs, was, either to obtain a chamber order, *ex parte,* directing security to be filed within twenty days, and in the event of security not being filed within twenty days, then requiring cause to be shown at the first special term to be held after the expiration of said twenty days, why security should not be filed, which order contained a stay of proceedings. On the return day of the order, if the security had not been previously filed, the motion for security was heard pursuant to the alternative of the order to show cause; if the motion was granted, a peremptory order to file security was made. This order operated as a stay of proceedings. If security was not filed within a reasonable time pursuant to the peremptory order, a motion was made for judgment of *non pros.*, or the party desiring security might apply in the first instance to the court on notice to the opposite party, in which event, if the motion was granted, a peremptory order to file security was made in the first instance. The proceeding in case of not filing security pursuant to the peremptory order was then by a motion for a *non pros.*

There is no enactment, either of the Code or otherwise, changing the practice.

In this case the order is a chamber order, without notice, and is a peremptory order to file security, and in default thereof to show cause why the complaint should not be dismissed.

This motion cannot be granted without introducing a new course of practice. Motion denied, without prejudice to defendants making a further application for security in a different manner.

SUPREME COURT.

Davison agt. Baker.

Where the *service of process* or *papers* upon a person is made by *violently thrusting them upon his person*, the service will be held *void*, although the person or officer making the service may have stated the nature of the papers, and the person upon whom they were intended to be served refused to receive them. In other words, a person or an officer has no right to commit an *assault and battery* upon an individual in trying to serve the papers upon him.

Where a person upon whom service of process or papers is desired to be made, *refuses to receive them*, the person or officer making the service should inform him of the nature of the papers and of his purpose to make service of them, and *lay them down at any appropriate place in his presence*.

Saratoga Special Term, *August*, 1862.

A motion is made, on an order to show cause, to set aside the service of the summons and all subsequent proceedings herein.

J. C. ORMSBY, *attorney for plaintiff.*
AUGUSTUS PRENTICE, *attorney for defendant.*

BOCKES, Justice. By the judgment roll it appears that the summons and complaint were served on the defendant personally, on the 7th May, 1861; that in June, 1862, an order was obtained—the defendant having neglected to appear—directing an assessment of plaintiff's damages under a writ of inquiry. The writ issued and was executed on the 5th July, 1862, and the damages were assessed at $500, for which sum, with costs, judgment was entered July 22d, 1862.

The defendant moves, on the roll and on his own affidavit, with that of James E. Brumley and of Augustus Prentice, to set aside the entire proceedings, and avers that no legal or valid service of the summons was ever made on him.

The plaintiff answers the application by his own affidavits, with those of Joseph Davison, Oliver Davison, Nelson Ostrander, George Ostrander, Alva Beebe and Josiah V. Loomis.

I have read carefully all the papers, and find, as I expected and intimated on the hearing of the motion, that the affidavits on both sides are made up principally of immaterial and unimpertinent matter. The details of the transactions alluded to in the papers, have no pertinency whatever to the question, whether the summons was or was not duly served—which question is the only one of moment here.

The defendant states that the pretended service was in this way: That he was present at a conversation between Brumley and Oliver Davison, in regard to matters of difficulty between them, as to which he, defendant, had acted as Brumley's agent. The conversation was spirited; whereupon Davison suddenly turned to defendant and thrust, or attempted to thrust, some papers into his bosom, which fell upon the ground. Soon after, defendant and Brumley made careful search for the papers where they fell, but were unable to find them. The defendant also swears that he did not then know, nor does he now know, what the papers were; and that the only remark made by Davison, in any way connected with such service was this: "I will fix for Baker," or words to that effect.

Brumley corroborates the defendant as to the transaction, in substance. He says, that near the conclusion of the conversation between him and Davison, which was an angry one, Davison said to the defendant: "You have been too officious, and I will fix you," and then thrust the papers into defendant's bosom, when they fell to the ground. That very soon after, he and defendant searched where the papers fell, but they were unable to find them. He says no person was there after the attempted service and the search, except Davison; and both defendant and Brumley charge in their affidavits, on their belief, that the papers were picked up or taken away by Davison.

If these persons have detailed all that occurred at the time of the alleged service, most clearly it was irregular, or rather there was no service. Instead of being a legal act, it was an assault and battery. As they state the case, Davison neither delivered to the defendant the papers, nor intimated to him that he wished to do so, but rudely and offensively thrust them upon him. The proceeding was uncivil and deserving rebuke, rather than favorable regard as a legal act.

Mr. Davison gives, however, a somewhat different version of the transaction. He says that he offered the papers to the defendant, and informed him that they were a summons and complaint, and that he refused to accept or receive them, and thereupon he quickly placed them in the defendant's bosom. If a party refuse to accept papers when decorously offered him, after being distinctly informed what they are, he should be held to the consequences of his own perverseness; and then if they should be laid down for him and before him, such offer, information, refusal to accept, and leaving of the papers for him and in his presence, should be deemed legal service. This would be in legal effect a delivery of the papers to the party and leaving them with him. It is not necessary that the papers be thrust into his bosom or upon his person. Such act is uncivil and offensive, and therefore irregular, to say the least of it. If not an actual breach of the peace, it tends to that end, and is reprehensible.

There is one charge in the moving papers which I think Mr. Oliver Davison should have met directly and distinctly. It is stated by both the defendant and Brumley, on their belief, that the papers were taken away, after they fell upon the ground, by Davison; and they state the circumstances on which they base their belief. I do not find any direct denial of this charge in Mr. Davison's affidavit. If he picked up the papers and carried them away, without informing the defendant that he had done so, or where they could be found or obtained, he did not act with entire fairness. But I shall not rest my decision on this point at all, as I am satisfied the service was irregular, not to say void, having been made by force. It may be asked, what shall be done in case a party will not accept papers offered him with a view to their service upon him? Suppose he reject them and turn away, how is service to be effected? The answer is ready and plain. The officer will inform him of their nature and of his purpose to make service of them, and lay them down at any appropriate place in his presence. This would be good service, undoubtedly, in case the party to be served refuses to receive them. It cannot be that the officer or person seeking to make service of a summons, must seize the party to be served, and compel him to take it; nor can he justify himself for any personal violence in order to make service Service may be effected, and in all cases should be, without personal violence or incivility, and in my judgment the dignity of the court, as well as the high privilege of personal immunity, which every individual has a right to insist upon, demand that this rule should be strictly adhered to.

In this case I should be quite willing, if I could do so consistently, to allow the service of the summons to stand, setting aside all subsequent proceedings in the action; for it cannot be said, I think, that the defendant conducted with entire ingenuousness. Mr. Davison says he informed him of his purpose to serve the papers, and that he refused to receive them. This he denies, but I cannot disabuse myself of the belief that he well understood at the time of the attempted service, and afterwards, that Mr. Davison sought to make service of papers on him as a party in some legal proceeding. Indeed, he so admitted in substance to Joseph Davison and to Nelson and George Ostrander, and in effect so states in his own affidavit. While I am satisfied that the service was irregularly made, I am also impressed with a conviction that the defendant is not wholly blameless. On the whole, I must hold the service irregular, and I think the best way will be to set aside the entire proceedings. This will best vindicate the rule as to the service of papers which I feel bound to recognize, and is in effect scarcely different from setting aside all proceedings subsequent to the service of the summons. But the motion must be granted without costs. As I have stated, I cannot regard the defendant entirely without fault, and, besides, his motion papers are stuffed with irrelevant and impertinent matters; and the costs of the motion should be denied him for that reason, if there were no other.

Motion granted, without costs.

SUPREME COURT.

George K. Roberts agt. John W. Carter and Edmund Terry.

An *assignee* of any thing but commercial paper, when he takes it *bona fide*, is liable to *all the equities* which exist against the demand while in the hands of the *assignor*.

In an action to *set off judgments*, one against the other, the statute of set-off must control; and the equities of the parties are paramount to the *attorney's lien for costs*.

New York General Term, May, 1862.
Ingraham, Clerke and Gould, *Justices*.

Statement of facts.

This was an action to set off judgments, one against the other. On the 21st of July, 1857, the plaintiff Roberts had a report of a referee in his favor for $820, and Carter had a report of a referee against Roberts for $149.17; and on same day Carter, without notice to Roberts or his attorney, assigned said report to Terry, his lawyer, who, on the 22d of July, 1857, by an *ex parte* order made by Justice Birdseye, (2d district,) was substituted plaintiff in place of Carter, and entered up judgment in his own name as plaintiff, instead of Carter's. (*See this case*, 15 *How. Pr. R.*, 65.) Plaintiff entered up his judgment against Carter for $1,040.12. Carter, as assigned to Terry, entered judgment against Roberts for $360.39. Excess of Roberts' judgment over Carter's, $679.73. The cause was brought to trial before the court at special term, Mr. Justice Mullin presiding, who, on the 19th November, 1859, ordered judgment for the defendants, and that the complaint be dismissed, with costs. From this judgment the plaintiff appealed to the general term.

John Fitch, *attorney and counsel for plaintiff.*

The assignment from Carter to Terry was *ex parte*. Roberts was not bound by it. The plaintiff was injured by it. (11 *How.*, 380.)

Terry, as an assignee of Carter, with full knowledge of the suits, must take the claim subject to all the equities. (5 *Cow.*, 376; 11 *How.*, 380; *Terry* agt. *Roberts*, 15 *How.*, 65.)

The court could not impose a condition. (6 *How.*, 220; 11 *How.*, 365.)

When, *pendente lite*, in an action on contract, the plaintiff sells and assigns the subject matter of the action to a third person, he will not be substituted as plaintiff on motion of the plaintiff to the record, and without notice to him. The alleged purchaser is the person to move for substitution, and he should do so on notice to the plaintiff as well as to the defendant. Even in such case, it is not a matter of course to order a substitution without imposing any conditions. (*Howard & Brown* agt. *Taylor*, 11 *How.*, 380.)

Where a party is substituted as plaintiff, without notice to the opposite party, the party so substituted stands in the shoes of the assignee, and is subject in equity, at least, to the same set off as the original party would have been. (This is in accordance with *Howard & Brown* agt. *Taylor*, 11 *How.*, 380; *see also Chappell* agt. *Potter*, *id.*, 365; *Terry* agt. *Roberts*, 15 *id.*, 65.)

The case of *Nash* agt. *Hamilton*, (3 *Abb.*, *p.* 35, *6th district general term*,) was where the party (defendants) had notice of the assignment. But in this case Roberts did not have any notice of the assignment; it was done *ex parte*; and in this case (3 *Abb.*) the court held, "that no set off could arise against it unless one in favor of the defendant. And in 1 *Cow.*, 56, 206; 4 *Hill*, 561, the court say, "if the right of set off exists at the time of the assignment, the assignee takes subject to all the equitable as well as legal claims which might be urged against the assignor at the time of the assignment." And the court say, (3 *Paige*, 365,) "that the right exists as against the attorney's lien, although the attorney be the assignee."

Judge MULLIN, who tried this cause, in his order for judgment makes the mistake of supposing that Terry (plaintiff, Carter's attorney) was substituted upon a regular motion on notice, because the cases to which he refers are cases where assignments were on notice. Here there was no notice. The order was *ex parte.* By his decision he in effect reverses the decision of this general term (1st district) in *Martin* agt. *Kanouse*, (17 *How.*, 146.)

The only fact necessary for Roberts to have his set off, as far as it would go, was that he and Carter both had equities. (Referee's report of judgments against each other at same point of time.) (2 *R. S.*, 354, § 18, 1*st ed.*; 5 *How.*, 339; 4 *id.*, 168; 10 *Abb.*, [*general term,*] 384.)

Where an action is brought for the purpose of setting off a judgment owned by the plaintiff, against a judgment for costs in favor of the defendant against the plaintiff, the attorney's lien for costs on the latter judgment cannot be protected or let in to obstruct the set off. It is otherwise where a motion is made to set off judgments. In the latter case the courts proceed without the statute, but in the former they are within it, and they must obey it. (*Martin* agt. *Kanouse*, 17 *How.*, 146; *Nicoll* agt. *Nicoll*, 16 *Wend*,, 446.)

The return of the execution unsatisfied, and Carter's imprisonment and discharge as a "poor debtor" under the statute, clearly proved him an insolvent at the time, and the court should have so held.

A new trial should be granted for the reasons set forth in the exceptions to the findings of the court, both law and fact, as are set forth in the case.

E. TERRY, *attorney and counsel for defendants.*

First.—Terry was not only the equitable assignee of that

portion of the judgment covering the costs, but he was the actual assignee for value of the whole judgment before the plaintiff Roberts had obtained his judgment, and before his equity arose to set off sufficient to liquidate this judgment againt him. (17 *How. Pr. R.*, 341.)

Second.—There is no proof of insolvency of Carter, at the time he assigned the judgment sought to be canceled by set-off to Terry, July 21st, 1857.

Third.—If there was insolvency of Carter, Terry's equity is as great as Roberts', and he was equally entitled to be paid.

Fourth.—There was no proof of fraud.

Fifth.—All the above points were submitted to the court on the evidence, and unless his decision is clearly against the weight of evidence, his decision is final.

Sixth.—The judgment should be affirmed, with costs.

By the court, GOULD, Justice. I do not see that in considering this case, we are necessarily to come in conflict with the decision of this court on a motion in the same matter (as reported in 17 *How.*, 341.) At page 343 of that case, Mr. Justice DAVIES expressly makes the distinction between a motion where the court will protect the attorney in his costs, and a suit to compel a set-off according to the provisions of the statute. And Mr. Justice CLERKE, though concurring in the result of denying the motion, does not concur in the ground upon which it is placed. And no other justice gives any opinion. We may therefore proceed untrammeled by that case.

Mr. Terry comes into this case as assignee of a claim of his client, (who, according to the subsequent proceedings to obtain his discharge as a poor debtor, must have been then insolvent;) Terry taking the assignment to protect himself, if he could legally, to which there is no objection.

But an assignee of anything but commercial paper, when he takes it *bona fide*, is liable to all the equities which exist against the demand while in the hands of the assignor. And, with a view to carry this out in case of an assignment, *pendente lite*, the case in 11 *How.* (381) seems to assign the principle that should govern courts in allowing such an assignee to be made party to the suit. "When a substitution cannot prejudice any right or remedy of the defendant, it would be almost a matter of course to permit it. When such a result would be produced by the change, the court would either refuse to permit it, or would grant it only on such terms as would protect the defendant from injury." While, in the case before us, the assignee of Carter was allowed to come in *ex parte*, to the manifest injury of Roberts the defendant.

The opinion of Justice Davies, in *Martin* agt. *Kanouse*, (17 *How.*, 148,) seems much sounder than his opinion above referred to; and the case he there cites (16 *Wend.*, 446) seems to be a binding one, decided in the court of last resort.

It would seem that the set-off should be allowed, and that therefore the decision of special term must be reversed.

Clerke, J. I concur.

SUPREME COURT.

John H. Morrell agt. E. Hoey.

The law as to *commissions* for the examination of witnesses is not altered by the Code. It is not applicable to witnesses in *supplementary proceedings*.

New York Special Term, November, 1862.

Ingraham, P. Justice. The plaintiff moves for a commission to examine a witness in supplementary proceedings. It is conceded that prior to amendment of the Code, in 1860, such a motion could not be granted. I do not think the amendment to the Code in section 399 alters that rule.

That section, as amended, only applies to the examination of the witness, and extends to special proceedings the right to examine a party, as in an action. It does not allow a commission to issue for such purpose. There is no other statute which makes such a commission proper. The Revised Statutes, under which commissions are issued, require issue to be joined. The law as to commission for the examination of witnesses is not altered, either by the amendments of 1860 or 1862. Motion denied.

SUPREME COURT.

James P. Ross agt. Alexander Longmuir.

In the *verification* of an answer *by an agent* of the defendant to an action upon a written instrument, where the allegations of the answer are stated *positively*, and without qualification, it is not necessary that the agent should state his *knowledge* or the *grounds of his belief* in the verification. That part of the verification which refers to matters in the answer, supposed to have been stated upon information and belief, may be treated as surplusage.

Monroe General Term, September, 1862.

Johnson, E. Darwin Smith and Welles, *J. J.*

Appeal from an order of special term, denying motion by defendant to set aside judgment.

H. R. Selden and Jno. McConvill, *for appellant.*
T. R. Strong and D. C. Hyde, *for respondent.*

By the court, Welles, Justice. The judgment was entered as for want of an answer to the complaint. An answer was served in due time, but was returned by the plaintiff's attorney to the defendant's attorney on the alleged ground that the verification was insufficient, the complaint having been duly verified, and the plaintiff perfected judgment. The verification was as follows:

"Monroe county, ss.:—Alexander Longmuir, junior, being duly sworn, says: that he is and has for a long time been agent for the defendant in this action; that the foregoing answer is true to his own knowledge, (except as to those matters therein stated on information and belief, and as to those matters he believes it to be true.) Deponent further says that the reason why the verification is not made by the defendant is, that all the material allegations in the answer are within the personal knowledge of deponent, and not within the personal knowledge of the defendant.

(Signed) "A. LONGMUIR, JR.

"Sworn before me, February 6th, 1862.

(Signed) "HIRAM L. BARKER, *Com. of Deeds.*"

This is nearly if not exactly in the language of that portion of § 157 of the Code, allowing the affidavit of verification to be made by the agent or attorney of the party in a case where the action or defence is founded upon a written instrument for the payment of money only, &c.

It is objected on the part of the plaintiff that the affidavit omits to set forth the knowledge or the grounds of belief of the agent who makes it. It is a sufficient answer to this objection that there is nothing in the answer stated upon information or belief, but each and every allegation is stated positively and without qualification. That part of the affidavit, therefore, which refers to matters in the answer supposed to have been stated upon information and belief, may be treated as surplusage. It is further objected that the answer contains no defence; but this, I think, is an error. The defence interposed is that of a recoupment. It may not be a full defence to the whole cause of action, but it is a full defence to the extent of the recoupment which the plaintiff may be able to prove on the trial. If it is true to any extent, the defendant had a right to set it up. Besides, the plaintiff has no right to treat it as a nullity on that ground, and enter judgment as for want of an answer. If frivolous, the only way he can take advantage of it is by application to a judge of the court, under § 247. The order of special term should be reversed, and the judgment set aside with $10 costs of appeal.

SAME agt. SAME.

Same facts, except that the affidavit of verification omits the clause in parenthesis in the affidavit in the foregoing case. Same order as in the other case.

SUPREME COURT.

EMMA L. UNDERHILL agt. SAMUEL G. TRIPP and others.

Construction of clauses in a will.—Personal property may be bequeathed *for life*, and then over, either absolutely or contingently.

A bequest by the testator to his daughter of $1,000, and then declares that this bequest is given to make his daughter equal with his other children who had been advanced; and after a residuary devise of all the residue of his real and personal estate, he says the bequest (of $1,000) which he has given to his said daughter, "she is to have and to hold during the term of her *natural life*, and at her decease is to be equally divided among her children,"

Held, that this last clause cut down the legacy of the daughter to a *life estate* or *usufructuary interest*; and that her *children* would take as *purchasers* on her death.

Dutchess Special Term, January, 1861.

AN action involving the construction of a will.

EMOTT, Justice. If this will and codicil contained an absolute bequest of one thousand dollars to the plaintiff in perpetuity, any directions or limitations inconsistent with such ownership would be void. This is the doctrine of numerous cases, among which are *Bradley* agt. *Peixotto*, (3 *Ves.*, 324,) and *Newton* agt. *Reid*, (4 *Sim.*, 141.) So if there were an absolute bequest in one part of the will, and an imperfectly expressed intention in a subsequent part that the legatee should take for life only, the plain language will not be cut down by the uncertain words in the residue.

This is the doctrine announced by the vice-chancellor of England, in *Billing* agt. *Billing*, (5 *Sim.*, 232.)

At the same time the whole will must be taken together, and all of it upheld if possible. Neither of the classes of cases just cited are applicable here, because the testator not only manifestly intended, but has clearly expressed his intention, that the legacy to the plaintiff should be for life only. I speak from the will only, and without referring to the codicil, which certainly could not cut down this bequest, if it were absolute and entire to the legatee by the will, although it may be referred to upon the question of construction and intention. But the will gives to the plaintiff $300 to buy furniture, which bequest she is to have and to hold absolutely at her own disposal. After certain specific bequests, in similar terms, to other relatives, the testator proceeds to say: "also I give and bequeath to my daughter, Emma L. Underhill, the farther sum of one thousand dollars." He then gives, in similar terms, a like sum to another daughter, and declares that these bequests are given to make these daughters equal with his other children who had been advanced. Then follows a residuary devise, of all his remaining real and personal property, to all his children, naming them and including the plaintiff, "to be equally divided among them, share and share alike." The next sentence is that upon which the present controversy turns: "the bequests which I have given to my daughter, Emma L. Underhill, excepting the three hundred dollars to buy furniture, she is to have and to hold during the term of her natural life, and at her decease is to be equally divided among her children." There is a clause in similar language in respect to the bequests to Hannah D. Tripp.

This language, in my opinion, cuts down the legacies of the plaintiff to a life estate, or the usufructuary interest. There is no doubt that personal property may be bequeathed for life, and then over, either absolutely or contingently.

In the case of *Norris* agt. *Beyea*, (3 *Kern.*, 273,) an executory devise upon a life estate in personal property was sustained, although the gift to the first legatee was express, and only limited by the subsequent contingent bequest. If the devise in that case had been absolute, and not contingent, would the case have been any stronger for the first taker? In *Paterson* agt. *Ellis*, the stress of the case was, as shown by Judge DENIO in *Norris* agt. *Beyea*, that the executory devise was void, because it was upon an indefinite failure of issues. There was also in that case, what is the material point in a number of the cases, an absolute power of disposing of the fund given to the legatee. This was the distinguishing feature of *Flanders* agt. *Clark*, (3 *Atk.*, 509,) where Lord HARDWICKE said that the power of disposing and spending the whole made the limitation one void. But he said, if it were not for this, the limitation being to issue living at the death of the first taker, he would sustain the devise and confirm the first legatee to an usufructuary interest. In the case of *Drake* agt. *Robinson*, decided by this court, there was an absolute bequest, with nothing to limit it but a direction to invest. On the other hand, in *Norris* agt. *Beyea*, although there was an express gift to Isabella Beyea, directed to be paid six months after the testator's death, yet as there was a valid contingent devise engrafted upon this, the court of appeals held that this limitation was not void for repugnancy, and that the first taker was only entitled to the use of the fund.

If the case rested upon a gift to the plaintiff, and at her death to be equally divided among her heirs, there would be at any rate a different question. But as I read the will, it is a bequest to the plaintiff for life expressly, and then to her children equally. The word heirs is not used, and there can be no question that children in such a connection in a gift of personal estate is a word of purchase and not of limitation. (*See Jarman on Wills*, *vol.* 2, 315; 1 *Dru. & W.*, 107; 2 *Sim.*, 485; 5 *Sim.*, 458.) It does not appear whether this legatee has children. The inference from the will is that she has. If so, I see no doubt that they take as purchasers at the death of their mother.

There is no repugnancy in the clauses of this will and codicil, fairly interpreted, and I cannot see any way to throw aside all the clauses of the will, except the first sentence relating to the plaintiff, in order to hold that she is absolutely entitled to this fund.

There must, therefore, be judgment for the defendants. The case is a fair one for costs out of the fund, if they can be given without interfering with the rights of other legatees who are not interested in the present question. The question of costs is reserved for consideration upon settling the judgment.

SUPREME COURT.

THOMAS S. BARLOW and another, executors agt. MIRA COFFIN and others.

An *inconsistent* devise or bequest in the *second* of two testamentary papers (a will and codicil) is a *revocation of the first.*

Thus, in case of a devise of the same lands to two persons, while if the devises are in the *same instrument*, the devisees may take jointly or in common; but if they are found in *distinct* testamentary instruments, the *latter* is a complete *revocation* of the former.

Dutchess Special Term, May, 1861.

AN action to settle the accounts of the plaintiffs as executors, to construe the will and determine the rights of the parties.

J. F. BARNARD, *for plaintiffs.*
MR. NELSON, *for defendants.*

EMOTT, Justice. The complaint in this case hardly states sufficient to authorize the court to entertain the suit. It does not appear when Thomas Barlow died, (the date of his death being left blank,) nor when Lucy Barlow, his widow, died, except that her death is stated to have occurred in 1860. I do not discover that the plaintiffs, as executors of Thomas Barlow, have anything to do with the real estate which he left, nor do I see how any judgment can be rendered in this action which can affect the lands devised by Thomas Barlow. I therefore exclude the real estate devised to Lucy Barlow, from the present consideration and judgment, and shall determine the rights of these parties in the personal estate only. In respect to this, the complaint states in general terms that Thomas Barlow left real and personal estate, and that his personal estate is undistributed. What the amount of personal estate is, or in what it consists, is not stated, nor does it appear why it still remains in the executors' hands.

If there is personal estate in the hands of the executors of Thomas Barlow, undistributed, and which is claimed by the legatees of Thomas Barlow on the one hand, and by those of Lucy Barlow on the other, a case is undoubtedly presented for the interposition of a court of equity, to settle the accounts of the executors, and to construe the will and determine the rights of the parties.

The counsel for the plaintiffs, representing the executors of Lucy Barlow, invokes the principles stated in *Underhill* agt. *Tripp*, (*ante p.* 51,) to show that the absolute gift in perpetuity to Lucy Barlow, in the will of her husband, can not be affected by the codicil. But the cases are widely distinguishable in more than one particular. If the will and codicil are to be treated as one instrument, they contain an absolute bequest to Lucy Barlow of one-third of the personal estate, and an equally express gift of the same third, after the death of Lucy Barlow, to the testator's four daughters. This is not the case of a mere direction or limitation inconsistent with an absolute bequest, as in *Bradley* agt. *Piexotto*, (3 *Ves.*, 324,) where there was an attempt to impose a condition that if the legatee attempted to dispose of the fund bequeathed to him, it should go over to another person. Nor is it the case of an absolute bequest, in one part of a will, and an imperfectly expressed intention in another part, to cut down the bequest to a life estate, as in *Billing* agt. *Billing*, (5 *Sim.*, 232,) where the property was first given to trustees to pay it to the testator's nephew, at such time as they saw fit; and there was also a clause that the trustees should pay him the interest after he became of age, weekly or quarterly during his life. This latter clause was not allowed to control the plain terms of a previous absolute bequest.

But here are two bequests, both explicit and necessarily repugnant. If they were both in the same instrument, one must fail altogether, or both must fail, or the will be construed so as to give effect to both by one modifying the other. If one of the bequests were to be rejected, it would not be the latter. The contrary is the old rule, and although somewhat modified in its application in more recent cases, it is a rule of law still, that of two repugnant clauses in a will, the last, while of two such clauses in a deed the first, shall prevail. (*Co. Litt.*, 112, *b;* 2 *Atk.*, 372; 2 *Saund.*, 103.) But where two devises or bequests are not totally irreconcileable, and such as cannot in any way of reading them stand together, one may modify the other, and both have effect, Thus, where lands were given to A. in fee, and in a subsequent part of the will the same lands to B. for life, both parts were allowed to stand, as if the devise were first to B. for life, and then to A. in fee. (*Cro. Eliz.*, 9.) So where the same lands are devised to A. in fee, and in another part of the will to B. in fee, they take jointly or in common. (2 *Atk.*, 486; *Plowd.*, 539.) Where one part of a will contains an absolute devise or bequest to one, and another part contains a clause giving a remainder to another, either absolutely or contingently, upon the death of the first devisee or legatee, it is plain upon principle and authority, that the two clauses are to be construed together, and the latter cuts down the former to a life estate. That conclusion was reached by Ld. BROUGHAM after a very able and satisfactory discussion of the authorities in his opinion in *Sherrat* agt. *Bentley*, (2 *Myl. & K.*, 149.) That case is very nearly in point upon the present question, assuming that this will and codicil are to be treated as one instrument. In *Norris* agt. *Beyea*, (3 *Kern.*, 273,) a contingent bequest over at the death of the first taker was sustained, although the first bequest was absolute and express, standing alone. I observed in *Underhill* agt. *Tripp*, that the case would have been no stronger for the first taker, if the bequest over had been absolute and not contingent, and that observation is fully justified by the authorities to which I have just referred. If the two bequests in the present case were contained in the same instrument, I should have no difficulty in holding that both should stand, and that the bequest to the children must cut down that to the widow to a life estate.

But the case is stronger for the defendants than this. The bequest to the widow is contained in a will which is dated January 12th, 1852. That to the children, under which the defendants claim, is contained in a codicil dated October 11th, 1862. The rule in such a case is well settled, that an inconsistent devise or bequest in the second of two testamentary papers is a revocation of the first. Thus, in the case already put, of a devise of the same lands to two persons, while if the devises are in the same instrument, the devisees may take jointly or in common; if they are found in distinct testamentary instruments, the latter is a complete revocation of the former. (3 *Mod.*, 206; *Brant* agt. *Wilson*, 8 *Cow.*, 56.) The opinion of Judge WOODWORTH, in the case of *Brant* agt. *Wilson*, has been reviewed and adopted in a controversy relating to the same lands, which was very recently before this court at general term. (*Wilson* agt. *Wilson*, 32 *Barb.* 328, 336; *S. C.* 20

How. Pr. R., 41.) The general principle is, that a subsequent testamentary disposition of lands or property already devised in an existing will, is a revocation of such previous will, absolutely or *pro tanto*, and at least as far as may be necessary to give effect to the last disposition. (*See Jarm. on Wills*, 156, 158, 161, *and cases cited.*) The codicil made by the present testator in October, revoked the disposition contained in his will of January, 1852, so far as was necessary to give effect to the provisions of the former. Lucy Barlow, therefore, took only a life interest in the one-third of the personalty, and the executors are accountable to the four daughters named in the codicil, for whatever of that share may be in their hands.

There will be judgment for an accounting and distribution accordingly; the costs to come out of the estate.

SUPREME COURT.

JAIRUS BEST agt. AMOS H. STARKS, impleaded with HENRY M. WEATHERBY.

Where the defendant denied that the claim in suit was for money received for the benefit of the defendant's *co-partnership firm*, but was money borrowed by his co-partner for his individual benefit, and that it was never appropriated to the use of the firm,

Held, that evidence to show that the money borrowed was not in fact used in the business of the firm, was properly excluded where the evidence was not sufficient to cast any suspicions upon the *bona fides* of the loan being for the firm. Also that evidence to show that on a final settlement of the partnership accounts by arbitration, this debt was not mentioned on either side, was properly excluded. Also, evidence to show that in the formation of the partnership, the partners arranged between themselves to procure what money they should want in their business from a particular source, was properly excluded. Also, evidence to show that no claim was made upon the defendant for the debt for a year and a half after the plaintiff knew of the insolvency of the other partner, was properly excluded.

Held, also, on the motion for a new trial, that the case belonged to that class of cases of conflicting evidence and doubtful facts, in which the verdict of a jury one way or the other is practically conclusive, and ought not to be disturbed.

Columbia Special Term, September, 1859.

MOTION for a new trial upon a case and affidavits, upon the ground of erroneous rulings of the court. Also, that the verdict is against the weight of evidence. Also, on the ground of newly discovered evidence.

P. W. BISHOP, *for defendant.*
H. N. WRIGHT, *for plaintiff.*

HOGEBOOM, Justice. This suit was originally brought by Jacob L. Best to recover against the defendants (who were a firm under the name of Starks & Weatherby) moneys paid by him, for their benefit, upon a note signed by him as their surety to Aaron Huyck. Best having *pendente lite* assigned the claim to plaintiff, the latter was substituted as the party plaintiff.

Starks defends the suit upon the ground that the money borrowed of Huyck was not borrowed for the firm but for Weatherby, who was a brother-in-law of Best; that it was never appropriated to the use of the firm; that by reason of transactions between Best and Weatherby, in which Best became the debtor of Weatherby, the former *assumed* the Huyck debt and became primarily responsible to pay the same.

These questions were litigated upon the trial, Best and Starks having both been sworn as witnesses, (Weatherby having removed to a western state,) and the result was that the plaintiff recovered by the verdict of a jury the full amount of his claim.

The defendant, among other things, moves for a new trial on the ground of newly discovered evidence. But that motion must be denied. The newly discovered evidence is not of itself very important; tends to establish precisely the same points as were litigated on the trial, and with reasonable diligence might have been discovered before the trial. (*People* agt. *Superior Court of N. Y.*, 5 *Wend.*, 115; *Graham & Waterman on New Trials*, 489.)

Jacob L. Best was examined as a witness on the trial against the defendants' objection—notice of his intended examination having been given while he was a party, but not repeated after the present plaintiff took his place. If a notice were necessary, I think the one originally given was sufficient, and operated through all the subsequent stages of the suit. This objection, therefore, cannot prevail. I do not discover that by the case he was objected to for any other reason; but if it was designed to object to him also as the assignor of the demand, I regard such objection as untenable. (*Alton* agt. *Franklin F. I. Co.*, 9 *How.*, 501; *Seymour* agt. *Peak*, 10 *How.*, 395.)

Best being a competent witness, and not interested in the event of the suit, there seems to be no reason why his wife was not a competent witness. I think she was properly admitted.

The offer to show that the money borrowed was not, in fact, used in the business of Starks & Weatherby, was, I think, properly overruled. The money was borrowed avowedly for the use of the firm by Weatherby. So it was stated to Best and to Huyck. They were merchants, and obtaining money for this purpose was within the legitimate range of their business. I discover no sufficient evidence which would have prevented Huyck from recovering against Starks as well as Weatherby, for the lender is not bound to see to the application of the money unless there be circumstances of suspicion. (*Church* agt. *Sparrow*, 5 *Wend.*, 223; *Whittaker* agt. *Brown*, 16 *Wend.*, 505; *Onondaga Co. Bank* agt. *DePuy*, 17 *Wend.*, 47.) Nor on the whole, upon the evidence of Mr. and Mrs. Best and Huyck, was there sufficient to cast suspicion upon the *bona fides* of the suretyship of Best, as being for the firm instead of Weatherby alone. Hence it was not material nor admissible to show that the money was misapplied, especially as the defendant did not accompany the offer of the evidence with such a claim, nor avow his intention to go to the jury upon that question.

I think, also, the offer to show that on a final settlement of accounts between Starks & Weatherby by arbitration, this debt was not mentioned on either side, was properly overruled. It was a very slight circumstance from which to infer that the loan was for the benefit of Weatherby alone. If Weatherby had not paid the debt, as in fact he had not, he had no claim for it as between him and Starks.

The offer to show that upon the formation of the partnership, the partners arranged between themselves to procure what money they should want in their business from a particular source, was also properly overruled. It would have very little weight in a litigation between Starks & Weatherby themselves. It appears to me to be entitled to none when the question is between Starks and a party not pretended to have been cognizant of such an arrangement, and therefore having no reason to suspect, on that account, the *bona fide* character of Weatherby's application as one to borrow money for the use of the firm.

I think, also, on the whole, that there was no error in excluding the evidence that Best became embarrassed in his pecuniary circumstances soon after his payment of this debt to Huyck, and that notwithstanding his knowledge of Weatherby's insolvency, he made no claim for payment against Starks till the commencement of this suit, nearly a year and a half afterwards. Can it be said that this should in law prejudice his claim or throw suspicion upon it? Was the evidence strong enough for that purpose? It seems to me it was of an altogether inconclusive character, which might well be explained upon a different hypothesis from that which should assume the invalidity of the plaintiff's claim. It belongs to that kind of evidence, of which I think there are more instances than is generally supposed, where it cannot be said to be positive error, either to admit or reject the evidence, where its unimportant character, if rightly weighed (and we must assume that the jury will put the right construction upon it) will not prejudice either of the parties by its admission or its exclusion.

On the whole, I am inclined to think that the present belongs to that class of cases of conflicting evidence and doubtful facts in which the verdict of a jury one way or the other, is practically conclusive and ought not to be disturbed. The parties have had a fair trial and we ought not to set aside the verdict merely because we may suppose that perhaps another jury, equally intelligent and equally honest, might consistently with the evidence reach an opposite conclusion.

The motion for a new trial must be denied with costs.

NEW YORK COMMON PLEAS.

Stewart agt. McCready.

The intent of the statute of 1860, (*Sess. Laws*, 771,) giving to the keeper of a *boarding house* a *lien* to the extent of the board due, is, to give them the same lien which an *inn-keeper* has upon the effects of a guest, without reference to the character of the guests, whether they are *transient* or *permanent boarders*.

New York General Term, August, 1861.

By the court, Daly, F. J. A boarding-house keeper, as contradistinguished from the keeper of an inn, should, in the sense of this statute, be regarded as one who furnishes accommodation for a definite period, as by the week or month, at a rate of compensation agreed upon. A guest, as distinguished from a boarder, is bound for no stipulated time. He stops at the inn for as short or as long time as he pleases, paying, while he remains, the customary charge. While he occupies the position of a guest, the inn-keeper has a lien upon his effects, and may detain them until he is paid for the accommodation which has been furnished; but if he and the inn-keeper enter into a special agreement for any fixed period, at a stipulated price, he ceases to be a guest, and becomes a boarder. The inn-keeper relies upon the special agreement, and has no longer a lien upon the effects. In modern times, and especially in cities, the practice has become very general of furnishing accommodation by the week or by the month, at a fixed rate, or as the parties may agree, and the persons who furnish accommodation in this way are distinguished as keepers of boarding-houses. Before the passage of this statute this class, now a very numerous one, had no lien upon the effects of the persons to whom they supplied entertainment, and it was evidently the intent of this statute to give them the same lien which an inn-keeper has upon the effects of a guest. The words, "to the same extent and in the same manner as inn-keepers have such a lien and such right of detention," was intended rather to indicate the general nature and character of the lien, than to specify any particular case or class of cases in which a boarding-house keeper might have a lien. If we did not so construe the statute, then it would have no meaning at all, and in interpreting a statute we must assume that the legislature intended something by the passage of the act.

Hilton, J., dissented.

Brady, J. The act of 1860 (*Sess. Laws*, 771) gives to the keeper of a boarding-house a lien to the extent of the board due. It provides that such keeper shall have the right to detain the baggage of "any boarder," and discards all distinction between transient and permanent guests, and further confirms this privilege by giving such lien for the amount "which may be due for board by such boarder," without reference to the manner in which, or the time for which, the board became due. This right is not qualified by the declaration which follows, that the lien is to the "same extent, and in the same manner as inn-keepers have such lien and such right of detention." These words apply to the character of the lien, and the extent and mode of exercising it. They designate the lien which the keeper has for the sum due, viz., the same lien as an inn-keeper, when he has any lien at all. This statute was drawn, doubtless, with reference to the rule applicable to inn-keepers in these cases; but the law-maker was either mistaken about the rule, or has been unfortunate enough to present an act which is obscure, and which it requires some reflection to understand. I think, however, that it becomes clear, as a matter of construction and intention, that the lien given to the boarding-house keepers is without reference to the character of the guests, and that it makes no difference whether they are transient or not.

The judgment should be reversed.

SUPREME COURT.

MORTIMER BROWN agt. ALLEN PENFIELD, JAMES M. PENFIELD and ALLEN P. HARWOOD.

Where the plaintiff, being in the *possession of negotiable paper* with *apparent title*, and no contradictory evidence to overthrow it, he shows a legal right as owner to recover.

Where a referee not only decides against the *weight of evidence*, but errs in the application of the *rules of law*, it is error of *fact and of law*. And a wrong result upon *undisputed evidence* is an *error of law*.

Albany General Term, March, 1861.

GOULD, HOGEBOOM and PECKHAM, *Justices*.

THIS action was commenced October 6th, 1853, to recover the amount of two drafts, each drawn and indorsed by Miles White, and accepted by the defendants, by their firm name of Penfield, Harwood & Co., each for $1,000; the one dated October 27th, 1852, at six months, the other dated September 10th, 1852, at eight months. The defendants answered, denying each and every allegation in the complaint. They deny that Miles White made the drafts or indorsed them, or that the defendants accepted them; deny the transfer and ownership by plaintiff; set up that defendants were acceptors, and that the drafts were used to pay precedent debts; allege payment; that the drafts were diverted from the purpose for which they were made; that the drafts were not negotiated until after they became due; that the plaintiff is not the *bona fide* holder, but White is, and that White got the acceptances by fraudulently pretending to be solvent when he was not so.

The plaintiff replied. The cause was referred to Gardner Stow, Esq., and tried before him. He reported in favor of the defendants, and judgment was entered against the plaintiff and for the defendants for costs, $169.61, November 28th, 1859. Plaintiff excepted to the report and appealed from the judgment.

Miles White was a manufacturer of axes at Cohoes, and the defendants were iron manufacturers at Crown Point, and in their business arrangements the defendants accepted the drafts in suit and many more for the accommodation of White. Miles White became embarrassed the last of November, 1852, and assigned December 3, 1852. The drafts in question were negotiated with H. Tator & Co., consisting of Henry Tator and George Eigenbrodt, for cash, one on the 29th October, 1852, and the other on the 30th November, 1852. Eigenbrodt swears that the firm of H. Tator & Co. did not hold the drafts in question at the time of signing the compromise paper. The compromise paper is dated March 23d, 1853. Penfield, Harwood & Co. compromised with their creditors for a large amount of liabilities on acceptances of Miles White's drafts, and intended to find and compromise all such liabilities upon the paper dated 23d March, 1853, mentioned above. In this compromise H. Tator & Co. included all the acceptances which they then claimed to own, *i. e.* two for $1,000 each. The holders of a portion of the acceptances did not sign the compromise paper. Penfield had his attention called before the date of the compromise paper, and in December, 1852, to the fact that the two acceptances in suit were outstanding and not included, and not proposed to be included in the compromise. In December, 1852, December 29th, 1852, or January 5th, 1853, H. Tator & Có., as Percy swears, and is not contradicted by any express evidence, sold and delivered these drafts to John T. Percy for $5. H. Tator was not examined as a witness at the trial, having previously died. Percy continued to hold them until September, 1853, when he sold them to R. W. Townsend, of New York, for $1,000, and took Townsend's note for that amount. A few days after that the plaintiff purchased these drafts of a man by the name of Gibbs, for $1,200, and gave his note at twelve months for that amount, and Percy advised him to make the purchase. These notes were still unpaid at the time of the trial. Percy appears to have been the principal actor and negotiator in the whole transaction. The purchase was September 20th, 1853. On the 22d the plaintiff sent the acceptances to Giles B. Kellogg, Percy's partner, to collect. Upon these facts the referee reported that the drafts were made by Miles White, and accepted by the defendants for the accommodation of Miles White. That the drafts were transferred to H. Tator & Co., in due course of dealing, for value before maturity. *But that H. Tator & Co. never sold or assigned the said bills of exchange, or parted or intended to sell or part with their interest therein, nor were the same transferred to the plaintiff, nor did he pay value therefor, nor purchase the same, nor had he any interest therein at the commencement of this action, and that the plaintiff was not entitled to recover.* The plaintiff excepted to so much of the report as is here printed in italics. Judgment having been perfected, the plaintiff appealed therefrom to the general term.

M. I. TOWNSEND, *for plaintiff, appellant.*

W. A. BEACH, *for defendants, respondents.*

By the court, HOGEBOOM, Justice. The sole question on the merits in this case is whether the plaintiff was at the commencement of the action the owner of the demand prosecuted. The referee has reported against him on this question.

The referee finds, and the undisputed testimony is, that Tator & Co. were at one time, and before maturity, the owners of the drafts in question for value. We may, therefore, take that fact for granted. It is equally clear that Tator & Co. did not compromise these demands, and that they did not attempt, intend or agree to compromise them. For although they had them when first spoken to about a compromise, they were not, in fact, embraced in the compromise, nor so supposed to be either by Tator & Co. or Penfield & Co. Nor was the compromise itself binding. It was not signed by Penfield & Co., nor by all the creditors.

The clear preponderance of evidence is, if not the undisputed fact, that at the time of the compromise, Tator & Co. did not own the demands. Tator himself was dead at the time of the trial. Eigenbrodt, his partner, expressly swears to such non-ownership, although perhaps he had no personal knowledge upon the subject. The books of Tator & Co. show the same fact. Penfield & Co. did not compromise upon the understanding that Tator & Co. then owned the drafts. In that particular, at least, they were not imposed upon, but acted with their eyes open. It is difficult to see how, under these circumstances, notwithstanding the report of the referee, Tator & Co. could now be listened to, if they claimed them, even if the statute of limitations was not in their way, for, as before stated: 1, the clear preponderance of evidence is against them; 2, they assumed not to be the owners, and so allowed Penfield & Co. to regard them; 3, they had at least authorized Percy to sell them.

They were, in fact, sold or parted with by Percy, by authority from Tator & Co., and in a manner to pass the title. It is obvious that Tator & Co. intended to part with them—to put them out of their hands so as not to have them subject to the compromise. Percy intended to purchase them—he did purchase them—such is the undisputed evidence. Percy so swears, and we must take the fact to be so, unless we are prepared to reject his evidence. The consideration was small, almost nominal, and inadequate to the real value of the drafts. But that is not decisive against the fact of transfer. I do not see but the transfer might have been gratuitous and still have been valid if the parties so clearly intended. (*Richardson* agt. *Mead*, 27 *Barb.*, 178; *Arthur* agt. *Brooks*, 14 *Barb.*, 533; *Robertson* agt. *Gardner*, 11 *Pick.*, 156; *Code*, § 111.) Whatever agreement, if any, existed between Percy and Tator, as to the ultimate proceeds, it is not proved, and we must not leave too much to mere inference. If there was any undisclosed understanding, it seems probable that it did not touch the *title* to the drafts, for Tator wanted the title out of him. The defendants should have added further evidence, if any they had upon this subject. As it stands at present, the evidence of fraud and collusion is unsatisfactory and insufficient, I think, legally to overthrow the apparent title of the plaintiff.

Nor was Percy the owner of the drafts at the time of the commencement of the action. By the uncontradicted evidence, he sold to R. W. Townsend. The consideration was adequate, and the story not improbable. It is not material, at least not decisive, that at the time of the trial Townsend's note, given for the consideration money, had not been paid. It was not then outlawed. It may have been collected afterwards or remained in *statu quo* to await an amicable adjustment after the result of this litigation. Percy was at least authorized to sell, and if he sold to Townsend, the title of Tator & Co. and of Percy passed by the act of sale.

So, also, I think it is sufficiently clear that Townsend

sold to Brown the plaintiff. Brown gave his note for the purchase money and immediately prosecuted this demand. Neither Brown's note nor Townsend's was outlawed at the time the testimony was taken. It is not improbable they may have been intended to be paid out of the proceeds of this litigation, or the payment postponed to await its event. And although there are circumstances of some suspicion arising out of this and other facts, they strike me as insufficient to overcome the case made by the plaintiff. The evidence of the transfer from Townsend to Brown is uncontradicted.

I think, therefore, the title of the plaintiff was sufficiently established, and that the referee should have reported in his favor, upon the evidence as it stood. The plaintiff had possession of the drafts; the evidence of transfer was satisfactory till contradicted. Tator & Co. do not claim the drafts; Penfield & Co. did not suppose they belonged to them; Percy does not claim the drafts, and would be estopped by his evidence if he did; Townsend makes no claim to the drafts. So far as the evidence shows, no one else claims them but the plaintiff—Penfield & Co. certainly owe them.

I think the evidence of the proposed compromise and agreement was properly admitted. The question was one of fraud and of actual transfer, and all evidence fairly bearing on that question was properly admissible. The participation of H. Tator & Co., in the compromise, was admissible: 1, to show that they had in fact compromised, and then owned the drafts; 2, to show a motive on their part for a fraudulent attempt to pass off the drafts to Percy, and thus avoid the effect of a compromise; 3, motives and probabilities are proper subjects of inquiry in cases of alleged fraud.

In my opinion the judgment entered upon the report of the referee should be reversed and a new trial granted, and under the circumstances I think with costs to abide the event of the action. 1. The referee not only decided against the weight of evidence, but erred in the application of the rules of law; 2, the plaintiff being in the possession of negotiable paper with apparent title, and no contradictory evidence to overthrow it, showed a legal right to recover; 3, a wrong result upon undisputed evidence is an error of law.

GOULD, J., concurred.

PECKHAM, J., dissented.

SUPREME COURT.

SUSANNAH B. YOUNG, administratrix, &c. agt. JAMES H. BRUSH and others, executors, &c.

Where the *domicil* of the testatrix was in New York—all the *personal estate* was in New York; the will was *proved* and letters testamentary *issued* in New York, *Held*, that the *legatees* of the personal estate were not chargeable with the expenses of proving and contesting the will in New Jersey, where the deceased had real estate. The decree of the court in New Jersey, directing such expenses to be paid out of the estate, had no force or validity here, and could not make these expenses chargeable to the legatees under the will, in this state.

Where, in an action for accounting against executors, the trust fund has been deposited in the *Trust Company*, *under the direction of the referee*, to be applied to the payment of any recovery in the action, the executors will not be charged with a higher rate of *interest* than that paid by the Trust Company.

New York General Term, *October*, 1862.

INGRAHAM, BARNARD and CLERKE, *Justices*.

By the court, INGRAHAM, P. Justice. The defendants, in the settlement of the account of their testator as the executors of Catharine Young, claim to be allowed the expenses of proving the will in New Jersey. All the personal estate was in New York. The will was proved in New York, and letters testamentary issued here. Afterwards Mr. Brush, the executor, submitted the will for probate in New Jersey, where the deceased owned some real estate. The probate was contested there, and a large amount of expense was incurred. These expenses were claimed by the defendants as a credit, and disallowed by the referee.

The referee has found that the domicil of the testatrix was in New York, and that the will was properly admitted to probate here, and that the decision on the will in New Jersey was only as to the real estate.

We see no reason for submitting the will to probate in New Jersey, excepting so far as the devisees of the real estate there might consider it necessary for establishing their title to the same. For this purpose the executor was not called upon to prove the will. Any party relying on it as the source of his title, could prove it on a trial, by witnesses, with the same effect as if admitted to probate, if not more.

There is no ground upon which such an expense should fall upon the legatees of the personal estate in New York.

The distribution of the personal estate was properly found to be according to the laws of New York, and the decree of the court in New Jersey, directing these expenses to be paid out of the estate, had no force or validity here, and could not make these expenses chargeable to the legatees under the will in this state.

The question of domicil was a question of fact for the referee. With his finding we would not interfere, even if we doubted the correctness of that decision. But we concur with him in that finding, because we consider the weight of evidence upon this point very much against the defendants.

The only point upon which we entertain doubt is, as to the charge of legal interest against the executor on the moneys deposited with the Trust Company.

Under ordinary circumstances where the defendant refuses to pay over moneys held by him in a fiduciary character, he should be charged with interest, and the fact of its being deposited for safe keeping in a bank or trust company, does not relieve the trustee from such liability, even though he receives a less rate of interest. (*DePeyster* agt. *Clarkson*, 2 *Wend.*, 77.) But where the money has been kept ready to be paid over, then interest is not to be charged. (11 *Paige*, 142.)

In the present case the money was deposited in the Trust Company under the direction of the referee, and with the consent of the defendants' counsel, as to the propriety of the place of deposit to be applied to the payment of any recovery in the action. As the defendants were executors, and the money was deposited under the direction of the referee, it is clear that the defendants could receive no benefit from the fund. Nor does it appear that any demand was made for the payment of this sum other than is to be inferred from the commencement of the suit which called for an accounting first. Under all the circumstances we think the defendants should not have been charged with a higher rate of interest than was received for the fund while it was deposited in the Trust Company.

The judgment should be corrected by the plaintiff's remitting the amount of interest charged on $3,700 over three per cent., and affirmed for the residue.

If the plaintiff refuse to remit the amount, the judgment must be set aside and case referred back to referee for correction in this respect.

Clerke and Barnard, J. J., concurred.

UNITED STATES COURT.

Betsey Cowen, administratrix of Esek Cowen, deceased, agt. David Banks and others.

Where an action for the infringement of a *copy right* of a publication was brought by the *assignees* thereof, and an issue of ownership was raised on the trial, upon which the author and assignor as a witness testified that by the agreement pro-

duced, "the intention was to convey deponent's whole interest in the copy right of the work; I supposed the book to belong to my assignees, as soon as made, including all that was in it,"

Held, that this testimony *estopped* the legal representatives of the author from subsequently claiming that the agreement was intended to be confined to the *first fourteen years' limitation of the copy right*, under which it was made, especially as the testimony was given after the expiration of such limitation to a portion of the work.

United States Circuit Court, New York, Nov. 1862.

THE bill is filed in this case by the complainant, to compel the defendants to account and pay over to her moneys received by them on the sales of the nine volumes of Cowen's reports since the expiration of the copy rights of Goulds & Banks, which, it is charged, expired on the 26th of April, 1838, 13th of November, 1843, and at various dates intermediate these two periods.

F. F. MARBURY, *solicitor for complainant.*

W. A. BEACH and WM. ALLEN BUTLER, *counsel.*

BANKS & ANDERSON, *solicitors for D. Banks.*

CHARLES O'CONOR, *counsel for Banks and ex'rs of A. Gould.*

OTIS ALLEN, *solicitor for W. Gould.*

JOHN K. PORTER, *counsel.*

S. D. LAW, *solicitor for ex'rs of Anthony Gould.*

NELSON, C. J. These copy rights were taken out under the act of 1790, which secured to the author or his assigns the exclusive proprietary right to the book or books during the term of fourteen years; and further provided, that if, at the expiration of the said term, the author be living, the same exclusive right should continue to him, his executors, administrators or assigns for the further term of fourteen years, provided he or they should take out a second copy right for the period.

The 16th section of the act of 1831 extended the term to the author or proprietor of the book, already copy-righted, to the period of twenty-eight years, unconditionally, if the author was living at the time of the passage of the act. Judge COWEN was living at the passage of the act, and the bill charges that, according to the true construction of the articles of agreement, transferring the copy right of these books to Gould & Banks, the proprietary right was limited to the first term of fourteen years, under the act of 1790; and that at the expiration of this period the right became vested in the author, under and by virtue of the 16th section of the act of 1831. The construction is denied by the defendants. On the contrary, they insist that the transfer embraced the contingent right to the additional term of fourteen years, under the act of 1790, which became absolute in them under the act of 1831.

We are satisfied, on a careful consideration of the provisions of this agreement, that the construction insisted upon by the complainant is the true one; and that if there was nothing else in the case, she would be entitled to the decree prayed for. But the defendants have filed a cross bill, in which they charge that, according to the true intent and understanding of the parties in the transfer at the time of the agreement, the assignees were to be entitled to the entire proprietary right, including the contingent interest of the author to the second term of fourteen years as well as the first; and hence, that they became the absolute proprietors of this term under the act of 1831, and they ask that the agreement be reformed so as to conform to the understanding and intent of the parties.

By a stipulation in the record, a deposition of Judge COWEN, taken 3d October, 1840, in a case pending between those claiming this proprietary interest in the reports, and one H. P. Hastings charged as violating their copy rights, is admitted as evidence. Judge COWEN was examined as a witness for the complainant; and an objection was taken to his testimony on the ground of interest. He was first examined on his *voire dire*, the agreement in question having been produced before him. He stated that this was the only contract between him and the assignees of the copy rights, and that "the intention was to convey deponent's whole interest in the copy right of the work." And on his examination-in-chief, he observes: "I supposed the book to belong to my assignees as soon as made, including all that was in it. I would not have taken the office of reporter, with its salary and duties, unless I was to have had a proprietary right which I could use or dispose of."

At the time of this examination, and the objection on the ground of interest taken to the witness, the first term of four of the first volumes had expired, and the proprietary right had become vested in him absolutely, unless parted with by the assignment. Judge COWEN's attention, therefore, was called directly to the fact of the understanding and intention of the parties at the time of the making the agreement of transfer. His testimony accords with his own practical construction of it, for, some two years had elapsed at the time after the expiration of the first term, as we have seen in respect to the four first volumes, and he had set up no claim to the copy right. He died 20th January, 1844, some three years after the expiration of the first term of the copy right of the last volume, and had all this time acquiesced in the claim of the assignees. Conceding, therefore, that, according to the terms of the written agreement of transfer, the assignees obtained a right to the term of fourteen years to the nine volumes of reports, yet, in view of the bill to reform the contract and make it conform to the true intent and understanding of the parties to the instrument at the time of entering into it, and the testimony of Judge COWEN, we do not see how we can avoid reforming the contract so as to give effect to the real agreement of the parties. The testimony of the witness is not an opinion expressed as to the construction of the instrument, but as to the question whether or not he was interested in the second term of the copy right of these books. He was not examined upon a question of law, but upon a question of fact; and in this view, and in the face of the claim of the complainants in that suit to a full title in the second term, then running, he testified that he had conveyed his whole interest to them. The evidence of Judge COWEN, under the circumstances in which it was given, is wholly inconsistent and irreconcileable with the idea that the parties, at the time the agreement was entered into, understood and intended a conveyance of a copy right only for the first fourteen years.

For these reasons we think a decree must be entered for the complainants in the cross bill, according to its prayer, to reform the contract, and for the defendants in the original bill.

COURT OF APPEALS.

THE REFORMED PROTESTANT DUTCH CHURCH OF WESTFIELD, STATEN ISLAND agt. SUSAN D. BROWN, executrix of DAVID BROWN, deceased.

Where the decision of a referee *on a question of fact* is affirmed by the court at general term, it is *conclusive;* that question cannot be reviewed by this court.

Where an individual at the formation of a *religious society*, promises by *subscription* to pay a certain sum towards the erection of a church edifice, and a further yearly sum for the support of the minister, the contract is binding, notwithstanding the society was not legally *incorporated* until some time afterwards, and the church edifice was not then completed.

It is not necessary that the *promise* by the subscription should be to or with the society in its *corporate capacity*. The society on becoming incorporated is, through its trustees, vested under the statute with authority to demand and receive the subscription.

September Term, 1861.

THIS action was brought against the defendant as executrix of David Brown, deceased, to recover $500 upon a subscription by the testator for the erection of the church edifice of the plaintiffs; also $100 subscribed by him towards the salary of the minister. The referee, by his report, found the following facts: That the plaintiffs are a religious society, duly organized and incorporated according to the laws of this state, as "The Reformed Protestant Dutch Church of Westfield, Staten Island." That David Brown was, on or about the 26th day of February, 1849, indebted to the plaintiffs in the sum of $600, as follows: $500 upon and as a subscription to build a house of worship for the plaintiffs, The Reformed Protestant Dutch Church of Westfield, Staten Island, which sum the said David Brown promised and agreed to give and pay towards the erection and building of the said church edifice, and a sum of $100 a year for the support and maintenance of a minister of the gospel for said church. That afterwards, and after the church edifice had become nearly completed, the said Brown again promised and agreed to give and pay towards the erection and building of the said church edifice the sum of $500, and the said sum of $100 a year for the support and maintenance of a minister of the gospel for said church, and expressly waived the operation and force of a clause in an article of agreement or statement made and signed on the 9th day of April, 1849, in relation to the indebtedness of the church. That the said David Brown was repeatedly called upon to pay the plaintiffs the sum of $600, but did not pay the same. That the plaintiffs were legally incorporated as a church, on the 11th day of September, 1849, and the act of corporation and certificate of election of officers of the church or society was duly and legally acknowledged, and was recorded on the 31st day of June, 1851, in the office of the clerk of Richmond county, and that the original formation of the said society and subscription was on the 26th day of February, 1849. That the said church was so completed and used, as was intended, for public worship, a minister employed, and the society was free from debt, within the meaning of the article of April 9, 1849, signed by David Brown and others. That said Brown had departed this life, leaving sufficient assets to pay all debts owing by him, and that on or about the 3d day of February, 1853, letters testamentary on his estate were granted and committed unto his widow, Susan D. Brown, executrix named in the last will and testament of said David Brown, deceased. And that such executrix entered upon her duties as such, was duly qualified, took possession of the goods, chattels and credits of said David Brown, deceased, according to law, and that she had sufficient money in her possession, arising from the estate of the said David Brown, deceased, to pay all debts due from the estate; and that the plaintiffs' demand, as set forth in the complaint, had been repeatedly presented to said executrix for payment, and payment demanded, previous to the commencement of this action, and that she had neglected and refused to pay the same; and that there is now due from Susan D. Brown, executrix of David Brown, deceased, to the plaintiffs, the sum of $959.33, for principal and interest, as claimed in the complaint. From the facts so found and reported by him, he decided and reported as matters of law, that the plaintiffs were entitled to judgment against the defendant, as such executrix, for the sum of $959.33, together with costs. For which sum judgment was entered, at a special term, in favor of the plaintiffs.

An appeal was taken by the defendant to the general term, where the judgment at special term was affirmed, (*see* 17 *How. Pr. R.*, 287, *and* 29 *Barb.*, 335.) From this judgment the defendant appealed to this court.

J. S. L. Cummins, *for appellant.*

1st. The referee erred in finding that David Brown, deceased, was indebted to the plaintiffs, on the 26th day of February, 1849, in the sum of $100, with interest from that day, which he had "promised and agreed to give for the support and maintenance of a minister of the gospel for said church."

Because there was no minister connected with the church

during the period laid in the complaint. (*See Com., fol.* 6–98; *Case, fol.* 59; *Martin* agt. *Hynd, Doug.*, 142; *Cowp.*, 437.)

2d. The referee erred in finding that plaintiff was legally incorporated as a church on the eleventh day of September, 1849.

In order to be legally incorporated, it was necessary that a certificate of incorporation should be signed, acknowledged and recorded, and then, and not until then, they became a corporation. (1 *R. S., chap.* 18, *title* 5, *art.* 1*st*, *sec.* 2, *last ed.*; *The First Baptist Society* agt. *Rapalee*, 16 *Wend., p.* 605.)

In this case the certificate was signed on the 11th of September, 1849, but not acknowledged or recorded until the thirtieth day of June, 1851.

3d. The church not being, at the time of the subscription incorporated, it could not be a party to a contract; therefore the contract with David Brown could not have been made with plaintiffs, nor has it been assigned to them.

4th. There was no act of David Brown, deceased, after the plaintiffs became incorporate, from which an implied request on the part of the testator to the plaintiffs could be raised to proceed on the faith of the original promise, or from which an implied promise to reimburse plaintiffs could be raised.

In all the cases relied on by the court below, there were such acts, or there was a promise to pay when the company was organized, and the cases turned upon such implied requests and promises. (*The Hamilton & Deansville Plank Road Co.* agt. *Rice*, 7 *Barb. S. C. R., p.* 159.)

The "certificate of stock was made out and delivered, and he accepted it," and the case turned upon such delivery and acceptance. (*Stanton, Pres.*, agt. *Wilson*, 2 *Hill*, 153.) In this case the articles "declared that the association should commence on 1st January, 1839," and the subscribers engaged "to pay to the directors or such person or persons as they should appoint."

The court held, Cowen, J., that "in legal effect, then, the contract of the defendant was made on the first of January, and was then to pay the corporation the amount subscribed." (*Trustees of Farmington Academy* agt. *Allen*, 14 *Mass. R.*, 172; *The Limerick Academy* agt. *Davis*, 11 *Mass.*, 113; *Scotts' Charitable Society* agt. *Shaw*, 8 *Mass.*, 532; *Comin's Dig.*, *tit. Action upon the case upon assumpsit*, *f.* 8; *Stewart* agt. *Hamilton Col.*, 2 *Denio*, 417.)

5th. There is no promise contained in the book of subscriptions for a Reformed Dutch Church in Westfield, Staten Island, to pay the corporation after incorporate, or, in fact, to pay any one. The subscription was not absolute, but merely "a preliminary step" to ascertain whether they would "be warranted in proceeding with the undertaking."

6th. By the terms of the agreement, they were not to proceed with the building unless they had "money in hand sufficient to cover the entire expense of the building." This they did not have, and therefore David Brown, deceased, was not bound to pay his subscription.

7th. By the terms of the agreement, the church was to be free from debt, but it was not at the time of its completion, and never had been.

John Fitch, *for respondent.*

I. The complaint shows the amount claimed,—the subscriptions,—the death of Brown,—the fact of leaving ample assets,—the fact that Susan D. Brown is executrix, &c., &c., with sufficient money in her possession, &c., &c., —the proper demand, &c.,—her refusal to pay; plaintiff an incorporation. The complaint, at folios 5 and 6, sets forth the way and manner the debt accrued,—the facts in relation thereto,—the promises and agreements of the said Brown in his lifetime,—the building of the church,—the employment of a pastor, and all that was requisite and necessary to do in the premises; the fact of the subscriptions, and the non-payment thereof, &c. &c., and all the necessary averments.

The answer is a general denial, as it were, of the several allegations set forth in the complaint.

II. The proof on the part of the plaintiff is perfect, complete and undisputed.

The documentary proofs are,—1. Proof of demand of plaintiff's account. 2. Original subscription books, in Brown's own handwriting. 3. Original subscription roll for a minister, &c., in Brown's handwriting. 4. The application for incorporation, &c., &c., the election of officers, &c., &c. 5. The organization as a church. 6. Memorandum, showing the way the account stood, and a statement of facts. 7. A request of the defendant's lawyer for a copy of the plaintiff's claim and demand in the suit, and to see the subscriptions, &c. 8. The death of Brown, and appointment of defendant as executrix, &c., and assets in the hands of executrix, all admitted. The estate of Brown was about eight hundred thousand dollars. 9. The exemplified copy of the appointment, &c., of the defendant as executrix.

The oral testimony of the witnesses, Jessup and Prall, is clear and positive, and shows the entire history of the transactions.

III. The fact of Brown's waiving all the reservations in regard to a debt on the church, and directing the officers to go on and finish the church, is clearly proved. This was after the filing of the article of incorporation. The church had become an incorporation, and all the work was done and paid for; the fact that the church was out of debt, Jessup footed the balance and paid all the bills, is clearly proven.

It was after all this had been done, that Brown frequently told those in charge of the erection of the church edifice "to go on and finish it, and he would pay his subscription."

On the 30th day of June, 1851, the articles of incorporation were duly acknowledged, filed and recorded in the office of the clerk of the county of Richmond, but made and executed 11th September, A. D. 1849, and acted upon by plaintiff as well as by Brown.

The church was finished in 1851, say 10th November, 1851. Brown left Staten Island in the fall of 1851. Jessup and Prall found him in New York, in Columbia street, the same fall after he left the Island, and then he again promised to pay up and settle the subscription.

After the 28th of October, when $1,898.75 had been paid out, for on the 2d November, 1851, only $1,222.40 had been collected, Jessup had paid all the bills, and he with Prall went in search of Brown for money; when Brown again (as he had done repeatedly before) promised to pay. Acting upon the faith of it, as they had done previously, they had purchased timber; and after the $1,000 were paid in by the Collegiate Church, Jessup footed the entire bill of $358.44, which Brown's subscriptions would have paid with everything, and a little surplus over. Brown told them, at the conversation in the fall of 1851, to "go on and get your subscriptions and build the church," &c. They did so. Jessup and Prall had a right to suppose Brown would pay his subscription. And with his subscription the church would have been clear of debt, with a little surplus over.

The purchasing the last bill of lumber, the obtaining the $1,000.00 from the Collegiate Dutch Church, the calling on Brown with Exhibit "No. 6," the paying up by Jessup of the $358.44, were all in the fall of 1851; Brown knew of, and approved, and assented to the whole of those transactions. He saw Exhibit "No. 6" about the month of September or October; he was pleased with what had been done, and promised to pay his subscriptions.

IV. The paper at folio 21 was a *preliminary* paper, without date, to be in force if money enough was raised, &c. Money enough was subscribed, and it must be considered as a paper bearing date as of the day the articles of incorporation were filed in the county clerk's office, June 30th, 1851: all the papers should be considered one instrument, and form the articles of incorporation, as in the case of the *Troy & Rutland Railroad Company.*

This case is similar to the case of "*Lake Ontario Railroad Co.* agt. *Mason,*" *at page* 463: "Until the incorporation of the Company (church) was perfected, the other subscribers had an interest in its execution and performance, of which they could not be deprived by the act of the defendant. After the articles were filed, and the church had a legal existence, it acquired a vested interest in the defendant's agreement. (9 *Barb.*, 202; 15 *id.*, 249; 1 *Kernan*, 102; 2 *id.*, 18; 2 *Hill*, 135.)

In *Small* agt. *Herkimer Manufacturing Co.*, (2 *Comstock*, 330,) the court of appeals held, "The subscription must be construed, therefore, as if all the provisions of the statute affecting the liability of the subscriber, or his title to the stock purchased by him, were by him incorporated in his agreement."

It was of no consequence to any one when the articles of incorporation were filed. For "a subscription made before a corporation is *in esse* with a view to a future incorporation is binding; and the corporation when organized can sustain an action upon it," 29 *Barb.*, 335; 7 *id.*, 157; *and at page* 153 *in* 2 *Hill, and at p.* 172 *in* 14 *Mass. R.*, the court held that "A recovery may be had on such subscriptions when no company or corporation was in existence at the time."

In the 7th *Barbour, at page* 165, the court says, "In the case of money subscriptions for charitable purposes, which embrace donations for religious or literary institutions, it has been held that there was no necessity for a personal pecuniary benefit to be derived by the subscription." The same doctrine is held in 6 *Pickering*, 427, and by the court of appeals, 2 *Kernan, p.* 24.

In 2 *Denio, page* 417, the court held, "The mutual promises of the several subscribers constitute the consideration;" and 2 *Denio*, 45, is cited to show that "The church to be created was a valid consideration, and the subscription binding," as in 2 *Hill*, 153; 14 *Mass. R.*, 172.

So far as Brown was concerned, he acted under the articles of incorporation from their date of execution, viz., September 11th, 1849, and frequently waived all reservations in the papers, and proceedings affirmed, and was pleased with all they did, and always intended to pay his subscriptions.

This subscription was for a religious society. It belongs to the church corporation; and the corporation is the legal owner and holder thereof, being the real party in interest. Therefore, this suit was correctly brought in the corporate name of the church. (*Code* § 111; 9 *Barbour, at p.* 206; 2 *Denio*, 417; 3 *Pickering*, 325.)

V. As to the consideration of the $100 subscription for the minister, they had preaching in 1849, in the schoolhouse, and for six months previous to the 4th day of May, 1849, the gospel had been preached for about six months, with steadily increasing attendance and interest.

Rev. J. A. M. Latourette was a brother-in-law of Mr. Brown. Another minister was called on the 9th September, 1851.

On the 10th of September, 1851, they called on Brown, and showed him the Exhibit "No. 6." He was then satisfied, and promised to pay his subscription; which would, as Jessup swears, have paid up all, and left a surplus in the treasury.

On the 10th day of September, 1851, they got $1,000 from the Collegiate Church; and that was the time they called upon Brown, as by Exhibit "No. 6." They received $358.44 more, and Brown's $500 would have paid up all and left a surplus.

The preaching of the gospel is a sufficient consideration to sustain the subscription of the sum of $100.00 yearly, for the support of the minister. (7 *Johnson*, 112; 20 *id.*,

12.) And Brown's signature to the original papers authorized, by statute, the giving of them in evidence. (*Laws* 1833, *ch.* 271, § 9; 20 *Johnson*, 12; 7 *id.*, 112.)

No objection or exception taken to the testimony of either of the witnesses, or to the introduction of any of the Exhibits.

VI. The referee found, as a matter of fact and law, that there was due to the plaintiffs, &c., by the defendant, &c., the sum of $959.33, and costs, and that the church was free from debt, within the meaning of the article of April 9, 1849, &c., and found all the facts as proven by the plaintiff.

This is a finding of the referee upon a question of fact, where the facts were undisputed; and the finding of the referee is in all respects in strict accordance with the admissions, proofs, exhibits, and for the amount proven to be due. It is, in all respects, the same as the finding of a jury; and there is no reason to disturb it. It comes within the rule laid down by the court of appeals, in *Davis* agt. *Allen*, (3 *Coms.*, 168, *and the cases there cited; see also*, 23 *Barb.*, 561.)

The costs in this case were given by authority of the court, under the Code, (§ 317;) see order of the special term, September 17th, 1857, in this cause. Such an order should have been appealed from, as an order of a special term, and cannot be reviewed or reversed on this appeal. (*See Code*, § 350.)

There was no departure, by the officers of the church, in the building thereof, as in any way or manner released Brown from either of his subscriptions; and his subsequent waiver of any such change or alterations of their agreement, not to have a debt upon them, and his express directions to them to "go on, and complete the church," brings this case within the rule laid down in *Troy & Rutland R. R. Co.* agt. *Kerr*, and in the case *Fort Edward & Fort Miller Railroad* agt. *Paine*, (17 *Barb. S. C. R.*, *pp.* 567 *and* 607, *and the great number of cases therein cited in each case; see also*, 23 *Barb.*, 436.)

The plaintiff was duly organized and incorporated, according to the laws of this state, by virtue of the act entitled "An Act for the Incorporation of Religious Societies," passed April 5, 1813, sess. 36, ch. 60, 3d vol. R. S., 2d ed., 206, § 2, as to Dutch churches. The certificate was properly acknowledged and recorded. (*Methodist Union Epis. Church* agt. *Picket*, 23 *Barb.*, 436; *New Clerk's Assistant*, *p.* 99, *as to the form of the certificate*; 11 *Wend.*, 604.)

By the court, LOTT, J. The decision of the referee having been affirmed by the supreme court, is conclusive on the question of fact in this case. (*Code*, § 272; *Borst* agt. *Spellman*, 4 *Coms.*, 284–289; *Dunham* agt. *Watkins*, 2 *Kern.*, 556–560; *Griffin* agt. *Marquardt*, 17 *N. Y. R.*, 28; *Hoyt* agt. *Thompson's ex'r*, 19 *id.*, 207–211; *Miller* agt. *Schuyler*, 20 *id.*, 522, *&c.*; *Carman* agt. *Pultz*, 21 *id.*, 547.) We must therefore assume the facts found by the referee to be correctly found; and as no exceptions appear to have been taken to any decision relative to the admissibility of evidence, or otherwise, during the process of the trial, the only question to be considered is, whether those facts justified the conclusion of law to which the referee arrived.

It appears by his finding, that a religious society was formed on the 26th day of February, 1849; that it was subsequently incorporated as a church in due form by the name of The Reformed Protestant Dutch Church of Westfield, Staten Island, and that the said corporation is the plaintiff in this action; that David Brown, the testator of the defendant, on the day of the formation of the society, promised and agreed, by subscriptions made by him, to give and pay the sum of five hundred dollars towards the erection and building of a church, and the further sum of one hundred dollars a year for the support and maintenance of a minister of the gospel for said church, and that he afterwards, and after the church building had been nearly completed, again promised and agreed to give and pay the said sums for the objects specified, and expressly waived the operation and force of a clause in an article of agreement, on a statement made and signed on the 9th day of April, 1849, in relation to the indebtedness of the church, (the nature of which does not, however, appear;) that Brown has departed this life, leaving sufficient assets to pay all debts owing by him, and that on or about the 3d day of February, 1853, letters testamentary on his estate were granted to the defendant; that she has assumed the duties of executrix; that the plaintiffs' demand, as set forth in the complaint, has been repeatedly presented to her for payment previous to the commencement of this action, and that she has neglected and refused to pay the same.

These are all the facts I deem pertinent or material to the question to be considered by this court. Whether the plaintiffs were incorporated on the 11th day of September, 1849, as found and decided by the referee, or on the 31st day of June, 1851, when the certificate of incorporation was acknowledged and recorded, as claimed by the counsel of the defendant, is wholly immaterial. They were in fact incorporated long before the commencement of this suit.

The facts above stated do not show, nor is it expressly found by the referee, to or with whom the promise or agreement of Brown was made; but it does appear that it was made at the time of the formation of the society, and that it was made by subscription. It will, therefore, in the absence of an express statement or finding, be presumed on appeal, that it was a legal subscription in and by which he, in some way, legally obligated himself to pay the sums subscribed for the use and benefit of the society, and in carrying out the objects contemplated. This presumption is fully warranted by the rule laid down by this court in *Carman* agt. *Pultz*, (*supra*,) "that error on the part of the court below will not be presumed, but must be made clearly to appear. Hence it is incumbent upon the appellant to take care so to present the facts upon which the case depends, as to show affirmatively that an error has been committed. This court will presume nothing in favor of the party alleging the error, but if compelled, through the imperfection of the statement of facts, to resort to presumptions at all, will adopt such only as will sustain the judgment;" and "where, as in this case, there is an evident omission of important facts in the statement or report, we must presume these facts to have been such as would warrant the judgment rendered."

I will only add, that it was not necessary that the promise or agreement should be to or with the plaintiffs in their corporate capacity. The general statute regulating the incorporation of religious societies, (3 *R. S.*, *p.* 282,) expressly provides by section 4, that the trustees of every church, after it is incorporated, are authorized and empowered to take possession of all the temporalities belonging to the church, whether given, granted or devised directly to the church, or to any other person for its use, and also in its corporate name to sue and recover, hold and enjoy all the debts, demands, rights and privileges belonging thereto, in whatsoever manner the same may be held, as fully and as amply as if the right or title thereto had originally been vested in the said trustees.

The plaintiffs, therefore, on becoming incorporated, became vested with the right to demand from Brown the amount of his subscription. (*See, also*, 2 *Hill*, 153; 7 *Barb.*, 157, *and* 14 *Mass. Rep.*, 172, *cited by the supreme court.*)

There is nothing in the facts disclosed by the referee's decision, which requires or demands the interposition of any technical rule of law to defeat the benevolent or religious intentions of the testator in forwarding the good work and enterprise to which he became a liberal subscriber.

Those facts, on the contrary, imposed a legal duty, and the referee has properly decided, and his decision and the judgment thereon should be affirmed, with costs.

SUPREME COURT.

THE REFORMED PROTESTANT DUTCH CHURCH OF WESTFIELD, STATEN ISLAND agt. SUSAN D. BROWN, executrix of DAVID BROWN, deceased.

No *term fees* ($10) can be allowed in a cause in the court of appeals, *before the return is filed.*

THE appeal to the court of appeals in this cause was taken, the undertaking and justification, &c. filed in the month of June, 1859, and the respondent's attorney noticed the same regularly, in good faith, seven terms consecutively, until it was argued. The respondent's attorney supposed, from a letter received from the clerk, that the return was duly filed with the clerk of the court of appeals, on the 13th September, 1859, until April, 1860, when he received another letter from the clerk, stating that he had given the respondent's attorney wrong information respecting the filing of the return in this cause; that it was another similar cause which he referred to in his first letter; that the return in this cause was not then filed. Whereupon, in April, 1860, the respondent's attorney served a notice on the attorneys of the appellant to file the return within ten days, &c.; which notice was complied with. After the decision of the cause in the court of appeals, in April, 1861, affirming the judgment of the supreme court, and after the filing the remittitur, the respondent's attorney served the adverse attorneys with a bill of costs in the court of appeals, in which he charged $50, five term fees, three of which terms were notices of argument before the return was filed. The sum of $30, for these three terms, was stricken from the bill on taxation, and the respondent appealed.

JOHN FITCH, *for plaintiff and respondent.*

I. The appeal in this cause was taken, and the bond filed, justified, &c. &c., in the month of June, A. D. 1859—in the same month that the notice of the judgment, &c. of the supreme court was given.

1. By rules 2 and 7 of the court of appeals, the appeal is perfected when the appeal and undertaking are both properly filed, &c. &c., as the facts may happen. The appeal absolute. The undertaking on stay of proceedings in certain cases—all of which had been done in this case. (*Rules* 2 *and* 7, *court of appeals; Thompson* agt. *Blanchard*, 4 *How.*, 210.)

2. By the 2d rule of this court, the return must be filed within twenty days after the appeal is perfected. And the court of appeals, in case of *Spoore* agt. *Fannan*, (2 *Smith's* 16 *N. Y. R.*, 620,) say: "The appellant must see to it, at his peril, that the return is actually filed in time."

3. The cause is necessarily on the calendar, so far as the respondent is concerned, when the appeal is perfected. The appellant must, at his own peril, attend to his own case. The respondent is not required to put it on the calendar. The cause was at issue. (16 *Smith's N. Y. R.*, 620; 9 *How. Pr. R.*, 333.)

4. It is and has been the uniform practice to allow the term fees from the time the causes at circuit are at issue and noticed. The cause on general term calendar and court of appeals, from time of perfecting the appeal. It is the appellant's duty to see that the appeal is ready to be argued as soon as it is at issue. Term fees begin when cause at issue. (9 *How. Pr. R.*, 333,; 2 *Abb.*, 255.)

5. A cause is on the calendar necessarily, when it is ready for trial. (*Code*, § 307, *sub.* 8; 9 *How. Pr. R.*, 332.)

6. The $15 and the $10 are both allowed, as it is on the final judgment in the court of appeals, before notice of argument, the same as before notice of trial. (*Phipps and others* agt. *Van Cott*, 15 *How. Pr. R.*, 110, *general term.*) Notice of argument is the same as notice of trial. (15 *How. Pr. R.*, 122.)

7. Respondent's attorney put the cause on the calendar,

so far as he could, by filing the notice of argument, with proof of service, with the clerk of the court of appeals; and the clerk thought that the cause "*Church* agt. *Brown*" was this cause.

8. The order of Mr. Justice BARNARD is irregular. No appeal from the taxation was ever made to the special term from the adjustment of the clerk.

J. S. L. CUMMINS, *for defendant and appellant.*

BARNARD, Justice. The Code makes no provision for taxing as costs in court of appeals, any other sums than $25, before argument; $50 for argument, and $10 term fees. The first two items in the bill were properly disallowed.

An appeal to the court of appeals is not properly or necessarily on the calendar till the return is filed. Until that is done, the court would not hear the case, and it could not be reached on the calendar till after the return is filed, because by rule 8 the date of filing of the return is the date of the issue. Rule 2 provides a remedy in case the appellent does not file his return, which is by motion to dismiss. This motion was not on the calendar. Unless a cause is in a situation to be heard when reached, it is neither necessarily nor properly on the calendar. Under the rule, a cause cannot be placed on the calendar until the return is filed.

For all the terms at which this cause was noticed prior to the filing of the return, no term fees can be allowed.

The bill as taxed must be reduced $30, charged for term fees prior to filing the return; also $4 for error, in addition by taxing officer, of $10 and $15. The items of $1 and $1.38 should also be deducted in case the costs be paid without entry of judgment.

Affirmed at general term, October, 1862, INGRAHAM, LEONARD and BARNARD, Justices.

SUPREME COURT.

SOPHIA JOSEPHINE ANABLE, an infant, by HIRAM W. DIXON, her guardian agt. JOHN C. ANABLE.

In an action for *divorce for adultery* by an infant plaintiff, the complaint is properly *verified by her guardian*. But the defendant may put in his answer *without verification*. Under the statute, he can not be compelled to be a witness in any case where he would be exposed to a *penalty or forfeiture*.

Albany Special Term, November, 1861.

THIS is an action by the complainant for a divorce from her husband on the ground of adultery of defendant, and plaintiff moves for a reference on the ground that defendant has made default. The complaint is on oath, and defendant has put in an answer without oath, claiming the right to do so. Plaintiff returned the answer because it was not verified. The complaint was sworn to by the guardian, and not by the infant.

C. P. COLLIER, *for motion*.
JOHN GAUL, JR., *opposed*.

PECKHAM, Justice. The first objection to this motion, that the complaint is not properly verified, being by the guardian instead of the infant, is not well founded. For this purpose, the guardian may be regarded as *the* plaintiff or *a* plaintiff. He is so as to the general proceedings in the cause. (*Hill* agt. *Thacter*, 3 *How.*, 407; *Van Santvoord's Pr.*, 374; *V. S. Eq. Pr.*, 111; *Whittaker's Pr.*, *vol.* 1, *p.* 333.) He verifies it in such case as a *party*, not as *agent* or *attorney* of the party.

It is next objected that the defendant is not compelled to be a witness, and cannot be compelled, therefore, to verify his answer. That he is privileged from testifying as a witness. I think this objection is well taken. It is provided by statute, that a witness shall not be required to "give any answer which will have a tendency to accuse him of any crime or misdemeanor, or to *expose* him to any penalty or forfeiture." (2 *R. S.*, 405, § 90 [§ 71.]) This is substantially the common law. (*People* agt. *Mather*, 4 *Wend.*, 230; *Sweet* agt. *Sweet*, 15 *How.*, 169, *and cases there cited.*) The loss of an estate in lands is a penalty or forfeiture within the meaning of this prohibition. By the act of 1860, if a wife die intestate, the husband will have the right to hold and enjoy all real estate left by his wife, till the youngest child becomes of age, and a life estate in one-third thereof thereafter; a life estate in one-third in any event, whether she die intestate or with or without children. (*Laws* 1860, *p.* 169, §§ 10, 11.) If his testimony "will have a tendency to expose him to a forfeiture" of this right, then he cannot be required to be a witness or to verify his answer. It is said, and perhaps correctly, that the statute which bars a wife's dower for adultery, does not apply to the husband, (3 *R. S.*, 5*th ed.*, 237, § 61,) and at common law adultery does not work a forfeiture. (*Reynolds* agt. *Reynolds*, 24 *Wend.*, 193.) But the Revised Statutes expressly provide that upon the dissolution of the marriage contract, at the instance of the wife for the husband's adultery, all her real estate, goods or things in action, however obtained, "shall be her sole and absolute property." (2 *R. S.*, 5*th ed.*, 237, § 59 [§ 46.]) This provision is entirely equal to the provision as to the forfeiture by the wife. It is left untouched and unrepealed by the new provisions for the husband by the act of 1860. It is insisted that a husband is compelled to testify, though his testimony will degrade him if it be material to the issue. This is true, probably, but has no application to testimony that may expose to a forfeiture. It is also insisted that the act of 1860 makes husband and wife competent as witnesses in cases of this character. Different courts have so held, and I think correctly. But they are competent witnesses against the other party, or in their own behalf, but cannot be compelled to testify, for the reason before given. It is also said that it does not appear that the wife has any property which the husband can forfeit. It is probably unnecessary that it should affirmatively appear she may or may not have property. Certainly she may earn or inherit it. It is enough that his testimony will have a tendency to "*expose* him to a forfeiture." The act of 1854 provides that "the verification of any pleading may be omitted where the party called upon to verify would be privileged from testifying as a witness to the truth of any matter denied by such pleading." (*Laws of* 1854, *p.* 153.)

If I am right, the defendant is privileged in this case from testifying. It follows that the answer was regular without a verification. The question being new under the present law, the motion is denied without costs.

SUPREME COURT.

RICHARD C. BEAMISH, receiver, &c. agt. WM. S. CONANT and others.

In an action to set aside an *assignment* for the benefit of creditors, for fraud, *held*, that there was not sufficient evidence of fraud to warrant an injunction and receiver, arising from the fact, 1st. That the assignor had continued in possession of the assigned property, and was employed by the assignee to sell the stock and assist in making collections at the store where the business was formerly carried on, and the amounts as collected were paid over to the assignee.

2d. That after about six months under such arrangement, the whole remaining stock was sold at 25 per cent. on the cost price to a brother-in-law of the assignor, who had paid a large portion of the purchase money, and was responsible for the balance. It also appearing that the sale was made for the full value of the goods.

New York General Term, November, 1862.

This was an appeal from an order granting an injunction and appointing a receiver of certain property during the pendency of the action. The facts are sufficiently stated in the opinion of the court.

Ira D. Warren, *for respondent.*
H. K. Hunter, *for appellant.*

By the court, Leonard, Justice. No complaint is made for constructive or legal fraud in respect to any matter arising from the face of the assignment. The fraud relied on to sustain the injunction and the order for the appointment of a receiver, arises from the acts of the defendants in relation to the assigned estate. These are:

1st. That there has been no change of possession in respect to the stock assigned, but the assignor, Conant, has had the control and management of it in the same manner as before the assignment.

2d. That the stock, at the time of the assignment, was worth $17,000, and after selling $3,000 to general customers, the residue was fraudulently sold for 20 per cent. of its value to Whitmore, a brother-in-law of the debtor, for the benefit of the debtor, and to enable him to continue the business; and the debtor still carries on the original business.

3d. That the debtor has fraudulently mortgaged and conveyed his real estate.

The first and second grounds are principally relied on by the plaintiff. The defendants explain the charges in relation to the alleged want of change in the possession, as I think, satisfactorily. Conant was employed by the assignee to sell the stock, and assist in making collections at the store where the business was formerly carried on. He continued in the employment of the assignee, in this manner, about six months, when a sale of the whole remaining stock was made to the defendant Whitmore, at 25 per cent. on the cost price, amounting to about $3,500. The purchaser has paid $2,700 on account of the transaction, to the assignee, and is a man of means sufficiently large to answer the full payment of the portion still remaining on credit. The price is shown, on an examination made by merchants acquainted with goods of the description sold, to be the full value. The sale to Whitmore appears to be an honest transaction, for a full price paid or sufficiently secured to the assignee. We have no further concern with the subsequent possession of the stock.

I advise the reversal of the order appealed from, as the defendant Dougherty appears to be responsible for any judgment the plaintiff may obtain against him.

INGRAHAM and PECKHAM, J. J., concurred.

COURT OF APPEALS.

MARTHA ERNST, executrix, &c. agt. THE HUDSON RIVER RAILROAD COMPANY.

A *defendant* may move for a *non-suit* when the plaintiff rests; or he may give testimony and rest, and then move for a non-suit. The refusal of the judge to grant such motion is equally, in either case, a good ground of *exception*.

After the testimony has been given by the defendant, and both parties have *rested*, and the defendant moves upon the whole evidence for a *non-suit*, it is *the right and duty* of the circuit judge to direct a non-suit at that stage of the cause, if the plaintiff is not entitled to recover, and a verdict in his favor could not be sustained.

Where there is a *disputed question of fact*—as, whether the engine bell of a railroad train was rung at the proper time before crossing a public highway, and evidence upon both sides is given, which is contradictory—it is especially and appropriately a question for the *jury* to determine the means of knowledge and credibility of the several witnesses, and where the weight of evidence rests upon this issue.

In an action for damages for injuries to the person, caused by *negligence*, the plaintiff must present a case of *unmixed* negligence;—a case where the injury is the result *exclusively of the defendant's negligence;*—where no negligence or fault of his own contributed in *any degree* to producing such injury.

In no case is it the duty of the circuit judge to submit a case to the jury, unless the evidence is so doubtful or conflicting that a verdict for the plaintiff or defendant could be sustained, and ought not to be disturbed, upon the principles governing *the review, by the courts, of the verdicts of juries.*

The doctrine that the courts should not *non-suit*, or set aside verdicts, as without or against evidence, in cases of *negligence*, because such verdicts, from the nature of the case, and the character of the facts and circumstances to be investigated, and going to establish negligence, are based so much upon mere opinion, that they cannot possibly be *reviewed*, wholly misconceives the theory upon which justice is administered in this country.

It is not the *jury*, but the *courts* which administer justice. The duty and responsibility of seeing that equal and impartial justice is meted out to all men, devolves, under the constitution, by the common law, upon the *judges of the courts*. Juries are mere *assistants* of the courts, whose province it is to aid them in the decision of disputed questions of fact. If there is no real *dispute* in a case, the court gives judgment.

In the judgment and opinion of a majority of men, *common prudence forbids* the attempt by any person to cross the track of a *railroad* in constant use, without first taking the precaution to *look both ways* upon the track, and see and ascertain that a train is not approaching in either direction; and the omission to do so is, *per se, gross negligence*, in view of the danger to be avoided, and the fatal consequences involved in any accident resulting from such omission.

As upon the whole issue in this case, it was impossible for the jury to find that the plaintiff had made out a clear, affirmative case of negligence on the part of the defendants, *unmixed* with any degree of negligence on the part of the deceased, contributing to the injury sustained, it was not the duty of the circuit judge to have submitted the case to the jury, and the motion for a *non-suit was properly granted. (Reversing the decision at general term supreme court,* 19 *How. Pr. R.,* 205.)

September Term, 1862.

THIS action was brought to recover damages of the defendants, for causing the death of Henry Ernst, deceased. The cause was tried at the Rensselaer circuit in May, 1859, before Mr. Justice GOULD and a jury. The judge declined to submit any question of fact to the jury, and directed a non-suit, and ordered the plaintiff's exceptions to be heard in the first instance at the general term. The following are the controlling facts as stated by the general term:

For half a century there has been a public highway leading from Sandlake to the city of Albany, passing through the village of Bath and over the Hudson river, by what is known as the Bath ferry.

The defendants, as is admitted by the pleadings, operate the Troy & Greenbush railroad, which is located on the east bank of the Hudson river, and crosses this public highway at Bath. The railroad crosses the highway upon the same level.

This company have a station-house at Bath, located east of the railroad track, and just north of the highway leading to the ferry, and ordinarily have a flagman stationed at the crossing.

When the accident happened, the deceased resided in the eastern part of the county of Rensselaer, some fourteen or fifteen miles from Bath. His family consisted of a wife (the plaintiff) and six daughters.

On the 29th day of December, 1855, the deceased, having a pair of horses attached to a sleigh, was passing upon this highway, bound for the city of Albany. On arriving at Bath, he stopped at a tavern about 158 feet east of the railroad track. As the ferry-boat was ready to start, and was only waiting for him, the deceased unhitched his team, seated himself upon the sleigh-bottom, facing the west, and drove at a quick pace directly towards the boat. Just as he approached the railroad crossing, he came in collision with the defendants' train of cars moving south, receiving an injury that caused his death.

The plaintiff's testator was a teamster, and for more than twenty-five years used the road to Albany, crossing at the Bath ferry, and very frequently crossed there. On the morning of the accident, he went to Bath by the Sandlake road, from which the cars were visible, if looked for, as far as the Nail factory, some miles distant, and might be seen nearly all the way from there to Bath crossing. He stopped at Dearstyne's tavern till the ferry-boat was ready to start; he then came out hurriedly, and drove towards the ferry-boat at a rapid rate of speed. He had a two-horse team and an empty sleigh. It was cold weather, and he had a shawl about his face. He had no bells on his horses. In going from the tavern to the boat, the road is nearly level, or a little ascending for 158 feet, when it is crossed by the railroad track. For the whole of this distance, except in passing the station-house, a building twelve or thirteen feet wide, there is no obstacle to seeing a train approaching from the north. The approach of a train can be heard without bell or whistle, from one to two miles. The noise of that train had been heard by one Ostrander, some time before deceased left the tavern. When deceased was at the middle of Mineral street, 125 feet from the track, Ostrander, whom he had nearly run into, heard the noise of the coming cars, looked round, and saw them coming.

The cars were moving at the rate of from thirty to forty miles an hour. Although in a situation to hear, no witness who was examined heard the bell or whistle before the collision. This omission on the part of the engineer in charge of the train, attracted the attention of the ferryman at the time of the collision.

Miller, the regular flagman, was absent, and no flagman or other person was present to warn travelers of the approach of the train. The flagman is ordinarily there for the purpose of signalizing the train when to stop for passengers.

Shortly before the collision, and as the deceased approached the track, some person on the ferry-boat made signals and motioned for deceased to come on. At the same time there was other hallooing in the street near the crossing. Other motions were made; one man motioned with his hand, waving it towards the east. The bystanders understood the meaning of these signals differently; one thought it meant to keep off; another thought it meant to come on the boat; while others did not understand the meaning at all.

The approach of the train was perceived by several persons near the crossing; some saw it, some heard it. The witnesses did not observe whether the deceased looked up or down the railroad track, as he approached the crossing, and it did not appear that he looked in either direction.

The appointment of the plaintiff as executrix of the last will and testament of her deceased husband, was shown in the case.

John H. Reynolds, *for defendants, appellants.*

R. A. Parmenter, *for plaintiff, respondent.*

By the court, E. Darwin Smith, J. The questions involved in this case are of much practical importance.

The case presents a single exception, upon the refusal of the circuit judge to direct a non-suit upon the whole evidence, after testimony had been given by the defendants, and both parties had rested. It was the *right and duty* of the circuit judge to direct a non-suit at that stage of the cause, if the plaintiff was not entitled to recover, and a verdict in his favor could not have been sustained.

The defendant may move for a non-suit when the plaintiff rests, or he may give testimony and rest, and then move for a non-suit. The refusal of the judge to grant such motion, is equally, in either case, a good ground for an exception.

The negligence imputed to the defendants, and on which the claim to maintain the action is founded, consisted in the omission, by the defendants' engineer, to ring the bell and sound the steam whistle, as required by the statute, for a distance of eighty rods before reaching the crossing. Upon this issue there was much conflicting testimony, and, so far as the proper determination of the action depended upon the single question of the negligence of the defendants' agents in charge of the train at the time of the accident, a verdict in favor of the plaintiff would, perhaps, be warranted by the evidence, or at least could not be disturbed as not founded on sufficient evidence, although the proof was positive from the defendants' agents and others on the train, that the bell was in fact rung and the whistle sounded at and for the requisite distance, yet quite a number of witnesses testified that they did not hear either the bell or whistle; and it was, therefore, especially and appropriately a question for the jury, to determine the means of knowledge and credibility of the several witnesses, and where the weight of evidence rested upon this issue.

The defence consisted in an attempt to prove that the plaintiff's intestate was also guilty of negligence, and that such negligence occasioned the collision of the train with his team, which caused his death. Upon this issue there is quite an amount of testimony, more or less conclusive, but certainly all tending to establish a case of gross negligence on his part.

He was familiar with the locality; knew of the existence of the railroad; that it was in use, and that trains upon it were constantly passing and re-passing. The train with which he came in collision, was a regular train on its stated and customary time. It was proved that he was a teamster, and had been engaged for about twenty-five years in teaming from Sandlake, where he resided, to Albany, and in going and returning, used to cross the road of the defendants at Bath, where this accident occurred; that he arrived at Bath on the morning of the accident, and stopped at a tavern there, about 150 feet east of the track, about the time the train was due, and after remaining there a few minutes, started for the ferry at a rapid rate of speed; that for most of the way from the tavern to the railroad, the track north of the place of crossing could be seen from the highway. Quite a number of persons at the same place, saw the train coming while he was passing from the tavern to the railroad, and several of them called to him and warned him to stop, and others beckoned to him to do so. These and various other particulars given in evidence, tended to show great carelessness and heedlessness on the part of Ernst, in attempting to cross the railroad at the time and in the manner he did. If the case had been reversed, and the collision between the locomotive and the team of the intestate had thrown the train from the track and killed the engineer, and this action had been brought by his representatives against Ernst, for his negligence in obstructing the train and thus throwing it from the track, and causing the death of such engineer, upon the evidence given on the trial in proof of such negligence, I think no judge would have deemed it proper to non-suit the plaintiff, and the jury would clearly have been warranted in finding a verdict for the plaintiff, which no court, I think, could have held unsustainable upon the evidence, or would have deemed it proper to set aside, independently of the question how far the negligence of such engineer contributed to his death.

And this, I conceive, presents the *true test* for the decision of the motion for a non-suit based upon the conducing and contributing negligence of the plaintiff, in cases of this kind. It was a clear, palpable, *prima facie* case of co-operative negligence. Practically, a duplicate issue arises on the trial in all this class of cases; and to recover, the plaintiff, it is held, must prevail upon *both* issues. But, in principle, there is but a single issue. The plaintiff must present a case of *unmixed* negligence;—a case where the injury is the result, *exclusively*, of the defendant's negligence;—where no negligence or fault of his own contributed in any degree to producing such injury. A party sueing for negligence must come into court faultless. He must not present a mere balanced case. The burden of proof is upon him, and he must satisfy the court, by the greater weight of the testimony, that without any carelessness or blame on his part, he has suffered an injury from the wrongful act, default or negligence of the defendant. For such injury, the law gives redress. This is the principle upon which the action for negligence at common law is based.

When the application for a non-suit was made on the trial of this action, did the plaintiff present such a case? Most clearly, it seems to me, he did not. It was at best, upon the undisputed evidence, a clear case of mixed negligence. It is impossible, I think, to hold or find otherwise upon the whole evidence. A verdict, finding that the death of the plaintiff's intestate was caused by the exclusive negligence of the defendants, and without any want of due care and caution on the part of the deceased, would, I think, be utterly unwarranted by the evidence, and unsustainable, according to the view in respect to the degree of care required of persons attempting to cross a railroad track, hereinafter more fully discussed. In this view, it was the clear duty of the judge to direct a non-suit.

In no case, as I understand the rule, is it the duty of the circuit judge to submit a case to the jury, unless the evidence is so doubtful or conflicting that a verdict for the plaintiff or defendant could be sustained, and ought not to be disturbed, upon the principles governing the review, by the courts, of the verdicts of juries.

But it is claimed quite urgently by counsel, and is assented to by some judges, in substance and effect, that these rules and principles do not apply to actions for *negligence*, and that negligence is purely a question of fact and of opinion, and belongs exclusively to the jury. I agree that negligence is always a *question of fact*. It is always to be inferred from, or imputed upon, *evidence* more or less direct, more or less positive or circumstantial: but I deny that it can be found or imputed without evidence, or that the verdict of a jury finding it will supply the place of evidence, or furnish a substitute for a cause of action. I deny that verdicts finding negligence are not just as much the subjects of review in the courts, as verdicts for any other causes of action. These must be found and predicated upon proper, legitimate and legal evidence, and of this the court must be the exclusive judge.

The argument upon this point, where the divergence of opinion upon these questions really begins, virtually assumes that the courts should not non-suit, or set aside verdicts as without or against evidence, in cases of negligence; that such verdicts, from the nature of the case, and the character of the facts and circumstances to be investigated and going to establish negligence, are based so much upon mere opinion, that they cannot possibly be reviewed. And it is said that the opinion of twelve men in a jury-box should control, (and the decision in such cases is better evidence of the truth,) rather than that of three or four men in bank in the supreme court, or eight judges of this court. This is the effect and substance of the argument constantly addressed to the courts in this class of cases.

This argument wholly misconceives the theory, as it seems to me, upon which justice is administered in this country. It is not the *jury*, but the *courts* which administer justice. The duty and responsibility of seeing that equal and impartial justice is meted out to all men, devolves, under the constitution, by the common law, upon the *judges of the courts*. Juries are mere *assistants* of the courts, whose province it is to aid them in the decision of disputed questions of fact. If there is no real *dispute* in a case, the court gives judgment.

Jury trial is justly regarded as a most invaluable mode of deciding disputed issues of fact, where there is contrariety and conflict in the evidence. But its value chiefly depends upon the fact that the trials are had under the direction and supervision of educated and experienced judges, who have devoted a lifetime to the study of the law and to the practical administration of public justice. Jurors, on the contrary, are selected from the body of the people, for a single occasion, and, as a general rule, are unfamiliar with the rules of evidence, and with the principles of law, and the processes of legal investigation. When the points in dispute are *simple* and *single*, and the facts are presented and discussed by able counsel, and the issues involved clearly presented by the presiding judge, the verdicts of juries are generally very satisfactory, and probably more so than the decisions of the courts on questions of fact, or any other mode of trial ever practiced among men.

But it is essential to the preservation of this noble institution, that juries be carefully confined to their legitimate province, and that the rights and interests of society be not jeopardized by capricious verdicts, rendered and depending upon uncertain principles. It is of infinite consequence to the community that the law be kept and preserved as certain, clear, known and stable as possible. This can only be done by the courts, and this duty is specially confided to them, and required at their hands by the people.

This necessity makes it the duty of the courts to regulate the conduct of juries, to pass upon the evidence submitted to them, and to decide all questions of law arising during the progress of a trial; and to review their verdicts, and to set them aside, if unwarranted by the evidence.

The court is necessarily the ultimate judge in all cases upon the evidence, and must decide whether in conformity with the rules of law it will warrant or sustain a verdict.

The argument that it belongs to the jury to pass conclusively upon the evidence, is fundamentally unsound and untrue, and the argument that the opinion of twelve men in the jury-box is of higher authority upon a question of fact, and better evidence of the truth than the opinion of the judges, is more specious than sound. So far as mere opinion is concerned, the opinion of twelve men of equal intelligence and capability, and means of knowledge and of judgment, is, doubtless, of superior weight to that of four or eight men, a smaller number than twelve. But that consideration does not meet the case.

The decisions of courts and juries stand upon a very different footing.

Aside from the difference in capacity to decide correctly, arising from professional education and practice, and judicial experience, the judges act and decide deliberately, after patient and careful investigation, and give the reasons for their decisions, which are open to the careful scrutiny of the parties, and the vigilant criticism of an educated and enlightened bar, and of the public.

Juries will certainly act and decide more or less hastily, without time, in most instances, for much reflection, and also act and decide in secret; and from this consideration, and their large number, they certainly act under much less personal and individual responsibility than the judges; and besides, common observation and experience show that they are far more liable to be swayed by passion and excitement, and other undue influences. Their verdicts are therefore notoriously many times founded upon mistakes, misconceptions and other errors, which make it indispensable, to secure to this mode of trial the public confidence, that a power of supervision and review of the verdicts should exist in the courts, and should be exercised with fidelity and firmness.

The *implication* from the argument, that negligence rests in matters of mere *opinion*, and may be imputed upon "*conjecture*" in respect to how men would act generally in given circumstances, is, that verdicts may be rendered by juries finding negligence, upon grounds, principles and conjectures beyond the control of the courts, and outside of the limits within which such verdicts are reviewed by them. Negligence consists in the violation or omission of some duty of positive legal obligation.

So far as the duty is clear and definite upon undisputed facts, it belongs to the courts to declare and apply the law. But when the duty depends upon the exercise or omission of *ordinary care*, or common prudence, the question, I agree, is one of *fact*, and belongs to the jury; but it is to be determined by them upon principles known and recognized by the courts. On an application for a non-suit in such a case, the circuit judge is called upon to apply to the evidence his observation, common sense and common experience, and to determine whether, allowing every legitimate inference which the jury might possibly draw from it, they would be authorized to find a verdict for the plaintiff; and the same rule applies in the review of this verdict, if the case should have been submitted to them and a verdict rendered.

What, in a given case, would be ordinary care, or *common prudence*, would be a question of *judgment*. It would be what, in the case supposed, would be the *conduct of a majority of men in like circumstances*. It would be for the jury to consider and decide this question with reference to the known and recognized interests of human nature, and the ordinary rules and principles of human conduct.

In asserting and obeying the primary instinct of every

human being to preserve and protect life, common sense and the law concur in declaring the rule of common prudence to be *such a degree of care and caution as will be in due proportion to the injury or damage to be avoided.* Persons riding, driving or passing in the crowded streets of a city, or driving horses upon a race course, will ordinarily exercise, and are bound and required to exercise, a much higher degree of care than travelers upon the common highways of the country. So with persons crossing a railroad track, where trains are constantly passing, propelled by the powerful agent of steam. Such collisions almost invariably and inevitably are attended with fatal consequences, and occasion more or less loss of life. Common prudence requires a much higher degree of care and caution.

We come, then, to the question, what is *common prudence*, or what kind or *degree of care* does common prudence enjoin and require in the crossing of a railroad track? This case illustrates the rule, and presents, as I conceive, a complete negative answer to this question. The conduct of Ernst, the intestate, in his attempt to cross the defendants' railroad, at the time of the collision which caused his death, shows most clearly, as I think, what is not *common prudence* in the crossing of a railroad track.

The question is, what would a majority of men of common intelligence, have done under like circumstances? Here was a man of fifty years of age, perfectly familiar with the locality at and about this railroad crossing, living at a distance eastwardly upon the highway intersecting said railroad at that place, which he was continually traveling in his business of teaming to and from Albany, knowing that said railroad was in constant use for the passing of trains propelled by steam, and knowing, also, or bound to know, the stated times for the passage of trains across said highway. With this knowledge, he arrives at the tavern in the village of Bath, distant about 150 feet eastwardly of said railroad, at about the time a train was notoriously due upon said railroad, stops a moment at the tavern, and then starts for the ferry across said railroad, at a trot of his horses, neither looking to the right or the left, although a train was then approaching from the north, and might have been seen by him at the distance of 100 rods from the said highway, for nearly the whole distance from said tavern to said railroad, and was in fact seen by quite a number of persons at the same place, and thus driving directly on to the railroad track just as the train reached the crossing, he comes necessarily in collision with the locomotive, and is killed. Was this *common prudence?* Did he exercise *ordinary care? Would a majority of men, with his knowledge, and under like circumstances, have attempted to cross this railroad at the time and in the manner he did?*

These questions, addressed to the eight judges of this court; to the learned judge who tried this cause at the circuit; to the three other judges of the supreme court who affirmed the judgment at general term, out of court, and calling, not for a judicial, but for an individual opinion as to how each of these would act under the same circumstances, and how, in their judgment, a majority of men of common intelligence would act under like circumstances,—would, as I believe, be answered by them, without exception, with an *unqualified negative.* The same questions, put to any one hundred men taken promiscuously from any town or city in the state, I think would be answered in the same way, by as large a majority as nine out of every ten, and the same questions put to the whole voting population of the county of Rensselaer, where the accident occurred, over thirty years of age, I think would be answered in the same way, by as large a proportion; and the jury who tried this cause, if they were men of the intelligence commonly found in the jury-box in this state; and if they were separately asked the same questions, away from the court and the excitement of the trial of such a cause, and the influences which sympathy for the friends of the deceased, and the just prejudices more or less engendered in the popular mind against corporations, by the harsh, heedless and oppressive course with which their corporate powers are many times used and exercised,—or a majority of them would, I believe, answer the questions in the same way.

If this be so, when, superadded to the facts above stated, it also appeared, as it does in the testimony in this case, that Ernst drank intoxicating liquors on his way, that morning, three times—brandy twice, and rum and sugar once; that he drove so carelessly by the way, that he nearly tipped over, and was cautioned at the time by the person riding with him, to drive more carefully; and it also appeared that other persons at the same place heard the train coming at quite a distance, before it reached the crossing; four persons, after he started from the tavern, respectively hallooed to him in a loud voice, *to stop*, several times each, and others beckoned to him to stop, with great earnestness of gesture—all of which was seen and heard by many persons in the vicinity—how much more would such questions be answered in the negative.

These facts also appearing, the whole facts together present a case where, upon the undisputed facts, I think a great majority of men would say that Ernst did not, in attempting to cross the railroad in the manner he did, exercise *common prudence*, and that he was guilty of a neglect of *ordinary care;* such as can only be accounted for, as a general rule, upon the assumption that he was intoxicated, or for some other cause was partially deprived of the use of his ordinary faculties.

Upon this question, therefore, thus illustrated by the facts of this case, I think the conclusion is rational and legitimate, that in the judgment and opinion of a majority of men, *common prudence forbids* the attempt, by any person, to cross the track of a railroad in constant use, without first taking the precaution to *look both ways* upon the track, and see and ascertain that a train is not approaching in either direction, and that the omission to do so is, *per se*, *gross negligence*, in view of the danger to be avoided, and the fatal consequences involved in any accident resulting from such omission.

As, therefore, upon the whole issue, it was impossible for the jury to find that the plaintiff had made out a clear, affirmative case of negligence on the part of the defendants, unmixed with any degree of negligence on the part of the deceased, contributing to the injury sustained, it was not the duty of the circuit judge to have submitted the case to the jury, and the motion for a non-suit should have been granted.

The judgment, therefore, should be reversed, and a new trial granted, with costs to abide the event.

SUPREME COURT.

Dexter B. Britton agt. Charles B. Phillips.

To sustain an action for damages for breach of a contract to sell land, it must appear that the parties' minds met in the proposed sale.

Where the proposed vendor submitted a proposition to sell the land in controversy—such proposition being in the form of a letter addressed from a banking house in Wall street to the proposed purchaser, containing at the bottom, "the above proposition is made for two days; after that subject to negotiation," it must appear on the part of the proposed vendee who brings his action to recover damages for breach of such alleged contract, that he accepted said proposition in writing, within the time specified, and brought to the knowledge of the proposed vendor such acceptance.

A mere deposit in the U. S. post-office (postage not prepaid) of a letter accepting such proposition, addressed to the proposed vendor, is insufficient.

It is not due diligence to excuse such deposit in the post-office, to prove that the proposed vendee was unable to find the proposed vendor within the time, where it also appears that the latter made no inquiries for the former at the banking house from which the proposition in form was addressed.

In case of an attachment issued under sections 227, *et seq*. of the Code, and also in case of a judgment recovered in such attachment suit, where it appeared that the judgment had been executed and paid, notwithstanding an appeal pending, the appellate court, under section 330 of the Code, have power to, and will order on reversal of the judgment below, a restitution to the appellant of the moneys so

collected, notwithstanding such reversal is accompanied by an order granting a new trial, and notwithstanding the attachment is so pending.

In such case, the restitution is effected by ordering a deposit of the moneys into court, to abide the result of the new trial, and subject to the lien of the attachment.

New York General Term, September, 1862.

INGRAHAM, *P. J.*, CLERKE and LEONARD, *Justices*.

THE appellant was the owner of five lots on the north side of Thirty-fifth street, between Second and Third avenues, on which were erected five brown stone houses, three stories high. The referee found the value of this property to be $34,000. On the premises were incumbrances amounting to $22,500, viz: $3,500 on each house and lot, and a $5,000 mortgage on the five. Besides, there was on them a mortgage for $10,000, given as security for some mortgages on the appellant's Chicago property, which liability was not absolute at the time.

The appellant desired to sell this city property, and he applied to John S. Christie, real estate broker, who introduced him to the respondent, and thereupon a negotiation ensued whereby the respondent sought to exchange with the appellant for the houses, in part payment, stock of the American Kaolin Company, $52,000, which value the appellant claimed they represented, so that money could be raised on it, of twenty-five cents on the dollar, *i. e.* in all $13,000, and also some other securities of the same kind. The referee found these securities never had any market value, although he found that there was no fraud on the part of the respondent. After proposals backwards and forwards, the appellant wrote a letter to respondent, in which he used these words:

"I will vend to you the five houses, about the title of which there will be no doubt, subject to the present mortgage incumbrances. I will take the Kaolin stock as per your offer; I will take the Beaver Dam mortgages and five hundred dollars in cash, if you wish to close the contract,"

&c., &c. "The above proposition is made for two days; after that, subject to negotiations."

In that letter the appellant made use of expressions which indicated either that he considered these securities equal to cash at the rate proposed, or that his mind had been imbued with that idea.

This was delivered to respondent 11th of December, 1858. The only acceptance of that proposition by respondent was by a letter addressed to appellant, and deposited in the New York city post-office, postage not prepaid, on the 13th December, 1858, and which was not shown to have been received by appellant, and which the appellant positively denied ever having received.

On the 14th December, 1858, the appellant declined further connection with the matter. The respondent brought an action for a specific performance and for damages. The referee awarded him $1,100 damages, and from that report this appeal was taken.

D. McMahon, *for appellant.*
A. R. Dyett, *for respondent.*

By the court, Clerke, P. Justice. It is not pretended in the negotiations between the parties in this action, that they arrived at any final understanding until after the defendant wrote the letter dated 11th December, 1858. In this letter he proposes to the plaintiff to sell him the five houses in Thirty-fifth street, on certain terms specifically set forth; and in a postscript he says: "The above proposition is made for two days; after that, subject to negotiation." Of course this letter, as the writer says in the postscript, contains nothing more than a proposition. It was not in itself an acceptance of previous propositions made by the plaintiff; there were negotiations indeed between the parties, and whatever offers may have been made on the part of plaintiff, this letter was no adoption of them, but it was merely a statement of terms which required a positive acceptance by the plaintiff before it could become an agreement binding on either.

Where is the evidence of an acceptance by the plaintiff?

He states that "he received defendant's letter on Saturday evening, December 11, and on Monday evening he sent a written communication to defendant, accepting his offer. He kept no copy of it; he sent the communication to defendant through the New York general post-office, inclosed in an envelope addressed to defendant, New York; he could not say whether the postage was paid." The defendant swears positively that he never received it. There is, therefore, not only no evidence that the acceptance was even received by the defendant, but direct and unmistakable evidence that it was not received by him. The plaintiff did not even exhibit ordinary diligence to comply with the requirement contained in the postscript to the letter of the 11th December. That letter was dated at the banking house of Bliss, Williams & Co., No. 4 Wall street; the plaintiff made no inquiries for the defendant at that place; never even called there; if he did, his acceptance probably would have reached the defendant in time. Mr. Williams, one of the firm of Bliss, Williams & Co., states "that the defendant transacted business at their house; was there, received his letters there, and did his correspondence there; had negotiations there with people about this property." If the plaintiff, then, failed to have the acceptance properly served on the defendant, he may blame his own want of care and diligence. It is, at all events, clear that no court would be justified in deciding that the defendant received the acceptance, and although the referee reports in favor of the plaintiff, he does not expressly find as a matter of fact that the defendant did receive it.

The judgment should be reversed, and a new trial ordered; costs to abide event.

On the settlement of the decree in this cause, the following question of practice arose: It appeared that pending the appeal, the plaintiff below went on and executed the decree, and collected the amount of the judgment appealed from. This collection was arrived at in this form: In the suit originally, an attachment was issued pursuant to sections 227, *et seq.* of the Code, and a levy made on certain moneys of the defendant in a banker's hands. After recovery of the judgment below, by proceedings in the name of the sheriff, the plaintiff below, under sections 232, 238 of of the Code, compelled the payment of the judgment.

A motion was now made for restitution, under section 330 of the Code; such restitution to be incorporated in the decree reversing the judgment below. Affidavits were read by the respondent, on the settlement of the decree of reversal, tending to show that after the attachment was levied, the appellant assigned over all his interest in the moneys in the banker's hands, to a third party, and that the appellant, after such assignment, disclaimed all interest therein. The appellant, however, introduced affidavits tending to show that the assignment in question was given as collateral security for moneys loaned, and that since the satisfaction of the judgment below, he had become re-instated with an interest in the moneys levied on, greater than the sum so levied on. Argument was heard on this point, before Justices INGRAHAM, LEONARD and PECKHAM.

Mr. McMAHON, *for motion*, made the following points:

I. After the respondent has satisfied his attachment and his judgment out of the moneys of the appellant pending the appeal, he ought to be estopped from setting up that such moneys were not the moneys of the appellant.

He collected *them as such* on the erroneous judgment. No pretence is set up that any one has called him to account for the moneys thus collected.

To allow him now to plead in answer to the right of the

appellant to have restitution, that he, the respondent, committed a greater outrage by collecting his judgment of somebody's else moneys, would be an evasion of all legal principles.

II. Section 330 of the Code provides that when the judgment is reversed or modified, the appellate court may make restitution of property and rights lost by the judgment.

III. We now claim that the moneys collected by the respondent, under his erroneous judgment, should be restored to the appellant, by being re-paid over to him. It was his money, on deposit with his banker, and should be restored to him.

IV. At any rate, the right of deposit and control of the appellant's moneys were affected and enjoined by the erroneous judgment reversed, and we submit that it is the right of the appellant to have said moneys so collected by the respondent, deposited in court or the Trust Company, to the credit of this cause.

V. The appellant, in his affidavits on the settlement of the order, has shown conclusively that the moneys so levied on by the respondent's proceedings, were his, the appellant's, own funds. We submit, therefore, that there can be no legal objection to a restoration of those funds to the proper custody, *i. e.* the appellant himself, or the Trust Company.

VI. Certainly, the respondent who has been decided to have no cause of action, has no right to retain those moneys.

Mr. Dyett, *opposed*, made the following points. The only authority for the motion is section 330 of the Code, and it should be denied, with costs.

I. This motion should be made at special term. This general term is not an "appellate court." It is the same tribunal that rendered the judgment.

II. The section in question applies to *all appeals*, and

only authorizes restitution where a judgment is reversed, *and it stops there.*

This does not apply to the case of a reversal, accompanied by the granting of a new trial with costs to abide the event.

In such a case restitution is not proper. (*Estas* agt. *Baldwin*, 9 *How.*, 80; *opinion*, 81.)

The true remedy is by an award of restitution on the record of reversal, (2 *Wend.*, 158,) or by action of assumpsit, (6 *Cow.*, 297.) But this can be only on a final reversal, which was the case in both the cases just cited. It cannot be where a new trial is ordered in the same court, on a case made, for there is no final judgment.

III. But in this case an attachment was issued, *and is still in force.*

The plaintiff, therefore, cannot have restitution. The money, if taken from the plaintiff, must go to the sheriff.

a. There is no authority for ordering the plaintiff to pay it to the sheriff, (and see next point.)

b. The sheriff should make that motion.

c. There is no authority for any order *paying the money into court.*

If it goes to anybody, it goes to the sheriff. If, as we show, restitution cannot be ordered because of the attachment, that is an end of the motion. The court should not make novel orders, or entertain these "fancy applications." There is no necessity of ordering *the money paid into court.*

IV. In the case of an attachment, the plaintiff cannot have any restitution of the property attached, unless he recover final judgment in his favor, (*Code*, § 239,) and until that time the defendant has no control over it.

V. But our affidavits show that the defendant has all along disclaimed any title to the money attached, and that a third party claims it as his, and both claim the money to have been assigned to such third party before the attachment was issued, which was February 26th, 1860, (see our affidavits.)

We have been obliged to give, and have given, a bond of indemnity to the sheriff and to the banker, against the claims of Wright.

The defendant does not now claim the money as his. He claims (fols. 2 and 3 of his affidavit) only a resulting trust after his assignments to two persons in whom the legal title to the money is; and at the end of his affidavit pretends to make the application as the attorney in fact of the last assignee. Such third party does not personally join in the application, and our bond of indemnity is still in force.

But if such assignees were both before the court, the court should not entertain such an application by a third party, and there is no precedent for it; and although we show conclusively, that the assignee had all along claimed the assignment to have been made to Wright previous to the attachment, (compelling us to indemnify,) for the purpose of preventing us getting the money, he now claims the assigment to have been made afterwards, for the purpose of getting it back.

The motion should be denied, with costs.

By the court, INGRAHAM, Justice. We think the order should direct the moneys to be paid into court, to abide event.

Thereupon, a decree was settled by the court, which, after providing for the reversal of the judgment below, contained the following provision, to wit:

" And it appearing to the court that, notwithstanding the appeal herein, the respondent executed and collected the amount of the judgment below, costs and sheriff's fees, to wit, the sum of $1,855.23, therefore it is further adjudged, ordered and decreed, that the said respondent make restitution to the said appellant, by paying into court, to the chamberlain of the city of New York, within ten days after service of this decree on him or his attorney, the said sum of $1,855.23, with interest from the date of said collection, by the said respondent, to abide the order of this court after such new trial is had."

SUPREME COURT.

THE PEOPLE *ex rel.* SAMUEL PLUMB agt. THE BOARD OF SUPERVISORS OF CORTLAND COUNTY.

If a *board of supervisors* disallow an account presented to them to be audited as a county charge, on the ground that *they have no power to allow it*—that the statute does not authorize the allowance; this precludes the *examination* contemplated by the statute under which the board act in the settlement of accounts, and the court can control the action of the board, in reference thereto, by *mandamus*.

It is otherwise where the board of supervisors enter into an *examination* of such accounts, and reject (or allow) them; they thus exercise their legal *discretion*, and their decision becomes *final*.

The *commissioners of excise* of a county are not, under the statute, limited in their services to *ten days* (at $3 per day.) This limitation is expressly confined to the time they shall spend in their meetings for the purpose of granting licenses.

It is their duty to *prosecute for penalties incurred*, and the members of the board have the right to charge for the time spent in the performance of that duty; and where they present their accounts to the board of supervisors, properly made out and verified, it is the duty of such board to receive and act upon them. If they refuse to do this, the authority of this court may be invoked to compel them.

Cortland Special Term, August, 1861.

MANDAMUS. The relator was one of the commissioners of excise of Cortland county. At the annual meeting of the board of supervisors of Cortland county, in 1860, he presented two bills to the board, for audit and allowance; one for $33, for eleven days' service—ten days in meeting the board to grant licenses, and one day to make report to the board of supervisors; the other for $143.62, for forty-two days' service performed as such commissioner of excise, in prosecutions for violations of the excise law, and $17.62 for disbursements incurred by him in such prosecutions.

The board of supervisors audited the first bill at $30 for ten days only, and the second bill at $17.62 for disbursements only, and claimed that the relator was only entitled to pay as an excise commissioner for ten days' service in any one year, at $3 per day, besides the disbursements necessarily expended by virtue of his office. This mandamus was brought to compel the board of supervisors to audit and allow the balance of said bills. The alternative mandamus was directed to "The Board of Supervisors of Cortland county," and was served upon their clerk only. Motion for a peremptory mandamus.

A. P. Smith, *for the relator.*
Horatio Ballard, *for defendants.*

Parker, Justice. This is an application for a peremptory mandamus to compel the defendants to allow the account of the relator, for services as one of the commissioners of excise of Cortland county.

An alternative mandamus was allowed and issued, which sets forth that the relator presented to the defendants, at their last annual meeting, an account, duly verified, for eleven days' service by him as such commissioner of excise, for the year 1860, and requested them to audit and allow the same at the sum of $33, but that they refused so to do; but did settle and allow the same at the sum of $30. And also, that at the same annual meeting, the relator presented to the defendants another account, in due form, and properly verified, for forty-two days' other services by him as such commissioner, during said year, and $17.62 disbursements, and requested them to audit and allow the same at the sum of $126 for said services, and $17.62 for said disbursements, but that they refused so to do; but did settle and allow the same at the sum of $17.62 for said disbursements, refusing to allow anything for said forty-two days' services. That both the eleven days' service charged in the said first account, and the forty-two days' service charged in the said second account, were actually and necessarily performed by the relator as such commissioner of excise, and the said sum of $17.62 necessarily expended by him in the discharge of his duties as such commissioner, during the said year.

To this writ the defendants return, that the relator did present his bill for services claimed to have been rendered as such commissioner, for eleven days' service, giving a copy of the bill, at $30, being for ten days' attendance of said relator at the board of commissioners of excise, as charged in said bill, disallowing $3 charged therein for one day making report to supervisors. Also, that the relator did afterwards, and during their session, present another bill, as set forth in the writ, (giving a copy of the bill in detail, consisting of services, from time to time, in attending justices' and other courts, traveling to get and serve subpœnas, and consult counsel, and attend to complaints, and settle with treasurer, and of expenditures in so traveling, and in and about various suits,) and that they allowed said bill at $17.62, for the disbursements charged therein, and that "the residue was examined, considered, rejected and not allowed by the said board of supervisors." The return further proceeds to deny the performance of the services, and charges in the bill, except as allowed by them; and that the relator performed more than ten days' service, by virtue of any requirement of any law of this state, or that any part of the second bill is legally chargeable against the county of Cortland.

The relator put in a plea to the return, reiterating the allegations of the writ above mentioned, and averring that no objection was made by defendants to either of said bills, except that defendants were not authorized to allow the relator for more than ten days' service, and that the portions of the bills not allowed were rejected for the reason that in the opinion of the defendants the law only authorized them to audit and allow the relator's bill for ten days' service as such excise commissioner, and for no other reason; also alleging that the second bill was audited and allowed at $99.63, but subsequently reconsidered and allowed at $17.62, as above stated.

To this plea the defendants put in a reply, admitting that the two bills were audited and allowed at $30 and $17.62, respectively, and that the relator was one of the commissioners of excise of said county, and denying every other allegation in the plea.

In connection with these pleadings, the parties submit a copy of the proceedings of the board of supervisors of Cortland county for the year 1860, in which appears the following: "Mr. Kingman offered the following preamble and resolution, which were adopted: Whereas it appears that a bill of Samuel Plumb (one of the excise commissioners of Cortland county) has been audited by this board for $99.63, for services and disbursements, which bill is contrary to the express provisions of the statute, which says, that 'in no case shall a greater compensation be allowed than three dollars ($3) per day, for ten days,' therefore resolved, that the said bill be referred back to this board for further action."

The bill was accordingly taken from the file and reviewed by the full board. "Mr. Kingman moved that the said bill of Samuel Plumb be rejected. By consent, the vote on the resolution was laid over until to-morrow morning, at nine o'clock." The minutes of the next day proceed: "The board took up the business of reconsidering Samuel Plumb's bill, which had been laid over by consent to this hour. Mr. Spencer offered an amendment to Mr. Kingman's resolution, previously offered, to reject the bill; that this board audit Mr. Plumb's bill at the sum of $17.63, that being the amount of his disbursements over and above his credits, as shown by his bill. The amendment was adopted. The question then recurred upon the original resolution as amended, which was adopted."

The case is thus brought before the court upon these pleadings and this evidence, at special term, and must be regarded as tried by the court upon waiver of a jury by the parties. As the case is presented upon the pleadings and evidence furnished by this extract from the proceedings of the defendants, I think it fairly appears that the portions of the bill rejected were disallowed on the ground that, in the opinion of the defendants, the statute prohibited their allowance; or, as stated in the resolution, the express provision of the statute is, that "in no case shall a greater compensation be allowed than three dollars per day for ten days." Whether they were rejected on this ground or not, was a fact properly in issue, and, it seems to me, the only issuable fact of those put in issue by the pleadings in this proceeding. It is of no consequence here, whether the time charged for, was *actually* or *necessarily* spent by the relator in the services alleged, or not. If the defendants were not satisfied as to either of those facts, and rejected the charges for such reason, their decision was final, however the facts might be; so that those facts cannot be inquired of here. But if the defendants rejected these items on the ground that the statute prohibited their allowance, that view precluded the *examination* contemplated by the statute under which the board of supervisors act in the settlement of accounts against their counties. That statute provides that boards of supervisors of each county in the state shall have power, &c. "to examine, settle and allow all accounts chargeable against such county." (1 *R. S.*, 367, § 4, *sub.* 2, 1*st ed.*) That is, in regard to accounts which are of *a kind* chargeable against their counties, they are to examine and decide whether they have been actually and properly incurred, and their decisions in these respects are final. (9 *Wend. R.*, 508;

26 *Barb.*, 118; 2 *Sandf. S. C. R.*, 472; 21 *How.*, 117.) Their jurisdiction in regard to accounts is limited to such as are by law chargeable to their counties. If they allow accounts which are not legally so chargeable, their decision is not only not conclusive, but of no force or validity. (*People ex rel. Kelly* agt. *Haws*, 21 *How.*, 117.) And on the other hand, if they decide that an account, which is legally chargeable against the county, is not so, and therefore reject it, their decision is of no binding force, and they may, notwithstanding, be compelled by *mandamus* to examine the account upon its merits, and reject or allow it, according to their judgment in that view of it. (*Hall* agt. *Supervisors of Oneida*, 19 *J. R.*, 259.)

In the case last cited, the court say: "The distinction recognized by us is, that when the inferior tribunal has a discretion, and proceeds to exercise it, we have no jurisdiction to control that discretion by *mandamus*. But if the subordinate public agents refuse to act, or to entertain the question for their discretion in cases where the law enjoins upon them to do the act required, it is our office to enforce obedience to the law by *mandamus*, in cases where no other legal remedy exists." And after showing that "the question raised before the board of supervisors was not, whether the applicant claimed more than a reasonable compensation for his services, but whether the account was legally chargeable against the county," and that "the supervisors denied that he had any legal claim which they were bound to audit and allow," the court proceeds to say: "Now this shows clearly, that the supervisors did not entertain the question whether $30 or any other sum was a reasonable allowance for the services rendered. That would have been a matter for their discretion, over which we exercise no control. The supervisors acted upon the principle that the applicant *had no legal claim*. * * If it be a legal claim, then we have no doubt of our jurisdiction to instruct and guide the supervisors in the execution of their duty, by *mandamus;* not to control their discretion in judging what is a reasonable compensation for such services, but to compel them to admit the claim as a county charge, and to exercise their discretion as to the amount." This view is fortified by the case of *The King* agt. *The Justices of Kent*, (14 *East.*, 395,) in which Lord ELLENBOROUGH said: "If the justices had rejected the application in the exercise of the discretion vested in them by the legislature, the court would not interfere; but if they had rejected it on the ground now stated, *that they had no power to grant it*, the court would interfere so far as to set the jurisdiction of the magistrates in motion, by directing them to hear and determine upon the application."

In the case at bar, as already stated, it appears that the defendants rejected the disallowed portions of the account on the ground *thut they had no power to allow them.* If they might legally have allowed them, *they refused to entertain the question of their discretion;* so that the case is made to turn upon the question whether, as the defendants assumed, the commissioners of excise are limited in respect to the services which they are to perform and charge for to ten days. I do not think they are; but that the act plainly contemplates that they shall not only control the granting of licenses, but also that they shall bring suits for such of the penalties as are not specially required to be sued for by other persons. The limitation is expressly confined to the time they shall spend in their meetings for the purpose of granting licenses.

The 22d section requires that the penalties imposed by the act, except those provided for in sections 8, 15 and 19, shall be sued for and recovered *in the name* of the board of commissioners of excise. There is in the act no other provision made for the bringing of the suits contemplated by this section, except the one in section 30, which is as follows: "In case the parties or persons whose duties it is by the provisions of this act to prosecute, shall neglect to prosecute for any penalty provided by this act, for the period of ten days after complaint to them that any provision of this act has been violated, accompanied with reasonable proof of the same, any other person may prosecute therefor in the name of the board of commissioners of excise." From these two sections, constituting as they do all the provisions of the act in regard to the duty of prosecuting for the penalties contemplated by the 22d section, the necessary implication is, that the board of commissioners of excise are charged with that duty, and that where suits are to be brought *in their name*, they are to be brought *by them*, except in the case provided for in the 30th section. If they are to bring suits, they are to be entitled to receive $3 per day for the time necessarily spent in the performance of this duty, according to section 5, as well as for that spent in granting licenses. The provision of section 5 on this subject is as follows: "No fee or reward shall be taken by any board of excise, or by any member thereof, for any license to keep an inn, tavern or hotel, or to sell strong or spiritous liquors, *or for any service required of such board;* nor shall any compensation be retained by any such board, or by any member thereof, or by any clerk thereof, out of the excise money, but the whole amount thereof shall be paid over to the county treasurers for the use of the poor in the several counties; but the persons composing such boards of excise shall be entitled each to receive the sum of three dollars per day for services actually performed, *to be allowed and paid in like manner as other county charges;* and no other or greater compensation shall be allowed."

I think, therefore, the relator is not confined in his right to charge *per diem* for services, to the ten days to which the board is restricted in the granting of licenses. It is the duty of the board to prosecute for penalties incurred, and the members of the board have the right to charge for the time spent in the performance of that duty; and where they present their accounts to the board of supervisors, properly made out and verified, it is the duty of such board to receive and act upon them. If they refuse to do this, the authority of this court may be invoked to compel them.

I think, therefore, the relator is entitled to a peremptory mandamus directing the defendants to examine the accounts *upon the merits.* But as was said by Lord ELLENBOROUGH, in *King* agt. *Justices of Kent*, (*supra*,) I "do not, by granting this mandamus, at all interfere with the exercise of that discretion which the legislature meant to confide to the" board of supervisors. I only say, that they have a discretion to exercise in deciding whether the relator has performed the services, and if so, whether the whole or any part of them ought to have been performed or ought to have been omitted, and consequently whether the account shall be allowed in whole or in part, or disallowed in whole or in part. To such effect must be the command of the writ.

I may here remark, that I do not agree with the defendants in the position taken by them, that the action does not lie against the *board of supervisors*, but should have been brought against the supervisors "individually, specifying in the process, pleadings and proceedings, their name of office," pursuant to 2 *R. S.*, 474, § 96, 1*st ed.* This is not an action against the "officers named in the preceding 92d section," to which the provision of the 96th section refers. It is made the duty of the *board of supervisors* of each county to examine, settle and allow all accounts chargeable against the county, as above shown. And it is to compel a performance of this duty by the *board*, and not by the supervisors individually, that this action is brought. Hence it is properly brought against the *board*.

A peremptory mandamus must issue, commanding the defendants to examine the said accounts, with the view above stated. The relator is entitled to his costs of this action.

UNITED STATES DISTRICT COURT.

Humphrey H. Crary agt. The Schooner El Dorado, her tackle, &c.

Meritorious services rendered by a steam-tug in our harbors, in saving a vessel beset with ice, cannot be placed on the basis of salvage services in their proper acceptation. A branch of the employment of steam-tugs, during the season of ice, is to aid vessels in moving their positions to all parts of the harbor.

A steam-tug aiding a vessel thus beset, is not regarded in the character of a volunteer governed by impulses of humanity, leaving her own pursuits and devoting herself to the rescue of another, with no view to compensation, but upon the final success of her efforts. Her services stand essentially on different grounds: 1. They impose no unauthorised or wrongful risks upon their owners. 2. They may have a reward, whether needed or not, and will not necessarily lose it because the services undertaken by them fail of being accomplished. 3. They differ from salvors, because they pursue and solicit the employment, and hold themselves prepared to fulfil a call to it, whenever made. They act notoriously as tow-vessels; as such, bargains made by them to render, for a compensation, services which otherwise might be salvage services, will be upheld, unless the case is clear that the bargain is a means of coercing an exorbitant price. In such case, the court will not permit the fears or weakness or ignorance of a party to be made the occasion of inequitable exactions from him.

In an action brought by the tug against a schooner and her cargo, to whom services of a salvage character were rendered by the tug in saving her from the ice by which she was beset, the court dismissed the libel against the cargo, but decreed against the bottom, with costs, for a reasonable compensation.

Before Hon. S. R. Betts, *District Judge.*

This libel was filed by the owners of the steam-tug C. P. Smith, to recover a salvage compensation for services rendered to the schooner. The libellants alleged that the schooner, with a cargo of molasses on board, was lying at anchor in the North river, surrounded by heavy ice, by reason of which she was in great danger, and those on board of her hailed the steam-tug, and agreed to give $1,000 to be towed to a place of safety, which the tug succeeded in doing, suffering great damage herself in the service, and they claimed to recover the sum of $1,000. It was proved that the tug had been employed in towing other vessels, which were near the El Dorado, on that morning; that she was engaged in the service only a few hours, and that the captain of the schooner was not on board, but the mate was, who, as the claimants alleged, could not make any binding agreement in the premises; that the customary compensation to tugs for aid of that description was $20 an hour, and no case was shown where more than $350 had been paid.

D. McMahon, *for libellant.*
E. C. Benedict, *for claimants.*

Betts, J. The recovery in this case cannot be justly placed on the basis of salvage services in their proper acceptation in law, nor on the footing of a specific bargain by the person in command of the schooner, to pay $1,000 for the towage undertaken to be performed on the part of the libellant.

The libellant's tug was employed in the towage business in this harbor, and out to and in return from the sea; and an essential branch of the employment of steam-tugs on those grounds, during the season of ice, is to aid vessels in moving their positions to all parts of the harbor, and from pier to pier along the docks on each face of the city.

The customary rate of compensation to these tugs, for aid of that description, is $20 per hour for the time they are engaged with a vessel and in going to her. The remuneration is enhanced in cases of great peril or extraordinary exertions, but no case was proved on the trial in which more than $350 had been received for this class of services rendered within the harbor.

Boats are built and equipped for this special business, and kept engaged in it at all periods of the year. The use of this kind of craft has grown to be one of the necessities of commerce and navigation in this port, and the demand for their services has brought into use a numerous flotilla of steam-tugs, who, like the pilots, are always to be had, to give vessels the advantages of their capacities in every season and under every circumstance in which they can be employed. The constancy of the demand guarantees also, in the average, a remunerative reward for the services they render, if it is not absolutely assured them in each individual case.

It has not as yet been attempted to measure that reward by an absolute scale of charges, it being probably found that the competition in business and the mutual interest of employers and employees will secure to this branch of industry an adequate compensation, and still restrain its exactions within reasonable limits.

A change so fundamental in inter-territorial and coast navigation, since the foundation of the principles of maritime jurisprudence, renders those rules defining the relation of helping vessels to those relieved by them in distress, in a great degree inapplicable. The new condition of things introduced by this modern agency, created for the conveniency and relief of vessels, either found in want of assistance, or in apprehension of needing it, no longer places the relieving vessel in the character of a volunteer, governed by impulses of humanity, leaving her own pursuits, and devoting herself to the rescue of another in peril, with no view to compensation but upon the final success of her efforts, attended with the hazard of sacrificing herself or her voyage in the adventure.

The courts apply their powers earnestly to encourage and stimulate salvage services of that grade, by payments for them, not restricted to the amount of benefit actually conferred, but measured also with a view to the meritorious motive of the acts, and considerations of public policy.

Steam-tugs stand essentially on different grounds. They impose no unauthorized or wrongful risks upon their owners. They may have a reward, whether needed or not, and will not necessarily lose it because the service undertaken by them fails being accomplished; and what differs vitally their aid from that of vessels casually coming upon one in distress, is, that the steam-tugs pursue and solicit the employment, or hold themselves prepared to fulfill a call to it whenever made.

Those considerations no way detract from their claim to an adequate recompense, nor impair the importance of their services to the interests and safety of navigation; but they demonstrate that the new relationship with other vessels, introduced by the establishment of this class of vessels, no longer entitles them to claim the character of salvors in most instances where it might, by maritime courts, be readily attributed to vessels not devoted to this special pursuit, having become a kind of public calling.

They act notoriously as tow-vessels. They seek that business, and undertake to assist vessels in that manner. When no other than towage service is performed, there can be no propriety, in respect to that craft, in characterizing and rendering it as a salvage. The courts possess ample authority to adapt the recompense for towage in extraordinary cases, to their exigencies, or it may, when not restrained by positive law, augment the ordinary amount of pilotage to meet the difficulties and merits of the service, without exalting it to a salvage compensation.

Parties, moreover, are free to bargain for themselves, and their agreements will be regarded as fair indicia of what might properly be claimed, when the case is clear of all overreaching or misapprehension, and will, as a common practice, decree in conformity with the agreement.

But they will not allow their powers to be used as means of covering the fulfillment of exorbitant or unconscionable bargains, however they may have been obtained. The court will be governed by the facts in proof, with a disposition always to uphold the agreement of parties, but with inflexible resolution not to permit the fears or weakness or ignorance of a party to be made the occasion of inequitable exactions from him.

I do not go over, on this occasion, the evidence in the cause; but I am satisfied from it, that the demand of $1,000 for the services rendered, whether placed upon the agreement of the master of the schooner or on the worth of the service, is unreasonably beyond what ought to be awarded the tug.

When the views of the court are fully expressed, it may be proper to notice the particulars of the transaction, and the reasons conducing to the adoption of the sum now decreed the libellant, differing so widely as it does from what the libellant contends he has proved—a positive contract to pay him, and that which the claimants suppose they establish to be a full recompense for the service.

The decree will be, that the libellant recover against the schooner, her tackle, &c., (in this cause,) $350, and his taxed costs. And it is further ordered, that the arrest and attachment of the cargo on board the said schooner be discharged, with costs to the claimants to be taxed against the libellant.

Decree accordingly.

SUPREME COURT.

Lucie N. Collins agt. Jane Heather.

Where, after a trial and verdict for rent due, judgment was entered and execution issued against the defendant, and the defendant moved to set aside the judgment and execution on the ground (disclosed for the first time) that she was a *married woman*,

Held, the evidence showing that her husband had been absent from the state a long time, and tending to show that she kept a boarding-house on her own account, that the motion *be denied, with costs.*

New York Special Term, June, 1862.

This was an action to recover rent. The defence was, surrender of the lease and payment. Upon the trial in March, 1862, before Mr. Justice James and a jury, a verdict was given for the plaintiff. Judgment was entered, and execution thereon was issued. A motion was then made by the defendant to set aside the judgment and execution, on the ground that defendant was a married woman when she hired the premises in question of the plaintiff, and still remained such; that she was not, therefore, personally liable for the rent, and that no action could be maintained or judgment given against her personally. The question of coverture was not raised at the trial, nor did the fact appear at any stage of the case prior to the motion. It was conceded that defendant's husband was, and for a long time had been, absent from this state. The opposing affidavits tended to show that defendant was keeping a boarding-house on her own account, and had occupied the plaintiff's said premises for that purpose.

RICHARD BUSTEED, *for the motion.*

EDWARDS & ODELL, *opposed, cited Code,* §§ 144, 147–8; 4 *E. D. Smith*, 125; 2 *Duer*, 679; 21 *How.*, 309; 13 *Abb.*, 13.

BARNARD, Justice, after consideration, denied the motion, with costs.

NEW YORK SUPERIOR COURT.

ALBERT G. LAWRENCE agt. FREEMAN DERBY and others.

Where it is apparent, by admissions in the answer, that it is sham or false, it will be stricken out as such, although *verified*.

Special Term, November, 1862.

ROBERTSON, J. The complaint alleges that the writ, by virtue of which the plaintiff was arrested, was caused to be issued by the defendants. The answer alleges that they have no knowledge or information sufficient to form a belief of the allegations of the complaint not therein admitted, or of either or any of them. The defendants must know whether they caused the writ to be issued. If their intervention be such as to render it doubtful whether it was causing the writ to be issued, they can state what they did, and deny that they in any other way caused it to be issued. If the facts stated show they did not cause it, a demurrer would determine it in their favor, or they would have the benefit of them, if denied and proved on the trial.

There is no such pleading as a general issue under the present system. A party is bound to verify his pleading, and if he does so, and any of his allegations are untrue, the plaintiff has a right to strike out his pleading as sham. (*The People* agt. *McCumber*, 18 *N. Y. R.*, 323.) This overrules all previous decisions to the contrary. The complaint is sworn to; there is nothing in the answer to contradict it, except the oath of one defendant, that none of them know anything about it. No additional affidavit is necessary. It is apparent, by the admission on the face of the answer, that it is sham or false.

It is not sufficient to strike out the ignoring of the allegation as to issuing the writ and leave the rest to stand, because there would be no defence left.

The answer must be stricken out as sham, with $10 costs to the plaintiff, with liberty to the defendants, within ten days, on filing and serving an affidavit of merits, to put in a new answer on stipulating to allow the date of issue to remain as it now is, and take short notice of trial.

GUNNING S. BEDFORD, JR., *for motion.*
LYON & PORTER, *opposed.*

SUPREME COURT.

LAFAYETTE D. HOLSTEIN agt. DAN RICE.

Where *supplementary proceedings*, having been commenced and continued before a *county judge*, until an order was issued for the defendant to show cause why an attachment for *contempt* should not be issued against him, and failing to show cause, the attachment was issued and put into the hands of an officer for service, and before the service the county judge *went out of office*, having previously transferred these proceedings to his successor in office,

Held, that the proceedings were properly *continued* before the successor in office.

An *order* of a *county judge*, dismissing proceedings on an attachment for *contempt* against the defendant in *supplementary proceedings*, is appealable to the general term.

Albany General Term, May, 1862.

HOGEBOOM, PECKHAM and MILLER, *Justices*.

APPEAL from order made by county judge of Albany county, in proceedings supplementary to execution. On the 11th of January, 1858, the plaintiff recovered a judgment in the supreme court, against the defendant, for $1,472.63, damages and costs. Execution having been issued thereon, and returned unsatisfied, the plaintiff, on the 7th of June, 1859, obtained an order for the defendant's examination, under section 292 of the Code. On the return day the defendant appeared, and the examination was commenced, and adjourned to a subsequent day. On the adjourned day the defendant did not appear, and an order was made on him to show cause why he should not be punished for a contempt. This order was personally served. At the time appointed, no cause was shown, and the proceedings were adjourned from time to time, on application of defendant's counsel. On the 20th of September, 1859, Judge ROBINSON issued an attachment for the arrest of the defendant. Unsuccessful efforts were made to serve the attachment. On the 30th December, 1859, Judge ROBINSON made an order transferring the proceedings to Judge WOLFORD, his successor in office, who took office on the first of January, 1860. On the 20th of January, 1862, notice of such substitution was served on the defendant. On the 25th of January, 1862, Judge Wolford issued an attachment for the arrest of the defendant, on which the defendant was brought before him by the sheriff of New York, on the 11th of February, 1862, and the judge ordered interrogatories to be filed. On the 12th of February, 1862, such interrogatories were filed and served on defendant, and proceedings adjourned to February 17th, to enable him to answer. On the 17th of February, 1862, the parties appeared, and the defendant moved for his discharge upon the ground that Judge Wolford had no jurisdiction. On the 18th of February, 1862, Judge Wolford made an order discharging the defendant from custody, on the sole ground that the proceedings had terminated with Judge Robinson's term of office, and that he therefore had no jurisdiction. On the 3d of March, 1862, the plaintiff appealed from this order to the general term.

Lyman Tremain, *for plaintiff, appellant.*
Anson Bingham, *for defendant, respondent.*

By the court, Hogeboom, Justice. The plaintiff, having a judgment on which an execution against the defendant had been returned unsatisfied, applied, in 1859, to Judge Robinson, then county judge of Albany county, for an order, under section 292 of the Code, to examine the defendant in regard to his property. The order was granted, duly served, the defendant appeared, and the examination was in part had, and adjourned to a subsequent day. On such day the defendant did not appear, and an order was issued and duly served, to show cause why an attachment should not be issued against him. No cause being shown, an attachment against the defendant was issued by Judge Robinson, but failed of service on account of inability to find the defendant. Meanwhile, on the last of December, 1859, Judge Robinson's term of office expired, and he made an order transferring the unfinished business to his successor, Judge Wolford, whose term of office commenced on the first of January, 1860. In 1862, Judge Wolford, on the application of the plaintiff, issued a new attachment on the old proceedings, against the defendant, on which the latter was arrested and brought before him. Interrogatories were filed, and time given to the defendant to answer. On the day appointed for answering he appeared, and moved to dismiss the proceedings upon the ground that the proceedings before Judge Robinson terminated with his term of office, and were not and could not be legally continued before his successor; that proceedings for contempt for disobedience of an order in supplementary proceedings, could be heard and the disobedience punished only by the judge issuing the original order, and were, in their nature, personal to that officer. The county judge dismissed the proceedings and discharged the defendant from arrest, holding that he had no lawful jurisdiction over him. From the order thus discharging the defendant, the plaintiff appeals to the general term.

1. I think the order is appealable, because it defeats the plaintiff of a substantial right. The object of the proceedings before Judges Robinson and Wolford was not simply to punish the defendant for a contempt of the judge's order, but to enforce the plaintiff's rights and collect his judgment. The attachment was issued at the instance of the plaintiff, and was a necessary proceeding to enable him to pursue the investigation before the judge. A contumacious refusal on the part of the defendant to answer before the judge, might be punished by the imposition of a fine fully vindicating the dignity of the tribunal for the contempt of its order or process, and fully indemnifying the prosecuting party for any pecuniary loss he had sustained thereby. (2 *R. S.*, *p.* 536; *People* agt. *Compton*, 1 *Duer*, 515, 532, 533; *Livingston* agt. *Swift*, *MS. opinion*, *third*

district.) It is not necessary now to determine whether the fine could equal the plaintiff's judgment, though I do not see why it could not, if satisfactory evidence was presented to the judge that the plaintiff had sustained that amount of loss by the contumacy of the defendant.

2. The considerations already referred to, show that the proceedings for the attachment of the defendant had a double object, to wit: 1. For the punishment of the defendant, and 2. For the indemnity of the plaintiff and the payment of his judgment. They should not, therefore, except for imperative and insuperable objections, be permitted to fall through or fail of their object, by the accidental circumstance of the expiration of the term of office of the incumbent thereof. The ends of justice require that the *continuity* of the proceedings should be preserved, if possible. Now, the proceedings under section 292 and subsequent sections of the Code, are either in continuation of the ordinary proceedings in the suit, and to be regarded as a part thereof, as has been held in some cases, (*Dresser* agt. *Van Pelt*, 15 *How.*, 23; *Bank of Genesee* agt. *Spencer*, 15 *How.*, 412,) or else they are special proceedings out of the ordinary course, but having the same general object in view, to wit, the collection of the judgment, as is held in several other cases, (*Davis* agt. *Turner*, 4 *How.*, 190; *see ex parte Ransom*, 3 *Code Rep.*, 148; *N. Y. Central R. R. Co.* agt. *Marvin*, 1 *Kern.*, 276; *Howard's Code, 2d ed., p.* 2.) If they come under the first head, then it would seem as if they were properly continued before the successor in office of the officer before whom the application was originally made. And as the suit itself in the supreme court, during its progress, would not abate by the death or expiration of the term of office of the justice before whom it was pending, or if he was the sole judge of the court, like the chancellor, by the death or expiration of his term of office, so the proceedings under section 292, which are in the nature of a creditor's bill, to enforce the judgment, (*Sale* agt.

Lawson, 4 *Sanf. S. C. R.*, 718,) ought not to be permitted to abate by the unavoidable occurrence of an event like the expiration of the term of office of the judge before whom the proceedings were first instituted,—an event not possible to be always foreseen as likely to occur during the pendency of the proceedings, and one over which the parties can have no control.

The propriety of such a rule would seem to be manifest in regard to the ordinary proceedings before the judge; and if such an event occurred while the examination of the case was going on, or during an adjournment of the hearing made for the convenience of the parties, I should have very little doubt, if, as before assumed, these proceedings were to be regarded as simply successive steps in the orderly progress of the suit towards its final consummation, that the subsequent proceedings might be appropriately pursued before the successor in office; and I have already endeavored to show that the proceedings to examine into the causes of a disobedience to the order of the judge requiring the appearance or further examination of a party, are in an important sense a part of the orderly proceedings under this section of the statute, inasmuch as they have in view (beside the punishment of the offender) the collection of the plaintiff's debt.

3. If these proceedings, however, are to be regarded as *special* in their nature—*extraordinary* in their character—*peculiar* in their object, and not to be classed among the ordinary proceedings in the actions or the ordinary methods resorted to for the consummation of those proceedings of which the summons is the first step,—then the question arises, whether, in the nature of things, or from any provisions of law, we can determine whether or not they die with the officer before whom they are commenced, or may be continued before his successor.

This question must be determined, I think, by the construction to be given to section 39 (51) of art. 2, tit. 2 of chap. 3 of part 3 of the Revised Statutes, (2 *R. S.*, *p.* 284.) This section provides that "in case of the death, sickness, resignation, removal from office, absence from the county of his residence, or other disability of any officer before whom any special proceedings authorized by any statute, may have been commenced, and where no express provision is made by law for the continuance of such proceedings, the same may be continued by the successor in office of such officer, or by any other officer residing in the same county, who might have originally instituted such proceedings," &c.

This provisiom being remedial in its nature, should be liberally construed to effectuate the object intended. That object apparently was to provide for the continnance of all judicial proceedings, except those in ordinary progress of an action—which would be continued of course—and those where special provision had already been made by statute. And I think it may, without violence to its language, be so construed as to embrace the present case. In a certain sense, "removal from office" may be said to embrace the displacement, departure or removal from office, consequent upon the expiration of the term of office of the incumbent, but more particularly, I think, the expiration of the term of office may be said to create a "*disability* of the officer before whom any special proceedings are instituted." If it be said that the term "disability" means a temporary one, or one applied to a particular cause or proceeding, I answer, it cannot mean that in the present case, because the language is, "removal from office" or "*other* disability," implying that removal from office and the permanent disqualification thereby induced, is one of the "disabilities" to which the statute refers. So also, it would not be a very latitudinarian construction (in order to promote the ends of justice) to read the words, "where no express provision is made by law for the continuance of such proceedings," by prefacing them with the words "in cases," and then they would plainly embrace the present proceeding.

It is said this section is inapplicable to the case in hand, because the statute is confined to "special proceedings," and this is not a special proceeding under the definition of the Code. I have already referred to several cases which hold this is a special proceeding within the definition of the Code; but I think it sufficient to say, that the term so designated in the Revised Statutes was employed before the enactment of the Code, and was evidently intended to designate all those which could not with propriety be classed under the *ordinary* proceedings in the action. In such a sense they are properly designated as *special*—that is, out of the ordinary course.

4. It is said that the power to punish for a contempt is *personal* to the judge or tribunal whose dignity or authority has been treated with disrespect; and *Shepard* agt. *Dean*, (13 *How.*, 174,) and *Wickes* agt. *Dresser*, (14 *How.*, 465, 470,) are cited in support of this position.

As to the first case, it must be remarked that *this* question was not before the court. The question *there* was, whether the *judge*, whose order was disobeyed, or the *court* of which he was a member, was the proper tribunal to enforce the proceedings for a contempt, and it was held that it belonged to the former. *Here*, the question is, whether the *successor* of the judge who has gone out of office, is in judgment of law the *officer or tribunal* before whom the proceedings were instituted. If he is not, the party is not punishable at all. Besides, Judge DALY's decision in *Shepard* agt. *Dean*, is directly opposed to that of Judge CLERKE in *Wickes* agt. *Dresser*, (13 *How.*, 331,) who holds that the *court* has the *inherent* power, in a general sense, of punishing as a contempt disobedience to orders made by *judges out of court;* and that it is a power essential to the efficacious existence of a judicial tribunal; and that the power has not been taken away from the court by any provisions of the Code relating to *supplementary proceedings;* and that, on the contrary, the Code, in the sections in reference to those proceedings, plainly recognizes such power.

The case of *Wickes* agt. *Dresser*, (14 *How.*, 465,) only decides that the application to punish for a contempt under supplementary proceedings, must be made to the *judge* whose order has been disobeyed, and not to the *court*, (in which respect it is directly contradicted by the case last cited,) but decides nothing as to the *continuity* of the proceedings before his successor in office, or the *legal identity* of the two. If, therefore, they are in legal effect the same person, and if the proceedings for contempt are but a mode of obtaining satisfaction of the judgment, then the last named objection to this process is unsupported by sound reason.

I think the order appealed from should be reversed, with ten dollars costs.

UNITED STATES COURT.

United States agt. Aylward.

In order to make counterfeiting an offence within the act of congress, (*Act of* 1825, *ch.* 65, *sec.* 20,) it is not necessary for the prosecution to show that the prisoner made the base in exact resemblance of the true coin.

The words "similitude" and "resemblance," as used in that statute, must be construed to mean, not an exact copy, but such a one as might deceive an ordinary observer.

If the spurious article had not a resemblance strong enough to deceive persons exercising ordinary caution, then the passing was not a public crime.

Before the Hon. A. T. Judson, *D. J.*

The prisoner in this case was indicted for passing a counterfeit coin, in the similitude and resemblance of an English sovereign, made current by the laws of the United States. He had pleaded guilty of passing the coin, but his counsel had taken exception, and called on the district attorney to bring into court the alleged base coin for inspection. This had been done. The coin on the one side bore a close resemblance to a sovereign, impressed with the likeness or head of the Queen of England, and the date 1849, &c.; but on the reverse side was a prince, mounted on a charger, with the words "To Hanover," and the figures 1837, in imitation, somewhat, of the sovereign of 1824 and of a double one of 1823. It was contended for the defence, D. McMahon, *of counsel*, that there was not such a similitude and resemblance between the genuine sovereign and this counterfeit, as to render the passing of it a crime within the act of congress; and the counsel referred to the *4th Washington Circuit Court Reports, page* 733, and the *1st Leach's Crown Cases,* (*page* 76,) *The King* agt. *Barley.*

J. Prescott Hall, *contra.*

The court, Judson, *D. J.*, now gave judgment. In support of the motion it might be stated as a principle, that if the spurious article had not a resemblance strong enough to deceive persons exercising ordinary caution, then the passing was not a public crime. The cases relied upon showed clearly that one ingredient in the crime was the tendency of the false coin to deceive and defraud the person to whom it was uttered; and in both those cases it was apparent that the coins could not deceive any one. So also, it had been held with regard to promissory notes. The important question arising here, was the true import of the terms "similitude" and "resemblance," as used in the act. In point of fact, these false coins had a decided resemblance to the genuine sovereign, in many particulars; but in others they wanted a strong similitude. He then stated the points of resemblance and dissimilarity; the latter was principally the difference between the George and the Dragon on the genuine sovereign of 1823 and 1824, and the prince galloping over the dragon, with the words

"To Hanover," and the date "1837" as appeared on the counterfeit coins in question; but these dissimilarities would only be known by those thoroughly conversant with those distinctions, and a very large portion of the community, who know nothing of these marks of resemblance, might easily be deceived; as in fact the persons were, to whom they were passed. It has been stated by counsel for the defence, that the similitude and resemblance should be strong and exact; but such could not have been the sense in which the words were used in the act. This construction would let loose every counterfeiter of coins, for an exact resemblance would extend to the metal itself. A reference to the best authors, (some of whom he quoted,) warranted him in saying that the terms, as used in the act of congress, did not mean an exact copy, but such a one as might deceive an ordinary observer; and such were those base coins.

The plea of guilty would require judgment to be entered against the prisoner, and he was sentenced to imprisonment, with hard labor, for the term of two years and eight months.

SUPREME COURT.

AARON C. GARNER agt. HORATIO N. WRIGHT, assignee of TUNIS H. SNYDER and PETER SHUFELT.

In an action against an *assignee* for the benefit of creditors, brought by a creditor for himself and all other creditors who might come in and avail themselves of the action, claiming an *accounting* by the assignee, and that the assignment be *reformed*, by substituting the proper name of an *indorser* with the plaintiff on a promissory note preferred in the assignment, instead of the name appearing in the assignment, which was alleged to have been mentioned or copied by mistake, *Held*, on demurrer to complaint for defect of *parties*, that the *indorser* of the note whose name was sought to be substituted by another, and the *assignors*, together with other *creditors*, standing in a lower class than that in which such note was stated, were necessary and proper parties, on a reformation of the assignment.

Columbia Special Term, January, 1862.

Demurrer to complaint for want of parties.

P. W. Bishop, *for plaintiff*.

H. N. Wright, *in person, for defendant*.

Hogeboom, Justice. This action is brought by the plaintiff, as well in his own behalf as in behalf of all the other creditors of Tunis H. Snyder and Peter Shufelt, who may choose to come in and avail themselves of the benefit of the action against the defendant as the general assignee of said Snyder and Shufelt, (insolvent debtors,) under an assignment dated the 22d day of November, 1856, to require *an account* of the property and effects which came into the hands of the defendant as such assignee, and to compel him to pay over and *distribute* the sum found due from him, upon such accounting, and to recover of the defendant the amount adjudged to be due the plaintiff on such accounting, and for general relief. The complaint, among other things, sets forth a copy of the assignment; alleges that certain specified accounts, demands and notes due to the assignors, have been paid to the assignee, and certain of their property has been sold and disposed of by the assignee; that a certain $1,000 note, due to the Union Bank of Kinderhook, first preferred in said assignment, has been paid as provided for therein; and that the defendant has realized out of the assigned property sufficient to pay a debt of $1,400, next preferred therein, over and above all previous charges and the expenses of the trust and debts previously preferred. In regard to this debt of $1,400, which is stated in the assignment as a note of $1,400, dated November 4, 1856, due to the Union Bank, payable two months from date, drawn by Snyder & Co., (the assignors,) and indorsed by Snyder and A. C. Garner, (plaintiff,) the complaint alleges that the plaintiff is the indorser upon said note, stated in the assignment as indorsed by *Snyder* and A. C. Garner; that said note is the only note mentioned in the second class of preferred debts; that said note was *in fact* indorsed by plaintiff and one *Shufelt;* and that the name *Snyder* is a clerical error, mistake or blunder of the draftsman or copyist; and that it was the true intent of the assignors that the aforesaid note should have been described as indorsed by said *Shufelt* and the plaintiff; "and this plaintiff asks that the same may be reformed in that particular, if necessary to protect the rights of the plaintiff under said assignment." The complaint then alleges that the plaintiff, as one of the indorsers of said note with Shufelt, has been compelled to pay the sum of $500 thereon, and that the defendant, although often requested to render an account as such assignee, has never done so, but refused to do so, until he was prosecuted for such purpose.

The defendant demurs to the complaint, because it seeks an account and appropriation of property "in which one Shufelt and others have an interest, and the said Shufelt and the other creditors are not joined as parties to this action."

The demurrer is not specific as to who are the other necessary parties besides Shufelt, or who are the other creditors of the assignors; and for that reason the demurrer is not entitled to a very favorable or liberal construction. But taking (as we must) the allegations in the complaint to be true, it is a part of the relief sought in the action, to *reform* the assignment by declaring that a note of $1,400, indorsed by *Shufelt* and the plaintiff, be substituted and incorporated in the assignment as a preferred debt in the second class, instead of a note indorsed by *Snyder* and the plaintiff. There is no allegation that there was in fact no note of that amount indorsed by *Snyder* and the plaintiff; and in the absence of such an allegation, I think we must presume that there was *such* a note, or at least one which *Snyder* is interested to protect. Snyder is not made a party to this suit, and may therefore be defeated of his just rights, without having an opportunity to be heard. I regard him as a necessary party, unless the complaint is amended by inserting some allegations rendering the addition of such a party unnecessary. Moreover, that would seem also to be a question in regard to which the assignors have a right to be heard. They have made a preferential assignment, as they had a right to do; and the instrument should not be altered or reformed, varying or disturbing the order of preference, without hearing them on the subject. There is also some doubt whether other creditors, who stand in a lower class than the one which prefers the $1,400 note in question, have not a right to be heard on the question, whether the assignment is to be reformed; for if it is not to be, and there is no such note as the one described, indorsed by *Snyder* and Garner, their debts may come in for a portion of the fund; whereas, if it is to be reformed, their debts may be excluded by the prior preferences absorbing the whole fund. There would seem, therefore, to be great propriety in hearing what they have to say on this subject.

The necessity of bringing in these parties, or some of them, is in no degree avoided by that provision of the Code which declares that "when the parties are very numerous, and it may be impracticable to bring them all before the court, one or more may sue or defend for the benefit of the whole. (*Code*, § 119; *McKenzie* agt. *L'Amoureux*, 11 *Barb.*, 516; *Bouton* agt. *City of Brooklyn*, 15 *Barb.*, 391; *Reed* agt. *The Evergreens*, 21 *How.*, 319; *Van Santvoord's Eq. Pr.*, 76, 77.)

There is nothing to show that the parties in this case come within the conditions of that section, either as to number or position. They occupy, or may do so, antagonistic positions and hostile interests, and are not, I think, so far properly represented, either by the plaintiff or defendant, as to exclude them from the right of being personally heard on the questions.

This is all which it is necessary to say, in order to dispose of this demurrer. I therefore forbear to express an opinion whether the complaint calls for a general account of the trust fund and its distribution among all the creditors entitled thereto, or only for a partial account, so far as the plaintiff's interests are involved, and whether, in the latter contingency, any other parties are necessary than such as are now before the court.

There must be judgment for the defendant on the demurrer, with leave to the plaintiff to amend on the payment of costs.

SUPREME COURT.

THE PEOPLE *ex rel.* WILLIAM BALDWIN and JOHN M. JAYCOX agt. ROBERT T. HAWS, comptroller of the city of New York.

The *fourth section* of the act passed in April, 1860, (*Sess. Laws*, 1860, *p.* 772,) to facilitate the taking of lands and building gate-houses, &c. in the city of New York, and which provides for an *arbitration*, and directs that it shall be held for the purpose of adjusting and determining the damages which the contractors, to whom the gate-houses were awarded, might be equitably entitled to recover of the city of New York, and if an award is made in their favor, directs the comptroller to pay the same, is *unconstitutional*.

When the law *compels* a party to *arbitrate* upon a claim, which properly should be the subject of an action, without his assent, such law deprives him of the right which is secured by the constitution, of a trial according to the course of the common law.

If this section was not unconstitutional, the provision, that if such report (of arbitrators) should be in favor of the party claiming such damages, such party should recover the same, &c., would give a remedy by *action on the award*, which would preclude a remedy by *mandamus*.

New York General Term, June, 1862.

Before INGRAHAM, LEONARD and CLERKE, *Justices*.

LUTHER R. MARSH, *for the relators.*

HENRY H. ANDERSON, *for the comptroller.*

By the court, INGRAHAM, P. Justice. The relators apply for a mandamus against the comptroller, to draw his warrant in their favor, for an award made against the corporation for damages sustained by the relators in consequence of the refusal of the common council to award them a contract for building a gate-house at the new reservoir.

This claim arises under the provisions of the 4th section of the act passed to facilitate the taking of lands and building such gate-house, &c., passed in April, 1860, (*Laws of* 1860, *p.* 772.) This section provided, among other things, "that for the purpose of adjusting and determining the damages that the contractors to whom the gate-houses and aqueducts, &c. were awarded by the Croton aqueduct board, &c., which they may be equitably entitled to recover of the city of New York, the same may be ascertained by arbitrators, one to be chosen by the mayor, one by the parties claiming such damages, and the third by the two arbitrators chosen as aforesaid;" and the same section, after directing the arbitrators to be sworn, to hear the case, and to make their award and file the same with the county clerk, allows an order of confirmation to be entered of course, and then adds: "If such report shall be in favor of the party claiming damages, such party shall be entitled to recover the same, and, upon presenting a certified copy of such report and order of confirmation to the comptroller of the city of New York, it shall be the duty of said comptroller to draw his warrant for the amount thereof, and to pay the same."

In pursuance of this act, three arbitrators were appointed in the mode directed by the statute. These arbitrators proceeded to hear the case. No notice of the hearing was served on the counsel of the corporation, and no appearance was made by him on behalf of the city. Notice, however, was served on the mayor and comptroller.

On such hearing the arbitrators awarded as damages, to

the relators, sixty-one thousand eight hundred and twenty-one dollars against the city of New York.

The report was filed, order of confirmation entered, a copy of the report and order served on the comptroller; a demand made of him for a warrant therefor, which he refused, and the relators moved, at a special term, for a mandamus. Which motion was denied.

The relators appealed from such order. In order rightly to understand the questions presented in this case, it is proper to remember that this claim is not one against the county, nor one which the supervisors have anything to do with, either as regards auditing or paying the same.

The contract was made, if made at all, in regard to property belonging to the city of New York; was under the direction and control of the Croton aqueduct department, a branch of the city government, and was to be paid for, when the work was completed, out of the city treasury. This was expressly held in regard to the work in question. The chancellor says the dam and the aqueduct must be considered the property of the defendants, and, as the owner of such premises, the corporation of New York is properly answerable for the damage which others have sustained thereby—and that case (*Bailey* agt. *The Mayor of New York*, 2 *Denio*, 433) was decided upon the ground that this work and the lands taken therefor belonged to the corporation of the city, and as the owners of property they were liable for any evils resulting from its improper construction or use.

The present claim is one of a similar character, arising out of an alleged contract for work on another portion of the aqueduct, to which the same principles are to be applied.

It is not material, in the examination of the questions which affect this appeal, to decide whether the relators had, by virtue of their offers to the Croton aqueduct board, to do the work on the reservoir, acquired any rights which entitled them to damages against the city.

Whatever claim of that kind they might have, could properly be enforced by an action.

The questions material to the decision of the present appeal are, 1st. Whether the statute providing for the appointment of appraisers was legal; and 2d. If it was, whether the remedy by mandamus is proper.

The statute, which provided for the arbitration, directs that it shall be held for the purpose of adjusting and determining the damages which the contractors to whom the gate-houses were awarded might be equitably entitled to recover of the city of New York, and if an award is made in their favor, directs the comptroller to pay the same.

It must be taken for granted that the intent of the statute was that the comptroller should pay the same out of the city treasury, although the provisions of law are such that he has not the power, without the concurrence of other officers, to draw from the treasury any moneys whatever. No one would suppose for a moment that the intent of the legislature was to compel the comptroller to pay such claim out of his own means, and yet, in fact, such a provision would be no more in opposition to the fundamental law of the state than to compel the corporation, by an act of the legislature, to pay a claim for damages for which they deny any liability, and which has not been adjudged by a legal tribunal to be a valid one.

It is contended by the relators, that questions of a similar character have been adjudged in their favor both in the supreme court and the court of appeals, and in support of these views they cite the case of *The Town of Guilford* agt. *Supervisors of Chenango*, (18 *Barb.*, 614, *and* 3 *Kern.*, 143,) and the case of *McSpedon & Baker* agt. *Haws, comptroller*, (21 *How.*, 178.)

But these cases, and many others of a similar character, which might have been cited, related not to the right or power of the legislature to compel an individual or corporation to pay a debt or claim, but to the power of the legislature to raise money by tax, and apply such money, when so raised, to the payment thereof. We could not, under the decisions of the courts on this point, made in these and other cases, now hold that the legislature had not authority to impose a tax to pay any claim, or to pay it out of the state treasury, and for this purpose to impose a tax upon the property of the whole state, or any portion of the state. This was fully settled in *The People* agt. *Mayor, &c. of Brooklyn*, (4 *Coms.*, 419,) but neither that case nor the case from 3 *Kernan*, 143, in any manner, gave a warrant for the opinion that the legislature had a right to direct a municipal corporation to pay a claim for damage for breach of a contract out of the funds or property of such corporation, without a submission of such claims to a judicial tribunal. In the case last cited, Denio, J., says: "The proceeding * * * is not aimed at, and cannot affect the corporate rights or corporate property in the town." Here, however, the act of 1860 directs that the claim of the relators, when adjusted by the arbitrators, shall be paid by the comptroller.

This is in direct violation of those provisions of the constitution, which say:

1. That no member of the state shall be deprived of any of the rights secured to a citizen, unless by the law of the land. 2. No person shall be deprived of life, liberty, or property, without due process of law. (*Constitution of State, secs.* 1 *and* 6; 1 *R. S., p.* 51.)

Both of these sections have been the subject of examination by the supreme court. (*Taylor* agt. *Porter*, 4 *Hill R.*, 138.) Bronson, J., says: "The words of the law of the land, as here used, do not mean a statute passed for the purpose of working the wrong. That construction would render the restriction absolutely nugatory, and turn this part of the constitution into mere nonsense." "The meaning of this section seems to be, that no member of the state shall be deprived of any of his rights, unless the matter shall be adjudged against him upon trial had according to the course of the common law. It must be ascertained judicially that he has forfeited his privileges, or that some one else has a superior title to the property he possesses, before either of them can be taken from him. It cannot be done by mere legislation." And the words "by due process of law" are defined in the same case as not to mean less "than a prosecution or suit instituted and conducted according to the prescribed forms for ascertaining guilt or determining the title to property;" and again, "when one man wants the property of another, I mean to say that the legislature cannot aid him in making the acquisition." The same doctrines were repeated by COMSTOCK, J., in *Wynehamer* agt. *The People*, (3 *Kern.*, 378, 393, *and* 12 *How.*, 238.)

If, by "due process of law," and by "the law of the land," is meant a suit instituted and conducted according to the course of the common law, then the legislature, by the passage of the act referring to arbitrators to decide the amount of damages the relators had sustained, deprived the corporation of a right to a trial according to the course of common law, and the provision referred to was in conflict with the constitution.

The conflict which has arisen in this case, as to who was appointed arbitrator by the mayor, shows the danger of selecting such a mode of trial which was not subject to any court, where such a proceeding could be controlled and questions of this character adjudicated. I do not deem it necessary to decide, even if there was sufficient evidence for that purpose, which was the arbitrator properly appointed.

Where parties agree to submit to arbitration any matters in controversy, such arbitration can be sustained, because it is the voluntary act of the parties; but when the law compels a party to arbitrate upon a claim, which properly should be the subject of an action, without his assent, such law deprives him of the right which is secured by the constitution, of a trial according to the course of the common law.

If, however, the views above expressed, as to the constitutionality of this section, are doubtful, still I am satisfied the remedy sought in this case is not the proper one. The same section says that if such report should be in favor of the party claiming such damages, such party should recover the same, &c. The remedy, then, could be enforced by an action on the award, if the same was valid. Where such a remedy exists, a party has no right to have a writ of mandamus. It is said the comptroller is directed to pay the amount. But with the knowledge that the moneys in the city treasury can only be used for the specific purposes to which they are appropriated; that other officers besides the comptroller must unite with him in the payment of moneys belonging to the corporation, and with the doubt, at least, which exists as to the validity of this statute, I think it is clear that the application for a mandamus ought not to be granted. (*See People* agt. *Brooklyn*, 1 *Wend.*, 318; *People* agt. *Judges of Oneida*, 21 *Wend.*, 20; *People* agt. *Supervisors of Chenango Co.*, 11 *N. Y. Rep.*, 563; *People* agt. *Burrows*, 27 *Barb.*, 89.)

The various cases referred to by the relator's counsel, on this point, were mainly cases in which the duty of auditing and paying depended on the action of the board of supervisors, and not of a corporation. The board of supervisors can be compelled in no other way, and where the application is to audit an account, or pay when the amount has been audited, this remedy is proper. The cases cited from 23 *Wend.*, 459; 10 *Wend.*, 393, as to corporations, were reviewed and disapproved of in *The People* agt. *Supervisors of Chenango Co.*, (1 *Kern.*, 563.)

The case of *Green* agt. *The Mayor, &c.*, (2 *Hilton*, 203,) is an authority for nothing except that a judgment may be recovered against the corporation for a claim for which no money has been appropriated, and if it has any relation to this case, it is to show that the remedy by mandamus is not proper.

The order appealed from must be affirmed, with costs.

LEONARD and CLERKE, J. J., concurred.

SUPREME COURT.

1. CORNELIUS HONLAHAN, JR., respondent agt. THE SACKETT'S HARBOR & SARATOGA RAILROAD COMPANY, appellants.
2. JAMES DRISCOLL agt. THE SAME.
3. CORNELIUS HONLAHAN, SEN. agt. THE SAME.
4. JOHN HORAN agt. THE SAME.
5. MICHAEL McMAHON agt. THE SAME.

Where the same *defendants* in several causes, sued by different plaintiffs claiming for labor and team-work done on defendants' railroad for sub-contractors, entered into a written stipulation in all of the causes, providing that all proceedings should be stayed in the above entitled causes, and that they should "abide the result of the final judgment rendered in the case of John Driscoll agt. The Sackett's Harbor & Saratoga R. R. Co., (defendants in these causes,) in which verdict is to be taken on written stipulation as to facts, subject to the opinion of the general term,"

Held, that the plaintiff in the John Driscoll case having subsequently obtained final judgment against the defendants, the plaintiffs in each of these cases were, on a reference for that purpose, *simply to prove the amount of their damages*, respectively, allowing the defendants to controvert their proof on that *single point only*.

If a party asks to have particular items considered in a court of review, and a report set aside for their allowance or disallowance, it is not demanding of him too much to require, that he shall,

1st. Bring the attention of the referee specifically to them.

2d. Make it manifest what disposition the referee has in fact made of them, by obtaining from him a specific report on that subject. And

3d. Except specifically to the report in those particulars.

Albany General Term, *May*, 1858.

WRIGHT, GOULD and HOGEBOOM, *Justices*.

THESE were appeals from judgments entered upon the report of a sole referee. The actions were brought to recover for labor and team-work performed by the plaintiffs, and in some cases by the plaintiffs' assignors, on the defendants' railroad, for sub-contractors. There was another action, brought by John Driscoll against the same defendants, in which certain leading facts were admitted, to wit: the incorporation of the defendants; the name of the contractor and sub-contractors upon the road, and that they had contracts and sub-contracts upon the same, and that the plaintiff was employed upon said road by one of the sub-contractors; that he performed work and labor upon said road, as stated in his complaint, and gave notice of indebtedness as therein stated.

On the same day of the date of the above stipulation, another stipulation was made in all of the above entitled actions, providing that all proceedings should be stayed in the above entitled causes, and that they should "abide the result of the final judgment rendered in the case of *John Driscoll* agt. *The Sackett's Harbor & Saratoga Railroad Company*, in which verdict is to be taken, on written stipulation as to facts, subject to the opinion of the general term."

The plaintiff in the John Driscoll case having subsequently obtained final judgment, the plaintiffs in the above entitled cases entered judgment in their favor on the above stipulation, for the amount claimed in the complaints respectively, which judgments, on motion, were set aside at special term, and orders made referring said causes to a referee "to hear, determine and assess amount of damages in each of said causes, and report thereon with all convenient speed." The referee reported in all of the causes for the plaintiffs, and exceptions were taken to his report by the defendants. The plaintiffs having perfected judgment, the defendants brought appeals to the general term. The remaining facts are sufficiently stated in the opinion of the court.

Geo. Van Santvoord, *for defendants.*
R. W. Peckham, *for plaintiffs.*

By the court, Hogeboom, Justice. The principal question presented on these appeals is, whether the plaintiffs, on the hearing before the referee, were obliged to establish their whole case, with the single exception of the legal question as to the liability of the defendants for work done for sub-contractors, which had been decided in a parallel case by the court of appeals, and in the John Driscoll case by the general term of this court; or whether the plaintiff was simply to prove the amount of his damages, allowing the defendants to controvert his proof on that single point. The former is the true rule, as claimed by the defendants' counsel, and the latter as claimed by the counsel for the plaintiff. Under the stipulations of the parties, we have no hesitation as to the rule which governs these cases. No question is open to the defendants, except the assessment of damages. They have precluded themselves, by their stipulation, from examining into any other part of the case. Effect must be given to every part of their stipulation. If they had merely intended to have the legal question of their liability for the acts of sub-contractors settled in one case for all others, it was easy so to have expressed themselves, and it would have been sufficient to have provided simply for a stay of proceedings in all the cases, until the pioneer case was disposed of. But they did not do so. They expressly agreed that the other cases should abide the result of the final judgment in that case, and thereby, I think, as a necessary consequence, bargained that the result—the final judgment—of that case, should govern the final judgment in the others. The subsequent order at special term, setting aside the judgments entered, without any assessment of damages, in the above causes, did not alter the case. The fair construction of that order is, in our judgment, to submit to the referee the simple question of damages; but if otherwise, he was, nevertheless, to hear and determine the cases, giving full effect to the stipulations of the parties. The result would be the same. The defendants had confessed their liability, provided they were ever liable in the case of sub-contractors. That question being decided against them, nothing remained for the plaintiffs, except to show the amount and value of the labor actually performed. The defendants might, perhaps, limit the recovery by counter evidence on this subject, by proof of payment, and by showing a notice on the plaintiff's part, restricting the claim to a less sum, Beyond this, I think, they could not go. All the questions, therefore, raised before the referee, in regard to the service of the notice; the person on whom the same was served; the time of service; the question whether the claim or notice of claim was for an original or an assigned demand, or a demand split up into several parts; and whether the suits were brought within thirty days after the service of the notices, were inquiries into which the defendants had, by their own acts, foreclosed themselves from entering. It is unnecessary more particularly to examine the action of the referee in regard to them.

The defendants claim that in James Driscoll's and in Cornelius Honlahan, senr.'s cases, the report is excessive in not allowing a deduction of $11 per month for board; but on recurring to the report of the referee, it appears that in point of fact such deduction was made.

The defendants further claim, that in John Horan's case the referee should have allowed only $59.60, instead of $85.94, as he has done. But to say nothing of the fact, that it does not appear that the referee's attention was drawn to this precise question, and that the exception to his report is not very specific on this point, it is sufficient to say, that this was a question of fact decided by him upon sufficient evidence; that he has in fact made a deduction of $31.61 from the plaintiff's claim; and that it does not clearly appear that the deduction should have been more. The defendants further claim several errors on the part of the referee, in McMahon's case, in not making sufficient deductions from the plaintiff's account; among the rest, an item of $50, sworn to by McMahon himself. But if we take McMahon's testimony, he was entitled to more than the referee allowed him, after making the deduction of $50. As to the other smaller items, it is enough to say, that it is not clear that the referee did not deduct them, nor that he was not entitled, upon the evidence, to disregard them. If a party asks to have particular items considered in a court of review, and a report set aside for their allowance or disallowance, it is not demanding of him too much to require that he shall in the first place bring the attention of the referee specifically to them; in the second place, make it manifest what disposition the referee has in fact made of them, by obtaining from him a specific report on that subject; and in the third place, except specifically to the report in those particulars. None of these things have the defendants done.

The judgments in all the cases must be affirmed.

WRIGHT, P. J., concurred. GOULD, J., dissented.

UNITED STATES COURT.

SYLVANUS G. CHASE and others agt. HUMPHREY H. CRARY and others.

Two vessels may be charged in a libel with joint negligence, where they jointly commit an act of collision which injures a third vessel, even though there is no apparent previous concert of action or navigation between the two colliding vessels.

Where the collision is occasioned by the joint negligence of those who have charge of the colliding vessels, as the servants of the owners, then a libel may be sustained against the owners jointly, as well as against the vessels.

Where the proof shows that only one of the colliding vessels charged, was guilty of negligence, the proper decree should be against that one, and in favor of the others, and not a dismissal of the libel because of the failure to prove the joint negligence.

The case of the *Samson*, (2 *Wallace*, p. 485,) approved of, and that of the *Moxey*, decided by Judge Betts, in 1847, distinguished from this.

In estimating the damages to the injured vessel, the court, on exception, rejected items claimed to be necessary to put her in good condition, because it did not appear that the vessel had been fully repaired.

The court also rejected an item of depreciation in the value, as being too speculative.

In Admiralty—Southern District of New York.

Before Hon. Charles A. Ingersoll, *D. J.*

This libel was filed by the owners of the lake boat Frank Carver, against the owners of the steam-tug Catharine, and the owners of the steam-tug Geo. Birkbeck, jr., to recover the damages occasioned to the Carver while in tow of the Catharine, by a collision with a lumber barge in tow of the Birkbeck, on the 8th of November, 1854, in the East river. The Carver was on the larboard side of the Catharine, and the barge was on the starboard side of the Birkbeck, her bow projecting beyond the steamboat's stern. The Catharine was coming from the Atlantic docks, bound to pier No. 17, East river, at the rate of about three miles an hour. The Birkbeck was bound to a pier in Brooklyn, and when first seen appeared to be coming across the Catharine's bows. When about ten yards apart, the pilot of the Catharine gave orders to slow and back. The Birkbeck had slowed and stopped before; and about the time when the Catharine slowed, the Birkbeck backed her engine, but her forward progress was not stopped, nor was her course changed. The Catharine had been stopped in the water, but when about fifty feet apart, the pilot of the Birkbeck motioned her to go ahead, which was done; but notwithstanding, the barge struck the Carver head on, a little aft midships;—and the libel is filed, alleging joint negligence and fault on the part of the two steamboats.

The respondents took the exception that there can be no joint negligence on the part of two steamboats, and that they would not be jointly liable even *in rem*.

C. Van Santvoord, *for libellants.*

D. McMahon, *for claimants and respondents.*

Held by the court, INGERSOLL, D. J., that the case of the *Samson*, in 2 *Wallace, jr.*, (*p.* 485,) is a case where a libel has been filed against two vessels *in rem*, without any such exception having been taken either by the counsel or by the court, which could hardly be, if there were any validity in the exception; and that in the case of the *Moxey*, decided by Judge BETTS, in 1847, was different from this, in that the libel that did not allege a joint negligence; that it must therefore be held that a libel against two vessels for joint negligence can be sustained.

That where the collision is occasioned by the joint negligence of those who have charge of the vessels as the servants of the owners, then a libel may be sustained against the owners jointly, as well as against the vessels.

That, as in the case of the *Samson*, a charge of joint negligence may be made against two vessels, and the proof show negligence against only one; and in such a case the decree must be against that one, and in favor of the others.

That on the evidence in this case, there was negligence on the part of the Birkbeck, in not changing her course; and if, as her pilot says, her engine was not strong enough to back against the wind, which was blowing, he was negligently exposing other vessels to be run down by having so weak an engine.

That there is no evidence of fault on the part of the Catharine. She slowed and stopped in time to enable the Birkbeck to avoid the collision, and had good reason to believe that the engine of the Birkbeck was strong enough to give her stern way against the wind, and that she would change her course, if necessary; that her going ahead was not the cause of the collision, which would have equally happened if she had not done so.

That there was no fault on the part of the Carver, either in not having a man at her helm, or in not properly using fenders. The pilot of the Catharine told the man at the helm that he was not wanted there, and the best was done with the fenders that could be done under the circumstances.

Libel dismissed as against Crary, the owner of the Catharine; and as against the owners of the Birkbeck, decree for libellants, with a reference.

On the reference as to the damages, the libellants proved that they had never fully repaired the vessel. Their witnesses proved the amount of repairs actually put on, and also testified that to make the vessel as good as she was before, she would need some brace clamps on the opposite side from the injury, which would cost $67.40; while witnesses for the respondents testified that she would not need such clamps.

The commissioner reported that the libellants should recover the amount of the repairs actually put on, and the cost of the brace clamps, and $100 for depreciation in the market value of the vessel, and $25 for her detention.

To this report the respondents excepted. The matter, on exceptions, was argued by

Mr. Van Santvoord, *for libellants.*
Mr. McMahon, *for respondents.*

Held by the court, Ingersoll, D. J., that to enable the libellants to enforce their right to be made good, they must submit such evidence as will enable the court to say what sum will make them good.

That the most satisfactory way of determining whether the brace clamps would be required, would have been to repair the boat fully. This, however, was not done, and the evidence is not sufficient to satisfy the court that they are required.

That the evidence of depreciation given, is not sufficient to support that item. It is too speculative and uncertain.

That the report must, therefore, be so modified as to strike out those two items.

SUPREME COURT.

ROBERT S. ROSS agt. CHARLES BRIDGE.
WINSLOW M. BURDICK agt. THE SAME.
WINSLOW M. BURDICK agt. THE SAME.

The right of a defendant to *offer judgment* under section 385 of the Code, in an action regularly commenced against him, is not limited to cases in which he would only confess *a part* of the plaintiff's claim. The offer may be for the *full sum* demanded in the plaintiff's summons and complaint.

The employment of the defendant, by the receiver, in supplementary proceedings, to make collections for him, where it appears no part of the assigned fund has been used for the benefit of the defendant, is not a sufficient ground for a removal of the receiver.

New York General Term, September, 1862.

INGRAHAM, LEONARD and ROSEKRANS, *Justices.*

THE facts will sufficiently appear in the following opinion.

By the court, ROSEKRANS, Justice. The plaintiff in the first above entitled action, whose judgment was obtained after the judgments in the other two cases above entitled, moves to set aside one of the judgments in favor of Burdick, on the ground that it was entered upon an offer served by the defendant, pursuant to section 385 of the Code, after the service of a summons and complaint upon him, the offer being for the full sum demanded in the plaintiff's summons and complaint. The special term has tried this motion. It was claimed on the part of the plaintiff Ross, that section 385 of the Code only applied to cases in which the defendant is willing to admit a part of the plaintiff's demand, and that when the defendant wishes to confess a judgment for the whole amount claimed by his creditors, he must comply with the requirements of sections 382 and 383 of the Code, and in case he does not the judgment may be set aside on the applications of subsequent judgment creditors. It has repeatedly been held that the proceedings under these various sections of the Code are entirely distinct and independent of each other; that the confession of judgment without action under sections 382 and 383 is analogous to confession by bond and warrant of attorney under the former system of practice, and that the proceeding under section 385 is analogous to the former mode of judgment upon cognovit. (9 *How. Pr. R.*, 130, 556; 10 *id.*, 293.) There is nothing in the language of section 385 which shows that it was the intention of the legislature to limit the right of a defendant to offer judgment in an action regularly commenced against him, to cases in which he would only confess a part of the plaintiff's claim. The titles of chapters three and four of the Code, in which these sections are found, show clearly that provision was intended to be made of a substitute for the former modes of confession of judgment without action, and when actions were commenced. Under the former system of practice, a party who had commenced an action was not compelled to receive a cognovit, but could proceed and take judgment by default. The Code has made it compulsory upon the plaintiff to accept the offer of the defendant, under the penalty of paying costs if he proceeds in the action and fails to obtain judgment for a more favorable sum than that for which judgment is offered.

There can be no doubt that the court have the power to set aside a judgment entered upon an offer of judgment, and would exercise it in a case in which it should be made to appear that such a proceeding was taken collusively between the plaintiff and defendant for the purpose of evading the provisions of sections 382 and 383. But in this case there is no suggestion of collusion or attempted evasion of those provisions, and the evidence before the court shows that such a suggestion would be unfounded. The order of the special term, denying so much of the motion as sought to set aside the judgment entered upon the defendant's offer, should be affirmed.

We think, also, that the order of the special term denying the motion of the plaintiff Ross to remove the receiver appointed upon proceedings supplementary to execution upon the two judgments in favor of Burdick, should also be affirmed. It is not suggested or proved that the receiver was appointed by collusion with the judgment debtor or for the purpose of protecting his property from other creditors. The explanation of the receiver's conduct in the particulars in which it is complained of by the plaintiff Ross, is full and satisfactory. The defendant has had no possession or control of the property which he assigned to the receiver, or of the place where the receiver has seen fit to keep it under his own control and that of the agents whom he has employed. The employment of the defendant by the receiver, to make collections for him of a portion of the assigned demands in the country, seems to have been a judicious exercise of his powers, and no part of the assigned fund has been used for the benefit of the assignor. The personal responsibility of the receiver is unquestioned, and his security ample. The plaintiff Ross and other creditors can at any time require the receiver to account, and the court will control the action of its officer.

The order of special term should be affirmed, with costs.

LEONARD, J. I concur.

NEW YORK COMMON PLEAS.

JOSE FRANCHERIS agt. DAVID M. HENRIQUES and THOMAS J. FERRIS.

Where the plaintiff in his complaint averred that Henriques was insolvent on the 17th Sept. 1857, and that by *fraudulently concealing* that fact from the plaintiff, and by *representing* to him that he was *prosperous* and *successful in business*, he led the plaintiff, on the 4th Sept., 1857, to consign to him $40,000 worth of segars:

And where the evidence of the plaintiff, among other things corroborative, disclosed that Henriques wrote to the plaintiff on the 17th Sept. 1857, saying that "business is good with me," and that "though money is very scarce, I do not suffer by it," and asking another large shipment of segars; and in *eight days* after such letter he failed, leaving $80,000 of indebtedness, upon his own showing, and $250 worth of effects to meet it, having by one stroke swept away the whole of the segars consigned to him by the plaintiff to pay $51,000 of indebtedness to members of his family,

Held, that upon such a state of facts, the plaintiff was entitled to *go to the jury* upon the question whether Henriques, by concealment and a false representation of his real condition, did not procure the shipment of the 4th of September to be made to him, neither expecting nor intending to pay for the goods, but designing to appropriate them in the way he did. The question was fairly raised, and it was a question of *intent*, which was not for the court, but the jury.

New York General Term, November, 1862.

Daly, Brady and Hilton, *Judges*.

The facts of this case will sufficiently appear in the opinion.

By the court, Daly, F. J. It is averred in the complaint that Henriques was insolvent on the 17th September, 1857, and that by fraudulently concealing that fact from the plaintiff, and by representing to him that he was prosperous and successful in business, he led the plaintiff to consign to him $40,000 worth of segars. That the representations were of the character alleged, sufficiently appears by Henrique's letters from the 17th of August to the 17th of September, 1857. Prior to that, on the 17th of August, 1857, the plaintiff shipped to him, from Havana, a large quantity of segars, amounting to $36,102. On the 4th of September, 1857, he made another shipment amounting to $33,234, and eight days before his failure Henriques wrote, hoping that he would have a good lot by the next shipment. On the 17th of August, 1857, he wrote, "I have money, but business is so dull that I am afraid to use it." On the 7th of September, that he had to pay a large sum in the month of August, but that it did not put him to any inconvenience. On the 12th, that the shipment of the 17th of August would turn out to be a very good one; that the segars were selling very well, and that all his customers were in very good circumstances; and on the 17th, he says that "business is good with me," and that "though money is very scarce, I do not suffer by it." Eight days after, he failed. During all the time, he was heavily embarrassed. By his own showing he had, in the July preceding, confessed a judgment to his brother-in-law for the very large sum of $34.675, This was alleged to be for money loaned in sums of $15,000, $6,000 and $4,075, from the 29th of June to the 8th of July, the day when the confession was given. He was further, by his own showing, indebted to his brother-in-law in $6,213, and to his mother and his aunt in $10,487; $4,029 of which latter amount was for money loaned from his mother in the February preceding, and $6,468 for money loaned by his aunt three years before. On the 20th of September, the last of the two shipments of $33,234 arrived. Five days after, he transferred the bill of lading to his brother-in-law, the brother-in-law then being in Europe, and made a bill of sale to him of the whole shipment, to secure the debt before referred to, of $34,675, and on the same day he confessed a judgment to his brother-in-law for $6,458, for money deposited with him. On the next day, the 26th, he confessed a judgment to his mother, she then being in Europe, for $4,029, and a judgment to his aunt for $6,458; and on that day, the 26th day of September, 1857, four judgments were entered up to his brother-in-law, his aunt, and his mother, amounting in the aggregate to $51,000. On the same day, four executions were placed in the hands of the sheriff, and a levy was made upon the same day, by the direction of the attorney of Henriques, upon segars in his store and in the bonded warehouse. There was but $100 worth in his store. The rest was in the bonded warehouse, and consisted of the two shipments made by the plaintiff, less $15,659 of the first shipment, which Henriques had previously withdrawn. Ten days after, he made an assignment for the benefit of creditors, preferring seven creditors whose debts amounted to $8,741. No property passed under this assignment, except outstanding claims consisting of protested paper and book accounts, amounting nominally to $100,000, but out of which the assignee realized only a very small sum, between $100 and $150. These claims and office furniture, worth less than $100, constituted, with the two shipments sent by the plaintiff, all that Henriques had at the time of his failure. The two shipments went to satisfy the judgment in favor of his brother-in-law, his mother and his aunt. What he had beyond these shipments to satisfy the creditors under his assignment, did not exced in value $150.

All that appeared in respect to the outstanding claims, amounting nominally to $100,000, was, that $10,000 of that amount had been due for six years, and $20,000 of it for two or three years; and that the remainder did not represent recent losses, is inferable from the statement of Henrique's brother, who was his clerk and assignee; that he knew of no particular losses he had met with between August and the 27th of September, except in the way of paying interest; that he paid a very large amount of interest between these dates, "heavier shaves" than he did before; and we have his own statement in writing in his letter to the plaintiff the day after his failure, that for the last three years he had met with very heavy losses in his business. His brother, in reply to a question to which the plaintiff objected, and which objection I think was well taken, said that all Henrique's embarrassments arose from the banks contracting their discounts. There was a serious commercial panic in New York, commencing with the failure of the Ohio Life and Trust Company on the 17th of August, 1857. To this he refers in his letter to the plaintiff, but declares that happily it did not put him to any inconvenience. This he says on the 7th of September, and on the 17th, (eight days before his failure,) he wrote that money was very scarce, but that he did not suffer by it. If any great and unexpected loss had occurred during the few days that intervened between that time and his failure, which suddenly changed his situation, and compelled him to stop payment, it may fairly be inferred that an event so important would have been known to his brother, and would have been brought out upon his cross-examination.

We have, then, in the evidence, these facts: That for three years he had met with very heavy losses in his business; that in July he was largely indebted, to an amount exceeding $51,000, and that he then confessed a judgment to his brother-in-law for $34,675; that from August to his failure, his clerk, brother and subsequent assignee knew of no particular losses he had sustained. That when he failed he had, in addition to what he owed to his brother-in-law, his mother and aunt, debts to the amount of $8,741; and how much beyond that, is not disclosed by his assignment, as that embraces only creditors of the first class, who were preferred. That his assets to meet this large indebtedness, leaving out the property shipped to him by the plaintiff from the 17th August to the 4th of September, was not worth $250. That after he had transferred the second shipment to his brother-in-law, Ferris, and executed to him a bill of sale for it, which he delivered to Ferris' agent, he made oath at the custom-house that he was himself the owner of the goods; and though the consideration of the transfer and bill of sale was the $34,000 owing to Ferris, a judgment for the same debt was upon the same day entered, and a levy made under it upon the same property. That ten days before his failure, he drew out of the custom-house $15,679 of the first shipment; that the residue of it and the whole of the second was turned over to his relatives, to satisfy judgments confessed to them, and that eight days before all this was done, he wrote to the plaintiff, urging a further shipment, with a request to send him a good lot of fine specified brands of segars, declaring that business was good with him, and adding, "thank God, that though money is very scarce, I do not suffer by it, because my payments this month have been very light, and happily my heavy payments took place last month;" and the plaintiff, in pursuance of the request, having made the shipment, Henriques' brother, as his assignee, now claims it, and has commenced a suit against the plaintiff to recover the segars thus consigned; to which may be added that which the letters of Henriques, written to the plaintiff during this period, abound in expressions of the greatest confidence and friendship. The plaintiff is not even placed among the preferred class in his assignment. The property consigned by him from the 1st of August to the 4th of September, has been disposed of by Henriques among his relatives, and the plaintiff, after $8,741 of preferred creditors, has the benefit of sharing in an estate the whole value of which is shown to be under $150.

This state of facts appearing on the part of the plaintiff, he was, in my judgment, entitled to go to the jury upon the question whether Henriques, by a concealment and a false representation of his real condition, did not procure the shipment of the 4th of September to be made to him, neither expecting nor intending to pay for the goods, but designing to appropriate them in the way in which he did. On the facts shown the question was fairly raised, and it was a question of intent, which was not for the court but for the jury. (*Smith* agt. *Acker*, 23 *Wend.*, 658.)

It is suggested that the business between Henriques and the plaintiff was one of long standing, and that the shipments were made in the regular course of business, without any new inducement being held out. It did not appear by the evidence whether the business was of long standing or not. It does appear that there were transactions before the two shipments referred to. It also appears that bills were drawn against each shipment, and that Henriques in each letter took occasion to refer to his circumstances; to declare, eight days before his failure, that his heavy payments took place before the panic; that his payments in the month of September were very light; that he did not suffer by the scarcity of money; although his brother testifies that he paid "heavier shaves" in September than he did before; that he paid a very large amount of interest during that month to Moses Taylor and other wealthy men.

His letters convey, and it is apparent were intended to convey, the impression that he was wholly free from embarrassment. He writes on the 17th of August that he has money, but that business is dull and that he is afraid to use it. In another, that the stoppage of the banks put him to no other inconvenience except to lock up $3,500 of his funds; the fact being that he had in the July previous procured loans from his brother-in-law to the amount of $34,000; and that his brother-in-law, in making this loan, looked upon his affairs as very critical, is evident from his taking a confession of judgment, and from his instructions to his agent, to watch Henrique's business very closely, and if there was any danger of his failing, to put the judgment immediately in the hands of the sheriff, and take every possible method of securing the debt. This was long before the panic, and nearly three months before the banks stopped pay. The facts disclosed warrant the presumption that he was then insolvent; that though he might go on for some time by getting discounts, his condition was then irretrievable, except by what he calls a "brilliant operation." That he had been brought to that state by three years' very heavy losses in business, and that the shutting off of discounts merely accelerated a result that was inevitable. The prosperous or safe condition portrayed in his letter was not true. In eight days after the flattering letter to the plaintiff, of 17th of September, asking another large shipment, he fails, leaving $80,000 of indebtedness, upon his own showing, and $250 worth of effects to meet it, having by one stroke swept away the whole of the segars consigned to him by the plaintiff, to pay $51,000 of indebtedness to members of his family.

If the question had been submitted to the jury, and they

were of opinion that he obtained the $33,000 worth of segars, shipped on the 4th of September, with a preconceived intention not to pay for them; that he obtained them by designedly misrepresenting his real condition, the conclusion would be that he acquired no title, and that having none himself, he could transfer none to the defendant Ferris. Nothing in such a case would pass by the indorsement of the bill of lading, the bill of sale, or by the seizure of the segars under the execution against Henriques. (*Mowrey* agt. *Welsh*, 8 *Cow.*, 238; *Ash* agt. *Putnam*, 1 *Hill*, 302.) It is suggested that the non-suit was right, the plaintiff having given no evidence to show that he was the owner, the presumption being that the goods belong to the consignee. The relation between the plaintiff and Henriques clearly appeared. The shipment was made against bills drawn upon Henriques in favor of the plaintiff. If the shipment was procured by fraud, this evidence was enough to show that the plaintiff was the owner.

I am not satisfied, moreover, even if the case is divested of the question of fraud, that the right of stoppage *in transitu* did not exist, but I forbear to discuss that question, deeming what is above stated sufficient to entitle the plaintiff to a new trial.

COURT OF APPEALS.

BENJAMIN KELLER, adm'r of RACHEL KELLER, his mother, agt. THE NEW YORK CENTRAL RAILROAD COMPANY.

No proof of *pecuniary* or *special damage* to the plaintiff or next of kin is necessary to sustain an action brought under the statute by the administrator of the deceased for injuries to the person. (*See to the same effect Oldfield* agt. *N. Y. Central R. R. Co.*, 14 *N. Y. R.*, 310.)

The question of *negligence* in all cases involves a question of *fact*, and it is only where the question of fact is *free from all doubt* that the court has a right to apply the law without the action of the jury; that is, the facts may be so clear and decided that the inference of negligence is irresistible; and in every such case it is the duty of the court to decide; but when the facts or the inference to be drawn from them are *in any degree doubtful*, the only proper rule is to submit the whole matter to the jury under proper instructions.

The *negligence* of the party, which will *defeat his action* in these cases, is nothing more than a *want of proper care;* and this question is always more or less affected by the conduct of the *opposing party*.

It is not always negligence to cross a railroad track. If the crossing is at a time when no train is due, and cannot be reasonably expected to pass, it is *not negligence*. It is not negligence when a person uses his faculties the best he is capable of under the circumstances.

In this case, the deceased mother and daughter, passengers on a mail train of the defendants' cars going west, left the cars at a station where they desired to stop, while the cars were on a slow move forward, getting off on the south side where there was another railroad track, over seven feet distant; they attempted to cross the latter track when an express train going east, at the rate of thirty or forty miles an hour, struck and killed them instantly. The two trains should have passed each other two and a half miles west of the station—the mail train being behind time,

Held, that the inference to be drawn from a pretty broad field of facts and circumstances, which legitimately belonged to the jury, rendered it a fit case to be submitted to the jury, and the defendants' motion for a *non-suit* was properly *denied*.*

September Term, 1861.

This action was brought by Benjamin Keller, administrator of Rachel Keller, to recover damages for injuries to her, and for killing her, by defendants, at Canastota, in the county of Madison, on the 29th day of August, 1854, under and in pursuance of the act of 1847, entitled "An act requiring compensation for causing death by wrongful act, neglect or default," as amended by chapter 256 of the Laws of 1849.

* If the case of *Ernst* agt. *Hudson R. R. R. Co.*, (*ante, p.* 97,) is to be followed, it would seem that the deceased in this case, both mother and daughter, were guilty of gross negligence in *omitting to look both ways upon the track* they were about to cross, to ascertain whether a train was approaching in either direction. If they had looked they would have seen it, and under the common instincts of humanity for the preservation of life, would have remained on the cars and been saved; or as in the case of *Wilds*, (23 *How. P. R.*, 492,) would have decided that they could cross uninjured and take the consequences. The presumption is, under this rule, that if they did look, they decided on the latter course; and what better or safer rule can be laid down in these cases than the one stated in *Ernst* agt. *Hudson R. R. R. Co.*; and that there is a necessity for some rule or settled direction on the subject is apparent, on looking over the many reported cases on this subject, most of which are injuries and death caused by undertaking to cross a railroad. As the latter case is the latest from this court, it ought to be considered binding. Rep.

The action was tried at the Madison circuit, in March, 1857, when the plaintiff obtained a verdict against the defendants for $1,700 damages.

The deceased was a widow, and left no child, surviving her, under the age of twenty-one years, or relative who was dependent upon her for support. Her heirs and next of kin were two sons and a daughter, all of whom were over twenty-one years of age. Another adult daughter was killed at the same time and in the same manner Mrs. Keller was.

Mrs. Keller and her daughter (Mrs. Dickens) arrived at Canastota, in the mail train from the east, which train was a few minutes behind time when it was stopped. That train was on the north track, which was about seven feet from the north rail of the south track, *i. e.* the south rail of the north track was about seven feet from the north rail of the south track. Mrs. Keller and Mrs. Dickens got off the mail train, on the south side, just previous to the passing of an express train at full speed, on the south track, from the west, and before they got across the south track that train struck them and killed both of them instantly.

The supreme court, at the general term, denied the defendants' motion for a new trial. (*See* 17 *How. Pr. R.*, 102; 28 *Barb.*, 44.)

The defendants appealed to the court of appeals, where the decision of the supreme court was affirmed.

The facts not stated above, which are necessary to a correct understanding of the points decided by the court of appeals, are contained in the opinion of that court, delivered by Judge Mason.

T. Jenkins, *for plaintiff.*
S. T. Fairchild, *for defendants.*

Mason, J. The first question which I propose to

consider in this case is, whether the judge at circuit was right in his refusal to grant the defendants' motion for a non-suit.

The grounds taken by the counsel on that motion, or that the complaint be dismissed, are: 1, because no damages were proved as contemplated by the statute, neither to the husband, nor to the next of kin, nor are any alleged in the complaint; 2, because no negligence or wrongful act on the part of the defendants is proved, but the contrary; 3, because the undisputed evidence in the case shows positive carelessness on the part of the deceased, which contributed to the accident. The case of *Oldfield, administrator of Downie* agt. *the New York & Harlem Railroad Company*, (14 *N. Y. R.*, 310,) and the complaint in the action furnishes a complete answer to the first objection. That case decides that no proof of resulting damages in such an action is necessary to sustain it, and it is alleged in the complaint that the next of kin of Rachel, the intestate, suffered great loss and damage by means of her death. There clearly was sufficient evidence upon the question of the defendants' negligence to submit the case to the jury. In the first place, it was negligence in the engineer of the express train to run his train past the station at the rate of thirty to forty miles an hour, when he knew the mail train was at the station discharging its passengers. In the second place, it was negligence in the conductor of the mail train to make so short a stop at the station. He should have given more time, and seen to it that his passengers were safely discharged. At least he should have given them reasonable time. In the third place, the station should have been announced in the car where the deceased was. I know there is a conflict in the evidence whether the station was announced in this car or not; that certainly belonged to the jury to decide, and we must assume it was found in favor of the plaintiff. In the fourth place, the defendants' servants, having in charge the mail train, knew that the express train was approaching at a rapid speed, and that there was great danger to be apprehended of injury to those who were to get off from their train, and they should have taken more precaution. The brakemen stationed to keep persons from getting off the south side were negligent in their duties, either in allowing these ladies to get off on that side or for leaving their posts before the apprehended danger was past. It seems this danger was apprehended and would have been guarded against if the brakemen had not been negligent in discharging their duty. The brakeman between the first and second car says, he knew the express train was coming and kept his station on the south side of the platform to prevent people getting off on that side. The deceased and her mother got off that platform on the south side, and yet this brakeman says he first saw them on the south track. He must have been asleep or else not attending to his duties.

The question of negligence in all cases involves a question of fact, and it is only where the question of fact is free from all doubt that the court has a right to apply the law without the action of the jury. (*Banker* agt. *Rens. & Sar. Railroad Co.*, 32 *Barb. R.*, 165–169.) When either the facts or the inference to be drawn from them are in any degree doubtful as to the question of negligence, it is the duty of the judge to submit the matter to the jury under proper instructions as to the law. (32 *Barb. R.*, 144.) The rule upon this subject was well stated by Judge JOHNSON, speaking for this court in the case of *Ireland* agt. *Plank Road Company*, (3 *Ker. R.*, 533,) where he said it by no means follows because there is no conflict in the testimony that the court is to decide the issue as a question of law. He adds, the fact of negligence is very seldom established by such direct and positive evidence, that it can be taken from the jury and pronounced upon as matter of law. On the contrary, it is almost always to be deduced as an inference of fact from several facts and circumstances disclosed by the testimony, after their connection and relation to the matter in issue have been traced and their weight and force considered. In such cases the inference cannot be made without the intervention of the jury, although all the witnesses agree in their statements. Deductions from facts and circumstances, from their very nature, are not strictly subjects of legal science, like presumptions of law. What constitutes negligence in such cases is determined by an inference of the mind from the facts and circumstances of the case, and as minds are differently constituted, the inference from a given state of facts and circumstances will not always be the same. I admit the facts may be so clear and decided that this inference of negligence is irresistible, and in every such case it is the duty of the judge to decide; but when the facts or the inference to be drawn from them are *in any degree doubtful*, the only proper rule is to submit the whole matter to the jury under proper instructions. The case at bar is one which the judge at circuit was clearly in the line of his duty in submitting the case to the jury upon the question of the defendants' negligence. There were so many facts and circumstances and such a variety of considerations to be taken into account in determining the question, the facts in regard to some of which being also in dispute, that the judge was right in leaving the inference or conclusion to be deduced from them to the jury; the facts were not so clear and decided that the inference was irresistible. My own opinion upon the trial was, that a case of negligence was proved, and if the duty had devolved upon me to decide, I should have so found. It is hardly a ground for interference with this judgment that another judge sitting in this court in review, comes to a different conclusion upon this question. The question to be determined in such a case is solved by the inference which the mind draws from the facts and circumstances of the case, and as minds are differently constituted, the inference from a given state of facts and circumstances will not always be the same. Here, then, you get a case which it is the province of the jury to decide. It would have been an error in the judge at circuit if he had refused to submit this case to the jury upon this question of negligence.

The remarks above made as to the submission of the question of the defendants' negligence, apply equally to the question of the negligence of the deceased. The negligence of the party which will defeat his action in such cases is nothing more than want of proper care, and this question is always more or less affected by the conduct of the opposing party. It is not always negligence to cross a railroad track. If the crossing is at a time when no train is due and cannot be reasonably expected to pass, it is not negligence. The passengers in this mail train had no reason to apprehend or expect that the express train would pass them at that station. Their time table required them to pass each other two and one-half miles west of Canastota, and such was their almost invariable custom. Mr. Toby, who kept the railroad house, there says that the trains do not usually meet there, and he did not know as they had that season. It was a thing unusual, and seemed to have alarmed the conductor of the mail train; and Rose, the ticket and freight agent, seemed alarmed that the express train was to pass while the mail train was receiving and discharging its passengers. The flagman, Weldon, says he was so flustrated and confused he could not tell how long the mail train did stop. It was an occurrence that semed to have alarmed Mr. Toby, who was familiar with all the dangers to be apprehended, and he was on the alert. Rose, the ticket agent, gave special instruction to the flagman. He sent Reese, the baggageman, around the south side of the mail train to see that no one got on the south track.

These two brakemen, R—— and Waterbury, saw the express train coming, and seemed fully to appreciate the danger. They voluntarily, without any directions, placed themselves on the south side of the platform of their cars to prevent persons getting off on that side, and Waterbury says he showed persons off the north side until he saw Miss White, who had got off on the north side, was passing around behind the cars to cross the track, and seeing her danger he started for her; but fortunately Mr. Toby saw her, and running after her caught hold of her, and drew her back when within three feet of the south track, and at that instant, says Mr. Toby, the express train came. The sequel demonstrated that these persons were not unnecessarily agitated in regard to the apprehended danger from the express train. If the deceased and her daughter knew that the express train was coming, it would have been a mere piece of recklessness in them to have got off on the south side. They did not know it, and therefore had no reason to apprehend it, and certainly the deceased was no more negligent in getting off the train on this side than on the other side, had not the express train been running in. The ground was smooth and hard where they got off, and there was a space between the north and south track of over seven feet in width, and where the passengers land who get off the down trains from the south track. It may have been, and I am inclined to think it was negligence in these ladies to get off while the train was in motion; and I think that we should hold that they assumed the risk of safely landing themselves from the cars. They did safely discharge themselves from the cars, and would have been all safe but for the unexpected approach of the express train. It was certainly not unlawful for them to get off the south side, and they were not negligent in doing so unless they had reason to expect a train to pass on the south track. Whether they were negligent or not depends upon the question whether they had reason to apprehend danger. Now it seems to me if she had been familiar with the locality and known the ground, and been familiar with it, they were not negligent in getting out on the south side; but these ladies were strangers there, and for aught that appears, were not aware that there was another track south of the one they were on. Was Miss White, the music teacher, negligent in attempting to cross this track at the time and in the manner she did? She had been accustomed to come upon this train, and cross the railroad to go to her music class, and knew that she had no reason to expect any train from the west at that time. She was not careless, because she had no warning of danger, and yet she would, beyond doubt, have been killed if Mr. Toby had not seized her and pulled her back just at the instant he did. And so young Fowler, who got off on the south side, would very likely have been killed if Mr. Toby and the flagman had not warned him of his danger in time to make his escape. Were they negligent in attempting to cross the track after they were safely landed? This depends upon many circumstances. They certainly were in great danger to remain where they were. The engineer of the express train swore that it would be difficult to stand where they got off, between the trains, when one was in full motion, although he thought it barely possible. Now, it does not appear from the evidence when they first learned the approach of the express train, whether before or after they had started to cross the track; if after, then it were safer to keep on. It does not make much difference, I apprehend, whether it was before or afterward. If they saw it as soon as they got upon the ground, they can hardly be charged with negligence in their best attempts to escape danger. Here was the express train coming towards them at the rate of thirty to forty miles an hour. Here was in their reach the train from which they had just alighted, and there was no escape that way unless they got back upon that train which had been increasing its speed. This could not have been done probably if they had tried. There certainly could have been no question in regard to their negligence had they been killed in attempting to get back upon the train from which they had just alighted. Had they stood still they would very probably have been killed. If they saw the whole of their danger after they landed, I am not prepared to say that the course they took was not the wisest. Had the mother but time to have taken one step more, and the daughter two, they both, probably would have been saved. But they had no time to reason and were undoubtedly greatly frightened, and if they did not exhibit sound judgment, or what we may think such, now in coolly looking the matter over, it is not such negligence as will deprive them of this action. It is not negligence when a person uses his faculties the best he is capable of under the circumstances. They were not negligent in remaining in the car so long as they did, unless the station was announced, and there is a conflict in the evidence in regard to this question which belonged to the jury to determine. There is also considerable discrepancy in the testimony as to the speed with which the train was moving when they got off, and Gen. Messanger says they had started with a slow motion, and others say they were at the speed of from five to eight miles an hour, and then again as to the time of the stop, the evidence varies from thirty seconds to two minutes. From all these facts and circumstances to which I have adverted, and many others which are to be found in the case, the deduction of negligence or not is to be ascertained. It is an inference to be drawn from a pretty broad field of facts and circumstances, and which legitimately belonged to the jury. It was a fit case to submit to the jury. It was so submitted, and they have found, from their verdict, that the deceased was not negligent. The supreme court, who had the right and were asked to set aside this finding of the jury, by their refusal, have approved it. If there was nothing to submit, I think it will demonstrate that both the jury and an intelligent court, which reviewed their finding, committed a pretty gross blunder; the one in rendering a verdict, and the other in sustaining it. This court has no power either to approve or disapprove of the verdict; all this court can determine is, whether as matters of law there is any aspect in which the case can be considered which would justify a verdict for the plaintiff; but the rule is, that if this rests in any degree of doubt, then the case must go to the jury for their verdict. They hold in Connecticut that negligence is so peculiarly a question of fact, that it shall be left to the jury, even on a conceded state of facts. (19 *Conn. R.*, 566; 2 *Smith & Bates Am. Railway cases*, 114.) There was no error committed in leaving this question of negligence to the jury. The general proposition was submitted on the motion for a non-suit that the evidence was not sufficient to entitle the plaintiff to recover, but it involved only the three propositions we have considered.

The point was also taken that the complaint did not state a cause of action; but the point is not made on this appeal, and there is nothing in the proposition, and it is not necessary to consider it. The first two propositions of the defendants' counsel, in his request to charge, are settled by this court against the defendants in the case of *Oldfield* agt. *The New York & Harlem Railroad Company*, (14 *N. Y. R.*, 310.) That case holds that no proof of pecuniary or special damage to the plaintiff or next of kin, in consequence of the death, was necessary to sustain the action. That case also holds that the existence of a widow to share in the damages, is not necessary to sustain the action; that the action lies in every case where the deceased could have sustained an action for the injury had she survived. The case of *Quin, adm'r* agt. *Moore*, (15 *N. Y. R.*, 432,) also affirms the latter proposition.

The third and fourth propositions in the defendants'

requests, to charge, involve simply the questions of negligence on the part of the deceased and the defendants, which we have already considered. The fifth proposition was charged as requested. The case of *Oldfield* agt. *The N. Y. & Harlem R. R. Co.*, (14 *N. Y. R.*, 310,) holds that it would have been an error for the judge to charge the latter branch of the sixth proposition, and it is not important, therefore, to inquire whether the first portion of the proposition is right or not; a request to charge the jury should be in such form that the court may charge in the very terms of the request, without qualification. (*Carpenter* agt. *Stilwell*, 1 *Kern. R.*, 61.) The judge is not required to separate a proposition of this kind and pick out what is good and refuse the rest. There was no error, therefore, in the refusal to charge the sixth proposition; but there is another answer to all of these propositions. They were submitted as a series of propositions for the judge to charge, and there is but a general exception which states that the defendants excepted to the judge's refusal to rule and decide as requested in the foregoing propositions. Now as several of the propositions are clearly erroneous, this general exception presents no question for review in this court. (*Caldwell* agt. *Murphy*, 1 *Ker. R.*, 416; *Jones* agt. *Osgood*, 2 *Seld. R.*, 233; *Hunt* agt. *Maybee*, 3 *Seld. R.*, 266–273.)

There are several answers to the defendants' objections, that the complaint did not state the names of the next of kin, &c. In the first place, it is not necessary to state them, and in the second place, the objection cannot be taken on a motion for a non-suit. If the defendant had desired to have the complaint more specific in this respect, his proper way was to move to have the complaint made more specific. And in the third place, as this objection was taken on the motion for a non-suit, it could not prevail, for this court has held in the two cases of *Quin* agt. *Moore*, and *Oldfield* agt. *The New York & Harlem Railroad Company*, above referred to, that the action depends on the right of the injured person to maintain an action for the injuries if he or she were living; and that the action lies in every case where the deceased could have maintained an action, were he or she living. This certainly settles the question that who are the next of kin is not material so far as the right to maintain the action is concerned.

The objection taken to the evidence of Davis and Wardecker cannot avail the defendant. The objection is a general one to the whole evidence. (*See case, folios* 36, 40, 124.) The most of this evidence was certainly wholly unobjectionable, and consequently the objection goes for nothing, If the counsel had called the attention of the judge to a particular portion of this evidence, by objecting to that specifically, very probably he would have excluded it. It is enough, however, that having objected to this entire evidence in gross, his objection cannot prevail for that reason.

The defendants' counsel proposed to ask the witness Rose, whether this train stopped ample time for all the passengers to get off, including these ladies. This was objected to, and excluded. This evidence was properly excluded. It presented one of the issues in the cause which the jury were to determine from all the evidence in the case, and the opinion of the witness was not competent evidence. It did not involve a matter of scientific opinion, or where the opinion of experts was competent. (*Cook* agt. *Brockway*, 21 *Barb. R.*, 331; *Morehouse* agt. *Mathews*, 2 *Comst.*, 514; *Merritt* agt. *Seaman*, 2 *Seld.*, 168; *The Jeff. Ins. Co.* agt. *Cathaal*, 7. *W.*, 72.) This witness had stated the time of the stop to be from one and one half to two minutes, while others had stated it to be thirty seconds to a minute; and there were other facts in the case upon which the jury were called upon to decide this question of fact. It is sufficient, however, that the evidence was not competent, for the opinion of the witness was not evidence upon such a subject. It was not competent for the defendant to prove by Cole and Woolever, although they were proved to have had experience in rail-roading, that in their judgment it was safer to run into the station, and discharge the passengers, than to stop either east or west of the station. It was a matter where the opinion of those men was not evidence. (21 *Barb.*, 331; 2 *Comst.*, 514; 2 *Seld.*, 168; 7 *W.*, 72.) The offer certainly went no further as a proposition, than to give the opinion of these men upon that subject, and was so treated and understood upon the trial. It was said by this court, in the case of *Daniels* agt. *Patterson*, (3 *Comst. R.*, 47–51,) that before a party excepts on account of the rejection of evidence, he must make his offer in such plain and unequivocal terms, as to leave no room for doubt about what was intended; and if he fail to do so, and leave the offer fairly open to two constructions, he has no right to insist in a court of review upon the construction which is most favorable to himself, unless it appear that he was so understood by the court which rejected the evidence. The offer was treated and understood, upon the trial, as but an offer to have the opinion of these men given to the jury upon that subject, and this it seems to me is but a fair construction. There is not a single fact stated which is offered to be proved to show that it was safer to go into the station; and besides, the offer of proof is based upon the distinct ground that these two witnesses were experienced men in railroading; Cole having been shown to be a conductor some eight years, and Woolever being an engineer upon the express train.

There is, however, another perfect answer to this offer of evidence, in any view which may be taken of the offer; the evidence was incompetent, as not being within the issue. There is not a single allegation, in the complaint, that it would have been safer to have stopped the mail train either east or west of the station. Nor is there any allegation that it was negligence for the conductor of that train to run into the station. Nor did the plaintiff adduce a single particle of evidence tending in the least to show that it was safer to stop short of, or go beyond, the station, nor was any such claim presented on the trial. The simple issue to be tried was, whether what was done afforded evidence of negligence, and not whether it would have been more negligent to have done something else. It is never error to confine the proof to the issue to be tried.

There are no other questions in the case, and where a trial and general verdict have been had, this court only deal with the questions of law, upon exceptions duly taken; we cannot consider whether the damages are excessive, or the verdict is against the weight of evidence, (4 *Kernan*, *R.*, 310.)

I advise the affirmance of the judgment. COMSTOCK, Ch. J. and LOTT, J., did not sit in the case. DENIO, HOYT, JAMES, and SELDEN, JJ., were for the affirmance of the judgment below; JAMES thinking that the negligence of the deceased was, if that question were examinable here, sufficient to bar the action, but that there was evidence on that subject enough to raise a question for the jury. DAVIES, J., expressed no opinion.

NEW YORK SUPERIOR COURT.

A. ALEXANDER ATOCHA, assignee, &c. agt. CLEMENTI P. GARCIA.

In all those actions, where the nature of the *cause of action* is such, that the defendant may be arrested under § 179 of the Code, it must be *stated in the complaint*; otherwise, an *execution* cannot issue against *the person*, unless an order of *arrest* has been served.

But where the action is one in which the defendant cannot be arrested, without some *extrinsic fact*, forming no part of the *cause of action*, but merely incidental to it, the fact must be stated in an *affidavit*, and an order of arrest must be obtained and served; and the averment of such fact in the complaint will not alone authorize an execution against the person. Hence the averment in the complaint is *immaterial*.

For instance, where the substantive cause of action alleged in the complaint, is the *debt* sought to be recovered, and allegations of *fraud* are also averred, the fraud being *incidental*, and only important to the plaintiff, as furnishing the ground for obtaining the provisional remedy of arrest; the allegations of fraud in the complaint are *immaterial* and *unnecessary*. The issue to be tried in the action is the *debt*, not the fraudulent contraction of it. The judgment recovered is for the debt, not for the fraud.

Such an action, where it involves the examination of a *long account*, although an order of arrest has been obtained, may be *referred*, under § 271 of the Code, without the consent of the parties.

Special Term, *July*, 1862.

The complaint alleges that the defendant boarded and lodged at the hotel of the plaintiff's assignor, with his wife and two children, from February 11, 1861, to January 27, 1862; during which time he was furnished by said assignor with board, lodging, and other necessaries, for himself, wife, and children, and that the same are worth the sum of three thousand two hundred and forty dollars. The complaint also alleges a demand of and refusal to pay. Allegations are also contained in the complaint, that the defendant made representations that he was in expectation of receiving large sums of money from the estate of his deceased father, and that upon the faith of which representations he was furnished with the board, &c. That about the 22d January, 1862, he did receive a large sum of money, as his share of his father's estate, and, thereupon clandestinely left the said hotel, and removed his property therefrom. The defendant denies each and every allegation in the complaint. The bill of particulars of the plaintiff's demand contains items covering upwards of fifty pages.

Monell, Justice. I cannot entertain a doubt that the trial of this action will require the examination of a long account, on the part of the plaintiff. The issues require the plaintiff to prove each item. The defendant, by his answer, puts him to this proof, and the action will fail, as to any part not sufficiently established by evidence. The case is brought, therefore, directly within § 271 of the Code. But it is objected by the defendant, that he has a right to a trial by jury, of the allegation of fraud contained in the complaint, and upon which an order of arrest has been issued, and executed by the arrest of the defendant, and that, therefore, the case is no longer referable.

I think, however, the defendant is mistaken in supposing such an issue can be tried at all. The action is to recover the value of board and lodging, &c., furnished the defendant, and for no other purpose. The allegations of fraud *in the complaint*, are not only unnecessary in order to procure the provisional remedy of arrest, but I think them to be improper, and should be stricken out, as irrelevant. Doubtless the plaintiff's attorney, in reading the amendment to § 288 of the Code, which provides that no execution shall issue against the person, unless an order of arrest has been served, or "unless the complaint contains a statement of facts, showing one or more of the causes of arrest, required by § 179," has supposed it necessary to allege the fraud, to secure the right to issue an execution against the person, if the plaintiff should not or could not procure an order of arrest. This, however, is not the correct construction of the amendment.

Subs. 1 and 2 of § 179, authorize an arrest, when the *action* is for the recoveries therein enumerated. In such actions the grounds of arrest must necessarily appear. They are a part, if not all, of the cause of action. Whereas in sub. 3, the grounds of arrest must as necessarily appear *after* the action is commenced. Sub. 4, which authorizes an arrest, where the debt has been fraudulently contracted, gives the provisional remedy in an action to recover the *debt;* and sub. 5 when the defendant has removed, &c., his property, with intent to defraud his creditors.

It is clear that in all that class of cases where the *substantive cause of action* is such, that the defendant may be arrested, it must be stated in the complaint, as in actions for injuries to the person or character, or for wrongfully taking, detaining, or arresting property, and the like. In these, the complaint, in alleging the *cause of action*, necessarily alleges the *grounds* which authorize an arrest; but where the substantive cause of action does not, of *itself*, warrant an arrest, and the arrest is an incident merely growing out of other facts, arising at the time, or subsequently, they become no part of the cause of action, and are unnecessary in the complaint. The true construction, therefore, of the amendment of the Code, referred to is, that in all those actions, where the nature of the cause of action is such, that the defendant may be arrested, it must be stated in the complaint, otherwise an execution cannot go against the person, unless an order of arrest has been served. But when the action is one in which the defendant cannot be arrested, without some extrinsic fact, forming no part of the cause of action, but merely incidental to it, the fact must be stated in an affidavit, and an order of arrest must be obtained and served, and the averment of such fact in the complaint will not alone authorize an execution against the person. Hence the averment in the complaint is immaterial. The grounds of arrest, in such cases, must appear by *affidavit*, and can only be met by affidavit. The issue to be tried in the action is the *debt*, not the fraudulent contraction of it. The judgment recovered is for the debt, not for the fraud. If the defendant fails to get the order of arrest vacated, he is liable to an execution against his person; and if no order has been obtained and served, he cannot be arrested, although the complaint alleges the fraud. In this view, if it be correct, no question of fraud can be tried in this action, and the only judgment the plaintiff can obtain is for the *demand* stated in his complaint.

But even if this view was incorrect, the case would still be referable. The necessary examination of a long account would make it so; that is, the substantive cause of action. The fraud is incidental and only important to the plaintiff, as furnishing the ground for obtaining the provisional remedy provided by law in such cases. That remedy has already been obtained, and the grounds for it cannot enter into the trial of the action.

The action must therefore be referred to a referee to hear and determine.

SUPREME COURT.

Jasper T. Van Vleeck agt. Myron H. Clark and others.
The Same agt. The Same.

Where the defendants in an action in this court, brought by a non-resident plaintiff, obtained judgment against the plaintiff, from which the plaintiff *appealed*, and filed security on appeal; and pending the appeal the defendants commenced an action against the plaintiff and his sureties, on the bond given as *security for costs*, in a district court, where the plaintiff appeared, and the action was tried and resulted in a judgment against the plaintiff, on which judgment the plaintiff moved for a stay of proceedings until his appeal was decided, which was denied, and he then appealed to the common pleas,

Held, that although the defendants should not be allowed to collect on the bond for security for costs, the moneys which they would not be allowed to collect directly on execution, until the appeal was decided, yet the plaintiff's remedy was not by action and an *injunction* to stay the proceedings on the judgment in the district court; but he should have moved this court before a judgment was recovered on the bond, for an order *staying any action* on the same until the *decision of the appeal*. Not having done this, his remedy by action and injunction was too late, as *judgment* had been rendered against him in a court over which this court had no control.

New York General Term, October, 1862.

'NGRAHAM, BARNARD and CLERKE, *Justices*.

.PPEAL by plaintiff from decision at special term granting a motion to dissolve an injunction and from an order denying a motion to stay proceedings.

By the court, INGRAHAM, P. Justice. The plaintiff, a non-resident debtor, on commencing an action against the defendants, was compelled to file security for costs. The action was tried and resulted in a judgment for the defendants. From this judgment the plaintiff appealed, and filed security on appeal.

The defendants commenced an action against the plaintiff and his surety in a district court upon the bond given as security for costs, and this action is brought to obtain an injunction against the prosecution of that action until the appeal is decided.

In the second action the defendant moved to stay proceedings on the judgment in the district court, recovered upon the bond given in that action for security for costs.

The motion to dissolve the injunction was granted, and the motion for the order to stay was denied, and plaintiff appealed.

The costs, which are the subject of controversy in these motions, were not payable, and could not be collected after the security on the appeal was perfected, until that appeal was decided. The defendants should not be allowed to collect, on the bond for security for costs, moneys which they are not allowed to collect directly by execution. The difficulty arises from the action on the bond being brought in a district court, where relief cannot be granted, unless appeal can be pleaded as a defence to the action on the bond.

The plaintiff might have moved in the original action, before a judgment was recovered on the bond, for an order staying any action on the same, until the decision of the appeal, as the parties were still suitors in this court, where the bond was given, and the bond was on file with the clerk of the court; such an order would have been binding on the defendants, and obedience to it could have been compelled. Instead of making this application, the plaintiff went to the district court and tried the cause there, and after a decision against him, seeks the aid of the court by way of injunction in this suit. This, we think, he cannot do. The remedy is as before intimated. It is not necessary here, to commence one action, to stay proceedings in another; and when a party has a remedy, which he neglects to apply for, until it is too late to obtain the relief he wants, he should not afterwards, without any excuse for his delay in the first instance, be allowed to resort to a new action for that purpose.

The second motion appealed from, is for a stay of proceedings on the judgment in the district court. By the recovery of judgment there, the case is beyond the reach of this court. We have no control over the judgments of the district courts. An order to stay proceedings on a judgment there would be inoperative. The court might order the bond to be canceled, but that would not affect the judgment recovered upon it in another court.

The motion for relief in this court is too late. As the plaintiff has pleaded the matter in the action in the district court, and appealed to the common pleas in that case, it is unnecessary for us to express any opinion on the sufficiency of the defence. The common pleas is the appropriate tribunal to decide that question.

We think neither of the remedies sought by the plaintiff was appropriate or proper, and that the decisions appealed from were correct and should be affirmed. We allow costs on one appeal, $10.

SUPREME COURT.

Robert S. Gallt agt. Charlotte E. Finch and Hotchkiss S. Finch.

An *order* made out of court, upon notice, must be first *entered with the clerk* before an *appeal* can be taken. (*Code*, § 350.)

And when an order is required to be entered with the clerk, and a party is required to give notice of the order, he *cannot give the notice until he has entered the order*.

Therefore, as regards all orders granted on notice, which are required to be entered with the clerk, the party has no right to give the written notice allowed by § 332 of the Code, until *after the order has been entered.*

Where the order was entered May 27th, and the notice of appeal was served on the 27th June, *held*, that the service of the notice of appeal was *in time*.

Rule 42 does not require the party *demurring to serve on the opposite party* any copy of the pleadings or other papers when the question to be decided arises on demurrer.

It is, to say the least, questionable whether *any court can extend the time to appeal*.

General Term, *July*, 1862, 6*th District*.

Present, Balcom, Campbell, Parker and Mason, *Justices*.

The facts will appear in the opinion of the court.

By the court, Mason, Justice. This case comes before us on a motion to strike the case from the calendar: First, upon the ground that no appeal in said action has been brought or is pending; secondly, that no papers upon the appeal have been served or furnished the attorney for the defendants; and thirdly, that the court will be then and there moved for such other or further order in the premises as may be just. This is an appeal from an order made by Justice Balcom, at chambers, on the 13th day of May last, on defendants' motion striking out the plaintiff's demurrer to the defendants' action as frivolous. Mr. McDowell swears that Justice Balcom made his decision on the 13th of May, and that on the same day he served a copy of the said decision, by delivering him personally a copy of said decision. It appears that this decision was not filed with the clerk nor any order entered until May 27th, and that the plaintiff never served any copy of the order entered, nor any notice of the entry of any order, and no paper in regard thereto, excepting the copy of the decision on the day it was made and before it was filed, or any order entered thereon. It appears also that the notice of appeal was not served on the clerk until June 27th, and that, although the plaintiff's attorney noticed this appeal for argument, he did not serve any copy of the papers on the defendants' attorneys. As I understand the practice, an order made out of court, upon notice, must be first entered with the clerk before an appeal can be taken. This is expressly required by section 350 of the Code. (2 *Whittaker's Practice*, 208; 3 *How. Rep.*, 276; 1 *C. R.*, 42, 119.) The question arises, then, was the notice of appeal in this case served in time? The 332d section of the Code declares that "the appeal allowed by the 4th chapter of this title must be taken within thirty days after written notice of the judgment or order shall have been given to the party appealing." (*Code*, § 332.) The only reasonable construction which can be put upon this section as prescribing a rule of practice on appeal is, that this notice must be of the order as entered with the clerk. I do not understand that the decision of the judge is the order. However this may be, I take it to be very clear when an order is required to be entered with the clerk, and a party is required to give notice of the order, he cannot give the notice until he has entered the order. This was the settled practice under our former system, and is the only proper practice under the present. I must confess that I never heard, before it was claimed in this case, that notice of an order which was required to be entered by the clerk, could be given until the order was entered. This 332d section of the Code gives the party thirty days after written notice of the order in which to appeal. Now, he cannot appeal until after the order is entered, and if his adversary can give notice of the order before he enters it, he may, by omitting to enter the order for thirty days, deprive the party altogether of his right to appeal. It is true he may be compelled to enter it, but it will frequently occur that he could not get a motion made, and a compulsory order on him, within the thirty days, for he must go to special term for the order; and even if the court order him to file the decision and enter the order, he may refuse, and submit to a contempt; or he may appeal from the latter order and delay it until the thirty days have expired. It is, to say the least, questionable whether any court can extend the time to appeal. I am of the opinion, therefore, that before the parties' right to appeal from the order can be cut off, there must have been thirty days' written notice given of the order entered with the clerk. This must be so in regard to orders that are required to be entered with the clerk. The case of *Bowman* agt. *Earle*, (3 *Duer's R.*, 691,) favors this view. This section of the Code is certainly susceptible of this construction; and this rule of practice is so reasonable and just, and the opposite so unreasonable and unjust, that we ought thus to construe it. I am, therefore, for holding that as regards all orders granted on notice, which are required to be entered with the clerk, the party has no right to give the written notice, allowed by section 332 of the Code, until after the order has been entered. This order was entered May 27, and the notice of appeal was served on the clerk June 27, and on the attorney before that. This was in time, under the rule prescribed by section 407 of the Code, which requires, in the computation of time, that the first day be excluded. This appeal, therefore, should be permitted to stand.

The next question which arises on this motion, is in regard to the plaintiff's omission to serve copies of the papers on which the appeal is to be argued.

The 40th rule of this court places appeals from orders sustaining or overruling a demurrer, amongst enumerated motions. The doubt in regard to this branch of the case arises from the language of rule 42 of this court. That rule was designed to prescribe who shall furnish the papers on enumerated motions, and in what cases they shall be furnished, what they shall contain or consist of, and when they shall be served. I am inclined to think that this rule 42 does not require the party demurring to serve on the opposite party any copy of the pleadings or other papers when the question to be decided arises on demurrer. The party demurring is required to furnish them to the court, but not to serve them on the opposite party. The rule reads as follows: "The papers to be furnished on such motion shall be a copy of the pleadings. When the question arises on the pleadings, or any part thereof, or of such parts only as relate to the question raised by the demurrer, or copy of the special verdict, return, or other papers on which the question arises; and the party whose duty it is to furnish the papers, shall serve a copy on the opposite party, *except upon trial of issues of law*, at least eight days before the time the matter may be noticed for argument; and the last part of the rule says the papers shall be furnished by the plaintiff when the question arises on special verdict, and by the party demurring in cases of demurrer, and in all other cases by the party making the motion." Thus it will be seen that the rule prescribes who shall furnish the papers, and what they shall be, &c.; and it also declares that the party whose duty it is to furnish the papers, shall serve a copy on the opposite party *except on the trial of issues of law*, at least eight days before, clearly implying that upon the trial of issues of law no service need be made.

The 249th section of the Code defines what is meant by an "issue of law." It says, "*an issue of law arises upon a demurrer to the complaint, answer or reply, or some part thereof.*"

This exception of issues of law in rule 42, I have no doubt

was intended to apply to cases of demurrer, and indeed there is little use in serving again a copy of the pleadings which the party already has; and it follows, therefore, if I am right in these views, that no copy of the pleadings in such cases need be served, and that this motion must be denied; but as the question has never been determined in this district, I think no costs should be given.

SUPREME COURT.

P—— agt. P——.

In the trial of an action for a *limited divorce*, husband and wife are competent witnesses against each other.

In this case, although the wife by living with the husband had condoned the cruelty and inhuman treatment by him towards her, so that she was not entitled to a judgment for a divorce from bed and board, yet as the husband was very penurious, and had declined to provide comfortably for her, the court, under the statute, adjudged that he should pay the wife's costs of the action, and provide for her suitable food and lodging in his own house, and pay her $200 per year, payable quarterly, out of which she could provide herself with clothing and such other articles as she might see fit to purchase.

It seems, that although the wife uses language calculated to irritate and provoke the husband, yet, if his treatment of her is *grossly disproportioned* to the provocation, she may nevertheless be entitled to a divorce.

It seems, also, that selling the husband's property to procure necessaries is no *justification* for *personal violence*.

Otsego Special Term and Circuit, June, 1862.

Action for limited divorce. It appeared, on the trial, that the parties were married about thirty-three years ago, and have ever since resided in Otsego county. During their married life there have been misunderstandings and slight controversies, but not of a serious character, until about four or five years ago, when the defendant was guilty of cruel and inhuman treatment toward the plaintiff; he used personal violence and did her bodily harm. The plaintiff, thereafter, freely and of her own will, continued to live and cohabit with the defendant, and has ever since continued so to do. The defendant, though comparatively poor at the time of the marriage, has become a man of wealth. He has been a man of close and penurious habits, and since he has acquired a competency has not afforded a suitable and proper maintenance to his wife and their children, (seven in number, three of whom are minors,) and has not, at times, provided them with the necessaries of life, especially with family groceries and suitable clothing. In consequence of defendant's penuriousness, the plaintiff, from time to time, contracted debts with different merchants for such necessaries, which defendant has been compelled to pay, and used some of the products of the farm on which the parties lived, without the knowledge or consent of the defendant, and sometimes used language calculated to irritate and provoke him. The facts proved on the trial, satisfied the court that there was no danger of future personal violence from defendant, if plaintiff should continue to live and cohabit with him. The court adjudged that plaintiff was not entitled to, and ought not to have a divorce or separation, in consequence of condonation and of there being no danger of future bodily harm, but that, in accordance with the provisions of the statute, the defendant provide, in his own house, suitable and necessary food and lodging for his wife and children, and pay the plaintiff $200 *per annum*, in quarter-yearly payments, from which she could provide her own clothing and defray her own personal expenses, other than her board, and that defendant pay the costs of the action made on the part of the plaintiff.

A. Becker, *for the plaintiff.*

E. E. Ferry, *for the defendant.*

Campbell, Justice. The charge of cruel treatment, and on which this action brought for a separation was predicated, was fully made out by proof, on the trial of the cause. A careful reading of the testimony has only served to strengthen the impressions which were made on my mind as the testimony was given. The defendant interposed two defences, recrimination and condonation. He did not claim that the plaintiff had used any violence towards him, but he insisted that her language had not always been chaste and becoming, and especially that she had appropriated his property in a clandestine manner, and had contracted debts, against his expressed wishes and without his consent, and which he had been compelled to pay. It is sufficient to say here, that the defence of recrimination was not established, and for reasons which will be more fully given hereafter. The fact was not controverted by the plaintiff, that she had secretly used the defendant's property, but it was made to appear that such property was only used by her to procure the necessaries of life for herself and children. The defence of condonation, I am inclined to think, was made out. It was not without some hesitation that I arrived at this conclusion. The question of fact on this point is not entirely free from doubt. The adjudicated cases might well authorize a finding, either that there was or was not a condonation, from the evidence in the case, which was uncontradicted. The hand of the husband was laid on the wife in anger and with violence, and that several times. On such occasions there was no justifiable cause; in one instance, hardly a palliating circumstance. Yet, after all this, the wife lived in the house and cohabited with the husband, and under circumstances which I think forbid the conclusion that she acted from fear or under compulsion. The true secret undoubtedly was, that she was unwilling to break up the family and to leave her daughters, some of whom were young and in feeble health, and needing a mother's care and attention. There can be no doubt, I think, that after the time when the *last* act of violence was committed by the defendant, there were periods when domestic harmony was restored. I have great confidence that such harmony may not only be restored, but continued, if the parties will, in good faith, execute the judgment which the laws of our state authorize me to make in a case like the present. The statute to which I refer is as follows: (3 *R. S.*, *5th ed.*, 238, § 68.) "Although a decree for separation from bed and board be not made, the court may make such order or decree, for the support and maintenance of the wife and her children, or any of them, by the husband or out of his property, as the nature of the case renders suitable and proper." This wise provision in our law meets the precise wants of this case. The history of these parties during their married life, as it was developed on the trial, satisfied me that the trouble between them arose chiefly, if not entirely, from the close, if not penurious habits of the defendant. That which may have been considered economy and thrift in early days, and when industry was required to procure the necessaries of life, may cease to be either when advancing years bring with them the infirmities of age; when the wearied body needs repose, and when the labor of the past has been rewarded with an abundance of this world's goods. And yet this defendant hardly seems to have realized such truths. As a man of wealth, and having reference to his habits and those of his wife, it may be added, a man of great wealth, he has not provided a "suitable and proper maintenance of the wife and her children." It would hardly be credited, that during the thirty years, and more, of married life, and many of which years have been to the defendant years of prosperity, he has never purchased a bonnet for his wife, and very few articles of clothing for her or their children. When those children were infants in her arms, seldom were any hired servants provided for her. She early opened a little account at the store, and procured, on her own credit, clothing for herself and children, and sometimes necessary articles of food for the family.

When the children were small and their wants few, she was enabled to meet and pay this account, with thread which she made herself, and with eggs and poultry which she raised. As the children grew up, and commenced going to school, and especially to sabbath-school, the wants for clothing increased and the account ran beyond her ordinary means, and other products of the farm were disposed of, and in some instances the defendant was sued and compelled to pay the accounts. I do not understand that any portion of the accounts were for anything except necessaries, either some articles of furniture for the house, articles of food, especially groceries, or clothing for herself or children. When sued on one of these accounts, the defendant posted his wife. Such conduct on the part of the father, who was known to all the family to be a man of wealth, had a tendency to alienate the affections of the children, and to cause them to gather round the mother, looking to her alone for their comfort and enjoyment. Several of the children were called as witnesses by the mother—none were called by the father. These children appeared well on the stand. The defendant is evidently a man of more than ordinary intelligence, a man of integrity and, it is believed, of unimpeachable moral character. This is true also of the plaintiff. I desire that these parties, the plaintiff and defendant, both now well stricken in years, may go down the hill of life hand in hand together. They owe it to themselves, to their children, and to society to do so. Several years have passed since any violence was done. In my judgment there is not the slightest danger of any in the future. The two hundred dollars a year will enable the plaintiff to purchase clothing and other necessaries for her personal comfort in her declining years. It is intended, of course, only for a partial maintenance. Her home will still be with her husband and children, and the defendant will, after this, I doubt not, see to it that there shall be no lack of at least the necessaries of life. The law of the state is, that I may make such order for her maintenance, as the nature of the case renders suitable and proper. In my judgment, it is suitable and proper that the defendant maintain his wife, under his own roof, that he furnish there the necessary food and other articles for living suitable to their condition in life, and that, in addition, he pay the two hundred dollars per year, to be expended by herself for her clothing, and such additional articles as she may need, or in any manner for the promotion of her own comfort and enjoyment, as she may see fit. I have made no order in relation to the minor children. I can hardly doubt that hereafter the defendant will make a suitable provision for them. At all events, I am disposed to give him the opportunity to do so. The judgment may provide that application, on the footing of it may be made, for a modification of it, if there shall be a failure to comply, or for an allowance for the maintenance of the children. I think the plaintiff and defendant were competent witnesses, on the trial of the action. I may add, however, that most, if not all, the material facts found, could have been found from the other evidence in the cause.

SUPREME COURT.

Edward F. Freyberg agt. Hilaire Pelerin.

An *infant plaintiff* cannot commence an action without the appointment of a *guardian.*

Where such an action is commenced without such appointment, the defendant may *move to set aside the summons, and complaint, &c., for irregularity.* He is not confined to his remedy by answer in the nature of a plea in *abatement.*

Kings Special Term, September, 1862.

Motion by defendant to set aside plaintiff's summons, and complaint, &c., for irregularity, in an action of slander, on the ground that the plaintiff was an infant, and had commenced the action in his own name, without the appointment of a guardian.

WM. E. CURTIS, *for defendant and the motion.*

1. The plaintiff is an infant, and sues in his own name. The Code requires him to appear by guardian. (*Code*, § 115.)

2. The motion to set aside the proceedings is the proper remedy for the defendant.

Judge WOODRUFF, in the case cited below, ruled "that infancy of a plaintiff cannot be proved as a ground of nonsuit on the trial. It must be pleaded in abatement, or the question be raised by motion to set the proceedings aside for irregularity in respect to the appointment of a guardian or next friend." (*Treadwell* agt. *Bruder*, 3 *E. D. Smith*, 597; *Code*, § 116 *and notes; Holmes & Disbrow's Practice*, 51; 1 *Burrill's Practice*, 115; 2 *id.*, 81; *Supreme Court, Rule* 65; 11 *How. P. R.*, 148.

AUGUSTUS B. KNOWLTON, *for plaintiff in opposition.*

LOTT, Justice. Motion granted, but without costs, as the question appears to be new under the Code. Although it would be competent to set up the infancy of the plaintiff by answer, in the nature of the old plea in abatement, I am of the opinion that the objection can be and is more properly taken by a motion like this. It was provided by the Revised Statutes (2 *R. S., p.* 446, § 2,) that before any process should be issued, in the name of an infant who was sole plaintiff, a competent and responsible person should be appointed as the next friend of the infant in the suit, who should be responsible for the costs thereof.

The Code has abolished the using of the term "next friend," not in terms, but by providing in section 115 that when an infant is a party, he must appear by guardian appointed by the court in which the action is prosecuted, or by a judge thereof, or a county judge; and the next section provides how the appointment shall be made. The guardian appointed for an infant plaintiff is made responsible by section 316 for the costs adjudged against the infant, and the payment thereof, and may be enforced by attachment.

Although there is a change in the designation of the party by whom the infant is to prosecute the action, yet I am of the opinion that no proceeding can be regularly commenced without the appointment of some person to act for him; and it is proper that the defendant should not be obliged to limit his objection to an answer. He is entitled to be indemnified against costs, and ought to be permitted to avail himself of the objection by motion, on the ground of irregularity, as was decided under the old practice. (*See Wilder* agt. *Ember*, 12 *Wend.*, 191; *ex parte Scott*, 1 *Com.*, 33; *since the Code*, *Hoftaling* agt. *Teal*, 11 *How. P. R.*, 188.)

NEW YORK SUPERIOR COURT.

THE BUTCHERS' & DROVERS' BANK agt. FREDERICK JACOBSON and others.

Where the *complaint* was drawn strictly under § 162 of the Code, which alleged an amount due to the plaintiffs from the defendants on a written instrument. Then followed a copy of a promissory note, signed by the defendants, for $3000, dated March 9, 1860, payable six months after date to the order of the makers, and by them indorsed in blank. A demand for judgment for the amount against the defendants,

Held, *sufficient*, under the decision of *Prindle* agt. *Caruthers*, (15 *N. Y. R.*, 425.)

April General Term, 1862.

Before BOSWORTH, Ch. J., BARBOUR and MONELL, J. J.

Argued April 14, 1862. *decided April* 26, 1862.

APPEAL from an order at special term, overruling a demurrer to the complaint, and directing judgment for the plaintiffs.

The complaint is drawn under section 162 of the Code, and alleges an amount due to the plaintiffs from the defendants on a written instrument. Then follows a copy of a promissory note, signed by the defendants for $3000, dated March 9, 1860, payable six months after date to the order of the makers, and by them endorsed in blank. A demand for judgment for the amount against the defendants.

W. B. LEEDS, *for defendants.*
C. BAINBRIDGE SMITH, *for plaintiffs.*

By the court, MONELL, Justice. I cannot distinguish this case, in principle, from *Prindle* agt. *Caruthers*, (15 *N. Y. R.*, 425,) which has since been followed by this court in *Price* agt. *McClave*, decided by the general term in December, 1860.

In *Prindle* agt. *Caruthers*, the complaint contained little if anything more than is contained in the complaint in this case. It did, however, allege that the defendant made the contract. There is no such allegation in this complaint. But looking at the section of the Code under which this complaint was drawn, in a spirit of liberal construction, with the light shed upon it by the court in *Prindle* agt. *Caruthers*, I cannot believe the legislature intended to give to it any other effect than its plain, unequivocal language imports. There is no doubt the legislature can prescribe the forms of pleading, and they can dispense with forms altogether. They can declare what shall be sufficient, and when they have declared that "*it shall be sufficient* for the party to give a copy of the instrument, and state that there is due to him thereon from the adverse party, a specified sum which he claims," it leaves no room for doubt that they intended to allow this seemingly informal and incomplete mode of pleading. In enacting the Code, it was designed to, as it does in terms, abolish all the forms of pleading as theretofore existing, and to allow such only as are therein prescribed. (*Code*, § 140.) In following those forms, the pleader is protected by an authority higher than the courts, and in my judgment, it is better to partake of the spirit of reform which the Code professes to have worked in the system of pleading, than by caviling to interrupt its harmonious action. I cannot entertain a doubt that the complaint in this action was perfectly intelligible to the defendants; and that without the aid of lawyers, they fully understood what they were sued for. Indeed, it was more apparent to their comprehension than if its meaning had been covered up and concealed under the useles verbiage of the old forms.

The complaint, we think, contained a sufficient statement of the cause of action; and it being upon an instrument for the payment of money only, was strictly within section 162 of the Code, and both upon reason and authority must be sustained.

The order appealed from must be affirmed with costs.

The case of *Prindle* agt. *Caruthers* cannot be distinguished from this. There the pleading was upheld, and *stare decisis*. J. M. BARBOUR.

SUPREME COURT.

CORNELIUS VAN DINE, assignee agt. JAMES C. WILLETT, sheriff, &c.

Where, at the time of the execution of the *assignment for the benefit of creditors*, a *contract* for the manufacture of goods in England had been made by the assignor, the order had been sent, and a subsequent delivery proved that the order had been *accepted*,

Held, therefore, that the assignor had a claim to have the goods manufactured, which he could enforce, and which contract he could assign; and that whatever interest he had under the contract *passed under the assignment to the assignee*.

The *assignee* having subsequently elected to accept the goods here in public store, by the payment of the duties and the purchase money, *held*, that a levy and taking of the goods afterwards by the *sheriff*, as the property of the assignor, made him a *trespasser*.

A direction in an assignment to the assignee to pay *rent* and *taxes* on the real estate until sold, *held*, not objectionable; it was only authorising the assignee to do what he would have been authorized to do without it, to preserve the property.

The assignment authorising the assignee to pay debts due and to grow due, *held* unobjectionable.

So the authority to employ an *attorney*, *held* unobjectionable.

New York General Term, October, 1862.

INGRAHAM, LEONARD and CLERKE, *Justices*.

MOTION by plaintiff for a new trial on a judgment dismissing the complaint.

By the court, INGRAHAM, P. Justice. The property in controversey in this action was ordered by the assignor to be manufactured for him in England, prior to the execution of the assignment. It did not arrive here till after that date.

On the arrival of the goods here, they were sent to the public store, and were afterwards entered in the name of the assignor, on behalf of the assignee, who paid the duties, and who subsequently paid the contract price for the goods to the manufacturer.

The defendant levied upon the goods, in behalf of a judgment creditor. The plaintiff claims the goods as assignee, and the defendant resists such claim:

1st. On the ground that no title passed to the assignee under the assignment.

2d. That the assignment was void.

At the time of the execution of the assignment, the contract for the manufacture of the goods had been made, the order had been sent, and the subsequent delivery proves that the order had been accepted. The assignor, therefore, had a claim to have the goods manufactured, which he could enforce, and which contract he could assign. Whatever interest he had under the contract passed under the assignment to the assignee.

The assignee was not bound to accept such an assignment,

and he might have undoubtedly refused to accept the goods, and would not, in such an event, have been liable to the manufacturer for the purchase money.

But he elected to accept the goods which is evidenced by his payment of the duties and the purchase money.

This election was before the levy by the sheriff, and whatever doubt there might have been if the levy had been made before the assignee had elected to take the assignment and comply with the terms of the contract, as soon as such election was made the interest of the assignor in the property was at an end, and the title was in the assignee. After that the sheriff was a trespasser in taking the property as the property of the assignor.

The facts as proven show the delivery by the manufacturer to the assignor on board of the vessel, subject, of course, to his right to stop the goods *in transitu*, bnt which right was not executed, and the goods reaching the place of destination.

Both parties must be considered as conceding that the assignor obtained title to the goods, as soon as they were placed on board of the vessel, in pursuance of the order before given for their manufacture, as both claim under his possession.

As to all the world, except the vendor, the title passed to the assignor, and no other person could dispute that title.

The assignment conveyed all the goods, chattels, merchandise, &c., and property of every name and nature whatever of the assignor. These words were sufficient to include all the property of the assignor, wherever it might be, and I see no reason why it did not include every property belonging to the assignor, on board of a ship as well as in his store.

If any measures had been taken to rescind the contract, that might have defeated the plaintiff's title; but as no such proceedings took place, the title of the assignor was not impaired, and whatever title he had passed to his assignee under the assignment.

The fact of the entry being made in the name of the assignor for the use and under the direction of the assignee, who paid the duties thereon, would not deprive the plaintiff of title to the goods, if that title had passed under the assignment previously. There is no ground for imputing any fraud to the assignee on that account.

The other ground alleged by the defendant for dismissing the complaint was that the assignment was void.

1st. The direction to pay the rent and taxes on the real estate until sold, was a necessary power to preserve the property, and the assignee would have been authorized to do it, if the authority was not included in the instrument itself.

It is true, as held in *Carter* agt. *Hammil*, (12 *Barb.*, 254,) that the assignee had a right to elect whether he would except an assignment of a lease so as to make himself liable for rent to the landlord, but if he refused to accept, the the authority to pay rent and taxes would become imperative, while the acceptance would make him liable until sale, whether the assignment authorized payment of the rent or not.

2d. It is objected that the assignment authorized the payment of debts due and to grow due.

The defendant's counsel admits, if this had been confined to debts for which the assignee (who was intended to be secured) was at the time liable, it would be good.

The assignment will bear no other construction. It authorizes the payment of debts, bonds, notes and sums of money due and to grow due, whether they were payable at the time or not would be immaterial. The assignment expressly confines the payment to debts, &c., for which the assignor was then liable to the assignee. It could not, in any way, be made to cover debts not then in existence.

3d. The authority to employ an attorney is also objected to.

The appointment of an attorney does not authorize the assignee to substitute any one in his place. He still remains liable, and bound to act as principal. Any discretion must be exercised by him and on his responsibility. Whatever an attorney does in the business is considered as done by the assignee. That he might employ an attorney without any express authority is undoubted. The authority given to do so does not, in any way, invalidate the assignment.

The case referred to in *Plank* agt. *Schermerhorn*, (3 *Barb. Ch. Rep.*, 644,) was a case where the assignee had a right to name a successor and not appoint an attorney.

I see no reason for holding the assignment void, as matter of law. If there was any fraud in fact, the question was for the jury and not for the court.

My conclusion is that the court erred in dismissing the complaint, and that the judgment should be reversed and a new trial ordered, costs to abide the event.

SUPREME COURT.

WILLIAM ALLGRO agt. WILLIAM E. DUNCAN.

Where, in an action upon a *promissory note*, the defendant interposes the defence and proves *infancy*, when the note was given, the jury should be *directed* to find a verdict for the defendant, although some facts may have come out on the trial tending to show that the defendant had been doing business for himself, and representing himself as of full age:

And where, in such case, the judge omitted to give such direction to the jury, but gave them particular instructions as to the law of the case, and they found a verdict for the *plaintiff*,

Held, that the verdict should be set aside on a motion made upon the minutes of the judge, under § 264 of the Code, if the awkward phraseology of that section could be applied to the case.

It must be assumed that a motion to set aside a verdict, and for a new trial "upon insufficient evidence," under § 264, means a motion for a new trial on the ground that the *verdict is against evidence*, as was the clear and plain language under the old practice.

A safe rule in such cases is, to apply the former practice, and interpret the obscurities and deficiencies of the Code by its light.

Kings Circuit and Special Term, November, 1862.

P. S. CROOKE, *for plaintiff.*
GEO. THOMPSON, *for defendant.*

EMOTT, Justice. This suit was upon a promissory note; the defence was infancy. The plaintiff proved the note, and rested; and the defendant proved, by his own testimony and that of another witness, that he was an infant when the note was made. Upon the cross-examination some facts came out tending to show that the defendant had been doing business for himself, and in certain particulars holding himself out, or allowing himself to be, considered of full age. This was all the evidence. When it closed, the defendant's counsel did not ask me to direct a verdict, as he might have done, since there was really nothing in the case for a jury. In the absence of any such request from counsel, I unwisely allowed the case to go to the jury, giving them very careful instructions. The result showed that I relied too much upon their intelligence or their firmness. They found a verdict for the plaintiff. If this verdict went upon the question of infancy, it was plainly contrary to the evidence; and if it went upon any notion of an estoppel against the defence of infancy, it was as plainly contrary to law. Either way it must be set aside, and the only question is, how or when.

The present motion is made upon the minutes of the judge, under section 264 of the Code. The phraseology which has been used by the codifiers gives rise to the only question in this, as it does in so many other cases. Section 264 allows a motion for a new trial upon the minutes, "upon exceptions, or for insufficient evidence, or for excessive damages." Before the Code, we had new trials granted when verdicts were contrary to the evidence, and when they were contrary to law. These expressions were sufficiently plain in themselves, or if there was any obscurity in the words, their meaning had been made entirely certain in the practice of the courts and the course of decisions. It seems, however, to have been a part of the scheme of codification not to continue the use of any term or phrase which had acquired a technical or precise meaning in the existing practice, but to introduce not only a new practice, but a new nomenclature, which, if it were much better than it is, would need time, controversy and decisions to define it. Instead of a motion to set aside a verdict as being contrary to evidence, we are introduced to a motion "to set aside a verdict and grant a new trial for insufficient evidence." What this awkward phrase means, may require judicial construction to determine. The astute counsel for the plaintiff in the present case, contends that a motion to set aside a verdict "for insufficient evidence," can only be entertained where the party succeeding had no sufficient evidence in his own behalf, and cannot be made where the jury have disregarded sufficient evidence offered by the defeated party to sustain an affirmative cause of action or defence. Thus, here the plaintiff's evidence consisted simply of the production and proof of his note, and was sufficient, standing by itself, to make out his case. The defendant put in the evidence of infancy. His evidence was also sufficient to establish his defence, and there was nothing to contradict it. If it had failed to make out the fact of infancy, and the jury had nevertheless given a verdict for the defendant, the argument of the counsel is, that a case would be presented for a motion like the present, but that a verdict against all the evidence, and founded upon no evidence, is not a verdict upon insufficient evidence. The argument is ingenious, but not sound. Perhaps if we were in the unhappy condition of the rising generation of lawyers, knowing nothing of practice but the Code, we might be embarrassed with the decision of this and similar questions. But a safe rule in such cases is, to apply the former practice, and interpret the obscurities and deficiencies of the Code by its light.

I shall therefore assume that a motion to set aside a verdict, and for a new trial, "upon insufficient evidence," means a motion for a new trial on the ground that the verdict is against the evidence. That I take to be the case. I am not required to assume that the jury found the fact of infancy in favor of the defendant, and then proceeded to a verdict against him upon some supposed legal ground of estoppel. There being no legal foundation or appearance of estoppel in the case, I shall not imagine any, but shall treat the verdict of the jury as given upon the question of infancy, and against the evidence on that issue.

It must therefore be set aside; but as the verdict and this motion would have been prevented by a proper application at the trial, to direct a verdict, the defendant ought not, in any event, to recover the costs of the late trial or of the motion.

The verdict is set aside and a new trial ordered, but the costs of the trial and of this motion are allowed to the plaintiff, to be costs of the cause, and to be recovered by him if he shall finally succeed; or if he is ultimately defeated, to be set off against the defendant's costs.

SUPREME COURT.

Griffin and others agt. Banks and others.

Where the *wife*, after her husband's absence for five successive years, and without her having known, during that time, that he was living, (*see* 3 *R. S.*, 227, *5th ed.*,) married a second husband,

Held, that the first marriage was only placed by the law in *abeyance*. It only temporarily suspended the rights of the first husband, unless, by his own neglect or acquiescence, he waived or abandoned them.

The first husband, in this case, having omitted or neglected to resort to the proper remedy, by filing a bill and proceeding in the manner prescribed by the statute,

to annul the voidable (second) marriage, the latter marriage continued in force after the death of the first husband, and had the same force and effect as if, when it was solemnized, the first husband *was not alive*.

A *deed of separation* between husband and wife, which is without consideration, and consequently void, does not affect the husband's rights in the property and business of the wife, or the debts contracted in her name; and such property passes to his assignee, in *an assignment for the benefit of creditors*

New York General Term, October, 1862.

INGRAHAM, BARNARD and CLEKE, *Justices*.

By the court, CLERKE, P. Justice. I. The justice who tried this action at special term has found as a matter of fact, "that on the 22d day of July, 1842, Mary McCullom married Bruce McKinney, at the city of New York; that such marriage was contracted by her in good faith, believing McCullom (her first husband) to be dead, and after McCullom had absented himself for five successive years, and without her having known, during that time, that McCullom was living."

This finding we see no reason to disturb; and we shall therefore assume its truth.

The statute (3 *R. S.*, 227, *5th ed.*,) provides that "if any person whose husband or wife shall have absented himself or herself for the space of five successive years, without being known to such person to be living during that time, shall marry during the lifetime of such absent husband or wife, the marriage shall be void only from the time that its nullity shall be pronounced by a court of competent authority." The second marriage in this case was not declared void by any court.

Had it, therefore, the same efficacy in all respects, as if the first husband was not alive at the time of its solemnization?

The language of the statute is very general and positive, without any reservation or exception, express or implied; and yet it would apparently be at variance with the plainest principles of justice, that the first husband should be deprived of his marital rights—of his right to the enjoyment of the society of his wife and of his interest in her property, merely by her mistake, arising from an absence which, under many circumstances, he could not avoid, and which, indeed, may have originated in an endeavor to promote the common benefit of both. If the second marriage is to be upheld, the first ceases to have any validity; both, certainly, cannot co-exist. Under our law, and under that of all christendom for many centuries, if not from the very origin of christianity, no man shall have more than one wife, and no woman more than one husband, at the same time. Does the law, then, provide no redress for the husband who has been thus injured by the act of his wife, committed under a mistake? I think it does. It places the first marriage only in abeyance. It only temporarily suspends the rights of the first husband, unless, by his own neglect or acquiescence, he should waive or abandon them.

The course pointed out by the chancellor, in *Valleau* agt. *Valleau*, (6 *Paige*, 207,) is open to every husband or wife in similar circumstances. He says: "The remedy of the former husband or wife, in such a case, is to file a bill, and proceed in the manner prescribed by the statute to annul the voidable marriage, and if the parties thereto continue to cohabit together, after a decree of nullity has been pronounced, the rightful husband or wife may then file a bill for a divorce on the ground of that adultery." This is the obvious and the only practicable course; and McCullom, the first husband in this case, having omitted or neglected to resort to it, the second marriage continued in force, and, after the death of McCullom, could not be disputed or invalidated by his representatives, or any other party.

I hold, therefore, that the marriage of Bruce McKinney and Mrs. McCullom has the same force and effect as if, when it was solemnized, McCullom was not alive.

Assuming, then, that this marriage was as legal in its origin and continuance as any other marriage, did the deed of separation, in 1844, or any other act of McKinney, divest him of all right to the property which then or afterwards belonged to his wife ?

On this point, I adopt the reasoning of the justice at special term, and agree with him that the deed of separation, being without consideration, was void; that the property and business remained the property and business of the husband; that the debts contracted in the business, although contracted in the name of Mary B. McKinney, were the debts of Bruce McKinney; that he, and not Langan, the trustee in the deed of separation, had the legal right and title in the property; that consequently he had the sole right to make an assignment for the benefit of the creditors, and that his assignees, and not the assignees of his wife, have a good title to the property in question and its proceeds.

The judgment of the special term should be affirmed, with costs.

SUPREME COURT.

THE PEOPLE *ex rel.* MICHAEL SCHMITT agt. SAINT FRANCISCUS BENEVOLENT SOCIETY.

Where a member of a *charitable and benevolent society*, organized under the statute of 1848, entitled "An act for the incorporation of benevolent, charitable, scientific and missionary societies," is *expelled* from such society for the non-observance of a by-law which is not authorized by the statute nor the constitution of the state, he will be restored to membership by *mandamus*.

Members of such society cannot be expelled therefrom upon charges made against them *without notice*, and an opportunity to be heard in their defence.

Erie Special Term, November, 1862.

THE respondents are a benevolent society in the city of Buffalo, organized under the laws of 1848, entitled "An act for the incorporation of benevolent, charitable, scientific and missionary societies."

The relator was a member thereof and was excluded, and

he made a motion for a peremptory mandamus, compelling the respondents to reinstate him to membership. The facts sufficiently appear in the opinion.

Motion for mandamus.

L. L. Lewis, *for relator.*
Eli Cook, *for defendants.*

Marvin, Justice. I think this motion must be granted. The relator makes a clear case of right to membership in the corporation, and the facts presented in opposition to the motion are not sufficient to justify the expulsion of the relator from the society. It is not my purpose to enter into a discussion of some interesting questions presented upon the argument; it will be enough to say that the relator, as one of the corporators, had rights which the law will protect. He states, that as a member of the corporation, he performed all the obligations and conditions required of him by the by-laws, rules and regulations of the society. He shows that he was expelled from the society in his absence, and without having had any notice in time of any intended proceedings against him, to enable him to attend and protect his rights. He states, upon information and belief, that he was expelled from the society by a vote of a majority of the members present, for the pretended reason that he had neglected to attend the confessional, that is to say, that he had neglected to attend before a catholic priest and confess his sins, as required by a by-law of the society. He states that he had fully complied with the by-law referred to during each and every year that he had belonged to the society, and that no notice had at any time been given to him that he had violated any of the laws or regulations of the society. These allegations are not put in issue or denied by the corporation. True, the affidavits read in opposition to the motion, were designed to show some notice of the intended proceedings against the defendant, or rather notices to attend certain meetings of the society. But it is not pretended that such notices came to the knowledge of the relator in time to enable him to attend the meetings indicated, at one of which he was expelled. The corporation takes and relies upon the position that no notice was necessary. Again, I cannot learn from the papers for what alleged cause the relator was expelled from the society. In the affidavit of the president of the society, (designed mainly to show that, though notice to the relator was not necessary, he directed notice to be given,) it is stated that the relator, "although a member of the association or society, having violated its constitution, by-laws and regulations, was, on the 17th day of July last, by a vote of a majortity of the members of the said association, expelled therefrom." What part of the constitution, or what by-law or regulation was it claimed that the relator had violated? This does not appear; it is added that there is no provision in the articles of association, constitution or by-laws requiring any notice to be served upon a member guilty of delinquency in attending the confessional; but in this case, for the purpose of enabling Schmitt to make a defence before said association, he, the president, caused notice to be left at the house of Schmitt, &c., in order that he might appear and explain before the said society the charges that were made against him. What charges?

It is said that no notice was necessary in a certain case, but it is not said that the charge against the relator was the one in which no notice was necessary. For aught that appears in these papers, the relator may have been charged with the violation of any other of the by-laws, &c., aside from the one relating to the confessional. There is another affidavit, made by the person who made some attempt to serve notice upon the relator to attend the meeting, "to answer certain charges which were preferred against him for a violation of the constitution, by-laws and regulations of the said association;" and in another place it is said, "for the purpose of answering the charges aforesaid." Thus it nowhere appears what the charge was, upon which the relator was expelled. The relator, after his expulsion, was informed that it was upon the *pretended* reason that he had neglected to attend the confessional, &c. And the papers read in opposition to the motion, do not show whether this was the reason or charge upon which he was expelled, or what the charge was. No good reason or cause is therefore shown for his expulsion. But if it is assumed that the relator was expelled upon a charge of violating article 4 of the by-laws, I think we shall come to the same conclusion.

The 2d subdivision of this article reads: "He is bound to receive the holy sacraments of penance and eucharist twice a year, and has to prove it before all the meeting that he has done the same, after he has been admitted in said society; without this, he shall not be considered a member." By article 2d, the society is to consist of members who profess the Roman Catholic religion, and who, at the same time, are church members of the St. John's church, and as such must have a pew or slip in said church. Thus it is seen that no one can become a member of the corporation, unless he professes the catholic religion and is a member of the St. John's church, and has a pew or slip therein; and after becoming a member of the corporation, he is to receive, twice a year, certain sacraments of that church, and is to prove such fact before the society, or he is not to be considered a member. It is argued that this clause of the 4th article is invalid; that it is not authorized by the statute under which the corporation is organized; that it is against the general policy of our laws and the constitution of the state, and that it is unreasonable. In my opinion, this by-law is not authorized by the statute, and it is in conflict with our constitution, which declares: Art. 1, sec. 3. "The free exercise and enjoyment of religious profession and worship, without discrimination or preference, shall forever be allowed in this state to all mankind."

The defendant was incorporated under the act of 1848, entitled "An act for the incorporation of benevolent, charitable, scientific and missionary societies." The act authorizes the corporation "to make by-laws for the management of its affairs, not inconsistent with the constitution and laws of this state, or of the United States." The purposes of the corporation in the present case, as declared in the charter or articles of association, were *charitable and benevolent.* Its general plan was to obtain money from its members, and use it for their benefit in times of the sickness or death of a member, and to render assistance to the widow of the deceased member, &c., &c. There is nothing said in the articles of association touching the religious character of its members. It may be that the society had the right to prescribe who should be members, and to require that the applicant for membership should be a professor of the catholic or any other religion, and that he should be a member of some particular church. The society may, I suppose, refuse to admit any one to membership, and such person would have no remedy. But once admitted, he will have all the rights and privileges provided by the charter under the statute; and the charter or articles of association can contain no provision in conflict with the statute. In the present case, the relator, who had been a member of the corporation for many years, and had paid in all dues, according to the charter and by-laws, has a legal right to be continued a member until he shall violate some rule or by-law authorized by law, and which justifies his expulsion. If the by-law in question, touching the sacraments, &c., is valid, then the relator will be deprived of a valuable right secured to him by the constitution. He cannot be permitted the free exercise and enjoyment of any other religion except the catholic. He must continue to profess that religion, and partake of the sacraments prescribed, &c., or forfeit his right as a corporator; a pecuniary right having no necessary connection with any particular religion.

It is not my intention to discuss this question at length; but in my opinion, the by-law in question cannot be sustained. The religious privileges which the constitution and the laws secure to all persons of this state, cannot in this way be infringed or abrogated. This position will, of course, have no relation to any rules and regulations, or articles of faith, adopted by any religious denomination or society, and for a departure from which the member is liable to punishment or removal. Our laws permit these societies to establish any rules, regulations or articles of faith, for the government of their own bodies, and he who becomes a member of such a religious society, agrees to the rules, regulations and articles of faith, and to the mode of discipline and trial provided by it, and the court will not interfere. But in this case the defendant was organized and incorporated for *charitable and benevolent* purposes, under a statute of the state, and it is possessed of property and funds in which the relator has an interest; and the law protects that interest, and he cannot be deprived of his rights by an unauthorized by-law, though he may have assented to it.

I am also satisfied that members of this society cannot be expelled upon charges made against them, until they have an opportunity to be heard in their defence. This is a general principle. It is a case of property of legal rights—but a case of voluntary association for purposes affecting no substantial property rights, in which the associates provide all their own laws, and may provide for expulsion, without notice, if they choose to do so. Here the relator had rights which the law will protect; and if there had been a by-law that any member might be expelled by a vote of the society, in his absence and without notice, I have no doubt such by-law would be illegal. It would be unreasonable. It would be an attempt to withdraw from the protection of law, the rights of a member.

Without further discussing the question raised, I think it clear that the relator is entitled to the relief he demands. He must be restored to membership, and if there should be charges made against him, he must have a reasonable notice of them, and an opportunity to make his defence.

Let a peremptory mandamus issue.

NEW YORK SUPERIOR COURT.

THE PEOPLE *ex rel.* JOSE VALIENTE and others agt. WILLIAM H. DYCKMAN.

The examination of a *party* at the instance of the adverse party, under § 391 of the Code, *before trial*, is conducted in all respects in the same manner as a *witness* examined conditionally under art. 2, title 3, chap. 7 of part 3 of the Revised Statutes.

That statute provides that if any witness attending before any judge, pursuant to a summons, shall, without reasonable cause, refuse to answer any legal and pertinent question, "the officer issuing such summons shall, by warrant, commit such witness to the common jail of the county;" there to remain until he submits to answer, or until he be discharged according to law.

Held, that it is the duty of the judge, where the witness refuses to answer a legal and pertinent question, to issue his warrant for the commitment of the witness; that an *order merely adjudging the witness to be in contempt*, is improper, and unauthorized by law. And an *appeal* from such order is for the same reason equally unauthorized.

It is not an open question, that a party examined as a witness, either at or before the trial, may be required, upon a *subpœna duces tecum*, to produce his *books* relating to or containing evidence pertinent to the issues in the action.

And where such party has produced a book of account and proved the same, and has pointed out and explained the charges in it, called for in evidence, he may be compelled to go further, and required *to read out of the book the specific items and charges to which he had referred and pointed*, to the end that the same may be incorporated in his deposition and preserved as evidence. For his refusal to thus read from the book, he may be punished for *contempt*, as before stated.

April General Term, 1862.
Before all the Justices.

Appeal from an order made at special term adjudging the defendant guilty of a contempt, and directing an attachment for his commitment to issue.

The defendant was under examination as a witness, upon a subpœna *duces tecum*, on the part of the plaintiff, before trial, under section 391 of the Code. The witness produced, under the subpœna, a certain *book*, which he testified contained charges made by Waydell & Co., for cooperage on the first shipment of cigars referred to in the pleadings, and which the witness testified he had paid. The witness pointed out to the plaintiff's counsel the charges in the book under date of May, 1860, and also entries made by Waydell or his clerk, under date of Sept. 7, 1860, of payments made by the defendant to said Waydell, of the said charges for cooperage, when the plaintiff's counsel propounded to the witness the following "*Question:* Now state the items as set forth in the book, to which you have pointed?"

The question was objected to by the defendant's counsel on the ground that the defendant, as a witness for the plaintiff, having produced the items, had done more than he was obliged to, and could not be examined so as to enable the plaintiff to incorporate into the deposition of the defendant, either copies or the substance of papers produced under the subpœna. The justice, before whom the examination was taken, overruled the objection, and decided that the witness must answer the question. To which ruling and decision the defendant's counsel excepted.

An attachment having been issued against the witness, he was brought before a justice of this court, and upon his refusal still to answer the question, the order appealed from was made.

H. A. Cram, *for appellant.*

I. T. Williams, *for plaintiffs.*

By the court, MONELL, J. The order appealed from, and all the proceedings subsequent to the refusal of the witness to answer, are so clearly irregular, that we might well dispose of the question on that ground, without looking into the merits.

The examination was of a party, at the instance of the adverse party, *before* trial. Such examination, though absolute, is conducted in all respects in the same manner as a witness examined conditionally under art. 2, title 3, chap. 7 of part 3 of the Revised Statutes. Section 61 of that title provides, that if any witness attending before any judge, pursuant to a summons, shall, without reasonable cause, refuse to answer any legal and pertinent question, "the officer issuing such summons shall, by warrant, commit such witness to the common jail of the county," there to remain until he submits to answer, or until he be discharged according to law. The power of the judge, under this statute, to compel a witness to answer, and to commit him if he refuses, is ample and free from doubt. The judge not only *may*, but the statute says *shall* commit the witness, if, without reasonable cause, he refuses to answer. The policy of conferring this power *exclusively* upon the judge before whom the examination is taken, cannot be questioned. No one is so well qualified to judge of the legality and pertinency of the question as he. No one can determine, as well as he, that the refusal to answer is without reasonable cause. It is, moreover, a contempt of his authority, and it would seriously impede the administration of justice, if the remedies to punish a contumacious witness were to be pursued through other and remote channels. The judge is to decide whether the question is legal and pertinent to the issue, and I am not aware that any statute or practice of the court has ever allowed his decision to be reviewed in the manner sought in this case.

It was obviously the duty of the judge, before whom the examination was taken, to have issued his warrant for the commitment of the witness; and hence the order he made, merely adjudging the witness to be in contempt, was improper and unauthorized by law. And the order appealed from was, for the same reasons, equally unauthorized.

It follows, therefore, that the order appealed from, and all proceedings subsequent to the refusal of the witness to answer, so far as the court has power to do so, must be reversed. Before compelling the witness to answer, the judge must be satisfied that the question propounded is legal and pertinent to the issue formed by the pleadings. Having determined this, his duty is plain. There is no force in the argument against this statute, that great injustice may be done; that a party may be compelled to answer impertinent questions; and that, especially, under the statute authorizing a party to be examined as a witness at the instance of the adverse party, the examining party may be allowed to pursue his investigations into the past history, business and career of the witness. No such danger exists. The law throws around the witness its ample protection; and the judge will see to it, that the examination is confined to subjects pertinent to the issue, and is not permitted for any purpose foreign to it. But while the law, thus administered, shields and protects the witness, it also imposes upon him the obligation of obedience, and forbids his contempt of its authority.

Enough has now been said to dispose of this appeal. Nevertheless, I deem it proper briefly to examine whether the question propounded to the witness was proper.

I think it may not be considered an open question, that a party examined as a witness, either at or before the trial, may be required, upon a subpœna *duces tecum*, to produce his books relating to or containing evidence pertinent to the issues in the action. That question has been put at rest by the decisions of nearly or quite all the courts. At any rate, it is the law of this court.

The witness under examination had produced his book

of account; had testified that it contained charges for cooperage on the first shipment of cigars referred to in the pleadings, and which he testified had been paid. *He then pointed out to the examining counsel the charges in the book*, and was asked to state the items as set forth in the book, to which he had pointed. The objection was not to the *form* of the question, but that the witness "could not be examined so as to enable the plaintiff to incorporate into the deposition either copies or the substance of papers produced." The objection did not go to the extent contended on the argument, that the witness could not be required to read the items out of the book, but rather, that it would be improper to compel the witness to do more, to enable the examining party to incorporate the items into the deposition. I have no doubt the question, in the form in which it was put, was understood by the witness as calling for the *reading*, by him, out of the book, of the items or charges to which he had pointed. The book produced by the witness, it would seem, remained in his hands. He was testifying from it, and it became important, as claimed, that the precise *words* and *figures* of the charges should be stated. To preserve them as evidence, they must be written into the deposition, which was subsequently to be signed by the witness and certified by the judge. Now, who was to state them? It was said the counsel might, or the judge, or the clerk; but I apprehend that in strictness neither could, under objection. That, however, is not the question. May it be made the duty of the *witness* to read the charges or state the contents of the book? or has *he* discharged all the duty that can be required of him, when he has produced the book, and said, this is my book of accounts? It is not doubted, he is obliged to go further, and to state whether it contains a particular account; in whose handwriting it is; on what page it commences, where it ends; to what part of the subject of the action it relates, and other similar questions to test its pertinency. But it is said, you cannot ask him to *read* from it. Why not? If not he, whom can you ask? Not, who may *volunteer* or *offer* to read it, but who can be required to read it? for read it must be, if it is to go into the deposition. How, then, are you to get the evidence, if the witness refuses, and cannot be compelled, and no other person, under objection, may read it?

It is conceded that if the book is kept in cypher, or in a foreign language, an expert or translator may be called to read it, and may be *compelled* to read it, if he is able to do so. May not the witness who produces it, equally be compelled to read it? May he not be treated as an expert, or does the absence of a necessity for an expert qualify or alter the rule? I apprehend not. The *practice* of counsel to read books and papers produced on the trial, does not aid or relieve the question. Counsel may refuse, and there is no power to compel *them*. The evidence is proper and important, and there must be some source from which it can be obtained, *ex necessitate rei;* the witness must furnish it. The book doubtless is the best evidence, and if produced on the trial and proved, could be read from to the jury by either party; but here the examination is *before* trial. The book could not be attached as an exhibit of the deposition, and afterwards brought into court, from the files, and read to the jury, and then returned to the files there to remain. A party or a witness is not to be deprived of his property. He is entitled to retain its custody. No; it must be extracted from, and the extract must be put into the deposition, and the book returned to the witness and retained by him. Should the counsel, or the judge, or the clerk read, it would be *testimony*, and testimony can only be given by a *witness.*

We are looking at an abstract question; not seeking if there be some *other* way in which the thing might be done; but endeavoring to determine whether a witness, without regard to other modes, ought to give the reading. We think he ought. He has not discharged his whole duty, until he has furnished the matter contained in his books of account, in such a form that it may be put and preserved in his deposition.

The question is new. It probably has never arisen before, and may never arise again. There is, therefore, no case like it to be found in the books; but as, *necessitas non habet legem*, so we may say necessity *makes* law.

The judge, having decided the question was proper, ought to have committed the witness for refusing to answer.

The order appealed from must be reversed.

SUPREME COURT.

PATTERSON KEIL, resp't agt. WILLIAM RICE, appel't.

Where the verdict of a jury is set aside and a new trial granted *on payment of the costs of the former trial*, the item of ten dollars, for proceedings *subsequent to notice and before trial*, is allowable under the order.

November General Term, Eighth District.

MARVIN, *P. J.*; DAVIS, GROVER and HOYT, *Justices.*

APPEAL from order of special term denying motion for readjustment of costs.

W. WOODBURY, *for appellant.*
C. C. TORRANCE, *for respondent.*

By the court, DAVIS, Justice. The verdict of the jury in this case was set aside and a new trial granted, on payment of the costs of the former trial. The question now presented is, whether the item of $10, for proceedings subsequent to notice and before trial, is allowable under this order. I have examined all the cases bearing on this question, and find that in every case where the precise point has been involved, this item has been allowed.

In *Mitchell* agt. *Westerwelt*, (6 *How. Pr. R.*, 265,) the verdict was set aside "on payment of the costs of the circuit." It was held that plaintiff was entitled to this charge. It "was intended," says the court, "as compensation of a notice of trial, issuing subpœnas, &c., preparatory to trial." This decision was affirmed on appeal, by the general term of the fourth district, WILLARD, HAND, CADY and ALLEN, JJ., being present. (6 *How.*, 311, *note.*)

In *Dewey* agt. *Stewart*, (6 *How.*, 465,) the plaintiff was allowed to withdraw a juror and move to amend his complaint, on payment of the costs of the term. SANFORD, J., with the concurrence of all the justices of the superior court, held that the charge for proceedings subsequent to notice of trial, and before trial, was taxable. "The fee," said he, "is provided as a compensation for the attorney's services intermediate the notice of trial and the trial, such as the subpœnas and tickets, their service, and procuring the attendance of witnesses, as well as brief for counsel."

In *Buckingham* agt. *Miner*, (18 *How.*, 287,) the defendant was let in to defend, after judgment, on condition that he pay "all the costs of the hearing before the referee, and of the proceedings subsequent thereto." The court ruled that the item now under consideration should be allowed to plaintiff as part of the costs to be paid by the defendant.

These appear to be all the cases where the point, presented by the facts of this case, seems to have been directly adjudicated.

It has also been held in many cases, that this item is taxable after judgment overruling a demurrer, where the demurrant is allowed to answer on payment of costs.

(*Collomb* agt. *Caldwell*, 5 *How.*, 336; *Hendricks* agt. *Bout*, 2 *Abb.*, 360; *Van Valkenburg* agt. *Van Schaick*, 8 *How.*, 271.)

There is a class of cases in which this item is not allowed. On postponing a cause at circuit, (*Noxon* agt. *Bentley*, 6 *How.*, 418; *Jackson* agt. *McBurny*, 6 *id.*, 408;) where the cause is necessarily noticed for trial more than once, (*Perry* agt. *Livingston*, 6 *How.*, 404;) and in *Jackett* agt. *Judd*, (18 *How.*, 385,) it was held that the item was taxable but once, when a judgment had been reversed on appeal and a new trial granted with costs to abide the event. In that case the learned justice relied on *Perry* agt. *Livingston*, (6 *How.*, 404,) and *Jackson* agt. *McBurny*, (*id.*, 408,) both of which were cases where the item was claimed for each time the cause had been noticed, though there had been but one trial.

The present case is distinguishable from *Jackett* agt. *Judd*, in the fact that here the motion for new trial was addressed to the favor of the court, and the costs were imposed as a condition of granting it. In such a case, the party obtaining the favor should be required to compensate the other party for such services attending the trial, and necessarily connected therewith, as must be repeated upon a new trial. The issuing and service of subpœnas, noticing and placing the cause on the calendar, and procuring the attendance of witnesses, are all to be repeated; and there is no good reason for saying that the party who asks this to be done as matter of favor, and not of strict right, should not be held to pay for the performance of those services of which he asks the repetition.

As before observed, the authorities on this point are uniformly in favor of allowing the disputed item in cases analogous to this; and it may also be remarked, that one of the justices, (ALLEN, J.,) who held that the charge was not proper when the cause had been noticed and put on the calendar, without trial, more than once, concurred in the general term decision that it was allowable where a new trial had been granted on payment of the costs of the former trial.

The order appealed from reversed, and order entered directing the allowance of the disputed item.

SUPREME COURT.

LIVINGSTON agt. PAINTER & BOYES.

In respect to *any agreement*, the non-fulfillment of which will not admit of *pecuniary compensation*, the court will afford relief by a *specific performance;* although it is chiefly with regard to *real property* that the substitution of damages by way of redress is generally insufficient.

Where the plaintiff, as owner of a first mortgage upon leasehold property, claimed that the defendant, who was owner of a second mortgage on the same property, had violated an agreement with him in bidding off the property at the sale thereof on the second mortgage, in the name of another person, who refused to pay certain expenses upon the property and a specified payment on the first mortgage, in pursuance of the agreement to waive the foreclosure of the first mortgage,

Held, that if the plaintiff had sustained any injury it was in consequence of the *delay* in not prosecuting a foreclosure of the first mortgage. The damages caused by the delay were capable of being measured and ascertained by a jury; that if the plaintiff was entitled to any redress under the agreement, it was by an *action for damages*.

New York Special Term, *December*, 1862.

THIS cause came on for trial on the 13th day of November, 1862, before Mr. Justice CLERKE.

LEWIS L. DELAFIELD, *of counsel for plaintiff.*
HARRINGTON & GRIEFF, *of counsel for defendants.*

The counsel for the defendants moved on the plaintiff's opening and the pleadings to dismiss the complaint.

Mr. DELAFIELD, in opposition, cited *Buxton* agt. *Lister*, 3 *Atk. R.*, 383; *Adderley* agt. *Dixon*, 1 *Sim. & St. R.*, 607; *Phillips* agt. *Berger*, 2 *Barb. R.*, 608; *Phillips* agt. *Berger*, 8 *Barb. R.*, 527; 2 *Parsons on Contracts*, 511, 529; 2 *Story Eq. Jur.*, §§ 716, 718.

CLERKE, Justice. This is an action to obtain the specific performance of an agreement.

The plaintiff alleges an agreement between the assignor of the plaintiff and defendant Painter, who was the owner of a second mortgage of a leasehold, (No. 84 Leonard street,) which mortgage was made by one Seabury Lawrence to one John Sniffen and others, to secure the payment of $12,340. The agreement recites that Painter had commenced proceedings to foreclose this mortgage; that Hamilton, the assignor of the plaintiff, was the owner of a first mortgage, made by the said Lawrence, on the same premises, to secure the payment of $12,000, which had become due at the option of Hamilton, according to a provision in the mortgage; but that he had agreed to waive this option, and that Painter in consideration of the sum of one dollar, and of the agreement made by Hamilton, agreed: 1st, to pay within forty-five days the semi-annual interest in arrear on the said first mortgage, and all taxes and assessments due upon the premises; 2d, to prosecute the foreclosure of the second mortgage to the earliest possible conclusion; and 3d, in the event of Painter's buying in his own name, or otherwise, at the sale under the said foreclosure, the said leasehold interest, subject to the first mortgage, he should reduce the same by payment on account of the sum of $3,000, within six months from date of the agreement.

The complaint alleges that Painter prosecuted the foreclosure of the second mortgage to judgment of foreclosure and sale; that under this judgment the leasehold was sold at public auction; that the same was purchased at the sale by the defendant Boyes for $2,000, and that the sheriff executed a decree thereof to Boyes, subject to the first mortgage.

The complaint further alleges that Painter purchased the leasehold at the said sale, in the name of Boyes, for the purpose of evading the terms (meaning the obligations) of said agreement, and that Painter is really the owner of the beneficial interest in the said purchase.

On this statement, the defendants move to dismiss the complaint, on the ground that it does not present a case for the equitable interposition of the court.

Although, generally, the subject in respect to which the court will give the specific relief sought in this action is realty, or things relating to the realty of a permanent nature, there are some few instances affecting personal property, in which, from the peculiar nature of the thing, arising either from an artificial value attached to it from its locality or other circumstances, a specific performance of the agreement would be the only adequate remedy. In other words, in respect to any agreement, the non-fulfillment of which will not admit of pecuniary compensation, the court will afford this relief; although it is chiefly with regard to real property that the substitution of damages by way of redress is generally insufficient. To mention instances supposed by Lord Chancellor Hardwicke, in *Buxton* agt. *Lister & Cooper*, (3 *Atk.*, 382,) a man may contract for the purchase of a great quantity of timber, as a ship carpenter, by reason of the vicinity of the timber, and this on the part of the buyer. On the part of the seller, suppose a man wants to clear his land in order to turn it to a particular sort of husbandry, there nothing can answer the justice of the case but the performance of the contract in *specie*. In the case of *John, Duke of Buckinghamshire* agt. *Ward*, a bill was brought for a specific performance of a case relating to alum works, and the trade thereof, which would be greatly damaged if the covenant should not be performed on the part of Ward. The covenants lay there in damages, and yet the court considered, if they did not make such a decree, an action afterwards would not answer the justice of the case, and therefore decreed a specific performance. Lord Hardwicke considered the case before him (*Buxton* agt. *Lister & Cooper*,) to be something of the like kind. Lister & Cooper had agreed with Buxton for the purchase of several large parcels of wood, (merely the timber,) standing within the township of Kirby, for the sum of £3,050, to be paid at six several payments, every Lady-day, for the six following years, Lister & Cooper to have eight years for disposing of the same; and that articles of agreement should be drawn and perfected as soon as conveniently could be, with all the usual covenants therein to be inserted concerning the same. Had not the merits of the case been against the plaintiff, Lord Hardwicke intimated that the memorandum appearing not to be a final contract, but to be made complete by subsequent articles—a bill to compel the execution of the subsequent articles would be allowed. The case of *Phillips* agt. *Berger*, (2 *Barb.*, 608; *id.*, 527,) to which I have been referred, was placed on especially the ground that, if the action had been brought by the defendant against the plaintiff, an award of damages would not put him in a situation as beneficial as if the agreements were specifically performed. The contract relative to the sale or compromise of a judgment, which Phillips had recovered against John C. and C. B. Morrison, in which a creditor's bill had been filed. During the pendency of that suit, Berger entered into a contract with the Phillips', agreeing to compromise the claim for $4,500. The court considered that an action at law would not afford to the defendant a complete and satisfactory remedy if the plaintiff had refused to assign or released the judgment according to his contract. They imagine many uses to which the defendant might have put the judgment, which could not be at all, except by very vague conjectures, measured or estimated; and if on this account he would have been entitled to a specific performance, then for the same reasons the plaintiff would be entitled to the same remedy. If a bill will lie in favor of one party to a contract, it will, according to the opinion in that case, also lie in favor of the other. The ground, then, of the interference of the court was, that the defendant might have applied the judgment to many uses, which could not be measured by damages; and that in order to render complete justice, if the defendant was in the plaintiff's place, the specific assignment of the judgment would be essential—that is, he must have the judgment to control in such a way as his interests may require. The thing itself would be necessary for him. In the case before us, the ownership or control of no specific thing is in question. The plaintiff does not ask for the sale or purchase of a thing, which from certain circumstances, or for certain purposes, or from the peculiar nature of it, arising from an artificial value attached to it from its locality or other causes, it is necessary for him to possess. He seeks for nothing but money; instead of bringing an action at common law for pecuniary compensation, he seeks our equitable interposition for the same purpose. The difference is that he demands a specific amount instead of damages, which a jury in a common law action may award him. In seeking pecuniary compensation, he resorts to the extraordinary instead of the ordinary jurisdiction of the court. In *Phillips* agt. *Berger*, the effect of the decree, indeed, was to compel the payment of a specific sum of money from the defendant to the plaintiff; but the court placed the decision, as we have seen, on the ground that if the defendant had brought the action, the assignment of the judgment would have been compelled; and the court maintained, as the obligation was reciprocal, so should the remedy be. Although I must say I have some misgivings as to this reciprocal right in relation to an action like this, which is addressed to the discretion of the court. In the present case, although if the plaintiff or his assignee attempted to violate this agreement by commencing an action to foreclose the mortgage, the court would probably enjoin him from doing so, on tender deposit of the $3,000. Still this alone is not sufficient to take the case out of the ordinary course. If the plaintiff has sustained any injury, it is in consequence of the delay in not prosecuting a foreclosure of the first mortgage. The damages caused by the delay are capable of being measured and ascertained by a jury. The fact that the damages may be so trifling as not to warrant the bringing of an action to recover them, so far from being a reason for the extraordinary interposition of a court of equity, is a conclusive reason against it. The mortgage is as effectual as ever; the non-fulfillment of the agreement has not in any respect impaired it, or interfered, except by delay, with the remedy under it; and it can, at any time, be foreclosed at the option of the plaintiff. In short, if the plaintiff is entitled to any redress under this agreement, that redress is by an action for damages.

The motion to dismiss the complaint is granted, and the complaint dismissed with costs.

SUPREME COURT.

WILLIAM F. McCARTY, appellant agt. ALFRED EDWARDS, respondent.

Actions seeking *equitable relief* are to be *tried by the court;* a party is not entitled as a matter of right to have the issues of fact in *such actions* tried by a *jury*.

After the time to settle the issues in a cause asking *equitable relief*, and for a money demand, to the settlement of which issues the plaintiff has lost his right, on the trial he is not entitled to have the issues settled instanter, or to *amend* his *complaint* instanter, and strike out of the prayer all except the money demand, and to proceed to a jury trial immediately, thus changing essentially the nature of the action and the mode of trial, apparently for the sole purpose of getting the cause before a *jury;* nor to *put the cause over the circuit* to enable him to move to amend the complaint and settle the issues, without showing a sufficient reason therefor. These matters are addressed to the *discretion* of the judge at the circuit, and cannot be reviewed at general term.

A non-resident *party* may be examined *on commission* as a witness in his own behalf.

It is not a valid objection that *cross-interrogatories* in a *commission* offered in evidence are not all answered, where it appears that some of them in whole or in part are answered by *reference to previous answers*, the latter being full and explicit.

Several objections were taken by the plaintiff in this case, to the *commissions* introduced by the defendant in evidence, which are specifically examined and passed upon by the court in their opinion; but with the remark, however, that they had seldom seen any objections to testimony *less specific* or *less significant* than these appeared to be, as presented on the bill of exceptions; and were inclined to think that all of them might with great propriety have been *summarily condemned for that reason.*

Albany General Term, December, 1861.

Gould, Hogeboom and Peckham, *Justices.*

This was an action in equity, tried at the Albany September circuit, 1860, before his honor Justice Gould. The decision was in favor of the defendant, upon which judgment was entered for the amount of his costs and disbursements. From this judgment the plaintiff appeals to the general term.

The action was commenced by service of summons and complaint on the 27th of July, 1858. The plaintiff was an engineer, engaged in running a locomotive on the New York Central Railroad. The defendant was an attorney-at-law, residing and practicing his profession, first at Clinton, and afterwards at Davenport, in the state of Iowa.

The summons was in form for "the relief demanded in the complaint," and not for the recovery of money. The complaint (fol. 4) alleged in substance, that on the 8th of April, 1856, the plaintiff delivered to the defendant at Albany, the sum of $335, which the defendant, as the agent of the plaintiff, was to take west with him, and invest the same, for and in the name of the plaintiff, in government lands in the state of Iowa, for which service he paid the defendant $35 in advance. That early in May following, plaintiff received a letter from the defendant, dated Clinton, April 28, advising a location in Minnesota, instead of Iowa, as at first contemplated, and that he would bring or send by mail, to plaintiff, the certificate of location, as soon as the same should be effected. That under date of the 27th of June, 1856, he received from defendant a second letter, to the effect that an advantageous location of land for plaintiff had been selected, and that by calling at the office of Mr. Meads in Albany, in the course of a few days, he would receive a certificate of location. That, notwithstanding such assurances and the original undertakings of the defendant, the defendant had theretofore neglected and refused, and still neglected and refused to deliver to plaintiff the said certificate of purchase and location, or any evidence of his having invested plaintiff's money for his benefit or on his account in Iowa, Minnesota or elsewhere, or refund the money.

The complaint then concluded with a demand for judgment. That the defendant be compelled to surrender and deliver to the plaintiff, said alleged certificate of location or title to the land alleged to have been purchased for the plaintiff, or in case defendant had not made such investment or purchase, then that the plaintiff have judgment for the $335, with interest from the 8th of April, 1856, with costs.

The answer of the defendant denies the material allegations of the complaint, and sets forth the facts as they were claimed by the defendant to exist, and which constituted his defence.

On the trial before Judge Gould, various rulings were made by him in regard to the mode of proceeding, and the admission and rejection of evidence, which were duly excepted to, and which are sufficiently stated in the opinion of the court. A large mass of testimony, mostly on commission, was introduced, which need not be given in detail, after which the judge made the following findings of fact and law:

That on the 8th day of April, 1856, at the city of Albany, the plaintiff paid to the defendant the sum of three hundred and thirty-five dollars, and that the defendant at the same time executed and delivered to the plaintiff an instrument in writing, in the words and figures following, and being the contract then entered into between the defendant and the plaintiff, to wit:

"Received, Albany, April 8th, 1856, from Wm. F. McCarty, three hundred and thirty-five dollars, to be given to agents in Iowa, and to be invested under my direction in government lands. (Signed) ALFRED EDWARDS."

That in pursuance of such contract defendant, with no unnecessary delay, did deposit in the hands of George L. Nichols & Co., on the 17th day of May, 1856, and in current funds, the sum of three hundred dollars, with instructions to invest the said sum in the purchase of government lands, in the name of and for the benefit of plaintiff, and that the said George L. Nichols & Co. were then residing and doing business as general land agents at Davenport, in the state of Iowa, and were then proper and responsible agents for that purpose.

That the plaintiff was duly informed by defendant of what had been done by the defendant in the premises, and assented thereto by making no objection.

That the money thus deposited by defendant with said agents has neither been invested by them, as directed, nor has any part thereof been prepaid by said agents either to defendant or plaintiff.

That said agents, George L. Nichols & Co., have become and are insolvent; that defendant has used all due diligence to have such investment made by said agents, or to obtain a return of said money to plaintiff, but without effect; that defendant has substantially, and in all respects, complied with his said agreement of April 8th, 1856, and that there has been no default by defendant in respect thereto.

That the sum of $35, retained by the defendant, of said $335 received by defendant of plaintiff, has been expended by defendant in and about his agency under said agreement, and is a reasonable sum to be allowed to and retained by defendant, for his expenses and services in said matter.

The said judge further found, as conclusions of law, that defendant has fully performed on his part, said contract of April 8th, 1856; that plaintiff is not entitled to the relief demanded in his complaint in this action; that plaintiff is not entitled to have or recover judgment against the defendant for any sum, by reason of the matter in said complaint alleged, and that the defendant is entitled to have judgment against the plaintiff for his costs and disbursements in said action.

The plaintiff's counsel duly excepted to the findings of fact and conclusions of law of the said judge; and thereupon, by direction of the judge, judgment was, on the 9th day of October, 1860, rendered for the defendant for his costs, ($106.68.) The plaintiff appealed to the general term.

HENRY SMITH, *for plaintiff, appellant.*
CLARK B. COCHRANE, *for defendant, respondent.*

By the court, HOGEBOOM, Justice. The plaintiff made several propositions and objections on the trial of the cause, which were overruled. It will be convenient to consider them in their order:

1. Plaintiff asked that the issues of fact be tried by a jury. He was not entitled to this as a matter of right, (*Code*, §§ 253, 254.) It was, therefore, a matter of *discretion*, and not reviewable. The discretion has not been abated. The action seeks equitable relief, and such are to be tried by the court. (*Cheesebrough* agt. *Houck*, 5 *Duer*, 125; *Wilson* agt. *Forsyth*, 16 *How.*, 448; *Moffatt* agt. *Van Doren*, 4 *Bosw.*, 610.)

2. The further applications then made by the plaintiff—*to settle issues instanter*, after the time to settle issues had

elapsed, and the plaintiff had lost his right thereto; *to amend the complaint instanter, and strike out of the prayer all except the demand to recover $335 and interest, and proceed to a jury trial immediately*—thus changing essentially the nature of the action and the mode of trial, and apparently for the sole purpose of getting the cause before a jury;—*to put the cause over the circuit to enable the plaintiff to move to amend the complaint or settle issues*, without any sufficient reason being given therefor, without any allegation or proof of surprise or want of preparation for the trial, were all, I think, properly overruled by the judge at the circuit, and were addressed to a discretion with which we cannot interfere.

3. The plaintiff also made several objections to the defendant's evidence, the most important of which I will notice:

1. "Plaintiff objected to the reading of letters addressed by defendant's agents to him." The objection amounts to nothing. It does not specify what *letters*, or what *agents*, or *why* the letters would be improper. If the objection refers to the letters of Nichols & Co. to defendant, it might be argued with some force that they were *plaintiff's* agents. If otherwise, their letters might, in a certain aspect of the case, be proper, as showing good faith on the part of the defendant, the course he took in investing the plaintiff's money, and reasons for delay in not prosecuting them for the money.

2. Plaintiff objected to the reading of defendant's testimony taken under commission: 1. "Because there is no authority to examine a party by commission, granted Feb. 18, 1859;" we have held the reverse in *Bigelow* agt. *Mallory*, (17 *How.*, 427.) 2. "Because the cross interrogatories are not all answered." On inspecting them, we find they are all answered—some of them, it is true, in whole or in part by reference to previous answers. This I am inclined to think not objectionable if the previous answers are full

and explicit, precise and definite, and the reference to them exact and specific. But whether so or not, no such objection was taken, nor would the court imagine that such a point was intended by the language in which the objection was couched. We cannot give effect to such a strained construction of language. (*Valton* agt. *National Fund Life Insurance Co.*, 20 *N. Y.*, 34.)

3. Plaintiff objected to the answer to the 4th interrogatory "as a conclusion of the witness."

On examining the answer, we find that it contains more than a page of printed matter, and a large number of specific facts which cannot, in any sense, be regarded as mere opinions or conclusions of the witness. The objection is, of course, wholly unavailable. It embraces matter wholly unobjectionable, and its generality and indefiniteness would be good cause for overruling it.

4. Plaintiff objected to the answer to the 8th interrogatory because it is hearsay and secondary, proving his declaration in his own favor.

A portion of this answer, which goes to show the efforts made by defendant to invest the plaintiff's money, and thus to resist the imputation of bad faith, delay and negligence on his part as the plaintiff's agent, was certainly pertinent and proper. Some of the letters referred to in this answer were lost and unable to be found after diligent search, and therefore not necessary to be produced. The objection, therefore, that it was secondary, would be unavailable to that part, and hence unavailable as to the whole, because embracing unobjectionable matter—unavailable also for the same reason, because a portion of the parol testimony was proper.

5. Plaintiff "objected to that portion of the answer to the 9th interrogatory, which states what defendant said in conversation with Nichols, and what he wrote to Nichols, because his reason for writing the letter is not a fact, and the letter itself is not produced."

The answer to the 9th interrogatory embraces about two pages of printed matter, and after perusing it, I do not discover that it states *any* thing of "what defendant said in conversation with Nichols," nor *any* thing "that he wrote to Nichols." The objection, therefore, seems to be without any point, if indeed we were authorized to give any consideration to an objection so general and indefinite as applied to an answer two pages in length. Some *letters* are mentioned in that answer; some written by the defendant to the plaintiff, which are produced; some written by Nichols & Co. to the defendant, one of which was produced; another not produced, the contents of which the witness did not disclose beyond alluding to a fact stated in it, that they would be able to enter plaintiff's land in a few days, which was a fact defendant would have a right to state on information, as a probable motive for the contents of his letter to the plaintiff, written shortly afterwards.

An objection is also taken to this answer, because it states that Nichols became embarrassed by the erection of a large block of buildings. I think this was not wholly irrelevant, inasmuch as it tended to show why defendant had not invested the plaintiff's money, and why, if not invested, he had not been able to get it back from Nichols; and why he wrote to plaintiff, requesting liberty to sue Nichols and attach his property.

6. Plaintiff "objected to part of the 14th interrogatory." This interrogatory is the general and usual one attached to interrogatories sent by commission. The objection is pointless, if not, in the manner it is made, ridiculous.

7. Plaintiff objected to the evidence of the other witnesses taken on commission, that the interrogatories are not all answered. This is incorrect in point of fact, and has been already fully considered.

8. Plaintiff further objected "to the 8th, 9th and 11th interrogatories as immaterial, and the answers to the same."

The 8th interrogatory related to letters written by defendant to plaintiff relative to the embarrassment and insolvency of Nichols & Co., and to the fact of ownership of any property by Nichols & Co., out of which plaintiff's debt could be made, and cannot be said to be wholly immaterial, as they tended to explain and justify the defendant's conduct, and repel the imputation of bad faith, negligence and delay, contained in the plaintiff's letters to the defendant. The answers to this interrogatory are pertinent for the same reason.

The 9th interrogatory inquired as to any offer made by Nichols to convey to plaintiff 240 acres of government land in Minnesota. This was also proper or admissible, as explanatory of defendant's conduct, to whom Nichols made the offer, and who communicated it to the plaintiff, and as tending to show diligence and activity on the part of the defendant in securing plaintiff against loss. The answers thereto are also proper for the same reason.

The 11th interrogatory was the usual general one, requesting the witness to state any other matter within his knowledge, beneficial to the defendant, and embraced within the issues in the action. Neither this nor any pertinent answers to it, (and so far as given they seem to be pertinent,) can with any propriety be said to be *immaterial.*

I have seldom seen any objections to testimony less specific or less significant than these appear to be, as presented on the bill of exceptions; and I am inclined to think that all of them might with great propriety have been summarily condemned for that reason. But on analyzing the testimony, with a view to see if the plaintiff would suffer from such a disposition of his objections, I am unable to discover, so far as our attention has been drawn to it, that the judge excluded any testimony which was material to the case, or admitted any erroneously, which tended to prejudice the plaintiff's case.

The weight of testimony on the merits is with the defendant, and appears to have abundantly justified the conclusions at which the judge arrived.

It is obvious that the plaintiff entertained an erroneous impression of the nature and legal effect of the contract between the parties.

The receipt of April 8, 1856, given by the defendant to the plaintiff, was in the nature of a contract between the parties, and was obligatory upon them. (*Creery* agt. *Holly*, 14 *Wend.*, 26; *Eggleston* agt. *Knickerbocker*, 6 *Barb.*, 458; *Wolfe* agt. *Myers*, 3 *Sandf.*, 7; *Niles* agt. *Culver*, 8 *Barb.*, 205.) It expressed the terms on which the defendant received the money, to wit: to be given to agents in Iowa, and to be invested in government lands under defendant's direction. This negatived the idea that he was to make the investment in person, or to be responsible for a neglect to do so on the part of others, provided he, as the agent of the plaintiff, exercised proper care and diligence in the selection of agents and in directing the investment. I am unable to see that he was guilty of laches or misconduct in this respect. It would seem that the *agents* intended by the parties, were mentioned at the time this writing was entered into, and they, or one of them, did reside in Iowa, although they did business also in Minnesota. These were the persons into whose hands the plaintiff's funds were promptly placed by the defendant.

It is a mistake to suppose that the contract required the investment to be made in Iowa lands. Such is not the construction to be given to it; and if it was the place of location, it was changed from Iowa to Minnesota, by the consent of the plaintiff.

It is matter of regret that the plaintiff's funds have been lost, but it appears to have been without the defendant's fault.

I think the findings of the court below were justified by

the evidence; and if it were a case of doubtful testimony, effect must be given to the principle which forbids a reversal after a fair trial before a competent tribunal hearing the testimony, and more able than any other to estimate its due weight and credibility.

The judgment of the circuit court should be affirmed, with costs.

SUPREME COURT.

TINKHAM agt. BORST.

A plaintiff, at whose solicitation a *receiver* has been appointed, cannot be allowed to prosecute a claim in this court for which a judgment has been already obtained for his benefit and on his behalf by the receiver, in *another court*.

New York Special Term, November, 1862.

DEMURRER to defendant's answer.

CLERKE, Justice. The second defence (to which the plaintiff demurs) sets forth, among other things, that the receiver, who recovered the judgment in the superior court, was appointed at the instance and request of the plaintiff, and that the action in which that judgment was recovered was commenced and prosecuted for his benefit and on his behalf, at his cost and expense, and for the purpose of obtaining satisfaction and payment of the debt and demand in the complaint in this action alleged and claimed.

It is contended in support of the demurrer, that as the plaintiff could not control the proceedings in the action in the superior court, he could not be bound by them, and that consequently a recovery in that action is no bar to this. This, however, is not the test.

If a person transfers his right of action to another, or if he authorizes another to sue for his benefit and on his behalf, or if he takes such proceedings in a court of justice, by which any officer of the law is authorized to sue for his benefit and on his behalf, he should be concluded by any legal action prosecuted in pursuance of those proceedings. In short, one is the privy of the other. The sense which the counsel for the plaintiff gives to the term "privy," is too limited. The books mention five kinds of privies;—privies of blood, such as the heir to the ancestor; privies in representation, as executors or administrators to the deceased; privies in estate between donor and donee, lessor and lessee; privies in respect of contract; and privies on account of estate and contract together. In this case, the receiver may be called the privy of the plaintiff by representation. He represents the interests of the plaintiff's estate, as far as the claim involved is concerned, as much as an executor or administrator represents the interests of a deceased person's estate. The authority to realize these interests is transferred from the original possessor to the person representing him, as effectually in the one case as the other; and to allow one at whose solicitation a receiver is appointed, to prosecute a claim for which a judgment has been already obtained for his benefit and on his behalf, by the receiver, would be multiplying unnecessary litigation, and encouraging what the law has always discountenanced.

The demurrer is overruled, with costs.

SUPREME COURT.

In the matter of George B. Webb.

The enlistment of a *recruit, under eighteen years of age*, in the *naval service* of the United States, without the consent of his parents or guardian, is not *binding or obligatory*, although he *took an oath*, when he enlisted, that he was twenty-one years of age. The oath can only be conclusive against the recruit, and not against others claiming a legal right to his services.

Kings Special Term, October, 1862.

On *habeas corpus*, for the discharge of George B. Webb, a recruit enlisted in the naval service of the United States.

G. T. Jenks and Augustus B. Knowlton, *for the petitioner.*

B. Frank Browne, *for the United States.*

Brown, Justice. The writ of *habeas corpus* in this case is prosecuted by James W. Webb, to procure the release and discharge of his son George B. Webb from the ship North Carolina, where he is detained in the service of the United States. The father resides at Winstead, in the state of Connecticut, and the return of Richard W. Mead, Esq., a captain of the navy, shows that George B. Webb enlisted as a landsman in the naval service on the 18th day of September last, in the city of New York. At the time he signed the articles of enlistment, he made oath that he was twenty-one years of age, and received the government bounty of thirty-six dollars. The proof taken at the hearing shows that he left his residence, which is his father's house, in Winstead, in June last, in company with his father, with a view to go to Pittsburg, in the state of Pennsylvania, and while so absent from home he enlisted as before mentioned. It also appeared by the proof, that he became sixteen years of age on the 9th of August, 1862. It is not claimed that he entered the naval service with the consent or approbation of his father, or that the latter had any knowledge of the transaction until some time after it was consummated.

No statute of congress has been referred to, and I presume none exists, authorizing the enlistment of boys into the naval service without the consent of their parents or guardians. The act of the 2d of March, 1837, seems to be still in force, and it is an authority for the enlistments of boys not under thirteen, nor over eighteen years of age, to serve until twenty-one; but the consent of the parent or guardian is expressly required to make the enlistment binding and obligatory.

I am referred, however, to the 2d section of the act of the 13th of February, 1862, which declares "that the 5th section of the act of the 28th of September, 1850, providing for the discharge from the service of minors enlisted without the consent of their parents or guardians, be and the same is hereby repealed, provided that no person under the age of eighteen years shall be mustered into the United States service, and the oath of enlistment taken by the recruit shall be conclusive as to his age." It is to be observed that the act of the 28th of September, 1850, the 5th section of which the 2d section of the 13th of February, 1862, is designed to repeal, is an act which relates exclusively to the army, and not the navy of the United States. It is also to be observed that the claim in regard to the oath of the recruit is contained in a proviso to the section quoted.

The office of a proviso is not to enlarge or extend the act, or the section of which it is a part, but rather to put a limitation and a restraint upon the language which the lawmaker has employed. The effect of the proviso in regard to the oath of the recruit must be therefore limited to the subject of the act of September 28, 1850, which is the army and not the naval service of the United States, and does not affect the present case.

But were it otherwise, who is it that should be concluded by the oath of the recruit? If this oath, taken at the time of the enlistment, as to his age, is to operate as an estoppel, whom shall it estop? Not the master or the parent who claims a legal right to services of the minor in opposition to the government. Congress has certainly not given any indication of an inclination to conclude this class of persons upon their right to the service of their minor sons or apprentices upon the mere act of the minors themselves, in the absence and without the assent of their parents and guardians. The section will receive a sensible and rational construction by declaring the oath of the recruit to be conclusive against himself, and not against others claiming a legal right to his services.

An order must be entered directing the United States officer having George B. Webb in his custody, to relieve him from further restraint, and deliver him over to his father, James B. Webb.

SUPREME COURT.

THE MANUFACTURERS' BANK OF TROY agt. THE MAYOR, RECORDER, ALDERMEN AND COMMONALTY OF THE CITY OF TROY.

By the *system of taxation* under the provisions of the statutes applicable to the county of Rensselaer and the city of Troy, a *banking corporation* located in that city, may be *exempt from taxation* as respects the county tax, under the law of 1853, (*Laws of* 1853, *chap.* 654, § 1, *amending* § 9 *of the former act*,) which entitles a bank to commutation, by paying a sum equal to five per cent. on their net annual income or profits, or to an exemption in case of no net profits or clear income at all; and yet be liable to a *city tax* on their *personal property*, although, by the provisions of the above law, *they have sworn they have none* liable to taxation, by reason of which they are exempt from the county tax.

Albany General Term, May, 1859.

WRIGHT, GOULD and HOGEBOOM, *Justices*.

THIS is an appeal by the plaintiff from a judgment rendered in favor of the defendants, pursuant to the directions of Mr. Justice GOULD, on the 5th day of November, 1858, for the sum of $85.06, being the amount of their costs in the action. The cause was tried before the said justice, without a jury, at the Rensselaer circuit, on the 16th of October, 1858. The plaintiff was a banking corporation in the city of Troy, and was assessed, in the year 1855, the sum of $187,873 upon its capital stock, as the personal property of said bank. The assessment roll containing this assessment was duly returned to the board of supervisors of the county of Rensselaer. At the annual meeting of said board, in 1855, and within two days of the commencement of their session, the bank presented to said board a petition, asking exemption from taxation under chap. 654 of the Session Laws of 1855, accompanying the petition with an affidavit that the plaintiff had not been, during the preceding year, in the receipt of net annual profits or clear income equal to five per cent. of the capital stock of said bank, paid in, or secured to be paid in, nor of any net profits or clear income at all.

The act of the legislature above referred to, provides that if any incorporated company named in the assessment roll should, through its proper officer, show to the satisfaction of the board of supervisors, at their annual meeting, within two days of its commencement, by the affidavit of such officer; that the company has not been, during the preceding year, in the receipt of net annual profits or clear income equal to five per cent. of its capital stock paid in, or secured to be paid in, after deducting from the amount of their capital stock the assessed value of their real estate, such company shall be entitled to commute for their taxes on such capital stock, by paying directly to the treasurer of the county, a sum equal to five per cent. on such net annual profits or clear income, and also the amount of the taxes on their real estate.

The board of supervisors referred said petition and affidavit to a committee, who reported in favor of exempting the plaintiff from taxation on personal property, pursuant to their petition; and the board subsequently resolved that the committee having charge of this subject, be authorized to expunge the assessment of The Manufacturers' Bank from said assessment roll. It was accordingly done. No tax was extended by the board opposite to said assessment, nor otherwise laid upon the capital stock. The real estate of the bank was duly assessed, and the tax thereon paid to the chamberlain.

The defendants proved the various acts of the legislature, having reference to the levy and collection of taxes in the city of Troy, and that under and in the manner required by said acts, the defendants, on the 4th of October, 1855, imposed a city tax for that year, to the amount of $2,250.67 on the capital stock of the plaintiff, and afterwards issued their warrant for the collection thereof, in the usual form. Under this warrant a levy was made under the direction of the defendants, by an officer, who seized and took of the plaintiff's property a sum sufficient to pay said tax, and the expenses of collection, and the proceeds thereof were paid to the chamberlain of the city. For the amount thus levied and collected, the plaintiff instituted this suit. The plaintiff contended that proof of the foregoing facts entitled it to exemption from the payment of the *city* as well as the *county* and *state* taxes. The defendants insisted upon the contrary, and having duly objected to the proof introduced as to the action of the board of supervisors upon the petition and affidavit of the plaintiff, as irrelevant and immaterial, moved to strike out such proof. The justice granted the motion, and the plaintiff excepted. The justice then decided that the defendant was entitled to judgment, and to this the plaintiff excepted. Judgment having been rendered accordingly, the plaintiff appealed to the general term.

David L. Seymour and W. A. Beach, *for plaintiff.*
John B. Gale and Martin I. Townsend, *for def'ts.*

By the court, Hogeboom, Justice. In this case, I have come to the following conclusions:

1. The petition and accompanying affidavit presented by the plaintiff to the board of supervisors, on the 3d of October, 1855, entitled it to commutation or exemption, under

the law of 1853. (*Laws of* 1853, *chap.* 654, § 1, *amending* § 9 *of the former act.*)

The affidavit was made by the proper officer—covered the contingency named in the act, and showed that the bank had not been in the receipt of any net annual profits or clear income, and of course not in the receipt of any equal to five per cent. of the capital stock paid in, or secured to be paid in, after deducting from such capital stock the assessed value of its real estate. This, by the terms of the act, entitled it to commutation, by paying a sum equal to five per cent. on such net annual profits or clear income, in addition to the assessment for taxes on the real estate. As there were no net profits or clear income at all, commutation was equivalent to total exemption.

2. The resolution and action of the board of supervisors upon this petition and affidavit, though slightly informal, sufficiently indicated their satisfaction that the bank had come within the provision above referred to, entitling it to commutation or exemption. The law pointed out no mode in which the supervisors should declare or manifest their satisfaction. When, therefore, they resolved that the assessment upon the capital stock of this bank should be expunged from the assessment roll, and it was accordingly done, we must assume that they extended no tax thereon, or if they did so, that it, like the assessment, was expunged from the roll, and they thereby virtually, and indeed in the most convincing manner, expressed themselves satisfied with the truth of the matters stated and shown by the bank. It would be exacting an unnecessary formality, to require a more strict compliance with the terms of the act.

3. The commutation or exemption in question was intended by the law to be confined to such taxes as the board of supervisors had a right to impose, review or collect.

We cannot suppose that the supervisors were intended to be clothed with power to abate or receive commutation for taxes over which they had no jurisdiction—which they did not create or impose—and as to which they were not entrusted with any supervisory power. At least we may infer that, if the law designed to confide to them, as a distinct body from the taxing power, the authority to supervise the taxes imposed by another tribunal, it would say so in express terms, or provide some mode by which its decision on the question of commutation should be certified to the body imposing the tax. As nothing of this kind appears in the law, we may reasonably infer that the jurisdiction of the supervisors on the subject of commutation of taxes, was designed to be limited to those taxes which they imposed, and which were contained in the assessment roll over which they had control and the power of correction.

4. The city taxes of the city of Troy, in distinction from the state and county taxes imposed upon the property of that city, do not come under the supervision or control of the board of supervisors, nor had they any power to lessen, increase, or in any way modify or remit the same, or receive any commutation therefor.

Troy, like some other cities in the state, has a system for the collection of taxes somewhat peculiar, and differing in many respects from the provisions of the general law. There are some features common to both systems. The original assessment roll is made by the same officers—the assessors—both for the city taxes, and the state and county taxes. When completed, it is delivered to the chamberlain, who is required to copy the same, and make out the city tax as soon as levied (imposed) by the common council, and then deliver the assessment roll to the order of the supervisors of the assessment districts, on or before the 15th day of October. This phraseology is not altogether unambiguous; but I understand it to mean that the chamberlain is to make a *copy* of the assessment roll, and to make out the city tax on the *copy* thus made, and then to deliver the *original* assessment roll to the supervisors; and such I understand to have been the practice under this act.

Thus two assessment rolls come into existence, upon one of which the city taxes are extended by the city officers, and upon the other of which the state and county taxes are extended by county officers, to wit: by the board of supervisors as a body. This idea is further confirmed by the *heading* of the different *articles* of this statute.; one of which, (article second,) from which the above provision is extracted, is denominated "Of the mode of collecting city taxes;" and another, (article third,) "Of the mode of collecting state and county taxes." Each of these articles contains the provisions of a distinct and complete system for the collection of the taxes. By article second, the city roll, after the taxes are extended thereon, is to have annexed to it a warrant under the hand of the mayor, and seal of the city, commanding the collection of the tax. The chamberlain is directed to collect the same, after public notice, before the last of January then next, and in the meantime to receive for the collection thereof, different per centages, according to the promptness with which the payments are made by the persons taxed. For the collection of such portion of the taxes as remains unpaid by the first of February, the chamberlain is to issue his warrant to the sheriff, or a constable or marshal, commanding a levy and sale of the property of the persons taxed. Somewhat similar, but not altogether identical, proceedings are required to be taken for the collection of the county taxes; but the warrant comes from the supervisors, and the times and modes of enforcing payment are slightly different.

There are other distinctions between the city system and the county system for the collection of taxes. The fiscal year of the first is from March to March; of the other, from October to October. The taxes of the one are payable, and the warrant issued to the chamberlain therefor, by the 15th of October; those of the other by the 15th of December. It is quite possible that the city taxes, or a portion thereof, may be collected before the actual meeting of the board which makes the commutation in question. Again: the commutation, when authorized to be made, is to be paid to the treasurer of the county, and no provision is made for the payment over to the city authorities of any portion of the commutation money, or of its equitable distribution between the city and the county taxes. Were they upon the same roll, there might be some reason for saying that a general commutation upon the property taxed ought to be ratably divided between the city and the county taxes for that property, according to their respective amounts.

It is objected to this view of the case that, after all, these several acts are part of one general system of taxation, and that the right of commutation should be regarded as applicable to all taxes, inasmuch as they have one general object in view—the support of the government; and that the reason for commutation applies in principle to each class of taxes alike, and that the terms of the act allowing commutation, are unrestricted, and comprehensive enough to embrace every species of tax. These considerations are not without force; but the difficulty, if not impossibility, of making the commutation in question applicable to the city taxes, and the improbability that where there are two distinct bodies vested with the power of taxation upon the same property, but for different purposes, that the one should be regarded as clothed with the power of remitting or diminishing the taxes imposed by the other, and the confusion which would thence arise, together with the other considerations before adverted to, have led my mind to the conclusion that the legislature intended to discriminate between the two cases, or else that the provision for commutation was inadvertently omitted from the system devised for the collection of city taxes. In either view, the plaintiff must fail.

An argument in favor of the plaintiff is also supposed to be derived from the allegation that the corrected assessment rolls, as finally perfected by the board of supervisors, form also the basis of taxation for the city taxes. But I think the allegation is not founded upon fact, or a proper apprehension of the provisions of the law. I do not understand that the *corrected* assessment rolls are those upon which the city taxes are extended, but that they are the *copies* of the *original* assessment rolls delivered by the assessors to the chamberlain. Hence the argument fails.

If these views are correct, they dispose of this case. The judge at the circuit was right in rejecting the evidence offered, inasmuch as it constituted no defence to the action, and also in determining that the defendants were entitled to judgment.

The judgment of the circuit court must be affirmed.

NEW YORK COMMON PLEAS.

James Lefferts agt. John Brampton and others.

Charles E. Borsdorf and others agt. John Brampton and others.

The right to the *inspection of books and papers*, with a view to the *discovery of evidence*, is distinctly recognised by statute, and is not to be confounded with the production of them as evidence *upon the trial*, or on the *examination of a party as a witness before trial*.

If there is reason to believe, upon the case as laid before the court, that the evidence in reality exists, and is material to the matter in controversy; if the other party admits the possession of the books or documents alleged to contain it; if he also impliedly admits the probability of its existence, *by not denying it*, and no great practical inconvenience will follow from allowing the other party to inspect it, the privilege ought to be *granted*.

Thus, where the plaintiffs brought their action to recover the possession of goods obtained from them by the defendants' assignors, upon *representations alleged to have been fraudulent*, and in their sworn *petition* stated that they were informed and believed that an examination of the books of the assignors, by a competent book-keeper, would enable the plaintiffs to show the assignors were, when they made their representations of solvency referred to in the complaint, hopelessly insolvent, and that they knew that the representations made by them were false,

Held, the defendants making no answer to the application, but moved to dismiss it on the ground that the discovery could not be allowed by the practice of the court, that the case appeared to be eminently one in which the court should lend its assistance to enable the plaintiffs to inspect documentary evidence which would show whether the representations made by the defendants' assignors *were true or fasle.*

New York General Term, November, 1862.

DALY, BRADY and HILTON, *Judges.*

THIS was an application on behalf of the plaintiffs, for an inspection of the books and papers of the defendants' assignors, in the possession of the defendants.

By the court, DALY, F. J. An inspection of books and papers will be granted, if facts and circumstances are shown which warrant a presumption that the book or document sought contains evidence which will prove, or tend to prove, some fact which the party applying has to establish. (*Rule XV of the Supreme Court; Davis* agt. *Dunham*, 13 *How.*, 425; *Commercial Bank of Albany* agt. *Dunham, id.*, 341; *Hoyt* agt. *American Exchange Bank*, 1 *Duer*, 652; *Jackling* agt. *Edwards*, 3 *E. D. Smith*, 539.) The applicant is not required to prove positively that the documentary evidence exists, as the right given is one of discovery; but he must show sufficient to satisfy the court that there is good reason to suppose that the opposite party has documentary evidence in his possession material to the matter in issue, and the presumption that he has, becomes a very strong one, if, with the means of knowledge in his power, he does not deny the fact.

The two actions in which the present application was made, were brought to recover the possession of goods obtained from the plaintiffs by the firm of Goldsmith & Gutman, upon representations alleged to have been fraudulent. It is stated in the petition, that the goods were sold to them upon a representation by them that they were solvent; that they had a capital of $17,000; had made money, and were doing a profitable business. That the sale was made in the months of June and July, 1857, and that, in the next month, Goldsmith & Gutman failed, and made an assignment to the defendants for the benefit of creditors.

It is averred that Goldsmith & Gutman kept, up to the time of their assignment, books of account, showing the amount of the capital invested by them in their business, their losses and profits therein, their debts, liabilities and assets, and their business transactions generally; showing the pecuniary condition of the firm before, since, and at the time when the sale above referred to was made; which books, it is averred, are now in the possession of their assignees, the defendants. That the petitioners applied to the defendants for liberty to see the books, and received for reply that no one should be allowed to see or inspect them.

The petitioners swear that they are informed and believe that an examination of the books by a competent bookkeeper, will enable them to show that Goldsmith & Gutman were, when they made the representations referred to, hopelessly insolvent, and that they knew that the representations made by them were false.

The defendants made no answer to the application, but moved to dismiss it, on the ground that the discovery sought could not be allowed by the practice of the court, and the motion was granted.

It may fairly be inferred that it will appear by their books what capital the firm had when they made the representations referred to, and whether, as they represented themselves to be perfectly solvent, and then doing a profitable business, these books constitute the written record which they kept of their business while engaged in transacting it; and if the books will show that the representations made by them were false, the evidence is not only material, but of a very conclusive kind. The fact that nothing which is stated in the petition is denied; the circumstance of Goldsmith & Gutman's failure in six weeks after these representations were made; and the statement of the plaintiffs, under oath, that they are informed and believe that an examination of the books by a competent book-keeper will enable them to establish that Goldsmith & Gutman knew what they represented, to be false, should, I think, be sufficient to warrant a well-founded suspicion that the evidence sought for exists, and will be obtained by an inspection of the books. Applications which contemplate a general investigation of the books of a party in business, are looked upon with great disfavor. It would be an abuse of the forms of judicial procedure, to allow them to be resorted to as a means of compelling a man to expose the whole of his business affairs to the prying curiosity of an adversary, actuated by no other motive than the hope that he may be able to discover something which he may use to his advantage in a legal controversy. To say nothing of the interruption, inconvenience and humiliation to a man in business giving up all his books, documents and papers to an investigation to be conducted by his adversary, there is the additional consideration that an exposition of the secrets of his business may prove detrimental to him. Such applications, therefore, are almost uniformly denied; for the case must be an exceedingly strong one—the facts and circumstances adduced in support of it, of the most conclusive kind—to justify a court's compelling a man who is in business, to expose all his books and papers for the discovery of evidence supposed to be contained in them. On the other hand, the right to the inspection of books and papers, with a view to the discovery of evidence, is distinctly recognized by statute, and is not to be confounded with the production of them as evidence upon a trial or on the examination of a party as a witness before trial. The Revised Statutes (*vol.* 3, *p.* 293, §§ 60 *and* 61, *5th ed.*) speak of compelling a discovery; of compelling a party to a suit in such cases as the court may prescribe by general rules to discover books, documents and papers in his possession or power, relating to the merits of the suit; and the Code, in the recognition of this right, is much stronger, by providing (§ 388) that "the court before which an action is pending, or a judge or justice thereof, may, in their discretion and upon due notice, order either party to give to the other, within a specified time, an inspection and copy, or permission to take a copy, of any books, papers and documents in his possession or under his control, containing evidence relating to the merits of the action or the defence;" an enactment in the Code which is merely auxiliary to and not a substitute for the previous provisions in the Revised Statutes. (*Gould* agt. *McCarthy*, 1 *Kern.*, 576.) The right here granted is coextensive with what could be obtained in equity by a bill of discovery. (*Townsend* agt. *Lawrence*, 9 *Wend.*, 458.) In equity the discovery was twofold; to discover the existence of written evidence assumed or believed to be in the possession of the other party; and then, if its existence and the possession of it was not denied, a discovery of its contents. (*Pollock on Courts*, 8.) It is the same under our statutes. There is a clear recognition that the ends of justice may be promoted by compelling a party to discover whether he has not writings in his possession tending to prove the matter in controversy; whilst at the same time, to guard against the abuse that would arise if parties were always allowed, under the form of a legal procedure, to pry into the private papers and books of their opponent, it is left to the sound discretion of the court, in every case, to say whether the privilege will be granted or not.

If there is reason to believe upon the case, as laid before the court, that the evidence in reality exists and is material to the matter in controversy; if the other party admits the possession of the book or document alleged to contain it; if he also impliedly admits the probability of its existence, by not denying it, and no great practical inconvenience will follow from allowing the other party to inspect it, the privilege ought to be granted.

Such is the case here. The plaintiffs have repossessed themselves of the goods; they must vindicate their right to retake them; and the case appears to me to be eminently one in which the court should lend its assistance to enable them to inspect documentary evidence which will certainly show whether the representations made by Goldsmith & Gutman were true or false. Neither the defendants nor Goldsmith or Gutman have undertaken to deny that the examination of the books will show that the representations were false. Not the slightest circumstance is given in explanation of the failure of the firm in six weeks after they had given such a flattering account of their business. The objections which might exist where liberty is asked to examine the books and papers of a merchant engaged in the ordinary prosecution of his business, do not exist in their case. Their business is at an end. Their affairs are in the hands of assignees for settlement, and no prejudice, injury or great inconvenience can arise from allowing the plaintiffs to inspect their books.

It is suggested that the examination asked for can be had at the trial or before it, by subpœnaing the parties or witnesses, and compelling the production of the books by a subpœna, *duces tecum;* and in *Breevort* agt. *Werner*, (8 *How.*, 321,) Justice Hand says that "a mere discovery, so called, as to books, documents and papers, should be in no other way than on the examination of the party." The answer to this suggestion is, that the statute gives the right to a discovery, and declares that, where the proceedings for that purpose are not therein provided, "the court shall be governed by the principles and practice of the court of chancery, in compelling discovery." There is nothing in the general rules which the supreme court have adopted, nor in the Code, to warrant such a conclusion as that the discovery can be had in no other way than upon the examination of the party. It was an existing remedy before the party could be examined. The party seeking the discovery may have nothing to ask the other party. The documentary evidence, if found, may be all that he requires, and he is not to be compelled to put his adversary upon the stand as a witness, when evidence that cannot be evaded, falsified nor contradicted may be obtained. The party applying, moreover, may wish to discover evidence that is against as well as for him. He may be satisfied, upon the inspection of documentary evidence in the possession of the other party, that he cannot maintain a defence, or that he must abandon his action; and such an inquiry, when made *bona fide*, is to be encouraged, as it may cut short the litigation and stop the increase of costs. The discovery of the evidence sought on the trial, or on the examination of the party, may be attended by great delay, which is avoided by an inspection out of court. The examination at the trial may prove very inconvenient, and to a certain degree impracticable, where the discovery sought depends, as in this case, upon the inspection of a set of mercantile books. A skillful accountant might be able to tell in a very short time whether the books do or do not show that the firm were hopelessly insolvent when they purchased the goods of the plaintiffs, or it might require on his part a very careful examination extending over many days. If the examination is to be allowed at all, it will economize time at the trial, and tend to elicit the fact with greater certainty, by permitting an inspection of the books out of court; and as there is nothing in the statute or in the general rules of the supreme court necessarily coupling this inspection with an examination of the party as a witness, it should be allowed in the way in which it has heretofore been allowed, if the facts and circumstances shown lead to the conviction that it may tend to promote the ends of justice. In my judgment, enough has been shown in this case to warrant a reasonable presumption that it will; and I think that the motion, to the extent of allowing the inspection of the books in the hands of the assignees, should have been granted.

SUPREME COURT.

Henry Mattice agt. Charles W. Lillie and Cecelia Lillie.

Where the *husband* purchased *lumber* for the building of a house on real estate which he *falsely represented* belonged to him, and on the *credit* of owning such property, when in fact the real estate at that time, and the house afterwards erected upon it with such lumber, belonged to *his wife*, and the house was built with her knowledge and approbation,—

Held, in an action in equity by the plaintiff against the *husband and wife* for the price of such lumber, that the facts thus established created an *equitable lien* in favor of the plaintiff *upon the real estate*, and it was thus decreed.

Albany General Term, March, 1862.

Hogeboom, Peckham and Miller, *Justices.*

Appeal by defendants from judgment at the circuit in favor of the plaintiff.

L. Tremain, *for plaintiff, respondent.*

H. Smith, *for defendants, appellants.*

By the court, Hogeboom, Justice. This is an equity suit, evidently designed, from the form of the complaint, to charge the real estate owned by the female defendant with the value of the plaintiff's lumber which went into the construction of the house upon it, upon the ground that the estate has had the benefit of the consideration thus furnished; that it was furnished for the express purpose of being so applied, and essentially upon the credit of such estate, being sold to the defendant, Charles Lillie, upon the faith of his assurance that he was the owner of the real property, and thus fraudulently procured from the plaintiff, and applied with the knowledge and consent of both of the defendants. These are substantially the allegations in the complaint, and, if sustained by the evidence, make a case I think where the plaintiff is entitled to recover. (*Yale* agt. *Dederer*, 18 *N. Y.*, 280; *S. C.*, 22 *N. Y.*, 450; *Colvin* agt. *Currier*, 22 *Barb.*, 371, 385.)

The judge who tried this cause at the circuit has not expressly found *all* of these facts, although I think they are, on the whole, inferable from the evidence, and perhaps has found some facts—some of which it might perhaps be claimed, with some plausibility, were not clearly deducible from the evidence—though I do not mean to say that the finding was on the whole erroneous.

Certain facts are I think sufficiently apparent, and among others the following:

1. That the plaintiff's lumber went into the construction of the defendants' house; and that this was with the knowledge and consent and *intent* of both the defendants. I think it also fairly inferable that this knowledge, consent and intent existed at the time the lumber was purchased; and that it was purchased for that express object. The female defendant has therefore had the benefit of the consideration, arising from the sale of the plaintiff's lumber; and there is nothing *inequitable* in compelling the property, thus *created in part* by the plaintiff's goods, to be answerable for his claim to the extent of their value.

2. It is not entirely clear that the wife authorized the misrepresentation of the husband, that he owned the real estate, although it would not be a very forced construction of the evidence to deduce such an inference from the facts proved. But it is sufficiently clear that he made such representation; that it was false and fraudulent on his part; that on the faith of it the lumber was sold;

that the wife knew of its appropriation for her benefit; that she did not repudiate or refuse the benefit of such appropriation; that she was aware, or at least supposed, that the plaintiff sold the lumber in the belief that the husband owned the house; that she took no pains to correct that impression; but recognizing the force of the equitable considerations which, under such circumstances, entitled the plaintiff to compensation, promised to make some provision for his benefit.

3. I am inclined to think the facts thus established create an equitable lien in favor of the plaintiff upon the real estate in question, and justify the decree which the court below made in the premises. The only defect in the findings of the judge, (if there be any,) to come fully up to the case made by the complaint, (which on a former hearing was adjudged sufficient,) is the absence of any finding that the defendants contemplated a *fraud* when the lumber was purchased. As I have before stated, I think the evidence justifies the inference of an *intent to defraud* on the part of the husband, and perhaps so also on the part of the wife. Although I do not deem the latter fact absolutely indispensable to the maintenance of the action, if she, with knowledge of the circumstances under which the lumber was obtained, chose to appropriate to her benefit the fruits of his fraud or misrepresentation, she thereby adopted his acts, and must be held responsible for them to the extent that she has been benefited by them.

The case presents strong equities on the part of the plaintiff, and I think no injustice will be done by affirming the judgment of the court below.

Some of the findings excepted to may not be borne out by the proof to the very letter, but it by no means follows that for that reason, in a case in equity, that a new trial should be granted. There appears to be no *direct* proof that the wife was in humble circumstances, nor that *both* husband and wife kept a candy and variety store. The defendants (in addition to the general question arising upon the merits of the whole case) rely mainly upon the exception to the judge's refusal to find that the lumber was sold to the defendant, Charles W., upon *his sole credit, without any other security or assurance than the said Charles W.'s promise to pay for the same.* I think the judge was warranted by the evidence in refusing so to find. The lumber was not sold upon the *sole credit* of Charles W. Lillie, but in part, at least, upon the credit of the real estate; nor was it sold without other security or *assurance* than his promise to pay for the same. On the contrary, it was sold upon the assurance that *he owned the real estate*, and it was doubtless in reliance upon that representation that the sale was made and the credit given.

On the whole, I discover no sound reason for disturbing the judgment at the circuit, and I think it should be affirmed with costs.

SUPREME COURT.

Middlebrook agt. The Merchants' Bank.

An *executor*, who has obtained probate and letters testamentary in a *sister state*, where he resides, can dispose (without action) of his testator's *personal property in this state*, without taking out letters ancillary here.

New York Special Term, *December*, 1862.

This was an action to compel the bank to allow the transfer of one hundred shares of their stock standing in the name of Robert Middlebrook, deceased, to his son, Louis N. Middlebrook, the plaintiff. The facts were as follows: The deceased was a resident of Trumbull, in the probate district of Bridgeport, Connecticut, and died in May, 1861. By his last will he gave $16,000 of bank stock to the plaintiff, to be selected by him and appraised, and he appointed three persons, all residents of Connecticut, his executors. The executors proved the will in the probate court for the district of Bridgeport; letters testamentary were granted to them, and they proceeded to settle the estate according to the will. The testator held stock in five or six other banks in this city. The plaintiff selected one hundred shares of the stock in defendants' bank as a part of his legacy. The shares were appraised, and the executors executed, in Connecticut, a transfer of the shares to the plaintiff, who applied to the bank for leave to transfer the item into his own name on the transfer books of the bank. The bank refused to allow the transfer, on the ground that the executors had no right to dispose of these shares without first taking out letters testamentary in this state.

E. SEELEY and WM. BLISS, *for plaintiff.*
B. W. BONNEY and ALFRED ROE, *for defendants.*

CLERKE, Justice. The simple question in this case is, whether an executor, who has obtained probate and letters testamentary in a sister state—the residence of the executor, and where the testator lived and died—can dispose of his testator's personal property, situated here, without taking out letters ancillary in this state.

It is certain that no person can maintain an action in our courts, as an executor or administrator, without first taking out letters ancillary in this state. That is, before he seeks the aid of our courts to enforce any legal right in this state, he must first be invested, recognized and commissioned, in his representative capacity, by the appropriate jurisdiction here.

But that is very different from saying that he cannot transfer any rights existing in this state—that he cannot sell any of his testator's estate, or release any interest therein, without first obtaining letters ancillary here.

In the language of Ashurst, J., in *Smith* agt. *Miles*, (1 *T. R.*, 480,) "the executor has the right immediately on the death of the testator, and the right draws after it a constructive possession."

The probate is a mere ceremony, but when passed, the executor does not derive his title under the probate, but under the will. The probate is only evidence of his right, and is necessary to enable him to sue; but he may release, &c., before probate. (*See, also, Valentine* agt. *Jackson*, 9 *Wend.*, 302; *Babcock* agt. *Booth*, 2 *Hill*, 181.) If the executor, then, can, before probate, dispose of his testator's property, situated or not in the place where his testator had resided, he certainly can dispose of it after probate, although he cannot enforce the possession of it under a foreign jurisdiction, without complying with the preliminary requirements of the laws of that jurisdiction.

The plaintiff, I think, is clearly entitled to judgment.

NEW YORK COMMON PLEAS.

Jules Jurgensen agt. James Alexander.

Where it is shown by evidence that the defendant has violated a well known *trade mark* of the plaintiff, he will be *perpetually enjoined and restrained* by the court from disposing of, selling, or causing to be disposed of or sold, any of the articles bearing the false, simulated or spurious stamp or mark.

And the defendant will be required to produce, before a *referee* appointed by the court, such spurious articles which at the time of the commencement of the action were in his possession, for the purpose of having the spurious trade mark *erased or liberated* therefrom, by or under the direction of the referee, at the *cost and expense of the defendant*, with the *costs* and *disbursements* of the action.

New York Special Term, Dec., 1862.

The plaintiff brought his action against the defendant for an infringement of his well known trade mark, "Jules Jurgensen," engraved on the cap or inside back of each of his own genuine watches.

The action was tried before the court without a jury, who, after hearing the proofs and allegations of the parties, found the following facts and conclusions of law thereon.

PLATT, GERARD and BUCKLEY, *Attorneys*, and THOMAS C. T. BUCKLEY, *Counsel, for plaintiff*.

J. VAN WINKLE, *Attorney and Counsel, for defendant.*

BRADY, J. *First.*—That at the time of the commencement of this action, and for twenty years previous thereto, the above named plaintiff was a manufacturer and vendor of watches, carrying on his business in Switzerland and Copenhagen.

That the trade mark used by him for the purpose of distinguishing and designating the watches manufactured by him was "Jules Jurgensen, Copenhagen," and that said trade mark was so used and employed by him on all such watches so manufactured or sold by him; being inscribed on the cap or inside back of each watch.

Second.—That said watches, so manufactured and sold by the plaintiff, bearing such trade mark or device, were at the time of the commencement of this action, bought, sold, and dealt in by dealers in watches and others, on the faith and credit of the said trade mark, and that the same had acquired a wide spread reputation, and an extensive sale.

Third.—That at the time of the commencement of this action, the defendant being a dealer in watches and other merchandise, had in his possession, at his place of business, in the city of New York, exposed for sale, four watches, purporting to be manufactured and made by the above-named plaintiff, and bearing the trade mark "Jules Jurgensen, Copenhagen."

That said watches were not, in fact, manufactured or made by the said plaintiff, but were of a much inferior quality and description, and that said trade mark thereon was false, simulated, and spurious.

And having in and by said decision determined, as a conclusion of law, that the plaintiff is entitled to the judgment hereinafter set forth, I direct the same to be entered accordingly:

First.—That the defendant, James Alexander, his agents, clerks, servants, and all persons employed under or in connection with him, be perpetually enjoined and restrained from disposing of, selling, or causing to be disposed of or sold, any watches bearing the false, simulated and spurious stamp or mark, "Jules Jurgensen, Cophenhagen."

Second.—That the said defendant do produce before Nathaniel Jarvis, Jr., Esquire, appointed herein referee for such purpose, the said watches, which at the time of the commencement of this suit were in defendant's possession, and had upon them the said false, simulated and spurious trade mark, to be erased or liberated therefrom, by or under the direction of the said referee, at the cost and expense of the said defendant.

Third.—That the said plaintiff, Jules Jurgensen, do recover against the said defendant, James Alexander, his costs and disbursements, adjusted at the sum of one hundred and twenty-five dollars and thirty-one cents, and that the said plaintiff have execution therefor.

SUPREME COURT.

ELKIN, plaintiff in error agt. THE PEOPLE, defendants in error.

Where on an indictment for *misdemeanor*, it appears that the offence consists of a *series of acts*, and a part of the series is a complete misdemeanor, there can be no *merger in a felony*, and the conviction for a misdemeanor will be sustained, although the evidence may show the commission of an act of felony.

But where, on such indictment, the act which is the gist of the indictment is a *single act*, and the evidence shows the commission of a *felony*, the misdemeanor may be merged in the felony.

New York General Term, *Oct.*, 1862.

INGRAHAM, BARNARD and CLERKE, *Justices*.

By the court, CLERKE, Justice. I. On an indictment for a misdemeanor, and where the act which is the gist of the indictment is a single act, and the evidence shows the commission of a felony, the former may be merged in the latter; and there are several authorities which maintain that the prisoner should be acquitted of the misdemeanor, in order that he may be indicted for the felony. (*Commonwealth* agt. *Roby*, 12 *Pick.*, 496, 508; *Same* agt. *Kingsbury*, 5 *Mass.*, 106; *Rex* agt. *Cross*, 1 *Ld. Raymond*, 711.) But, where the offence consists of a series of acts, and a part of the series is a complete misdemeanor, there can be no merger, and the conviction for a misdemeanor will be sustained. (*The Queen* agt. *Button*, 63 *Eng. C. L. R.*, 947, 112, *D.* 929.)

In the case under consideration, as well as in the case to which I have just referred, the indictment was for a conspiracy, which is a misdemeanor and nothing more, whatever may have been done by the conspirators in pursuance of it. Conspiracy may be followed by a series of overt acts; but the offence is distinct from them, and complete without them. The misdemeanor of which the defendant was convicted cannot be made identical with any felonious act, even if the indictment expressly set forth or the evidence showed that the conspiracy was consummated by a felonious act.

In the words of Lord DENMAN, in *The Queen* agt. *Button*, we are of opinion that this conviction for a misdemeanor ought to be sustained, even if the evidence proving it proved also that it was part of a felony, and that such felony had been completed.

II. The indictment contains all necessary words to make it conform to the legal definition of the offence. It alleges a conspiracy, and then sets forth that the conspirators, well knowing that Laube was not guilty of the offence which they charged against him, they procured one Josephine Westerdoff to appear before a police justice and falsely swear, &c.

The counsel for the prisoner objects, that the words "falsely and maliciously" are in the wrong place, as they precede and relate exclusively to the conspiracy, and do not, in any degree relate or attach to the object of the conspirators—the arrest. If these words were absolutely indispensable at all, the counsel would probably be right; it was not necessary that they should precede and relate to the conspiracy, which would be sufficiently alleged without them; and as to the purpose—the arrest—the falsity and malice of this are sufficiently shown by stating, that the conspirators well knew that he was not guilty of the offence. The statement of this fact is much more effective and satisfactory than if the words averring falsity and malice were employed, without this statement; and to employ them, in addition to the statement of their knowledge of Laube's innocence, would be superfluous. So that the indictment could dispense altogether with the words complained of; and their insertion in any part of the indictment does not vitiate it. They are only harmless surplusage.

The judgment should be affirmed.

SUPREME COURT.

JOHN OSTELL agt. WILLIAM BROUGH.

Where consignments of lumber are made by the consignor to the consignee under a contract between them that the consignee is to sell the same on *commission*, at eight per cent., which is to include a premium for *guaranty of sales*, and to account for the net proceeds, after deducting charges and commissions, the consignee acts in a *fiduciary capacity*, and is liable to *arrest* for not paying over the proceeds received from purchasers.

It seems, that where the purchaser does not pay, and the consignor or owner of the lumber sues the consignee for the price upon the *contract of guaranty*, the latter is to be considered as a *mere debtor*, and not liable to arrest.

Albany Special Term, April, 1860.

MOTION by defendant to vacate order of arrest or reduce the amount of bail, which was originally fixed at $10,000.

W. A. BEACH, *for defendant.*
IRVING BROWN, *for plaintiff.*

HOGEBOOM, Justice. The defendant moves, upon the pleadings and papers in this action, to vacate the order of arrest, or, if that be denied, to reduce the amount of bail.

The plaintiff was a lumber dealer in Montreal, and according to the defendant's answer consigned lumber to the defendant at West Troy, to be by him sold on commission, such commission being eight per cent., which included a premium for guaranteeing sales, and to account for the net proceeds, after deducting charges and commissions.

Independent of the question of guaranty, money received by the defendant for sales made under such an agreement, was, according to several adjudications, money received by a person in a fiduciary capacity, and rendered the party liable to arrest for misappropriating it. (*Frost* agt. *McCarger*, 14 *How.*, 131; *Stoll* agt. *King*, 8 *How.*, 298;

Holbrook agt. *Homer*, 6 *How.*, 86; *Turner* agt. *Thompson*, 2 *Abbott*, 444; *Schudder* agt. *Shiells*, 17 *How.*, 420.)

Is the relation of the parties in this particular substantially altered by the fact that the consignee guarantees the sales made by him, receiving an additional compensation therefor? Is he any the less the consignee of the lumber, receiving it for the purpose of sale, and bound to account for the proceeds? It is true the consignor has an additional security in the personal responsibility of consignee for the sales made; but I think that circumstance does not destroy the fiduciary relation. The property sold is still, until sold, the property of the consignor; and when sold, the proceeds of the sale belong to him. If received by the consignee, he is bound, according to his own statement of the contract, to return or account for them to the consignor; and so bound I think by the obligations of this peculiar relation. He received the goods upon the special trust and confidence that he would do so; and he receives an extra compensation for making the sales to trustworthy and responsible purchasers. Where the purchaser does *not* pay, and the vendor (the original owner) sues the consignee for the value or price upon the contract of guaranty, it may be that he is to be treated as a mere debtor, and not liable to arrest; but where the purchaser does pay, and the proceeds of sale come into the hands of the consignee, I think he holds them as a trustee for his principal, and is subject to arrest for their misappropriation. Suppose by the conditions of the sale the purchaser had agreed to pay, and had paid in certain commodities, instead of money, is there any doubt that if the defendant had received them, he would hold them for the benefit of the plaintiff, and that they would belong to the latter, and would be recoverable by him under the terms of the original fiduciary relation? I think this is the most fair and reasonable construction of the contract between the consignor and consignee, and that the contract of guaranty is merely superadded to the other and does not destroy the fiduciary relation, unless it be in the single case where the vendor prosecutes upon the guaranty.

As to that part of the application which seeks to reduce the bail, I confess to some difficulty in ascertaining the true amount which the plaintiff will be entitled to recover. The parties are directly at issue on this point, and the evidence is sufficient I think, on this preliminary investigation, to entitle the plaintiff to such security as an order of arrest will give him, to the amount of $8,000. The bail may be reduced to that amount. The cost of making and opposing the motion may abide the event of the action.

SUPREME COURT.

THE PEOPLE agt. JOHN MAUCH.

On an indictment for *keeping a disorderly house*, the character of the house cannot be proved by *general reputation*.

No one should be convicted of any criminal offence upon *mere reputation* or rumors.

New York General Term, Nov., 1862.

WRIT OF ERROR to the general sessions on exceptions taken to a judgment of conviction for keeping a disorderly house.

NELSON J. WATERBURY, *for people.*
E. W. DODGE, *for defendant.*

By the court, INGRAHAM, P. Justice. The prisoner was indicted for keeping a disorderly house. On the trial, the prosecution offered to show the character of the house in which the defendant lived, from reputation. This was objected to, but admitted, and the prisoner's counsel excepted.

The point involved is whether the character of the house can be proved by general reputation. Formerly, the rule was settled by *Radcliff, Mayor, in Rathbone's case,* (1 *vol. City Hall Recorder*, 26,) that particular acts were not admissible to prove a house disorderly, but that it must be proved by general reputation of the house.

This decision has, I believe, been very generally followed in this city since.

In Pennsylvania, in *Commonwealth* agt. *Stewart*, (1 *Sergeant & Rawle*, 342,) the contrary doctrine was held.

I have never been able to understand the principle upon which such a rule was established. Where the question is as to character, there the rule has been settled, that it is to be proven by the reputation in which a person is held by his neighbors. Yet there is no judge who has not at times seen the injustice of this rule, in cases where witnesses have become exasperated at individuals from some private cause, often of mere non-payment of debts, and who on cross-examination, have shown their opinion of a man's character has been formed from such causes rather than from his general reputation. There is no other offence in which general reputation is considered sufficient to convict a man of crime, and when we reflect how such reputation is made up, not from proof of facts, nor from the relation of actual occurrences, but rather from gossip, tale-bearing, prejudices, and other similar means, we may well hesitate at the propriety of permitting such evidence to be sufficient to blast a man's character, or to consign him to a prison. The difficulty seems to be in ascertaining a proper mode of proving such facts as will make out the character of a house. I see no difficulty in submitting to the jury under oath the same evidence upon which individuals out of doors, not under oath, make up a man's general character. One hears one story, another hears another story, and these are repeated from one to another until they become changed into proof of general reputation. Instead of taking it second, third, or fourth hand from others, it would be better to submit to the jury the series of occurrences at the house, from which they could form the opinion, whether the occurrences there were such as to warrant the conclusion that the general management of the house was such as to bring it within the description of a disorderly house.

Such was in fact the course of the evidence in this case. The prosecution proved that prostitution and fighting occurred there, and the defendant produced evidence to the contrary.

If a house was proved to have been used for such purposes, that rows and fights were of frequent occurrence, that noise sufficient to disturb the neighborhood was often permitted, or matters of a similar character, a jury would be much better able to form the opinion as to the character of the house, than from opinions of policemen who had no personal knowledge of the occurrences from which they formed their opinions.

In the case of receiving stolen goods, the general reputation of the house, that it was frequented by thieves, has been held inadmissible. The rules of evidence in criminal are generally the same as in civil cases, and whatever difference exists, it is that the caution in criminal cases requires a stricter rule to be enforced than in civil actions.

In civil suits, reputation is not sufficient to sustain a cause of action. It will not prove a partnership or a custom, without knowledge on the part of the witness of such custom being acted upon, nor of agency, and many other matters which might be enumerated.

In the *People* agt. *Carey*, (4 *Park. C. Rep., p.* 238,) may be found a case where a keeper of a disorderly house was convicted upon proof of the various occurrences from which the opinion as to the character of the house is formed, and such opinion may be much better formed from witnesses who testify, than from the opinions of those who give no reasons therefor.

No one should be convicted of any criminal offence upon mere reputation or rumors, and the evidence in this case should not have been admitted.

In *Wharton Cr. Law, sec.* 661, it is said that evidence of general reputation as to a gaming house, or disorderly house, is not admissible, and at section 3,290, it is said that proof of the character of the women who frequent such a house, the character and behavior of the men, and the effects upon the neighborhood, is admissible. The 2,393d section does not establish any different rule. It says that the particular acts need not be proven, but that common reputation as to the defendants and the character of the houses they keep, and the persons visiting them, is admissible. This rule is stated to be on the case of *United States* agt. *Stevens*, (4 *Cranch, C. C. Rep.*, 341;) an examination of that case will show that no other evidence than reputation of the character of the persons who frequented the house was admitted; and in the *United States* agt. *Jardine*, (4 *Cranch, C. C. R., p.* 338,) it was expressly held that such general evidence was not admissible.

The conviction should be reversed and a new trial ordered in the sessions.

NEW YORK COMMON PLEAS.

THE MAYOR, &c. OF NEW YORK agt. CHARLES V. LYONS and WM. H. CHARLOCK.

In an action on a *constable's bond*, in the city of New York, the plaintiff is *irregular* to enter up a *general judgment* for the sum mentioned in his complaint, where the defendants' answer has been adjudged frivolous.

He should enter up judgment for the *penalty of the bond*, and then move this court, under the act of 1813, for an order directing so much money to be levied upon the judgment as shall be sufficient to pay the plaintiff his debt or damages recovered, with costs.

If the defendants *appeal* to the general term, from such an irregular judgment, they *waive the irregularity;* and if judgment is given against them on the appeal, they cannot afterwards move to have the judgment set aside for the irregularity.

An error in the mode of entering up a judgment cannot be reviewed on appeal.

But the defendants, having lost the right to move, upon the ground of irregularity, to set aside the judgment, cannot complain of an order of the court directing that the judgment be *entered up properly;* that other suitors, if any there should be, may be enabled to have the amounts recovered by them levied under this judgment in the way in which the statute provides.

General Term, January, 1863.

DALY, BRADY and HILTON, *Judges*.

APPEAL from judgment at special term.

By the court, DALY, F. J. This judgment was undoubtedly irregular. The condition of the bond upon which the action was brought was, that the defendant Lyons would well and faithfully execute the office of constable; and the mode of proceeding in an action upon bonds of this nature is regulated in part by the 147th section of the act to reduce several laws relating to the city of New York, into one act, (*Rev. Laws of* 1813, *p.* 396,) and in part by art. 2, title 4, chap. 6, part 3 of the Revised Statutes, pointing out the mode of proceeding in action upon bonds for the performance of covenants. It is not, in the sense of the fifth section of the article referred to in the Revised Statutes, a bond for the payment of money. The description of bond there meant is for the payment of money in gross, the amount and the time for the payment of which is fixed by the condition of the bond, and in which no assessment of damages is necessary, as nothing remains but to compute the amount of interest, which may be ascertained by the clerk, (*Graham's Pr.*, 803, *2d ed.*;) but it comes under the general class there referred to, in which the plaintiff must set out in his complaint the specific breaches for which the action is brought. This article in the Revised Statutes is not repealed; the only modification that it has undergone being the provision of the Code which allows the court to take the proof, or to order a reference to ascertain the damages, when a judgment is taken in an action upon such a bond by default.

The 147th section of the act of 1813 declares that where a recovery is had against a constable by a party aggrieved through the officer's default or misconduct, that such party may obtain an order in this court that the bond be put in suit, and if judgment is recovered, the act directs that this court shall, upon motion, direct so much money to be levied upon the judgment as shall be sufficient to pay the party the debt or damages so recovered, with costs to be paid to the party aggrieved. If there has been an appearance in the cause, this motion must be made upon notice to the opposite party, (*King* agt. *Stafford*, 5 *How.*, 30;) and since the Code, (§ 246,) the court, instead of directing an assessment, as was formerly the practice, or a reference, may hear the proof in the recovery of the judgment against the officer, and if satisfied of the fact, make the order provided for in the act referred to. Instead of doing this, the plaintiff, upon its being adjudged that the answer was frivolous, took a general judgment for the sum mentioned in his complaint, which was erroneous. He should have entered up judgment for the penalty of the bond, and then moved the court for the order provided for by the act of 1813.

But although the mode in which the judgment was entered was irregular, the defendants waived the irregularity by appealing from the judgment to the general term; and judgment having been given against them on the appeal, they could not afterwards move to have the judgment set aside for irregularity. It is a general and long-established rule, in all applications to set aside proceedings for irregularity, that the party complaining of it must make his application at the first opportunity after he has knowledge of the fact, and before any further proceedings have been had. It is, said Lord KENYON, in *Pearson* agt. *Rauling*, (1 *East*, 77,) "the universal practice of the court, that when there has been an irregularity, if the party overlook it and take subsequent steps in the cause, he cannot afterwards revert back to the irregularity and object to it;" and to the same effect are *D'Argent* agt. *Vivant*, (1 *East*, 330;) *Fox* agt. *Money*, (1 *Bos. & Pul.*, 250;) *The King* agt. *Perry*, (5 *T. R.*, 464;) *Petrie* agt. *White*, (4 *id.* 10.) At first it was questioned whether the rule was not confined to cases where the party complaining of the irregularity had taken some subsequent step, but in *Downs* agt. *Witherington*, (2 *Taun.*, 243,) it was held to apply equally, where the party, with knowledge of the irregularity, remained passive, and allowed the other party to take a subsequent step; and in *Thorpe* agt. *Beer*, (2 *Barn. & Ald.*, 548,) as indicating the general policy of the courts upon the subject, it was held that, where a party moves for irregularity, he is bound to state every irregularity of which he wishes to take advantage, and is considered to have waived all those which he does not state at the time. The principle of this rule applies equally, whether the motion is made before or after judgment. In *Jones* agt. *Dunning*, (2 *John. C.*, 74,) the defendant moved after judgment, and the court denied the application upon the ground that they had suffered two terms of the court to go by, when it was to be presumed that they had notice of the proceedings against them; and to the same effect are, *Sharp* agt. *Pell*, (10 *John.*, 497;) *Rowan* agt. *Lytle*, (4 *Cow.*, 91;) *Graham's Practice*, (702,

2*d ed.*) The defendants in the present case knew of the irregularity, as they appealed from the judgment; and if they wished to avail themselves of it, they should have moved to set the judgment aside, instead of taking an appeal from the order directing the entry of the judgment, and from the judgment. The error in the mode of entering up the judgment could not be reviewed upon appeal. *Whitehead* agt. *Allen*, (28 *Barb.*, 661;) *King* agt. *Stafford*, (5 *How.*, 30.) The appeal, therefore, must have been brought upon other grounds, or for delay; and it is not to be tolerated that a party, knowing that the judgment is irregularly entered up, shall be at liberty to appeal from it to the general term; and if he fails there, go to the court of appeals; and ultimately failing to get the judgment reversed, be permitted to do then, what he ought to have done in the beginning without putting the other party to the expense and trouble of the appeal; that is, to move the court to set the judgment aside as irregularly entered. It may be said that as the error consists in the way in which the judgment was entered, that the court ought, for the benefit of other parties who may recover judgment against the same officer, see that it is properly entered up for the penalty. We do not know that any other parties will have occasion to bring suits against this officer, and we can see that no injustice has been done, as this judgment is for the amount which the party would in any event be entitled to; or, as was done in *Martin* agt. *Lott*, (4 *Abb. R.*, 365,) the defendants' application could have been denied, with costs, upon the ground that they had lost the right to make it; and for the benefit of other parties, should any recover judgments against the officer for official misconduct, and that the defendants may not be made liable in any event beyond the penal limits of their bond, the plaintiff could, and under the circumstances should, have been permitted to amend his judgment by entering it up for the penalty, with a further judgment that he have execution for the amount recovered against the officer, and costs.

The order appealed from should, in my opinion, be modified to that effect. The defendants having lost the right to move, upon the ground of irregularity, cannot complain of an order directing that the judgment be entered up properly; that other suitors, if any there should be, may be enabled to have the amounts recovered by them levied under this judgment in the way in which the statute provides. (*Davies' Laws*, 549.)

SUPREME COURT.

JOSEPH ABELS agt. ISAAC N. WESTERVELT and HENRY CAMP.

The *property of a copartnership* cannot be seized and sold on an *attachment* issued against *one* of the partners only. It is only the *interest* in the property of the partner in the attachment that can be seized and sold, which is his share in the *surplus* of the property, after payment of the partnership debts.

The other partner has a right, as against such an attachment, to *retain* the property for the purpose of paying the debts of the partnership.

New York General Term, September, 1862.

INGRAHAM, LEONARD and ROSEKRANS, *Justices*.

APPEAL from an order of special term.

By the court, ROSEKRANS, Justice. The order of the special term should be affirmed.

Westcott obtained a judgment in the marine court against the defendants upon a debt which they owed as partners. A transcript of this judgment was filed on the first day of October, 1860, in the office of the clerk of the city and county of New York, and an execution issued on the same day to the sheriff of that county, who levied upon the partnership property of defendants, and sold it, and realized the fund which is the subject of this motion. The plaintiff in this action obtained his judgment several days after

Westcott's execution was issued. He claims, however, the money in the sheriff's hands should be applied to the payment of his judgment, because, in September, 1860, he obtained an attachment in his action against Westervelt & Camp, directing the sheriff to attach the property of Westervelt alone, the attachment having been issued upon an affidavit that Westervelt was a non-resident of the state, and that by virtue of that attachment the sheriff seized the property sold on Westcott's execution, several days before Westcott obtained his judgment. Now, it is well settled, that upon an attachment against the property of one partner, the sheriff can only seize the interest in the property of the defendant in the attachment, and that interest, in the case of partnership, is the share of the partner in the surplus of the property after the payment of the partnership debts. The sheriff could not, under Abels' attachment, take the property of the partnership, which was sold on Westcott's execution. Camp, as partner, was entitled to retain it for the purpose of paying the debts of the partnership. (*In the matter of Smith, an absconding debtor*, 16 *John. R.*, 102; *Stoutenburgh* agt. *Stoutenburgh & Vanderburgh*, 7 *How. Pr. R.*, 229; *Sears* agt. *Gearn*, *id.*, 383.)

The execution of Westcott has a priority over the attachment of Abels. All of the defects in the execution of Westcott, which are urged by Abels, are amendable, and cannot be raised by any one except the defendant in the execution.

The order of special term is affirmed, with costs.

INGRAHAM and LEONARD, JJ., concurred.

SUPREME COURT.

HENRY THOMPSON agt. DUDLEY G. CULVER.

A *motion* to set aside an *attachment*, may be made *after judgment* in the action. The judgment does not *supersede* the attachment. (*This is adverse to Scheib agt. Baldwin*, 22 *How. Pr. R.*, 278.)

New York General Term, *November*, 1862.

INGRAHAM, LEONARD and PECKHAM, *Justices*.

THIS is an appeal from an order made at special term, denying a motion made by the defendant to set aside the attachment issued by the plaintiff. The attachment was issued on the ground that the defendant had absconded or kept himself concealed, to avoid the service of civil process. The attachment issued on the 12th of February last—served on the 14th of February. On the 12th of March following, an order was granted to show cause why the attachment should not be vacated. On the 25th of same month, the facts involved in the hearing of the motion on the order to show cause was referred to a referee, to hear and report the evidence, with his opinion thereon. The hearing was had, and on the 21st of April last, the referee reported the evidence, with his opinion substantially that the facts did not sustain the attachment. The defendant sought to have the time extended for entering judgment till after the decision of the motion to set aside the attachment, but ultimately failed, and judgment was perfected on the 10th of April against him. On the 10th of May, the sheriff sold the attached property on the execution issued on the judgment.

WM. FULLERTON, *for appellant*.
GILBERT DEAN, *for respondent*.

By the court, PECKHAM, Justice. Two points are made by plaintiff against the motion:

First.—That it comes too late—judgment having been perfected prior to the hearing of the motion.

Second.—That the defendant did, in fact, keep himself concealed with intent, &c.

As to the first point. If the position be sound, that such a motion cannot be made after judgment, yet this motion having been noticed and actually made confessedly in time, the extension of time caused by the reference will not make it irregular, though the hearing be not completed till after judgment. But in my opinion, it is not indispensably necessary that the motion should be made before judgment. A very learned and respectable court has declared that the attachment is discharged *ipso facto* by the entry of the judgment. But I can find no provision in the Code to that effect; on the contrary, there are provisions entirely inconsistent with such a position.

Among other provisions, the statute declares that "until the judgment against the defendant shall be paid"—not recovered—but until it "shall be paid," the sheriff may proceed to collect the notes and other evidences of debt, and the debts that may have been seized or attached under the warrant of attachment, * * * and apply the proceeds thereof to the payment of the judgment." (*Sub.* 4 *of* § 237 *of the Code.*)

It is clear that the sheriff has no such power under the execution. He has it obviously under the attachment, which, therefore, cannot be said to be superseded by the judgment.

The facts as disclosed by the affidavits, and the evidence before the referee, show that there was no ground for the attachment. The order appealed from should therefore be reversed, and the attachment discharged with $10 costs.*

* NOTE.—Perhaps this question may be further illustrated by another reference to § 237 of the Code, which says: "In case judgment be entered for the plaintiff in such action, the sheriff shall satisfy the same out of the property attached by him, if it shall be sufficient for that purpose: 1. By paying over to such plaintiff the proceeds of all sales of perishable property, and of any vessel, or share or interest in

any vessel sold by him, or of any debts or credits collected by him, or so much as shall be necessary to satisfy such judgment. 2. If any balance remain due, and an *execution* shall have been issued on such judgment, he shall proceed *to sell under such execution so much of the* ATTACHED PROPERTY, real or personal, except as provided in subdivision 4 of this section, as may be necessary to satisfy the balance, if enough for that purpose shall remain in his hands," &c. Subdivision 4 says: "Until the judgment against the defendant shall be paid, the sheriff may proceed to *collect* the notes, and other evidences of debt, and the debts that may have been seized or attached under the warrant of attachment, and to prosecute any bond he may have taken in the course of such proceedings, and apply the *proceeds* thereof to the payment of the judgment," &c. And § 238 shows how these notes, &c. are to be collected by the sheriff. It says: "The actions herein authorized to be brought by the sheriff, may be prosecuted by the plaintiff, or under his direction, upon the delivery by him to the sheriff of an undertaking executed," &c. Thus showing that the notes and evidences of debt, &c. mentioned in subdivision 4, cannot be collected under the *attachment*, nor indeed under the *execution*; otherwise there would have been no necessity for an *exception* in subdivision 2; but must be collected by *action*. The result, then, seems to be, that *after judgment* the attached property, real and personal, must be sold on *execution*, except the notes and other evidences of debt, which must first be collected by *action*, to satisfy the judgment, leaving no office whatever for the attachment to perform after judgment.

REP.

☞ Page 95, line 6, for H. K. HUNTER, read R. H. HUNTLEY.

SUPREME COURT.

IN THE MATTER OF THE PEOPLE agt. JOSHUA HART.

The statute (*Laws* 1862, *p.* 476) declares that "it shall not be lawful to sell or furnish any wine, *beer* strong or spirituous liquors to any person in the auditorium or lobbies of such place of exhibition or performance mentioned in the first section of this act."

***Held*, that where the *warrant* charged the defendant with having sold *lager beer*, instead of "beer," it did not charge an *offence* on its face.**

New York General Term, November, 1862.

INGRAHAM, LEONARD and PECKHAM, *Justices*.

By the court, PECKHAM, Justice. This is virtually an appeal from the decision of Mr. Justice BARNARD, who discharged the defendant on the ground that no offence was charged against him in the warrant of arrest. The case was before Judge BARNARD on *habeas corpus*, and comes here for review on a *certiorari*.

The statute declares that "it shall not be lawful to sell or furnish any wine, beer, strong or spirituous liquors to any person in the auditorium or lobbies of such place of exhibition or performance mentioned in the first section of this act," &c. (*Laws of* 1862, *p.* 476.)

The principle has been settled in substance, that "beer," in statutes of this character and in such connection, must mean "strong liquor, that is, strong enough with the inebriating principle or element, whether obtained by distillation or fermentation, to produce intoxication." (*Board of Excise* agt. *Taylor*, 20 *N. Y. R.*, 178.)

The warrant in this case charged the defendant with having sold "lager bier."

It may be made to appear by proof, possibly, that "lager bier" is a kind of beer forbidden by the act. But that is not sufficient in a warrant, without other averments. The court cannot take judicial notice that "lager bier" belongs to the prohibited character or class. The warrant should charge an offence on its face; what the court can see is an offence; should distinctly state the fact that showed the violation of the statute. It would have been sufficient to charge that the defendant had sold "beer" in the prohibited place, and then sustained that charge by proving the sale of lager bier, if lager be, from its properties, within the prohibition; or the warrant might have charged by averment, that lager was of that character of beer. But there is nothing now in the warrant that shows either by fact or averment, that "lager bier" is within the prohibition of the act.

The order for defendant's discharge was therefore right, and is affirmed.

NEW YORK COMMON PLEAS.

M. & E. Meyer and others agt. Harnden's Express Company.

The right of a *common carrier to limit his liability* is well settled in the affirmative.

And when a special contract is made, the relations of the parties are changed, and the carrier becomes as to that transaction an ordinary *bailee and private carrier for hire.*

Where the plaintiffs *directed E. & Co.* to ship goods by Harnden's express, it authorized E. & Co., at least so far as the defendants were concerned, to make any *contract* which the defendants insisted on.

Consequently, where E. & Co., on the delivery of the goods, presented a printed *receipt* in a receipt book of the defendants in their possession, which the driver of the express company signed, *held,* that E. & Co. had *authority,* as the agents of the plaintiffs, to make the contract contained in the receipt.

To hold that when goods are delivered, the carrier, who chooses to limit his responsibility, should be compelled to stop and examine the authority of the person presenting the goods, to make the contract, would virtually destroy the utility of the express business.

New York General Term, November, 1862.

Daly, Brady and Hilton, *Judges.*

Appeal from judgment at special term.

By the court, BRADY, J. The defendants agreed to carry from this city to Selma, Alabama, two cases of goods marked M. & E. Meyer & Co. At the time the goods were delivered, a receipt "was filled up" by I. Emanuel & Co., who were acting for the plaintiffs in forwarding the goods, and given to the defendants' driver, who signed it. That receipt was produced and put in evidence by the plaintiffs, after they had rested, and a motion for nonsuit had been made on the ground that it appeared from the evidence that there was a written contract which the plaintiffs had not produced. After its introduction the witness, who had identified it, was asked the question: "Was your attention ever called to the printed matter of this receipt?" The question was objected to, but allowed, and an exception was taken. The witness was the bookkeeper of I. Emanuel & Co., and it was wholly immaterial whether his attention had been called to the printed matter or not. The evidence had disclosed the fact that Emanuel & Co. had a receipt book of the defendants in their store, from which the receipt in question was adopted by them, and without any application on the part of the defendants. It was filled up and given to the driver of the defendants, and signed by him. The witness was also asked: "What authority had you from Meyer & Co. relative to the shipping of the goods?" and the question was allowed, although objected to. The answer was: "Our directions were to ship the goods by Harnden's express; we had no other authority or direction from the plaintiffs in respect to the shipment." Upon this evidence the presiding judge charged the jury as follows: "If you find that I. Emanuel & Co. had no other authority or direction in regard to the goods than merely to purchase and ship them in the ordinary way, then no contract exists between the plaintiffs and defendants, limiting the liability which the law imposes upon common carriers in case of non-performance of their agreement to deliver property in a safe condition." And further, " that unless Emanuel & Co. had authority to make such a contract, the plaintiffs are not bound by any such condition in the receipt in respect to the defendants' liability in the event of fraud or gross negligence." This was substantially telling the jury that, unless Emanuel & Co. had the power to make the contract contained in the receipt, the defendants were liable. The charge was erroneous. The right of the carrier to limit his liability is no longer subject to discussion. (*Dorr* agt. *Steam Nav. Co.*, 1 *Kern.*, 490; *Wells* agt. *Steam Nav. Co.*, 4 *Seld.*, 381.) And when a special contract is made, the relations of the parties are changed, and the carrier becomes as to that transaction an ordinary bailee and private carrier for hire. (Parker, J., *in Dorr* agt. *N. J. Steam Nav. Co.*, *supra.*)

The directions given by plaintiffs to ship goods by Harnden's express, authorized Emanuel & Co., so far at least as the defendants are concerned, to make any contract which the defendants insisted upon. If the agents transcended their power, the innocent party should not suffer. There was nothing in the case to call upon the defendants for an examination or investigation of the authority of Emanuel & Co. It was enough that they delivered the goods to them, and asked for their carriage; but in this case they did more. They drew the contract and presented it for signature. It would virtually destroy the utility of the express business, which has become a very important part of our commercial system, to hold that when goods are delivered, the carrier, who chooses to limit his responsibility, should stop to examine the authority of the person presenting the goods to make the contract which he exacts. It would in this case, in my judgment, be erroneous to sustain the proposition that Emanuel & Co. had not authority to make this contract. They had possession of the goods, and delivered them for carriage. The possession was a lawful one, and the person selected to transport them in accordance with instructions received. Not only that, but the plaintiffs introduced the contract to sustain their case, and then sought to avoid it by proving instructions in relation to the carriage, by the bookkeeper of Emanuel & Co. If the doctrine be tolerated that in cases similar to this, the contract can be avoided for want of power to make it, the proof on the part of the plaintiff should be ample.

I think the rule is not a sound one, and that its annunciation was error.

The judgment should be reversed.

DALY, J., concurred.

SUPREME COURT.

SAMUEL S. TIFFANY agt. RICHARD S. WARREN and others.

No *conveyance* can be sustained on the ground of *good faith*, as against a *prior unrecorded* mortgage or deed for value, unless made for a *valuable consideration*.

An honest *existing demand* is a valuable consideration; but a conveyance on such consideration is not in *good faith* when coming in conflict with a *prior* conveyance given for value. It is the want of good faith, and not the want of a valuable consideration, which prevents full effect from being given to a subsequent conveyance made on account of an *antecedent debt*.

It was well established on principle and authority, when the statute in relation to filing mortgages of personal property was passed, that subsequent purchasers and mortgagees, on account of *pre-existing indebtedness*, were not holders in *good faith*, when their claims were brought in conflict with a *prior unrecorded* mortgage or conveyance otherwise valid.

New York General Term, November, 1862.

INGRAHAM, LEONARD and ROSEKRANS, *Justices*.

THE plaintiff claims the title to a large amount of personal property sold to him by Garner & Co., who held as mortgagees thereof in possession, or by transfer from Seaman & Muir, the former owners, and also the mortgagors, voluntarily made in consideration of an antecedent debt due to, and liabilities previously incurred by Garner & Co.

for Seaman & Muir. The mortgage covered the whole stock of the debtors.

At the time the bill of sale and the delivery of the stock to Garner & Co. was made, the mortgagors, Seaman & Muir, and the plaintiff and defendants, as well as Garner & Co., were present, and it was well understood by all the parties, including the plaintiff, that defendants Warren, Moran & Co. held a chattel mortgage against the same stock of goods for a large sum, made by the same debtors, Seaman & Muir, prior to the mortgage held by Garner & Co., which was wholly unpaid; and that the defendants then claimed their prior right by virtue of their mortgage, and challenged the right of Garner & Co., under the subsequent mortgage held by that firm. During this interview, and prior to the bill of sale and the delivery of the stock, the mortgagors had, with the knowledge of the plaintiff, offered to divide the stock between the two mortgages, which offer Garner & Co. consented to accept, but the defendants declined it. The mortgagors having ascertained that Warren, Moran & Co. refused to divide the security as proposed, executed the bill of sale, and delivered the stock of goods so mortgaged, of which Garner & Co. then took possession. Neither the mortgage of Garner & Co. nor of the defendants had been filed in the office of the register.

With the knowledge of these facts, the plaintiff immediately afterwards purchased the whole stock from Garner & Co., and gave his promissory note therefor, falling due, by arrangement, in such manner as to enable Garner & Co. with the proceeds to meet certain bills which they had accepted for the accommodation of Seaman & Muir, drawn by a French house, of which the plaintiff was the agent, for the security of which liability so incurred, the said mortgage to Garner & Co. was in part executed.

A few hours after these transactions, Warren, Moran & Co. caused judgment to be perfected in their favor against

Seaman & Muir, on confession previously executed, for a large demand, not included in their mortgage, and issued execution thereon to the sheriff, and also delivered to him a power of attorney to take the mortgaged stock under their mortgage and sell it; and by virtue of the execution and this power of attorney, the sheriff seized the property and took it into his possession. The plaintiff thereupon replevied the stock in this action, without joining the sheriff as a party, his possession being considered, by agreement, that of the defendants.

At the trial the judge charged that the possession of Garner & Co., being prior to the entry of the defendants' judgment, and there being no dispute that the mortgage to Garner & Co. was taken to secure an honest debt, without any fraudulent intent on their part, the levy of the defendants' execution was unlawful and inoperative. Also, that Garner & Co., although their mortgage was given for an indebtedness previously existing, were mortgagees in good faith, and entitled to preference and priority in respect to their mortgage, if they received it fairly for an honest debt of Seaman & Muir to the full amount, without notice of the prior mortgage of Warren, Moran & Co., and without any actual intent to defraud; and there being no dispute as to the absence of such notice, and of any such intent, and as to the fairness of the mortgage debt claimed by Garner & Co., there was no question of fact for the jury, and that they were bound by law to find a verdict for the plaintiff. The counsel for the defendants excepted to each of these propositions.

By the court, LEONARD, Justice. The statute declares that mortgages of goods and chattels, not accompanied by an immediate delivery, and followed by an actual and continued change of possession of the things mortgaged, shall be absolutely void as against the creditors of the mortgagor and as against subsequent purchasers and mortgagees in good faith, unless the mortgage or a true copy thereof shall be filed (if the mortgagor resides in the city of New York) in the office of the register.

The mortgage to Warren, Moran & Co. not having been filed, and no delivery or change of possession of the things mortgaged having been made, they are not in a position to claim any advantage from the provisions of the statute.

The question has then to be considered, whether Garner & Co. or the plaintiff here are in a condition to be benefited by the laches of the defendants, or the provisions of the statute in favor of the creditors of the mortgagors, and subsequent purchasers and mortgagees in good faith.

It is not, nor indeed can it be, claimed that Garner & Co. were creditors of Seaman & Muir, within the meaning of the statute. They had not a judgment and execution in their favor, and were in no situation to claim or enforce any rights or title provided by law for the collection of debts. Such only are the creditors referred to in this statute. (17 *N. Y. R.*, 583.)

Garner & Co. must make title, if at all, by virtue of their possession under their mortgage, or as subsequent purchasers under their bill of sale. Theirs was not a title which the law has provided for the collection of debts. Unless they were purchasers or mortgagees in good faith, the priority of the defendants' mortgage will give them the preference in obtaining satisfaction out of the property mortgaged.

The words "in good faith," or *bona fide*, have acquired in the law a certain well-known signification.

A person having knowledge of the existence of a prior right to property in favor of some other person, cannot be considered a purchaser or mortgagee in good faith. (*Far. L. & Trust Co.* agt. *Hendrickson*, 25 *Barb.*, 488.)

It can never be truly said, that it is good faith to disregard the well-known rights of another.

A purchaser or mortgagee on account of a pre-existing

indebtedness parts with nothing, and is not considered as having acquired title, or the right to hold property as security, against a prior deed or mortgage not recorded.

Such subsequent purchaser sustains no injury by being postponed in right to the prior unrecorded deed or mortgage. He is placed in no worse condition than he was before he received his deed or mortgage, and ought not to disturb any prior acquired rights.

It was well established on principle and authority, when the statute in relation to filing mortgages was passed, that such subsequent purchasers and mortgagees were not holders in good faith when their claims were brought in conflict with a prior unrecorded mortgage, or conveyance otherwise valid. The words were used in the same sense in the present statute. (*Dickerson* agt. *Tillinghast*, 4 *Paige*, 220; *Van Heusen* agt. *Radcliff*, 17 *N. Y. R.*, 580.)

We were referred to the case of *Baskins* agt. *Shannon*, (3 *Com.*, 310,) to establish a different rule for the interpretation of the words "in good faith," occurring in the statute referred to. I am unable to perceive that any such conclusion is warranted. The learned justice there says, that before the second mortgagee can show good faith, so as to question the rights of the prior mortgagee, or of the creditors of the mortgagor, he must prove that his mortgage was given for a vauable consideration or for an honest debt. This observation falls very much short of an assertion that an existing honest demand is a sufficient consideration to sustain a junior over a prior chattel mortgage, given to secure an equally honest debt. The purport of that decision is, that the second mortgage, being without consideration, so far as appeared from the evidence, the holder thereof could not, for that reason, object to the sufficiency of the prior mortgage, in any respect. The case of *Hanford* agt. *Artcher*, (4 *Hill R.*, 271,) is the authority cited to sustain the remark of the learned justice above mentioned, in *Baskins* agt. *Shannon*.

The question in *Hanford* agt. *Artcher* was between a vendee of goods, where there had been no change of the possession of the thing sold, and an execution creditor. To rebut the presumption of fraud in such a case, the party claiming under the sale must make it appear that it was made in good faith, and without the intent to defraud creditors. Senator HOPKINS remarks, at page 295, that "proof of a valuable consideration or an honest debt, is essential to show good faith;" being the same words used in *Baskin* agt. *Shannon*.

In the case of *Hanford* agt. *Artcher*, an honest debt was sufficient as a consideration to uphold the sale, as between the vendee and a creditor, under a subsequent judgment and execution.

But certainly it does not appear from either case, that it was the intention of the court to overthrow the well-established legal rule, that a subsequent purchaser or mortgagee, on account of an existing debt, does not hold in good faith, so as to disturb the rights of a prior mortgagee for an equally fair consideration.

Where both securities are given on account of antecedent debts, nothing can be alleged against the equity of the rule giving a preference to the first in time.

So learned and careful a judge as the author of the opinion of the court in *Van Hoeson* agt. *Radcliff*, above referred to, would never have stated the rule in this respect to be well settled, and in force, if the prior decision of the same court in *Baskin* agt. *Shannon* (3 *Coms.*, 310) were to be understood as holding a contrary principle. The analogous rule applied to commercial paper is supposed to have been shaken by the decision of the court of appeals in *Youngs* agt. *Lee*, (2 *Kern.*, 551,) and the judge at the trial here, may have felt himself justified, on this authority, in holding that an honest debt was a consideration in good faith, although the prior mortgage was in equal good faith, and the effect will be to give a preference to a mortgagee who has parted with no present consideration.

I am unable, however, so to understand the decision in *Youngs* agt. *Lee*. Prior decisions, sustaining the rule, are there referred to with approbation. There is also a clear and emphatic distinction mentioned in the opinion in that case, taking it out of the operation of the principle referred to.

The learned justice delivering the opinion in *Van Hoesen* agt. *Radcliff*, evidently so regards it, and refers to that case as an acknowledgment and repetition of the previously existing rule.

I am not willing to add my voice in overruling well settled principles of law, as they have been administered in the courts of this state, either by encroachment or judicial legislation. If a change or advance has occurred in the times, creating a necessity for an alteration in any of the rules upon which justice has been administered, the appeal ought to be made to the legislature for the proper change. It is not the province of the judiciary.

The case of *Dickerson* agt. *Tillinghast*, above referred to, arose under the recording act, which declares that every conveyance of real estate, not recorded, shall be void as against subsequent purchasers in good faith, and for a valuable consideration, whose conveyance shall be first recorded.

This, and a large class of similar cases arising under the recording act, are strictly analogous, and in point here. The additional words, requiring a valuable consideration, do not diminish the force of the statute in its operation against prior unrecorded conveyances.

No conveyance can be sustained on the ground of good faith as against a prior unrecorded mortgage or deed for value, unless made for a valuable consideration.

An honest existing demand is a valuable consideration; but a conveyance on such consideration, in the numerous reported cases arising under the recording act, are held not to be in good faith when coming in conflict with a prior conveyance given for value. It is the want of good faith, and not the want of a valuable consideration, which prevents full effect from being given to a subsequent conveyance made on account of an antecedent debt.

Those who doubt the existence and force of the principle of law here referred to, and its application to the present case, may profitably refer to the opinion of the court of appeals in *Wood* agt. *Robinson*, (22 *N. Y. R.*, 564, 567.)

The court there say: "It is well settled that a grantee or incumbrancer who does not advance anything at the time, takes the interest conveyed subject to any prior equity attaching to the subject."

I am of the opinion, therefore, that Garner & Co. were not purchasers or mortgagees in good faith as against the mortgage held by the defendants. Also that the title of the plaintiff cannot be sustained, he having become a purchaser with full knowledge of the mortgage held by the defendants and the claim which they made to a preference over the mortgage of Garner & Co. The charge of the judge, in this respect, was erroneous.

The judgment and execution of the defendants was, however, subsequent to the possession of the stock by the plaintiff under his purchase from Garner & Co. The levy was, as stated by the judge, unlawful.

There should be a new trial, with costs to abide the event.

INGRAHAM, J. I am of the opinion that the consideration of the mortgage to Garner & Co. was good, and that they were to be considered *bona fide* holders for value.

I am in favor of affirming the judgment.

ROSEKRANS, J. Within the cases cited by Justice LEONARD, Garner & Co. were not *bona fide* mortgagees of the property. They took their mortgage, it is true, without notice of the unrecorded mortgage previously executed to the defendants, but the consideration of their mortgage was a precedent debt, and no security was surrendered, or other act done by which they were placed in a worse position by reason of not having notice of the previous mortgage. It is impossible to sustain the judgment in this case without overruling the uniform current of decisions on this subject. I concur in the conclusions of Justice LEONARD.

The precise point was decided in *Ray* agt. *Birdseye*, (5 *Den. R.*, 619,) by the court of errors.

SUPREME COURT.

THE PEOPLE OF THE STATE OF NEW YORK agt. CORNELIUS VANDERBILT.

Where an act of the legislature vested in the corporation of the city of New York the title to the soil under the water, and the right to fill in and extend the battery into the river, not exceeding six hundred feet, with a *limitation on the use of the land*, so to be made out of the water, for any purpose except certain *public purposes* therein expressed,

Held, that any grant or other conveyance of the land to an individual *for the purpose of* widening a pier and to extend it to the permanent or exterior line, or for any such *private use*, would be void, and would justify the state in claiming an *injunction* to prevent such violation of the conditions imposed upon the corporation.

The power to compel a *removal* of an obstruction after it has been erected, does not prevent an application to the court to *prohibit the erection* of such obstruction before it is completed.

Held, also, that if there was no legal authority for the erection of the pier, it was a *nuisance*, and no *evidence* was admissible to show, that though illegal, it would do no harm.

New York General Term, *October*, 1862.

INGRAHAM, BARNARD and CLERKE, *Justices*.

THIS action was brought to restrain the defendant from enlarging a pier known as No. 1, North river, adjoining the battery.

By the court, INGRAHAM, Justice. The right of the defendant to make such enlargement, is claimed under a resolution of the common council, passed in 1853, granting permission to the defendant to widen the pier and to extend it to the permanent or exterior line. The right of the corporation to grant such a permission depends upon their title to the land upon which the pier was to be erected. This claim of title in the corporation is based upon the act of March, 1821, which authorized the corporation to extend the battery into the river not exceeding 600 feet. This act vested in the corporation the title to the soil under the water so to be filled in. If this were all, there would be no question as to the right of the defendant to enlarge the pier, except so far as it might afterwards be restrained by the act of 1857, establishing a new exterior line, and which prohibited the building of piers beyond that line. But the same act which gave the right to fill up to the extent of 600 feet, also contained the limitation on the use of the land so to be made out of the water, by limiting the same "for a public walk, and for erecting buildings and works of defence thereon, but without any power to dispose of the same for any other use or purpose whatever, and without any power of selling it or any part thereof."

This restriction upon the use of the land for any but public purposes of a public walk, or for defence, prevented the corporation from selling or otherwise disposing of any part of the land so to be acquired for any private purpose whatever. Any grant or other conveyance of the land for any such private use would be void, and a breach of that condition by the corporation would justify the state in any legal measures to prevent its violation. Wherever any such attempt is made to use the land for purposes forbidden by the grant, the grantor would have a right to interfere, and an application to the court to prevent such misuse of the land, would clearly be within the province of a court of equity.

This view of the question at issue is independent of the act of 1857, establishing an exterior line and prohibiting the extension of any piers beyond that line. If it be held that the state could interfere to prevent the breach of the condition in the grant, independent of that law, the passage of that act does not deprive the plaintiffs of such right. It is true that a way is provided by which, after the pier has been erected, it may be removed, but the remedy sought in this action is to prevent the injury to the navigation by prohibiting the erection of the pier. The power to compel a removal of an obstruction after it has been erected, does not prevent an application to the court to prohibit the erection of such obstruction before it is completed.

It is urged for the defendant that this was only filling a portion of the land under water, which was authorized by the act of 1821. The act of 1860 prohibited the filling beyond the exterior line, and was of itself enough to prevent this obstruction of the river. But independent of that statute, it is idle to say that this was the filling up contemplated by the statute, when all the authority of the defendant was under the resolution of the common council, which granted permission to the defendant to widen a pier, and the injunction granted was against erecting the pier which the court found to be unauthorized and a nuisance.

It is also contended that the judge erred at the trial in excluding the evidence offered by him to show that the proposed pier would not be an actual nuisance, but no such question was involved in the issue. It was immaterial whether it would have been an actual nuisance or not. The real question was, whether the erection of the pier was authorized or not. If there was no legal authority for the erection of the pier, it was a nuisance, and no evidence was admissible to show that, though illegal, it would do no harm. In the language of the learned justice, before whom the case was tried, "any encroachment upon a public stream was a purpresture, that is, the making of that private, which ought to be common to many, and an obstruction in a public river is a nuisance, and may be dealt with as such." Such an erection is a nuisance *per se*, and needs no evidence to prove that as a matter of fact, after the erection of it is shown to be in violation of the law.

I see no ground for interfering with the decision below. The judgment must be affirmed with costs.

SUPREME COURT.

WM. C. RHINELANDER and others agt. THE MAYOR, &c. OF NEW YORK.

When the law authorizes the common council of a city to impose the expenses of paving streets, or other improvements, by assessment upon the *owners of property benefited*, the assessment becomes a *lien* upon the lots benefited; and it is an undue assumption of power in the common council to incur the expense and attempt its collection from *tax-payers at large*, even under a prior ordinance which required them thereafter to keep such streets repaved and kept in repair *at the expense of the corporation*.

New York Special Term, *November*, 1862.

DEMURRER to complaint.

EDWARDS PIERREPONT, *for plaintiffs*.

HENRY H. ANDERSON, *for the corporation*.

LEONARD, Justice. The complaint states that Fifth avenue was opened under the authority contained in section 177, and was regulated and paved under section 175 of the general act of April 9, 1813, reducing several laws relating particularly to the city of New York into one act. The common council are authorized by section 177 to open any street or avenue whenever they desire; and by section 175 to pave, alter, amend, &c., any street, &c.

The corporation of said city adopted an ordinance in 1824, declaring that whenever the owners of lots fronting on the streets should pay the expense of paving the carriage way, &c., for a distance not less than one block, under the orders of the common council, and the work should be approved, such part of the street should forever thereafter be repaved and kept in repair at the expense of the corporation.

The owners of certain lots fronting on Fifth avenue allege in this complaint that this avenue was subsequently opened, paved, &c., and the expense paid in the manner contemplated by this ordinance; that the common council, in disregard of the obligation of this ordinance, repaved the avenue with the Belgian pavement, and assessed one-half of the expene thereof in 1860 on the owners of lots fronting on the carriage way so repaired, amounting to over $98,000, from which assessment they now demand to be relieved.

I think there can be no doubt that the act of 1813, section 175, authorized the improvement in question; indeed no suggestion to the contrary was indulged at the argument.

The statutes authorize the common council to impose the expenses for the improvements mentioned in these actions by assessment upon the owners of property benefited. It became the duty of the common council, by virtue of this authority, to raise the expenses incurred for the purposes contemplated, by the sections referred to, in the manner authorized by that act.

The amount for paving, &c., in 1834, was assessed, and became a lien upon the lots benefited.

The corporation had no inducement by way of consideration to bind themselves not to exercise the power conferred upon them, so far as we can ascertain from the plaintiffs' statement of their case.

Assuming that the corporation had the authority to direct the laying of the Belgian pavement, derived by the act of 1813, aside from the question of consideration, the common council could not, in 1824, abrogate the duty which the law imposed, to assess the expenses of it upon the lots benefited thereby. We must also hold that it was the lien upon the land which the assessment created in 1835 and 1845, that induced the payment then, and not the ordinance of 1824.

When the law authorizes the expenses of such an improvement to be assessed in a particular manner, it is an undue assumption of power to incur the expense and attempt its collection from tax-payers at large; and I must doubt the obligation or validity of any ordinance or contract that has for its object the release of that source of payment which alone is authorized by the law that permits the improvement.

Judgment upon the demurrer for the defendants with costs.

SUPREME COURT.

William Brown agt. Jacob Weber, Jr.

H. having made a contract with the defendant to build him a saw mill on his lands, after part performance, made a sub-contract with the plaintiff to complete the job. The plaintiff commenced work accordingly, but a few days after went to the defendant, informed him he had learned H. was irresponsible, and declined going on with the job. The defendant, to induce the plaintiff to go on and finish the mill, promised that "he would see that plaintiff did not lose anything by it," and that "he would see that plaintiff got his pay." *Held*, that the promise was a collateral undertaking, and not being in writing was void by the statute of frauds. Campbell, J., dissented.

And it appearing further that while the plaintiff was finishing the job, he and his hands boarded with defendant, under a contract between the parties, and that the defendant furnished some materials to be used in the work, which, under the original contract, H. and plaintiff were to find. *Held*, also, that the defendant was entitled to recover the value of such board and materials in this action of the plaintiff.

——— *General Term*, 1862.

Balcom, Parker and Campbell, *Justices*.

The defendant entered into an agreement in writing, under seal, with William W. Horton, bearing date the 13th day of December, 1855, by which the latter bound himself to build a saw-mill for the defendant on *his lands*, in the town of Roseboom, in a manner therein specified, and furnish all the materials therefor, and complete and have it ready "for running, in a good workmanlike manner, by the 25th of August, 1856." The defendant was to pay Horton $600 for building the mill and furnishing the materials—$300 when the frame was up, and $300 on the 1st day of November, 1856. Horton and the defendant altered said agreement in some respects, by writing under seal executed by them, bearing date the 2d day of July, 1856. Horton framed and raised the mill, and afterwards on the 17th day of July, 1856, entered into an agreement in writing, under seal, with the plaintiff, whereby the plaintiff bound himself to Horton to go on and finish and fully complete said mill, ready and fit for business, so far as the carpenters' and mill-wright work was included, in a good workmanlike manner, on or before the 25th day of August, 1856, Horton agreeing to furnish all the materials for the same, for which Horton was bound to pay the plaintiff $110 on the 1st day of November in the same year, by passing over to the plaintiff an obligation in writing executed by the defendant for $110, payable on the first day of November aforesaid. On the 18th day of July, 1856, Horton and the plaintiff, by a writing under seal, signed by them and dated that day, changed their said agreement, bearing date the previous day, so as to bind the plaintiff to furnish all the materials necessary for finishing the saw-mill and flume, and to cover the mill, except such as were then on hand, and the castings named in Horton's contract with the defendant; and in consideration thereof, Horton was to pay the plaintiff the further sum of $90, making $200 in all the plaintiff was to receive of Horton; and it was stipulated that the whole $200 should be paid by Horton to the plaintiff, by defendant's note payable the 1st day of November, 1856. The plaintiff commenced work upon the mill about the 17th day of July, 1856, under the contracts with Horton, bearing date July 17th and 18th of that year. He continued to work on the mill until about the 15th day of September, 1856, when it was ready to run, and the defendant commenced sawing in it.

The plaintiff sought to recover in this action of the defendant for the work performed by him (plaintiff) in building the mill. He claimed that he did the work under a promise of the defendant to pay him therefor; and that he had performed his contracts with Horton, and built the mill in accordance with the contracts between the defendant and Horton, except in some respects, of which the defendant approved.

The action was tried before a referee, who found that the plaintiff commenced work on the mill under the contracts he made with Horton of July 17th and 18th, 1856; that "after said commencement on the said mill, the plaintiff became fearful that Horton was not responsible for the performance of the contracts aforesaid, on his (Horton's) part, which he communicated to defendant Weber;" "that the defendant, to induce the plaintiff to go on and finish the mill according to the contract, did promise the plaintiff that if he would go on and finish the mill according to contract, he would see that plaintiff did not lose anything by it. Also, that defendant told plaintiff that he would see that plaintiff got his pay, if plaintiff finished the mill according to contract,"—meaning the contract between the defendant and Horton, dated December 13, 1855, as altered on the 2d day of July, 1856; "that plaintiff went on and finished the mill according to the contracts between said defendant and Horton, with the following exceptions, viz: the said mill was not all inclosed; that some of the sheeting on the roof were more than one foot apart. There were no trap doors for saw-dust to pass down; the hinges to the fall doors were not of sufficient strength and size to hold them; the main water wheel was from four to six inches higher than in the old mill; the carriage was not made long enough to saw a twenty-four foot log; that the mill was not completed by the 25th of August, 1856;" "that the plaintiff and his hands quit work about the 15th day day of September, 1856, and did not after that work on said mill; that during the time plaintiff and his hands were at work, the defendant was often at the mill, and expressed his approbation of the work as it progressed up to the time Brown and his hands left the mill, except the single instance of the hinges to the fall doors. Also, that defendant about the time plaintiff and his hands left the mill, and afterwards, used the mill for sawing purposes;" but that he used the mill pursuant to an understanding or agreement between him, Horton and the plaintiff, "that it should not be regarded as an acceptance of the mill." The referee also found that there was affirmative evidence that plaintiff regarded his contracts with Horton as being in full force. The referee held that the plaintiff could not recover upon the defendant's promise that he would see that plaintiff had his pay for his work, or should lose nothing if he would go on and finish the mill according to contract, because such promise was void by the statute of frauds. The plaintiff and his hands boarded with defendant while they worked on the mill, under an agreement (as found by the referee) by which the plaintiff was to pay defendant therefor $2 per week for each person boarded; and for this board and some other account, the referee found the plaintiff was indebted to the defendant the sum of $49.66. Judgment was entered against the plaintiff for that sum with costs. The plaintiff's counsel took exceptions on the trial, and also excepted to the findings of the referee. The plaintiff appealed from the judgment to the general term of the court.

E. COUNTRYMAN, *for appellant.*

A promise cannot be collateral within the statute of frauds when a party simply answers for what accrues to *his own individual benefit.* So long as the promisor is *the* person interested, his promise cannot be to answer for *another person* within the meaning of the statute, although such other person may have also made a like engagement with the promisee. Indeed, the rule may now be considered settled in this state, that where the new promise is founded on a consideration of *benefit or advantage to the promisor,* who is directly *interested in the performance* of the contract, it is valid, although the original debt be still subsisting, and the liability of the original debtor remaining in full force. (*Leonard* agt. *Vredinburgh,* 8 *Johns.,* 23–31; *Harrison* agt. *Lawtell,* 10 *Johns.,* 242; *Myers* agt. *Morse,* 15 *Johns.,* 424; *Farley* agt. *Cleveland,* 4 *Cow.,* 432; *id.,* 9 *Cow.,* 639, *in Court of Errors*; *Gardner* agt. *Hopkins,* 5 *Wend.,* 23; *King* agt. *Despard,* 5 *Wend.,* 277; *Meech* agt. *Smith,* 7 *Wend.,* 318, 319; *Rogers* agt. *Kneeland,* 13 *Wend.,* 114; *Mather* agt. *Perry,* 2 *Denio,* 162; *Colgan* agt. *Aymar, Lalor's Sup. to Hill and Denio,* 27; *Flanders* agt. *Crolius,* 1 *Duer,* 206; *Stilwell* agt. *Otis,* 7 *Abb.,* 431; *Brown* agt. *Curtis,* 2 *Coms.,* 225; *Mallory* agt. *Gillett,* 21 *N. Y.,* 412; *See also Nelson* agt. *Boynton,* 3 *Metcalf,* 396; 2 *Parsons on Contracts,* 305; *Quintard* agt. *De Wolf,* 34 *Barb.,* 97; *Devlin* agt. *Woodgale, id.,* 252.)

JAMES E. DEWEY, *for respondent.*

The promise is incontestably "to answer for the debt, default or miscarriage of another," and is *within all the mischiefs* which the statute to prevent frauds and perjuries was designed to remedy. (3 *R. S.,* 221, *5th ed.,* § 2; *Barber* agt. *Fox,* 1 *Stark.,* 270; *Mallory* agt. *Gillett,* 23 *Barb.,* 610, *affirmed in court of appeals, September term,* 1860; *Lar-*

son agt. *Wyman*, 14 *Wend.*, 246; *Carrille* agt. *Cram*, 5 *Hill*, 485; *Brown* agt. *Bradshaw*, 1 *Duer*, 199; *Curtis* agt. *Brown*, 5 *Cush.*, 488–492; 14 *Barb.*, 570.)

1. The expressions used, "would *see* that plaintiff did *not lose anything by it*," and "would *see* that plaintiff *got his pay*," plainly import an intent to guarantee performance by another, not that the promissor himself will pay. (*Smith* agt. *Harris*, 2 *Stark.*, 48; *Thompson* agt. *Bond*, 1 *Campb.*, 6; *Keate* agt. *Temple*, 1 *Bos. & Pull.*, 158; *Watkins* agt. *Perkins*, 1 *Lord Raymond*, 224; *Matson* agt. *Wharam*, 2 *Term R.*, 80; *Brown* agt. *Bradshaw*, 1 *Duer*, 199–201; *Cahill* agt. *Bigelow*, 18 *Pick.*, 369–372; *Brown's Statute of Frauds*, 198, § 199.)

2. If *any* credit was given to Horton, the promise was collateral and void. (*Brown's Statute of Frauds*, 195–7; *Anderson* agt. *Hayman*, 1 *H. Bl. R.*, 120; *Brady* agt. *Sackrider*, 1 *Sandf.*, 514.)

3. Whether credit was given to Horton or to the defendant, was exclusively a question of fact, (*Brown's Statute of Frauds*, 199, § 199,) which has been found against the plaintiff.

By the court, Balcom, Justice. The referee did not commit any error in the case, unless it was in holding that the plaintiff could not recover upon the promise of the defendant, to see the plaintiff did not lose anything or should get his pay, if he would go on and finish the mill according to the contracts between Horton and the defendant. After the plaintiff commenced working on the mill, he became fearful that Horton was not responsible for the performance of those contracts, and communicated that fact to the defendant. The defendant, "to induce the plaintiff to go on and finish the mill according to those contracts," then made the promise to the plaintiff which I have mentioned. The referee held this promise was void by the statute of frauds, (2 *R. S.*, 135, § 2, *sub.* 2.) The controlling question in the case, therefore, is, whether this was a "special promise to answer for the debt, default or miscarriage of another person." If it was such a promise, it was void, because it was not in writing. The plaintiff's counsel insists that the promise made was not collateral but original; that the consideration for it was beneficial to the defendant, and therefore binding upon him. If the referee had found that the plaintiff abandoned his contracts with Horton, or refused to go on under them, and that thereupon the defendant promised him if he would go on and finish the mill, in the manner specified in the contracts between Horton and the defendant, he would see the plaintiff did not lose anything, or should be paid for his work, and that the plaintiff relying upon such promise did go on and complete the mill, the defendant would be bound to pay the plaintiff for all the work he performed subsequent to such promise. But the referee has not found that the plaintiff abandoned his contracts with Horton or refused to go on under them; and has found there was affirmative evidence that the plaintiff regarded those contracts as being in full force. It therefcre seems to be very clear, if the plaintiff completed the mill so the defendant was satisfied it answered the contracts between him and Horton, he could have recovered of Horton the price he agreed to pay the plaintiff therefor. And it is equally clear that the promise of the defendant "to see the plaintiff got his pay," or should not lose anything if he would go on and complete the mill, was collateral, and a special one to answer for the debt, default or miscarriage of Horton. The most that can be claimed on the part of the plaintiff, is that the promise of the defendant induced the plaintiff to go on and perform his contracts with Horton; and that the defendant assumed to be surety for Horton's performance of those contracts. The plaintiff was still in the employ of Horton, and was not at any time servant or employee of the defendant. Horton remained the principal debtor of the plaintiff. It follows that the defendant is not liable on his promise, because it was not in writing.

I have not thought it necessary to cite authorities to sustain any of the foregoing views, or deemed it profitable to comment upon any of the decisions relied upon by the counsel for either party. I will only say, I have examined all the authories cited upon the points of the counsel in the cause.

The judgment in the action should be affirmed with costs.

PARKER, J., concurred. CAMPBELL, J., dissented, and delivered a dissenting opinion.

Judgment affirmed with costs.

SUPREME COURT.

HELENA CRAIG agt. HIRAM HYDE and others.

Where the plaintiff in his complaint claims *specific relief* purely equitable, against the defendants, and makes no demand for money or damages, and the facts show that the relation of debtor and creditor exists between the plaintiff and defendants, and that the latter are alone responsible to the plaintiff in an action for a *money demand*, the plaintiff will not be allowed to *change his remedy* by obtaining an order that the issue be tried by a jury as a *money demand*. The complaint must be *dismissed*.

New York Special Term, January, 1863.

THE defendants in this action were Hiram Hyde, James C. Cogswell, and The American Telegraph Company. The complaint set forth an agreement between Hyde and D. H. Craig, whereunder Hyde subscribed for 330 shares of the capital stock of the telegraph company, 210 of which were to belong to Craig, and the remaining 120 shares to Hyde. The plaintiff, the wife of D. H. Craig, became the assignee of his interest in the agreement, and subsequently received transfers of the 210 shares.

Certificates for 120 shares were issued by the company

to Hyde, who afterwards (in the fall of 1857) transferred them to Cogswell as collateral security for a loan, and a new certificate for the same was issued to Cogswell.

Mrs. Craig, the plaintiff, in 1858 sold to the company certain property for the sum of (about) seventeen thousand dollars, for which she was credited on the company's books. At the time the credit was made, her account was charged with the sum of $3,661.23—the amount then appearing to be unpaid, and due upon the 120 shares held by Cogswell, and that sum was credited to Cogswell's account.

The plaintiff claimed that the transfer of the said sum was made by the officers of the company wrongfully and without her knewledge or consent, and she asked for relief, principally "that it be adjudged that said credit of $3,661.-23, with interest thereon from May 10, 1858, is the property of the plaintiff, and that the officers and agents of the American Telegraph Company be required and compelled to withdraw said credit of $3,661.23 from the stock of said Cogswell, and to re-transfer the same to the credit of the personal account of plaintiff."

The action was defended by Hyde & Cogswell. The telegraph company did not appear.

WILLIAM LAWSON and DAVID DUDLEY FIELD, *for pl'ff.*
WALTER EDWARDS, Jr. and HAMILTON ODELL, *for def'ts Hyde and Cogswell.*

CLERKE, Justice. Even assuming that the plaintiff did not, in person or by her agent, authorize the American Telegraph Company to transfer the amount in question ($3,661.23) to the credit of the stock held in Cogswell's name, yet this was nothing more than the misapplication of that sum by the company, for which the latter alone are responsible to the plaintiff in an action for a money demand. The relation between the plaintiff and the company was that of creditor and debtor, and there is no reason why the liabilities pertaining to such a relation should, in this case, be enforced by any specific form of relief. If the company fail or refuse to pay this amount to the plaintiff, the remedy is plain and adequate, and the questions which may arise are to be tried, as the constitution prescribes, before a jury, unless both parties expressly waive that mode of trial. No legal liability to the plaintiff has been proved against Cogswell and Hyde, and the complaint must be dismissed against them. The only question upon which any doubt can arise is, whether as the company may be liable to refund this money to the plaintiff, still although she has mistaken her remedy, may not the court, instead of dismissing the complaint as against the company, order the issue, as a money demand, to be tried before a jury.

I do not understand the court of appeals in *Emory* agt. *Pease* to go to this extent. In that case the complaint, without averring that the parties had stated an account, set forth a state of facts showing that the plaintiff was entitled to an account, and tending to show an account stated. It demanded judgment for a sum certain as an ascertained balance. It was held the complaint should not be dismissed, but that the action should proceed as if the plaintiff had prayed an accounting and judgment for the amount which should thereupon be found due. Thus he stated facts showing that he was entitled to an account, and that the court allowed him instead of allowing the specific sum to which he claimed he was entitled.

In the present case the plaintiff claims specific relief, purely equitable, against the company and two other defendants, and makes no demand for money or damages. She asks nothing but *relief*. The remedy she seeks is so dissimilar to that to which she can prove herself entitled, that I think it would be productive of confusion and inconvenience in the administration of justice to allow a plaintiff in such a case to establish a remedy so entirely different from, and almost inconsistent with, the redress which she has attempted in the first instance to obtain, and which she has failed to obtain after protracted proceedings, a long and tedious trial, and serious expense to the parties concerned.

The complaint must be dismissed as to all of the defendants with costs.

SUPREME COURT.

RUFUS L. LORD agt. HARTMAN VREELAND, executor of ELIZA LEWIS, deceased; HARTMAN VREELAND, executor of DANIEL W. GAUTIER, deceased; and HARTMAN VREELAND in his individual capacity.

The acceptance of a *renewal lease*, under an original lease of premises, satisfies only the *covenant to renew;* it does not satisfy any of the other covenants in the original lease.

On *demurrer*, where facts are stated in a complaint showing that the plaintiff has *two contracts* which are broken, so that an action might be maintained on either, but are not stated separately, as several causes of action, the action must be considered founded on that contract upon which it can be sustained as to some or all of the defendants, and not upon the contract where the action must fail unless *new parties* are brought in.

The allegations of the complaint showing a cause of action in such case, which cannot be sustained for want of proper parties defendant, must be treated as *irrelevant* or *immaterial*, and upon motion should be *stricken out*.

Where an *executor* receives property in his own right as a gift, from the testator, it involves the same equitable liability to satisfy the damages arising from the breach of covenants in a lease given by the testator, as when held by the testator.

The person to whom was bequeathed the *personal estate*, or his legal representatives are proper and necessary *parties*, to conclude any claim hereafter to the estate of the testator, in the hands of his executor.

A demurrer must reach the *whole of a cause of action*. A paragraph cannot be expunged on demurrer, unless it amounts to a *separate cause of action*, and is so stated.

New York General Term, November, 1862.

INGRAHAM, LEONARD and CLERKE, *Justices*.

THIS is an appeal from an order overruling a demurrer to the complaint.

WM. CURTIS NOYES, *for appellant.*

DANIEL LORD, *for respondent.*

By the court, LEONARD, Justice. This is an appeal from an order overruling a demurrer to the complaint.

1. The first objection to the complaint is, that the renewal lease, having been accepted by the plaintiff, constitutes a satisfaction of all the covenants of the original lease.

The objection is not well taken. The renewal lease satisfies only the covenant to renew. It is no satisfaction of the other covenants.

2. The second objection relates to the liability of Vreeland as executor of Gautier, and individually. The demurrer assumes that the complaint contains two causes of action. In this, I think, the defendant is mistaken.

Some of the subsequent objections also assume the same ground.

There is but one injury, and but one satisfaction is sought by the complaint.

The pleader has unnecessarily stated the covenants in the renewed lease and the breach of them, as well as the covenants of the original lease and their breach, and has claimed to recover damages by reason of certain covenants in each of these leases, which are alike.

A statement of the covenants of the two leases, and of their breach, is consolidated in the complaint, as if the two constituted a single cause of action.

The complaint does not purport to state two causes of action separately.

A reference to the renewed lease was necessary only so far as to show that the plaintiff was in lawful possession, as against the defendants, at the time he was ejected, which was after the expiration of the term granted in the original lease, and as the foundation for claiming certain expenses sustained in obtaining the renewed lease, and in defending possession against those demanding it by a paramount title. But this reference gave no occasion for stating the covenants of the renewed lease, or what breaches of them had occurred.

The defendant is right in asserting that, in an action for breaches of the covenants of the renewed lease, the proper parties defendant are not before the court, inasmuch as there are others who executed that lease jointly with the defendant, but are not made parties here.

There are, however, sufficient parties, and all the proper parties before the court here, in an action founded on the original lease.

As an action on the renewed lease, it would fail altogether, without the addition of other parties, while, as an action on the original lease, there is no want of parties defendant.

It must be held on demurrer, where facts are stated in a complaint, showing that the plaintiff has two contracts which are broken, so that an action might be maintained on either, but are not stated separately, as several causes of action, that the action is founded on that contract upon which it can be sustained as to some or all of the defendants, and not upon that contract where the action must fail unless new parties are brought in. The allegations showing a cause of action in such case, which cannot be sustained for want of proper parties defendant, must be treated as irrelevant or immaterial, and upon motion should be stricken out.

For these reasons, as well as that the intent of the pleader is manifest to pursue the representatives of the original lessor, Eliza Lewis, deceased, it must be held that this action is brought to recover for the breach of certain covenants contained in the original lease.

The arguments in favor of a contrary decision are drawn from the inartificial, redundant and irrelevant matter contained in the complaint, considered as an action on the original lease only. Such defects in pleading are reached by a motion to expunge or strike out, but are not the ground of a demurrer.

Having arrived at the conclusion that the action is upon the original lease, is there any capacity in which Vreeland is made defendant, in which, upon the allegations of the complaint, he will not be liable to respond, or will not be a proper party defendant?

His liability as executor of Eliza Lewis has not been disputed. It will be necessary to consider only his liability, or the propriety of his joinder here, as a party defendant, as executor of Daniel W. Gautier, deceased, and in his individual capacity.

1st. As to the liability of Vreeland in his individual capacity.

The allegations of the complaint are not entirely harmonious as to the manner by which the real estate devised by Eliza Lewis to Gautier came from him to Vreeland. It is averred in one part of the complaint that Gautier conveyed to John Leveridge all the real estate devised to him by Eliza Lewis in trust to convey it to Vreeland upon the death of Gautier, and that Leveridge, in pursuance of the trust, conveyed it to Vreeland. Subsequently it is alleged that the specific property devised by Eliza Lewis to Gautier, was by him devised to Vreeland, and that Vreeland received it.

In either case it came to Vreeland as a gift from Gautier, without the payment of any consideration, and involves the same equitable liability to satisfy, to the extent of the property or estate so received, the damages arising from the breach of the covenants of Eliza Lewis, deceased.

2d. As to the liability of Vreeland as the executor of Gautier, deceased.

It is averred that a large amount of personal estate came to the hands of Vreeland as the executor of Eliza Lewis, deceased, and still remains in his hands.

The personal estate was bequeathed by her to Daniel W. Gautier, deceased. His executor would be entitled to take after the estate of Eliza Lewis was settled. The executor of Gautier is properly a party to conclude any claim hereafter to the estate of Eliza Lewis, deceased, in the hands of her executor on behalf of Gautier's representatives. He is a necessary party in the settlement of the rights of the various claimants of the fund, and also to reach any personal estate received by his executor, from the estate of Eliza Lewis, deceased, or to which the executor of Gautier is now entitled. It is also insisted in this second ground of demurrer that certain expenditures are mentioned as damages for which the plaintiff claims that the defendant is liable in addition to the natural damages arising from the breach of the covenants in the lease, and that the complaint does not in this respect state a cause of action.

This amounts to a demurrer only to a portion or paragraph in a cause of action set forth in the complaint.

A demurrer must reach the whole of a cause of action. A paragraph cannot be expunged on demurrer unless it amounts to a separate cause of action, and is so stated.

The third ground of demurrer relates to the averments respecting the renewed lease, supposed to be a second cause of action, and the omission of several of the joint covenantors therein as parties defendant, and to the improper joinder of an action on the renewed lease with an action on the original one.

These grounds, as has been before shown, depend on the mistaken assumption that more than one cause of action is stated in the complaint, and require no further comment.

The only remaining cause of demurrer relates to all other causes of action in the complaint, besides those founded on the two leases.

This can hardly be considered as a general demurrer, for the want of facts sufficient to constitute a cause of action.

There is no cause of action in the complaint except such as arises from the lease or leases.

Considered as a general demurrer, there are sufficient allegations to show a breach of the covenant that the renewal lease should be executed by the parties lawfully entitled, and of that providing against a compulsory surrender of the premises until payment has been made or tendered for the building erected by the lessee. Under the circumstances of the eviction averred in the complaint, the presumption of non-payment or tender is in favor of the plaintiff.

The order appealed from should be affirmed with costs, with liberty to the defendant within twenty days to answer upon payment of the costs of the demurrer, and of this appeal, to be adjusted by the clerk.

SUPREME COURT.

Charles O. Richardson agt. The Brooklyn City & Newtown Railroad Company.

Where it is alleged by the plaintiff's *attorney*, that subsequent to the entry of judgment in favor of the plaintiff, he assigned it without the knowledge of his attorney, with a view to defraud him out of his fees for services in the action; on motion, the attorney may have a *reference* to ascertain his *lien* or *right*, if he has any, beyond the *taxable costs*, on or to the judgment on the final recovery to be had in the action, as against the assignee.

And such a reference will be allowed, although it does not appear, except by the attorney's claim, on the motion that there was any *special agreement*, between the plaintiff and his attorney, that he should receive more than the *taxable costs*.

Kings General Term, December, 1862.

This cause was tried January 31, 1862, and a verdict rendered for the plaintiff. On the 8th of March, a judgment was entered for $1,377.24, from which an appeal was immediately taken by the defendants to the general term. Subsequently, the plaintiff it is alleged, with the view of defrauding his attorney out of his fees for services, assigned the judgment to one William Cutler, without the knowledge of his attorney. The cause was called on the calendar of the general term, at Brooklyn, December 10, 1862, and counsel on both sides were ready to argue it, though the attorney for the plaintiff, knowing nothing of the assignment, was not present. On the *ex parte* motion of A. H. Hitchcock, who said he was the attorney for the assignee, and without notice to the attorney for the plaintiff, the court granted an order to the effect that it be referred to Hon. George G. Reynolds, to take proof and ascertain the amount of costs as taxed in the suit, and report thereon; and on the coming in of the report, and on the payment by said Cutler to said attorney the amount of said costs, that then said A. H. Hitchcock be substituted as the attorney for the plaintiff, and that he deliver up the papers in this suit. An agreement had been made, it was alleged, between the attorney and the plaintiff for a much larger sum than the taxed costs. This was a motion on the part of the attorney for the plaintiff to amend or modify said *ex parte* order, so as to authorize the referee to take proof and report the full extent of the lien which the attorney for the plaintiff may have for his fees for services as attorney and counsel, fees of associate counsel, disbursements paid, &c. On this motion the plaintiff made an affidavit, denying that any agreement between him and his attorney had been made.

Mr. Wheeler, *in person, cited Wilkins* agt. *Batterman*, 4 *Barb.*, 47, (*G. T.;*) *Sherwood* agt. *The Buffalo & N. Y. R. R. Co.*, 12 *How.*, 136; *Creighton* agt. *Ingersoll*, 20 *Barb.*, 541, (*G. T.;*) *Ward* agt. *Wordsworth*, 1 *E. D. Smith R.*, 598, (*G. T.;*) (*approved and concurred in by the court of appeals, in* 18 *N. Y. R.*, 368;) *Easton* agt. *Smith*, 1 *E. D. Smith R.*, 318, (*G. T.;*) *McKenzie* agt. *Rhodes*, 13 *Abb. P. R.*, 337;

Ackerman agt. *Ackerman*, 14 *Abb. P. R.*, 229; *Hall* agt. *Ayer*, 9 *Abb. P. R.*, 220; *Hoffman* agt. *Van Nostrand*, 14 *Abb.*, 336; *Garr* agt. *Mairet*, 1 *Hilton R.*, 498; *Stowe* agt. *Hamlin*, 11 *How.*, 452; *Moore* agt. *Westervelt*, 3 *Sand.*, 726; *Code*, § 303.

LOTT, Justice. Motion denied without costs, but without prejudice to the lien or right of Mr. Wheeler, if he has any beyond the taxable costs referred to in the order of December 10, 1862, on or to the judgment on the final recovery to be had in the action, as against the assignee of the judgment or claim; and the order may be amended by inserting a provision therein to that effect, or by the entering of a new order declaratory thereof. The weight of the authorities cited by Mr. Wheeler is, to declare that the lien or right of an attorney may by agreement extend beyond the taxable costs to any sum or amount stipulated, but that, in the absence of such agreement, the taxable costs are *prima facie* the measure of his compensation. (*Keenan* agt. *Dorflinger*, 19 *How. P. R.*, 158; *Hall* agt. *Ayer*, *id.*, *p.* 91; *Rooney* agt. *The Second Avenue R. R. Co.*, 18 *N. Y. R.*, *p.* 368,) where it is said by Judge HARRIS: In the absence of any agreement on the subject, I suppose the sum recovered by the party as an indemnity for his expenses would be the measure of compensation allowed to the attorney. This, then, would be the extent of his lien. And Judge COMSTOCK says, if there is a special agreement, that will take the place of the pre-existing statutory rates, but does not express any definite opinion as to the rule if there be no such agreement. (*See also Creighton* agt. *Ingersoll*, 20 *Barb.*, *p.* 541.) No special agreement is alleged by Mr. Wheeler. It is true that he says that he has a *bona fide* and actual lien upon the judgment in this action for much more than the taxable costs for counsel fees, disbursements and the expenses already incurred; but he does not state how it has been acquired, and I can only look upon and treat the statements as his opinion in relation to his legal rights. The plaintiff, on the contrary, swears that at the time he employed said Wheeler, or at any other time, no agreement was made or entered into between said Wheeler and this deponent respecting the compensation of said Wheeler for his services in said action, or the amount thereof, or when or how he was to be paid. Under such circumstances, I am of the opinion that the order of 10th December last, is as favorable to Mr. Wheeler in reference to the amount to be paid to him, on substitution of another attorney, as he is entitled to. (*Stevenson* agt. *Stevenson*, 3 *Edw. Ch. R.*, 340; *Trustee* agt. *Roper*, 15 *How. P. R.*, 570.) The provisions I have directed to be made for his benefit, will fully protect his rights as to a larger claim.

SUPREME COURT.

JOSEPH COLWELL, respondent agt. HERBERT LAWRENCE, JR. and JOSEPH FOULKS, appellants.

The objection that an *assignment for the benefit of creditors* was not executed by *all the parties*, should be taken at the *trial*; it is too late to raise such an objection, to defeat the assignee's title on *appeal*.

A *referee's* finding on questions of *fact* is conclusive—the court will not disturb it on appeal—such facts, as the performance of a contract; the waiver of that performance; extension of time for its performance; and the value and amount of defendant's set-off.

The claim for a *stipulated sum* as *liquidated damages*, for the non-performance of a *contract*, cannot be enforced under the law, as it must be construed at the present time, where the contract is for doing a piece of work, the defect in the completion of which might be a very trifling matter, which a very little expense would remedy, and consequently a very small amount of damage (compared with the stipulated sum,) would be the result.

The court of last resort will probably have to, sooner or later, settle definitely, the precise question whether where parties have agreed, *in any case, on a sum which they say shall be liquidated damages, they should or not be held to their contract as they make it.*

New York General Term, November, 1862.

INGRAHAM, LEONARD and PECKHAM, *Justices.*

This was an appeal from a decision of Hon. H. P. Hunt, referee, who had rendered a judgment in favor of the respondent, who was the assignee of Birkbecks & Hodges, a manufacturing firm, which formerly existed in this city.

Various points of law were raised on the appeal, among which were the following:

It appeared that the assignee claimed title to the demand under an assignment of the general partners in that firm—which was a limited partnership under the statute—the special partner not having joined in the assignment, although he assented to it.

Another point arose on this state of facts. It appeared that the firm of Birkbecks & Hodges had entered into a contract with the appellants to construct for the latter a double engine for a new vessel, which the appellants were building for the Spanish government. In this contract was a provision imposing on the contracting parties $100 per day forfeiture in case the same was not completed by the contract time.

The referee overruled both of those points, and rendered judgment for the assignee. From this judgment appeal was taken to the general term.

John S. McCulloch and Nathaniel J. Wyeth, *for appellants.*

D. McMahon, *for respondent.*

By the court, Ingraham, P. Justice. This action was brought by the assignee of an insolvent firm to recover moneys due upon contracts with the firm for work, &c.

The case was referred, and the referee has reported for the plaintiff. The various exceptions taken by the defendants will be noticed in the order in which they were submitted in the defendants' points.

1. The defendants object to the plaintiff's title under the assignment, upon the ground that the assignment was not executed by all the parties.

Whatever force there would have been in this objection, if properly presented, the defendants cannot receive any benefit from it in this action. When the assignment was offered to be proved, its execution, as averred in the complaint, was admitted. This admission concludes the defendants. The objection is also one which should have been made on the trial, because the want of signature of one of the defendants might have been remedied by proof of his assent to the signature of the firm, and which was, in fact, proven.

2. It is objected that there was an implied warrantee that the article should be fit for the purpose contemplated, and that they were entitled to recover a claim for extra charges caused by the non-performance of the assignor's contract. There is no special finding of the referee as to this item. He allowed the defendants an offset of $781.68. Of what this sum was composed it is not easy for us to discover, nor is it material.

The evidence as to the performance of the contract by the plaintiff's assignors, of the waiver of that performance, and extension of time for performance, as well as the value and amount of defendants' set-off, raised questions of fact for the decision of the referee. Even if we differed from him on such finding, the evidence is of that character as to render his finding conclusive.

3. It is objected that the damages for non-performance of the contract within the stipulated time were liquidated damages, and that the defendants were entitled to recover those damages at one hundred dollars per diem.

Independent of the provision of the contract making this a forfeiture, I think the cases do not warrant the conclusion that this amount was to be considered as liquidated damages.

The case which throws most doubt upon this question, is that of *Cotheal* agt. *Talmadge*, (5 *Selden*, 551,) but in that case the contract was of that particular character which could not be separated as to performance, so as to assess damages for a breach of one part and not the other. The judge said, in referring to that case: "from the nature of the adventure, the amount of gain by a strict performance of the contract could not be foretold, and the amount of loss could not be ascertained by proof; the liquidation of the damages by contract between the parties was therefore prudent and reasonable."

Here the contract was for doing a piece of work in building a vessel. The defect in completion might have been a hinge or a lock, or some trifling matter which a very little expense would remedy, and consequently a very small amount of damage would be the result.

To hold, under such circumstances, this to warrant the recovery of the amount of damages named as liquidated, would operate very severely, and should require a clear expression of the intent of the parties.

The distinction between this and the case above referred to is, that here the damage can be easily ascertained, and should have been remedied by the defendants, instead of asking for a daily penalty for the non-performance. RUGGLES, J., says, in *Cotheal* agt. *Talmadge:* "The only plausible ground for withholding the doctrine (of liquidated damages) is, that the party might be made responsible for the whole amount of damages for the breach of an unimportant part of his contract, and so be made to pay a sum by way of damages grossly disproportionate to the injury sustained by the other party." This I suppose to be the true rule, as it is to be drawn from the cases, and the application of this rule to the present case would sustain the finding of the referee. I am free to say that I have never been able to see the propriety of denying to the parties, in any case, the right to fix the amount of damages to be recovered in case of non-performance of a contract, and have always thought, where the parties have agreed on a sum which they say shall be liquidated damages, that they should be held to their contract as they make it.

There will now and then be an apparently hard case, but the establishment of such a rule, when clearly understood, would make parties more careful in making contracts, and would relieve the courts from many gross contradictions, which now exist in the cases on this subject.

We do not feel at liberty to adopt this as the rule in all cases with the decisions before us, and must leave it to the higher court, if they should think it best to overrule these decisions.

4. Whether or not there was an adjustment of the amount due between the parties, was a question of fact for the referee. His finding is consistent with the evidence.

5. The same remarks apply to the alleged counter-claim for extra charges of work on "The Virginia."

6. The ruling of the referee as to the conversations in regard to the Cornelia, prior to the written contract, was not erroneous.

Those conversations were merged in the written contract. They were in no sense admissible, unless to explain some terms which would not be otherwise understood. No such object was avowed, and it is clear that no such reason existed to admit the testimony.

7. The question put to Belknap was one put to an expert on a matter with which the court or jury could not be supposed to be conversant, and as such was admissible.

Such evidence is admissible to explain technical terms in a contract, and also, as in this case, to explain the meaning of provisions used in a specification.

My conclusion is that the referee committed no error which will call for a reversal of this judgment.

Judgment affirmed with costs.

SUPREME COURT.

Mattoon agt. Baker.

An *appeal* lies from an order overruling a demurrer to one of several alleged defences, with liberty to reply to that part of the answer demurred to.

Where the complaint alleged a cause of action on contract for goods, wares, and merchandise sold and delivered; for work, labor and services done and performed, and for money paid, laid out and expended, as one cause of action; and for an accounting and a balance due the plaintiff, and a promise to pay, as a second cause of action, and the defendant put in first a general denial; second, a set-off or counter-claim for goods sold and delivered, money paid, laid out and expended, &c., and for a general balance on account; and third, a *multifarious defence of a legal and equitable* character, to which last defence the plaintiff *demurred*,

Held, that if the last defence, although containing a set-off, and matter of purely an equitable nature, and therefore multifarious, contained allegations of *fact* sufficient to make out a proper case for a *set-off*, it must be held good as a *counter-claim*, notwithstanding it might also contain other statements of no value as a defence—no objection having been taken on that ground—the remedy being by motion to strike out, not by demurrer.

Held, also, that should the third defence contain no sufficient ground for a set-off, but matter for *equitable relief only*, having no connection with the subject of plaintiff's action, the demurrer would be well interposed, although the latter defence was pleaded as a counter-claim.

A *counter-claim*, to be available to a party, must afford to him protection in some way against the plaintiff's demand for judgment, either in whole or in part. It must, therefore, consist in a set-off or a claim by way of recoupment, or be in some way connected with the subject of the action stated in the complaint; and an answer which does not meet these requirements is *insufficient*.

Schenectady General Term, January, 1863.

Potter, Bockes and James, *Justices*.

This is an appeal from an order overruling a demurrer to the third count of the defendant's answer.

Armstrong & Palmer, *for plaintiff*.

S. M. Weed, *for defendant*.

By the court, Bockes, Justice. The complaint is on contract, and contains two causes of action. The first for goods, wares and merchandise sold and delivered; for work, labor and services done and performed; and for money paid, laid out and expended. The second alleges an accounting between the parties, and a balance due the plaintiff with a promise to pay.

The defendant interposed three defences: first, a general denial; second, a set-off or counter-claim for goods, wares and merchandise sold and delivered; for money paid, laid out and expended; for rent and board, and for a general balance on account; third, a multifarious defence of a legal and equitable character.

To the third alleged defence the plaintiff demurred.

1. The objection that an appeal does not lie in this case is not well taken. The demurrer was interposed to one of several alleged defences, and the order overruled the demurrer, with liberty to reply to that part of the answer demurred to. The appeal was, therefore, properly taken from the order declaring the decision. (*Code*, § 349, *sub*. 2.)

2. It does not appear from the pleadings that the matters stated in the third defence have any connection with either alleged cause or ground of action. They must, therefore, be considered as wholly distinct from the contracts and transactions set forth in the complaint as the foundation of the plaintiff's claim. Nor are they pleaded as a defence to the action, except by way of counter-claim. The question therefore is, whether those matters are well pleaded as a counter-claim.

This defence is informally stated, and requires a careful examination in order to understand the bearing and import of the facts alleged. But on analysis it will be found to contain matter of set-off, and also matter of an equitable nature, cognizable only by a court of equity. In this aspect the pleading is multifarious. It includes distinct subjects in the same alleged defence. No objection is taken, however, to the pleading on this ground, nor could it here prevail if taken, as the remedy in such case is by motion, not by demurrer. If, therefore, the pleading contains allegations of fact sufficient to make out a proper case for a set-off, it must be held good as a counter-claim, notwithstanding it may also contain other statements of no value as a defence. Such statements may be treated as useless and redundant. In this view, I think the pleading will be found to be sufficient and admissible under the provisions of the Code. If these be stricken from it, the various allegations on which the defendant bases his claim for equitable relief, enough will remain to show a money demand, or cause of action in favor of the defendant against the plaintiff, arising on contract. This being so, the demurrer was properly overruled. The remedy of the plaintiff was by motion to strike out portions of the alleged defence, and to make it more definite.

3. Should the defence demurred to be deemed to contain no sufficient allegation to establish a set-off, or money demand in favor of the defendant and against the plaintiff, and be held to state grounds for equitable relief *only*, having no connection with the subject of plaintiff's action, then in my judgment the demurrer would be well interposed. Suppose the defendant had set up those facts, and those only, which would entitle him to a claim against the plaintiff to the effect that he held the lands embraced in the sheriff's deed for the defendant, and that in equity he was bound to convey them to the defendant, and directing a conveyance accordingly. Would this constitute a defence to plaintiff's action for goods sold, &c., and for balance due on settlement of accounts? Clearly not; nor would it be such a counter-claim as the defendant would have a right to interpose by way of answer to plaintiff's alleged grounds of action. Such equitable claim for relief would afford no answer to the plaintiff's claim for judgment. He would still be entitled to recover according to the allegations of his complaint without any deduction, even on account of the matters stated in the answer. A counter-claim to be available to a party must afford to him protection in some way against the plaintiff's demand for judgment, either in whole or in part. It must, therefore, consist in a set-off or

claim by way of recoupment, or be in some way connected with the subject of the action stated in the complaint. It must present an *answer* to the plaintiff's demand for relief, must show that he is not entitled, according to law, or under the application of just principles of equity to judgment in his favor, as or to the extent claimed in the complaint. It must, therefore, contain not only the substance of what is necessary to sustain an action in favor of the defendant against the plaintiff, but it must also operate in some way to defeat, in whole or in part, the plaintiff's right of recovery in the action. An answer which does not meet this requirement is insufficient, whether regarded as a defence or counter-claim. If a person be sued on a promissory note, he cannot set up by way of defence or counter-claim a contract with the plaintiff for the purchase of lands, and allege payment of the purchase price, and claim a decree in the action for specific performance; nor could he in such action on promissory note have a foreclosure of a mortgage against the plaintiff, especially if he were not personally liable for the mortgage debt.

But I think the defence demurred to contains a counter-claim by way of set-off or money demand, and hence the order of the special term overruling the demurrer was properly granted.

The order appealed from must be affirmed with $10 costs and disbursements of the appeal, with liberty to the plaintiff to withdraw the demurrer and reply within twenty days after service of the order of affirmance, and on paying the costs of the demurrer and of the appeal, but without prejudice to other proceedings already had in the case.

SUPREME COURT.

Oliver H. Clark and others agt. The Mayor, &c. of New York.

On a motion for a *new trial* in an action for damages caused by *negligence*, where the plaintiff has been *non-suited* at the trial, and where he submitted without objection, to have the question of negligence passed upon by the court instead of the jury,

Held, that he is precluded on such motion from insisting that the question of *negligence was one exclusively for the jury*.

New York General Term, February, 1863.

Ingraham, Leonard and Peckham, *Justices*.

This was an action to recover damages against the city by reason of certain obstructions in the channel of the Harlem river, between Manhattan Island and Ward's Island, whereby the plaintiffs claim their steamboat was wrecked and lost.

The cause was tried before Mr. Justice Hogeboom and a jury, on the 3d day of October, 1861.

The case shows that after the plaintiffs rested, "the defendants moved to dismiss the complaint. The court granted the motion, and the plaintiffs duly excepted." Upon what ground the motion was made, what points were presented or decided, the case does not show.

A statute was passed in 1807 authorizing certain persons to build a bridge across a part of Harlem river to Great Barn Island—in other words, between Manhattan and Ward's Islands; and when finished, the bridge was by the statute required "to be forever thereafter kept and maintained in good repair at the sole expense of the proprietors and inhabitants of said island (Ward's Island) for the time being."

The bridge was built, but in 1815 was swept away, leaving a part of the stone constituting its abutment still there. Upon that stone, it was proved, the injury occurred to plaintiffs' boat in July, 1858.

The plaintiffs also proved that the defendants owned a part of this island from 1851, and at the time of the injury their portion of the island was occupied by some fifty of its employees.

The plaintiffs sought to establish that the injury would not have occurred if the bridge had been kept in good repair, and they claimed (I infer from the evidence given) that the city was bound to keep it in good repair, from its proprietorship and occupancy of the island.

They also claimed (as I infer from the argument here) that the city was bound by its charter to remove from the river obstructions of this character, and not having done so, whereby this loss had been sustained, the defendants were liable for omitting their duty in that behalf.

D. DUDLEY FIELD, *for plaintiffs*
HENRY H. ANDERSON, *for defendants*

By the court, PECKHAM, Justice. From the course of the trial I infer and shall assume that the court conceded the liability of the defendants for this injury in case it occurred without negligence on the part of the plaintiffs. If not, the complaint should have been dismissed when the cause was opened. If the defendants were not liable and could not be so held under my proof, either as proprietors and occupants of the island, or by reason of the obligations imposed by their charter, the testimony was entirely supefluous and immaterial. I assume, therefore, that the court placed its decision in fact upon the negligence of the plaintiffs contributing to the injury.

The case presents a good deal of evidence bearing upon this point of negligence on the part of the plaintiffs.

1st. As to the condition of the boat. She was about or a little over a quarter of a century old when she was lost, but she had had a new boiler put in her since 1852; as the witness, Boatman, her former owner, expresses it, "she was a good boat for her age." She was staunch and well built. But the immediate or direct cause of the accident was the breaking of what is called the "tap screws," which both broke and fell into the fire below, together with the "guide," to which they were attached. This had the effect to stop the engine, and before she could be put in order again this injury occurred.

These "tap screws," two in number, were, one witness (Franklin, the fireman,) says, about three-eighths of an inch in diameter, and another (Browley, an engineer,) "about half an inch in diameter—a light affair."

In answer to the question, what would be likely to cause the breaking of both tap screws at once, this witness said, "they might by a continual jar—iron loses its tenacity by continual vibration." By his further cross and direct examination, the witness then proved that these screws must have been defective or they would not break. This he modifies, and then modifies the modification. There could be no sudden strain on them, he says, "the strain at any time must be very trifling."

It would seem from this testimony that the iron in these screws, from twenty-five years' vibration, had lost its tenacity and broken; and as they were so material, so vital to the working of the steamer, was it not negligence that they should have been changed in that time? No government inspector would, or perhaps could, detect such a defect. It would be the duty of her owners, knowing her age, at the proper time to exchange these old for new materials. A government certificate can give no impunity to negligence so far as respects civil remedies.

2d. As to the management of the boat. This boat had been running to Ward's Island for many years, and those on board of her well knew of these stones, the "butments," as the witness called them. They were quite familiar, and obviously dangerous to run upon. At the time of this accident the wind was blowing "very hard" towards this abutment, and the tide and current were then setting "very strong" in the same direction. Both had the effect to drive her on the rocks as soon as she was disabled. If the accident had not occurred the steamer would have gone within about fifteen or twenty feet of this sunken pier.

If they had kept forty feet from the pier she would have cleared the stone when disabled.

In view of the age of this boat and her liability to accidents, was it careful and discreet management to run her under such a wind and tide so near to so dangerous a point?

No difficulty was alleged or pretended in going farther from the point. The map of the harbor commissioners showed there was width of channel enough.

It was proved by the plaintiffs that the course pursued by the boat was the usual one she had before taken.

The counsel for the plaintiffs insists here that negligence was a question for the jury.

The court of appeals, in its latest decision, has held the other way; that the court may properly non-suit for that cause; and that court, in the same opinion, has utterly abolished all the former well-known and well-settled degrees of negligence. It is thus announced that "the party injured must have been entirely free from any degree of negligence which contributed to the injury."

If this be the law, (23 *How. Pr. R.*, 492,) can it be claimed that the very highest care and caution were exercised in this case, either as to these screws or in the navigation of the boat?

Again, the counsel for the plaintiffs insists here that this question was one exclusively for the jury. But the difficulty is, he does not seem to have requested to go to the jury at the trial. He seems to have submitted without objection to have the question passed upon by the court instead of the jury. In such case it is held he cannot complain here. (28 *Barb.*, 157; *Winchell* agt. *Hicks*, 18 *N. Y. R.*. 558.)

This view of the case renders unnecessary the examination of questions as to the admissibility of evidence tending merely to show the liability of defendants, provided the plaintiffs were free from fault.

If the question were proper for the jury, their verdict would not ordinarily be set aside. On this evidence, I do not think it would. A new trial should therefore be denied.

SUPREME COURT.

NANCY C. BURRITT agt. LORINDA SILLIMAN and others.

The supreme court has no power, either at special term or on appeal at general term, to *allow extra costs* (*Code*, § 309,) on the trial of a *feigned issue*, made up to try the questions of the *validity or execution of will*, under the provisions of the Revised Statutes.

A *new trial* of such issue might be granted by the supreme court; but no discretionary power exists in the court to award extra costs, or in fact *any costs at all* for making up such issue and its trial. Cases of this kind are not affected by the Code, they are governed by a special statutory provision.

Third District General Term, September, 1861.

APPEAL from an order of special term granting extra allowance of costs. The facts appear fully in the opinion.

JOHN L. FLAGG, *for plaintiff.*
J. A. MILLARD, *for defendants.*

By the court, WRIGHT, Justice. The surrogate of the county of Rensselaer having made a decree refusing to admit the will of Abigail Clapp to probate, Mrs. Burritt appealed therefrom to this court. The supreme court, at general term, reversed the decision of the surrogate upon a question of fact, and directed an issue to be made up to try the questions arising upon the application to prove the will. The questions made by the feigned issue were tried at a circuit court held in the county of Rensselaer, in February, 1861, and the determination was in favor of the validity of the will. At the succeeding May general term of this court, its direction was asked in respect to the costs which had accrued, not only of the last appeal but of a former appeal, which had been taken to the court of appeals. An order was made and entered that the costs of the plaintiff arising on the last appeal from the decision of the surrogate, and also ten dollars costs of the motion, be allowed to her, and be paid out of the personal estate of the testatrix. This order has not been appealed from, and the question of the power to make it is not open for discussion in this court, collaterally or otherwise.

It appears that at the trial of the issue as to the validity of the will, and after the rendition of the verdict of the jury sustaining it, an application was made to the court at special term for an extra allowance of costs. The application was considered as made at the conclusion of the trial to be heard at some future time; and it was heard on the 15th July following—the attorneys for and against the application appearing before the judge upon notice. An order was made and entered that the plaintiff have six hundred dollars costs as an extra allowance. The present appeal is from this order.

The order would not be appealable if this court had power to make it. Any power in the premises is supposed to be conferred by the concluding clause of the 309th section of the Code, which provides, that "in difficult and extraordinary cases, when a trial has been had, except in any of the actions or proceedings specified in section 308, the court may also, in its discretion, make a further allowance to any party, not exceeding five per cent., upon the amount of the recovery or claim or subject matter involved." (*Code*, § 309, *amended in* 1859.)

The exercise of power under this provision is a discretionary one, from which there would be no appeal, unless possibly in a case of palpable abuse of the discretion. But

I am of the opinion that there was no power in the court to make the order. This was not an action or proceeding under the Code, in which a trial had been had, but an appeal from a decree of a surrogate's court, not affected in any way, but in terms excepted from the operations of the Code.

The appeal was taken pursuant to the provisions of the Revised Statutes, and the feigned issue directed to be made up and tried in the same manner as issues awarded by the court of chancery. Any power to impose costs must have been conferred by statute, or existed in the court, independent of the Code of Procedure. The costs and expenses of making up an issue in a case like this, and of the trial thereon, and all subsequent costs therein, are charged by statute on the party appealing in case of his failure to impeach the validity or execution of the will, to be collected in a suit on the bond directed to be given on filing the appeal; and if the appellant succeeded in impeaching the validity or execution of the will, the party maintaining such validity or execution might be required by the surrogate to pay the costs and expenses of the proceedings, either personally or out of the property of the deceased, such payment to be enforced by process of attachment. (3 *R. S.*, *5th ed.*, *p.* 150, §§ 71, 72, 73, 74, 75, 76, 77, 78.) These costs and expenses were not those fixed by the Code and given to the prevailing party, but were to be taxed according to the fee bill, as it existed before and apart from the Code. There was no power in the court of chancery or in the supreme court, in their discretion, to make an additional allowance of costs to those given by statute. When a feigned issue had been made up to try the questions of the validity or execution of a will, under the provisions of the Revised Statutes, a new trial of such issue might be granted by the supreme court; but no discretionary power existed in the court to award extra costs, or in fact any costs at all, for making up such issue and its trial. In this case, all that the court assumed to do at the May term, was to order the costs of the last appeal from the decision of the surrogate, to be paid out of the personal estate of the testatrix. No direction was given or order made in respect to the costs and expenses of the feigned issues; and most clearly if the order had embraced both the costs of the appeal and the feigned issue, and there was any power to allow additional costs beyond those fixed by law, that power could only be exercised by the court to which the appeal was taken. The discretion could not be exercised by the special term or circuit court, that never had jurisdiction of the case. But the appellate court would be equally without authority to make the order appealed from. It is not pretended that there is any power given except by the Code, and that enactment does not touch or relate to a case arising in a surrogate's court. The Code especially provides that appeals of this character shall not be affected by it, (*Code*, § 471,) and such appeals are wholly without its purview. Its provisions in respect to costs control only actions or proceedings under it. It establishes a new system in regard to costs in actions or appeals affected by it. Costs are given to the prevailing party by way of indemnity for expenses in the action. In cases where costs are allowed, the amounts are fixed; and then follows the provisions giving the power to the court, in its discretion, to make a further allowance of costs in difficult and extraordinary cases, when a trial has been had, (*Code*, § 303 *to* 309.) This, of course, means in a civil action or proceeding brought under, and affected by, the Code, and when a trial has been had. The circuit court never had cognizance of the present case, except to try certain issues involved, and that not in pursuance of any authority derived from the Code, but from the direction of the supreme court, deriving its authority from a special statutory provision. The special term never had any cognizance of it. The case is to be regarded as in the supreme court until the verdict in the feigned issue is received and remitted to the surrogate for his action.

I am clearly of the opinion that the special term was not authorized to make the order, and that it should be reversed.

GOULD, J., and HOGEBOOM, J., concurred.

SUPREME COURT.

THE PEOPLE agt JOHN FELLINGER.

Where an *indictment*, charging *burglary in the first degree*, complies with all the requisites of the statute in describing the offence, except that it omits to state the *mode of entry into the premises*, (by forcibly bursting or breaking the wall or outer door, window, &c.,) it is *fatally defective*, and the defect is *not cured by verdict*.

Where the allegations in the indictment charged only *burglary in the second degree*, the jury have no right to find the prisoner guilty of burglary in the *first degree*, because evidence was furnished sufficient for that purpose.

It seems, that before the decision of the court of appeals in the *People* agt. *Hartung*, the law was settled, that if a *wrong judgment* be given against a defendant, which is reversed on error, the court of review *can neither give a new judgment against the prisoner, nor send the case back to the court below for the proper judgment. The judgment, being erroneous, must be reversed. A venire de novo can only be awarded where the judgment is* REVERSED ON BILL OF EXCEPTIONS.

New York General Term, November, 1862.

INGRAHAM, PECKHAM and LEONARD, *Justices*.

THE prisoner was indicted for burglary, was tried and convicted of burglary in the first degree, and sentenced to state prison for life. The case comes up on writ of error.

A. OAKEY HALL, *district attorney, for the people.*

S. H. STEWART, *for prisoner.*

By the court, INGRHAM, P. Justice. The alleged error is in the indictment. This indictment charges that the prisoner, on a certain day during the night of the same day, did break and enter the dwelling house of one Reinhardt, whilst there were human beings within the said house, with intent to commit some crime therein.

The prisoner's counsel contends that this indiciment does not charge the crime of burglary in the first degree.

The statute defines this crime to be the breaking and entering into the dwelling house of another in the night time, in which there shall be at the time some human being, with intent to commit some crime therein, by forcibly bursting, or breaking the wall or outer door, window or shutter, or the lock or bolts of the door or fastening of the window, or breaking in any other manner, armed with a dangerous weapon, or with the aid of one or more confederates, or by unlocking a door with false keys, or picking the lock, &c.

It will be seen by comparing the allegations of the indictment with the provisions of the statute, that the pleader has complied with all the requisites of the statute in describing the offence, by stating those matters which generally apply to the offence of burglary in the first degree, and which must exist in each case to constitute this offence, but has omitted to state the mode of entry into the premises, which is also a requisite to make out this offence in the first degree.

The mode of breaking into the house, as stated in the statute, is just as necessary to be proved to make out the offence, as that it was in the night time, or that there was at the time a human being in the house. Without proof of one of these modes of entering the house, the offence is only burglary in the second degree.

If the indictment only contained the first count, and a general verdict of guilty had been rendered, it could not, for a moment, be supposed that the prisoner was guilty of the highest grade of burglary, because in such a case all the proof necessary to sustain the indictment would only make out a case of burglary in the second degree, and under such a verdict the punisment could only be for the minor offence. It does not alter the rule to say that on the trial the other ingredients necessary to make out the offence were proven. There is no proof that such evidence was furnished. The case comes before us simply upon the record, and that shows no evidence whatever. The jury, on an indictment charging a lesser offence, have no right to find the prisoner guilty of the greater, because evidence was furnished sufficient for that purpose.

It is conceded that the indictment must describe the offence in the language of the statute. In doing so, it is necessary to aver every affirmative matter which goes to make out the offence. It is not necessary to negative exceptions, unless in some special cases, but in such cases the exceptions do not make out the offence. Chief Justice SAVAGE says: "it is sufficient if all the circumstances necessary to describe and render the charge intelligible in its legal requisites appear on the face of the proceedings," (*People* agt. *Phelps*, 5 *Wend.*, *p.* 1; *see also People* agt. *Biggs*, 8 *Barb.*, 547;) and in *The People* agt. *Allen*, (5 *Denio*, 76,) BEARDSLEY, chief justice, says, an indictment upon a statute must state all such facts and circumstances as constitute the statute offence, so as to bring the party indicted within the provisions of the statute. If the statute is confined to * * * acts done at some particular time or place, the indictment must show, &c., that the time and place where the alleged criminal acts were perpetrated were such as to bring the supposed offence directly within the statute. If the statute creates an offence or declares a common law offence, when committed under particular circumstances, not included in the original offence, punishable in a different manner from what it would have been without such circumstances, the indictment should be drawn in reference to the provisions of the statute creating or changing the nature of the offence. (*People* agt. *Enoch*, 13 *Wend.*, 159–173; *People* agt. *Allen*, 5 *Denio*, 76;) and in *The People* agt. *Dediere*, (22 *N. Y. R.*, *p.* 178,) DENIO, judge, says, "if any of the ingredients contained in the statute definitions are omitted, the indictment is fatally defective, and the defeat is not cured by verdict." (*See also The People* agt. *Davis*, 4 *Parker*, 67.)

The cases cited from the English books refer to the offence of burglary as it existed at common law, and under those cases the indictments might be sustained for the common law offence, but under our statute different grades have been established, depending not only on the fact that there shall be a human being in the house, and that the offence shall be committed in the night time and with intent to commit a crime, but also connects with it the mode by which the burglary is effected to be by breaking into the house, either armed or with a confederate, or by the use of false keys. These, or one of these acts, are just as necessary to constitute burglary in the first degree, as that it should be a dwelling house or that a human being should be in it. The case of *Thompson* agt. *The People* does not lay down any other rule. There the indictment alleged the breaking and entry "into the house of one Eleanor B. Padgett," and the objection was that it was not called a dwelling house. The learned justice who delivered the opinion, put his decision as to the sufficiency of the indictment, upon the ground that the word "house" with us in common parlance, meant dwelling house. (*Thompson* agt. *The People*, 3 *Parker C. R.*, 213.)

The offence has been so altered by our statute from the common law, that, to find out the degree of the offence, it is necessary that the words or substance of the statute should be used in its description, and if not, then the indictment is fatally defective if it is intended to charge burglary in the first degree, because it omits an essential part of the statutory description of the felony. (*People* agt. *Lohman*, 2 *Barb.*, 216–219.)

I think it is apparent that this indictment did not charge any higher offense than burglary in the second degree, and that unless some matters were proved which were not alleged in the indictment, the prisoner could not have been convicted of any higher offence.

It was urged, however, upon the argument, that these defects were cured by the verdict. No defect in substance can be so cured. It is only matters of form not affecting the substantial rights of the prisoner, which can be disregarded after verdict. If it appear that the prisoner has suffered wrong by the verdict, no one can sustain the proposition that such wrong should be continued, because the jury, by their verdict, have inflicted it. Such is this case. The indictment only charged the offence of burglary in the second degree. The verdict found the prisoner guilty of the offence of burglary in the first degree. Certainly, this is something more serious than error in matters of form. The defect is not cured by verdict. (*People* agt. *Dediere*, *supra.*)

In the words of Judge DENIO, in the last case, the prisoner has been convicted and sentenced for an offence of which the grand jury never indicted him.

In *The People* agt. *Powers*, (2 *Selden*, 50,) the defects in the indictment were held to be cured by the verdict. But those defects were in alleging generally, that the court before which a prior conviction of the prisoner had taken place, had jurisdiction of the subject matter and of the prisoner, by stating that the court had competent power and authority to try and to convict him for the offence. The defect was in form, merely, in not showing how the court had jurisdiction, instead of stating the same fact in general terms. Such an error was cured by the statute.

Under the present statute, classifying the crime of murder into the first and second degrees, a person might be indicted for murder in the second degree. This would be by omitting the allegation of its being premeditated, or being committed in the perpetration of some other offence. If, under such an indictment, the jury should find the prisoner guilty of murder in the first degree, the conviction could not be sustained, nor would the defect be cured by the verdict. The prisoner has no opportunity to make the objection before the verdict. The indictment was good for the lesser offence, and it is only when he is convicted of a higher grade of crime than that charged, that he is injured. If the defect is cured by the verdict, then the prisoner has been damnified without any remedy. He could not object to the indictment before trial, because it was good for the lesser offence, and he could not object to the verdict for the defect in the indictment, because it would be cured by the verdict. Such a rule cannot be sustained.

The remaining question is, what judgment we should render in reviewing the proceedings of the court below.

In *People* agt. *Taylor*, (3 *Denio*, 97,) the rule is stated. If a wrong judgment be given against a defendant, which is reversed on error, the court of review can neither give a new judgment against the prisoner, nor send the case back to the court below for the proper judgment. (*Rex* agt. *Brown*, 7 *A. & E.*, 58.)

The prisoner was sentenced for life, when by law the offence charged in the indictment was to be punished by imprisonment not exceeding ten years.

The judgment here rendered was erroneous, and must be reversed.

Peckham, J. The opinion is sound. I concur, except on the authority of *People* agt. *Hartung*, in court of appeals; I go for a reversal and for awarding a new trial.

There the case went up on bill of exceptions. The court held there was no error in the bill, but there was error in the judgment. Such is substantially this case.

Leonard, J., concurred.

NEW YORK COMMON PLEAS.

ANDREW FASH agt. MARTIN KAVANAGH.

Where a *monthly tenant* occupies rooms of a landlord, with an agreement to pay *rent in advance*, and leaves the premises the latter part of the month, he is not liable for the rent of the *subsequent month*, which has not become due.

Where it appeared that the filth from a privy, either *on* or *adjoining* the premises, flowed over the apartments occupied by the tenant, without any fault on his part, and rendered them unfit to occupy, the tenant was justified in *abandoning* them under the provisions of the "act in relation to the rights and liabilities of owners and lessors, and of lessees and occupants of buildings," passed April 13, 1860.

The injury to the premises contemplated by this act, to authorise a surrender of possession, must be of a physical nature, such as if done by the landlord would amount to an *eviction* of the tenant from the whole or part of the demised premises.

The occupant of *apartments* in a *tenement house*, is not bound either to see to the erection of a proper *sink or privy* upon the premises, or to cause it to be *emptied* to prevent an overflow. This is a matter which the *landlord* is required to look after and prevent, or else to stand to the consequences.

General Term, March, 1861.

DALY, BRADY and HILTON, *JJ.*

By the court, HILTON, J. The defendant occupied rooms in the plaintiff's building, under a hiring by the month, the rent being payable in advance. This action is brought for the month's rent, payable August 1st, and the defence seems to be twofold: 1. That he removed from the premises in the month of July, and before the rent claimed became due. 2. That before he left, the contents of the privy attached to the house overflowed his apartments, rendering them untenantable and unfit for occupancy; and having been on this account obliged to abandon them, he was not thereafter bound or liable to pay rent.

I think the proof at the trial entitled him to judgment on both grounds. The defendant testified positively that he left on the 23d July, and then offered the keys to the plaintiff's agent, who declined to receive them. That at the time, the filth from the privy had flowed over his apartments, rendering them untenantable and unfit to occupy. The plaintiff swore that he was told the defendant had left the latter part of July, and his agent testified that the defendant offered the keys before the 1st of August. In addition to this, Donahue, a tenant in the same house, stated, that at the time defendant left, the filth was ankle deep in his apartments, which appear to have been on the basement floor; that he took the keys to the plaintiff's house about a week thereafter, and thinks the keys were then taken by him, from about 10th to 15th August. It is perhaps proper to add, that the plaintiff's agent testified that the filth of which defendant complained, came from the adjoining premises; also, that the plaintiff, in his direct examination, stated that the defendant was in possession of the premises on the 15th August; but I think it must be assumed that this was rather a conclusion of his mind than a statement of a fact within his knowledge, as it appears he did not live on the premises. If this view was not correct, he would not have closed his testimony with the remark, that he "was told the defendant had left the premises the latter part of July last," without explanation or comment.

I feel bound, therefore, to conclude from the testimony at the trial, that the defendant left before the 1st of August, and as his hiring was only for the month, he terminated his tenancy before the rent sued for accrued.

The reasons he gave for leaving were, in this view of the case, unnecessary; but I think there can be no doubt of their sufficiency; and that they would have justified an abandonment under the provisions of the "act in relation to the rights and liabilities of owners and lessors, and of lessees and occupants of buildings," passed April 13, 1860, (*Sess. Laws*, *p.* 592,) which declares that the occupant of any building which shall without any fault or neglect on his part be destroyed, or be so injured by the elements or any other cause, as to be untenantable and unfit for occupancy, shall not be liable or bound to pay rent after such destruction or injury, unless otherwise expressly provided by written agreement or covenant; and the occupant may, therefore, quit and surrender possession of the premises so leased or occupied.

The injury here contemplated must obviously be of a physical nature, such as if done by the landlord would amount to an eviction of the tenant from the whole or part of the demised premises. It must be to the building occupied, and not caused by the privity or procurement of the tenant, or by his neglect or want of proper care. If it be of the nature the present case discloses, I have no doubt it would fall within the class of injuries which the law was passed to meet.

As an occupant of apartments in a tenement house, the defendant was not bound to either see to the erection of a proper sink or privy upon the premises, or to cause it to be emptied, to prevent an overflow.

This was a matter which the landlord, who by maintaining a building of this class—one of those so called modern improvements which the necessities of the present day have required to be erected in the compact portion of our city, where rents are high and the poor abound—was required to look after and prevent, or else stand to the consequences.

I do not mean to be understood as holding that a landlord is required, after he has rented a house, to attend to the emptying of the sinks and cesspools attached to it; on the contrary, that duty ordinarily devolves upon the tenant, who is bound to see that the premises are not injured by any inattention to his duties in this respect; but I do mean to say, that modern improvements require appropriate rules; and as, in a tenement house, no occupant of a single room, renting direct from the landlord for a short and may be uncertain term, generally from month to month, can be required to perform this duty, it follows of necessity that it must fall upon the landlord to attend to.

On the other hand, if, as the plaintiff's agent testified, the filth came from the adjoining premises, and as it is not contended it thus came through any fault, procurement or neglect of the defendant, it was equally an injury to the building within the provision of the law referred to. It will probably be said that if this view be correct, a landlord may be left without remedy against the acts of those who covertly furnish his tenants with excuses for abandoning demised premises. I can only answer, that the statute is certainly extraordinary in its character, and may give rise to great abuses being practiced under it by unwilling tenants upon landowners; but it is our duty only to construe its provisions, and not speculate upon the injustice it may produce, leaving to future legislatures to remedy any of the evils which may spring from it.

Judgment reversed.

SUPREME COURT.

William Williams agt. The People.

An *indictment* for unlawfully, willfully, maliciously and mischievously driving the horses attached to a freight car, on the Fourth avenue railroad, against another railroad car, then and there being, and then there injuring the last mentioned car, he so intending, &c., does not set up or include the common law offence of *malicious mischief*. The defendant can be considered as guilty of nothing beyond a *hurtful trespass*.

A trespass upon property, although it may be willful and malicious, is not within the offence of *malicious mischief at common law*, unless it was in the *night time, or secretly, without the hope of gain*; or unless it consisted of some act of *cruelty to domestic animals*.

New York General Term, November, 1862.

Ingraham, Clerke and Barnard, *Justices*.

The plaintiff in error was indicted for unlawfully, willfully, maliciously and mischievously driving the horses attached to a freight car, on the Fourth avenue railroad, against another railroad car then and there being, then and there injuring the last mentioned car, he so intending, &c.

The prisoner was convicted.

Charles W. Sandford, *for plaintiff in error.*

A. Oakey Hall, *district attorney.*

By the court, Ingraham, P. Justice. It is sought to sustain this indictment upon the ground that it sets up the common law offence of malicious mischief. Unless the act complained of comes within the definition of that offence, the prisoner was guilty of nothing beyond a hurtful trespass. *Blackstone* defines this offence as being perpetrated not *animo furandi*, or with an intent of gain, but out of wanton cruelty, or black and diabolical revenge. In the *People* agt. *Smith*, (5 *Cowen*, 258,) it is said that the offence is distinguishable from an ordinary trespass as being a violation of private right, without color or pretext, and without the hope or expectation of gain.

Many of the cases on this subject are cited in *Kilpatrick* agt. *The People*, (5 *Denio*, 277,) in which case it was held that willfully, unlawfully and maliciously breaking and destroying two windows of a house, was not within the description of this offence.

The distinction is noted in that case between acts done openly and those done secretly, or in the night time, and between acts done to property and injuries to domestic animals.

From the cases there cited, I think the rule may be stated to be that a trespass upon property, although it may be willful and malicious, is not within the offence of malicious mischief at common law, unless it was in the night time, or secretly, without the hope of gain, or unless it consisted of some act or cruelty to domestic animals.

The act is not indictable because it is willful, or simply because it is malicious. There must be other circumstances, such as secresy, cruelty or public injury, to make out the offence.

The present case does not come within either class. The prisoner was driving a car at a point where two roads met, and in trying to get ahead of a car, on the other road, he ran into it. We are bound to consider it done maliciously, because the jury have so found, but that is not enough.

The counsel for the people sought to make out a distinction between the present case and those before referred to, because the word "mischievously" is used in this indictment, but that does not alter the rule. It was so held in *State* agt. *Wheeler*, (3 *Vermont*, 344,) where the word mischievously was used in the indictment, and yet the killing of a beast of another under such circumstances was held to be only a civil injury, and not indictable. I think the definition of the offence, as stated above, is quite as comprehensive as the cases warrant, and more so than some of them would sustain.

The plaintiff in error has not committed an offence coming within these rules, and the judgment should be reversed.

CLERKE, J., concurred.

BARNARD, J., *dissenting*. The act complained of being one against the safety of the public, turns what might otherwise be a mere trespass into an indictable offence. This is the principle on which the case of the *Commonwealth* agt. *Eckert*, (2 *Brown Rep.*, *p.* 291,) was decided, when the act complained of was the cutting down of a tree useful for public convenience, ornament and shade. The element of cruelty to an animal, or of secresy in the commission of the crime, has also been held to turn what otherwise would be a mere trespass, into an indictable offence.

Judgment affirmed.

SUPREME COURT.

WALRATH and wife agt. HANDY and others.

Misjoinder of parties plaintiffs is ground of *demurrer* to the complaint.

In such case the complaint does not state facts sufficient to constitute a cause of action.

In an action to obtain *construction of a will*, the complaint should state that the testator left property, and also whether real or personal or both.

If there be no *trust* declared or raised by the will, and the legatees and devisees take absolutely, they must vindicate their rights by an action or actions at law —not by an action in equity for its construction.

A person who is *not executor* nor in any sense a *trustee* is not entitled to ask instruction or advice from the court.

In case a *trust* be declared by will, and questions of doubt arise as to its true meaning, any person having an *interest* in the property *held in trust* may apply by action to have the will construed or its validity determined.

Saratoga Special Term, Feb., 1863.

THIS action was brought to obtain construction of a will.

MCMARTIN & PLANTZ, *for plaintiffs.*
SMITH & CARROLL, *for defendant, Handy.*

BOCKES, Justice. It seems plain that the wife of Wm. Walrath is an unnecessary party plaintiff. She obtains her only right—an inchoate right of dower—through her husband, and this right attaches to those lands to which her husband is entitled under the will. A judicial determination of his right under the provisions of the will, if necessary, would conclude her as to any claim for dower. She would have dower in the lands devised to him, according to the true construction of the will.

But it is insisted that a misjoinder of parties plaintiff, cannot be urged on demurrer. It has been often held that a misjoinder of parties defendant, is not ground of demurrer. (23 *How.*, 396; 12 *How.*, 134; 17 *N. Y.*, 592;) and very general language has been used in some of the cases, to the effect, that a demurrer to a complaint for an *excess* of parties cannot be allowed. It was so stated in *Davy* agt. *Betts*, (23 *How.*, 396;) also in *Gregory* agt. *Oaksmith*, (12 *How.*, 134.) So it has been said that a demurrer must be sustained or fail to the whole extent to which it is applied; and that where a demurrer is to the whole complaint, if one of the plaintiffs might have judgment separately, it is bad. But in *Brownson and wife* agt. *Gifford*, (8 *How.*, 389,) it was held on demurrer that the action should have been brought by Mrs. Brownson alone, and that her husband was improperly joined as plaintiff. In this case, Judge HARRIS allowed the demurrer to use his own language—"*solely on the ground that the husband of Mrs. Brownson ought not to have been joined as a co-plaintiff with her*," (*page* 397.) In *Mann and wife* agt. *Marsh*, (35 *Barb.*, 68 *same case*; 21 *How.*, 372,) it was held, that when two or more plaintiffs unite in bringing a joint action and the facts stated do not show a joint cause of action in them, a demurrer will lie upon the ground that the complaint does not state facts sufficient to constitute a cause of action. In *Barstow* agt. *Draper*, (5 *Duer*, 130,) it was held that in an action by husband and wife, they must recover jointly or not at all. (*See also* 16 *How.*, 195; *also cases cited in Mann* agt. *Marsh*, 35 *Barb.*, *on page* 73.) According to these authorities Mrs. Walrath is an unnecessary and improper party. The case of *Mann* agt. *Marsh* is well considered, was decided at general term after full argument, and is the latest decision on the point. I feel bound to follow it at special term. It seems to me too, that the remarks of Judge ALLEN are well made. He says, (*page* 72,) "it is true, that when all the parties plaintiff do not show an interest in the cause of action, this is in one sense a misjoinder of plaintiffs, but in a more important sense it is a failure to make a case entitling the plaintiffs to recover against the defendant." And he adds, "the demurrer was necessarily to the whole complaint, and to the cause of action as then alleged in favor of both plaintiffs. A demurrer could not be interposed as against one plaintiff and an answer as to the other." So he holds that in such case judgment should be given for the defendant on the demurrer with liberty to amend the complaint. This decision sustains the demurrer, not solely on the ground that there is a misjoinder of parties plaintiff, but on the ground that in such case the complaint does not state a cause of action in favor of the plaintiff.

The complaint is however fatally defective in this: it is not alleged that the testator died seized or possessed of any property whatever, real or personal; without an allegation that there was property on which the will could take effect, certainly, the complaint does not state facts sufficient to constitute a cause of action.

But it is difficult to see how the complaint could be held good, even if it contained an averment that the testator died seized and possessed of both real and personal property, and the action was by William Walrath alone. He is not the executor of the will, nor in any sense a trustee, hence he is not entitled to ask instruction or advice from the court—nor does it appear from the complaint that he has been in any way injured or in any danger of being injured either in his person or property by the defendants, or by either of them.

The plaintiffs rest their case on the authority of *Bowen* agt. *Smith*, (10 *Paige*, 193,) when it was held, that where the executor takes the legal estate *as trustee*, any person having an interest in such property (*so held in trust*) may file a bill, to have the construction of the will settled, or to have the question as to the validity of its provisions determined, so far as concerns the interest of the complainant in the property, and to have a decree against such executor for such parts or portions of the property as he is legally and equitably entitled to recover. In this case the bill of complaint was dismissed for want of equity, and on the ground that the plaintiff had a remedy, if any, at law by a common law action. The chancellor remarked, "I am not aware of any case in which an heir at law of a testator, or a devisee, who claims a mere legal estate in the real property where there was no trust, has been allowed to come into a court of equity for the mere purpose of obtaining a judicial construction of the provisions of the will. On the contrary, the decision of such legal questions belongs exclusively to the courts of law, except when they arise incidentally in this court in the exercise of its legitimate powers; or where the court has obtained jurisdiction of the case for some other purpose."

So, in the case under consideration, there is *no trust* as regards the real property devised by the will. The legal title is not given the executor or to any one in trust. Whatever rights William Walrath gets by the provisions of the will, are absolute and unconditional. He takes a legal estate disconnected with any trust. So, as was remarked by the chancellor in the case cited, the decision of all legal questions in regard to it, belong, therefore, exclusively to the courts of law, and it follows that his rights must be protected in the usual proceeding by an action at law, if any one attempts, improperly and unlawfully, to interfere with them.

As regards the personal estate, perhaps a case might be made calling for a decision as to the true construction and meaning of the will. As to the personal property the executor is a trustee, and William Walrath is *cestui que trust*. If, therefore, a case be made in other respects proper for the action of the court, the complaint might be upheld. No case is made out, however, on the complaint, in any view, and the demurrer must be held to be well taken.

Judgment is ordered for the defendant, Handy, on the demurrer with costs, but with liberty to the plaintiff to withdraw the demurrer and to serve an amended complaint on payment of costs of the demurrer

SUPREME COURT.

WALTON agt. BRYENTH.

The provision of the United States Internal Revenue Act, of July 1, 1862, requiring a *stamp* upon every *summons* or *original proceedings*, issued by state courts, is *illegal and unconstitutional*.

New York Special Term, February, 1863.

AN order had been obtained to vacate the proceedings in this case, on the ground that the summons had been filed without an adhesive stamp, as required by the United States Internal Revenue Act, approved July 1, 1862.

EDMON BLANKMAN, defendant's counsel, contended that the provisions of the statute rendered all original proceedings invalid and of no effect unless stamped.

EDWIN JAMES, plaintiff's counsel, argued that congress had no power to interfere with the proceedings of the state courts. It was doubtful whether they had the power to impose the penalty of $50; but if they could render the proceedings in state courts invalid, they usurped a power that was illegal and unconstitutional. If they could impose a duty of six cents upon a summons, they could, upon the same principle, lay a duty which would amount to a prohibition, and thus paralyze the whole system of administering justice in the state tribunals.

BARNARD, J., decided to dimiss the order. Congress had no right to interfere with the proceedings of the state courts. In his judgment, the provision was illegal and unconstitutional. Congress might impose a penalty, but could not invalidate the proceedings of the state courts; he would facilitate any appeal from his decision, upon a question of so much importance.

NEW YORK SUPERIOR COURT.

The Mayor, &c. of the City of New York agt. Henry Erben and The New York Life Ins. & Trust Co.

Exceptions to findings of *fact* are not required.

Where exceptions to the *conclusions of law* are not made within *ten days after judgment*, none can be sustained upon an *appeal*, and the case is heard solely upon the exceptions taken at the *trial*.

Where the complaint averred the payment of a certain sum of money, as "an excess of an amount awarded, and not of right due and payable to the defendant; and that said payment was made under a mistake of fact on the part of the plaintiffs," &c.,

Held, that *evidence*, as to the validity and correctness of the proceedings of the commissioners of estimate and assessment, and as to the sufficiency of the award made by them to the defendant, was properly allowed under the issue tendered by defendant to such allegations.

The rule with respect to *voluntary payments* is, that if a party has actually paid what the law would not have compelled him to pay, *but what in equity and good conscience he ought*, he cannot *recover it back* in an action for *money had and received*.

General Term, February, 1863.

This action was commenced on the 29th of January, 1858, to recover of the defendants $9,000, and interest from the 10th day of May, 1855, for an alleged over-payment to the defendants as owners and mortgagees of the lots Nos. 158, 164 and 166 Centre street, upon the proceedings for the extension of Canal street and the widening of Walker street.

The defence was a denial of over-payment, and an averment that the amount paid was the true value of the property taken by the city, as estimated by the commissioners of estimate and assessment in the proceedings referred to, and that any statement in their report in conflict with this fact, was the result of a clerical error in making up the formal report.

The case was on the calendar from April term, 1858, until November term, 1859, when the same was referred by the court to George W. Stevens, Esq., as referee.

The trial was commenced on the 2d of December, 1859, and was finished on the 31st of July, 1861. The referee held the matter under advisement until November 9, 1861, when he reported in favor of the defendants. On the 18th of November, 1861, judgment was entered for the defendants, and on the 20th of November, 1861, appeal was taken by the city to the general term of this court.

GREENE C. BRONSON, R. F. ANDREWS and G. R. THOMPSON, *counsel for the city.*

MATHEWS & SWAN, *counsel for the def't* HENRY ERBEN.

BETTS & ROBINSON, *counsel for the def'ts, The New York Life Insurance & Trust Company.*

By the court, MONCRIEF, J. This action was brought in the year 1858, to recover from the defendants the sum of nine thousand dollars, and interest from May 10, 1855, upon an allegation that said sum "was an excess of an amount awarded, and not of right due and payable to the defendant Erben; that said payment was made under a mistake of fact on the part of the plaintiffs," &c.

The action was referred by consent of parties to a referee, who reported in favor of the defendants in November, 1861. Judgment was entered upon this report on the 18th day of November, 1861. Exceptions to the conclusions of fact and law, found by the referee, appear to have been filed in the month of January, 1862.

Without attempting to give in detail the testimony sustaining each of the findings of fact, as set forth in the case upon this appeal, it must suffice that in my opinion no error was committed by the referee in that regard. Exceptions to findings of fact are not required. (*Hunt* agt. *Bloomer*, 3 *Kern. Rep.*, 341; *Johnson* agt. *Whitlock*, *id.*, 346.)

Where exceptions to the "conclusions of law," found by the referee, are not made by the making of a case, or by the filing of written exceptions within ten days after judgment, none can be sustained upon an appeal, and the case is heard solely upon the exceptions taken at the trial. (3 *Kernan*, *supra*; *Magie* agt. *Baker*, 4 *id.*, 435.)

The appellants argued, "as one of the principal questions on this appeal, the exceptions to the ruling of the referee in allowing evidence as to the validity and correctness of the proceedings of the commissioners of estimate and assessment, and as to the sufficiency of the award made by them to the defendants."

The complaint averred the payment of a certain sum of money, "not of right due and payable, and a payment made under a mistake of fact on the part of the plaintiffs." There is no pretence that the defendant Erben was guilty of a wrong in accepting the amount actually paid to him, or that he believed or had reason to suppose he was taking what was not of right due and payable to him. True it is, the commissioners in their report awarded to him a sum of nine thousand dollars less than the sum he actually received, but it is also true that he had inquired and had been advised, and had no reason to doubt, that he would be awarded the just and fair value of his property; that he would be entitled to receive the exact sum actually paid to him, the commissioners told him; the sum paid was the fair and actual value of the land taken from the defendant Erben; the rule adopted by the commissioners for measuring the valuation of property to be taken, entitled the defendant Erben to a larger sum than was paid to him. He was advised at the office of the street commissioner, when he called for the perpose of inspecting the report, and upon inquiry therefor, that the amount awarded to him was the sum paid to him; he was thereby induced to omit filing objections to the report, which as a matter of fact is conceded to have awarded to him only the sum of $15,805, the plaintiffs resting upon their claim to recover back a supposed over-payment for about a period of three years.

The answer of the defendant Erben apprised the plaintiffs that he should interpose these several matters as a defence to their claim. The defence was a just and reasonable one. To have sustained the objection and precluded the defendant Erben from showing this defence, would have been manifest injustice. If the plaintiffs had paid more than was stated as the award to him, and did so, having possession of the report, under a mistaken notion that he was awarded the sum paid, yet they had not paid to him more than of right and in justice was due and payable to him, and they had misled him and lulled him into silence until long after the period when he could correct the only mistake which was made, the stating a clearly inadequate compensation for what was taken from him.

Their proposition seems to be this: the land we took from you was worth more than we have paid; the commissioners and the street commissioner's officers advised you of being entitled to the sum paid; you could not have filed objections against the award actually inserted in the report, and corrected it by inserting the amount we have paid. We have your land, and although you innocently and without fault have accepted what we voluntarily paid, and less than as strict right you might have claimed, yet we claim that the report being confirmed, and it being manifest that in and by it you were awarded only $15,805, the excess on that amount should be refunded.

The adoption of this rule works plain wrong and injustice.

The least that the plaintiffs should be required to do would be to reinstate him in the position he was when the mistake was made by the commissioners in inserting an incorrect amount of award to him, or to enable him now to have the same advantage of showing error in the report that he would have had if the commissioners and others had not misled him.

The evidence was properly received; it established an issue tendered by the defendant Erben.

The rule with respect to voluntary payments is, that if a party has actually paid what the law would not have compelled him to pay, but what in equity and good conscience he ought, he cannot recover it back again in an action for money had and received. The objections taken at the trial were properly overruled, and the exceptions thereto untenable.

Upon the merits, as presented by the case upon appeal, we then have a payment made on behalf of the plaintiffs voluntarily, without fraud or deceit, or knowledge of the fact on the part of the defendant Erben, more than two years before reclamation is attempted or an assertion of error or mistake on their part—the fact that he was misled by those acting on behalf of and for the plaintiffs, and prevented from correcting the real mistake that was made in not inserting the amount he received; and that the plaintiffs have received and been in the enjoyment of his property, of the value, if not greater than, of the amount that was paid to him; and applying the rule just given, the plaintiffs having voluntarily paid what the report in terms did not require them to pay, but an amount which in equity and good conscience they should have paid, the plaintiffs cannot recover it back again.

It would be in the highest degree an injustice to permit the plaintiffs to assert their claims of payment under a so-called mistake, under the circumstances detailed in the evidence, and found as matters of fact in the present case.

The action against the defendants, the New York Life Insurance and Trust Company, could not under any circumstances have been maintained.

The company was a mortgagee having a lien for the sum awarded to it; the company received only the amount due to it. The fact that the checks were payable to the joint order of the defendants, perhaps, might create the company a disbursing agent of the plaintiffs to liquidate their claim and transfer the residue of the amount to the defendant Erben, which the company did. There was no mistake in the payment to it, nor in my opinion was there paid to the defendant Erben any sum of money "not of right due and payable to him."

We think the judgment is correct and should be affirmed.

SUPREME COURT.

J. Franklin Peck agt. Anthony Yorks and others.

When an *injunction order* has been allowed, and the same has been served, and the parties in the suit have appeared and taken steps in the action, and acquiesced in the injunction, no judge has authority to *modify it ex parte*.

Section 324 of the Code was designed to allow a judge who had hastily or improvidently granted an order to rectify the error, *if applied to immediately, and before any steps are taken in the action*. It was not intended to give an unlimited right to vacate orders granted *ex parte*.

Monroe Special Term, January, 1863.

This case is a creditors' suit, brought against the judgment debtor, Anthony Yorks, with his son Theodore D. Yorks, his brother-in-law Zimri Cook, and others, and the charge is fraud in the transfer of the property of the judgment debtor to the other defendants. The action was commenced in November, 1861, and an injunction order was granted on the 22d day of that month, by George Hastings, county judge of Livingston county, in which county the action was brought. This injunction was served on all the defendants, between the 10th day of December, 1861, and the 21st day of January, 1862, and all except Cook (who resides in Ohio) appeared and answered in the action. On the 29th day of December, 1862, and after proceedings had been commenced by the plaintiff against the judgment debtor and his son, Theodore, for violating the injunction order, the defendants, without notice to the plaintiff, obtained from Judge Hastings a modification of the injunction order, which he had originally granted, and this motion is made to set aside the order of modification.

On the argument, the defendants insisted that section 324 of the Code authorized the modification of an injunction granted *ex parte*, without requiring notice to the plaintiff, and cited *Bruce* agt. *Del. & Hud. Canal Co.*, (8 *How.*, 440,) but the plaintiff claimed that the case quoted could not be sustained, as it was entirely inconsistent, and would make section 225 a mere nullity, which was never intended by the framers of the Code—that section 324 was only intended to apply to the various orders arising in the progress of a suit, while section 225 was a special enactment, applicable to provisional remedies, citing *Mills* agt. *Thursby*, (1 *Code Rep.*, 121.)

J. F. Peck, *plaintiff in person, for the motion.*
Geo. F. Danforth, *opposed.*

E. Darwin Smith, Justice. I do not think the order of Judge Hastings, modifying the injunction issued in this case, properly made. It was not made till more than a year had elapsed after its service upon the defendants or some of them, and not till after all of them, except Cook, had appeared and answered in the cause. If section 324 applied to injunction orders, I don't think it will justify the order made in this instance. That section was designed to allow a judge who had hastily or improvidently granted an order, to rectify the error if applied to *immediately*, and before any steps are taken in the action. It was not intended to give an unlimited right to vacate orders granted *ex parte*. It is very rarely, indeed, when a judge should modify an injunction *ex parte*. I did it in one instance, when it had not been served upon all the parties, and before appearance, and when I thought it was improperly used or abused, but I doubted much and still do the general right to modify an injunction order, without notice to the parties. Important rights depend upon them, and they should not be allowed or vacated without care. When an injunction order has been allowed, and the same has been served, and the parties in the suit have appeared and taken steps in the action, and acquiesced in the injunction order, as in this instance, I do not think the county judge or judge of this court should modify the injunction; and I go further—I do not think he has any authority to do so, within the spirit and intent of the sections 225 and 324 of the Code, or that it was ever intended to confer any such power. If this order had been granted by myself, or any other judge of this court, I should deem it my duty to set it aside as improvidently granted, if not unwarranted. I cannot sanction any such practice on the part of any judge, either of this court or of the county court. If application had been made to Judge HASTINGS immediately on the service of this injunction, and it appeared that the injunction was improvidently granted, or too extensive, and he had modified it, and it appeared that such modification was right and worked no injustice, I do not think the court would interfere with the order upon the single ground of irregularity, but it would look at the merits of the modification, and affirm it if proper.

I regard the present motion as in the nature of an appeal from this order of Judge HASTINGS, and that I am called upon to see whether it ought in fact to have been entertained and made *ex parte*. I think it was clearly improper to grant it without notice, and for that reason shall direct that it be set aside, and the original injunction order reinstated, and if the defendants think proper, they may apply to the court upon motion for such modification as may be just.

SUPREME COURT.

Hewit agt. Mason.

In a complaint for *slander*, where the words charged were, "nothing ails him but the pox; he is rotten with it, he got it," &c., *held* that the words are actionable *per se*.

If the allegations of *special damage* by reason of the words spoken are not sufficiently *specific*, the objection cannot be raised by *demurrer*; the remedy is by motion under the Code, (§ 160.)

Demurrer to the complaint. The words charged were, "nothing ails him but the pox: he is rotten with it, he got it," &c.

J. Covill, *for plaintiff*.
J. S. L'Amoreaux, *for defendant*.

Bockes, Justice. Demurrer to the complaint. The action is slander. The plaintiff states in his complaint, that he is twenty-two years of age, and unmarried; that in February, 1862, he was ill, whereupon the defendant falsely and maliciously charged him with having an infectious disease, known as *lues venerea*, by reason of which he was injured in his good name and business, and excluded from the society of his friends and neighbors, to his damage of $2,000, for which he demands judgment. The defendant interposed a general demurrer, and insists that the words are not actionable *per se*, and that no special damages are alleged.

Blackstone, in speaking of words which, upon their face, and according to common acceptation, import such defamation as will, of course, be injurious, includes those which may exclude the person of whom they are spoken from society, as to charge a person with having an infectious disease. (3 *Black. Com.*, 123, 124.) It is laid down in *Com. Dig.*, that words are actionable which charge an infectious disease—as to say of a person, he has the leprosy, plague, &c.; and very many cases are there cited, in which it was held slanderous to charge a person with having the disease known as *lues venerea*. (*Com. Dig.*, *Act. Def. D.* 28.) In a note to *Blackstone*, it is said, there are only three disorders which the law deem it slanderous to report that a person labors under, viz: the plague, the leprosy and the *lues venerea*. The cases are numerous in England in which charges of the latter disease have been decided slanderous. There are one or two cases holding an adverse doctrine, but Ashhurst, J., in speaking of them, said they were loosely reported, unintelligible and not to be relied on. Many of the English cases are cited by Mr. Justice Mason, in *Williams* agt. *Holdridb*, (22 *Barb.*, 396,) quite enough to sustain the remark that the law is well settled in England, and has been for centuries, that it is actionable to charge a person with having the *lues venerea*. Mr. Starkie remarks: "actions for words of this description seem, in the absence of special damage, to have been confined to charges of leprosy and *lues venerea*," and he adds, "it seems, however, that though the reason has in some degree ceased to operate, an action will, even at this day, be sustainable for a charge of either of the diseases alluded to." (*Stark. on Slan.*, 114.) This rule obtains in several of our sister states.

It has been said in many cases that words, to be actionable *per se*, must impute a crime involving moral turpitude punishable by indictment. This general language will be found in several reported cases, and, indeed, in some of the text-books. But, when used, it was with reference to a charge of criminality.

This general observation should be considered as applicable to the class of cases where some charge of a criminal nature is made, and admits of the exception spoken of by Judge Woodworth in *Burtch* agt. *Nickerson*, (17 *John.*, 217.) He says, "the general rule is well settled, that slanderous words are not actionable unless the charge, if true, will subject the party charged to an indictment for a crime involving moral turpitude, or subject him to an infamous punishment. The exceptions to the general rule are words spoken of a person *in his office, profession or trade, or which impute to him an infectious disease.*" This exception or qualification should be understood as applying to the general statement of the rule in *Wright* agt. *Paige*, (36 *Barb.*, 438.)

The case of *Williams* agt. *Holdridge*, (22 *Barb.*, 396,) is directly in point. It is there settled that the rule of law in the English courts obtains in our own state. It must, therefore, be deemed as settled on authority, that words are actionable *per se*, which charge a person with having the infectious disease known as *lues venerea*. The reason of the rule is stated by Judge MASON, in the case last cited. The words, to be actionable, however, must be spoken in the present tense, and impute a continuance of the malady. The averments in the complaint that the plaintiff is aged twenty-two and unmarried, are of no value as a matter of pleading. Those facts may possibly be competent matters of evidence, but if so they could be proved on the trial under the material allegations of the complaint. Whether the plaintiff is twenty-two years of age or eighty, married or unmarried, does not determine the right of action, although such facts might be very proper matters of consideration on the question of damages. On this question, his age and social condition may be of some importance.

But if the words charged are not actionable *per se*, the complaint alleges special damage resulting from their utterance by the defendant.

The complaint states that by reason of the speaking of the words, the plaintiff was injured in his good name and business, and excluded from the society of his friends and neighbors, to his damage of $2,000. The injury to his business and exclusion from society are damages of a special character. Perhaps the plaintiff should have been more specific; certainly he should as to the charge in regard to the injury to his business; but this objection cannot be raised on demurrer. The remedy of the defendant was by motion, under section 160 of the Code of Procedure.

Judgment must be ordered for the plaintiff on the demurrer, with costs; but with liberty to the defendant to withdraw the demurrer and answer the complaint within twenty days after service of a copy of the order, on payment of the costs of the demurrer, to be adjusted by the clerk of Saratoga county.

COURT OF APPEALS.

The People *ex rel.* Andrew J. Hackley agt. John Kelly, Sheriff, &c.

The first article, § 6 of the Constitution, which says, "no person shall be compelled, in any criminal case, to be a witness against himself," does not protect a witness, in a criminal prosecution against another, from being compelled to give testimony which disgraces him or tends to convict of a crime, if he has been protected by statute against the use of his testimony on a trial against himself.

December Term, 1861.

The relator was committed to prison by the court of general sessions of the peace of the city and county of New York, on the 23d of April, 1861, for a contempt of court in refusing to answer, before the grand jury then empanneled in that court in a matter pending before them against certain aldermen for feloniously receiving a gift of money to influence their votes in an official capacity, the following question, viz: "What did you do with the pile of bills received from Thomas Hope, and which he told you amounted to over $40,000?" Hackley alleged, that when the interogatory was propounded, that any answer which he could give to that question would disgrace him, and would have a tendency to accuse him of a crime.

He demurred to the question, referred to the common law rule that no man is held to accuse himself, and to the sixth section of the first article of the Constitution. The grand jury came into court before the recorder, where Hackley attended and made complaint of his contumacy. The court decided that the question was a legal and proper one, and that the reasons offered by Hackley were insufficient, and ordered him to answer it; he still contumaciously refusing, the court adjudged him guilty of a criminal contempt, and committed him to prison in the county jail for thirty days. Hackley applied on *habeas corpus* to be discharged from custody. The general term of the supreme court decided that there was no evidence before them of a want of jurisdiction or authority to pronounce the decision which the court of general sessions did pronounce, and there was no irregularity or defect on the face of the commitment. The writ of *habeas corpus* must be discharged, and the prisoner remanded to the custody of the sheriff. (*See* 21 *How. Pr. R.*, 54.)

From this decision the relator appealed to this court.

James T. Brady and Amasa J. Parker, *for appellant.*
John H. Anthon, *for respondent.*

Denio, Justice, after reviewing the question and deciding that the contempt was committed in the presence of the court, although the refusal to answer was before the grand jury, said: There seems, therefore, to be nothing to preclude us from examining the main question, whether the relator could lawfully refuse to answer the interrogatory put to him. The bribery act of 1853 declares the giving to or receiving money, &c., by any of divers public officers named, including any member of the common council of a city, with a view to influence their action upon any matter which may come officially before them, an offence punishable by fine and imprisonment in a state prison. For the purpose of enabling the public to avail itself of the testimony of a participator in the offence, the fourteenth section provides as follows: "Every person offending against either of the preceding sections of this article shall be a competent witness against any other person so offending, and may be compelled to appear and give evidence before any magistrate or grand jury or in any court, in the same manner as other persons; but the testimony so given shall not be used in any prosecution or proceeding, civil or criminal, against the person so testifying." (*Ch.*, 539.) A similar provision is found in an act to amend the charter of the city of New York, passed in 1857. The fifty-second section relates to bribes of the members of the common council and the officers of the corporation, making the giving and the receiving of bribes highly criminal, and concluding with an enactment substantially similar to the fourteenth section of the act of 1853. The design was to enable either party concerned in the commission of an offence against the act to be examined as a witness by the grand jury or public officer entrusted with the prosecution. The question to be determined is, whether these provisions are consistent with the true sense of the constitutional declaration, that no person shall be compelled, in any criminal case, to be a witness against himself. (*Art.* 1, § 6.)

The primary and most obvious sense of the mandate is, that a person prosecuted for a crime shall not be compelled to give evidence on behalf of the prosecution against himself in that case. It is argued that no such narrow and verbal construction could have been in the view of the authors of the article, for the reason that no such atrocious procedure, as that supposed, has been tolerated in civilized countries in modern times. But constitutional provisions are not leveled solely at the evils most current at the times in which they are adopted; but while embracing these, they look to the history of the abuses of political society in past times and in other countries, and endeavor to form a system which shall protect the members of the state against those acts of oppression and misgovernment which unrestrained political or judicial power are always and everywhere most apt to fall into. (*See the observations of Chief Justice* SPENCER *on this subject, reported in* 18 *Johns.*, 202.) The history of England in early periods furnishes abundant instances of unjustifiable and cruel methods of extorting confessions; and the practice at this day in the criminal tribunals of the most polished countries in continental Europe, is to subject an accused person to a course of interrogatories which would be quite revolting to a mind accustomed only to the more humane system of English and American criminal law. It was not, therefore, unreasonable to guard by constitutional sanctions against a repetition of such practices in this state; and it is not at all improbable that the true intention of the provision in question corresponds with the natural construction of the language. But there is great force in the argument that constitutional provisions devised against governmental oppressions, and especially against such as may be exercised under pretence of judicial power, ought to be construed with the utmost liberality, and to be extended so as to accomplish the full object which the author apparently had in view, so far as it can be done consistently with any fair interpretation of the language employed. The mandate, that an accused person should not be compelled to give evidence against himself, would fail to secure the whole object intended, if a prosecutor might call an accomplice or confederate in a criminal offence, and afterwards use the evidence he might elicit to procure a conviction on the trial of an indictment against him. If obliged to testify on the trial of the co-offender to matters which would show his own complicity, it might be said upon a very liberal construction of the language, that he was compelled to give evidence against himself, that is, to give evidence which might be used in a criminal case against himself. It is perfectly well settled, that when there is no legal provision to protect the witness against the reading of the testimony on his own trial, he cannot be compelled to answer. (*The People* agt. *Mather*, 4 *Wend.*, 229, *and cases there referred to.*) This course of adjudication does not result from any judicial construction of the constitution, but is a branch of the common law doctrine which excuses a person from giving testimony which will tend to disgrace him, to charge him with a penalty or forfeiture, or to convict him of a crime. It is, of course, competent for the legislature to change any doctrine of the common law; but I think they could not compel a witness to testify on the trial of another person to facts which would prove himself guilty of a crime without indemnifying him against the consequences, because I think, as has been mentioned, that by a legal construction, the constitution would be found to forbid it.

But it is proposed by the appellant's counsel to push the construction of the constitution a step further. A person is not only not compellable to be a witness against himself in his own cause, or to testify to the truth in a prosecution against another person when the evidence given, if used as his admission, might tend to convict himself if he should be afterwards prosecuted; but he is still privileged from answering, though he is secured against his answers being repeated to his prejudice on another trial against himself. It is no doubt true that a precise account of the circumstances of a given crime would afford a prosecutor some facilities for fastening the guilt upon the actual offender, though he were permitted to prove such account upon the trial. The possession of the circumstances might point out to him sources of evidence which he would otherwise be ignorant of, and in this way the witness might be prejudiced. But neither the law nor the constitution is so sedulous to screen the guilty as the argument supposes. If a man cannot give evidence upon the trial of another person without disclosing circumstances which will make his own guilt apparent, or at least capable of proof, though his account of the transactions should never be used as evidence, it is the misfortune of his condition and not any want of humanity in the law. If a witness objects to a question on the ground that an answer would criminate himself, he must allege, in substance, that his answer, if repeated as his admission on his own trial, would tend to prove him guilty of a criminal offence. If the case is so situated that a repetition of it on a prosecution against him is impossible, as when it is forbidden by a positive statute, I have seen no authority which holds or intimates that the witness is privileged. It is not within any reasonable construction of the language of the constitutional provision. The term "criminal case," used in the clause, must be allowed some meaning, and none can be conceived other than a prosecution for a criminal offence. But it must be a prosecution against *him;* for what is forbidden is, that he should be compelled to be a witness against himself. Now if he be prosecuted criminally touching the matter about which he has testified, upon the trial of another person, the statute makes it impossible that his testimony given on that occasion should be used by the prosecution on the trial. It cannot, therefore, be said, that in such criminal case he has been made a witness against himself by force of any compulsion used towards him to procure, in the other case, testimony which cannot possibly be used in the criminal case against himself. I conclude, therefore, that the relator was not protected by the constitution from answering before the grand jury.

A similar question has been before the former court of chancery and the late court of errors. By the usury act of 1837, it was made a criminal offence to take usurious interest, and by a provision of the same act, a plaintiff in an action at law, brought on a contract alleged to be usurious, might be examined by the defendant as a witness to prove the usury, and the alleged usurer was likewise obliged to answer a bill of discovery on oath; but it was provided that neither the testimony so given, nor the sworn answer of the defendant in chancery, should be used against the party who had so testified or answered, either before the grand jury or on the trial of an indictment. (*Ch.*, 430.) In *Perine* agt. *Striker*, (7 *Paige*, 598,) the defendant had demurred to the plaintiff's bill, which was filed to enjoin proceedings at law on a note alleged to be usurious, and which required a discovery of the usury by the defendant's oath. The chancellor considered the statutory provision that the answer should not be used against the party before the grand jury, or on the trial of an indictment against him, as an answer to the objection taken, on the ground now under consideration; but the case was decided against the plaintiff on another ground. The case of *Henry* agt. *The Bank of Salina*, (5 *Hill*, 323; *S. C. in the supreme court*, 1 *id.*, 555,) approaches very near to a judgment of the court of errors upon the precise point. On the trial, the defendant had offered to call the real plaintiff to prove the usury in an action at law, pursuant to the act of 1837, though the plaintiff on the record was another person, who had no interest in the demand. The main question was, whether one for whose benefit the action was brought, but who was not the plaintiff on the record, was within the scope of the statute. The supreme court held he was not; and hence, that not having the protection of the statute, he could not be compelled to prove himself guilty of a misdemeanor. The judgment, which was for the plaintiff, was reversed in the court of errors, where it was held that a plaintiff in interest was within the statute, and that the supreme court had committed an error in not compelling the plaintiff to be sworn. Such a decision of course assumed that the statute requiring the plaintiff to be sworn was constitutional, on the ground that it afforded a sufficient protection to the plaintiff, who was thus compelled to be a witness. This would be entirely conclusive upon the point now under discussion, but for the fact first mentioned by the chancellor, that the case did not disclose whether the usury, on account of which the defendant sought to avoid the note, had been actually taken, or only secured to be taken. If the latter was the case, he held that the usurer would not be indictable, as the section of the statute creating the criminal offence applied only to those who actually received the usurious premium. No protection would be required in such a case; at all events the constitution would not stand in the way. But the learned chancellor added: "In the case now under consideration, I think the witness was compelled to testify, he being the real plaintiff, even if he had received a portion of the usurious premium, so as to subject him to indictment under the act of 1837; and provided he was not the real plaintiff, but a mere witness, he was bound to testify if he had made a usurious contract merely, without having actually received the usurious premium." None of the other members of the court spoke particularly of the point now in question; but the case, if not a precise authority, shows at least considerable weight of judicial opinion in favor of the judgment of the supreme court in the present case. My conclusion is, that both the judgments appealed from ought to be affirmed. All the judges concurring,

Judgment affirmed.*

* NOTE.—It will be seen that the court of appeals take a more liberal view of the constitutional provision in question in this case, than the general term of the supreme court. The latter court took the ground that this constitutional protection did not apply to a witness unless the prosecution was against himself. In other words it did not apply to a *witness*, but merely to a *party defendant*. The court of appeals, however, say: "If (the witness is) obliged to testify on the trial of the co-offender to matters which would show his own complicity, it might be said, upon a very liberal construction of the language (of the Constitution), that he was compelled to give evidence against himself, that is, to give evidence which might be used in a criminal case against himself."

Again, the court say: "The common law doctrine excuses a person from giving testimony which will tend to disgrace him; to charge him with a penalty or forfeiture, or to convict him of a crime. It is, of course, competent for the legislature to change any doctrine of the common law; but I think they *could not compel a*

SUPREME COURT.

F. M. St. John agt. Orin Beers.

Where the action was upon *promissory notes* assigned to the plaintiff, and *for goods sold*, *held*, that the plaintiff might properly allege in his complaint that, on his "information and belief," the notes were executed by the defendant, and on his "information and belief," the goods were sold to the defendant.

Albany Special Term, December, 1862.

The complaint set forth three separate causes of action: 1st. A note payable to E. L. B., or bearer, made by defendant and assigned to Plaintiff.

---

witness to testify on the trial of another person to facts which would prove himself guilty of a crime, without indemnifying him against the consequences, because, I think, as has been mentioned, that by a legal construction, the constitution would be found to forbid it."

Why would the constitution forbid it? Evidently because the constitutional provision is declaratory of the rule of the common law in criminal cases. Therefore, the court hold, that any statute which would violate this rule, *without indemnifying the witness against the consequences*, would be unconstitutional. The *violation* of this constitutional rule by the legislature, then, is made to depend upon a *condition*. If the *condition* is inserted at the time the statute is passed, which would otherwise violate the constitution, it is held to be no violation. Now, is there any provision in the *constitution* that its mandate for the protection of a witness shall not apply, if this or any other condition is inserted in a statute compelling the witness to testify against himself in a criminal case? Not any. Every witness, in a criminal case, by the common law, is excused from giving testimony which will tend to disgrace him, to charge him with a penalty or forfeiture, or to convict him of a crime; and by the decision of this court, this common law principle cannot be changed absolutely by the legislature without violating the same principle in the constitution. Now, in the passage of these bribery and other similar acts of the legislature, is not the common law rule as to witnesses as completely changed as though no indemnity to them for the consequences was inserted in the acts? The violation of the constitution consists in compelling a witness *to give his testimony;* the indemnity may not be sufficient to protect him from the consequences of such violation. Take the question of *disgrace*, for instance: how is an exoneration from a criminal trial to restore the witness to the standing and favor he was in, before being compelled to testify? The simple question appears to be, has the legislature power to deliberately change the common law and violate the constitution as to the privilege of witnesses in criminal cases, by attempting to protect them from such violation? If they can do so in one case, why can they not violate any constitutional provision, where personal rights are involved, by assuming to protect the subject from such violation? Rep.

2d. A note payable to J. W. H., or bearer, made by defendant and assigned to plaintiff.

The plaintiff stated, on his *information and belief*, that the defendant executed these notes, &c.

The 3d count was for goods sold and delivered by plaintiff to the defendant, upon the *information and belief* of plaintiff, on which the plaintiff claimed a balance.

The defendant moved to strike out the words, "information and belief," wherever they occurred; also to make the complaint more certain by stating the time when the notes were assigned, and the time of the sale of the goods, and the kind of goods, with costs of motion.

C. V. R. Ludington, *for the motion.*

A. C. Niven, *opposed.*

Hogeboom, Justice. The plaintiff has very properly stated the making of the two notes on his "information and belief." They being payable to other persons and assigned to him, he could properly only state the making of them on his "information and belief."

There is no objection to stating the sale of the goods on "information and belief," as they may have been sold by his clerk or agent, and not by himself personally; and as to the time of sale and the specific articles sold, it was not necessary to make a motion for that purpose, as an application for the particulars of plaintiff's demand would have attained the object.

Motion denied, with ten dollars costs.

SUPREME COURT.

PETER O'HARA, respondent agt. STEPHEN B. BROPHY, appellant.

The allowance or refusal of *costs* in actions for the *strict foreclosure of mortgages*, is in the *discretion of the court*.

Where the *notice* prescribed by § 131 of the Code has not been served, it does not deprive the court of the power in equity cases to *award costs* for unreasonably defending, against defendants upon whom a copy of the *complaint* has been served.

It is not necessary to the *commencement* of any action that a copy of the *complaint* be served upon the defendant; he is brought into court by the *summons alone*.

Where the *jury*, on conflicting evidence in a justice's court, found that the defendant (an attorney at law,) put in an answer for the plaintiff in an action for strict foreclosure, *without authority* from the plaintiff,

Held, that there being evidence to sustain the finding of the jury, and the evidence against it not so preponderant as to create the conviction that it must have preceded from passion, prejudice, corruption or palpable mistake, the verdict must be sustained.

Brooklyn General Term, February, 1863.

IN May, 1860, an action for a strict foreclosure was brought by James Wood, in which action the plaintiff was joined as defendant. The plaintiff and his then co-partner, Peter McLaughlin, held a mortgage subsequent to the one in suit and upon the same premises. They were therefore made parties defendants, with the usual allegations that no personal claim is made against these defendants.

When the process was served upon Mr. O'Hara he took it to D. P. Barnard, Esq., of Brooklyn, for advice, and was then and there advised that no defence could be successfully interposed by him.

He then took the papers and met Mr. Brophy, to whom he handed them with instructions to see the plaintiff's attorneys and ascertain if they would pay him anything upon the mortgage, agreeing to give Brophy one-third of all that was made by the settlement, at the same time informing him that he would not defend, or would have "no law."

Brophy called on plaintiff's attorneys, and being unable to effect a settlement, he prepared and served upon the plaintiff's attorneys an answer in behalf of Peter McLaughlin and Peter O'Hara, which purported to have been sworn to by Mr. O'Hara.

The verification to the answer purported to have been made before R. J. Todd, a commissioner of deeds in Brooklyn.

Mr. O'Hara swears positively that he never swore to a paper in the case; that he never took an affidavit or swore to one of any kind before R. J. Todd; that he not only never authorized defendant to put in an answer in the case, but repeatedly forbade him doing so. Brophy did not produce the original answer upon the trial, although notified to do so.

The plaintiff's attorneys saw Mr. Brophy and informed him that unless he withdrew the answer they would apply, when the case should be reached and tried, for a judgment against the defendants, McLaughlin and O'Hara, for costs for unreasonably defending the foreclosure suit. Brophy firmly refused to withdraw his answer unless plaintiff would pay him a fee for so doing, which plaintiff declined to do.

The cause was placed upon the special term calendar in New York city, and remained there until June term, 1861, when it was called in its order and tried.

Brophy did not appear, nor did any one appear in behalf of McLaughlin or O'Hara.

Judgment was then taken for a strict foreclosure, and that the defendants, McLaughlin and O'Hara, pay costs for unreasonably defending the case.

Brophy did not inform O'Hara of the fact that the suit was on the calendar, nor that a defence was put in.

Nor did Mr. O'Hara know anything of it until an execution was presented to him by the sheriff of Kings county. Mr. O'Hara paid the amount of judgment ($166.33) and $9 sheriff's fees.

This action was brought in a justice's court by the plaintiff to recover the amount paid in said suit, caused by disobedience of the defendant.

The jury found a verdict for the plaintiff for the said amount ($175.38).

The above facts, substantially, appeared upon the trial.

An appeal was taken to the county court and the judgment affirmed.

S. B. Brophy, *defendant in person*.

1. Plaintiff brought this action against defendant "for unreasonably defending an action wherein he appeared without authority, and unskillfully conducted the defence." He failed to prove either of these averments.

The Wood suit, being the action referred to, was for a strict foreclosure of several mortgages. No relief was asked, personally, against the defendants.

No notice of object of action was served with the copy complaint in the foreclosure suit, under section 131 of the Code.

2. There being no impeachment of defendant's witnesses, he is entitled to the benefit of his uncontradicted testimony. (*Newton* agt. *Pope*, 1 *Cow.*, 109; 3 *E. D. Smith*, 121.)

3. O'Hara had a legal right to put in the answer and defend that action without any liability for costs.

From the terms of the agreement, Brophy had a right to put in an answer.

4. The answer was shown to be in plaintiff's possession, yet he refused to account for it on the trial.

For the purpose of this action, it makes no difference whether the answer was sworn to by the plaintiff or not; if it was put in with his consent, that concludes him.

The plaintiff having retained the defendant and served an answer, and then having stayed his proceedings, plaintiff is not entitled to any remedy against the defendant. It would be otherwise if defendant was not stayed and had neglected to defend the action.

5. The justice erred in refusing to charge the jury as requested.

The verdict is against law and fact on the evidence. Judgment should be for defendant. (*Code*, § 366.)

"Wherever the finding of a jury or referee is clearly against the body of evidence, although there be some evidence to support it, a new trial will be granted. (6 *Barb.*, 141; *Thompson* agt. *Manck*, 22 *How. P. R.* 431; *Dobson* agt. *Arnold*, 10 *How. P. R.*, 528; *Tracy* agt. *Hartman*, 1 *Hilt.* 350.)

The plaintiff did not prove any cause of action.

H. C. PLACE, *for plaintiff.*

1. This court will only review the questions raised by the grounds in the notice of appeal from the justice's court to the county court. (2 *Sand. S. C. R.*, 632; 15 *Howard*, 32; 16 *Howard*, 18; 16 *Howard*, 471; 14 *Howard*, 307; 6 *Abbott*, 183.)

2. While the court will throw around its officers a shield of protection in the discharge of those honest and legitimate acts which are peculiarly the duties of an attorney, it will at the same time guard the community with a like protection against the improvident, negligent, or dishonest acts of attorneys.

The evidence was conflicting, and the jury having passed upon it, this court will not review their findings upon questions of facts. (15 *Wendell*, 490; 21 *Wendell*, 305; 3 *Hill*, 75; 18 *Barbour*, 347; 22 *Barbour*, 134; 1 *E. D. Smith*, 318.)

3. There was only one exception taken upon the trial which is open to review, and that is the exception to the judge's refusal to charge the jury as requested. It is now well settled by authorities in this state that the justice is

not bound to charge the jury at all, and if he does charge, is only bound to charge correctly so far as he goes.

At all events, the county judge has well said, that there is no error in the justice's refusal to charge in this case. (12 *Abb.*, 44.)

By the court, SCRUGHAM, Justice. Actions for the strict foreclosure of mortgages are not among those mentioned in section 304 of the Code, in which costs are allowed of course, but their allowance or refusal in such actions is in the discretion of the court. (*Code*, § 306.)

The provision that a defendant upon whom the notice prescribed by section 131 is served, shall pay costs if he unreasonably defend the action, does not deprive the court of the power in equity cases to award costs for unreasonably defending against defendants upon whom a copy of the complaint, but no such notice, has been served.

It is not necessary to the commencement of any action that a copy of the complaint be served upon the defendant; he is brought into court by the summons alone. In equity cases this gives him no information of the cause of action or of the nature of the relief sought against him; a copy of the complaint would afford it, but as the complaint may be, and in such cases generally is, voluminous, the notice is provided as a short substitute calculated to convey to the defendant all the information necessary to acquaint him with the nature and object of the action, and of the extent to which his rights will be affected by it, and upon which a defendant, against whom no personal claim is made, may safely determine whether it will be necessary for him to take any proceedings in the action.

The complaint furnishes this information more fully than the notice, which is nothing more than an abstract of it, and it is not necessary to serve the notice in case a copy of the complaint is served with the summons; for it would certainly be as improper for a defendant in that case unreasonably to defend the action as it would be if, instead of a copy of the complaint, a notice of the object of the action had been served upon him, and the court, exercising its discretion in the awarding of costs, would doubtless award them against him in the one case as freely as in the other.

The justice therefore was right in refusing to charge that O'Hara and McLaughlin, as defendants in the action for strict foreclosuse, had a right to defend it without any personal liability to costs.

No costs would have been awarded against the present plaintiff in the foreclosure suit if the answer had not been interposed, and the jury have found that the answer was put in by the defendant as attorney for the plaintiff, without authority from him.

Upon this question there was conflicting evidence; and in passing upon the verdict of a jury in a justice's court, the question with us is not whether the evidence would lead us to the same conclusion, but only whether there is any evidence to sustain the finding of the jury, and if so, whether the evidence against it is so preponderant as to create the conviction that it must have proceeded from passion, prejudice, corruption or palpable mistake.

As there is no such extreme preponderance in this case, the verdict must be sustained, and the judgment of the county court affirming the justice's judgment should be affirmed.

ERRATA.

The case of *Brown* agt. *Weber*, *ante*, *p.* 306, was decided at Broome General Term, January, 1861—BALCOM, CAMPBELL and PARKER, Justices.

In *Jurgensen* agt. *Alexander*, *ante*, *p.* 259, in the case and head note, for the words "erased or liberated, read "erased or *obliterated*."

In *Klen* agt. *Gibney*, *ante*, *p.* 32, for the words "*The Duchess of Magazine*," read "*The Duchess of Mazarine*."

SUPREME COURT.

PETER G. FOX, executor, &c. of ARCHIBALD FOX, deceased agt. LAWRENCE M. FOX.

Where an application for an *extra allowance* of costs under § 309 of the Code, has been made after trial, and *denied*, on the ground that it was not a difficult *and* extraordinary case; and after a *second trial* a like application is made, the first order denying the application is no *bar* to the second application, where the facts and circumstances on the second trial are *materially different* from those on the first trial.

Where a case has been litigated on the trial on both sides, with unusual pertinacity, by distinguished counsel, and occupying an unusually long period, without appearing to have been unnecessarily protracted—the examination of a large number of witnesses, and difficult questions of law and evidence, raised and discussed, and the recovery of a large amount *in favor of the defendant*, it comes within the plain meaning and intent of § 309 of the Code, in being both *difficult and extraordinary*, and an extra allowance will be granted.

Saratoga Special Term, July, 1862.

MOTION by defendant for an extra allowance of costs, under section 309 of the Code. The facts sufficiently appear in the opinion of the court.

HENRY C. ADAMS, *for the motion.*
PHILO GRIDLEY, *opposed.*

BOCKES, Justice. Motion by the defendant for an extra allowance of costs under section 309, Code.

The case has been twice tried. On the first trial the defendant recovered, on the report of a referee, $2,123.71 damages, besides costs.

On appeal, the judgment was reversed and a new trial ordered. The case was again tried before another referee, who has reported in favor of the defendant, and against the plaintiff, as executor, for $1,862.24. It is not denied that the defendant is entitled to the ordinary taxable costs against the plaintiff as executor, as a matter of course, without motion or application to the court. (22 *How. Pr. R.*, 453; 14 *How. Pr. R.*, 481; 4 *Sandf.*, 719.) Nor is it denied that a further or extra allowance for costs may be made by the court, in its discretion, in a case prosecuted by an executor or administrator, too, in which the defendant recovers.

But it is urged: *first*, that a similar motion in this case was denied, (22 *How. Pr. R.*, 453;) and *secondly*, that the case is not "difficult and extraordinary," within the provision of section 309.

After the first report in this action was delivered, an application was made to the court for an extra allowance; the motion was denied. The facts on which it was based, and its ultimate decision, will be found in the case cited, (22 *How.*, 453.) That decision would be conclusive of this motion, were this grounded on the same facts. But this motion is materially different from the former, as regards the facts on which the application is founded, in many important particulars. Since the former motion was made, the pleadings have been amended and new issues formed. Numerous motions and various proceedings have been made and taken, for which there is no adequate compensation prescribed by the fee bill. A second protracted trial has been had, and, as the papers show, an immense amount of labor has been performed, in the conduct of the cause, since the new trial was ordered. Indeed, in no aspect of the case can it be fairly or justly said, that this motion stands on the same footing as did the former one. Such former motion cannot, therefore, be interposed as a bar to this application.

Secondly. Is the case, as presented by the papers on this motion, "difficult and extraordinary," within the provision of section 309?

As a general rule the courts have inclined to a very liberal construction of these terms; in many instances a construction quite too liberal to accord with the plain purpose and intent of the statute. All the cases, I believe, assume to proceed on the ground that it was the intent of the legislature to confer upon the court the power to give an additional sum as costs in difficult and extraordinary cases, when a trial has been had, as a compensation or indemnity for the performance of unusual duties and services in the conduct of the cause.

So it has been held that the term "difficult and extraordinary" should be deemed to apply to the nature of the action, and the mode of prosecution and defence, with a view of affording to the prevailing party compensation for extraordinary labor and unusual expense. In this view, the case before me is obviously both difficult and extraordinary.

Few cases have ever fallen under my observation in which so great an amount of labor has been performed as in this. The case has been litigated on both sides, with unusual pertinacity. Distinguished counsel were employed, who labored assiduously, and, as I must infer, from their high professional character, with no purpose to complicate or enhance in importance a simple and ordinary case.

The last trial occupied an unusually long period of time, nor is it suggested that it was unnecessarily protracted. Many witnesses were examined, and difficult questions of law and evidence were raised and discussed. The recovery is for a larger amount in favor of the defendant.

If this case does not come within the plain meaning and intent of section 309, in being both difficult and extraordinary, it is impossible, I apprehend, to conceive of any that will.

The motion must be granted. An order allowing the sum of $75, for extra costs, may be entered.

COURT OF APPEALS.

JAMES SHEPHERD, plaintiff in error agt. THE PEOPLE, defendants in error.

A *law* which makes an act punishable *in a manner in which it was not punishable when committed,* or *which increases the punishment with which the act was punishable when committed,* is *ex post facto* and *void.*

The plaintiff in error was convicted of *arson in the first degree,* committed in 1857, which, under the Revised Statutes, was punishable with *death,* and was sentenced under the act of 1860, which substituted *imprisonment for life* for the punishment of death, to imprisonment in the state prison for life.

Held, that the provisions of the act of 1860, changing the *punishment* of arson in the first degree, were intended to apply only to offences *thereafter committed;* but if it should be held otherwise, then that those provisions are *ex post facto* and *void,* so far as they were intended to apply to a *crime* of arson in the first degree, committed *before the passage of the act.* In either view of the act and upon either holding, the judgment of the court below must be *reversed.*

Where a judgment against a prisoner is reversed upon the *ground alone that a wrong judgment was given,* upon a lawful and regular trial and conviction, he cannot constitutionally be *tried again:* he must be *discharged.*

(*This law would seem to fully meet and settle Mrs. Hartung's case; for although there was no bill of exceptions in this case, and there was one in her case, yet the judgments in both cases were reversed on the ground alone that there was a wrong judgment given. It is difficult to see how the court can look into a bill of exceptions when there is a wrong judgment brought up by the record, and the error being created by a statutory law.*—REP.)

September Term, 1862.

SUTHERLAND, J. When the crime of which the prisoner was convicted was committed, it was punishable with death. The prisoner was sentenced to imprisonment in the state prison, at Sing Sing, for life. The prisoner must have been sentenced on the theory that the provisions of the act of April 14, 1860, substituting imprisonment for life, for death, as the punishment of arson in the first degree, were intended to apply not only to an offence committed after that act took effect, but also to the offence of which the prisoner had been convicted, committed in 1857, before the passage of the act.

The first section of the act of 1860 declared, that no

crime thereafter committed, except treason and murder in the first degree, shall be punished with death in this state. The second section makes two degrees of the crime of murder, defining them. The sixth section declares that every person convicted of murder in the second degree, shall be sentenced to imprisonment in one of the state prisons for life. By the seventh section it is declared that section one, of title one, of chapter one, of part four of the Revised Statutes, shall be amended so as to read as follows:

"Section 1. Every person who shall hereafter be convicted, first, of treason against the people of this state; or second, of murder.; or third, of arson in the first degree, as those crimes are respectively declared in this title, shall be punished as herein provided."

The first section of title one, of chapter one, of part four, of the Revised Statutes, thus amended, originally read thus:

"Section 1. Every person who shall hereafter be convicted, first, of treason against the people of this state; or second, of murder; or third, of arson in the first degree, as those crimes are respectively declared in this title, shall suffer death for the same."

By the 9th section of the act of 1860, it is declared that the provisions of the act "for the punishment of murder in the first degree, shall apply to the crime of treason; and the punishment of murder in the second degree, as herein provided, shall apply to all crimes now punishable with death, except as herein provided." The 10th section is: "All persons now under sentence of death in this state, or convicted of murder and awaiting sentence, shall be punished as if convicted of murder in the first degree under this act." The eleventh and last section of the act repeals section 25, and eleven other sections of the title of the Revised Statutes before referred to—section 25 being the section which prescribed the manner of executing capital punishment by hanging. The other repealed sections contained certain regulations in respect to the execution of capital punishment in certain cases, or under certain circumstances.

It is perfectly plain that the legislature, by the act of 1860, intended to punish crimes of arson in the first degree thereafter committed, with imprisonment in a state prison for life; for section 6 of the act provides that punishment for murder in the second degree; and section 9 declares that the punishment of murder in the second degree "as herein provided, shall apply to all crimes now punishable with death, except," &c.; and arson in the first degree was then by the Revised Statutes punishable with death.

The prisoner was sentenced under the act of 1860, and upon a construction of that act that the provisions of the act changing the punishment for arson in the first degree from death to imprisonment for life, were intended to apply to a crime of arson in the first degree, committed before the passage of the act, and when the provision of the Revised Statutes punishing the crime with death was in full force. I doubt whether such is the true and reasonable construction of the act. What particularly distinguishes the question in this case from that in the case of *Hartung* agt. *The People*, (22 *N. Y. R.*, 95,) is, that by the 10th section of the act, it is expressly declared, that all persons then under sentence of death, or convicted of murder and awaiting sentence, should be punished as if convicted of murder in the first degree under the act. This section applied to Mrs. Hartung's case. She was under sentence of death for murder when the act of 1860 was passed. The question was whether she could be punished under the act; and it was held that she could not; that so far as the act attempted to subject to the new punishment of death and previous imprisonment at hard labor, persons who had been convicted of murder, it was *ex post facto* and void. The act does not expressly declare that the provisions of the act changing the punishment of arson in the first degree should apply to offences committed before the passage of the act. In the absence of express words showing an intention that these provisions should be retroactive, it is not to be presumed that they were intended to be so. (2 *Dwarris on Statutes*, 540; *Tillman* agt. *Lansing*, 4 *John.*, 45; *Dask* agt. *Van Bleek*, 7 *John.*, 477; *Johnson* agt. *Burrell*, 2 *Hill*, 238; *Lawrence* agt. *Miller*, 2 *Comst.*, 245.) Certainly, it is not to be presumed that the legislature intended to pass an unconstitutional *ex post facto* law, and if the provisions of the act changing the punishment of arson in the first degree should be construed to apply to offences committed before the act, it will hereafter be shown that it must also be held that, so far, it was *ex post facto* and unconstitutional.

The first section of the act is exclusively and expressly prospective. The words are "no crime hereafter committed," &c. I find nothing in the subsequent provisions of the act except, perhaps, the 11th section, repealing certain sections of the Revised Statutes, regulating the execution of capital punishment, going to show, that the provisions of the act changing the punishment of arson in the first degree were intended to be retrospective. The fact that the 10th section expressly declares, that persons who were then under sentence of death, or convicted of murder and awaiting sentence, should be punished as if convicted of murder in the first degree under the act, certainly goes to show that the provisions of the act preceding the 10th section were intended to be prospective merely. The 10th section would probably not have been inserted in the act if the preceding provisions of the act had been intended to be retroactive.

The passage of the act of April 17, 1861, reviving and undertaking to re-apply the punishment for murder and for arson in the first degree, in force at the time the act of April 14, 1860, was passed, to offences committed previous to the day that act took effect, certainly does not show that the act of 1860 was not intended to have a retrospective operation; but the passage of the act of April 17, 1861, must certainly be deemed a conclusive legislative construction of the act of 1860, to the effect that that act presently abolished or repealed the provisions of the Revised Statutes prescribing the punishment of murder or of arson in the first degree, so that the prisoner (who was sentenced prior to the passage of the act of April 17, 1861) could not have been sentenced to suffer death under the provisions of the Revised Statutes in force when his crime was committed, whatever may be deemed to be the force or effect of the act of 1861. Nor does it follow that the provisions of the act of 1860, changing the punishment of arson in the first degree to imprisonment for life, should be construed as intended to have a retrospective operation, if that act should be deemed to have repealed the provisions of the Revised Statutes punishing that crime. If the legislature, by the act of 1860, carelessly or unintentionally repealed the law punishing the prisoner's crime, that is no reason why reasonable and well-settled principles of construction should be disregarded, for the purpose of punishing it under that act. If the act of 1860 presently repealed the provisions of the Revised Statutes prescribing the punishment of death for arson in the first degree, and the provisions of the act of 1860, changing that punishment to imprisonment for life, were intended to apply only to offences thereafter committed, the consequence was, that the prisoner's crime was left without any law to punish it. (*Dwarris*, 676, 677; *State* agt. *Daley*, 29 *Conn.*, 272; *and cases cited by Judge* DENIO *in the case of Mrs. Hartung.*)

As the prisoner was sentenced before the passage of the act of April 17, 1861, considering that the first section of the act of 1860 was expressly prospective, that there are no words of express repeal in the act, except the 11th section, that the words of the 7th section are: "section 1, of title 1, &c., of the Revised Statutes, shall be amended," &c.,

I think the question was, whether the prisoner could not have been sentenced under the provisions of the Revised Statutes, in force when his crime was committed, upon the construction of the act of 1860, that it did not repeal the provisions of the Revised Statutes as to offences committed before its passage; that the amendment by the 7th section, and the other provisions of the act changing the punishment of arson in the first degree, were intended to apply only to offences thereafter committed, leaving offences committed before the passage of the act to be punished under the Revised Statutes. If the legislature had expressly declared that the amendment, by the 7th section, was to apply only to offences thereafter committed, such, I think, would have been the construction and effect of the act. I think the question was, from the whole act, whether that was not its reasonable construction, in the absence of any such express declaration. Certainly, my doubt would have been, independent of the act of 1861, whether it could properly be said, that the act of 1860 does repeal the provisions of the Revised Statutes, punishing treason, murder and arson in the first degree, except so far as the act, by the 10th section, attempts to apply the new punishment under the act, of imprisonment for at least one year previous to the execution of the death penalty, to persons then under conviction for murder, and except so far as the 11th section expressly repeals the sections of the Revised Statutes regulating the manner of the execution of the death penalty, &c.

In *State* agt. *Daley*, (29 *Conn.*,) before cited, it would appear from the report of the case, that section 6 of the act prescribing the original punishment, was not only altered, but expressly repealed by the new act. So in most, if not all, of the cases cited by Judge DENIO, in *Mrs. Hartung's* case, except that of *Commonwealth* agt. *Devane*, (1 *Binney*, 601,) the original act was expressly or plainly impliedly repealed by the subsequent act prescribing the new punishment or penalty, and the case of *Commonwealth* agt. *Devane*, I think was wrongly decided.

No doubt the act of April 17, 1861, was passed upon the careless assumption that this court, in *Mrs. Hartung's* case, had decided that the act of 1860 had repealed the provisions of the Revised Statutes punishing treason, murder and arson in the first degree, and that offences committed previous to the passage of the act of 1860 could not be punished under it; when, as I think, that the only point that can be said to have been decided in that case was, that so far as that act attempted by the 10th section to subject to the new punishment of death and previous imprisonment at hard labor, persons already under conviction for murder, it was *ex post facto* and void. The act of 1861, having been passed upon an erroneous assumption, has increased the doubts and complications resulting from the extraordinary act of 1860, and one might be almost excused for thinking that both acts were mainly designed to punish judges who should unfortunately be called upon to construe and apply them. But the question presented by the record in this case is, not whether the prisoner might have been sentenced under the provisions of the Revised Statutes to suffer death, or whether, if the judgment should be reversed, and the court can and should award a new trial, and he should be tried and convicted again, he could be sentenced to suffer death under the Revised Statutes, or the act of 1861, or both; but the question presented by the record is, whether the sentence to imprisonment for life, which was pronounced upon him under the act of 1860 was legal. I think it was not, because, for reasons before stated, I think the provisions of the act changing the punishment for arson in the first degree to imprisonment for life must be deemed to have been intended to apply only to offences committed after the act should take effect.

If, however, the provision of the act changing the punishment of arson in the first degree should be held to have been intended to apply to offences committed before the passage of the act, in my opinion, so far the act should be held to be *ex post facto* and void.

I think this is shown conclusively by Judge DENIO in his opinion in the *Hartung* case; but I will add, that a law which increased the punishment with which an act was punishable when committed, would be plainly *ex post facto*, although it might be said, perhaps, that the new law did not change the manner of the punishment, as for instance, if when the act was committed, it was punishable with thirty days' imprisonment, and the new law declared that it should be punished with forty days' imprisonment; for, as to the number of days' imprisonment by which the punishment was increased, the case would be precisely the same as if the act when committed had not been punishable at all, and under the new law the criminal could not be sentenced to any less number of days than were prescribed by it.

So, also, if an act when committed was punishable by thirty days' imprisonment, a subsequent law changing the punishment of the act to thirty stripes or thirty dollars fine, would be plainly *ex post facto;* for, when the act was committed, it was not punishable in that manner, and in view of the constitutional prohibition of *ex post facto* laws, the case would be precisely the same as if the act had not been punishable at all when committed. If you do not hold a law punishing an act in a different manner than it was punishable when committed to be *ex post facto*, irrespective of the question whether the new punishment is or is not more merciful or lenient, you will leave it to the discretion of the legislature or of judges to say whether the new punishment is or is not more merciful or lenient than the old; and such a construction of the constitutional prohibition would impair its value and certainty of protection.

A law, the effect of which is simply to reduce or diminish the punishment with which an act was punishable when committed, cannot be an *ex post facto* law, because it inflicts no new or additional punishment. In *Fletcher* agt. *Peck*, (6 *Cranch*,) Chief Justice MARSHALL defined an *ex post facto* law to be one which makes an act punishable "in a manner in which it was not punishable when committed." Add to this, "or which increases the punishment with which the act was punishable when committed," and I think the definition will be as complete, and certain, and safe, as can well be made.

It is plain, then, that the moral or philosophical disquisition as to whether imprisonment for life, at hard labor, is better or more desirable, or less severe than death, has really nothing to do with the question whether the act of 1860, assuming that it was intended to have a retrospective effect, is so far *ex post facto* or not. Imprisonment for life, at hard labor, is an entirely different kind or manner of punishment from punishment by death. The act of 1860 entirely changed the punishment for arson in the first degree. It changed it from death to imprisonment for life; the two punishments have no elements in common. If it should be held that the act of 1860 merely diminished the punishment wherewith the prisoner's crime was punishable when committed, because imprisonment for life, at hard labor, is generally considered a more lenient punishment than death, or one which the criminal would prefer to suffer; then it could be held that a law changing the punishment of an act from imprisonment for a certain number of days or months to a fine, or from a certain number of stripes to imprisonment for a certain number of days, was not *ex post facto*, because the court might think the new punishment more lenient than the old, or that the criminal would prefer to suffer the new punishment. Indeed, as I have before said, if you depart from the principle that a law is *ex post facto*, because it punishes the offence in a different manner, or by a different kind of punishment than it was punishable with when committed, the question whether the law is *ex post facto* is left to judicial discretion;

for the decision of the question must depend upon the opinion of judges as to whether the new punishment is more severe than the old, or whether the new punishment would or would not generally be preferred by criminals to the old.

The construction of constitutional limitations should be left as little as possible to either legislative or judicial discretion.

My conclusion is, then, that the provisions of the act of 1860, changing the punishment of arson in the first degree, were intended to apply only to offences thereafter committed.* But if it should be held otherwise than that, those provisions are *ex post facto* and void, so far as they were intended to apply to a crime of arson in the first degree, committed before the passage of the act. In either view of the act, and upon either holding, the judgment of the court below must be reversed.

But an important question remains to be considered, which is, ought this court, upon reversing the judgment, to order a new trial or the discharge of the prisoner? In looking at this question, I think we must assume that the prisoner, if a new trial is ordered, might be sentenced to suffer death under the Revised Statutes or the act of April 17, 1861, or both, if he could be lawfully tried again, and was tried and convicted. For we must assume that no opinion that this court might now express upon the question, whether if the prisoner should be again tried and convicted he could be sentenced to suffer death, would prevent such sentence; that question not being raised by the record before us.

Section 24 of the article of the Revised Statutes relating to writs of error on judgments, and *certioraris* in criminal cases, (2 *Rev. Stat.*, 741, § 24,) provides, "if the supreme

* As to this point, DENIO, Ch. J., was of a contrary opinion. SELDEN, J., expressly reserved himself upon the point, and none of the other judges expressed an opinion.—*Reporter Court of Appeals.*

court (upon a writ of error) shall affirm such judgment, it shall direct the sentence pronounced to be executed, &c. If the supreme court shall reverse the judgment rendered, it shall either direct a new trial, or that the defendant be absolutely discharged."

There was no bill of exceptions in this case; but if there had been, it is very clear that if the supreme court had reversed the judgment upon the ground that a wrong sentence had been pronounced, that court could not have directed the general sessions to proceed and pronounce the proper sentence. By the statute the supreme court, on reversing the judgment, could only grant a new trial or absolutely discharge the prisoner.

Upon reversing the judgment, this court must either direct a new trial or the discharge of the prisoner; it cannot direct any other judgment to be given on the conviction. This would have been so, had there been a bill of exceptions *a fortiori* where there is none.

Previous to the law giving a defendant in a criminal case a right to a bill of exceptions, (2 *Rev. Stat.*, 738, § 21,) a new trial could not be granted on the merits by any court in any case of felony. (*The People* agt. *The Judges of Dutchess Oyer and Terminer*, 2 *Barb.*, 286; *The People* agt. *Comstock*, 8 *Wend.*, 549, *and authorities there cited.*)

But by the common law a new trial could be granted in a case of felony, when there had been a *mis-trial* relating to the regularity of the organization of the court, or of the impanneling of the jury, or, perhaps, conduct of the jury.

Thus in *Arundel's* case, (6 *Coke*, 14,) where the defendant had been tried by a jury returned from a certain city, instead of a certain parish, and had been convicted, and moved in arrest of judgment, on that ground, it was adjudged that the jury ought to have come in from the parish and not the city, and that the trial was insufficient, and a new *venire* was awarded to try the issue again.

So in the case of the *People* agt. *McKay*, (18 *John.*, 212,) where the defendant was indicted, tried and convicted of murder, and moved in arrest of judgment, on the ground that the *venire* which had been issued was a nullity, and the court adjudged that it was a nullity, a new trial was ordered.

In his opinion in this case, Ch. J. SPENCER refers to a case as having occurred within his knowledge, where the defendant was tried and convicted of murder, and a new trial was granted, on the ground of the misconduct of the jury in separating after agreeing and before rendering their verdict. So in *Cancemie's* case, (18 *N. Y.*, 128,) since the Revised Statutes, where the defendant, with his own consent, was tried and convicted by a jury consisting of but eleven jurors, the judgment was reversed and a new trial ordered. There was a bill of exceptions in this case, but the judgment was reversed and a new trial ordered on the record alone.

In all these cases the new trial was awarded on the ground that there had been no lawful trial; on the ground of irregularity in the impanneling, or conduct, or organization of the jury, and on the record alone.

In the principal case the indictment was sufficient; the court at which the defendant was tried was a court of competent jurisdiction; the jury was regularly impanneled, and rendered a lawful verdict; and the judgment, if reversed, must be reversed upon the record alone, and upon the ground alone that a wrong judgment was given upon a lawful and regular verdict; and the question is, whether, in such a case, the court should order a new trial? In view of the provision of the Revised Statutes, above referred to, expressly authorizing the court, upon reversing the judgment, to either direct a new trial, or that the prisoner be discharged, I think the court should not direct a new trial if the prisoner could plead his former regular trial, and conviction in bar of another trial. The circumstance that the counsel of the prisoner, on moving in arrest of judgment, also asked for a new trial, I regard as of no consequence. The constitutional provision is, "No person shall be subject to be twice put in jeopardy for the same offence." (*Constitution of State, art.* 1, § 6.) This provision may be considered as addressed to courts; and if the prisoner is within its protection, he ought to be discharged, though his counsel did personally ask for a new trial. The question is, then, whether the prisoner, if the judgment is reversed upon the ground alone that a wrong judgment was given upon a lawful and regular trial and conviction, can constitutionally be tried again? It is clear to me that he cannot. In the case of *The People* agt. *Taylor*, (3 *Denio*, 97,) Judge Bronson said: "If a wrong judgment be given against a defendant, which is reversed on error, (there being no bill of exceptions,) the court of review can neither give a new judgment against him, nor send the case back to the court below for a proper judgment;" (*citing The King* agt. *Brown*, 7 *Add. & Ell.*, 58; *Sheppard* agt. *Commonwealth*, 2 *Metc.*, 419; *Christian* agt. *Commonwealth*, 5 *id.*, 530; *and The King* agt. *Ellis*, 5 *Barn. & Cress.*, 395.)

These cases fully establish the rule as stated by Judge Bronson. In the case of *O'Leary* agt. *The People*, (4 *Park. Crim. R.*, 187,) where the prisoner was regularly tried, and the jury rendered a verdict which would have authorized a judgment as upon a conviction for a simple assault and battery, but did not authorize the judgment that was rendered, as upon a conviction for felony, the supreme court upon reversing the judgment, on writ of error, discharged the prisoner, referring to Judge Bronson's opinion in *The People* agt. *Taylor*.

These cases are probably sufficient to show that a new trial should not be directed in this case; but in view of the provision of the statute which was not referred to either in *People* agt. *Taylor* or the case last cited, and in view of the great importance of the question in this case not only, but in other capital cases in which the question has arisen, since the act of 1860, I shall examine the question further. In 1st *Inst.*, 391, *a.*, it is said: "The difference between a man attainted and convicted, is, that a man is said convict before he hath judgment, as if a man be convict by confession, verdict or recusance; and when he hath his judgment upon the verdict he is said to be attaint." It is further said: "By a conviction of a felon, his goods and chattels are forfeited; but by attainder, that is, by judgment given, his lands and tenemants are forfeited, and his blood corrupted, and not before." So in *Jacobs' Law Dict.*, (*Attainted*,) it is said: "Attainder of a criminal is larger than conviction; a man is convicted when he is found guilty or confesses the crimes before judgment had, but not attainted till judgment is passed upon him." This shows the technical common law definition of the word *convict* or *convicted;* a felon was convicted by the verdict of a jury, he was attainted by the judgment rendered on the verdict.

One would think from this common law definition of the word convict or convicted, that by the common law the plea of *autrefois* convict implied merely a regular trial and verdict of guilty, or a confession upon a sufficient indictment. I think the books show this was so. In *Daly's* case, (4 *Coke*, 40,) one Wetherel brought an appeal against Darby of murder; the defendant pleaded not guilty, and was found guilty of homicide, and had his clergy; and afterwards was indicted for murder, and he pleaded his former conviction in the appeal at the suit of the party, and it was adjudged a bar, and thereupon he was discharged, "because a man's life should not be twice put in jeopardy for one and the same offence."

In *Vaux's* case, (4 *Coke*, 45,) it is said, "if a man is convicted either by verdict or confession upon an insufficient indictment, and no judgment thereupon given, he may be again indicted and arraigned, because his life was never in jeopardy, &c." This implies, if the indictment is sufficient, that the conviction is a bar, though no judgment is given upon it. The same case shows that a lawful conviction by verdict on an insufficient indictment, followed by a judgment, is a bar to a second trial until the judgment is reversed. *Hawkins* (*P. C. Book* 2, *ch.* 36, § 10,) says: "The plea of *autrefois* convict seems chiefly to depend on the reason that the party ought not to be brought twice into danger for the same crime; upon which ground it seems agreed that a conviction, upon an appeal or indictment, of burglary or other felony may be pleaded to an indictment or appeal for the same felony." Again, he says, (§ 15, *same ch.*,) "But it seems clearly settled that whenever the record on which a man is convicted of manslaughter, and admitted to his clergy, on an indictment or appeal of murder, is erroneous either in respect of insufficiency in the indictment, or for a mis-trial, so that his life was not in danger at the trial, he cannot plead such conviction and clergy thereon in bar of a second indictment or appeal."

Blackstone says, (4 *Black. Com.*, 336,) citing *Hawkins:* "The plea of *autrefois* convict, or a former conviction for the same identical crime, though no judgment was ever given, or perhaps ever will be, (being suspended by the benefit of clergy or otherwise,) is a good plea in bar."

Chitty says: "In order to plead this plea (*autrefois* convict) with effect, the crime must be the same for which the defendant was before convicted, and the conviction must have been lawful on a sufficient indictment. And if he has neither received sentence nor prayed the benefit of clergy, this plea is said not to be pleadable if the former indictments were invalid." (1 *Chitty Crim. L.*, 462.)

In the case of the *People* agt. *Barrett*, (2 *Caines Rep.*, 304,) where the prisoner had pleaded to the indictment, the jury been sworn and evidence offered, and the public prosecutor, without the prisoner's consent, had withdrawn a juror, because he was unprepared with his evidence, it was held that the prisoner could not afterwards be tried on the same indictment. Held, that he might be tried on another indictment for the same offence, in 1 *John. R.*, 66, where it appeared that the first indictment was defective.

In the case of the *People* agt. *Casborus*, (13 *John.*, 351,) it was held that the former indictment and trial was no bar where the judgment had been arrested, but this was upon the ground that it was presumed that the judgment was arrested upon the ground that the indictment was defective.

In *State* agt. *Benham*, (7 *Conn.*, 414,) where the judgment was suspended, it was held that the verdict constituted the bar.

In *State* agt. *Merrell*, (2 *Serg.*, 24,) that the verdict was a bar when the judgment was improperly arrested upon a good indictment.

In *Dyer* agt. *Commonwealth*, (23 *Pick.*, 404,) there was a special verdict which did not authorize the judgment entered on it, and the judgment was reversed, and the prisoner discharged.

In the *People* agt. *Goodwin*, (18 *John.*, 202,) Ch. J. SPENCER said that the rule that no person shall be subject for the same offence to be twice put in jeopardy of life or limb, meant that no man shall be twice tried for the same offence.

The prisoner, James Shepherd, having been regularly and lawfully tried, and convicted on a good indictment, and there being no bill of exceptions, the authorities leave no room for doubt that he is entitled to the protection of this common law and constitutional rule.

In *Mrs. Hartung's* case there was a bill of exceptions, and there was a new trial ordered. It must be conceded that the judgment was not reversed on the bill of exceptions, but it is not probable that the question whether the prisoner should be discharged or a new trial ordered was much considered in that case.

My conclusion is, that the judgment against the prisoner, James Shepherd, should be reversed, and he should be discharged.

DENIO, Ch. J., SELDEN, WRIGHT and ALLEN, JJ., concurred.

SUPREME COURT.

William Radley, appellant agt. Robert Fisher and another, administrators, respondents.

Where a claim against *executors* or *administrators* is *referred* under the Revised Statutes, and the report of the referees is adverse to the plaintiff, and in favor of the defendants, (executors or administrators,) they are entitled to *costs* against the plaintiff, *as in an action under the Code.*

In such cases, it is *irregular* to *enter judgment* upon the report without *an application to the court.*

The amount of such costs are those given by the Code in an *action* between party and party, prosecuted and defended in accordance with the provisions of the Code. The provision of the Revised Statutes, authorizing the court to adjudge costs as in actions against executors, is in *full force.*

Erie General Term, September, 1862.

Marvin, *P. J.*, Davis, Grover and Hoyt, *Justices.*

Appeal from order of special term that defendants recover their costs and disbursements, as in an ordinary action in that court.

C. Henshaw, *for plaintiff.*

Peck & Willetts, *for defendants.*

By the court, Marvin, P. Justice. The claim of the plaintiff against the defendants as administrators, was referred under and in pursuance of the Revised Statutes, (*vol.* 2, *p.* 88–9, §§ 36, 37.) The report of the referee was adverse to the plaintiff and in favor of the defendants; and the question is, what costs and disbursements the defendants are entitled to against the plaintiff? The Revised Statutes, *supra*, authorize the court to set aside or confirm the report of the referees and "adjudge costs," as in actions against executors. The next three sections provide for actions in cases where the claim is disputed or rejected, and not referred, or where the claim has not been presented in time; and then § 41 provides that in such suit no costs shall be recovered against the defendants; nor shall any costs be recovered in any suit at law against any executors or administrators, to be levied of their property or of the property of the deceased, unless, &c. These provisions relate to actions against executors, except the provision in § 37, empowering the court to adjudge costs as in actions against executors.

By the Code, (§ 317,) the law relating to costs in actions, prosecuted or defended by executors, &c., is somewhat changed. It is declared that "whenever any claim against a deceased person shall be referred, pursuant to the provisions of the Revised Statutes, the prevailing party shall be entitled to recover the fees of referees and witnesses, and other necessary disbursements, to be taxed according to law."

This provision is imperative in favor of the prevailing party.

In *Avery* agt. *Smith*, (9 *How. Pr. R.*,) it was decided, in view of the provision of the Code just cited, that the defendants were only entitled to the fees of referees and other necessary disbursements; that this provision had changed the law. In *Van Sickler* agt. *Graham*, (7 *How.*, 208,) it was held that the reference was not an action within the definition of the Code, and that the defendants, administrators, were not entitled to costs under the general provisions of the Code; that they were, by the Code, entitled to recover the fees of referees and witnesses, and other necessary disbursements. The court waived the consideration of the question whether the defendants were entitled to costs, according to the old fee bill of the Revised Statutes.

In *Boyd* agt. *Bigelow*, (14 *How.*, 511,) decided in this district, it was necessarily decided that such a reference was not an action, as understood and defined by the Code, but a proceeding, in which it was necessary to apply to the court for judgment upon the report of the referees. The question of costs was not up in the case.

In *Linn* agt. *Clow*, (14 *How.*, 508,) there was a reference under the statute, and the claimant recovered against an administrator; and upon an application to the court to confirm the report, and for costs, Justice HARRIS came to the conclusion that the claim of the plaintiff had been unreasonably resisted or neglected, and awarded costs to be taxed against the defendant, and he held that the costs were the costs given by the Code in an ordinary action.

In *Munson* agt. *Howell*, (20 *How.*, 59,) the administrators defeated the claim and had a report in their favor, and it was held that they were entitled to costs against the plaintiff, as in an action under the Code. This was a general term decision in the 7th district. I have come to the conclusion that the decisions touching costs, in the two last cited cases, were correct. It is supposed by the counsel for the defendants in this case, that it was decided in *Munson* agt. *Howeli* that the proceedings were an action, so that the provisions of the Code relating to costs *in actions* necessarily applied. I do not so understand the decision. It is true that the defendants had their costs adjusted by the clerk, and entered up judgment upon the report, without application to the court. The plaintiff only appealed from the *adjustment* of costs. He made no motion so set the judgment aside for irregularity. As the court were of the opinion that the defendant was entitled to costs as in an action, the adjustment was affirmed. I make this explanation, as I have no doubt the proper practice is to apply to the court for judgment upon the report, and that it is irregular to enter judgment without such application to the court. We shall, in this district, adhere to the practice as indicated in *Boyd* agt. *Bigelow*, *supra*. Let us again turn to the statutes. As we have seen, by the Revised Statutes, "the court may set aside the report of the referees, or appoint others in their places, and may confirm such report and adjudge costs, *as in* actions against executors."

In *an action* against executors or administrators, costs were not given, of course; but the statute contained some special limitations; hence if there be a recovery now against the executors, &c., in one of these cases of reference under the statute, the question of costs must be determined in the light of the special limitations, as in *Linn* agt. *Clow*, *supra*, except so far as the Code has modified the statutes, to be hereafter noticed. When the claimant failed, and there was a report against him, he was *always* liable to pay costs, as in an action, and the court had the power to adjudge them, and I suppose always did so, as the special restrictions relating to costs were applicable only to executors or administrators in actions *against* them. From this view it follows that the claimant or plaintiff, who is defeated in these reference cases, must pay costs, and the question has been started, what costs? Justice BARCULO, in *Van Sickler* agt. *Graham*, *supra*, decided that the administrator could not recover the costs given in an action under the Code, and declined to decide whether he was entitled to the costs according to the old fee bill. In my opinion he was wrong. The costs are those given by the Code in an *action* between party and party, prosecuted and defended in accordance with the provisions of the Code. The provision of the Revised Statutes authorizing the court to adjudge costs, as in actions against executors, is in full force.

Now, in actions against executors, as I have already said, the plaintiff failing in his action was liable for costs, of course, and those costs were such as the statutes existing at the time had fixed for costs between party and party. The statutes relating to costs have been frequently changed, and new fee bills established, and the costs, in these reference cases, have followed these changes. The Code has made an additional change in the items of costs, and we must resort to it to ascertain how much and what the defeated party to a reference, under the Revised Statutes, is liable to pay, as the costs are to be those "in an action against executors."

I have spoken of a modification made by the Code of the

system of costs in these cases. It is found in the clause in §317, herein above quoted, viz: "Whenever any claim against a deceased person shall be referred pursuant to the provisions of the Revised Statutes, the prevailing party shall be entitled to recover the fees of referees and witnesses, and other necessary disbursements, to be taxed according to law." The effect of this provision is, that now the claimant, plaintiff, will, where the report is in his favor, recover these items of costs without any regard to the fact whether the claim was "unreasonably resisted or neglected." (*See opinion of* HARRIS, *Justice, in Linn* agt. *Clow*, 14 *How.*, 510.) As I have already shown, the plaintiff failing was always liable to pay costs, including, of course, the fees of referees, &c.; hence the word "*prevailing*," before "party," was unfortunately used. It should have been the plaintiff or claimant, leaving the executor, &c., to his full claim for costs when he succeeded.

Justice C. L. ALLEN was embarrassed with this provision of the Code, inserted as an amendment, and held that no costs could be allowed except those mentioned in this clause. He does not remark upon the word *prevailing*, but he expressed the opinion that the intention was to exclude all other costs. This conclusion must have been reached by supposing that the clause in question repealed the provision of the Revised Statutes touching the power of the court to adjudge costs in these reference cases. If such effect is to be given to this clause, it must be by *implication* only, and I am unwilling thus to repeal an important provision of the statute. It is not necessary, nor was it, as I think, so intended by the legislature.

The order appealed from in this case must be affirmed with $10 costs.

SUPREME COURT.

PETER G. FOX, executor, &c. of ARCHIBALD FOX, deceased agt. LAWRENCE M. FOX.

An *attorney* has a *lien* on the *judgment* obtained by him for his client, to the extent of his claim for *services and disbursements* in the action, whether the amount of his compensation is *agreed upon or depends upon a quantum meruit.*

The attorney is entitled to such a *sum* as shall have been *agreed upon* between him and his client; and the *lien* will attach to the judgment to *the extent of the amount thus agreed upon.*

Payment of the judgment to any other person after notice of the lien, will be of no avail against the attorney's right *to enforce it for the amount of his claim.*

When there is a *dispute* as to what the *contract is*, or in regard to the *amount* which the attorney is entitled to *demand under it*, and also when the amount of compensation is by express agreement made *to depend on the value of the services, and unliquidated*, the remedy of the attorney is by *direct action* against all the parties. There cannot be a *compulsory reference* on these questions. The case of *Haight* agt. *Holcomb*, (16 *How. Pr. R.*, 173,) settles this point.

Saratoga Special Term, January, 1863.

MOTION made on an order that the plaintiff show cause why he should not pay to Henry C. Adams, the attorney and counsel for the defendant in this action:

1st. The amount of the defendant's taxed bill of costs and disbursements, as the same were entered in the judgment in this action, together with the interest thereon from the date of the judgment, (July 24, 1862.)

2d. The amount justly due to said Adams for his general services and disbursements rendered by him for his client, the defendant, as his attorney and counsel in this cause, as the same are specified or indicated in his bill against the defendant, a copy of which was served with the papers for this motion.

3d. Why the payment or satisfaction, if any has been made, of such judgment, should not be set aside and vacated to the extent of said Adams' claims and lien, referred to in said motion papers, and the said Adams, defendant's attorney, have leave to issue execution upon the judgment in this action for a sufficient amount to cover the claims and demands he holds against the said defendant, as stated in said motion papers, or for such other relief in the premises as the court shall see fit to grant.

In the 22*d How. Pr. R.*, 453, and 24 *How. Pr. R.*, 385, many facts appear, showing the nature and character of this suit, and the extent of labor, services and disbursements rendered by Adams as attorney and counsel for defendant in this cause.

The judgment referred to was entered July 24, 1862, upon the report of Geo. A. Hardin, Esq., sole referee upon the second trial, for $1,862.24, and for costs and disbursements, $681.83. This includes referee's fees, $187.75, and witnesses' fees, $72, paid by the defendant. On the 7th of October Adams was informed by the plaintiff that the defendant left that day at noon for Michigan, to reside there.

On the 8th of October, Adams served a written notice upon the plaintiff, claiming a lien on the judgment for his whole bill, and should look to the plaintiff to arrange the same with him, and that the plaintiff should not pay the amount of Adams' bill to any but him.

It also appeared that defendant was worth nothing except what was involved in this suit, and that he frequently promised to Adams that he should be amply rewarded for his services and disbursements out of the avails of the suit; and that upon those promises Adams rendered those services, and made the large advances of money to carry on the suit.

The defendant, in his affidavit, denies that he ever made such promises. This affidavit was taken before a notary public at Detroit, Mich., which the clerk certified as to the notary.

A preliminary objection was taken to it on the ground that it was not properly certified. (*See* 3 *R. S.*, 5*th ed.*, 677–8, (396) § 25.) This question was reserved and the affidavit was read on the motion.

Henry C. Adams, *for the motion.*

1. Upon the entry of the judgment the defendant's attorney became the equitable assignor of the judgment to the amount of his claims and demands for services and disbursements in this cause. (*See* Harris, *J.*, *Rooney* agt. *Second Avenue R. R. Co.*, 18 *N. Y. R.*, 371, *and cases there cited.*)

2. The costs in the judgment went to the defendant, not to his attorney. The Code, § 303, says in terms, that the party shall recover "certain sums by way of indemnity for his expenses, &c., termed costs."

The attorney's claims are of a different nature. They extend in every direction, for which the fee bill has made no provision, and for which he holds against his client and has a lien, not simply upon the costs in the judgment but upon the whole judgment for his entire bill. (*See* Harris, *J.*, *id.*, 370.)

How much his claims against his client shall be, depends upon the contingencies of the case, and the measure shall depend upon "the agreement, express or implied, of the parties." (*Code*, § 303; *See* Comstock, *J.*, 18 *N. Y. R.*, 373.)

3. If no express agreement be made, there is still an agreement which the law will imply from the nature of the case, for no party can foresee where his cause will go to; and no professional gentleman can foresee the extent of the services he must necessarily render. If the attorney has earned, by his labor and expenditures for his client, say $100, or half the amount of the judgment, or the whole of it, or more than the judgment, whatever may be the *quantum meruit*, there is an agreement that it shall be paid, even though no words pass, for the law implies it from the nature and extent of the services and disbursements. If words pass, fixing a stipulated sum, they shall be the restriction or limitation as to amount. If no words

pass, then the amount agreed upon, as the law implies, rests upon a *quantum meruit*. This is the plain import of § 303, and the fair construction of the decisions.

If the bill be the rates fixed by § 307, and the attorney has earned five times that bill, shall the attorney have no more than the bill? If so, then why was the term *implied* employed in § 303? (*See* COMSTOCK, *J.*, 18 *N. Y. R.*, 373.)

4. In this case the defendant, who was in indigent circumstances, repeatedly agreed with his attorney and counsel that he should be amply rewarded out of the avails of the suit, which was a large judgment. This is shown by the positive affidavit of the attorney, and is corroborated by various undisputed contemporaneous circumstances, and the defendant's attempt to deny such agreements should receive no countenance. Had the defendant failed in his precarious counter-claims, the attorney would have got nothing from the empty pocket of his indigent client.

Having won the cause, shall it be said, even in the absence of any words passed, that the attorney shall have only the $422, when he has expended more than half that for cash advances, besides enormous labor, not included in the bill?

If the attorney can recover more than the taxed bill upon a *quantum meruit*, in the absence of any words passed, it must necessarily be upon an implied agreement, and the law makes his lien co-extensive with it.

Such is the palpable meaning of § 303, and such is evidently the drift of the decisions. If not, then the word *implied* should be wiped out of § 303 as of no force, and only calculated to tantalize and mislead the profession.

5. This application is in the most essential respects like the case of *Rooney* agt. *The Second Avenue R. R. Co.*, (18 *N. Y. R.*, 368;) that was an application to protect the attorney's rights, so is this; there the judgment debtor was required to show cause, &c., so here; there the judgment creditor was not a party to the application, nor is he here;

there the court protected the attorney's rights, so it should here.

The only essential difference between the cases is, that there the amount was limited, here it rests upon a *quantum meruit*. There the plaintiff made an honest affidavit, tending to support the application; here the defendant makes one corruptly tending to defeat it.

The equities, too, of this case preponderate over all others, for the defendant has absconded, manifestly with intent to defraud his attorney and counsel of his pay for enormous labor and expenditures, (*see ante*, 24 *How.*, 410,) and the relations between the plaintiff and defendant go to prove that the plaintiff is a party to this corrupt combination to defraud the attorney out of his bill.

6. In such a case as this, with such circumstances as surround it, the attorney ought not to be put to any expensive, laborious or prolix action or proceedings to obtain his remedy. He should have it by this short and simple proceeding, as in the case 18 *N. Y. R.*, 368, and should not be compelled to earn a single dollar over again to get what is his due. The bill in this case is made up of specific items, and is proved *prima facie* to be correct and just, and an order should be made that the plaintiff pay it, or that the attorney be at liberty to issue execution for the amount, unless the plaintiff or defendant shall desire a reference to ascertain the correctness of the bill. Then the order should stand for the amount so reported due to the attorney. (14 *Abbott's P. R.*, 229.)

HENRY B. CUSHNEY, *opposed*.

This motion cannot be entertained for the following reasons:

1. The court cannot, on this motion, determine how much L. M. Fox is indebted to his attorney for services in this cause *exclusive of the taxable costs*. The defendant, L. M.

Fox, has an undoubted right to contest any pretended claim over and above the taxable costs, in the ordinary way, by *action;* and the court has no power to *order a reference* without his consent on this motion. (16 *How. Pr. R.*, 173.)

2. The attorney asks leave to issue execution on the judgment. His papers do not show the judgment satisfied, and a motion for that purpose is not necessary. This is an undoubted right he has, and this seems to me to dispose of the other proposition in the case, viz: That the plaintiff pay him the amount of his taxed bill of costs, as the same are entered up in the judgment.

3. The lien of the attorney in this case extends to the taxable costs as they appear on the judgment roll, and no further. (16 *How. Pr. R.*, 173, *&c.;* 18 *N. Y. R.*, 368, *&c.*)

The case of *Carpenter* agt. *Sixth Avenue R. R. Co.*, decided in the superior court of New York in March, 1862, I think reported in *Abbott's P. R.*, decides every question in this case against the attorney Adams.

The plaintiff offered to pay, before the service of the motion papers on him, the taxable costs to the attorney, amounting to over $400, which he refused to take. The money in his hands belonged to an estate which he represented as executor, and was paid over to the assignee of the judgment by direction of the surrogate—done to avoid accumulation of interest.

4. The only remedy of the attorney Adams is by action, and not by motion against this plaintiff.

The motion should be denied with costs.

Bockes, Justice. It is well settled now that an attorney has a lien on the judgment, obtained by him for his client, to the extent of his claim for services and disbursements in the action. To that extent he is to be deemed the equitable assignee of the judgment.

The law is so declared in *Rooney* agt. *The Second Avenue R. R. Co.*, (18 *N. Y. R.*, 368.) There are many other cases to the same effect in this court. (20 *How.*, 39; 16 *How.*, 160–173; 12 *How.*, 136; *see also* 9 *How.*, 16, *and* 14 *Abb.*, 229, *in N. Y. common pleas.*)

The lien exists, too, whether the amount of the attorney's compensation is agreed upon, or depends upon the *quantum meruit.* (*See above cases.*)

The question, then, is: What is the amount to which the attorney is entitled for services and disbursements? for when that is determined, the case is relieved from all difficulty as regards his lien.

1. The attorney is entitled to such sum or amount as shall have been agreed upon between him and his client. This was decided in *Rooney* agt. *The Second Avenue R. R. Co.*, *supra.* It was there held that the compensation and lien was a subject of agreement between the attorney and client, and might be more or less in amount than the allowance for services specified in the Code. Judge Harris says, that the effect of the Code is "to leave the attorney free to agree with his client for a greater or less amount than that which he may recover, according to circumstances." Judge Comstock says, in the same case, that since the Code the compensation of the attorney is left "to the agreement of the parties, express or implied." This being so, it follows, according to the above authorities, that the agreement, by determining the amount of compensation, also determines the extent of the attorney's lien. There can be no difficulty, then, in a case where the amount the attorney is to receive is agreed upon, and stands uncontradicted. He has a lien on the judgment for such amount, and may enforce it by taking the proper steps for that purpose. Payment of the judgment to any other person after notice of the lien will be of no avail against his right to enforce it for the amount of his claim.

2. An attorney is entitled, on a general retainer in a cause, without any agreement fixing the measure of his compensation, to be remunerated according to the allowance for

services and disbursements specified in the Code. This is decided in *Haight* agt. *Holcomb*, (16 *How.*, 173.) Perhaps this was not actually adjudicated in *Rooney* agt. *The Second Avenue R. R. Co.*, but the principle was advanced with the apparent approval of the court. Judge Harris (*page* 371) says: "In the absence of any agreement on the subject, I suppose the sum recovered by the party as an indemnity for his expenses would be the measure of compensation allowed to the attorney. This, then, would be the extent of his lien."

On this point, the two cases cited are not at all in conflict. On another point, it seems to me, they are not in entire consonance. Still, the former case is cited by Mr. Justice Harris, in his opinion in the latter case, without intimating any point of difference whatever. I think it plain, however, that the main question, decided in *Rooney* agt. *The Second Avenue R. R. Co.*, is in conflict with that part of the decision in *Haight* agt. *Holcomb*, whereby it is decided that the attorney's lien is in all cases restricted to or measured by the taxable costs. As was stated above, it may be more or less, in case the parties see fit to make an agreement in regard to the compensation; but it seems that the case of *Haight* agt. *Holcomb* is not overruled, in so far as it decides that the attorney's lien, in the absence of any agreement, is restricted to what appears as costs on the judgment roll. His general retainer raises an implied promise to pay the fair value of the attorney's services, which Judge Harris supposes would be the sum authorized by law to be recovered by the party as an indemnity for his expenses in the action.

3. If it be agreed between the attorney and client that the attorney shall be entitled to a fair and reasonable compensation beyond, or over and above the taxable costs, then the lien will attach to the judgment to the extent of the compensation thus stipulated for. This, I am aware, is in conflict with the decision of *Haight* agt. *Holcomb;* but I

understand this proposition to be maintained as sound law in the case cited in the court of appeals. (18 *N. Y. R.*, 368.) It is there distinctly stated that the attorney may agree with his client as to how much he shall receive for his services, and may thus fix beforehand the amount for which he shall have a lien upon the judgment when recovered. It was supposed by the court in *Haight* agt. *Holcomb*, that no lien could be maintained, because of the indefiniteness of the agreement as to the amount of compensation; and for the further reason that there was no short remedy by which the attorney could determine the amount of his lien. But there is no difficulty in settling the amount and in having it declared a lien on the judgment. If there be no short way of accomplishing this, there remains the usual way by direct action for that purpose. Indeed, this seems to me the true mode of proceeding, when there is a dispute as to what the contract is, or in regard to the amount which the attorney is entitled to demand under it, and also when the amount of compensation is by express agreement made to depend on the value of the services and unliquidated.

It was held in *Haight* agt. *Holcomb* that in case of dispute on these points, there could not be a compulsory reference.

The decision of that case in this regard has not been overruled. It is a general term decision in this court, and I am unquestionably bound by it. The New York common pleas held otherwise. (14 *Abbott*, 229.) But I must, at special term, follow the decision in our own court, made at general term, in preference to that.

There seems to be a difficulty in proceeding by motion to try matters in controversy between one of the parties to an action and his attorney. Those matters are not in issue in the cause, nor do they bear on the issues therein, nor do they relate at all to the practice or conduct of the cause as between the plaintiff and defendant. The proceeding, in all its material bearings, is by the attorney against his client; yet how is the client (the defendant in this case) before the court on this motion? The motion papers were not served on him, nor has he appeared on the motion. True, his affidavit is read, but it is read by and in behalf of the plaintiff. This motion is by the attorney in hostility to the interests of the client. It follows that he has a right to be heard, and I think he may insist on being heard in the usual mode, by which the rights of parties are determined. A claim is made against him as to what sum or amount he shall pay his attorney. If he admit his liability, in other words, if there be no controversy as to the terms of the contract, nor as to the amount he ought to pay under such contract, the difficulty might be settled on motion. Even if he had been served with the motion papers, as regards him, it would then be a motion to determine his liability, or, what is equivalent, a claim against him for services, by a reference without action. This cannot be done. An attorney can no more determine his claim for services by a reference without action, than could any other laborer for hire.

There is no difficulty in securing the lien by direct action for that purpose against all parties, and this is the course to be adopted when there is a controversy as to what the contract is, or in regard to the amount payable under it.

It follows from the above considerations that the motion in this case must be denied. In my judgment, the proper way for the attorney to proceed, with a view to a determination of the matters in controversy in a case like this, is by an action to determine the amount or extent of the lien, and have a decree declaring the judgment subject to the lien, and for liberty to issue execution therein for the amount due him by virtue of his contract with his client. Then issue may be framed and a trial had in a way to secure the rights of all parties.

An objection is made to the affidavit of the defendant, L. M. Fox, on the ground that it is not duly authenticated.

But I do not deem the objection of importance, for even if the affidavit should be excluded the motion should be denied, if I am correct in the conclusions at which I have arrived on the law and practice.

The motion will be denied without costs, and without prejudice to any action or other proceeding to attain the end sought by the motion.

I do not understand that there is any objection to paying the costs and disbursements taxed and included in the judgment, except the referee's and witnesses' fees, which were paid by the defendant himself and not by the attorney. Indeed, the plaintiff has offered to pay such costs and disbursements, and still holds the amount ready for the attorney whenever he will accept that amount. To this extent the plaintiff admits and recognizes the attorney's claims and lien. The motion was, of course, unnecessary as regards those costs and disbursements. I presume the attorney can have this amount by calling for it, or if payment should be refused he could issue execution therefor, without any order or application to the court.

Motion denied.

COURT OF APPEALS.

Edwards Pierrepont, executor of Alfred H. P. Edwards agt. Mary G. Edwards and others.

Construction of a will.—Where the testator, in the second section of his will, directed in these words: "That my executors pay out of the income of my estate to my wife $8,000 per annum, if I shall leave a child or children by her, so long as she shall live and remain my widow;" and then in the third section declared, "if there shall be no child or children, then I direct that my said executors do pay unto my said wife $7,000 per annum so long as she shall live and remain my widow, and pay the residue of the income of my said estate in equal portions unto my brother, John M. Edwards, my sister Frances, wife of William S. Hoyt, and my sister Henrietta, wife of Worthington Hooker;" and in the fourth section directed that in case he left a child or children, his entire estate should remain in trust for their benefit, until such children should arrive at majority, when it should be equally divided between them, "reserving in trust $8,000 per annum for my wife, so long as she lives and remains my widow," and he left no children;

And it appeared in evidence, that at the time of his death he supposed himself possessed of a clear income sufficient to pay the largest of the annuities bequeathed to his wife, and to have a surplus for the benefit of his brother and sisters, but owing to a depreciation of the estate, the income proved inadequate to pay the widow's annuity of $7,000,

Held, that the bequest to the wife, although *demonstrative* as pointing out the fund from which it was to be paid, *was not specific*, so that it failed or abated in consequence of the inadequacy of such fund; but was *general and payable at all events* out of the *corpus* of the estate.

Each case of this nature must depend upon a consideration of the material provisions of the will, and the extrinsic circumstances of the testator's family and estate, which may be fairly brought to bear upon the question of *intent*.

A separate and independent intention to bequeath a sum of money or an annuity at all events, will not be permitted to be overruled merely by a direction in the will, that the money is to be raised in a particular way or out of a particular fund.

The provision for his widow was the primary and most material portion of the testator's intent, while that for his brother and sisters was incidental and subordinate to that.

September Term, 1862.

THIS was an appeal from the judgment of the supreme court in the first judicial district, giving a construction to the will of the late Alfred H. P. Edwards.

That court decided that under the will the widow's annuity was payable only out of the income of his estate; and that the income having proved insufficient to pay it, she was not entitled to payment of the deficiency out of the body of the estate.

The facts appear sufficiently in the opinion of Chief Judge DENIO.

EDWARDS PIERREPONT, *for the executor.*

WM. BLISS, *for the defendants, Hooker and wife.*

A. W. BRADFORD and THOMAS H. RODMAN, *for Mrs. Edwards.*

DENIO, J. The only question which I think it necessary to consider in this case is, whether the bequest of the annuity of $7,000 a year to the testator's wife was specific in the sense that if it could not be paid out of the fund indicated, namely, the income of the trust estate, it was to fail or to abate in the proportion that the indicated fund should prove deficient; or on the other hand whether it was intended by the testator that it should be paid at all events—the income of his property given to the trustees being pointed out by way, as it is called, of demonstration. I am of opinion that the last mentioned construction is the one which we are bound to place upon the instrument. The authorities upon the question are very numerous, and the most prominent of them have been referred to by the counsel for Mrs. Edwards, the appellant. It will be seen by an examination of them that no positive rule of ready application to every case can be laid down, but that each case will depend upon a consideration of all the material provisions of the will to be construed, and of the extrinsic circumstances respecting the testator's family and estate, which may be fairly brought to bear upon the question of intent. The leading principle of the cases is, that when the testator bequeaths a sum of money, or which is the same thing, a life annuity in such a manner as to show a separate and independent intention that the money shall be paid to the legatee at all events, that intention will not be permitted to be overruled merely by a direction in the will that the money is to be raised in a particular way or out of a particular fund. (*Sir James Wigram, in Dickin* agt. *Edwards*, 4 *Hare*, 273.)

There is in this will a positive direction to the executors (who are also made trustees) to pay to the testator's wife eight thousand dollars ($8,000) per annum if he shall leave children, and seven thousand dollars ($7,000) per annum if he shall not; but, as to the first mentioned sum, it is parcel of the direction that it is to be paid out of the income of the estate, and it is plausibly argued that the same qualification is annexed by implication to the direction to pay the seven thousand dollars per annum, in the event which has happened, of there being no children. The evidence and the admissions of the parties show that the testator supposed himself to have a clear income, arising upon invested property, sufficient to pay the largest of the annuities, and to have a considerable surplus of income, which he destined for the benefit of his brother and sisters. But their right to participate was to be subordinate to that of the wife, who has to be paid her $8,000 or $7,000, as the case might be, before anything should be paid to them. It now appearing that he was mistaken as to the sufficiency of his revenue to pay continuously even the smallest of the annuities, which the event has shown to be the only one which can be claimed, and that only a portion of it can be paid from the income, the question arises, which was the primary and most material portion of the testator's intent, and which was, in his mind, the incident to such primary intention? Manifestly, it seems to me, it was that his widow should receive one or the other of the alternate sums mentioned, according to the event.

In the first place, this annuity was the only provision made for her in any part of the will. He contemplated that there might be issue of the marriage between himself and his wife, for he graduated the amount of the annuity by that circumstance; but if the provision is to be strictly conditioned upon his estate continuing to yield income, it might happen that his wife and children would be without any means of support derived from his estate, while the estate itself might be of vendible value to a large amount. It was shown that a large amount had been invested in unproductive lands, from which, of course, no revenue could be expected. It is not suggested but that the personal property, stocks, vessels, &c., may be converted into money at some reasonable price. It is shown, indeed, that in the present condition of the property, sufficient income will not be realized to pay the annuity in full. Whether this would be so if it were converted into money, does not appear from the case.

But it is argued on behalf of the brother and sisters that

the testator is to be considered as equally solicitous to bestow a pecuniary benefit upon his brother and sisters, as upon his wife, or his wife and children, if he should have children. Hence it is suggested that his wishes and intentions will not be altogether disappointed if, upon the failure of income, the body of the estate is kept unemployed during the lifetime or widowhood of his wife, for the benefit of his brother and sisters. This view seems to me very unreasonable. The brother and sisters were not the primary objects of these dispositions. They were only to participate in the income, provided it should be so large as to produce a surplus after applying to the wife and children the sum which he thought it necessary for them to have. There failing to be any such surplus, the benefits intended for them were to be postponed until after her death; but it was only in a contingency that they were then to have any interest, for if the testator should leave children, the brother and sisters would be wholly excluded from participation. Again, in the event of there being no children, the brother and sisters did not occupy so favorable a position as that of devisees in remainder after the death of his wife, for it was their children and not themselves who, upon the event of the extinction of his own family, were to become the final beneficiaries of the estate.

Again, the first paragraph of the fourth division of the will proves beyond question that the testator had no such intention as is attributed to him, of confining his widow strictly to a participation, and of preserving the whole of the principal for the benefit of the brother and sisters and their issue. The provision is, that if there should be children, upon their attaining their majority, the sum of eight thousand per annum should be reserved for the benefit of his wife. It cannot be pretended that this provision was limited to the case of his investments, yielding income to the required amount, for the direction is positive and unconditional that such a sum should be reserved for her.

If the property, as invested, was unproductive of income, it would be the duty of the trustees, by the purchase of a life annuity, or in some other way, to secure the payment of the yearly allowance mentioned.

If we were to hold that the widow was to have nothing unless the property or securities in which the estate happened to be invested yielded income, and that she was not to be paid the full seven thousand dollars per annum, directed to be paid to her, unless the investments should happen to yield that sum, we should, in my opinion, sacrifice the substance and primary intention of the will for the sake of an incidental provision, inserted for the convenience of the estate, and not intended to limit or control, or to render uncertain or conditional, the provision in her favor; and I think, moreover, that the case is within the spirit of the authorities which have been referred to by the counsel for the appellant. To these may be added, for the purpose of presenting an early and a recent case, *The Attorney General* agt. *Parkins*, (*Ambler*, 566,) and *Colvelle* agt. *Middleton*, (3 *Kernan*, 570;) and also for a recognition of the doctrine in this court, *Teft* agt. *Porter*, (4 *Seld.*, 516,) *Giddings* agt. *Seward*, (16 *N. Y. R.*, 365,) *De Nolblach* agt. *Oster*, (3 *Kernan*, 104–5.)

I see no reason for interfering with or attempting to regulate the discretion of the trustees upon the subject of the sale of the unproductive or the unsafe property. The right of the widow to the annuity does not, in my opinion, depend upon such sales. The trustees should be guided by the circumstances of the property and the necessities of the estate. There are not sufficient facts before us to show whether at present a sale would or would not be judicious.

I am of opinion that the judgment of the supreme court should be reversed, and of entering a judgment in conformity with the foregoing views, to be settled before one of the judges.

SUPREME COURT.

JOSEPH HART agt. JOHN A. KENNEDY, THADDEUS C. DAVIS and DE WITT C. SMITH.

By §60 of the *rules* of the *commissioners of the Metropolitan police*, of the city of New York, passed under and in pursuance of 27th section of the act of the legislature, of April, 1860, it is provided that the superintendent, inspectors, captains and sergeants of police, will be deemed to be *always on duty*.

By the 34th section of the act of April, 1860, it is declared that "no person holding office under this act shall be liable to military or jury duty, nor to arrest on civil process, or to service of subpœnas from civil courts, *whilst actually on duty*."

Held, that the 60th section of the rules of the commissioners must be considered as a mere rule or matter relating to discipline, as between the commissioners and those holding office under them. It cannot be deemed to affect in any manner *the rights of third parties* under the 34th section of the act, when persons holding office under the act *are not actually on duty*.

Though they may be deemed to be on duty, yet if they are not *actually on duty*, these officers are liable to *arrest and to be served with subpœnas*.

New York General Term, March, 1863.

SUTHERLAND, INGRAHAM and CLERKE, *Justices*.

APPEAL from an order at special term vacating and discharging an order of arrest. The facts will appear in the opinions of the court.

By the court, SUTHERLAND, J. This is an action for two several alleged illegal arrests and false imprisonments of the plaintiff by the defendants.

The defendant Kennedy is the superintendent, the defendant Davis a captain, and the defendant Smith a patrolman of the Metropolitan police.

An order of arrest was granted by a justice of this court, holding the defendants to bail, each in the sum of $1,000.

This order of arrest was, on motion of the defendants, by an order made at special term, vacated and discharged as to the defendants Kennedy and Davis, and modified as to the defendant Smith, by reducing the amount of bail required of him to $250.

The case comes before us by the appeal of the plaintiff from the order vacating and discharging the order of arrest as to the defendants Kennedy and Davis, and modifying it as to the other defendant.

I infer from the papers that neither of the defendants had been arrested when the order vacating and modifying the order of arrest was made; that the return day of the order of arrest as originally granted had been extended by an order, for the purpose of enabling the defendants to make the motion to vacate the order before the defendants should be arrested.

By the twenty-seventh section of the act passed April 10, 1860, to amend the Metropolitan police act, passed April 15, 1857, the commissioners of the Metropolitan police, "in furtherance of the police government of the said Metropolitan police district, and for the promoting and perfecting the police discipline of subordinates and of the members of the Metropolitan police force, are empowered to enact, modify and repeal, from time to time, rules and regulations of general discipline, wherein, in addition to such other provisions as may be deemed expedient by said commissioners, there shall be particularly defined, enumerated and distributed the powers and duties of the superintendent of police force, and of the inspectors and captains of police force, etc., provided that such rules or regulations shall not conflict with any of the provisions of this amended act, or with the constitution of the United States, or of this state."

By the thirty-fourth section of the same act it is declared that "no person holding office under this act shall be liable to military or jury duty, nor to arrest on civil process, or to service of subpœnas from civil courts, whilst actually on duty."

It appears from the affidavit of the defendant Kennedy in this case, that under section twenty-seven of said act the commissioners of the Metropolitan police enacted or passed certain rules and regulations of general discipline, and that by section sixty of said rules it was provided that the superintendent, inspectors, captains and sergeants of police will be deemed to be always on duty.

It appears from the opinion of the learned justice who made the order at special term, vacating and modifying the order of arrest in this case, and it was conceded on the argument before us, that the order of arrest was vacated and discharged as to the defendants Kennedy and Davis, on the ground that the one was the superintendent and the other a captain of the Metropolitan police when the alleged arrests and false imprisonments of which the plaintiff complains took place, and that being such officers, by the thirty-fourth section of the act, and the sixtieth section of the rules and regulations enacted or passed by the commissioners under the twenty-seventh section of the act, they were as such officers free from arrest on civil process, at all times and under all circumstances.

It is difficult to see upon what other theory the order vacating the order of arrest as to the defendants Kennedy and Davis, and modifying and retaining it as to the defendant Smith, could have been made.

It is plain that it was an error to vacate and discharge the order as to the defendants Kennedy and Davis on this ground.

The thirty-fourth section of the act, by declaring that no person holding office under the act shall be liable to arrest on civil process, or to service of subpœnas, etc., whilst actually on duty, plainly impliedly declares that persons holding office under the act shall be liable to arrest on civil process or to service of subpœnas, etc., whilst not actually on duty.

This section impliedly declares that no person holding office under the act shall be deemed to be actually on duty at all times and under all circumstances, so as never to be liable to arrest or service of subpœna whilst holding the office.

The police commissioners had no power under the twenty-seventh section of the act to enact any rule or regulation in conflict with the thirty-fourth section. The twenty-seventh section contains an express proviso to that effect, and independent of such proviso they would have had no power to enact or pass a by-law or regulation inconsistent with an express provision of the act conferring on them their powers.

But I do not think the sixtieth section of the rules or regulations enacted by the commissioners was intended to interfere with the thirty-fourth section of the act. It was intended to be, and is, a mere rule or matter relating to discipline, as between the commissioners and those holding office under them. It was not intended, and cannot be deemed to affect in any manner the rights of third parties under the thirty-fourth section of the act, when persons holding office under the act are not actually on duty.

It would be an extraordinary thing to hold, that the superintendent or a captain of the Metropolitan police can at no time or under any circumstances be served with a subpœna, or compelled to appear and testify in a civil court; and yet the thirty-fourth section of the act places the same restriction on the right to subpœna as it does on the right to arrest.

The order at special term should be reversed, so far as it vacated the order of arrest as to the defendants Kennedy and Davis; but I do not see why the other part of the order should not be affirmed.

Clerke, J. The judge at special term gave no effect whatever to the sixtieth section of the general rules adopted by the commissioners, declaring that the superintendent, inspectors, captains and sergeants shall "be deemed always on duty." It is emphatically denied in the opinion, delivered at the special term, that any rule or regulation of the commissioners can interfere with the right of a court of justice to determine the fact according to the evidence.

But it was contended that, from the nature and extent of the duties of the superintendent and captains, the statements in the affidavit of Kennedy must be assumed as true, "that he has always since his appointment as superintendent of police been, and ever is, on duty as such superintendent at all times of the day and night," and that "all the captains in his district are also on duty at all times, day and night, without intermission." It was thought that this should be assumed until the contrary be shown; so that, after this positive statement, the burden of proof should devolve on the plaintiff to show that, at the time of the arrest on civil process, the party arrested, if the superintendent or a captain, was engaged in some pursuit of business or pleasure not within the sphere of his public duties.

In the language of the opinion below, "the patrolmen have certain intervals of remission from duty fixed and known, during which they are not liable to duty; but this can scarcely be affirmed of the superintendent. No doubt he has certain hours for taking his meals and taking sleep; but, as he has a general and unremitting supervision over the operations of the whole force, and as his directions and advice in a city like this may be necessary at any time, he is liable to be called to active duty at any hour of the day or night, so that it is not at all unreasonable to say that he is always actually (though not actively) on duty."

In such a case, to be prepared for duty is to be on duty. When, either in his office or in his house devising plans and thinking of instructions for the large force under his command; when he is awaiting applications for these instructions, ready to give them during every hour of the twenty-four, if required; and when, not thus engaged, he is visiting the numerous stations in the city; I repeat, it is not at all unreasonable to acquiesce in his sworn statement, until the contrary be proved, that "he is at all times actually on duty." It would indeed be erroneous to hold that the superintendent or a captain of the police cannot, at any time or under any circumstances, be served with a subpœna or any other process. On a careful perusal of the opinion of the judge at special term, I cannot discover that he held any such thing. But he did hold, that those endeavoring to compel a superintendent or captain to appear and testify, or those at whose suit he is arrested in civil process, should show that he was otherwise engaged than on duty at the time of the service of the process; the clear presumption being, from the nature and extent of his duties, and from his own sworn statement, that, like the sentinel in his sentry-box, he is always actually on duty.

I think that a regard for the efficient government of the police force of this populous city, and a desire for the public safety and comfort render it expedient to establish this presumption in favor of the superintendent and captains, particularly when we consider that it is only raised in the case of a provisional remedy, the allowance of which, in any case, rests in a great measure in the sound discretion of the judge, who may refuse it altogether if he thinks the arrest is not necessary to secure the presence of the defendant to answer to the final judgment of the court. It is not at all probable that a public officer holding a position and performing duties, like those of the superintendent of police, will not render himself amenable to any process which may be issued to enforce any judgment that may be rendered against him.

Nevertheless, I am not in favor of affirming the order of the special term, as far as the superintendent and captains are concerned. No arrest of these persons was actually made; the motion was made to set aside the order of arrest—not to release them from arrest.

Therefore, the plaintiff had no opportunity of having them arrested when not on actual duty, so that the principles on which the decision of the special term is founded are not applicable to the present motion.

The order at special term should be reversed so far as it vacated the order of arrest as to the defendants Kennedy and Davis, but should be affirmed as to the other defendant.

INGRAHAM, J. I concur in reversing the order below as to Kennedy and Davis.

The commissioners may have power by rules to provide that, for reasons of their own, officers in their employ shall be deemed always on duty; but no such regulation can alter the meaning of the terms used in the statute, "actually on duty." Though they may be deemed to be on duty, yet, if they are not actually on duty, the officers are liable to arrest, and to be served with subpœnas. We must look at the object of the provision to ascertain the intent of the legislature. That evidently was to prevent an arrest, etc., while the officer was actually discharging his public duties, so as to prevent the possibility of arresting one of their officers while actually in the public employ. But when some other officer has temporarily taken his place, it cannot be said that he is actually on duty, although for police purposes they provide that they shall be deemed to be so.

The reduction of the bail by the justice at chambers was a matter of discretion, with which, under ordinary circumstances, we do not interfere.

NEW YORK SUPERIOR COURT.

MATILDA C. GRAY, administratrix, &c. agt. JOHN COOK, JR., administrator, &c.

An order or decree of the court, entered after trial on a reference, that the plaintiff have judgment for a certain amount against the defendant as administrator, and that he pay said moneys into court, *to await the further order of the court, and to be distributed according to law*, is a *final judgment* against the defendant as between the parties.

The defendant may be proceeded against upon such judgment by *execution* to collect such moneys, under § 285 of the Code; but a proceeding by an order, as for a *contempt* and *attachment* against him, is *unauthorized.*

Where a copy of a decree or judgment, for the payment of money, is served on the defendant without any *demand* for payment being made, he cannot be convicted as of a *contempt* in not paying over the money—there must be a *demand* and *refusal*, to authorize proceedings for a contempt.

Special Term, January, 1863.

THE parties were this day heard on the matter of the alleged contempt of the defendant, in not paying into court the sum of money which he was so ordered to pay by the judgment or an order made in this action, on the 12th of December, 1859.

That contains, among others, these provisions, viz: "It is therefore ordered and adjudged and decreed that the plaintiff have judgment against the defendant for said sum of $6,259.39, with interest thereon from said 2d day of June, 1859, together with $133.47, costs of this action, and an allowance of $200 dollars; and that John Cook, Jr., do forthwith pay said moneys into court to await the further order of the court, and to be distributed according to law."

It was entered in an action after a trial of it upon pleadings and proofs, and a decision thereupon by the court, that the defendant should account for the moneys alleged in the complaint to have been received by him; and that he had received them as administrator of an estate of which the plaintiff was also administratrix; and after the report of a referee, appointed to take an account of the balance of the moneys in defendant's hands, which he had thus received, had been made and confirmed, stating such balance to be the sum for which judgment is given. This judgment or order disposes, as between these parties, of every issue made by the pleadings.

A certified copy of this order or judgment was served on the defendant personally on the 26th of June, 1860, with a notice dated December 24th, 1859, that it was a "certified copy of a decree made in within entitled action, on which decree judgment was this day rendered."

No demand or request has been made of the defendant that he should pay such money into court or to the plaintiff, and he has not paid any part of it, and is insolvent and was when the judgment was entered.

An attachment was issued against the defendant to answer to an alleged contempt in not having paid said money. He was arrested, and has answered interrogatories filed and served upon him; and the interrogatories, answers and affidavits, on which the attachment issued, show the facts to be as above stated.

P. G. GALPIN, *for plaintiff.*

B. C. THAYER, *for defendant.*

BOSWORTH, Ch. Justice. The decision of the 12th of December, 1859, is a judgment. It is the final detemination of the rights of the parties in this action. (*Code*, § 245.) No questions, as between them, are reserved for further consideration or left open. The plaintiff insists it is an *order*, because it requires the defendant to pay the moneys into court to await the further order of the court, and to be distributed according to law. The decision made allows to the defendant his commissions on the moneys received, and he has no right, in reference to the moneys to be paid, nor any duty to perform, except to pay the amount for which judgment is ordered. There is nothing in the allegation or proofs before me suggesting any matter affecting these moneys, which can become a subject of litigation between these parties. The judgment itself, neither in terms nor by the import of its provisions, suggests the existence of any matter of further litigation. I therefore regard it a judgment within the meaning of the Code.

It directs the payment of money and only that, and section 285 prescribes the mode of enforcing it. Although a judgment may require the performance of acts specified in it, yet if it also requires the payment of money, it may be enforced in that respect by execution; § 285 so declares. But this judgment requires nothing besides the payment of money; and if an execution can issue to collect it, that is the only proceeding that can be resorted to, in the first instance, to compel payment.

Proceedings cannot be had under 2 *R. S.*, (*5th ed.*,) 849, § 1, *sub.* 3, because that, in terms, excludes all cases where by law execution can be awarded for the collection of the sum ordered to be paid. It excludes them, because this remedy "for the non-payment of any sum of money ordered by such court" is authorized only "in cases where by law execution cannot be awarded for the collection of such sum."

No authority for this proceeding is found in section 4, (*id.*, 850,) for that applies only to a "rule or order of court."

Another fatal objection is, that no demand has been made of the defendant to pay the money to the plaintiff or into court. Under § 4 *of* 3 *R. S.*, *5th ed.*, and § 285 of the Code, there must have been *a refusal* to comply with the order, to justify a conviction as for a contempt. (*Lorton* agt. *Seaman*, 9 *Paige R.*, 609.)

The judgment was entered on the 12th December, 1859, and a copy of it was served on the 26th of June, 1860, with a notice that it was a certified copy of a decree entered on the 24th of December, 1859. No other notice nor any demand accompanied the service, and no demand of payment has since been made.

The decree having been served, and not having been performed, there has been a neglect to obey it; but it cannot be said that there has been *a refusal* to obey it, when performance of its requirements has not been requested.

The necessary conclusion from these views is, that the defendant is not guilty of the misconduct alleged against him.

I think the plaintiff has proceeded in good faith, but under erroneous views of her rights.

Nothing was said on the question of costs, as to which the parties may be heard on the settlement of the order to be entered.

SUPREME COURT.

WILLIAM G. SANDS, Receiver of the Ætna Insurance Company, of Utica, respondent agt. BRADLEY TILLINGHAST, appellant.

THE SAME, respondent agt. JOHN GRIFFITHS, appellant.

The "act to facilitate the closing up of insolvent and dissolved mutual insurance companies," passed April 21, 1862, is *not unconstitutional*, as impairing the *right of trial by jury*. A *compulsory reference*, therefore, may be ordered in these cases.

Broome General Term, January, 1863.

Present, BALCOM, CAMPBELL and PARKER, *Justices*.

APPEAL from orders made at chambers appointing a referee in these proceedings.

The receiver of the Ætna Insurance Company, after personal demand of payment of notes made to said company, and refusal to pay the same, applied to Mr. Justice CAMPBELL under the act entitled "An act to facilitate the closing up of insolvent and dissolved Mutual Insurance

Companies," passed April 21, 1862, to appoint a referee to hear the proofs and allegations of the parties.

The leading point against the application was that the said act was unconstitutional, as impairing the right of trial by jury.

Orders were made and entered with the clerk of Chenango, appointing a referee, from which orders an appeal was had to the general term in the sixth district.

The appeal was argued at the November term, 1862, and decided at the January term, 1863.

WARD HUNT, *for the appellants.*
HENRY R. MYGATT, *for the respondent.*

By the court, PARKER, Justice. The principal question presented in these cases is, whether the provisions of the act entitled "An act to facilitate the closing up of insolvent and dissolved Mutual Insurance Companies," passed April 21, 1862, (*Sess. Laws*, 1862, *p.* 743,) by which parties controverting any demand made against them by receivers of such companies, may be compelled to a submission of such controversies to the decision of a referee, to the exclusion of a jury, is constitutional.

It is claimed by the defendants that it is in conflict with section two of article one of the constitution of this state, which is as follows: "The trial by jury, in all cases in which it has been heretofore used, shall remain inviolate forever," etc.; that the alleged liability of the defendants being upon promissory notes, the question of their liability, under the ordinary defences which they may set up, belongs to that class of cases in which trial by jury has been heretofore used, and hence that it is not competent for the legislature to deprive them of that right thus guaranteed by the constitution.

The plaintiff's counsel replies that references as broad as those provided by this act were sanctioned by statute and practiced long before and up to the time of the adoption of the present constitution, and refers to the provisions contained in the Revised Laws of 1813, similar to those in this act, (1 *Rev. Laws*, 161, § 16,) which are carried into the Revised Statutes, (2 *R. S.*, 45, § 19, 1*st ed.*,) and were the law in 1846, when the constitution was adopted, and also refers to the provisions of the Revised Statutes in the article relating to the voluntary dissolution of insolvent corporations, giving receivers the same powers conferred by law upon trustees of insolvent debtors, (2 *R. S.*, 469, §§ 68, 73,) including the power to compel references in any controversies which shall arise between them and creditors or debtors of the corporation.

These references show that, as the law stood when the constitution was adopted, the persons representing insolvent debtors might, instead of bringing suits in court to settle controversies between themselves and the debtors of the insolvent, compel references of such controversies to referees, and that receivers of insolvent corporations might in the same manner compel references of controversies between themselves and the debtors of the corporations.

The powers conferred on receivers by the act in question are very similar to those conferred on trustees of insolvent debtors, and receivers of insolvent corporations, by the Revised Statutes; and it may with truth be said, that in cases like this now before the court, the trial by jury had not "been heretofore used" as the only mode of trial; but that trial by referees was also a mode of trial in use and authorized.

An action involving the examination of a long account might be tried by a jury or by referees under the law as it existed at the adoption of the constitution. Hence, a reference in such cases is constitutional. *Lee* agt. *Tillotson*, (24 *W. R.*, 337,) Judge COWEN said in that case "but the seventh article (§ 2) of our constitution declares that 'the trial by jury, in all cases in which it has been heretofore used, shall remain inviolate forever,' and the case before us is supposed not to come within the exception. It is a satisfactory answer, however, that references as broad as that now contended for by the plaintiff were sanctioned by statute, and practiced by the courts long before the adoption of the constitution."

The same may be said in answer to the objection made to this statute.

I am of the opinion that it is not in conflict with the constitution, and that the orders appealed from should be affirmed with costs.

SUPREME COURT.

John F. Butterworth, receiver, etc. agt. James O'Brien.

The *right of action* to claims for *dividends* improperly declared by an insolvent banking corporation is in the *creditors* and not in the receiver.

Where the complaint by the receiver averred that the defendant (former president of the bank) used *fictitious notes* in lieu of money of the bank, which he fraudulently used and disposed of, and that such notes were among the assets of the bank,

Held, that these facts, if proven, would be sufficient to put the defendant on his defence, and showed a cause of action in favor of the receiver.

Under the late decisions in the court of appeals, courts of original jurisdiction are not to *pay any attention to forms*, if they can find in the complaint any allegations which, under any view of them, may give the plaintiff a right to recover. *(Ergo, books of forms must be considered as calculated to mislead and confuse.)*

This action is brought by the receiver of the Island City Bank against the defendant, who was president and director, to recover from him certain moneys for wrongful acts charged against him.

The defendant answered to the complaint, denying all the allegations made against him.

The case was referred and the referee has dismissed the complaint as insufficient and containing no cause of action.

By the court, INGRAHAM, J. The referee was clearly right as to all the causes stated in the complaint, excepting that contained in the fourth clause of the complaint.

The claim for dividends improperly declared belongs to creditors and not to the receiver. The right of action is in them, and the receiver cannot collect such moneys for the benefit of stockholders. Nor was it a cause of action, that such dividends were paid to persons who were indebted to the bank.

The allegation that the defendant parted with notes of the bank as security for loans made to him in the name of the bank, without an averment that anything was due to the bank, or that the loans had not been paid, showed no cause of action against the defendant.

In the fourth clause of the complaint it is averred that the defendant used fictitious notes in lieu of money of the bank, which was fraudulently used and disposed of by the defendant; that such notes were among the assets of the bank, and amounted to $27,000.

Under the ruling of the referee we must consider these allegations to be admitted, and then we have the following as facts:

That the defendant put in the bank two notes signed by a fictitious drawer; that the notes were used by the defendant in lieu of so much money of the bank; that the money was fraudulently disposed of by the defendant, and that the notes are now among the assets of the bank. It appears to me that these facts, if proven, would be sufficient to put the defendant on his defence. The possession of the notes by the receiver is presumptive that the moneys have not been repaid. If paid, the onus is on the defendant to show it. If the notes were the defendant's, there would be no doubt of sufficient facts to make out the plaintiff's case. If the notes were fictitious, quite as good a cause of action exists against him. The claim is also one which would belong to the receiver, and may be collected by him.

The complaint as to this claim, as well as to the others, is very loosely and informally drawn, and may subject the plaintiff to a motion to have it made more specific; but, under the present system, is not so bad as to be demurrable, so far as relates to this clause.

In fact, under the late decisions in the court of appeals, we are not to pay any attention to forms if we can find in the complaint any allegations which, under any view of them, may give the plaintiff a right to recover.

I think the referee erred in this respect, and that the judgment should be reversed and a new trial ordered, costs to abide the event.

Clerke, J., concurred.

Sutherland, P. J. I dissent; I think the judgment below should be affirmed.

It does not belong to the plaintiff or receiver to correct or prosecute for the frauds and illegal acts complained of in the complaint.

The other grounds stated in the opinion of the referee appear to me also to justify the dismissal of the complaint.

SUPREME COURT.

David H. Gould agt. E. B. Gager, Wm. P. Libby and others.

Same agt. Wm. A. Woodward, William P. Libby and others.

Same agt. Henry Mathews, William P. Libby and others.

Same agt. Alice C. Lawler, William P. Libby and others.

Same agt. Clement Kain, William P. Libby and others.

A *sale of mortgaged premises will be set aside* where the owner of the equity of redemption *appealed in good faith* from the judgment of foreclosure of the county court, but owing to *imperfect justifications of his sureties* in the undertakings

given on the appeal, the sale was not stayed, and the plaintiff proceeded and sold the premises, without notice to the owner or return of the undertakings, bidding off the same himself or by his agent for one-third less than their real value, and taking a decree against the owner for the balance.

Brooklyn General Term, February, 1863.

APPEAL by plaintiff from the decision of the county court of Kings county, granting an order for a re-sale of the mortgaged premises in this case.

D. P. BARNARD and W. M. INGRAHAM, *for plaintiff.*

J. W. GILBERT, *for W. P. Libby.*

BROWN, Justice. The court will not interfere and set aside a sale under a judgment or decree of foreclosure for mere inadequacy of price. But where there has been fraud or collusion, or the parties having an interest as owners or creditors have been prevented from attending the sale by the representations of the master or referee, or by sickness or inevitable accident, then it will exercise its power and order a re-sale. In *Collier* agt. *Whipple,* (13 *Wendell,* 224,) a re-sale was granted and affirmed on appeal, upon the ground that the judgment creditors were prevented from attending the sale in consequence of impressions received by their agent, from a conversation with the master, that the sale would not take place. In *Tripp* agt. *Cook,* (24 *Wend.,* 143,) it was held that a re-sale will be ordered where the mortgaged premises have been sold below their real value, and bought in by the mortgagee, if the mortgagor or those representing his interest have been misled by the mortgagee, or even by a third person in reference to the foreclosure of the mortgage, and in consequence do not attend the sale. In *Requa* agt. *Rea,* (2 *Paige,* 339,) a re-sale was ordered, because the master, mistaking his duty, sold the premises for $1,000 to a purchaser who was aware at the time that the master had written instructions from the complainant's solicitor not to sell for less than $2,600. It was also held that the purchaser at such a sale submits himself to the jurisdiction of the court as to all matters connected with the sale. In *Billington* agt. *Forbes and Marsh*, (10 *Paige*, 487,) a re-sale was ordered where a co-defendant of the mortgagor took advantage of the absence of the latter from illness and prevented a postponement of the sale, and then became the purchaser himself at one-third of the real value of the premises. To the same effect is the case of *May* agt. *May*, (11 *Paige*, 201.) The papers disclosed improper interference and management to prevent competition at the sale, and the chancellor ordered a re-sale upon the application of a judgment creditor who was not present when the sale was effected. (*Vide, also, Dunning* agt. *Smith*, 3 *Johns. Ch. R.*, 332; *Powell* agt. *Tuthill*, 3 *Comst. R.*, 396.)

The five cases in favor of David H. Gould, of which the titles are given above, were actions brought in the county court of Kings county, each to foreclose a mortgage upon premises in Brooklyn. William P. Libby was not the mortgagor in either, but he was made a party as the owner of the equity of redemption in each case. The complaints charged that he had assumed and become personally chargeable with the payment of the mortgage debts, and on that account the complaints prayed in addition to the usual relief a judgment against him personally for the deficiency. This claim was put in issue and resisted by the defendant Libby, and upon the trial, judgment was rendered against him. He thereupon appealed to the supreme court on the 1st of August, 1861. These appeals were regular in all respects, and were designed by him to operate as a stay of all the proceedings in the actions until the appeals could be heard and determined. They did not have that effect, however, in consequence solely of the affidavits of justification of the sureties to the undertakings being in the amounts stated therein, and not in double those sums, as required by the practice. The undertakings, with these imperfect affidavits of justification, were filed and served on the 1st day of August, 1861, and on the 3d of that month the plaintiff proceeded to a sale of the mortgaged premises, Libby not being present, and without returning the undertakings or intimating to him or his attorney the defect which he must have observed. In the first named action, the property was struck off to and purchased by the plaintiff for $500. He assigned his bid to one Henry I. Powers for $1,000, and the referee conveyed the premises to Powers, the plaintiff settling with the referee for the purchase money. This was on the 6th of August. On the same day judgment was entered against Libby for the difference of $1,953.69. In October thereafter, Powers mortgaged the premises to one Philo W. Titus. The premises in the second named action were also struck off to and purchased by the plaintiff at the sale for $800. On the 5th August he also sold this bid to one Nicar for $1,000, who, on the 6th of August, took the referee's deed. Judgment in this action for $1,645.88 deficiency was also entered against Libby. In the third named action, the premises were purchased by the plaintiff at the sale for the sum of $500, for which he took the referee's deed on the 6th of August, and entered his judgment against Libby for $1,947.41, the deficiency therein. In the fourth entitled action, the premises were bid in at the sale by the plaintiff, as the agent of Edwin A. Brooks, for $500. He also settled the consideration money with the referee, and took the deed to Brooks August the 5th. Judgment in this case was entered against Libby for $1,945.88, the deficiency therein. In the fifth and last of the above entitled actions, the premises were struck off to and purchased by the attorney for the plaintiff, as agent of one Mary B. Jackson, for $600. He settled with the referee for the purchase money on the day of the sale, and took the deed to her. The deficiency in this action was $1,850.22, for which judgment was entered against Libby. Mary B. Jackson afterwards mortgaged this lot to one Cowenhoven. Four things are worthy of observation here: 1st. Each of the five lots were bid in at the sale by the plaintiff, or by his attorney in the actions, for himself or as the agent of other persons. 2d. In each case the plaintiff or his attorney settled with the referee for the purchase money. 3d. The deeds were all executed and delivered on or before the 6th of August, within three days of the time of the sale. 4th. The entire proceeds of the sales is $2,900, and the deficiency for which judgments are entered, $9,313.08. The proof as to the value of the mortgaged premises is, as usual, conflicting; but there are two facts of some significance in this connection. Libby is the purchaser and owner of the equity of redemption, with an agreement to pay the several mortgage debts, as the plaintiff alleges. And as a part of the papers upon which the county court granted the order to re-sell, there is the offer of Libby's brother, who is thought to be of ample ability, to bid $1,500 upon each lot at the re-sale. I can hardly doubt that the property was sold at a ruinous sacrifice. The affidavits of justification were amended and corrected on the 3d of October, 1861, under an order of the county court. Libby then moved the county court for a re-sale, which was granted upon terms from which the plaintiff has appealed in each case to this court.

I arrive at the conclusion, from a perusal of the papers, that Libby intended in good faith to bring an appeal in each of these actions—an appeal which should stay the plaintiff's proceedings and arrest the further progress of the sale. It follows as a corollary to this proposition that the defect in the affidavits of justification, which rendered the appeals ineffectual to stay the sale, was an inadvertance—a mere accident, a thing which will occasionally occur in the present transition state of the practice, whatever may be the care and skill employed. The defendant Libby confided, as he certainly had a right to confide, in the efficacy of the appeal papers to stop the sale, and did not, therefore, attend or give himself any concern therewith. The defect in the papers was unknown to Libby, but it was well known to the plaintiff, and having the contract of the sale he was armed with power to work great mischief to his adversary. He was not bound under any rule of practice to return the undertakings as insufficient, and to give the owner of the property notice that the sale would proceed. The question is not so much what he was bound to do, as what he was in equity and good faith bound not to do. His only legitimate object in prosecuting the actions was to collect his money. He knew his adversary was laboring under a delusion, and that one word from him would make him aware of the peril and danger of his position. If his omission to speak that word resulted in irreparable injury to his adversary and large benefit to himself, he cannot complain if the court exerts its power to redress the injury, doing him no wrong at the same time. In *Billington* agt. *Forbes and Marsh, supra*, the mortgagor was unable to attend the sale from illness. A co-defendant interfered and prevented a postponement, and became the purchaser of the property himself at one-third of its real value, and a re-sale was ordered. In this case the owner of the property was not physically ill; he was, however, laboring under a misapprehension, a delusion, as to the sale of his property. This was well known to the plaintiff, who, notwithstanding, proceeded with the sale and bid in the property for himself and others at one-third of its real value. The two cases are not dissimilar in principle, and the one should be open to the same relief as the other. There was accident and surprise upon the one side, and advantage taken of it upon the other, and unless the court can afford relief, the loss will be irreparable. I am influenced somewhat by the haste with which the plaintiff had the conveyances executed and the sales perfected, and by the speed with which others became interested as purchasers and mortgagees. It looks like the execution of a purpose to place barriers between the owner and the relief he now seeks. The circumstances are peculiar and unusual, certainly. The transfers and charges referred to form no insurmountable impediment to a re-sale of the property. The persons having these claims are not purchasers without notice, so as to entitle them to hold against the equities of the owner. All the lots were bid in by the plaintiff and his attorney, either for the plaintiff or the others, and notice to the agent is notice to the principal. Besides, purchasers under a judgment or decree of the court submit themselves to its jurisdiction in respect to the property purchased, and take it subject to its power to vacate the sale under proper limitations, and to promote the ends of justice.

The orders of the county court should be affirmed and modified so as to protect the purchasers at the sales and the subsequent mortgagees, and insure the application of the proceeds of any sales of the mortgaged premises, to be made hereafter, to the payment of the moneys advanced by them; and to that end the purchase money upon such sales should be held and not distributed until the further order of the court, and with leave to the parties interested to apply for further directions. The orders to be settled upon notice by the justice who delivers this opinion.

NEW YORK SUPERIOR COURT.

CHARLES H. WINFIELD, respondent agt. SAMUEL B. POTTER, appellant.

It was *held* no error for the judge at the trial to deny a motion to *dismiss the complaint*, where the application was made *during the progress of the examination of a witness;* and where the application appeared in the double character of an *objection to evidence*, and on the ground that there was *no consideration in the agreement* upon which the action was brought.

It was also *held*, that the *written agreement* signed by the defendant, on which the action was brought in this case, taken together with an agreement signed at the same time by the plaintiff's assignor, was not void under the statute; construed together a sufficient *consideration* was expressed; and it could not be treated as an undertaking to *pay the debt of another*.

Heard General Term, January, 1863, *before* MONCRIEF *and* MONELL, *Justices. Decided January* 31, 1863.

FREDERICK F. BETTS & Co., on the 24th day of August, 1861, obtained an order or contract from the United States government for the manufacture and delivery to the government of five thousand sets of military equipments.

Frederick F. Betts & Co. proceeded under this order or contract, and manufactured and delivered to the government, at Governor's Island, a large portion of the goods agreed to be delivered under that contract, when, on the seventh of October, 1861, Frederick F. Betts & Co. sold out to the defendant all their assets, including the equipments so manufactured and delivered, and all their right, title and interest under their contract, for the sum of $8,000, which Potter had previously loaned them, and an agreement that Potter should pay the debts of Frederick F. Betts & Co.

At the time of the transfer of the property to Potter, on the seventh of October, the firm of Frederick F. Betts & Co. were indebted to H. B. Hart, for money which Hart had previously loaned them to carry on this business, in the sum of $1,125, for which Hart held the firm note; and, as collateral security for its payment, he also held at that time quartermasters' receipts for fifty cases of goods which the firm of Frederick F. Betts & Co. had delivered to the government under their contract.

On the tenth day of October, 1861, three days after Potter bought this contract and property of Frederick F. Betts & Co., and while the contract was in full force, for it was not canceled until the fourteenth of October, he applied to Hart to get these receipts, which Hart held as collateral security for the payment of the money he had loaned. Hart agreed to give Potter the collateral receipts, upon Potter's giving him a writing to pay the debt due from Frederick F. Betts & Co. to him, and Potter gave him the agreement upon which this suit is brought, and took the receipts, and Hart agreed to aid Potter in getting the goods inspected to the best of his ability.

Without these receipts Potter could not have obtained possession of the property delivered, nor could he have obtained the certificates therefor.

The agreement upon which the suit is brought is as follows:

"NEW YORK, *October* 10*th*, 1861.

I, Samuel B. Potter, agree that whenever I receive a certificate or certificates from the government of the United States, or its officers, under or in pursuance of a contract between Frederick F. Betts & Co. and the government of the United States, for the making and delivery of five thousand sets of military equipments, for the whole or any portion of the sum agreed to be paid by said government, or the whole or any portion of the property so furnished, then I will deliver to said H. B. Hart, Esq., eleven hundred and twenty-five dollars, provided I receive certificates to that amount, which is in consideration that said Hart shall aid me in procuring the inspection and acceptance of said military equipments without charge, less disbursements.

$1,125. SAMUEL B. POTTER."

The agreement given by Hart to Potter to aid in getting the goods inspected is as follows:

"NEW YORK, *October* 10*th*, 1861.

I hereby agree to aid and assist Mr. S. B. Potter, the representative of F. F. Betts, to the best of my ability in getting his goods examined, as per contract with the United States government, for (5,000) five thousand sets military equipments made by said U. S. to Messrs. F. F. Betts & Co., without charge. H. B. HART."

On the 14th of October, 1861, four days after Potter had given this agreement to Hart, upon which this suit is brought, he gave up the order or contract of Frederick F. Betts & Co. with the government, which he purchased on the seventh of October, and had it canceled, and took an order directly to himself.

It does not differ from the order canceled in any respect, except running to Potter instead of Frederick F. Betts & Co. By its terms the government agree to take the goods already manufactured and delivered under the first order of Frederick F. Betts & Co., in fulfillment of "*the order.*"

After Potter obtained this order, he expended between $3,000 and $4,000 to complete the goods already nearly finished under the first order, and in November, 1861, he received from the government a certificate for $17,412.50, which certificate included all the goods delivered to the government by Frederick F. Betts & Co., on their order, before they sold out to Potter, and also the fifty cases which Hart gave Potter the receipts for.

All the goods, therefore, for which Potter received a certificate, except between $3,000 and $4,000, were manufactured and delivered under the order of Frederick F. Betts & Co., viz., $14,000.

On the 26th of December, 1861, H. B. Hart assigned the contract upon which the suit is brought to Frederick B. Betts, which assignment was in writing.

On the 21st of April, 1862, Frederick B. Betts sold and assigned the contract in suit to the plaintiff in this action; the assignment was in writing.

This action was commenced on the 26th of April, 1862, and came on for trial on the eighth day of October, at a trial term, before the Hon. Joseph S. Bosworth, chief justice, and a jury. The jury found a verdict for the plaintiff for damages $1,195.83, and costs. A motion for a new trial was made upon the judge's minutes, and denied. The defendant thereupon appealed to the general term, from the judgment of $1,299.37 damages and costs, entered

November 26th, 1862, in favor of the plaintiff, and also from the order denying a motion for a new trial.

The defendant took a number of exceptions to the exclusion of testimony; to the decision denying his motion to dismiss the complaint, and to a portion of the charge of the judge.

D. M. Porter, *for defendant and appellant.*
Ira D. Warren, *for plaintiff and respondent.*

By the court, Moncrief, Justice. This is an appeal from a judgment in favor of the plaintiff, entered upon the verdict of a jury, and also from an order denying a motion for a new trial.

There was no error in denying the motion to dismiss the complaint. The application was made during the progress of the direct examination of a witness, (the assignor of the plaintiff,) interrupting the orderly administration of justice in the trial of a cause. It appears in the double character of an objection to evidence which had been given, tending to show performance of the agreement on the part of the assignor of the plaintiff, (Hart,) and of a motion to dismiss the complaint on the ground that no consideration is named in the agreement.

The agreement was not void under the statute; taken together, the two instruments constituting the contract, one signed by the defendant and the other by Mr. Hart, a consideration is expressed. Besides, the agreement cannot, in a just sense, be treated as an undertaking to pay the debt of another; it partakes more of the character of the vendee of personal property upon becoming the possessor of the instrument claimed to be indicia of title assuming and agreeing to pay to the extent of the alleged lien. The expression of opinion by the learned chief justice, in his charge to the jury, is well sustained by the testimony, and was not error: the question was submitted to the jury. (*Coyles* agt. *Hurtin*, 10 *J. R.*, 85, 88; *Bulkly* agt. *Keteltas*, 4 *Sandf. R.*, 450, 454.) The case was fully and fairly submitted to the jury, who rendered a verdict for the plaintiff, doing, as I think, justice between the parties to the action. The other objections and exceptions are embraced by the views expressed with reference to the first exception, or so plainly untenable as not to require discussion.

The judgment and the order denying the motion for a new trial must be affirmed.

SUPREME COURT.

THE PEOPLE agt. JOHN OSMER.

The public keeping of intoxicating liquors on Sunday is not a *misdemeanor* under the police act of 1860.

New York General Term, March, 1863.

By the court, INGRAHAM, J. The question submitted to us in this case is whether the violation of the 42d section of the police act of 1860, which prohibits the public keeping of intoxicating liquors on Sunday, is a misdemeanor.

The statute imposes a penalty of $50 for each offence, to be sued for by the district attorney, and does not declare the offence to be a misdemeanor.

It is well settled that where any act is prohibited, and a penalty imposed for its violation, and the offence was not criminal before the passage of the statute, no other punishment than the penalty can be imposed, and the provision in the Revised Statutes, 3d ed., (5th ed.,) p. 980, which makes the violation of a statute containing such prohibitions a misdemeanor, only applies to cases in which no penalty is provided for its violation.

In this act there are provisions as to other violations,

in which such offences are declared to be misdemeanors, but no such provision is contained as applicable to this offence.

The only ground on which it is attempted to sustain this indictment is, that the police force are directed to enforce this section and to proceed in the manner provided by law for the arrest of offenders.

In the absence of any other enactment relating to this subject, I do not think this sufficient to warrant us in saying that the legislature intended to make the offender liable both to the penalty and to indictment. I am not in favor of making out crimes by mere inference, and where the penalty imposed is, as in this case, a heavy one for offences of this kind, the court should require a clear expression of the intent of the legislature before they add to that penalty the liability of prosecution for a criminal offence.

As the legislature in other parts of this act have declared the cases of violations of the act which they intended should be punished criminally, and have omitted any such declaration as to the acts prohibited in this section, the fair presumption is that they did not intend to apply to such acts any other punishment than the penalty.

We concur with the recorder in his views on this question.

Judgment affirmed.

COURT OF APPEALS.

JOHN J. HAYES, plaintiff in error agt. THE PEOPLE, defendants in error.

In this state there may be a *valid marriage*, though not formally solemnized by a *clergyman*, or *consent declared before a magistrate*.

If parties competent to contract, in the presence of witnesses, agree together to be husband and wife, and afterwards cohabit and recognize each other as such, it is a sufficient marriage to sustain an indictment for *bigamy*, in the event of one of the parties having before that time married another, who is still living.

September Term, 1862.

WRIT OF ERROR to the supreme court, by the plaintiff in error, to bring up a conviction for bigamy.

JAMES T. BRADY, *for plaintiff in error.*
S. B. GARVIN, *for defendants in error.*

WRIGHT, J. To convict of bigamy, a marriage in fact must be proved, and reputation and cohabitation alone are not sufficient. The fact of marriage may be proved by a witness present at the celebration, and this is the ordinary way of proving it. In this state marriage is a civil contract, and may exist without any formal solemnization by minister or magistrate.

The fact of the marriage of the prisoner to Sarah E. Blair in February, 1845, and that she was living at the time of the trial, was proved. To establish the fact of a second marriage in September, 1860, to Jane White, she was called and examined as the principal witness for the prosecution. She testified in substance, that the prisoner made her acquaintance in May, 1860, and that in August following, and whilst she was at work as a servant in a hotel at Middletown Point, they entered into an engagement to be married in September. She was to come to New York for that purpose at the expiration of her month's service. On the 12th September the prisoner met her at the steamboat landing in the city, and conducted her to a house in Thompson street, where he had taken rooms. That night she staid at her father's house in Brooklyn, and in the afternoon of the next day came over to the city and met the prisoner at the house in Thompson street. They were together until about seven o'clock in the evening, when the prisoner went out and returned in a few minutes with a person represented to be a minister. He was dressed like one, and had on a white necktie. She did not ask his name. The marriage ceremony was then performed by this person. He used the form of marriage of the Protestant Episcopal Church. He inquired of the witness if she would take the prisoner for her husband, and she replied in the affirmative; and the prisoner was asked if he would have her for his wife, and upon his replying affirmatively, the minister declared them man and wife. The person officiating gave her a certificate, using a partly printed form, and filling in the blanks by writing. The certificate was taken by the prisoner and put in his trunk, and was afterwards seen by a sister of the witness when the parties were living together as man and wife. This marriage ceremony was followed by cohabitation, which continued for about a year.

It was shown by other witnesses that the prisoner called her his wife, and wrote letters to her as such, and admitted that he had been married to her in September, 1860.

If this evidence was to be credited, a marriage in fact, as contradistinguished from one inferrable from circumstances, was proved. It is true that the authority or official character of the person performing the marriage ceremony was not affirmatively shown, and there was some proof in the case to excite at least a suspicion that the prisoner had procured the man who officiated, to falsely represent himself as a clergyman. If, however, to constitute a valid marriage, it must be solemnized by a minister or magistrate, the evidence was sufficient *prima facie* to prove a marriage in fact. A person appearing in the character of a clergyman performed the ceremony, using the marriage service of the Protestant Episcopal Church. The marriage was followed by cohabitation, and the prisoner distinctly admitted to others that he was married at the time. If the person officiating was not a clergyman it was for the prisoner to show that fact after a *prima facie* case was made out against him. (*State* agt. *Rood*, 12 *Vt. Rep.*, 296; *Rex* agt. *The Inhabitants of Trampton*, 10 *East*, *R.*, 282.) But the recorder was right in his charge to the jury. In this state there may be a valid marriage, though not formally solemnized by a clergyman, or consent declared before a magistrate. If parties competent to contract in the presence of witnesses agree together to be husband and wife, and afterwards cohabit and recognize each other as such, it is a sufficient marriage to sustain an indictment for bigamy, in the event of one of the parties having before that time married another, who is still living. It was not error, therefore, for the judge to instruct the jury that if the prisoner and Jane White agreed, in the presence of the man represented to be a minister, to be man and wife, and afterwards lived together as such, that was in the eye of the law a sufficient marriage to sustain an indictment for bigamy (the fact that the prisoner had before that time married Sarah E. Blair, and she was then living being admitted), and it was of no consequence whether the man represented to be a minister was such or not. It is only claimed that the latter branch of the charge is erroneous; but marriage in this state being a civil contract, and not requiring the intervention of minister or magistrate to make it legal, this part of the charge was manifestly correct.

The judgment of the supreme court and court of general sessions should be affirmed.

NEW YORK COMMON PLEAS.

CHARLES A. BUCKLEY and others agt. GEORGE P. LORD, SAMUEL N. BROWN, ABIEL B. MARKS and EDMUND C. BRAMHALL.

Where a person under a *private agreement* with a *special partner* in a limited copartnership furnishes a certain portion of the capital which the special partner puts into the business of the firm in his own name, and is to have a certain portion

of the income or profits which the special partner derives from the business, with a privilege of examining from time to time into the business matters of the firm, he and the special partner become thereby *general partners.*

They are made so by the operation of the statute, which declares that all persons interested in the partnership shall be liable as general partners, if any *false statement* is made in the *certificate* or *affidavit* by which the limited copartnership is formed.

A *published notice* of a *limited partnership* does not operate under the statute as an *actual dissolution* until *four weeks* after the publication.

General Term, March, 1863.

DALY, BRADY and HILTON, *Judges.*

APPEAL from a judgment at special term. The facts will appear in the opinion of the court.

C. BAINBRIDGE SMITH, *for plaintiffs.*

BENEDICT & BOARDMAN, *for defendants.*

By the court, DALY, F. J. On the 31st of December, 1860, the defendants Lord, Brown and Marks entered into an agreement for the formation of a limited copartnership, to commence on the first of January following, and to continue for four years thereafter, of which Lord and Brown were to be the general partners and Marks a limited partner; Lord to contribute $5,000, Brown $1,000, and Marks $20,000 in cash; and on that day the certificate and affidavit required by the statute was filed to the effect that Marks had contributed the sum of $20,000 as special partner, and that the same had been actually and in good faith paid in to the common stock in cash. The usual notice was published, and at the time designated the parties commenced business. Brown did not contribute the $1,000, having been disappointed in obtaining it, and Lord contributed but $3,000 instead of $5,000.

Eight thousand dollars of the $20,000 paid in by Marks was received from the defendant Bramhall. Bramhall was an old acquaintance of Lord and of Marks, and shortly before the formation of the partnership he introduced Marks to Lord. Lord, who was examined as a witness, testified that Bramhall told him previous to its formation, after he had introduced Marks to him, and while negotiations were pending for the formation of the partnership, that he had agreed to take an interest with Marks in the business, and had agreed to do so for the purpose of assisting Lord, and that Lord must keep it strictly private; that he was to contribute $8,000 of the $20,000 that Marks was to furnish, and was to receive two-fifths, and Marks three-fifths of the profits resulting from advancing the $20,000 capital contributed by Marks; that he had a written agreement between himself and Marks in regard to his interest, drawn up by Mr. Boardman, the defendant's attorney, and that the agreement was so drawn that in case Marks should, by any action of his, make himself liable as a general partner, he, Bramhall, would be entirely exempt from liability; and that he had Marks tight; that he requested that his interest in the business should be kept strictly private, and said that the object in so arranging matters was to enable him to advise and assist the firm more than could be done in a limited copartnership under the laws of New York; that the law relating to special partnership was so stringent that the special partner could hardly go into the store without making himself liable as a general partner, and that by this arrangement he could advise with and assist the firm.

There was a clause in the articles of copartnership in these words: "As a matter of courtesy to Mr. E. C. Bramhall, of Jersey City, for the interest he has manifested in the welfare of this copartnership and his assistance in the advancement of its interests, we invite him, at all times, or at such times as may suit his convenience, to examine into our business affairs." Lord testified that when he saw the clause in the article of copartnership he objected to it as unnecessary, and Marks answered that he, Lord, knew that Bramhall had an interest, and that he had desired that article to be inserted. Lord testified further that after the copartnership was formed Bramhall told him that he had contributed $8,000 of the $20,000 capital furnished by Marks, and that he was to receive from Marks two-fifths of all that Marks received from the firm; and he requested that in giving the notes of the firm as dividends of profits, that they should be so drawn as that he might receive his share of them without waiting until they had become due; that he was to receive two-fifths of all that Marks received, whether he received it as interest or capital, or as dividends of profits, or as dividends of the capital at the time when the copartnership should terminate. Lord also testified that Marks knew of Bramhall having an interest or share in the profits of the firm; that he knew of it from Bramhall before the copartnership articles were signed, and that he introduced the article before referred to, so as to allow Bramhall to have a supervision over his interest; that Marks frequently told him that Bramhall owned a share of his interest in the business.

It appeared that an agreement in writing was executed between Bramhall and Marks, bearing date the third day of January, 1852, two days after the copartnership was to commence, by which it was agreed, in consideration of $8,000 received by Marks from Bramhall, that Marks would account for and pay over to Bramhall two-fifths of all sums of money, securities, or evidence of debt or other property, during the continuance of the copartnership, which Marks might receive therefrom as interest, profits or increase, and two-fifths of all that he might receive on the winding up thereof, Marks agreeing to account to Bramhall for two-fifths thereof, the same as if he, Bramhall, was a special partner in the house by the investment of the said sum of $8,000; but that Marks was not to be liable to Bramhall beyond two-fifths of all he received from the firm, in any event.

Admitting this state of facts to be true, it is apparent

that the whole arrangement was a flimsy contrivance to evade the statute, a device by which Bramhall meant to secure all the benefits of a limited copartnership to the extent of $8,000, with a more active interference in the business of the firm than the law will allow, without becoming responsible as a general partner. This is apparent from the written agreement between him and Marks, and from the insertion of the clause before referred to in the article, which Marks himself testified was inserted "simply because Bramhall was a good business man and could advise with Lord." This agreement operated as a transfer of two-fifths of Mark's interest, not only of the profits but of the capital invested by him. By the language of the agreement, he was to have everything that he could have had as a special partner investing $8,000, and, upon a dissolution, he would have been entitled to claim that interest. Having been transferred to him by Marks, the other partners would have been bound to pay it over to him. He could not become a special partner without complying with the provisions of the statute. As a special partner, he would have had the right from time to time to examine into the state and progress of the partnership concerns, and to advise as to their management. (2 *R. S.*, 51, § 17, 3*d ed.*) He sought to secure the right and all the benefit of a special partner without becoming one, and thereby made himself a general partner. He is made so by the operation of the statute, which declares that all persons interested in the partnership shall be liable as general partners if any false statement is made in the certificate or affidavit by which the limited copartnership is formed. (1 *R. S.*, *p.* 765, §§ 7, 8.) The statement in the certificate and affidavit was that Marks had contributed $20,000 of the capital. By Lord's testimony, $8,000 was contributed by Bramhall, with an understanding and under an arrangement by which he was to have all the benefit of a special partner without becoming one. Such is the legal effect of the written agreement between him and Marks. Such was the understanding of Lord both before and after the copartnership was formed; and though Brown, the other general partner, testifies that he knew nothing of it, the arrangement was carried out by the firm for three years, the notes for profits and interest on capital being drawn, as Bramhall had suggested, for two-fifths and three-fifths. This was proved by the defendants' witnesses. The clerk of the firm, Clusman, and the defendant Marks, testified that all the notes received by Marks were divided up in this way, and this is a fact with which Brown, as a general partner, is chargeable with the knowledge of. Lord conducted the financial business, but in his absence it was attended to by Brown. It was a matter which Brown could have known. It would appear upon the payment of the notes, and if he did not know it, it must be deemed to have been done with his assent. The fact that the $8,000 was in reality invested in the firm for the benefit of Bramhall, rendered the statement in the affidavit that it was contributed by Marks untrue, and the effect of this false statement was to make Bramhall and Marks general partners.

Both Bramhall and Marks denied that they had made the statements sworn to by Lord. They, however, contradict each other, and are in turn contradicted by the agreement. Marks swore that he borrowed the $8,000 from Bramhall. The agreement shows that it was not borrowed; that it was not a loan in any sense, which is an agreement to repay a sum received, with interest, if it is retained beyond the time when it is payable back. So far from being a loan, it was to be used in merchandising, and Bramhall was to receive all the profit that might grow out of its use in that way as part of the capital of a mercantile firm. Bramhall swore that he told Marks that he would loan him the $8,000 with the understanding that he could, if he so desired, have the privilege of taking two-fifths of what Marks should receive from the business of the firm in lieu of the $8,000; that he finally concluded to avail himself of that privilege, and that the arrangement was made when he entered into the written agreement; that was according to its date, on the 3d of January, 1852. Marks swore that, about the time of the formation of the partnership, Bramhall told him that he could loan him $8,000 for a time, but could not spare it from his business permanently; that it was finally left at his option that he might take two-fifths of what Marks should receive, or have the $8,000 repaid to him; and that, finally, in the summer following, they made a definite agreement that Bramhall was to have two-fifths of all profits; and in the last statement he is contradicted, both by Bramhall and by the agreement; in addition to which, the testimony of Marks throughout, and that of Bramhall to a certain extent, was evasive and shuffling.

So far, therefore, as the testimony of these witnesses was in conflict with the statement of Lord, it was for the jury to decide which they would believe; and as the judge left it to the jury to find as a question of fact whether Bramhall was interested in the partnership at the time of its formation, and the jury having found that he was, they must be regarded as having pronounced in favor of the truthfulness of Lord.

The special partnership could not be dissolved by the act of the parties until four weeks after the publication of notice of the intended dissolution, (*Beers* agt. *Reynolds*, 12 *Barb.*, 288; 1 *Kern.*, 100,) which in this case would be on the 17th of September, 1854. Before that time Marks withdrew all his capital by the transfer to him of certain interests, profits and notes which the statute forbids. (1 *R. S.*, *p.* 766, § 15.) He had nothing in the firm after the 14th of August, 1854. He could not by that act terminate his limited copartnership, but continued liable until the actual dissolution—that is, until the 17th of September, 1854—for all engagements which the firm might make in the prosecution of their business up to that time. One of the notes in suit was given for merchandise sold to the firm on the 18th of August, 1854, and for the payment of that note he is liable. He is liable upon that as well as upon the note given on the 19th of March, 1854, as a general partner, by reason of the false statement in the certificate and affidavit as to the amount contributed by him to the capital stock.

The answer as to the purpose of Bramhall's visit to the store was properly allowed. The witness spoke as to a general fact which he might well know. The same remark applies to the answers to the fifth and sixth interrogatories; the witness answered as to facts within his knowledge. The answers to the forty-eighth, fifty-third, fifty-seventh, fifty-ninth, sixtieth and forty-third cross-interrogatories in the last depositions read were all properly excluded. The testimony was totally irrelevant, and had no bearing upon the questions under consideration. There was no positive evidence that the plaintiff had received actual notice of the intended dissolution. The boy who served the circulars could remember but a few of the firms with whom they were left. The plaintiff Buckley admitted that he had seen circular, but could not recollect whether he had received a copy of it in August, 1854, or not, and that he did not recollect whether, when he sold the goods, he knew of the dissolution or not.

Marks and Bramhall, to be released from liability as general partners for the debt incurred by the sale of the goods on the 18th of August, 1854, were bound to show that the plaintiffs had notice of the dissolution before that sale; and there was no positive evidence that they had.

The published notice, moreover, was of the dissolution of a limited partnership, which did not operate under the statute as an actual dissolution until a month after this sale was made, and persons dealing with the firm had a right to rely upon the continuance of the partnership until the dissolution, as the notice expressed it, took "effect according to law." (*Beers* agt. *Reynolds*, 12 *Barb.*, 291; 1 *Com.*, 100.) The amount of the notes and the interest having been admitted by the counsel for Marks and Bramhall, there was no occasion for an assessment of the amount due.

The judgment should be affirmed.

SUPREME COURT.

Alfred Field and others agt. Isaac L. Hunt and others.

John Askham and others agt. The Same.

Each member of a copartnership has a right to dispose of his interest in the partnership property, in good faith, and for a valid consideration, unless some creditor has acquired a *lien* thereon. And the right of the creditor is subordinate to this power of the partner to dispose of the property *until it is subjected to the creditor's lien.*

Where one partner thus transfers his interest in the partnership assets to his copartner, the property so transferred cannot be reached by execution on a judgment recovered against the firm, where the *latter has not been personally served with process.*

The remedy at law has not been exhausted as against the partner not served with process, and of course a *creditor's suit* against the defendants cannot be maintained. (*This affirms the decision S. C. at special term, 22 How., 329.*)

It is *held* in the first judicial district that it is not necessary to wait sixty days—the return day of an execution—before commencing equitable proceedings on a judgment at law, if the execution has actually been returned before the sixty days have expired. (*There are adverse decisions in other districts.*)

New York General Term, February, 1863.

Ingraham, Leonard and Barnard, *Justices.*

Appeal by plaintiffs in each action from a judgment of the special term. The facts of this case will be found in full in the report of the case at special term. (22 *How. Pr. R.*, 329.)

GEORGE N. TITUS, *for plaintiffs.*

WM. CURTIS NOYES and CHAPMAN & HITCHCOCK, *for defendant Chapman.*

LEONARD, J. Each member of a copartnership may require the assets of the firm to be applied to the satisfaction of the partnership debts. Each member may also dispose of his interest in the partnership property in good faith, and for a valid consideration, unless some creditor has acquired a lien thereon. The right of the creditor is subordinate to this power of the partner to make a *bona fide* disposition of the property until it is subjected to the creditor's lien. (3 *Kent's Com.*, 65, *and note; Story's Eq. J.*, §§ 675, 1243, 1253; *Story on Partnerships*, §§ 373, 402; *Gow on Partnerships*, 275; *Ex parte Rowlandson*, 1 *Rose R.*, 416, 419; *Greenwood* agt. *Brodhead*, 8 *Barb. S. C.*, 593; *Crippen* agt. *Hudson*, 13 *N. Y. R.*, 161; *Sage* agt. *Chollar*, 21 *Barb. R.*, 596; *Ketchum* agt. *Durkee*, 1 *Barb. Ch. R.*, 480; *Kirby* agt. *Schoonmaker*, 3 *Barb. Ch. R.*, 46.)

In the present case Hunt transferred to Julia M. Chapman all his interest in the partnership assets. There is no allegation that this transfer was fraudulent. No creditor had any lien to prevent it. Hunt has made no stipulation for the benefit of the creditors of the firm, requiring Julia to pay the partnership debts, and she came under no obligation to her partner Hunt to apply those assets to any particular purpose, or to indemnify him against the partnership liabilities. The creditors have no equities here to be worked out through the retiring partner. That partner reserved none for them or for himself. His disposition of the assets was absolute and complete, and Julia became vested with the entire and separate ownership thereof.

This property so transferred cannot be reached by execution on a judgment recovered against the firm composed of Hunt and Julia M. Chapman, where she has not been personally served with process. The property belongs to her individually, and the execution to be issued on such judgment must direct the sheriff not to levy on her separate property.

It is quite clear that in such a case the remedy at law has not been exhausted as against Julia, and that creditors having judgments recovered by the service of process on Hunt only, with executions thereon, cannot maintain an action to inquire into or set aside any transfer made by her of such partnership property or assets as were conveyed to her by her former partner, Hunt, in the manner above mentioned.

The order appealed from should be affirmed.

INGRAHAM, P. J. There can be no doubt that the judgment in this case would not be sufficient to warrant an execution against the defendant Chapman, who was not served, so as to reach her individual property.

Nor would it form the foundation of an action against her if she had been sued upon it; that would only furnish the amount of recovery after her liability was established by other evidence. (*Mervin* agt. *Kumbell*, 23 *Wend.*, 293; *Oakley* agt. *Aspinwall*, 4 *Comst.*, 513.)

Nor would it be a cause of action upon which an attachment against the debtor not served could be issued. (*Id.*)

In the *Commercial Bank, &c.* agt. *Meach*, (7 *Paige*, 468,) the CHANCELLOR held that, upon a joint judgment against several defendants, some of whom were not served with process, all must be made defendants in a creditor's bill, to enable those whose property was taken to satisfy the debt to claim contribution against their co-defendants; and in *Howard* agt. *Sheldon*, (11 *Paige*, 558,) he held that in an action on a judgment against joint debtors, where process was not served on one defendant, but an execution issued against the joint property of all and the separate property of the one served, the creditor had not by such execution exhausted his remedy at law so as to entitle him to a creditor's bill against the defendant who was served with process in the last suit.

In that case it was also held that the complainant had not exhausted his remedy at law for the recovery of his debt until execution had been issued against each of the defendants as to their individual property as well as the joint property of the firm.

This rule, applied to the present case, shows that the order appealed from was correct. (*See, also, Childs* agt. *Brace et al.*, 4 *Paige*, 309.)

There is no force in the objection that the execution was returned before sixty days had expired. All the judges in this district have held that it was not necessary. The CHANCELLOR also so held in *Platt* agt. *Cadwell*, (9 *Paige*, 386.)

NOTE.—As there is considerable diversity of opinion in reference to this question, perhaps it may not be considered out of place, or improper, to briefly review some of the decisions of the late court of chancery on this point. In this *same case* at special term, (22 *How. Pr. R.*, 329,) W. F. ALLEN, J., said: "Had the objection been urged that sixty days had not elapsed between the issuing of the executions upon the judgments at law and the commencement of these actions, I should have felt constrained to hold the objection well taken, following the decision at general term in the fifth district, and the construction given by the CHANCELLOR to the statute regulating this equitable remedy." (*Cassidy* agt. *Meacham*, 3 *Paige*, 311; *Strange* agt. *Longley*, 3 *Barb. Ch.*, 650.)

In the case of *Platt* agt. *Cadwell*, (9 *Paige*, 386,) the CHANCELLOR said: "This court does not inquire into the regularity of the proceedings of courts of co-ordinate jurisdiction. And the return of the executions in this case, even if they were liable to be set aside for irregularity by the court out of which they issued, were not void. The complainant, therefore, *after the return day was past, had a right to consider his remedy at law exhausted,* and to file his bill here to reach the effects of the defendant, which could not be levied on by the sheriff. And if the filing of the executions, with the return indorsed thereon, before the expiration of sixty days, was irregular, the defendant must apply to the court of law to set aside the returns. (*Williams* agt. *Hogeboom*, 8 *Paige*, 469.) All that this court can do in such a case is to compel the complainant *to wait until after the return day of the execution is past* before he files his bill here. (*Cassidy* agt. *Meacham*, 3 *Paige*, 311.) And it will, when necessary, stay the proceedings here a sufficient length of time to give the defendant an opportunity to apply to the court of law for relief, where there is a probability that such relief will be granted.

To the same effect is the case of *Williams* agt. *Hogeboom*, *supra*, where the execution was made returnable on a day certain, which was only five days after its

SUPREME COURT.

Daniel Gardner agt. Hiram Barney and Charles Butler.

Where an appeal is taken from the judgment of the special term to the general term, and the proper *undertaking* executed by the appellant and his sureties, under and in pursuance of § 335 of the Code, the *obligation of the sureties* is not fulfilled, and the undertaking satisfied by a reversal of the judgment at the general term, *where the judgment of the general term has also been reversed in the court of appeals.*

That is, the *sureties* are not limited in their liability to the judgment of the *general term.* The *affirmance* mentioned in their undertaking, is an affirmance by the legally constituted tribunal having cognizance *finally* of the subject of the litigation. The *reversal* by the court of appeals, when effect is given to it in the court below, is in fact an *affirmance by the general term* of the judgment at the *special term.*

Nor are the liabilities of the sureties at all affected or changed by the fact that when they executed the undertaking there was no law in existence that authorized an appeal to the court of appeals from an order of the general term *granting a new trial;* but before the decision of the general term a law was passed which authorized such an appeal, and under which the appeal in this case was taken.

When an appeal is from a judgment against two defendants, the sureties upon a joint undertaking are liable if the judgment is *affirmed against one.* (*To the same effect is Seacord* agt. *Morgan*, 17 *How. Pr. R.*, 394.)

---

teste; the Chancellor says: "I am satisfied that a neglect to make an execution returnable at the end of sixty days, from the receipt thereof by the sheriff, renders it irregular merely; and that the execution is not void, so as to make the attorney issuing it, and the party in whose favor it is issued, trespassers, without the necessity of an application to the court to set aside the execution for the irregularity."

In *Cassidy* agt. *Meacham, supra*, the Chancellor said: "Perhaps a return made by the sheriff on an execution before the return day, may be valid by relation, after the expiration of the time the execution has to run. *Until the return day, however,* it would be the duty of the sheriff to seize and sell any property of the defendants which could be found within his bailiwick. *The execution cannot, therefore, be considered as legally returned unsatisfied until after the return day.* The creditor must, in his bill, set out the issuing of the execution, the time at which it was returnable, and the actual return of the sheriff thereon, in such a manner that the court can see that the remedy at law has been *legally exhausted.* The intention of the legislature was to adopt the principle settled by the court for the correction of errors in *Hadden* agt. *Spader*, (20 *John. R.*, 554,) and not to establish an arbitrary rule, by which the defendant might be harassed by a suit in chancery when he had sufficient property which could be reached at law *during the life of the execution.* In the case under consideration the court cannot legally know, or presume, *previous to the return day of the execution,* that the judgment will not be satisfied. Although the sheriff cannot now find property, the defendants may, before that time, satisfy the execution out of the equitable funds in their hands, which cannot be levied on by him."—Rep.

Brooklyn General Term, February, 1863.

BROWN, LOTT and SCRUGHAM, *Justices*.

APPEAL by defendants from a judgment at special term. The facts will appear in the opinion of the court.

WM. CURTIS NOYES, *for the plaintiff*.
SAMUEL J. TILDEN, *for defendants*.

By the court, BROWN, Justice. In April, 1856, Daniel Gardner recovered a judgment at the special term of this court, held at Troy, in the county of Rensselaer, against Henry Smith and William B. Ogden, for the sum of $15,000 and interest thereon with the costs of the action, with a provision that the reconveyance of certain lands mentioned in the judgment, and within the time therein prescribed, should be deemed a satisfaction of the judgment or decree, so far as damages and interest were concerned. From this judgment an appeal was taken to the general term, and thereupon the defendants in this action entered into and executed the undertaking upon which this action is brought, which was duly acknowledged and filed in the proper office. The judgment was afterwards reversed at the general term and a new trial ordered. This was in December, 1857. In January, 1858, Gardner appealed to the court of appeals from the order granting a new trial, and in December, 1860, the court of appeals gave judgment in favor of the defendant Ogden, and against the defendant Smith—that is, the court of appeals reversed the judgment of the general term, and affirmed that of the special term against the defendant Smith. The judgment of the court of appeals was perfected in this court upon the remittitur against Smith; an execution against him was duly issued thereon, which was returned *nulla bona*, of which the defendants in this action had notice, but they omitted to pay the judgment. Thereupon Gardner brought this action against them upon the undertaking. The action was put at issue and tried before Mr. Justice LOTT, without a jury, at the Kings circuit, in 1862, where the foregoing facts were found by him, and he rendered judgment against the defendants in this action for $23,104.41, besides costs. The defendants excepted and then appealed.

The undertaking is given in conformity with § 335 of the Code. It recites the recovery of the judgment at the special term, giving the amount thereof, and states that the defendants have appealed therefrom to the general term of the supreme court. It then asserts that the defendants "undertake that the appellants will pay all costs and damages which may be awarded against them on appeal, not exceeding $250;" and also, "that if the said judgment so appealed from, or any part thereof, be affirmed, the appellants will pay the amount directed to be paid by said judgment, or the part of such amount as to which the said judgment shall be affirmed, if it be affirmed only in part, and all damages which shall be awarded against said appellants on the said appeal." The defendants claim that the meaning and effect of their agreement is not to be enlarged by construction, so as to charge them as sureties for the defendants in the judgment appealed from; and that the recital in the words, "have appealed to the general term," is to be regarded as a limitation, restraining and limiting their liability to the appeal to the judgment of the general term. The judgment appealed from was entered upon the order of a single judge, and the only appeal that could be taken was that to the general term. In no other way could the defendants review what had been done. The undertaking would, therefore, have been quite as effective for all the purposes of perfecting the appeal and staying the collection of the money, mentioned in the judgment or decree, had the words "general term" been omitted. They are to be regarded as merely descriptive of what had been done to give point and effect to the words that follow, and not to limit the liability of the sureties to such order or judgment as might be rendered by the general term. Besides, the subsequent words are explicit, that if the judgment was affirmed without limitation as to time or form, the appel lants would pay it. The affirmance spoken of is an affirmance by the legally constituted tribunal having cognizance finally of the subject of the litigation. Any other construction would be at variance with the decisions of the courts in analogous cases. In *Gelston* agt. *Codwise*, (1 *John. Ch. Rep.*, 194,) the CHANCELLOR says: "It is the acknowledged doctrine of a court of review to give such decree as the court below ought to have given; and when the plaintiff below brings the appeal, the court above not only reverses what is wrong but decrees what is right, and models the relief according to its own view of the ends of justice and the exigencies of the case. The court above, therefore, acts on appeals in a given case with all the plentitude of a court of equity of original jurisdiction, and the special terms of the decree, whatever they may be, become to this court the law of that case, and no other or further relief can be administered to the party." The general term committed an error in reversing the judgment or decree against Smith, and when this error was corrected in the court of appeals, the judgment of the latter court then became the law and the judgment of the supreme court. In *Traver* agt. *Nichols*, (7 *Wend.*, 434,) the question was, whether the security required to be given by a non-resident plaintiff, upon applying for a warrant, is confined to such sum as may be adjudged against him by the justice, or whether it also extended to the final determination of the cause when it was carried to the court of common pleas by appeal. The court, after citing the statute, said: "There is nothing in this act which restricts the security to the costs before the justice. It extends in terms to any sum which may be adjudged against the non-resident plaintiff in the cause. It is the same cause, although carried by appeal to the court of common pleas. No new pleadings are put in, and it is considered but a counter-action of the original suit." Various cases are referred to in support of the opinion. In *Ball* agt. *Gardner*, (21 *Wend.*, 270,) the question was, whether the condition of a bond taken on suing out an attachment, before a justice of the peace, extended to, and is controlled by, the final result in the common pleas—in other words, whether a condition was kept by a recovery of judgment before the justice. The court adjudged not, and say: "The reasons given for the judgment of the court in *Traver* agt. *Nichols*, *supra*, apply with the greater force to the case before us. The plaintiff in the attachment binds himself to pay all damages and costs that the defendant may sustain by reason of the issuing of it, if he fail to recover judgment thereon. Now, it is clear that he has failed. The reversal in the common pleas, on the certiorari, has at least vacated the judgment before the justice, and if it proceeded upon the merits, has finally disposed of the subject matter of the litigation. (*Vide also Smith* agt. *Crouse*, 24 *Barb. S. C. R.*, 433; *Bennett* agt. *Brown*, 20 *N. Y. R.*, 99.) There is nothing in the section of the Code, under which the undertaking was given, nor in the language of the undertaking itself, which restricts the liability of the sureties to the action of the general term; and I therefore conclude that their duty and obligation is not fulfilled and the undertaking satisfied by showing a reversal of the judgment at the general term, where it also appears that its judgment has also been reversed in the court of appeals. This reversal by the court of appeals, where effect is given to it in the court below, is in fact an affirmance by the general term of the judgment rendered at the special term.

The judgment of the general term reversed that rendered at the special term and ordered a new trial. It is to be observed that the undertaking bears date on the 26th of July, 1856. At this time there was no right of appeal to the court of appeals from an order of the general term of this court granting a new trial. In 1857 the practice was modified and the following provision inserted in the Code of Procedure: "But no appeal to the court of appeals from an order granting a new trial shall be effectual for any purpose, unless the notice of appeal contain an assent on the part of the appellant that if the order be affirmed, judgment absolute shall be rendered against the appellant. If the court of appeals shall determine that no error was committed in granting the new trial, they shall render judgment absolute upon the rights of the appellant." (2 *Laws of* 1857, *pp.* 551, 552.) It is quite apparent that but for this action by the legislature there would have been no substantial ground upon which this action could have been maintained; because, without the amendment to the law which I have quoted, the error made by the court at general term could not have been corrected by a direct appeal to the court of appeals. The cause must have been remitted upon the order granting a new trial to the circuit or the special term, there to be retried upon the law as announced by the general term, and subject to a new appeal by the party thinking himself aggrieved by the judgment upon the new trial. Thus the undertaking and the obligation of the defendants in this action would have been satisfied and extinguished. They now claim and insist that this change in the practice of the courts upon appeal has enlarged their liability and changed the nature of their contract as sureties, and that consequently, upon well known principles, they are discharged; or, to state the proposition in another form, that their contract does not extend to an affirmance of the judgment rendered under the new provisions of the Code. The defendants undertook that if the judgment was affirmed the appellants would pay. There is nothing in the undertaking which qualifies the word "affirmed." It was not to be affirmed in any prescribed manner nor in any given tribunal. It was not to be affirmed according to the practice of the courts existing at the time the undertaking was executed. The obligation was, that the appellants should pay if the judgment was affirmed generally. The defendants' argument is in effect a claim that the mode of procedure existing at the time is to be regarded as incorporated into and made a material stipulation of the undertaking; that the contract is made with express reference to such modes of proceeding, and any change effected therein by the legislature or the rules of the court relieves the parties to the undertaking from their obligation. Such a rule would render all amendment and improvement in the practice of the courts attainable only at the hazard of impairing the obligation of undertakings previously given as security for the payment of moneys and the restoration of property in the numerous instances in which such instruments are required by the practice. A more sensible rule would be to hold that such undertakings are given with reference and subject to the power of the legislature to change the practice, provided such legislation does not impair absolute rights or stipulations material and essential to the security and protection of the parties who execute them. Thus a provision that a party recovering a judgment upon appeal, shall exhaust his remedy against the judgment debtor before he resorts to the sureties upon the bond or undertaking upon appeal, as in the statutory provision referred to in the case of *Hamilton* agt. *Averill*, (11 *Wend.*, 625,) is made for their benefit and protection, and of which they cannot be deprived by legislation or otherwise, without at the same time impairing the obligation of their contract. Such a change in the law acts directly upon the contract as well as upon the proceedings in the action, because the issuing of an execution against the judgment debtor is the most efficient means of collecting the debt without resort to the sureties upon the bond or undertaking; but a change in the mode of hearing the appeal and of affirming or reversing the judgment appealed from stands upon very different grounds. The sureties upon the undertaking can have no interest whatever in having the proceedings conducted or heard in any particular mode. If the appeal is heard and determined by the constitutional tribunals of the state, created for that purpose, the process by which that end is attained is not material to the contract of the sureties upon the undertaking, and forms no part of it. Let it be assumed that the judgment had been affirmed at the general term when it rendered its judgment, which was in December, 1857, and there had been no other appeal, could there have been any real doubt of the liability of the sureties upon the undertaking? What good reason could have been given for their exoneration? None whatever, that I can imagine. There is their written agreement that the appellants should pay if the judgment should be affirmed, and there would have been the judgment of affirmance at the general term and no further appeal. The liability of the sureties would, under such circumstances, have been irrevocably fixed. If the sureties would have been liable, then they must be liable now, because if their contract is impaired or broken by force of the act of the 17th April, 1857, it was impaired and broken the moment the act passed into the form of a law, which was eight months before the decision of the general term was rendered. The undertaking and the defendants' obligation under it, cannot be valid and in force up to the time the decision of the general term was rendered, and of no force or effect after that time. These reasons lead me to conclude that the right of the plaintiff to maintain this action is not affected by the amendment to the law giving an appeal from an order made at the general term of this court granting a new trial. We have already determined (*Seacord* agt. *Morgan*, 17 *How. Pr. R.*, 394) that when there is an appeal from a judgment against two defendants, the sureties upon a joint undertaking are liable if the judgment is affirmed against one.

The judgment of the special term should be affirmed.

NEW YORK SUPERIOR COURT.

Sally Ann Howell agt. The Knickerbocker Life Insurance Company.

A motion under § 160 of the Code, to strike out irrelevant matters, cannot prevail to strike out a *whole complaint*.

Whether matters set up in a complaint, which are intended to constitute a cause of action, do or do not constitute a cause of action, must be *tested by demurrer*.

Where matters alleged in the complaint, by way of excuse for not paying the premium on a life policy of insurance on the day it fell due, were proposed to be stricken out under § 160,

Held, that if they did not furnish a legal excuse the plaintiff had no cause of action to recover on the policy; but they were not so *palpably immaterial* in making out a good cause of action as to be disposed of summarily, and to justify the court in pronouncing the complaint bad. The defendants must be put to their *demurrer*.

New York Special Term, March, 1863.

In the year 1853, as appeared in this case, George R. Howell, of this city, as agent for his wife, insured his life for her benefit and the benefit of his children in the Knickerbocker Life Insurance Company, of this city, in the sum of $5,000. The premiums were paid regularly and punctually, as claimed from that time until 1861. On the morning of the 15th of July, 1862—that being the day upon which the premium became payable—Howell left his residence in perfect health and proceeded to his place of business, where he made memoranda of several things to be done on that day, and among them was the payment of the premium on this policy of insurance. But before noon of that day he was suddenly struck with paralysis, and lingered in a state of stupor, incapable of speech or action, until the next day, when he died.

The fact of the non-payment of the premium was not discovered until a day or two after his death, when the same was tendered to the company. The company, however, declined receiving the premium, and claimed that the policy was forfeited.

This action was thereupon brought, and the complaint

set out a number of facts to relieve the plaintiff from the consequences of omitting to pay the premium on the day fixed. Motion was made to strike out such allegations as irrelevant.

Robertson, Justice. It is conceded that if the parts proposed to be stricken from the complaint be so stricken out, no cause of action on the policy will be set out.

The motion is made under the 160th section of the Code to strike out irrelevant matters. Under this a motion could not prevail to strike out a whole complaint. The irrelevancy must therefore be to the cause of action as the plaintiff claims it to exist, and not as the defendant supposes it to be constituted. Possibly all the matters set up in the complaint may not furnish a legal excuse for not paying the premium on the day it was fixed to be paid; if they do not, the plaintiff has no cause of action. But whether they do or not should be tested by demurrer, otherwise such a motion might be made always to take the place of a demurrer by attacking any allegation of a complaint, upon the ground that it did not aid in constituting an available legal cause of action.

But the allegations proposed to be stricken out are not so palpably immaterial in making out a good cause of action as to be disposed of summarily. It is not so clear that the policy is not an insurance for the life of the party mentioned in it, defeasible on the failure of the assured to pay the premiums on the day fixed. It is a sealed instrument; the payment of the annual premiums may not be intended to make a new agreement, but only to sustain the fixed one, otherwise the provision that the parties could make a new agreement is superfluous, since they necessarily have that right. If a new contract is to be made on the payment of each premium, many of the representations contained in the application for insurance might be untrue at the time of such payments, and thus avoid the new contract. Premiums or policies of life insurance are concluded according to the age of the subject insured. If the defendants had a right to refuse a policy at the end of each year on the same terms, the assured would have paid his premium in vain. (*See Peacock* agt. *The New York Life Ins. Co.*, 3 *Bosw. Sup. Ct. Rep*,, 293.)

It is also specified in the policy that all premiums shall be forfeited in case there shall be found any misrepresentations or concealment in the representations; this tends to show that the representations were to apply to the continuance of the policy by all furure payments of premiums. All such considerations have a tendency to show the payment of premiums annually to be a condition subsequent, and capable of having these rigorous terms relaxed.

The policy also provides that a payment on the 15th of July, in each year of the premium, keeps the policy alive. The assured have consequently the whole day to pay it in, although the time fixed in the body of the policy expires at noon. If the subject of insurance died in the afternoon, a tender of the premium before midnight might make the company responsible. This rather gives color to the construction that precise time was not of the essence of the contract. Any understanding of the company with the plaintiff's husband, or usage on their part, might perhaps sustain a deviation by her from the rigorous terms of the contract, if the payment of premiums were only conditions subsequent.

It is possible, also, the act of God in striking down the plaintiff's husband, agent, and sole reliance in paying the premium, may excuse the want of exact performance of the contract. (*See Wolfe* agt. *Howes*, 20 *N. Y. R.*, *and cases cited by* ALLEN, *Justice; and Baldwin* agt. *New York Life Insurance & Trust Company*, 3 *Bosw.*, 530.)

There is enough in the case to justify me in not pronouncing the complaint palpably bad, and compelling the defendants to demur. The motion must be denied with $10 costs to abide the event.

SUPREME COURT.

JOHN BELL agt. JACOB NOAH and others.

Upon an application for judgment on account of the frivolousness of the pleading under § 247 of the Code, the weight of authority is against allowing a *trial fee* of $15. Costs of a motion, $10 only, can be allowed.

Erie General Term, November, 1862.

MARVIN, *P. J.*, DAVIS, GROVER and HOYT, *Justices*.

APPEAL from an order allowing a trial fee upon an application for judgment, under § 247 of the Code, upon the ground that the demurrer to the complaint was frivolous.

WM. ROBERTSON, *for plaintiff*.
HUMPHREY & PARSONS, *for defendants*.

By the court, MARVIN, Justice. The weight of authority is against this allowance of $15 for a trial fee. In *Gould* agt. *Carpenter*, (7 *How. Pr. R.*, 97,) Justice HARRIS decided that the hearing of such application was not a trial. In *Lawrence* agt. *Davis*, (*id.*, 354,) Justice ROOSEVELT decided that the full costs of a trial were recoverable. The same decision was made in *Roberts* agt. *Morrison*, (*id.*, 396,) by MORRIS, Justice.

In *Roberts* agt. *Clark*, (10 *How.*, 451,) Justice WELLES held such application to be a motion, and that the prevailing party could only have motion costs. In *Marquiser* agt. *Bingham*, (12 *How.*, 399,) Justice BALCOM, upon a motion for judgment upon the ground that the answer was frivolous, held that the costs of a motion, $10 only, could be allowed.

In the *Rochester City Bank* agt. *Rapelje*, (12 *How.*, 26,) it was decided by the general term in the 7th district that upon such an application there was no trial of an issue as defined by the Code; that if the judge does not see the demurrer, answer or reply to be frivolous, he makes no decision of the issue. but simply decides that it is not frivolous. Justice Welles examines the various provisions of the Code bearing upon the question, and I fully concur in the opinion. (*See also The People* agt. *McCumber*, 18 *N. Y. R.*, 324–5.)

The order of the special term must be reversed, and the trial fee, $15, disallowed.

SUPREME COURT.

Ann E. Leggett agt. William D. Sloan.

A judgment creditor having *supplementary proceedings* pending, is not entitled to *eight* days' notice of an application for a receiver by *another creditor*. A less notice is sufficient.

New York General Term, February, 1863.

Sutherland, Ingraham and Clerke, *Justices*.

This was an appeal by Charles Brower from an order appointing a receiver in supplementary proceedings in above action, on the ground that, as a judgment creditor having supplementary proceedings pending, he was entitled to eight days' notice of an application for a receiver, by another creditor, and that a less notice was insufficient.

E. C. D. Kittridge, *for appellant.*

Daniel W. Baldwin, *for respondent.*

By the court, Clerke, Justice.—As to the objection that the notice to the other judgment creditors was too short:

The application to appoint a receiver under supplementary proceedings is not a motion, within section 402 of the Code. Section 298, which authorizes the judge to appoint a receiver under these proceedings, directs him, if practicable, to ascertain if other supplementary proceedings are pending against the judgment debtor; and if such proceedings are pending, the plaintiff therein shall have notice to appear before him, &c.

This notice is not a notice of motion to the plaintiff in the other proceedings, but a notice to appear, in order that he may have an opportunity of showing that a receiver in his proceedings has been appointed, and that the judge may be governed accordingly in the selection of a receiver in the proceedings pending before him.

Order affirmed with costs.

SUTHERLAND, P. J., concurred.

NOTE.—In the case of *Richardson* agt. *Brooklyn City & Newtown R. R. Co.*, *ante*, *p.* 321, the *head note* was made hastily, and is broader than the decision of the court will authorize. All that the court decided in that case, and which should be considered as the correct head note, is as follows:

On substitution of attorneys, where the plaintiff has assigned the judgment without notice to his attorney, an order of reference has been made by the court to ascertain the amount of the original attorney's lien on the judgment to the amount of his *taxed costs*, and the attorney moves to amend the order of reference by extending it to his claim for a lien beyond the taxed costs, but does not show any *special agreement* with the plaintiff to that effect, his motion to amend will be denied, without prejudice to his lien or right, if he has any beyond the taxable costs, on or to the judgment on the final recovery, as against the assignee of the judgment.

SUPREME COURT.

THE PEOPLE *ex rel.* PATRICK E. DILLON agt. THE BOARD OF METROPOLITAN POLICE.

When the *jurisdiction of an inferior tribunal* depends upon *evidence* to be taken before it, this court, upon *certiorari* will examine such evidence in order to determine the question of *jurisdiction, but for no other purpose.*

An order was given to the *relator* as a member of the Metropolitan police by one of its sergeants to proceed to Hamilton Avenue, Brooklyn, and either kill a dog which had bitten a child, or bring the dog to the station house. The *relator* did neither, alleging that the order was *illegal.* After a trial before the board of police, he was removed for *disobedience of orders,*

Held, that the order was a *legal and proper* one, which the *relator* was bound to obey.

Such a case is not one in which this court should interfere. The discipline of the police force of a large city to be effectual must be sharp and severe, and vigorously applied. Disobedience of orders is an offence which should not be extenuated.

Brooklyn General Term, December, 1862.

EMOTT, BROWN and LOTT, *Justices.*

CERTIORARI, to remove proceedings on an order of the defendant's removing the *relator* as a member of the Metropolitan police.

WINCHESTER BRITTON, *for the relator.*

A. J. VANDERPOEL, *for the defendant.*

By the court, BROWN, Justice. On the 6th of August, 1860, the relator was a member of the Metropolitan police force of the Metropolitan district of the state, and on the 11th of the same month was removed from his office by an order made by the defendant. This writ of certiorari is brought to remove the proceedings into this court for review and reversal, upon the ground that the board of Metropolitan police exceeded its authority, and that its proceedings were illegal and erroneous.

The 10th section of the act of the 10th of April, 1860, to amend the act concerning the Metropolitan police district, provides for the appointment by the board of the superintendent and other officers and members of the police force whenever vacancies occur therein, and confers upon it authority to promulgate all regulations and orders through the superintendent of police, who shall be the executive head of the whole police force of the Metropolitan district, with the direction and control of the force, subject to the rules and regulations of the board of police. The 13th section of the act also directs that each member of the force shall hold office during good behavior, and shall be liable to be removed only after written charges shall have been preferred against him according to the rules and regulations of the board of police, and the same shall have been publicly heard and examined after notice to him thereof by the board in the manner prescribed by such rules and regulations. These two sections briefly prescribe the mode of appointment to office, the duration of the time thereof, and the manner of removal therefrom. Written charges are to be preferred against the member charged with delinquency. Notice is to be given to him of the hearing before the board of police, and the same are to be publicly heard; that is, there is to be a public trial upon written charges, of which the accused is to have due notice, with an opportunity to be present at the examination of the witnesses, and to offer such defence as he may have to make.

The return to the writ of certiorari is full and explicit upon all these points. It appears that charges of disobedience of orders were duly preferred against the relator. A copy thereof was duly served upon him, which he was required to examine and answer. A notice was also given to him of the time and place appointed for the hearing. He was also at the same time served with a copy of rule No. 7 of the rules of the board of police, which directs that where charges are filed the chief clerk shall notify the accused to call and examine and answer the same either in writing or orally, to be taken down by such clerk. The rule also directs, that the trial may be had at any subsequent meeting of the board of which the accused shall be advised. But he may waive such trial, and submit the case and answer upon affidavits, after two days' notice has been given to the complainant of such waiver, and opportunity for the latter to procure witnesses, or to furnish affidavits in support of his complaint. The return further shows that on the 11th day of August, 1860, the trial was had before the board of police at their office in the city of New York. Four witnesses were sworn and examined on behalf of the complainant, and the relator was then and there also sworn in his own behalf; and after hearing the proofs and allegations of the parties, the board made the order that the charge of disobedience of orders was established and made out, and that the relator was guilty thereof, and that he be removed from his office as a member of the Metropolitan police force.

It is not claimed that there is any irregularity in the proceedings themselves which the relator seeks to review. The errors alleged are: First, the want of sufficient proof to establish the charge of disobedience of orders. Second, that the order referred to required the relator to do an illegal act which he was under no obligation to obey. The sufficiency of the evidence to sustain the charge is not open to question and examination in this proceeding. The office of a common law certiorari is to bring up the record from the inferior tribunal, and if it appears to have had jurisdiction, this court will not examine the evidence for the purpose of reviewing the decision upon the merits. (*Carter* agt. *Newbold*, 7 *How. Pr. R.*, 166; *The People* agt. *Goodwin*, 1 *Selden*, 568; *The People* agt. *Van Alstyne*, 32 *Barb. S. C. R.*, 131.) When the jurisdiction depends upon evidence to be taken before the inferior tribunal, this court upon certiorari will examine such evidence in order to determine the question of jurisdiction, but for no other purpose.

The order given to the relator was from one of the sergeants of police. It directed him to proceed to Hamilton avenue, Brooklyn, and either kill a dog which had bitten a child, or bring the dog to the station house. The specification was that he did neither. He did not kill the animal, or bring it to the station house. It is going very far, I think, to say that such an order issued to a policeman by his superior officer in a populous city is illegal. A dog, *per se*, is not a nuisance; but a dog with certain habits and propensities—such as flying at persons and biting children upon the public streets—is a nuisance of the worst kind, which it is clearly the duty of the police to suppress. If he did not kill the dog, the order was to bring him to the station house. Freedom from arrest and detention at the station house is not one of the privileges and immunities of dogs. The order, I think, was clearly a legal and proper order, and one which the policeman was bound to obey.

In conclusion, this is not a case in which we should interfere. The discipline of the police force of a large city to be effectual must be sharp and severe, and vigorously applied. Disobedience of orders is an offence which should not be extenuated.

The proceedings should be affirmed with costs.

NEW YORK COMMON PLEAS.

John C. Baxter and others, respondents agt. Robert R. Wallace, appellant.

A person whose real interest is that of a *mortgagee*, and who has *never taken possession of the vessel*, is not answerable for *supplies*, though he holds a *bill of sale* vesting in him the *legal title*, and though the vessel may be *registered in his name* at the custom house accompanied by his oath that he is the true and only owner.

To make a mortgagee responsible for supplies, it must be shown either that he was *in possession of the vessel*, or that they were furnished *at his request*, or by the direction of some person *authorized to contract on his behalf*.

General Term, February, 1863.

Daly, Brady and Hilton, *Judges*.

APPEAL by defendant from judgment for plaintiffs rendered at special term.

D. & T. McMAHON, *for appellant.*
A. S. DIOSSY, *for respondent.*

By the court, DALY, F. J. The plaintiffs sought to charge the defendant Wallace as owner of the brig Hope for supplies furnished to the brig in the port of New York, where the vessel belonged. To charge the defendant personally, it was necessary to show that the supplies were furnished either by his expressed authority, or under circumstances from which an authority would be implied. The supplies were furnished at the request of the mate of the vessel and one Webster. Webster introduced the mate to the plaintiffs, and told them to deliver what goods he might order for the brig, and to present the bill on board, and that it would be paid. The plaintiffs produced no evidence to show that either Webster or the mate had any authority from the defendant to order the supplies, and the defendant swore expressly that he had never authorized any person to present the bill to him; that he did not know the mate; had never had any transactions with him; that he never had possession of the vessel; had never seen her but once; had nothing to do with the loading of her; did not control her running in any way; had no interest in her profits, and had never employed any officer or any one on board of her. This was decisive upon the question of authority, but the plaintiffs recovered simply upon the ground that the defendant held a bill of sale of the brig, and had made the usual affidavit at the custom house that he was the owner of the vessel.

The nature of his interest was this: Webster bought the brig at a marshal's sale, and to complete the purchase he borrowed $800 of the defendant upon an agreement that the title should be taken in the defendant's name as a security for the loan. The bill of sale was accordingly made out in the name of the defendant, and a written instrument in the nature of a defeasance was executed by both parties, setting forth that Wallace had loaned Webster $800 for the purpose of enabling him to purchase the brig; that it was agreed that the title should be in Wallace, and that Wallace, upon the payment to him of the $800 and interest, was to transfer the vessel to Webster or his order. This was not such an ownership as would make the defendant responsible for supplies furnished to the vessel, though the bill of sale was made out in the name of the defendant. The transaction, as shown by both instruments, was, in legal effect, a mortgage. He held the bill of sale merely as security for the eight hundred dollars; and though the legal title was vested in him, his interest was no greater than that of a mortgagee.

It is well settled that a person whose real interest is that of a mortgagee, and who has never taken possession of the vessel, is not answerable for supplies, though he holds a bill of sale vesting in him the legal title, and though the vessel may be registered in his name. (*Noartyman* agt. *Hart*, 1 *Starkie's R.*, 366; *Hasketh* agt. *Stevens*, 7 *Barb.*, 488; *Leonard* agt. *Huntington*, 15 *Johns.*, 288; *McIntyre* agt. *Scott*, 8 *id.*, 159; *Abbot on Shipping*, *p.* 35 *to* 40, 132, 8*th Lond. ed.*)

The registration of a vessel at the custom house under a bill of sale, although accompanied by the oath of the person in whose name it is registered that he is the true and only owner, is not conclusive as to the ownership, the object of the registry being simply to determine the national character of the vessel; and though the bill of sale is absolute upon its face, it may be shown that it was intended, in fact, to operate as mortgage. (*Sharp* agt. *United States Ins. Co.*, 14 *Johns.*, 201; *Weston* agt. *Penniman*, 1 *Mason*, 318; *Ring* agt. *Franklin*, 2 *Hall R.*, 1; *Dey* agt. *Dunham*, 15 *Johns.*, 555.)

To make a mortgagee responsible for supplies, it must be

shown either that he was in possession of the vessel (*Miles* agt. *Spinola*, 4 *Hill*, 177,) or that they were furnished at his request, or by the direction of some person authorized to contract on his behalf. Nothing of the kind having been shown here, there was no ground whatever for the judgment.

Judgment reversed.

SUPREME COURT.

LUCIUS M. BANGS, receiver, &c. of the Genesee Mutual Insurance Company agt. HENRY W. BARTO.

By the "act to facilitate the closing up of insolvent and dissolved mutual insurance companies," passed April 21, 1862, it was intended to limit the *costs, besides disbursements, to twenty dollars*, in all cases where actions had been commenced, and *had not proceeded to judgment*, whether they should be referred under the fifth section to a referee, or the issues joined should be tried by the court or a jury.

Wyoming Special Term, December, 1862.

MOTION for readjustment of costs. The action was tried by the court at the Genesee November circuit, 1862, and decision of the court was in favor of the plaintiff for $196. The bill of costs, containing charges for *term* and *trial* fees, amounting to $70, was presented to the clerk for adjustment. These items were rejected and $20 substituted. The action was upon a premium note given for a policy of insurance.

A. N. WELLES, *for plaintiff.*
C. HENSHAW, *for defendant.*

MARVIN, Justice. Whether the clerk was right, depends upon the construction to be given to the act of April 21, 1862, entitled "An act to facilitate the closing up of insolvent and dissolved mutual insurance companies." (*Sess.*

Laws 1862, 743.) The first section of the act provides for a reference to a sole referee of any controversy or disagreement in the settlement of any demand or claim against a member or stockholder.

The 2d, 3d and 4th sections relate to the powers and duties of the referee and the practice, including an appeal to the supreme court. It is declared in the fifth section that " the supreme court shall have power to refer all actions now pending therein, wherein any such receiver is a party, and when any controversy arises, as mentioned in the first section of this act. Such reference shall in no way prejudice the proceedings already had." The sixth section provides: " The prevailing party shall recover the disbursements to the controversy only. This act shall not affect the costs already made in actions pending, and the costs now incurred in actions pending shall abide the event of the action, not to exceed $20 in cases where no judgment has been entered. Costs on appeal may be allowed in the discretion of the court, and may be absolute or directed to abide the event of the action."

The supreme court has power to refer actions pending when the parties to the action and the controversy are such as are specified in the first section of the act. This is so provided by the fifth section. The first sentence in the sixth section is: " The prevailing party shall recover the disbursements to the controversy only."

If the act stopped here, it would be clear that disbursements only could be recovered in the case of a reference under the fifth section. It provides, however: " This act shall not affect the costs already made in actions pending, and the costs now incurred in actions pending shall abide the event of the action, not to exceed $20 in case where no judgment has been entered."

The counsel for the plaintiff argues that these provisions apply only to actions pending at the time the act was passed, and which have been actually referred under section five. That the entire act relates to references and to cases that have been referred; and that all that is said touching costs relates to such cases. I think such is not the true construction of these provisions of the act. It was intended by the legislature that in pending actions the prevailing party's right to costs should not be affected, but that the costs incurred in such actions should abide the event of the action, not, however, to exceed twenty dollars. If there could have been any doubt as to the proper construction, it would be removed by the words, "in cases where no judgment has been entered." It was the intention to include all pending cases that had not gone to judgment.

There had been no judgment in cases referred pursuant to this statute, as there could have been no such references.

Unless these provisions touching costs include all cases pending, whether they should be tried by jury, the court, or a referee appointed under the act, the words, "in cases where no judgment has been entered," would be certainly meaningless. I think it was the intention of the legislature to limit the costs, besides disbursements, to twenty dollars, in all cases where actions had been commenced and had not proceeded to judgment, whether they should be referred under the fifth section to a referee, or the issues joined should be tried by the court or a jury. The clerk was right and the motion must be denied.

SUPREME COURT.

Skinner and others agt. Stuart and others.

A plaintiff cannot maintain an equitable action in his own name against any *debtor* of the defendants in an *attachment suit*, to collect and receive the debts, credits and effects of such defendants alleged to be in the possession of their debtor, without complying with the provisions of § 238 of the Code, which requires an

undertaking, &c., to be given by the plaintiff to the sheriff, who has levied the attachment.

And where there is nothing stated in the complaint to show fraud or collusion, or combination obstructing the ordinary processes of the law, and that the lien of the attachment cannot be enforced without the intervention of the court, in the exercise of its equitable powers, such an action cannot be maintained by the plaintiff, even by the compliance with the provisions of § 238 of the Code.

New York General Term, March, 1863.

INGRAHAM, LEONARD and PECKHAM, *Justices.*

DEMURRER to complaint. The facts will sufficiently appear in the opinion of the court.

By the court, CLERKE, Justice. At common law, when personal, tangible property was levied upon under an execution, it forthwith vested in the sheriff—the plaintiff in the execution could not meddle with it; if it was converted or concealed or taken away, none but the sheriff could retake it, or by action recover it, or the value of it. The property when once levied upon, was in the custody of the law, and its minister, the sheriff, was bound to preserve it against all the world for the purpose of satisfying the judgment. To him alone could the plaintiff look for the application of the property to this purpose.

The law now allows a provisional remedy in certain cases to secure the application of property to the satisfaction of an alleged debt, immediately after the commencement of an action, and, of course, before the claim is established. By this provisional remedy, a warrant of attachment is issued; if it is tangible personal property, the sheriff shall keep the property seized by him, and all debts, credits and effects of the defedant, he shall collect and receive into his possession. He may take such legal proceedings, either in his own name or in the name of the defendant, as may be necessary for that purpose. (§ 232 *of Code.*) This section certainly does not authorize the plaintiff in the action in which the attachment is issued, to commence an action to take possession of the tangible property levied upon, or to take legal proceedings to collect, or receive into his possession debts, credits and effects of the defendants. He is precisely under the same disability in that respect, in which the plaintiff in an execution was placed, before the legislature gave the right to this provisional remedy. He can no more meddle with or claim possession of the property under it, than he could at any time under an execution. The property is in the same manner in the custody of the law, and he can only look to the sheriff, who is responsible to him for its application to any judgment which he may recover. The only provision in the Code, or in any statute, which admits of any proceedings directly by the plaintiff, is contained in section 238, which says that the actions authorized in the chapter to be brought by the sheriff, may be prosecuted by the plaintiff, or under his direction, upon the delivery by him to the sheriff of an undertaking executed by two sufficient sureties, &c. So that, by complying with the conditions of this section, the plaintiff may undoubtedly prosecute, in his own name, any action which the sheriff could have prosecuted; that is, if there are debts, credits and effects, he may, in his own name, take such legal proceedings as may be necessary to collect and receive them into his possession. If it is a promissory note belonging to the defendant, he may sue the parties liable on the note, in his own name, or he may sue any debtor of the defendant, or any person, who, like the defendants Stuart in this action, have moneys, bills, notes or other evidences of debt, or other property belonging to the defendant in the attachment. But certainly he cannot do this under the provisions of the Code, without complying with the conditions which it prescribes. It is nowhere alleged in the complaint that he has executed an undertaking to the sheriff; and he has no such right at common law, he must strictly comply with the terms upon which the statute gives him this new right. As I have already shown, he has no more right at common law, or by any previous statute, to mmence such a suit than he had to commence a suit to collect and receive into his possession debts, credits and effects of the defendant under an execution, before the provisional remedy was authorized by law.

2. But, even if he did comply with the conditions prescribed by the Code, could an action of this kind be maintained? This is an action requiring the equitable interposition of the court, seeking its extraordinary instead of its ordinary remedies. The complaint sets forth that the defendants Stuart & Company have a large amount of personal property, consisting of moneys, bills, notes and other evidences of debt and property deposited with them, by and belonging to Shepherd & Moore, the defendants in the attachment suit. It shows no fraud, collusion or combination obstructing the ordinary processes of the law; it does not show that those processes have been exhausted. Indeed, it does not show that they have ever been resorted to, for they could not have been resorted to without first bringing a common law action. There is nothing stated in the complaint, as is erroneously supposed by the court below, to show that the lien cannot be enforced without the intervention of the court in the exercise of its equitable powers. If the defendants, Stuart & Co., withhold the statement required of them by the Code, a summary method is provided by which they can be compelled to furnish that statement, and if they refuse to deliver the property to the sheriff, the remedy afforded by an ordinary action will be ample for the plaintiffs, if they think proper to resort to it, by first complying with the conditions which the Code prescribes.

It is, in my opinion, a great mistake to say that the remedies afforded by the chapter of the Code relating to attachments are merely cumulative. They are the only remedies known to the law in such cases. Where a lien was obtained on personal property under a judgment previous to the enactment of the Code, no one but the sheriff could have enforced the lien by virtue of the execution. As I have shown, where the property was levied upon, it vested in him, and he was responsible to the plaintiff for the faithful performance of his duties.

The sheriff alone could sue for its recovery when converted, concealed or taken away. Where, indeed, the execution was returned unsatisfied, the plaintiff was entitled to his creditor's bill; or where an execution was issued, and the enforcement of the execution was obstructed by fraud, collusion or combination, the extraordinary aid of a court of equity would be afforded to remove the obstruction. But this case does not fall within either of these classes of equitable remedies. Neither will the pretence of settling priorities among the attaching creditors warrant the court in assuming extraordinary jurisdiction. If the sheriff sued and received possession of the property, he would satisfy the attaching creditors in the order of their priority. If any attaching creditor commences an action under section 238 of the Code, and, as in this case, prays to have the property delivered to the sheriff, that officer will do precisely the same as if the action was prosecuted in his name.

The complaint cannot be sustained: 1st, because the plaintiffs have not complied with the condition of the section of the Code (§ 238) which authorizes the plaintiffs to commence an action; and 2d, if they did comply with it, the complaint does not state a sufficient cause to sustain an action of this nature.

There should be judgment for the defendants on the demurrer with costs.

SUPREME COURT.

CHARLES E. BENSON agt. JOHN TILTON.

A decree for *specific performance* to convey real estate by deed will be made after the day fixed in the agreement for its delivery, and the payment or delivery of the consideration therefor, where the *time fixed* appears to have been disregarded by the parties as of the *essence of the contract.*

A *strong evidence* of such disregard by the parties in this case appeared from the fact that the leasehold premises and personal property to be given by the plaintiff as a consideration for the deed of real estate, to be delivered by the defendant, had been for several days, both before and after the day fixed for performance, *in the possession of the defendant by his agents.*

THE plaintiff seeks by this action to compel the specific performance of a contract dated 24th September, 1860, whereby the defendant agreed to convey to him, on the ninth day of October following, two parcels of land in New Jersey, subject to a mortgage described in the contract, in consideration of receiving from him on that day the stock of goods and fixtures of a certain store in Brooklyn, then kept and occupied by the plaintiff, with the horse, harness, and grocer's wagons used in the business, and the assignment of the lease by or under which the plaintiff held possession of the store. The defendant claims that he was exonerated from all obligations under the contract because of the failure of the plaintiff to assign and deliver to him the lease on the ninth day of October, as he had agreed to do by the contract—thus assuming that time was of the essence of the contract.

JOHN M. MARTIN, *for plaintiff.*
HARRINGTON and GRIEFF, *for defendant.*

SCRUGHAM, Justice. In determining this question, a court of equity, while carefully regarding the expressions of the contract upon the principle that in general the parties must be considered as intending what they express, will also inquire into the conduct of the contracting parties to ascertain whether they have not so acted as to enable the court to give to the contract a meaning different from its *prima facie* obvious import, or whether they have not disregarded the appointed day, and dealt together on the footing that the contract should be construed as a contract to complete in a reasonable time. (*Parkin* agt. *Thorald*, 11 *Eng. Law and Eq.*, 277.)

To decide whether the day fixed in the agreement for its completion was disregarded by the parties, it will be necessary to determine whether either of them performed, or offered to perform, his part of the contract on that day. Upon this question, as upon almost every question of fact presented on the trial, there is much conflicting evidence; and as the rights of the parties in the view which I have taken of the case depend mainly upon its solution, it is proper that I should state briefly the considerations which have led to my conclusion upon it. It would be a circumstance corroborative of the evidence produced by the defendant to show that he tendered and demanded performance on the day fixed, if the object of the contract or the intentions he had in view in making it would be defeated, or in any manner injuriously affected by a failure to complete it on that day. The object of the contract was to effect an exchange of the lands in New Jersey for the stock of goods in the store and other property, and so much of the term demised by the lease as should be unexpired on the ninth day of October, 1860. To effect this object, it was not necessary that a formal assignment of the lease should be executed and delivered on the ninth of October; but it was essential that the defendant should have possession on that day of the premises demised by the lease—for otherwise he would not enjoy the whole of the term which was to be assigned to him; and as before, and on the ninth day of October, 1860, he, by his agents, had possession of the stock of goods, fixtures, and store, and was conducting the business there with the consent of the plaintiff, he would not probably be prejudiced by the neglect of the plaintiff to deliver to him an assignment of the lease on that day, or by a delay in that respect for a reasonable time. The intention of the defendant in making the contract appears to have been to procure the store with its fixtures, stock of goods, and other property used in the business for the benefit of his brothers, Wm. H. Tilton and Robt. L. Tilton, that they might be established in business there. In pursuance of this intention, the defendant authorized Wm. H. Tilton to make the agreement with the plaintiff, and generally to manage the business growing out of it. Wm. H. Tilton, believing that the lease was not transferable without the consent of the lessor, called with the plaintiff upon the agent of the landlord to see whether such consent or a new lease would be given. This was on the tenth of October; and it is a circumstance scarcely consistent with the proposition that the defendant had, through the same Wm. H. Tilton, rescinded the contract on the day before. The defendant claims that the deed was tendered, and the assignment of the lease demanded by Wm. H. Tilton, as his agent, at an interview between him and the plaintiff in the presence of Robert L. Tilton and Robert T. Smith, in the office in the back part of the store. William H. Tilton testifies that this interview was on the ninth of October, and Smith states that he thinks it was on the ninth, but is not certain; and this same witness also testifies to another interview between William H. Tilton and the plaintiff, which he says took place on the day before that at which the deed was exhibited, and at which first interview William H. Tilton told the plaintiff "he would be ready, and that he wanted him to have the lease." William H. Tilton does not state that any interview took place between him and the plaintiff before the ninth, but he mentions one as having occurred on the morning of that day, at which he told the plaintiff that the defendant was ready to complete the contract on his part. If this was the same interview of which Smith speaks as occurring on the day before that at which the deed was exhibited, it would fix the time of the latter as of the tenth of October. Robert L. Tilton testifies that he was present at but one interview between William H. Tilton and the plaintiff at the store; that it was in the back office; that he went into the office with them, and that he "thinks it was on the 10th; the day after the agreement was to be consummated." The plaintiff fixes the time of the interview in the back office at which the deed was exhibited as the evening of the 10th of October, and he states that he and William H. Tilton immediately thereafter went from the store to the office of Mr. Mackey, the agent of the landlord, and had the interview with him to which I have referred, and which all agree occurred on the tenth of October.

Edward K. Edlin, who was a clerk in the store at the time of the interview between the Messrs. Tilton and the plaintiff in the back office, and who noticed it, testifies that on that occasion William H. Tilton and the plaintiff went from the store together to Mr. Mackey's office, and afterwards returned together.

Considering this testimony in connection with the circumstances to which I have alluded, I have concluded that the interview between the plaintiff and the Messrs. Tilton at which the deed was exhibited occurred on the tenth, and not on the ninth of October, 1860; that the time fixed for the delivery of the deed and the assignment of the lease was not regarded by the parties as of the essence of the contract, is evidenced by the fact that neither of them performed, or offered to perform, on the day fixed in the agreement; and that the defendant, by his agents, continued in possession of the store for five or six days thereafter. If the delivery of the assignment of the lease on the particular day fixed was a material condition of the contract, the defendant, on restoring to the plaintiff all that he had received from him under it, might have rescinded it on that day, on the failure of the plaintiff to make such delivery. He could not, however, continue in possession of the premises after that day, and then rescind the contract for having had an intermediate possession of the premises under the agreement; he could not restore the plaintiff to his original position. (*Hunt* agt. *Silk*, 5 *East*, 449; *Mason* agt. *Borst*, 1 *Denio*, 69.) The defendant, it is true, claims that he never had possession of the store; but that his agents went in under an agreement that one of the plaintiff's sons (Alexander Benson) should take charge of the premises until the time for the delivery of the deed. The only witness who testifies to such an agreement is William H. Tilton; and the plaintiff being examined as a witness in his own behalf, contradicts all of his statements in that respect. I do not consider it important to determine this question, for it appears that the defendant's agents were in possession after Alexander Benson left, and so continued after the time fixed for the completion of the contract. By so continuing in possession of the store and of the property received from the plaintiff, the defendant must be considered as having waived his right to a delivery of the assignment of the lease on the day mentioned for that purpose in the agreement; and no other time having been fixed by notice or otherwise, his subsequent acts did not affect the right of the plaintiff to complete the performance of the contract on his part, and demand its fulfillment by the defendant. He did this within a reasonable time, to wit, on the 31st of October, 1860, by the tender and demand made on that day.

In adjudging specific performance, provision should be made to compensate the plaintiff for the loss he has sustained by the delays. In estimating this, it will not be proper to consider the depreciation in the value of the lands; but only the value of their use during the period that they have been kept from him. Damages resulting from such depreciation would be speculative, and are not such as would necessarily result from the failure of the defendant to deliver the deed at the time appointed—for they are calculated entirely upon the presumption that the plaintiff would have sold the lands if he had possessed the title; while it is equally reasonable to presume that he would have retained them. Such estimates are proper in regard to contracts respecting leasehold estates—for in such cases the property itself being the term wastes by delay; and all of the authorities which the plaintiff cites to sustain his claim for such damages refer to leasehold property. The plaintiff is entitled to judgment that the defendant convey to him the lands mentioned in the complaint pursuant to the agreement, and subject to the payment of the principal sum secured by the mortgage therein mentioned, and that he pay the plaintiff such sum as upon a reference to be ordered for that purpose shall be found to be the fair value of the use and occupancy of the premises from the 31st day of October, 1860, to the date of the referees' report in that respect, after deducting all taxes upon the lands that have been or may be paid during that period; and also that the defendants pay the costs of this action.

SUPREME COURT.

JOHN F. FENTON, respondent agt. ELZI FLAGG, appellant.

Where an *execution* has been duly issued and duly returned by the sheriff unsatisfied in whole or in part, and the plaintiff has in no wise interfered, he may safely act upon the return of the sheriff, to institute *proceedings supplementary to execution*. And the question whether there was property which the sheriff ought to have taken and sold for the purpose of satisfying the judgment in whole or in part, *cannot be raised*.

Erie General Term, *May*, 1861.

MARVIN, DAVIS and GROVER, *Justices*.

APPEAL from order appointing a receiver in proceedings supplementary to execution.

A. SHELDON, *for plaintiff.*
WM. H. HENDERSON, *for defendant.*

By the court, MARVIN, P. J. It appeared from the examination of the defendant that he owns and is in possession of 1,000 or 1,100 acres of land in Cattaraugus county, worth about $10 an acre, incumbered by a mortgage to one Dow of $2,100, and a judgment in favor of the plaintiff of $3,100, and perhaps some $400 or $500 of interest, &c., besides the judgment upon which the proceedings in question are had. This judgment was for $1,514.81, a portion of which, by stipulation, was not due; the amount due, and to collect which the execution was issued, was $514.81, and interest from July 5, 1860. The execution was issued November 2, 1860, and was returned by the sheriff on or before the 1st day of December. No call was made upon the defendant by the sheriff, nor was he aware that execution had been issued until the institution of these proceedings.

The defendant had some personal property, all of which was incumbered by chattel mortgages. This proceeding was under the first branch of section 292 of the Code, providing for those cases in which an execution has been returned unsatisfied in whole or in part. The position of the defendant's counsel is that the plaintiff must make an effort in good faith to collect his debt by execution, and must exhaust that remedy before resorting to this proceeding, and that in this case such effort has not been made, and the remedy by execution has not been exhausted.

The language of the Revised Statutes relating to the jurisdiction of the court of chancery is: "Whenever an execution against the property of a defendant shall have been issued on a judgment at law, and shall have been returned unsatisfied, in whole or in part, the party suing out such execution may file a bill in chancery, &c." (2 *R. S.*, 173,

§ 38.) It will be seen on consulting the Code (§ 292) that the same language touching the return is used, when the execution " is returned unsatisfied, in whole or in part, the judgment creditor, at any time after such return made, is entitled to an order, &c."

Under the Revised Statutes it was constantly held that the complainant must have exhausted his remedy at law before filing his bill. (4 *Paige*, 309; 7 *Paige*, 663; *McElwain* agt. *Willis*, 9 *W.*, 548-560.) The execution must have been duly issued to the sheriff of the proper county, and then duly returned, or it was held that the remedy at law was not properly exhausted. (1 *Barb. Ch. R.*, 402.)

When the execution has been duly issued and duly returned by the sheriff unsatisfied, in whole or in part, and the plaintiff has in no wise interfered, I am not aware of any case permitting the question to be raised that there was property which the sheriff ought to have taken and sold for the purpose of satisfying the judgment in whole or in part. And I apprehend that this question, under such circumstances, cannot be made. The plaintiff having done all that the law required of him, may act safely upon the return of the sheriff. If the plaintiff acted in good faith, and the sheriff made a false return, the plaintiff was not to be deprived of his creditor's bill, and so now, of his order from a judge requiring the debtor to appear and answer concerning his property. The question is one of jurisdiction. The statute says, when the execution shall have been returned unsatisfied, in whole or in part, the party may file his bill in chancery, and by the Code, when the execution is returned unsatisfied in whole or in part, the judgment creditor is entitled to an order from a judge.

It seems that such return is made the evidence upon which the jurisdiction depends, assuming, of course, that the judgment creditor has performed all that the law requires of him, and has not improperly interfered with the sheriff. In *McElwain* agt. *Willis*, (9 *W.*, 560,) Justice

NELSON, in the court for correction of errors, says, after citing the Revised Statutes: "The ground upon which the jurisdiction of the court rests in such cases is, that the legal remedy has been exhausted without satisfaction of the judgment, and certainly the best evidence of the fact is the official return of the sheriff that no goods or chattels, lands or tenements, can be found, out of which he can levy the debt by virtue of the execution. Upon any other view, the question, whether there was property subject to an execution or not, would be open to be litigated by the parties in every proceeding of the kind in question, and to be decided by the court upon the testimony produced. The return of the officer is now considered conclusive, and if the defendant is injured by his misconduct, the law affords an ample remedy."

The cases cited by the defendant's counsel are not in point. The proceedings in *Sackett* agt. *Newton*, (10 *How.*, 560,) were under the second clause of section 292 of the Code. The execution had not been returned. In *Pudney* agt. *Griffith*, (15 *How.*, 410,) the plaintiff gave directions to the sheriff as to the time of the return, and instructed him not to proceed to serve the execution. In *Spencer* agt. *Cuyler*, (17 *How.*, 158,) the plaintiff or his attorney interfered with the sheriff and requested him to return the execution immediately, and he did so. The court regarded the return as the act of the party and not the official act of the sheriff. *Farqueharson* agt. *Kimball*, (18 *How.*, 33,) is an authority for the position I have taken.

The order appealed from must be affirmed with $10 costs.*

* NOTE.—It would seem that the question, whether the sheriff's return to an execution before the return day, sixty days, is an *irregularity*, which the supreme court, now clothed with equitable as well as legal powers, *is bound to take notice*, on the institution of supplementary proceedings, will probably have to be settled by the court of appeals.—[REP.

SUPREME COURT.

Daniel Penn agt. George Remsen, late sheriff of Kings County.

Where the plaintiff has the right to take the *persons of all the defendants* in satisfaction of his judgment, it carries with it the right to proceed against the *bail of one of them*, as to whom there may be a return of *non est inventus*.

Brooklyn General Term, December, 1862.
Emott, Lott and Brown, *Justices*.

Mr. McAdam, *for plaintiff*.
J. W. Gilbert, *for the defendant*.

By the court, Brown, Justice. In June, 1858, the plaintiff commenced an action in this court against William C. Annan and James W. Embury to recover the proceeds of certain goods sold by them as his agents and for him. He obtained an order of arrest from one of the justices of this court, directed to the sheriff of the county of Kings—the amount of the bail to be taken being fixed at $600. The order was delivered to the defendant, who was then sheriff of the county of Kings, to be executed. On the 15th June, 1858, he arrested James W. Embury under the order or warrant, held him to bail, and afterwards returned the order with his certificate of the service, and a copy of the undertaking of the bail. The defendant Annan was not arrested on the order. Within ten days the plaintiff gave due notice that he did not accept the bail taken by the sheriff. The bail never justified, and thus the sheriff became liable as bail to the plaintiff.

On the 29th of November, 1858, the plaintiff recovered a judgment in the action against Annan and Embury for $672.67. It was duly docketed in Kings county. An execution against the property of the defendants was issued, and returned unsatisfied. An execution against the bodies of the defendants was then issued to the sheriff of Kings county, which was returned not found. A like execution was issued to the sheriff of the city and county of New York, on which the defendant Annan was taken, but which, as to the defendant Embury, was also returned not found. This action is brought charging the defendant as bail. The answer sets up as a defence the taking of the defendant Annan's body in execution, and insists that it is a satisfaction and discharge of the judgment. The cause was tried before Mr. Justice Lott without a jury at the January circuit, 1862, in Kings county, where the foregoing facts were proved or admitted. Judgment was rendered for the plaintiff for $635, besides costs, upon which judgment was entered, and the defendant appealed.

In *Wakeman & Andrews* agt. *Lyon & Evans*, (9 *Wendell*, 241,) it was decided that a plaintiff in a judgment who had taken notes as collateral security for its payment cannot maintain an action upon the notes, if, after he took the same, he issues an execution and imprisons the defendant in the judgment. Lyon was the judgment-debtor, and the notes in suit were made by Evans and him as collateral security for the payment of the debt. The action upon the notes was a joint action, and whatever was a good defence to Lyon was also good as to Evans. The former was already in execution upon the judgment, and if the action could have been maintained, there would have been two judgments against him upon the same cause of action. The court, therefore, held that the right of action upon the notes was suspended so long as the judgment-debtor remained in custody upon the execution, which, *pro hac vice*, was to be deemed a satisfaction of the debt which the notes were given to secure. To the same effect is the case of *Sunderland* agt. *Loder, impleaded with Lockwood*, (5 *Wend.*, 58.) Lockwood was the judgment-debtor, and Loder had given a bond as collateral security to stay the execution. The court here distinguish between cases when there are several defendants all liable for the judgment debt, and cases where there is but one judgment-debtor, and another person or persons liable upon a collateral undertaking. The latter are not liable to an action, while the person of the judgment-debtor is in custody in satisfaction of the judgment; while in the case of a judgment against several defendants, the taking of one does not affect the plaintiff's right to pursue the others until there is a payment in fact. This is said to be a qualification of the general rule, that a *capias ad satisfaciendum* is an execution, and a full satisfaction by force and judgment of law. (*Vide also Chapman* agt. *Hatt*, 11 *Wend.*, 41.) The theory of the defendant is, that where there are several defendants liable to imprisonment in satisfaction of the debt, the taking of one upon the execution is a satisfaction for the time being as against the others. This is not the law. The plaintiff has the right to take the persons of all the defendants in satisfaction of his judgment, and this carries with it the right to proceed against the bail of one as to whom there may be a return of *non est inventus*. The point in regard to the sufficiency of the affidavits upon which the order of arrest was granted, taken at the time of the trial, seems to have been abandoned on the argument, and I forbear to consider it.

The judgment should be affirmed.

NEW YORK SUPERIOR COURT.

JOSEPH W. HARTLEY, respondent agt. BENJAMIN TATHAM and wife, impleaded, &c., appellants.

An *assignee of a mortgage* takes it subject to the same *equity* that it was subject to in the hands of the *assignor*, and the rule that it is only an equity residing in the *original debtor*, and not the latent equities of third persons against the assignor that have this effect, does not exclude any one who so far stands in the place of the debtor *as to have acquired his equity*. It does not exclude a judgment creditor of the debtor claiming to redeem.

Where a defendant in a mortgage foreclosure suit has succeeded to the rights of the mortgagor, by taking a deed of the premises subject to the mortgage, he may insist upon the fact of an *actual partial payment to the mortgagee,* while he owned the mortgage—a fact which ordinary precaution would have brought to the knowledge of the *assignee,* whether he had inquired of the mortgagor or of the grantee.

New York General Term, March, 1863.

BOSWORTH, *Ch. J.*, MONCRIEF and ROBERTSON, *Justices.*

APPEAL from judgment at special term. The facts will sufficiently appear in the opinion of the court.

Mr. CLARKE, *for appellants.*
Mr. PORTER, *for respondent.*

By the court, BOSWORTH, C. J. This action is brought to foreclose a mortgage dated May 30, 1861, executed by Michael Cunningham and wife to Samuel W. Dunscomb, and by the latter assigned to the plaintiff May 13, 1862.

The defence is founded, in part, on the allegation, that while Dunscomb owned the mortgage, one Alfred A. Aiment, who, by a written contract with one Higginson, to which Dunscomb was a party, had contracted for a deed of the premises in question, subject to this and a prior mortgage of $4,000, by agreement between him and Dunscomb, performed work and labor to the amount of $490.03, in part payment of this mortgage; that, in execution of said written contract, the deed, at Aiment's request, was executed to Tatham instead of Aiment, January 26, 1862. The *habendum* clause of this deed is, "to have and to hold * * * subject, however, * * * to a certain other indenture of mortgage for $1,500, dated May 30, 1861, and recorded," &c., being the mortgage in question. The deed does not declare that Tatham is to pay this mortgage, nor did the agreement between Higginson and Aiment require him to do it. That stipulates for a deed of the premises to Aiment, free and clear of all incumbrances, "except the said sum of $5,500." Aiment was to do plumbing work to the amount of $3,600 for Higginson, as a consideration for such conveyance, and did the work. The agreement between Aiment and Dunscomb for doing the work, &c., amounting to $490.03, was made prior to January, 1862, and was completed as early as April, 1862, and on the 3d of May, 1862, Aiment assigned to Tatham this claim for work, amounting to $490.03. The assignment recites that the work, &c., creating the debt, was done for Dunscomb upon his agreement to credit the amount on this mortgage. The assignment of the mortgage to the plaintiff was made on the 13th of May, 1862. The important question is, whether Tatham is entitled to be credited with this sum on the mortgage.

A finding by the court, or the verdict of a jury to the effect that this work was done by Aiment, under an agreement between him and Dunscomb, that the amount of it should be in payment of the mortgage *pro tanto*, could not be disturbed as contrary to evidence given, and substantially stricken from the case against the objection and exception of Tatham.

If the mortgagor had paid $490.03 on the mortgage before it was assigned, the assignee would necessarily have taken it subject to such payment. That position is not controverted.

But it is insisted that this equity in behalf of Aiment and Tatham is a latent one, in a third person, and one existing between him and the mortgagee only, and that the assignee cannot be affected by it.

It was necessary for Aiment to pay off the mortgages or suffer the property to be sold to satisfy them. He was not personally liable to pay them, because he never agreed to do so. If he had agreed to pay them off, he would be personally liable to pay them, (*Burr* agt. *Beers*, 24 *N. Y. R.*, 178,) and as between himself and the mortgagor, would have been, in equity, the principal debtor.

Aiment, at the time he agreed with Dunscomb to do work, in payment, to the extent of the value of such work, upon this mortgage, had a valid contract for a deed of the premises in question. To this contract Dunscomb was so far a party that he assented to it, and in such wise that the deed, when executed, was to be executed by him or by some one holding the title for him; and Aiment was either to pay the mortgages in discharge of the liability of the mortgagor, or lose all he paid on the premises, by a foreclosure and sale of the mortgaged premises.

It is said, in the opinion, (*in James* agt. *Morey*, 2 *Cowen Rep.*, 298,) that "the assignee can always go to the debtor and ascertain what claims he may have against the bond or other chose in action, which he is about purchasing from the obligee; but he may not be able with the utmost diligence to ascertain the latent equity of some third person against the obligee. He has not any object to which he can direct his inquiries, and for this reason the claim of the assignee, without notice, of a chose in action, was preferred in the late case of *Redfearn* agt. *Ferrier and others*, (1 *Dow Rep.*, 50,) to that of a third party setting up a secret equity against the assignor."

The right application of these rules to the present case cannot produce a result adverse to Tatham. An inquiry of the mortgagor would presumptively have informed him of the fact of this payment. If the plaintiff did not have notice of it when he took the assignment, he obtained it the same evening and within a few hours thereafter.

The deed from Smith to Tatham was recorded over two months before the mortgage was assigned to the plaintiff, and as that deed was subject to this mortgage, it pointed out Tatham as a person interested to pay the mortgage, and one who had a right to pay it, even though he may have been under no legal obligation to do so. He was a proper person to ask whether he had made any payments upon it or not.

The case of *James* agt. *Morey* (*supra*) is unlike this in its essential particulars. In that case the mortgagee, before assigning the mortgage, had become the owner of the equity of redemption, and might at his election treat his estate, as mortgagee, as merged in the legal estate, or preserve it as a separate estate.

After assigning the mortgage he quit-claimed the mortgaged premises to the respondent. The latent equity was that of the respondent under such deed, who took it ignorant of the previous assignment of the mortgage. (*Id; 2 Cowen Rep.*, 283.) The mortgage was enforced in behalf of the assignee as a valid and subsisting security.

Assuming the fact to be that Aiment paid to Dunscomb upon this mortgage, while the latter owned it, the sum of $490.03, it is difficult to conceive of any sound considerations of justice or equity which will make it less efficient than if the same sum had been paid at the same time by Cunningham. Payment by the latter before the assignment would be allowed, and so would a payment subsequent to the assignment and before notice of the assignment. (*James* agt. *Morey*, 2 *Cow. R.*, 297; 3 *R. S.*, *5th ed.*, *p.* 59, § 74, [*sec.* 41].)

The gist of *Redfearn* agt. *Ferrier* (*supra*) may be stated thus: On the books of a stock company one Stewart appeared to be the owner of a certain number of its shares. By the rules of the company such shares could be owned by individuals only, not by firms as such. He assigned the shares to Redfearn as security for moneys advanced *optima fide*, and it was sought to be shown, to defeat the claim of such an assignee, that Stewart, in fact, held the stock for a firm who were the true equitable owners. The question was whether this latent equity of the firm against the assignor could defeat such an assignee's title, and on the facts and circumstances of the case it was held that it could not.

That case, too, is essentially unlike the present.

The true rule deducible from the cases I understand to be this: The assignee of a mortgage takes it subject to the same equity that it was subject to in the hands of the assignor, and the rule that it is only an equity residing in the original debtor, and not the latent equities of third persons against the assignor that have this effect, does not exclude any one who so far stands in the place of the debtor as to have acquired his equity. It does not exclude a judgment creditor of the debtor claiming to redeem. (*Roosevelt* agt. *Bank of Niagara*, *Hopk. R.*, 579; *United States* agt. *Sturges*, 1 *Paine R.*, 525.)

By force of the contracts between Higginson and Dunscomb, (of the 23d of April, 1860, and of the 24th of April, 1860,) and of the contracts between Higginson and Aiment, (of the date of March 30, 1861,) and Dunscomb's written assent and cotemporaneous agreement in relation thereto, and of Aiment's assignment to the Bull's Head Bank, and through the bank to Tatham, of the right to a deed of the premises in question, and of the execution of such deed to Tatham, and the payment by Aiment of the $490.03 on the mortgage, and the formal assignment, May 3, 1862, by Aiment to Tatham of this claim, and of his right to have it applied as a payment, Tatham was substituted in place of the mortgagor and Aiment, with all their rights, equitable as well as legal.

As between him and the mortgagor, the property was a security for the payment of the amount due on the mortgage, because it had been, and, by the aforesaid agreements, was to be conveyed subject to this and the prior mortgage of $4,000. The mortgage debts, as between the mortgagor and Aiment, or as between the mortgagor and Tatham, Aiment and Tatham were in equity bound to pay, if the premises were an adequate security for their payment. Such being the position of Tatham, he did pay $490.03 on the mortgage while Dunscomb owned it. He at that time stood in the place of the mortgagor, and was clothed with all his rights, and his equity to be protected in such payment is as clear as that of the mortgagor would have been if he had made the payment personally.

From the time of the recording of the deed to Tatham, the record disclosed him as the person having the right of being under an equitable obligation to pay the mortgage in exoneration of the personal liability of the mortgagor. He was, therefore, a person of whom it was as proper and as much the duty of one about taking an assignment of the mortgage, to inquire as to the fact of payments as the mortgagor himself.

It is not, therefore, the case of a defendant attempting to set up against the assignee of a mortgage the latent equity of a third person against the mortgagee, but the case of one who has succeeded to the rights of the mortgagor, and entitled to the same protection that the law extends to him, insisting upon the fact of an actual partial payment to the mortgagee, while he owned the mortgage, a fact which ordinary precaution would have brought to the knowledge of the assignee, whether he had inquired of the mortgagor or of Tatham.

It is insisted, however, that taking the deed, subject to the mortgage, estops Tatham from questioning the fact of its being a valid security for the face of it.

The deed does not state that no part of it has been paid; and no authority has been cited which tends to the support of the proposition, that taking a deed in the form of the deed to Tatham precludes the grantee from showing that the mortgage had been in part paid before the deed was given and accepted.

If the deed had not only in terms been subject to this mortgage, but had also declared that the whole amount was unpaid, and that the grantee assumed the payment of it, he might possibly be precluded from showing, as between himself and a *bona fide* assignee of the mortgage, the fact of a partial payment. (*Burr* agt. *Beers*, 24 *N. Y. R.*, 178; *Hailey*, *exr.* agt. *Harrison*, *id.*, 170.)

But no such question arises here. I think, therefore, that the decision at special term, excluding evidence of the defence consisting of the facts before stated, and striking from the case the evidence that had been given in support of it, was erroneous, and that the judgment should be reversed and a new trial granted, with costs to abide the event.

SUPREME COURT.

The People agt. William A. Boardman and another.

Where a justice of the peace issues a warrant on a complaint for *bastardy*, and the defendant is arrested and brought before the said justice and *another justice* called to his aid, pursuant to the statute, and the defendant not being ready for examination applies for an adjournment and executes the proper *bond* for his appearance on the adjourned day, there is no *breach of the bond* by the failure of the defendant to appear on the adjourned day before the said justice and a *different associate justice*, the former associate justice being absent.

Steuben County Circuit, 1*st Monday of January*, 1863.

Action on bond to appear on adjournment of examination before two justices, on charge of bastardy. The following facts were proved upon the trial: The warrant was issued on a proper complaint by William H. Doty, a justice of the peace of the town of Wayne, in said county, and the defendant was arrested and brought before the said justice, who thereupon called to his aid and associated with himself Levi Knox, another justice of the same town. The defendant not being then ready to proceed to the examination, applied for an adjournment thereof to another day, which was granted, and the bond in question was executed for the appearance of the defendant Boardman at the adjourned day. On the adjourned day the associate justice, Knox, was absent from the county, and Doty, the justice who issued the warrant, called to his aid Robert Bigger, another justice of the said town, and these two justices appeared at the time and place designated, and were ready to proceed with such examination. The defendant Boardman refused to appear in person before these justices, but sent his attorney, who objected that they had no right to enter upon or make the examination. The said justices, after waiting nearly two hours, dissolved their court or sitting, and handed over the bond for prosecution.

C. BELL, *for people.*

G. B. BRADLEY, *for defendants.*

JOHNSON, Justice. Unless the tribunal before which the defendant Boardman undertook to appear on the adjourned day met, and had a session for the purpose of an examination, according to the statute said defendant was not in default for not appearing, and there has been no breach of the bond; and if there has been no breach, no action can be maintained upon it. If the court did not meet and sit, there was nothing before which he could appear, and his presence at, or absence from, the place, merely, is of no consequence whatever.

This presents the question whether the defendant Boardman was obliged to appear and answer before any other justices than those first associated, and who are named in the bond. I am clearly of the opinion that he was not. The language of the statute is precise and explicit upon this point.

When a party is arrested on such a warrant, and is brought before the justice who issued it, such justice is required immediately to call to his aid any other justice of the same county; "and the said two justices shall proceed without unnecessary delay to make the examination of the mother."

It is then provided by § 12 of the act, that "if the said justices shall not be prepared to proceed, or the person charged shall require delay," they may adjourn such ex amination for any time not exceeding six weeks, and take a bond with sureties from such person for his appearance at such time "before them."

That was the bond given in the present case. The two justices thus associated had then jurisdiction of the person of the defendant, and of the subject matter of the examination. No other magistrates or tribunal had such jurisdiction; nor could it be obtained without a new process, or the express consent of the defendant.

Section 13 of the statute provides that "the said justices shall determine who is the father of such bastard, or of such child likely to be born a bastard," and points out the method to be pursued by them.

Thus by statute the said "justices" are to constitute the tribunal to make the examination, and to determine the matter before it; and I do not see how any other justices, or any other body, could take cognizance of it without the defendant's consent.

It is urged in behalf of the people that the justice, Bigger, was eligible, and might as well have been called in the first instance as the other Justice Knox. This is true, but he was not so called until after the tribunal to try the matter had been formed, and it was then too late.

The statute provides that the justice who issued the warrant, and the justice who is called to his aid, where the person arrested is brought before him, "shall determine" the matter. It is a tribunal of special and limited powers, and must proceed according to the statute, or it has no authority whatever. As there was no sitting or appearance of the court or tribunal before which the defendant undertook to appear, his appearance in the manner and for the purpose contemplated by the statute and by the bond, was impossible, and there is no breach, and no action can be maintained.

The defendants must, therefore, have judgment for their costs of their action.

SUPREME COURT.

NORMAN S. WASHBURN agt. JOSEPH F. FRANKLIN.

Where the defence to a contract is given by a statute founded on grounds of public policy (against stock jobbing), the *repeal* of the statute since the contract was made takes away the *defence of illegality the same as if such statute never existed.*

New York General Term, October, 1861.

CLERKE, INGRAHAM and LEONARD, *Justices*.

MOTION for a new trial, on appeal from a judgment at special term.

By the court, INGRAHAM, Justice. In *Key* agt. *Goodwin*, (4 *Moore & Payne*, 341,) it is said: "I take the effect of a repealing statute to be to obliterate it as completely as if it had never passed, and that it must be considered as a law that never existed, except for the purpose of those actions or suits which were commenced and concluded while it was an existing law." (*See Butler* agt. *Palmer*, 1 *Hill*, 324.)

A repealing clause is such an express enactment as necessarily divests all inchoate rights which have arisen under the statute which it destroys.

The principle that a repeal of an act which made a contract illegal on grounds of public policy, repealed also the consequences of the act, even as to contracts entered into while it was in force, was distinctly held in the *Central Bank* agt. *Empire Stone Dressing Co.*, (26 *Barb.*, 23.)

In *Curtis* agt. *Leavitt*, (15 *N. Y. Rep.*, *p.* 9–85,) Mr. Justice COMSTOCK says of the statute of the state which prohibits a corporation from setting up the defence of usury: "The act must be construed as a repeal of the statute of usury as to all contracts of corporations stipulating to pay interest, thus leaving the contract in full force, according to its terms; and such an act is liable to no constitutional objection." In that case it was held that the defence of usury could be taken away after the defence was pleaded. Mr. Justice SELDEN says: "Usury being a mere statutory defence, not founded on any common law right, either legal or equitable, it was clearly within the power of the legislature to take it away (*p.* 254.)

And Justice BROWN also says: "The borrower can have no vested interest in the forfeiture which follows proof of usury," (*p.* 153.)

Chief Justice SAVAGE, in the *People* agt. *Livingston*, (6 *Wend.*, 526,) says: "It cannot be denied that the legislature possess the power to take away by statute what was given by statute, except vested rights;" and refers to the statute against gaming, the repeal of which would take away all means of receiving back moneys previously lost by gaming.

The principle in all these cases is, that a cause of action or defence given by a statute, founded on grounds of public policy, conferred no vested right which could not be taken away by a similar statute, and that a repeal of a law which gave such right of action or defence, terminated all claim to such recovery or defence, although the contract was made previously.

Applying this rule to the present case, the defence to the contract was given by the statute against stock jobbing. That statute was repealed since the contract was made. The repeal of the statute has taken away the defence of illegality, the same as if such statute never existed.

The judge at the trial held that the defence was still good, notwithstanding the repeal of the statute, and made the distinction between this case and the case in 26 *Barbour*, because in that case the statute did not declare the contract void.

It will be seen from the decisions before cited, in regard

to the defence of usury, that this distinction does not exist.

The judge erred in this rule, and a new trial must be ordered, costs to abide event.

LEONARD, J. I concur in the above opinion. The case of *Curtis* agt. *Leavitt*, (15 *N. Y. R.*,) opinions of J. J. COMSTOCK, at *p.* 85, of BROWN, *pp.* 152, 153, and SELDEN, *p.* 254, are directly in point, and in my opinion are entirely conclusive as authority in support of the plaintiff's action herein.

SUPREME COURT.

PHILO STEVENS and others agt. THE PHŒNIX INSURANCE COMPANY OF HARTFORD.

A *foreign insurance company* created by the laws of another state, but doing business in this state, under and in compliance with our laws, on being sued by a citizen of this state, cannot remove the cause into the circuit court of the United States, on the ground that it is a *citizen of another state.*

Oneida Special Term, March, 1863.

MOTION by defendant to remove cause to circuit court of the United States for the northern district of New York, upon the ground that the plaintiffs are citizens of the state of New York, and the defendant is a corporation created by the laws of Connecticut, and located and doing business in that state.

Mr. KERNAN, *for the motion.*
Mr. TOWNSEND, *contra.*

ALLEN, Justice. The petition and security of the defendant for the removal of the action from this court to the circuit court of the United States are in due form, and in conformity with the federal judiciary act authorising the proceeding. (1 *Story Laws of U. S.*, 57, § 12.) If the defendant, therefore, is within the act a citizen of the state of Connecticut, this court has no discretion, and it is a matter of course to grant the order for the removal. (*Vandevoort* agt. *Palmer*, 4 *Duer*, 677; *Norton* agt. *Hayes*, 4 *Denio*, 245.) Before the case of *The Louisville, Cincinnati & Charleston R. R. Co.* agt. *Letson* (2 *How. U. S. R.*, 497,) it was supposed that the citizenship could not be predicated of a coporation, so as to give the federal courts jurisdiction of actions to which it might be a party, unless all the corporators were citizens of the same state. That is, the corporation, as such, was regarded as having no citizenship but the citizenship of the several associates and corporators, which was alone regarded in determining the question of jurisdiction. (*Curtis* agt. *Strawbridge*, 3 *Cranch*, 267; *Bank U. S.* agt. *Devaux*, 5 *id.*, 84; *Commercial & R. R. Bank of Vicksburg* agt. *Slocomb*, 14 *Peters*, 60.) But a more reasonable and convenient rule was adopted in the case first cited. Corporators, as individuals, were held not to be parties to the action as suitors, but merely parties having an interest in the result represented by the corporation—an artificial person created by authority of law, having for the purposes for which it was created many of the powers and capacities of a natural person, including the power of suing and being sued. The court did not decide that a corporation, created by the laws of a state, must necessarily be treated as a citizen of that state for all purposes of suing and being sued. The decision was guarded and carefully qualified, and was merely to the effect that a corporation, created by, and transacting business in a state, is to be deemed an inhabitant of the state *capable of being treated* as a citizen for such purposes, and that an averment of the facts of its creation, *and the place of its transacting business*, was sufficient to give the circuit courts jurisdiction. This is the language of Judge WAYNE, by whom the decision was pronounced, and at the close of the opinion he says: "Where the corporation exercises its powers in the state which chartered it, that is its residence, and such an averment is sufficient to give the circuit courts jurisdiction." Although a corporation cannot migrate, they may, by the comity of other states, transact business in such states; and although they cannot by force of their organization have an extra territorial existence, they may be, and are, recognized as corporations capable of suing and being sued beyond the limits of the state of their creation. When they avail themselves of this comity and of the privileges thus conferred, and transfer their business, or any part of it, to another state, and establish agencies within such state, although they remain inhabitants of the state of their incorporation, for the reason that the "artificial, invisible and intangible being," the "mere creation of law," and of a positive law which has no force *ex proprio vigore* beyond the limits of the state jurisdiction, cannot migrate; they *quoad* the business thus transferred, lose their citizenship, and become to that extent citizens of the state under whose laws they transact their business, and of whose governmental protection they avail themselves. The corporation is an "invisible, artificial" existence, represented and acting by agents, and may as well be thus represented and thus exist in one place as another, and by one set of agents as another, and is not necessarily confined to any one place or state, or to personation by agents of any particular character. It is truly restricted as to its liability, which is imaginary at the best, by the terms of its charter, and the jurisdiction and authority of the power by which it is brought into existence.

But the defendant in this action has gone further, and has expressly submitted itself to the jurisdiction of this state, and consented to do business here, not solely in virtue of its charter and incorporation by the legislature of Connecticut, but under and by authority of the laws of this state. By the "act to provide for the incorporation of fire insurance companies" in this state, (*chapter* 466 of *Laws* of 1853,) the business of fire insurance by foreign corporations is regulated and restricted, and such corporations doing business in this state must conform to that law and the regulations therein prescribed. The defendant in this action has complied with these regulations, and is doing business within this state under the authority conferred by that act, and was sued with process in this action through an agent appointed under that law for that purpose. Sections 23 and 24 of that act, (2 *R. S.*, *5th ed.*, 762, 764,) contain the important provisions upon this subject. By these sections, foreign insurance companies taking risks or transacting business of insurance in this state, must possess the capital required of similar companies chartered within this state; they must appoint an attorney in this state, upon whom process of law can be served, and must file annually a detailed statement of their capital, their assets, securities and liabilities, and must procure from the comptroller a certificate of their having complied with the provisions of the act. They are also subject to the visitation and examination of the comptroller, and the authority to insure in the state may be revoked by him.

Saying nothing of the other acts of the defendant, by which it has submitted itself to the jurisdiction of this state, and consented to do business under its authority, the appointment of an agent to represent it and accept the service of process issuing out of the courts of this state, is a surrender of the right to be treated as a citizen of Connecticut as to actions thus commenced. They have stipulated as to the jurisdiction of the courts of this state, and cannot revoke such stipulation. It would be contrary to the spirit of the act under which they have engaged in business here, as well as a breach of faith toward those who have insured with them, under the idea that for all the purposes of being sued they occupy the same position as a domestic corporation. To appoint an agent to be served with process, and through whom they may be sued, is inconsistent with and repugnant to the idea that they may repudiate the jurisdiction of the court, and avail themselves of the plea of a foreign citizenship. I think the case is clearly within the qualification of the rule plainly implied in the *Louisville, &c. R. R. Co.* agt. *Letson*. The defendant is an inhabitant of Connecticut, but it has yielded its *quasi* or qualified citizenship, which is the most that it can have in that state, *qua* the business of its agencies in this state.

The motion is denied without costs.

SUPREME COURT.

JAMES S. SANDFORD and others agt. ELISHA RUCKMAN.

MORTIMER PORTER agt. ELISHA RUCKMAN.

It is not necessary to refer to a *fee bill*, to ascertain what is a proper compensation to be paid by a *client to his attorney;* and if it is referred to, although the items would be deemed erroneous by the taxing officer, still, if the *whole amount* does not exceed what the attorney is entitled to as a fair compensation from his client, no error is caused by allowing that amount.

New York General Term, March, 1863.

SUTHERLAND, INGRAHAM and CLERKE, *Justices.*

THESE actions were brought to recover for professional services. In the first case the plaintiffs sued as surviving partners of Edward Sandford, for services in his lifetime, and for their own services after his death in September, 1854, and up to January, 1856. The second suit was brought by one of the partners for services from January, 1856, when he became the sole attorney for the defendant, to the summer of 1858. The services for which compensation was claimed in the first suit, were rendered between 1851 and 1856, in ten suits in the supreme and superior courts, and two in the United States district court. The services claimed in the second suit were rendered after January, 1856, in continuing seven of the suits in the superior and supreme courts.

The bill of particulars in the first case gives first, the gross charges in the several suits, and then the items of such charges. The whole claim is $2,791.57. The referee allowed the whole bill, except one deduction amounting to $225, and another amounting to $155. The rest of the plaintiffs' claim is for costs, counsel fees and disbursements in nine suits upon policies of insurance, brought by them as attorneys for the defendant, in 1851 and 1852. The items are set out in detail in the bill of particulars. The services in these nine suits, their value, and the disbursements made by the plaintiffs, and the whole bill, were proved by the plaintiff Porter, and confirmed by six other witnesses.

The defendant's defence to the first item in the first bill of particulars (the costs in the Radius case) was, that the defendant did not employ the plaintiffs. The defendant offered no evidence to disprove the services in the second case, or to diminish the estimate of their value. The defence to the claim for services in the insurance cases rested upon the alleged negligence of the plaintiffs in the management of the business, from which damages resulted, and a counter-claim for such damages.

LYON & PORTER, *for plaintiffs.*
E. A. DOOLITTLE, *for defendant.*

By the court, CLERKE, Justice. The questions of fact in these cases were, whether the plaintiffs, as the attorneys of the defendant in certain actions, were guilty of negligence; and whether, even if they were not guilty of negligence, the finding in their favor was not for too large an amount. As to the first question, evidence to a considerable extent on behalf of the plaintiffs and the defendant was taken before the referee; and we can see no reason for the assertion that his conclusions from that evidence were against the weight of evidence.

As to the second question, even admitting that the charges for term fees were not taxable as between the parties, yet it was proved that the aggregate amount of these fees was not an unreasonable compensation for the services rendered. This is all that is necessary to justify the finding of the referee. It is not necessary to refer to the fee bill at all, to ascertain what is a proper compensation to be paid by a client to his attorney; and if it is referred to, although the items would be deemed erroneous by the taxing officer, still, if the whole amount does not exceed what the attorney is entitled to as a fair compensation for his client, the referee does not err by allowing him that amount. No legal exception taken in either case is tenable.

The judgment in both cases should be affirmed with costs.

ERRATA.

Page 397, line 12 from top, after word otherwise, for "*than*" read "*then*."
Page 400, 7th line from top, for "*personally*" read "*formally*."
Page 403, for "2 *Serg.*, 24," read "2 *Yerg.*, 24."

DIGEST

OF THE

POINTS OF PRACTICE

AND

OTHER IMPORTANT QUESTIONS,

CONTAINED IN THE FOLLOWING REPORTS:

24 Howard's Pr. R.; 36 Barbour's R.; 24 N. Y. R.; 7 Bosworth's R., and 14 Abbott's R.

ACCOUNT.

1. If an account is payable in specific articles, upon demand of the creditor, no action will lie upon it for the recovery of money, nor can the account be used as a set-off, until after a demand and refusal to pay in the specified articles, and in the manner stipulated in the contract. And where a creditor has agreed to receive payment of his debt in specified articles, there is no duty to pay in money, until the creditor has made his election to receive his pay in those articles, and has demanded payment accordingly. (*Smith* agt. *Tiffany*, 36 *Barb.*, 23.)

ADMIRALTY.

1. Meritorious services rendered by a steam-tug in our harbors, in saving a vessel beset with ice, cannot be placed on the basis of salvage services in their proper acceptation. A branch of the employment of steam-tugs, during the season of ice, is to aid vessels in moving their positions to all parts of the harbor. (*Crary* agt. *Schooner El Dorado*, *ante*, 128.)

2. A steam-tug aiding a vessel thus beset is not regarded in the character of a volunteer governed by impulses of humanity, leaving her own pursuits and devoting herself to the rescue of another with no view to compensation, but upon the final success of her efforts. Her services stand essentially on different grounds: 1. They impose no unauthorized or wrongful risks upon their owners. 2. They may have a reward, whether needed or not, and will not necessarily lose it because the services undertaken by them fail of being accomplished. 3. They differ from salvors, because they pursue and solicit the employment, and hold themselves prepared to fulfill a call to it, whenever made. They act notoriously as tow-vessels; as such, bargains made by them to render, for a compensation, services which otherwise might be salvage services, will be upheld, unless the case is clear that the bargain is a means of coercing an exorbitant price. In such case, the court will not permit the fears or weakness or ignorance of a party to be made the occasion of inequitable exactions from him. (*Id.*)

3. In an action brought by the tug against a schooner and her cargo, to whom services of a salvage character were rendered by the tug in saving her from the ice by which she was beset, the court dismissed the libel against the cargo, but decreed against the bottom, with costs, for a reasonable compensation. (*Id.*)

4. Two vessels may be charged in a libel

with joint negligence, where they jointly commit an act of collision which injures a third vessel, even though there is no apparent previous concert of action or navigation between the two colliding vessels. (*Chase* agt. *Crary*, *ante*, 159.)

5. Where the collision is occasioned by the joint negligence of those who have charge of the colliding vessels, as the servants of the owners, then a libel may be sustained against the owners jointly, as well as against the vessels. (*Id.*)

6. Where the proof shows that only one of the colliding vessels charged was guilty of negligence, the proper decree should be against that one, and in favor of the others, and not a dismissal of the libel because of the failure to prove the joint negligence. (*Id.*)

7. The case of the *Samson*, (2 *Wallace*, *p.* 485,) approved of, and that of the *Moxey*, decided by Judge BETTS, in 1847, distinguished from this. (*Id.*)

8. In estimating the damages to the injured vessel, the court, on exception, rejected items claimed to be necessary to put her in good condition, because it did not appear that the vessel had been fully repaired. (*Id.*)

9. The court also rejected an item of depreciation in the value, as being too speculative. (*Id.*)

10. A person whose real interest is that of a *mortgagee*, and who has *never taken possession of the vessel*, is not answerable for *supplies*, though he holds a *bill of sale* vesting in him the *legal title*, and though the vessel may be *registered in his name* at the custom house, accompanied by his oath, that he is the true and only owner. (*Baxter* agt. *Wallace*, *ante*, 484.)

11. To make a mortgagee responsible for supplies, it must be shown either that he *was in possession of the vessel*, or that they were furnished *at his request*, or by the direction of some person *authorized to contract on his behalf*. (*Id.*)

12. The owner of a ship, having chartered her for a voyage, effected insurance upon the freight, earned or not earned. The ship was wrecked near her port of discharge, and the insured abandoned the freight to the underwriter. The seamen saved from the rigging, etc., enough to pay their wages, and also part of the cargo, on which the freight was enough to pay their wages: *Held*, that the seamen were entitled to wages for the voyage, and not merely from the time of the casualty. They take their pay as wages, and not as salvage. (*Daniels* agt. *Atlantic Mutual Insurance Company*, 24 *N. Y. R.*, 447.)

13. The wages, upon the abandonment, became a charge upon the ship and owner, in exoneration of the freight. (*Id.*)

14. All owners of a vessel who assent to the employment of the vessel, and share the proceeds of such employment, are, as a general rule, *prima facie* liable for repairs and supplies to the vessel, and for seamen's wages while the vessel is employed for their benefit. (*Kohler* agt. *Wright*, 7 *Barb.*, 318.)

See DAMAGES, 5.

See DEFENCE, 1.

AFFIDAVIT OF MERITS.

See SERVICE, 1. 2.

AGREEMENT.

1. A promise is to be interpreted in that sense in which the promisor knew that the promisee understood it. (*Barlow* agt. *Scott*, 24 *N. Y. R.*, 40.)

2. Accordingly where the vendor of land undertook to execute such a conveyance as he had received from his grantor, which he said was a warranty deed —the same in fact containing only a covenant against the acts of the grantor—the purchaser, although he saw the deed under which the vendor held, understood it to be, and understood the vendor to promise, a deed with general warranty, and the vendor knew that such was his understanding, *held*, that the vendor was bound to convey with general warranty. (*Id.*)

3. An agreement between the payee of a note and the maker, made with the assent of the latter's partner, to apply the indebtedness of the payee to such maker and his partner in payment of the note, operates *in presenti* as a satisfaction of the note *pro tanto*. (*Davis* agt. *Spencer*, 24 *N. Y. R.*, 386.)

4. Whether the assent of the partner was necessary or material: *Quere*. (*Id.*)

5. No right can be derived from any agreement made in express opposition

to the laws of the place where it was made. (*Otis* agt. *Harrison*, 36 *Barb.*, 210.)

6. An agreement to convey land to another, upon the consideration that the latter shall give all the aid in his power, spend his time, and use his utmost influence and exertions to procure the passage of a law pending before the legislature, conferring upon the covenantor a valuable public franchise, is illegal and void. It is against public policy. (*Mills* agt. *Mills*, 36 *Barb.*, 474.)

7. In an action on a written agreement made between the plaintiff and defendants, all directors of a corporation, by which the plaintiff claimed to recover of the defendants their aliquot shares of the amount of certain promissory notes which the plaintiff had indorsed under the agreement, and had been compelled to pay for the benefit of the corporation, *held*, that on putting the material allegations in issue, the defendants might show by parol that such notes were not indorsed by the plaintiff under the alleged agreement; but were indorsed upon a subsequent contract between the plaintiff and some other directors of said company of the one part, and the said company of the other part. And on the alleged agreement being produced, and the signatures being proved, the defendants might show that they never delivered said agreement, but signed it on the express condition that it was not to be delivered as an executed instrument until it was signed by all the directors of the company, and that all of the latter had not signed it. (*Burnham* agt. *Wilbur*, 7 *Bosw.*, 169.)

See Will, 35.

See Bills of Exchange and Promissory Notes, 7. 9.

AMENDMENT.

1. The mistakes which may be amended under section 173 of the Code, do not include judicial errors in rendering judgment. In an action involving the construction of a will, the court have no power to amend the judgment after it has been entered, by inserting an allowance to certain of the parties, in addition to that given by section 308 of the Code, by way of indemnity to the expenses of the suit. (*Hotaling* agt. *Marsh*, 14 *Abb.*, 161.)

See Appeal, 1.

See Trial, 1. 2. 3.

See Slander, 3. 4.

ANSWER.

1. Where it is apparent, by admissions the answer, that it is sham or false, will be stricken out as such, althou *verified*. (*Lawrence* agt. *Derl ante*, 133.)

2. An *appeal* lies from an order ove ruling a demurrer to one of several leged defences, with liberty to reply that part of the answer demurred (*Mattoon* agt. *Baker*, *ante*, 329.)

3. Where the complaint alleged a cau of action on contract for goods, war and merchandise sold and delivere for work, labor and services done a performed, and for money paid, la out and expended, as one cause of a tion; and for an accounting and a ba ance due the plaintiff, and a promise pay, as a second cause of action, and t defendant put in first a general denia second, a set-off or counter-claim f goods sold and delivered, money pai laid out and expended, &c., and for general balance on account; and thir a *multifarious defence of a legal an equitable* character to which last d fence the plaintiff *demurred*. (*Id*

4. *Held*, that if the last defence, a though containing a set-off, and matt of purely an equitable nature, a therefore multifarious, contained all gations of fact sufficient to make o a proper case for a *set-off*, it must held good as a *counter-claim*, notwit standing it might also contain oth statements of no value as a defence no objection having been taken on th ground—the remedy being by moti to strike out, not by demurrer. (*Id*

5. *Held*, also, that should the third d fence contain no sufficient ground for set-off, but matter for *equitable reli only*, having no connection with t subject of plaintiff's action, the d murrer would be well interposed, a though the latter defence was plead as a counter-claim. (*Id.*)

6. A *counter-claim*, to be available to party, must afford to him protection some way against the plaintiff's d mand for judgment, either in whole in part. It must, therefore, consist a set-off or a claim by way of recoup ment, or be in some way connecte

with the subject of the action stated in the complaint; and an answer which does not meet these requirements is *insufficient*. (*Id.*)

7. What answers or defences forming parts of an answer, and what matter in an answer or defence, forming part thereof, or of a defence therein, may be treated as irrelevant, and what are sham and frivolous, considered. (*Lee Bank* agt. *Kitching*, 7 *Bosw.*, 664.)

8. An answer is not frivolous merely because it denies the several allegations of the complaint conjunctively, instead of denying them disjunctively. The Code permits any material allegation of a complaint to be put at issue, by an answer that the defendant has no knowledge or information thereof sufficient to form a belief as to its truth. When any material allegation of a complaint is thus controverted, the answer cannot be treated as frivolous, or held bad on demurrer, merely because such allegation is of the recovery of a judgment, or of some other fact, the truth of which can be ascertained by inquiry. If the answer is believed to be sham, the remedy is a motion, on affidavit, to strike it out as sham. (*Livingston* agt. *Hammer*, 7 *Bosw.*, 670.)

9. Where an answer states new matter as a defence, it must state facts which if true will bar the action, or so much of it as is attempted to be answered. (*Carter* agt. *Koezley*, 14 *Abb.*, 147.)

10. Where the defendant after service of an amended complaint under an order allowing him to elect to let his answer stand, or to serve a new answer, suffered the trial to proceed on the issues raised by his first answer, his time to serve a new answer not having expired, *held*, that he did not thereby waive his right to serve a new answer. (*Low* agt. *Graydon*, 14 *Abb.*, 443.)

See Verification, 1.

See Contract, 8. 9.

See Judgment, 14.

See Defence, 1. 2.

See Assignment for the Benefit of Creditors, 12.

See Corporations, 1.

See Appeal, 17.

See Motion, 4.

APPEAL.

1. Where a party has given *notice of appeal* by *service thereof* on the opposite party, but *not on the clerk*, he is not authorized to *amend* under § 327 of the Code. (*Ellsworth* agt. *Fulton*, *ante*, 20.)

2. In case of an attachment issued under sections 227, *et seq.* of the Code, and also in case of a judgment recovered in such attachment suit, where it appeared that the judgment had been executed and paid, notwithstanding an appeal pending, the appellate court, under section 330 of the Code, have power to, and will order on reversal of the judgment below, a restitution to the appellant of the moneys so collected, notwithstanding such reversal is accompanied by an order granting a new trial, and notwithstanding the attachment is so pending. (*Britton* agt. *Phillips*, *ante*, 111.)

3. In such case, the restitution is effected by ordering a deposit of the moneys into court, to abide the result of the new trial, and subject to the lien of the attachment. (*Id.*)

4. *Held*, that the proceedings were properly *continued* before the successor in office. An *order* of a *county judge*, dismissing proceedings on an attachment for *contempt* against the defendant in *supplementary proceedings*, is appealable to the general term. (*Holstein* agt. *Rice*, *ante*, 135.)

5. An *order* made out of court, upon notice, must be first *entered with the clerk* before an *appeal* can be taken. (*Code*, § 350.) (*Gallt* agt. *Finch*, 193.)

6. And when an order is required to be entered with the clerk, and a party is required to give notice of the order, he *cannot give the notice until he has entered the order*. (*Id.*)

7. Therefore, as regards all orders granted on notice, which are required to be entered with the clerk, the party has no right to give the written notice allowed by § 332 of the Code, until *after the order has been entered*. (*Id.*)

8. Where the order was entered May 27th, and the notice of appeal was served on the 27th June, *held*, that the service of the notice of appeal was *in time*. (*Id.*)

9. It is, to say the least, questionable whether *any court can extend the time to appeal*. (*Id.*)

10. An *appeal* lies from an order overruling a demurrer to one of several

alleged defences, with liberty to reply to that part of the answer demurred to. (*Mattoon* agt. *Baker*, *ante*, 329.)

11. The granting of a new trial in a suit before a justice of the peace, under section 366 of the Code, is matter of mere discretion, not reviewable on appeal. (*Wavel* agt. *Wiles*, 24 *N. Y. R.*, 635.)

12. This rule applies where the application for a new trial was on the ground that the summons had never been served and the justice did not obtain jurisdiction. The County Court having denied a new trial except upon terms, the Supreme Court cannot review its order. (*Id.*)

13. The court can review the findings of the jury on the facts, or set aside the verdict as against the weight of evidence, only when there is no evidence to sustain the verdict, or when it is against the clear and decided weight of the evidence. (*Smith* agt. *Tiffany*, 36 *Barb.*, 23.)

14. When a court of review is satisfied, from the general scope and tenor of the proceedings on the trial, that a particular fact was not a matter of contest nor a ground of objection there, but was assumed or taken for granted in the conduct of the cause, it may and should conclude that the fact was as it was assumed to be. (*Paige* agt. *Fazackerly*, 36 *Barb.*, 392.)

15. When an appeal is moved in its order on the calendar, the court will presume that the case therein has been settled, unless moved to interfere on affidavits alleging the contrary. On appeal from a judgment entered on report of a referee, the appellant may be heard on exceptions taken to the referee's conclusions of law upon the facts found, although the printed case does not contain any of the evidence; but in such case he cannot be heard upon his exceptions to the findings of fact. It will be assumed that they are found upon competent and sufficient evidence. (*Frost* agt. *Smith*, 7 *Bosw.*, 108.)

16. On appeal from a judgment on the decision of a referee, where the case stated that the cause was submitted, "the counsel for the defendants admitting that the defendants were liable for the payment of a bill" which was one of the bills of which the plaintiff claimed to recover, the defendants on appeal cannot question the correctness of the decision of the referee allowing such payment, although the defendant, after such submission, handed to the referee written points assailing the plaintiff's claim in that respect. (*Kohler* agt. *Wright*, 7 *Bosw.*, 318.)

17. On an appeal from a judgment rendered against a defendant on account of the frivolousness of the answer, the question is, whether the judgment is right on the merits of the case made by the pleadings, and not whether the answer is frivolous. (*East River Bank* agt. *Rogers*, 7 *Bosw.*, 493.)

18. An order made by a judge is not appealable until it is entered. That there is at the foot of it a written direction of the judge to enter it, does not alter the case. But where an appeal has been argued without any objection or suggestion that the order has not been entered, the court will not assume that it has not been entered, but will decide the appeal upon the merits. (*Whitaker* agt. *Desfosse*, 7 *Bosw.*, 678.)

19. Whether a default should be opened on excuse, and as to the sufficiency of the excuse, are matters of judicial discretion, and the decision of a judge thereon is not appealable. (*Id.*)

20. An order of reference is appealable, when made in a case where a reference is not authorised by law. (*Id.*)

21. An order of reference on appeal will be treated as compulsorily made, where it recites that the motion was opposed, and there is nothing in the papers showing that it was assented to, although the order contains directions affecting the proceedings, otherwise than by referring the cause. (*Id.*)

22. On appeal from judgments in actions tried by the court, if the case contain no findings of fact, it is the practice of the general term of the first district to dismiss the appeal, unless the parties consent before the appeal is submitted, to have the case sent back for correction. (*Mathews* agt. *The Mayor, &c. of New York*, 14 *Abb.*, 209.)

23. On appeal from the special to the general term of the marine court of the city of New York, the appellant has ten days after written notice of the entry of judgment, to prepare a case or exceptions. If no written notice of the judgment is served, the appellant's time to serve his case is not limited,

The New York common pleas, on reversing the judgment, remitted the case to the marine court for argument. (*Whitlock* agt. *Joseph*, 14 *Abb.*, 342.)

24. Where the sureties proposed in an undertaking given on an appeal to the court of appeals, fail to justify when excepted to by the respondent, the appeal becomes a nullity. It is no bar to an appeal to the court of appeals, that a prior ineffectual appeal has been undertaken by the appellant. (*Kelsey* agt. *Campbell*, 14 *Abb.*, 368.)

25. An appeal under section 344 of the Code, to the supreme court from an inferior court, is ineffectual, unless security for costs be given as on an appeal to the court of appeals. *Held* applicable to an order of the city court of Brooklyn, overruling a demurrer. (*Jones* agt. *Decker*, 14 *Abb.*, 391.)

26. Irregularities not referred to in the papers upon which a motion is made at special term, are not available on appeal from the order made thereon. (*Shipman* agt. *Shaffer*, 14 *Abb.*, 449.)

See INJUNCTION, 1. 2.
See EVIDENCE, 3.
See CONSTABLE'S BOND, 1. 2. 3. 4. 5.
See ASSIGNMENT FOR THE BENEFIT OF CREDITORS, 6.
See REFEREES AND REPORTS, 9. 10.
See EXCEPTIONS, 2. 3.
See JUDGMENT, 17.
See HIGHWAYS, 11.
See UNDERTAKING, 1. 2. 3. 4.
See RECEIVERS, 8. 9.

ARBITRATION.

See CONSTITUTIONAL LAW, 1. 2. 3.

ARREST.

1. In all those actions, where the nature of the *cause of action* is such, that the defendant may be arrested under section 179 of the Code, it must be *stated in the complaint*; otherwise, an *execution* cannot issue against *the person*, unless an order of *arrest* has been served. (*Atocha* agt. *Garcia*, *ante*, 186.)

2. But where the action is one in which the defendant cannot be arrested, without some *extrinsic fact*, forming no part of the *cause of action*, but merely incidental to it, the fact must be stated in an *affidavit*, and an order of arrest must be obtained and served; and the averment of such fact in the complaint will not alone authorise an execution against the person. Hence the averment in the complaint is *immaterial*. (*Id.*)

3. For instance, where the substantive cause of action alleged in the complaint is the *debt* sought to be recovered, and allegations of *fraud* are also averred, the fraud being *incidental*, and only important to the plaintiff, as furnishing the ground for obtaining the provisional remedy of arrest; the allegations of fraud in the complaint are *immaterial* and *unnecessary*. The issue to be tried in the action is the *debt*, not the fraudulent contraction of it. The judgment recovered is for the debt, not for the fraud. (*Id.*)

4. Such an action, where it involves the examination of a *long account*, although an order of arrest has been obtained, may be *referred*, under § 271 of the Code, without the consent of the parties. (*Id.*)

5. Where consignments of lumber are made by the consignor to the consignee under a contract between them that the consignee is to sell the same on *commission*, at eight per cent., which is to include a premium for *guaranty of sales*, and to account for the net proceeds, after deducting charges and commissions, the consignee acts in a *fiduciary capacity*, and is liable to *arrest* for not paying over the proceeds received from purchasers. (*Ostell* agt. *Brough*, *ante*, 274.)

6. *It seems*, that where the purchaser does not pay, and the consignor or owner of the lumber sues the consignee for the price upon the *contract of guaranty*, the latter is to be considered as a *mere debtor*, and not liable to arrest. (*Id.*)

7. A motion to vacate an order of arrest cannot be made after the entry of judgment in the action. (*Barker* agt. *Wheeler*, 14 *Abb.*, 170.)

8. The fact that a creditor has accepted the promissory note or check of his debtor for money received in a fiduciary capacity, is no bar, after the dishonor of the note or check, to an arrest in an action on the original indebtedness, where the note or check is

offered to be returned. (*Shipman* agt. *Shaffer*, 14 *Abb.*, 449.)

See METROPOLITAN POLICE, 1. 2. 3. 4.

ASSIGNMENT FOR THE BENEFIT OF CREDITORS.

1. In an action to set aside an *assignment* for the benefit of creditors, for fraud, *held*, that there was not sufficient evidence of fraud to warrant an injunction and receiver, arising from the fact, 1st. That the assignor had continued in possession of the assigned property, and was employed by the assignee to sell the stock and assist in making collections at the store where the business was formerly carried on, and the amounts as collected were paid over to the assignee. (*Beamish* agt. *Conant*, *ante*, 94.)

2. 2d. That after about six months under such arrangement, the whole remaining stock was sold at 25 per cent. on the cost price to a brother-in-law of the assignor, who had paid a large portion of the purchase money, and was responsible for the balance. It also appearing that the sale was made for the full value of the goods. (*Id.*)

3. Where, at the time of the execution of the *assignment for the benefit of creditors*, a *contract* for the manufacture of goods in England had been made by the assignor, the order had been sent, and a subsequent delivery proved that the order had been *accepted*. *Held*, therefore, that the assignor had a claim to have the goods manufactured, which he could enforce, and which contract he could assign; and that whatever interest he had under the contract *passed under the assignment to the assignee*. (*Van Dine* agt. *Willett*, *ante*, 206.)

4. The *assignee* having subsequently elected to accept the goods here in public store, by the payment of the duties and the purchase money, *held*, that a levy and taking of the goods afterwards by the *sheriff*, as the property of the assignor, made him a *trespasser*. (*Id.*)

5. A direction in an assignment to the assignee to pay *rent* and *taxes* on the real estate until sold, *held*, not objectionable; it was only authorizing the assignee to do what he would have been authorized to do without it, to preserve the property. The assignment authorizing the assignee to pay debts due and to grow due, *held*, unobjectionable. So the authority to employ an *attorney*, *held*, unobjectionable. (*Id.*)

6. The objection that an *assignment for the benefit of creditors* was not executed by *all the parties*, should be taken at the *trial*; it is too late to raise such an objection, to defeat the assignee's title on *appeal*. (*Colwell* agt. *Lawrence*, *ante*, 324.)

7. An assignment in trust for creditors is not rendered void by a provision giving the assignees (one of them being a lawyer) "a just and reasonable compensation for labor, time, services, and attention," in the business of the trust. (*Campbell* agt. *Woodworth*, 24 *N. Y. R.*, 304.)

8. This language is to be construed as meaning no more than the commissions fixed by law. (*Id.*)

9. A provision in an assignment executed by a debtor in trust for the benefit of his creditors, directing the payment of a fictitious demand to the wife of the assignor, renders the assignment void; on the ground that it is intended to hinder and delay creditors. (*American Exchange Bank* agt. *Webb*, 36 *Barb.*, 291.)

10. An insolvent debtor cannot do by concealment what he may not do openly, therefore he cannot, by a secret agreement with a portion of his creditors, compel them to agree to his release on condition of his executing an assignment for the benefit of creditors giving them preferences. (*Spaulding* agt. *Strang*, 36 *Barb.*, 310.)

11. An assignment by a manufacturing corporation formed under the act of February 17, 1848, of all its property in trust for the benefit of all its creditors *pro rata*, made in contemplation of insolvency, is void. (*Loring* agt. *U. S. Vulcanized Gutta Percha Co.*, 36 *Barb.*, 330.)

12. A creditor of an assignor, when sued by the assignee for taking the assigned property on an attachment against the assignor, may set up as a defence that the property was assigned with intent to hinder, delay, and defraud the creditors of the assignor; and his attorney directing the levy may avail himself of the same defence. (*Fallon* agt. *McCunn*, 7 *Bosw.*, 141.)

13. An assignee for the benefit of creditors acquires no better title than the assignor had, and therefore is not entitled to the same favor in equity as a purchaser for a valuable consideration. (*Scheiffelin* agt. *Hawkins*, 14 *Abb.*, 112.)

14. The provisions of the act of April 13, 1860, (*Laws of* 1860, 595, *ch.* 348) which require general assignments for the benefit of creditors to be acknowledged by the assignor before delivery, and schedules to be made within twenty days thereafter, are directory merely. (*Fairchild* agt. *Gwynne*, 14 *Abb.*, 121.)

15. Under the act of 1860, (*Laws of* 1860, 594, *ch.* 348, § 1) requiring assignments for benefit of creditors to be in writing and duly *acknowledged* before delivery, an assignment which is *proved* by a subscribing witness is not effectual. (*Cook* agt. *Kelly*, 14 *Abb.*, 466.)

See PARTIES, 1.

See ATTACHMENT, 4.

See HUSBAND AND WIFE, 14.

See PARTNERS AND PARTNERSHIPS, 12. 13.

See SET-OFF, 2.

ASSIGNEE.

1. An *assignee* of anything but commercial paper, when he takes it *bona fide*, is liable to *all the equities* which exist against the demand while in the hands of the *assignor*. (*Roberts* agt. *Carter*, *ante*, 44.)

See ASSIGNMENT FOR BENEFIT OF CREDITORS, 3. 4. 5. 13.

See MORTGAGE FORECLOSURE, 5. 6. 7. 8.

See CREDITOR'S SUIT, 11.

ATTACHMENT.

1. A *motion* to set aside an *attachment* may be made *after judgment* in the action. The judgment does not *supersede* the attachment. (*This is adverse to Scheib* agt. *Baldwin*, 22 *How. Pr. R.*, 278.) (*Thompson* agt. *Culver*, *ante*, 286.)

2. The statutes relating to the process of attachment, issued by the marine court in the city of New York, stated and considered by HOFFMAN, J. (*Fallon* agt. *McCunn*, 7 *Bosw.*, 141.)

3. Where the plaintiffs sued out an attachment against P. on contract, with a view to get the proceeds of flour sold in Liverpool, England, by the defendants, and charged in their affidavits that they sold and delivered the goods to P., in New York, on his promise to pay cash on the delivery; and the defendants subsequently sold the flour which they received from P. and paid the proceeds, over the specified advances and charges, to plaintiffs, who accepted the same and gave a receipt therefor, expressed to be "in full of proceeds of sales of flour, as per your acceptance of P.'s order in our favor," *held*, that the plaintiffs could not subsequently maintain an action against the defendants, either for a conversion of the flour, by reason of their having sold it, or to recover the moneys obtained for it, as for so much money had and received by the defendants to the plaintiffs' use. (*Wilmot* agt. *Richardson*, 7 *Bosw.*, 570.)

4. An attachment may issue under the Code against the property of a debtor, who has made a fraudulent assignment for the benefit of creditors, although the assignment is valid on its face under the law of 1860. (*Skinner* agt. *Ottinger*, 14 *Abb.*, 109.)

5. It is unnecessary that the plaintiff in the attachment suit should be a judgment creditor. (*Id.*)

6. Before a justice of the peace, or a district court of the city of New York, can acquire jurisdiction to proceed to trial in an action commenced by attachment, the return of the officer serving it must show a strict compliance with the statute; especially when the defendant has not appeared. Service of the attachment and inventory upon a person in charge of the property attached is insufficient, unless it appears affirmatively that the defendant has no place of residence within the county. (*Marshall* agt. *Canty*, 14 *Abb.*, 237.)

See PARTNERS and PARTNERSHIPS, 4. 5.

See JUDGMENT, 2. 3. 4.

See ATTORNEY, 10.

See CREDITOR'S SUIT, 5. 6.

See ASSIGNMENT FOR THE BENEFIT OF CREDITORS, 12.

ATTORNEY.

1. On substitution of attorneys, where the plaintiff has assigned the judgment

without notice to his attorney, an order of reference has been made by the court to ascertain the amount of the original attorney's lien on the judgment to the amount of his *taxed costs*, and the attorney moves to amend the order of reference by extending it to his claim for a lien beyond the taxed costs, but does not show any *special agreement* with the plaintiff to that effect, his motion to amend will be denied, without prejudice to his lien or right, if he has any beyond the taxable costs, on or to the judgment on the final recovery, as against the assignee of the judgment. (*Richardson* agt. *Brooklyn City & Newtown R. R. Co.*, *ante*, 480.)

2. An *attorney* has a *lien* on the *judgment* obtained by him for his client, to the extent of his claim for *services and disbursements* in the action, whether the amount of his compensation *is agreed upon or depends upon a quantum meruit*. (*Fox* agt. *Fox*, *ante*, 409.)

3. The attorney is entitled to such a *sum* as shall have been *agreed upon* between him and his client; and the *lien* will attach to the judgment to *the extent of the amount thus agreed upon*. (*Id.*)

4. *Payment* of the judgment to any other person after notice of the lien, will be of no avail against the attorney's right *to enforce it for the amount of his claim*. (*Id.*)

5. When there is a *dispute* as to what the *contract is*, or in regard to the *amount* which the attorney is entitled to *demand under it*, and also when the amount of compensation is by express agreement made *to depend on the value of the services, and unliquidated*, the remedy of the attorney is by *direct action* against all the parties. There cannot be a *compulsory reference* on these questions. The case of *Haight* agt. *Holcomb*, (16 *How. Pr. R.*, 173,) settles this point. (*Id.*)

6. Reasonable counsel fees incurred in the defence of a suit to restrain the payment of an award, are recoverable upon a bond conditioned for the payment of all costs and damages arising from the obligor's obtaining an injunction or from his contesting the payment. (*Corcoran* agt. *Judson*, 24 *N. Y. R.*, 106.)

7. The attorney in an execution, who refused to state whether he directed the sale of particular chattels by instruction of his client, and challenged a suit against himself, is estopped from denying that he acted on his individual responsibility. (*Ford* agt. *Williams*, *id.*, 359.)

8. The owner of such chattels, who states his claim and forbids the sale, may purchase the property without impairing his right of action for the trespass. (*Id.*)

9. A statement made by a client to an attorney, about two years and a half after the latter had obtained a judgment for the former against a defendant, and several months after the judgment had been assigned by the plaintiff to another person, as to the payment of that judgment, *held*, not to be a privileged communication between attorney and client; that relation in respect to such judgment had ceased. If a statement made to an attorney has no reference to the professional employment, it falls within the exception to the rule of exclusion, although made while the relation of attorney and client exists. (*Marsh* agt. *Howe*, 36 *Barb.*, 649.)

10. An attachment will not be granted against an attorney, for the non-payment of money collected by him for a client, after the remedy by action has been barred by the statute of limitations. The court will not compel payment in any form of proceeding, when it is made to appear that there is nothing due by the law of the land. (*People* agt. *Brotherson*, 36 *Barb.*, 662.)

11. The power of a court of equity to direct the payment of counsel fees out of a common fund belonging to the parties in the action, can be made only by the judge who tried the cause. (*Hotaling* agt. *Marsh*, 14 *Abb.*, 161.)

12. An attorney has an equitable right to be paid for his services and the amount of his lien, out of the proceeds of the judgment or other proceeding obtained by his labor and skill, which the court will compel to the extent of its equitable power. Under the Code the lien is not limited to the taxable costs; but the attorney, unless the proceeds have come into his hands, must invoke the equitable aid of the court to ascertain the existence and amount of the lien before he can enforce it. (*Ackerman* agt. *Ackerman*, 14 *Abb.*, 229.)

13. Payment by a judgment debtor to a judgment creditor, of the amount of the judgment, is valid against the lien of the attorney, unless the debtor has notice of the attorney's claim by way of lien to a portion of such judgment. (*Id.*)

14. The lien of the attorney attaches not merely to the costs in the judgment, but to the whole judgment—damages and costs. (*Id.*)

15. An action commenced and prosecuted in the name of the plaintiff for the benefit of another person, where the attorney did not claim costs from the plaintiff, but from the real prosecutor, *held*, that the plaintiff could not change his attorney without satisfying the attorney's claim for costs. A party has no right to change his attorney without leave of the court; who will consult the rights of the attorney, and will not allow the change until the just claims of the latter are discharged or secured. (*Hoffman* agt. *Van Nostrand*, 14 *Abb.*, 336.)

See Set-off, 1.

See Costs, 9. 10. 17. 18. 19.

See Assignment for Benefit of Creditors, 3. 4. 5.

See New Trial, 6. 7. 11.

See Principal and Agent, 2.

See Verification, 3.

See Excise Law, 3.

BAIL.

1. Where the plaintiff has the right to take the *persons of all the defendants* in satisfaction of his judgment, it carries with it the right to proceed against the *bail of one of them*, as to whom there may be a return of *non est inventus*. (*Penn* agt. *Remsen*, *ante*, 503.)

BANK CHECK.

1. A *bank check* drawn by the president of the bank in his individual name, payable to another person, and certified "good" by the drawer *as president*, renders the acceptance *void* in the hands of the drawer, irrespective of the question whether or not he has funds in the bank. (*Claflin* agt. *Farmers' and Citizens' Bank of Long Island*, *ante*, 1, *court of appeals*.)

2. The want of authority in the president as agent, to bind the bank, appears upon the *face of the check*; of course there can be no *bona fide holder* of the check. (*Id.*)

3. And it does not alter the case that a general authority to certify checks had been conferred by the bank on the president. The question is one of agency, where the president cannot act as the agent of both parties to the contract, nor as agent in regard to a contract in which he has any interest, or to which he is a party, on the opposite side to his principal. (*Id.*)

BANKING CORPORATIONS.

1. The act (*ch.* 654 *of* 1853), allowing corporations which have not received net annual profits equal to five per cent. upon their capital, to commute for taxes is applicable only to corporations which have been in existence for a full year before the assessment is made. (*Park Bank* agt. *Wood*, 24 *N. Y. R.*, 93.)

2. Held, accordingly, that a bank which had been organized only three months was liable to be taxed for the full amount of its capital, though its income and profits were less than five per cent. (*Id.*)

3. A provision in the articles of a banking association that the shares of its stock shall not be transferable until the shareholder shall discharge all debts *due* by him to the association, includes liabilities of the shareholder which have not matured. (*Leggett* agt. *Bank of Sing Sing*, 24 *N. Y. R.*, 283.)

4. Such a provision creates a valid lien as against an assignee of the stock, who takes with knowledge thereof, while the shareholder is under a contingent liability as indorser, and gives no notice to the bank of his claim until after the indorser's liability has become fixed. (*Id.*)

5. A dividend of the profits of a banking association, declared by the directors "payable in New York State currency," is payable in cash. The directors have no authority to declare it payable otherwise. (*Ehle* agt. *Chittenango Bank*, 24 *N. Y. R.*, 548.)

6. Evidence of an understanding by the cashier that "State currency" meant country bank notes current in New York city at a discount of a quarter of one per cent., but not showing a general

usage in that sense, is inadmissible. (*Id.*)

7. Where the cashier of a bank is authorised to indorse a note or other negotiable paper for the sole purpose of transmitting to other banks for collection, such indorsement does not make the bank liable as indorser. The cashier of a bank has no power to make a contract for the bank in his own name, unless the corporation has authorized him to do so on its behalf, and with the intention that it should be bound. (*Bank of the State of New York* agt. *Farmers' Branch of the State Bank of Ohio*, 36 *Barb.*, 332.)

8. Where the court of chancery of New Jersey adjudges a bank, created under the laws of that State, to be insolvent, and appoints a receiver, the validity of the appointment cannot be questioned collaterally, provided enough was alleged and done on initiating the proceeding to give that court jurisdiction of the subject matter. The order is not void merely because no officer of the bank had notice of the application, it having been proved to the satisfaction of the court, before making it, that no such officer could be found within the State. (*Dayton* agt. *Borst*, 7 *Bosw.*, 115.)

9. A subscriber to the certificate, filed to organize a bank, is liable to pay for the number of shares therein stated to have been subscribed by him, and payment can be enforced at the suit of a receiver, appointed on its becoming insolvent, to satisfy the creditors of the bank. In a suit by such receiver, against an original subscriber, a judgment in favor of a third person against the bank, in a court of record, in an action in which the bank appeared and defended, is *prima facie* evidence that the bank owes the amount recovered. The fact that a subscriber assigns all his interest in the bank, does not discharge his liability upon his subscription, and it can be enforced for the benefit of one who subsequently becomes a creditor of the bank. (*Id.*)

10. The act to restrain unauthorised banking is inapplicable to obligations, not payable on demand. (*Hubbard* agt. *N. Y. & Harlem Railroad Co.*, 14 *Abb.*, 275.)

See Bank Check, 1. 2. 3.

See Receivers, 3. 4.

See Taxes and Assessments, 1.

BILLS OF EXCHANGE AND PR(MISSORY NOTES.

1. Where the maker of a promissory no within this state removes therefrо and continues to reside abroad until i maturity, the indorser may be charg without a demand of such maker presentment at his last place of res dence within this state. (*Foster* ag *Julien*, 24 *N. Y. R.*, 28.)

2. A note given to a mutual fire ins rance company, organised under t general law, as one of the notes r quired by the statute (*chap.* 308 1849) to make up its capital, is, in l gal effect, payable on demand, *i. e at its date*, though by its terms pa ment was to be made at such times a in such portions as the directors mig require. (*Howland* agt. *Edmond* 24 *N. Y. R.*, 307.)

3. No actual demand is necessary in r spect to such a note. The statute u der which it is given fastens on it t character of a note payable absolutel or at the mere will of the holder. (*Id*

4. The statute of limitations begins run against such a note at the time is given, and is a good defence at t expiration of six years from that tim (*Id.*)

5. An agreement between the payee o note and the maker, made with t assent of the latter's partner, to ap the indebtedness of the payee to su maker and his partner in payment the note, operates *in presenti* as satisfaction of the note *pro tanto.* (*Davis* agt. *Spencer*, 24 *N. Y. R* 386.)

6. Whether the assent of the part was necessary or material: *Que* (*Id.*)

7. Where a bill or note having time run, is received from a party primar liable on a bill or note then over-du the receipt of such note or bill does operate to discharge an indorser on t bill or note over-due, unless there is agreement express or implied that t note or bill thus received shall be payment of the former, or extend the time of payment in favor of so party who is liable thereon, prior such indorser. If a new draft or n is taken by the holder of a protes note, as collateral to such note, t will not prevent him from enforc payment of the note. (*Taylor* a *Allen*, 36 *Barb.*, 294.)

8. Where the maker of an instrument in writing promises to pay to the order of another a specified sum, at his store or in goods on demand, for value received, it is a negotiable promissory note. (*Hosstatter* agt. *Wilson*, 36 *Barb.*, 307.)

9. In an action by an indorsee against his immediate indorser of a promissory note, or by the payee against the maker, the defendant cannot prove a verbal agreement, cotemporaneous with the indorsing or making of the note, by which the note is not to be paid or become payable until the defendant has realized the amount thereof from specified sources, where the alleged agreement and facts connected with it do not show a failure of consideration, or that there was no consideration for indorsing or making the note. (*Lewis* agt. *Jones*, 7 *Bosw.*, 366.)

10. A bill of exchange that has been negotiated by the indorsement of several parties, the holder has, the next day after receiving notice of dishonor, to notify any prior indorser whom he desires to charge; and each successive indorser who receives notice, has at least one day thereafter to give notice to any antecedent indorser. And this rule is not confined to holders for value, but applies to an agent or banker. Where the party giving the notice, and the party to whom it is given, do not reside in the same town, the notice may be sent by mail. (*West River B'k* agt. *Taylor*, 7 *Bosw.*, 466.)

11. To charge the indorser upon a promissory note, payable at a particular place, the complaint must contain an averment to the effect that payment was demanded at such place. The complaint averred that at maturity the note was duly presented for payment to the makers, *held*, a sufficient averment of presentment at the place named. (*Turner* agt. *Williams*, 14 *Abb.*, 215.)

See Guaranty, 2.

See Complaint, 8. 9.

See Manufacturing Corporations, 1.

See Foreign Corporations, 2.

See Partners and Partnerships, 19.

See Banking Corporations, 7.

See Usury, 3. 7.

See Principal and Agent, 7.

See Defence, 1. 2.

BILL OF LADING.

1. A shipping bill, executed by the owner of property and of the canal boat on which it is laden for transportation, stating that it is to be delivered as addressed, viz: "Account J. F. M., care of Dows & Cary," though not signed by the master of the boat, nor containing any words of negotiability, is substantially a bill of lading, and affects the title to the goods in the same manner as if it were in regular form. (*Dows* agt. *Greene*, 24 *N. Y. R.*, 638.)

2. Under such a bill, Dows & Cary are the consignees, and have a lien under the factor's act (*chap.* 179 *of* 1830) in respect to any money advanced by them to J. F. M. (*Id.*)

3. *It seems* that, at common law, and independent of the factor's act, the transfer of a bill of lading to a *bona fide* holder would transfer the title in the same manner as a transfer of the goods, although the bill had been obtained from the owner of the property by fraud. *Dows* agt. *Perrin*, (16 *N. Y.*, 325,) in this respect questioned. (*Id.*)

4. The master of a vessel who signs a bill of lading, by which he acknowledges the receipt on board, of goods of a designated kind and specified quantity, and agrees to deliver the same to the shipper or his assigns, on payment of freight, at a specified rate per ton, is bound to deliver to one purchasing the goods *in transitu*, and taking from the shipper an assignment of the bill of lading, in good faith and relying thereon, goods of the kind so designated, and the specified quantity thereof. (*Byrne* agt. *Weeks*, 7 *Bosw.*, 372.)

5. In an action by an assignee of the master's claim for freight, where the assignment is made after a part delivery of the cargo, and a refusal to deliver the residue of it, the assignee of the bill of lading may deduct from the amount of the freight payable upon the goods delivered, the value of the goods not delivered pursuant to the contract in the bill of lading. (*Id.*)

BOARDING HOUSE KEEPERS.

1. The intent of the statute of 1860, (*Sess. Laws*, 771,) giving to the keeper of a *boarding house* a *lien* to the extent of the board due, is, to give them the same lien which an inn-

keeper has upon the effects of a guest, without reference to the character of the guests, whether they are *transient* or *permanent boarders*. (*Stewart* agt. *McCready*, *ante*, 62.)

BONDS.

1. A bond issued by a railroad company acknowledged the receipt of $1,000 from ——, and in consideration thereof the company promised and agreed to pay to ——, or assigns, the sum of $1,000 ten years after date, &c. *Held*, that any lawful holder by delivery or transfer was authorised to fill his own name in the blanks as the payee. And that averments in the complaint that the corporation received the money from some person unknown to the plaintiff, and delivered the bond to such person for the purpose and with the intent that the same should be assignable and transferable by delivery from hand to hand; that before maturity it came lawfully into the possession of the plaintiff for value, and that he was the owner and holder, *held*, that the complaint was sufficient, and that the action would lie against the company. (*Hubbard* agt. *New York and Harlem R. R. Co.*, 36 *Barb.*, 286.)

2. An indemnifying bond given by the defendants to the plaintiffs, with a condition that if the plaintiffs should pay a specific sum of money as therein designated, the defendants would "indemnify and save harmless the plaintiffs from all actions and suits, both in law and in equity, and from all loss, cost and damage, by reason of the payment of said sum of money as aforesaid," *held*, to be an indemnity against actual damage only. (*Bridgeport Fire and Marine Insurance Co.* agt. *Wilson*, 7 *Bosw.*, 427.)

BREACH OF CONTRACT.

See CONTRACT.

See SPECIFIC PERFORMANCE, 1. 2. 3.

BREACH OF PROMISE.

1. In an action for breach of promise, evidence, drawn out by the plaintiff, of declarations by the defendant, tending to prove that his failure to marry the plaintiff proceeded from no want of respect or attachment to her, is for the consideration of the ju mitigation of damages. (*Johns* *Jenkins*, 24 *N. Y. R.*, 252.)

2. The defendant in such an ac entitled to prove the truth of declarations, and to show th mother, a woman in infirm healt strenuously opposed to the r (*Id.*)

CANAL BOARD.

1. The canal board, upon revers modifying an award of the can praisers, must state the grou reversal or modification in their r tion. The statute (*ch.* 752 *of* § 4) is imperative, not merely tory. (*People*, ex rel. *Barne* *Gardner*, 24 *N. Y. R.*, 583.)

2. The offering by one of the cana missioners, at a meeting of the board of a resolution, in writin an appeal be reheard, is an appli in writing for such rehearing. (

CAUSE OF ACTION.

1. Where the plaintiff, being in th *session of negotiable paper* *apparent title*, and no contra evidence to overthrow it, he sh legal right as owner to recover. (agt. *Penfield*, *ante*, 64.)

2. The *right of action* to claims fo *dends* improperly declared by an vent banking corporation is *creditors* and not in the re (*Butterworth* agt. *O'Brien*, 438.)

3. That a complaint, under the states fraudulent representati the defendant, by which the pl was induced to pay him money, he seeks to recover back, do necessarily stamp the action as tort, or show that the cause of is not assignable. (*Byxbie* agt. 24 *N. Y. R.*, 607.)

4. It is no objection to a recovery i a case that fraud is not proved, i cient facts appear to warrant a re as for money had and received.

5. Nor is it an objection to the ability of the cause of action th party paid the money under a agreement, and signed admissio the several accounts upon wh made payments were correct. (

6. A cause of action for the conversion by the defendant of funds intrusted to him as an agent, for which he has not accounted to his principal, is assignable. Such a cause of action would survive to the personal representatives. (*Gould* agt. *Gould*, 36 *Barb.*, 270.)

7. Under § 167 of the Code, a plaintiff may unite a claim to recover the possession of land with a claim for damages for withholding the same, and for the rents and profits; but this provision gives no new rights of action; and the plaintiff is not bound to elect, as between those causes of action, which he will adopt. (*Hotchkiss* agt. *Auburn & Rochester R. R. Co.*, 36 *Barb.*, 600.)

8. The payment by the plaintiffs of a specified sum of money, not made voluntarily merely, and if not to be deemed as made at the defendant's request, but made for his benefit and in discharge of a liability on his part, it is a sufficient consideration for the defendant's subsequent promise to repay the amount so paid. (*St. Nicholas Ins. Co.* agt. *Howe*, 7 *Bosw.*, 450.)

See Complaint, 2. 3.

See Executors and Administrators, 5. 6.

See Demurrer, 2.

See Fraudulent Representations, 5.

See Slander, 1. 2.

See Bills of Exchange and Promissory Notes, 9.

See Will, 26.

See Public Office, 2.

See Account, 1.

CERTIORARI.

1. When the *jurisdiction of an inferior tribunal* depends upon *evidence* to be taken before it, this court, upon *certiorari*, will examine such evidence in order to determine the question of *jurisdiction, but for no other purpose*. (*People ex rel. Dillon* agt. *Metropolitan Police*, *ante*, 481.)

2. A common-law *certiorari* to review a summary conviction under a penal statute brings up, not only questions affecting the jurisdiction of the magistrate and the regularity of the proceedings, but the question whether there was any evidence to warrant the conviction. (*Mullins* agt. *People*, 24 *N. Y. R.*, 399.)

3. In such cases the evidence must appear on the face of the record, or the conviction will be quashed. (*Id.*)

4. The act in relation to the sale of bottles, &c. (*ch.* 117 *of* 1860), imposes no penalty for the secreting of a bottle, though subjecting a dealer in bottles to a search-warrant. (*Id.*)

5. The return of a justice of the peace to a certiorari, under the Code, must contain all the testimony received by him. (*Orcutt* agt. *Cahill*, 24 *N. Y. R.*, 578.)

6. Where a justice's return sets forth evidence in detail, it is to be considered as stating the whole testimony, unless the contrary distinctly appears. (*Id.*)

CHARITABLE AND BENEVOLENT SOCIETIES.

1. Where a member of a *charitable and benevolent society*, organized under the statute of 1848, entitled "An act for the incorporation of benevolent, charitable, scientific and missionary societies," is *expelled* from such society for the non-observance of a by-law which is not authorised by the statute nor the constitution of the state, he will be restored to membership by mandamus. (*People ex rel. Schmitt* agt. *Saint Franciscus Benevolent Society*, *ante*, 216.)

2. Members of such society cannot be expelled therefrom upon charges made against them *without notice*, and an opportunity to be heard in their defence. (*Id.*)

CHATTEL MORTGAGE.

See Mortgage of Personal Property.

CITY COURT, BROOKLYN.

See Jurisdiction, 2.

See Appeal, 25.

COMMISSIONERS OF EXCISE.

1. The *commissioners of excise* of a county are not, under the statute, limited in their services to *ten days* (at $3 per day.) This limitation is expressly confined to the time they shall

spend in their meetings for the purpose of granting licenses. (*People ex rel. Plumb* agt. *Supervisors of Cortland*, *ante*, 119.)

2. It is their duty to *prosecute for penalties incurred*, and the members of the board have the right to charge for the time spent in the performance of that duty; and where they present their accounts to the board of supervisors, properly made out and verified, it is the duty of such board to receive and act upon them. If they refuse to do this, the authority of this court may be invoked to compel them. (*Id.*)

COMMISSIONS.

1. The law as to *commissions* for the examination of witnesses is not altered by the Code. It is not applicable to witnesses in *supplementary proceedings*. (*Morrell* agt. *Hoey*, *ante*, 48.)

2. A non-resident *party* may be examined *on commission* as a witness in his own behalf. (*McCarty* agt. *Edwards*, *ante*, 236.)

3. It is not a valid objection that *cross-interrogatories* in a *commission* offered in evidence are not all answered, where it appears that some of them in whole or in part are answered by *reference to previous answers*, the latter being full and explicit. (*Id.*)

4. Several objections were taken by the plaintiff in this case, to the *commissions* introduced by the defendant in evidence, which are specifically examined and passed upon by the court in their opinion; but with the remark, however, that they had seldom seen any objections to testimony *less specific or less significant* than these appeared to be, as presented on the bill of exceptions; and were inclined to think that all of them might with great propriety have been *summarily condemned for that reason*. (*Id.*)

5. A paper issued by a court of record in the form of a commission to take testimony, but without a seal, is a nullity, and depositions taken under it are not admissible as evidence. (*Ford* agt. *Williams*, 24 *N. Y. R.*, 359.)

COMMON CARRIERS.

1. The right of a *common carrier to limit his liability* is well settled in the affirmative. (*Meyer* agt. *Harnden's Express Co.*, *ante*, 290.)

2. And when a special contract is made, the relations of the parties are changed, and the carrier becomes as to that transaction an ordinary *bailee and private carrier for hire*. (*Id.*)

3. Where the plaintiffs *directed E. & Co.* to ship goods by Harnden's express, it authorized E. & Co., at least so far as the defendants were concerned, to make any *contract* which the defendants insisted on. (*Id.*)

4. Consequently, where E. & Co., on the delivery of the goods, presented a printed *receipt* in a receipt book of the defendants in their possession, which the driver of the express company signed, *held*, that E. & Co. had *authority*, as the agents of the plaintiffs, to make the contract contained in the receipt. (*Id.*)

5. To hold that when goods are delivered, the carrier, who chooses to limit his responsibility, should be compelled to stop and examine the authority of the person presenting the goods to make the contract, would virtually destroy the utility of the express business. (*Id.*)

6. The carrier of a boat-load of wheat lost or converted a portion of it, and discharged the residue into a barge provided by an intermediate consignee for transporting it to its ultimate destination. The intermediate consignee refused to pay freight for the quantity delivered, unless the carrier would allow and deduct the value of the wheat lost. *Held*, that no contract to pay the freight was to be implied under these circumstances, and that an action therefor would not lie against the intermediate consignee. (*Davis* agt. *Pattison*, 24 *N. Y. R.*, 317.)

7. An intermediate consignee is, in virtue of that character, authorized to adjust and receive damages from a loss of part of the property. (*Id.*)

8. The rights and duties of intermediate consignees discussed, *per* ALLEN, J. (*Id.*)

9. If a passenger in a vehicle upon a city street voluntarily assumes a position which is not intended and ordinarily used for the conveyance of passengers and which is exposed to danger, he contributes to an injury which he sustains by a collision produced by the

willful or negligent acts of a third party, without any fault in the management of the vehicle which carries him, and he cannot recover against the carrier for injuries received. (*Spooner* agt. *Brooklyn City R. R. Co.*, 36 *Barb.*, 217.)

See RAILROAD COMPANIES.

See EXPRESS COMPANIES.

See NEGLIGENCE, 4.

COMPLAINT.

1. Where the *complaint* was drawn strictly under § 162 of the Code, which alleged an amount due to the plaintiffs from the defendants on a written instrument; then followed a copy of a promissory note, signed by the defendants, for $3,000, dated March 9, 1860, payable six months after date to the order of the makers, and by them indorsed in blank; a demand for judgment for the amount against the defendants, *held, sufficient*, under the decision of *Prindle* agt. *Caruthers*, (15 *N. Y. R.*, 425.) (*Butchers' & Drovers' Bank* agt. *Jacobson, ante*, 204.)

2. On *demurrer*, where facts are stated in a complaint showing that the plaintiff has *two contracts* which are broken, so that an action might be maintained on either, but are not stated separately, as several causes of action, the action must be considered founded on that contract upon which it can be sustained as to some or all of the defendants, and not upon the contract where the action must fail unless *new parties* are brought in. (*Lord* agt. *Vreeland, ante*, 316.)

3. The allegations of the complaint showing a cause of action in such case, which cannot be sustained for the want of proper parties defendant, must be treated as *irrelevant* or *immaterial*, and upon motion should be *stricken out*. (*Id.*)

4. Where the action was upon *promissory notes* assigned to the plaintiff, and for *goods sold, held*, that the plaintiff might properly allege in his complaint that, on his "information and belief," the notes were executed by the defendant, and on his "information and belief," the goods were sold to the defendant. (*St. John* agt. *Beers, ante*, 377.)

5. The allowance or refusal of *costs* in actions for the *strict foreclosure of mortgages*, is in the *discretion of the court*. Where the *notice* prescribed by § 131 of the Code has not been served, it does not deprive the court of the power in equity cases to *award costs* for unreasonably defending, against defendants upon whom a copy of the *complaint* has been served. It is not necessary to the *commencement* of any action that a copy of the *complaint* be served upon the defendant; he is brought into court by the *summons alone*. (*O'Hara* agt. *Brophy, ante*, 379.)

6. Where the complaint by the receiver averred that the defendant (former president of the bank) used *fictitious notes* in lieu of money of the bank, which he fraudulently used, and disposed of, and that such notes were among the assets of the bank, *held*, that these facts, if proven, would be sufficient to put the defendant on his defence, and showed a cause of action in favor of the receiver. (*Butterworth* agt. *O'Brien, ante*, 438.)

7. Under the late decisions in the court of appeals, courts of original jurisdiction are not to *pay any attention to forms*, if they can find in the complaint any allegations which, under any view of them, may give the plaintiff a right to recover. (*Ergo, books of forms must be considered as calculated to mislead and confuse.*) (*Id.*)

8. The ownership of a promissory note by the plaintiff is sufficiently shown by the averment of its making, indorsement and delivery to him before maturity, for a valuable consideration, though coupled with the statement that it was, "by the Bank of Commerce, in the city of New York, which then held the same," presented for payment at another bank in that city, where it was payable. (*Farmers' & Mechanics' Bank of Genesee* agt. *Wadsworth*, 24 *N. Y. R.*, 547.)

9. The statement in respect to the Bank of Commerce imports only a holding as the plaintiff's agent for collection, and not ownership. (*Id.*)

10. When it appears that the defendant was not, and could not have been misled by a variance between the complaint and the proof, the variance may be disregarded without amendment. (*Craig* agt. *Ward*, 36 *Barb.*, 377.)

11. Where in an instrument for the payment of money, the name of the payee is left blank with the intention that such instrument may be transferred by delivery, the holder may plead it in an action thereon as having been delivered to some persons unknown for a valuable consideration received from them, and as having therefore come lawfully into plaintiff's possession, and that he is owner thereof. (*Hubbard* agt. *New York & Harlem R. R. Co.*, 14 *Abb.*, 275.)

12. In an action upon a policy of insurance for the amount of the loss, the complaint must allege that the plaintiff had an interest in the thing insured at the time of the loss; unless the claim was assigned to him afterwards, or unless he sues as trustee of an express trust. If the plaintiff sues as trustee or agent, he must allege in his complaint the existence of such trust, and show his authority to collect the amount of the insurance. (*Freeman* agt. *Fulton Fire Insurance Co.*, 14 *Abb.*, 398.)

See Verification, 2.
See Arrest, 1. 2. 3. 4.
See Answer, 7. 8.
See Public Office, 1. 2.
See Trial, 1. 2. 3.
See Parties, 2. 3.
See Will, 6. 7. 8. 9.
See Irrelevant and Redundant Matter, 1. 2. 3.
See Cause of Action, 3. 4. 5. 7.
See Slander, 3. 4.
See Bonds, 1.
See Bills of Exchange and Promissory Notes, 11.

CONSIDERATION.

See Mortgage of Personal Property, 1. 2. 3.
See Bills of Exchange and Promissory Notes, 9.
See Usury.
See Married Women, 12.
See Complaint, 11.

CONSIGNEE.

1. The carrier of a boat-load of wheat lost or converted a portion of it, and discharged the residue into a barge provided by an intermediate co[nsignee] for transporting it to its ultim[ate des]tination. The intermediate co[nsignee] refused to pay freight for the q[uantity] delivered, unless the carrie[r would] allow and deduct the value [of the] wheat lost. *Held*, that no [obligation] to pay the freight was to be [implied] under these circumstances, a[nd that] an action therefor would not lie [against] the intermediate consignee. [...] agt. *Pattison*, 24 *N. Y. R.*, 3[...]

2. An intermediate consignee is, i[n a case] of that character, authorized t[o sue for] and receive damages from a los[s or conversion] of the property. (*Id.*)

3. The rights and duties of inter[mediate] consignees discussed, *per* Al[...] (*Id.*)

See Bill of Lading, 1. 2. [...]

CONSTABLE'S BOND.

1. In an action on a *constable's* [bond in] the city of New York, the pla[intiff is] *irregular* to enter up a *genera[l judg]ment* for the sum mentioned [in the] complaint, where the def[endant's] answer has been adjudged fr[ivolous.] (*Mayor, &c., of New York* agt. [...] *ante*, 280.)

2. He should enter up judgment [for the] *penalty of the bond*, and the[n apply to] this court, under the act of 1[...] an order directing so much m[oney to] be levied upon the judgment [as shall] be sufficient to pay the plai[ntiff the] debt or damages recovered, wit[h costs.] (*Id.*)

3. If the defendants *appeal* to the [general] term, from such an irregular jud[gment,] they *waive the irregularity*; [and if] judgment is given against them [on the] appeal, they cannot afterward[s move] to have the judgment set aside [for the] irregularity. (*Id.*)

4. An error in the mode of enteri[ng up] judgment cannot be reviewed on [appeal.] (*Id.*)

5. But the defendants, having l[ost the] right to move, upon the gro[und of] irregularity, to set aside the jud[gment,] cannot complain of an order [of the] court directing that the judg[ment be] entered up properly; that oth[er credit]ors, if any there should be, [may be] enabled to have the amounts re[covered] by them levied under this judg[ment, in] the way in which the statute pr[ovides.] (*Id.*)

CONSTITUTIONAL LAW.

1. The *fourth section* of the act passed in April, 1860, (*Sess. Laws*, 1860, *p.* 772,) to facilitate the taking of lands and building gate-houses, &c. in the city of New York, and which provides for an *arbitration*, and directs that it shall be held for the purpose of adjusting and determining the damages which the contractors, to whom the gate-houses were awarded, might be equitably entitled to recover of the city of New York, and if an award is made in their favor, directs the comptroller to pay the same, is *unconstitutional*. (*People ex rel. Baldwin* agt. *Haws, ante*, 148.)

2. When the law *compels* a party to *arbitrate* upon a claim, which properly should be the subject of an action, without his assent, such law deprives him of the right which is secured by the constitution, of a trial according to the course of the common law. (*Id.*)

3. If this section was not unconstitutional, the provision, that if such report (of arbitrators) should be in favor of the party claiming such damages, such party should recover the same, &c., would give a remedy by *action on the award*, which would preclude a remedy by *mandamus*. (*Id.*)

4. The provision of the United States Internal Revenue Act, of July 1, 1862, requiring a *stamp* upon every *summons* or *original proceedings*, issued by state courts, is *illegal and unconstitutional*. (*Walton* agt. *Bryenth, ante*, 357.)

5. The first article, § 6 of the Constitution, which says, "no person shall be compelled, in any criminal case, to be a witness against himself," does not protect a witness, in a criminal prosecution against another, from being compelled to give testimony which disgraces him or tends to convict of a crime, if he has been protected by statute against the use of his testimony on a trial against himself. (*People ex rel. Hackley* agt. *Kelly, ante*, 369, *and* 24 *N. Y. R.*, 74.)

6. The "act to facilitate the closing up of insolvent and dissolved mutual insurance companies," passed April 21, 1862, is *not unconstitutional*, as impairing the *right of trial by jury*. A *compulsory reference*, therefore, may be ordered in these cases. (*Sands* agt. *Tillinghast & Griffiths, ante*, 435.)

7. The tolls imposed, at the time of the adoption of the constitution of 1846, on freight carried on railroads, were not, within the meaning of that instrument, part of the revenues of the state canals, though payable to the commissioners of the canal fund. (*People* agt. *N. Y. Central R. R. Co.*, 24 *N. Y. R.*, 485.)

8. The act (*ch.* 497 *of* 1851), repealing the laws imposing such tolls is, therefore, consistent with article 7 of the constitution, which irrevocably pledges the revenues of the canals to the payment of certain debts, and to their completion; and the act is valid. (*Id.*)

9. The acts of April 19, 1859, and March 3, 1860, authorizing an assessment by the city of Brooklyn for the purpose of compensating the Long Island Railroad compay for the relinquishment of its rights to use steam power within said city, &c., are not in conflict with the 16th section of the 3d article of the constitution; nor are they in conflict with the constitution, on the ground that they authorize the taking of private property for a purpose not sanctioned by the constitution. (*People ex rel. Crowell* agt. *Lawrence*, 36 *Barb.*, 177.)

10. The act of April 13, 1861, amending the Revised Statutes in regard to judgments in actions of ejectment does not act retrospectively, so as to apply to judgments rendered prior to its passage. Retrospective laws, which do not impair the obligation of contracts, or affect vested rights, or partake of the character of *ex post facto* laws, are not prohibited by the constitution. (*Bay* agt. *Gage*, 36 *Barb.*, 447.)

See Criminal Law, 10. 11. 12. 13. 14.

See Agreement, 6.

CONTEMPT.

1. Where a copy of a decree or judgment, for the payment of money, is served on the defendant without any *demand* for payment being made, he cannot be convicted as of a *contempt* in not paying over the money; there must be a *demand* and *refusal* to authorize proceedings for a contempt. (*Gray* agt. *Cook, ante*, 432.)

2. The refusal of a witness to answer a proper question before a grand jury is punishable as a contempt under the statute (2 *R. S.*, *p.* 534, § 1, *p.* 735,

Digest.

§ 14), as committed in a proceeding upon an indictment. (*People ex rel. Hackley* agt. *Kelly*, 24 *N. Y. R.*, 74.)

3. When the refusal was reported by the grand jury to the court in the presence of the witness, who did not deny but justified the same, and reiterated the refusal, the contempt is one "in the immediate view and presence of the court," and no affidavit or further evidence is requisite to a commitment. (*Id.*)

4. The appellate court, before which the propriety of a commitment for contempt is brought by *certiorari*, or even collaterally on *habeas corpus* is bound to discharge the prisoner where the act charged as criminal is necessarily innocent or justifiable, or where it is the mere assertion of a constitutional right. (*Id.*)

5. The adjudication of the court in which the alleged contempt occurred, while conclusive that the party committed the act whereof he was convicted, and of its character when that might, according to the circumstances, be meritorious or criminal, cannot establish as a contempt that which the law entitled the party to do. (*Id.*)

6. To punish for contempt where interrogatories have been administered to the party accused, the moving party may read affidavits to contradict his answers. In order to bring a party into contempt for disobedience of an order of the court which has been entered with the clerk, delivery of a copy of the order, showing him at the same time a copy certified by the clerk, is a sufficient service. (*Smith* agt. *Smith*, 14 *Abb.*, 130.)

7. To bring an action against a receiver, without leave of the court which appointed him, is a contempt; and the proceedings in such an action will be stayed. (*Taylor* agt. *Baldwin*, 14 *Abb.*, 166.)

8. On an order to show cause why a party should not be punished for contempt, a conviction may be had and punishment imposed upon the party, without issuing an attachment or filing interrogatories against him. (*Id.*)

See Witnesses, 2. 3. 4. 5. 6.

See Judgment, 2. 3.

CONTRACT.

1. To sustain an action for damages for breach of a contract to sell land, it must appear that the parties' min[ds] met in the proposed sale. (*Britt[on]* agt. *Phillips*, *ante*, 111.)

2. Where the proposed vendor submitt[ed] a proposition to sell the land in contr[o]versy, such proposition being in t[he] form of a letter addressed from a ban[k]ing house in Wall street, to the pr[o]posed purchaser, containing at the bo[t]tom, "the above proposition is ma[de] for two days; after that subject [to] negotiation," it must appear on t[he] part of the proposed vendee who brin[gs] his action to recover damages for brea[ch] of such alleged contract, that he accep[t]ed said proposition in writing, with[in] the time specified, and brought to t[he] knowledge of the proposed vendor suc[h] acceptance. (*Id.*)

3. A mere deposit in the U. S. post-offi[ce] (postage not pre-paid) of a letter ac[]cepting such proposition, addressed [to] the proposed vendor, is insufficien[t]. (*Id.*)

4. It is not due diligence to excuse suc[h] deposit in the post-office, to prove th[at] the proposed vendee was unable to fi[nd] the proposed vendor within the tim[e] where it also appears that the latt[er] made no inquiries for the former at t[he] banking house from which the propo[]sition in form was addressed. (*Id.*)

5. A *referee's* finding on questions [of] *fact* is conclusive; the court will n[ot] disturb it on appeal; such facts, as th[e] performance of a contract; the waiv[er] of that performance; extension of tim[e] for its performance; and the value an[d] amount of defendant's set-off. (*Col[d]well* agt. *Lawrence*, *ante*, 324.)

6. The claim for a *stipulated sum* [as] *liquidated damages*, for the non-per[]formance of a *contract*, cannot be en[]forced under the law, as it must b[e] construed at the present time, wher[e] the contract is for doing a piece [of] work, the defect in the completion o[f] which might be a very trifling matte[r] which a very little expense woul[d] remedy, and consequently a very sma[ll] amount of damage (compared with th[e] stipulated sum) would be the result[.] (*Id.*)

7. The court of last resort will probabl[y] have to, sooner or later, settle definitel[y] the precise question whether, whe[n] parties have agreed, *in any case, on* [a] *sum which they say shall be liqui[]dated damages, they should or n[ot] be held to their contract as they mak[e] it.* (*Id.*)

Digest.

8. To avoid a contract as against the stock-jobbing act, (1 *R. S.*, *p.* 710, § 6,) the burden of proof is upon the party alleging a violation. *Stebbins* agt. *Leowolf*, (3 *Cush.*, 143,) overruled on this point. (*Dykers* agt. *Townsend*, 24 *N. Y. R.*, 57.)

9. In an action by the vendor of stocks against a vendee refusing to perform his contract to purchase, it was a defence that the vendor did not own, nor was authorised to sell, sufficient stock to fulfill the contract in suit and his previous outstanding contracts. But evidence falling short of this, as merely showing contracts sufficient to absorb all the stock which the plaintiff had *proved* himself to own, is inadmissible. (*Id.*)

10. A contract between a railroad corporation and a gratuitous passenger by which the former is exempted from liability under any circumstances of the negligence of its agents for any injury to the passenger, is not against law or public policy and is valid. (*Wells* agt. *N. Y. Central R. R. Co.*, 24 *N. Y R.*, 181.)

11. It is immaterial whether the negligence of the agents be slight or gross. The supposed distinction between different degrees of negligence, in respect to the liability of common carriers, discarded as illusory and impracticable. (*Id.*)

12. A railroad corporation cannot, by contract, exempt itself from liability to a passenger for damage resulting from its own willful misconduct or recklessness which is equivalent thereto. (*Perkins* agt. *N. Y. Central R. R. Co.*, 24 *N. Y. R.*, 196.)

13. But in respect to a gratuitous passenger it may contract for exemption from liability for any degree of negligence in its servants, other than the board of directors or managers who represent the corporation itself, for all general purposes. (*Id.*)

14. Whether the corporation is liable to a free passenger, so contracting, for negligence in the construction of the road, as upon an implied guaranty of its security, when the misconduct from which the injury resulted was that of a trackmaster, who knowingly used rotten material in building a bridge, there being no evidence that it was known to the superior managing officers. *Quere.* (*Id.*)

15. *It seems* that the owner of cattle, transported for hire on a railroad, and who goes along in charge of them, under a contract that "the persons riding free to take charge of the stock do so at their own risk of personal injury from whatever cause," is not to be regarded as a gratuitous passenger. Per Wright, Denio, and Davies, JJ. (*Smith* agt. *N. Y. Central R. R. Co.*, 24 *N. Y. R.*, 222.)

16. Whether, as to one who, in the manner stated, gives some consideration for being carried, a contract is valid which aims to exempt the carrier from liability for damages resulting from the negligence of his servants. *Quere.* (*Id.*)

17. The owner of cattle traveling in charge of them, under such a contract, and paying no independent consideration for the conveyance of himself, was injured by the gross negligence of an agent of the carrier in using an unfit and dangerous car. The carrier was held liable by a divided court, four of the judges going on the ground that the contract for exemption from liability was void, as against public policy; and the fifth, that the negligence, as it respected the machinery of transportation, is imputable to the carrier himself. (*Id.*)

18. A writing in this form, "F. bought of W. one horse, $150. Received payment. W.," given upon the purchase of and payment for the horse, is a mere receipt, and not a contract or bill of sale, so as to exclude parol evidence of a warranty of soundness of the horse by the vendor. (*Filkins* agt. *Whyland*, 24 *N. Y. R.*, 338.)

19. A contract for the publication of an advertisement in a newspaper to be issued and sold on Sunday, is void. (*Smith* agt. *Wilcox*, 24 *N. Y. R.*, 353.)

20. The rule as to contracts is that the *lex loci contractus* governs, as to the nature, validity, construction and effect of the contract, and the *lex fori* as to the remedy. (*Gans* agt. *Frank*, 36 *Barb.*, 320.)

21. Where a sealed contract has been entered into between an employer and a laborer, by which the latter is to serve the former in a specified business for a term of years, at a fixed sum yearly, and the laborer gives a bond with sureties for the faithful performance of the contract, and the employer subsequently forms a partnership with

third persons, and the laborer, by a verbal agreement between him and the firm, for a different compensation, agrees to serve the firm, and in pursuance thereof does serve the firm for nearly two years, the sealed contract and bond are thereby abandoned, and no action will lie thereon for an alleged breach, after the service under the verbal agreement. (*Bagley* agt. *Clark*, 7 *Bosw.*, 94.)

22. Where a defendant contracts to make and deliver from time to time, as required, six engines, and he delivers only two, and on request to deliver another refuses, without cause, the contract may be treated as rescinded, and any moneys advanced to him, over and above the worth or contract price of the two delivered, may be recovered back. (*Frost* agt. *Smith*, 7 *Bosw.*, 108.)

23. In an action brought against M. & R. to recover of them, as joint contractors with the plaintiff, the value of materials furnished and work done by him in erecting a building, where it appears that the work was done and materials furnished under a written contract to which the plaintiff and M. were alone parties, R. cannot be held liable, even if the building was erected on his land; and he performed acts of supervision and indorsed M.'s notes for the purpose of making payments on account. (*Alger* agt. *Raymond*, 7 *Bosw.*, 418.)

See SPECIFIC PERFORMANCE, 1. 2. 3.
See ARREST, 5. 6.
See USURY, 4. 6.
See COMMON CARRIERS, 1. 2. 3. 4. 5.
See STATUTE OF FRAUDS, 1. 2. 3.
See ATTORNEY, 1. 2. 3. 4. 5.
See PARTNERS AND PARTNERSHIPS, 6. 7. 8.
See GUARANTY, 1.
See STATUTES, 1.
See VENDOR AND VENDEE.
See RAILROAD COMPANIES, 26. 27. 28. 29.
See WILL, 35.
See MORTGAGE FORECLOSURE, 9.
See INSURANCE COMPANIES, 6. 7.

CONVERSION.

1. In an action, under the Code, for damages for the conversion of a billiard table, the plaintiff is entitled to recover upon proof of the detention of tables, assumed to be of equal v to *some* one of which the plainti title, though the particular one h no manner been designated, e upon the notion that the defe must have taken some three of before removing the fourth, and selected those three as his own. (C agt. *Griffith*, 24 *N. Y. R.*, 595.)

See ATTACHMENT, 3.

COPY-RIGHT.

1. Where an action for the infringe of a *copy-right* of a publication brought by the *assignees* thereof, an issue of ownership was raise the trial, upon which the author assignor as a witness testified th the agreement produced, "the in tion was to convey deponent's v interest in the copy-right of the w I supposed the book to belong to assignees, as soon as made, inclu all that was in it." *Held*, that testimony *estopped* the legal repre tatives of the author from subsequ claiming that the agreement wa tended to be confined to the *first f teen years' limitation of the c right*, under which it was made, e cially as the testimony was given the expiration of such limitation portion of the work. (*Cowen Banks*, *ante*, 72.)

CORPORATIONS.

1. In an action by a plaintiff, with w the defendant has contracted as b a corporate body, the plaintiff ca be required to prove the fact of incorporation, merely because the fendant states in his answer that ' is informed and believes" the plai is not a corporation. (*East R Bank* agt. *Rogers*, 7 *Bosw.*, 493.

2. In an action by a creditor of a co ration to recover the amount of debt from a stockholder under a sta provision making stockholders joi and severally liable in case of a ficiency in the cash capital, it is a defence to the action that such cred himself, at the time of acquiring demand against the corporation, w stockholder therein. (*Wait* agt. *F gusen*, 14 *Abb.*, 379.)

See MANUFACTURING CORPO TIONS.

See AGREEMENT, 7.
See MUNICIPAL CORPORATIONS.
See RELIGIOUS CORPORATIONS.
See INSURANCE COMPANIES.
See BANKING CORPORATIONS.
See FOREIGN CORPORATIONS.

COSTS.

1. Where, in an action for the recovery of money, the plaintiff enters judgment against the defendant for the amount (over $50) which the defendant offered that plaintiff might take judgment, and the parties go to trial for the balance of the plaintiff's claim, and the verdict of the jury is for the plaintiff, but for a sum less than $50, the plaintiff is nevertheless entitled to *costs*. (*Hoe* agt. *Sanborn, ante*, 26.)

2. Because, the *judgment roll*, (and there should be but one,) if properly made up, containing the whole history of the case, including the verdict of the jury, shows that the plaintiff recovered over $50, and an amount *greater* than the sum mentioned in the offer of judgment served by the defendant. (*Id.*)

3. No *term fees* ($10) can be allowed in a cause in the court of appeals, *before the return is filed*. (*Reformed Protestant Dutch Church* agt. *Brown, ante*, 89.)

4. Where the verdict of a jury is set aside and a new trial granted *on payment of the costs of the former trial*, the item of ten dollars, for proceedings *subsequent to notice and before trial*, is allowable under the order. (*Keil* agt. *Rice, ante*, 228.)

5. The supreme court has no power, either at special term or on appeal at general term, to *allow extra costs* (*Code*, § 309,) on the trial of a *feigned issue*, made up to try the questions of the *validity or execution of will*, under the provisions of the Revised Statutes. (*Burritt* agt. *Silliman, ante*, 337.)

6. A *new trial* of such issue might be granted by the supreme court; but no discretionary power exists in the court to award extra costs, or in fact *any costs at all* for making up such issue and its trial. Cases of this kind are not affected by the Code, they are governed by a special statutory provision. (*Id.*)

7. Where the *jury*, on conflicting evidence in a justice's court, found that the defendant (an attorney at law,) put in an answer for the plaintiff in an action for strict foreclosure, *without authority* from the plaintiff. (*O'Hara* agt. *Brophy, ante*, 379.)

8. *Held*, that there being evidence to sustain the finding of the jury, and the evidence against it not so preponderant as to create the conviction that it must have proceeded from passion, prejudice, corruption or palpable mistake, the verdict must be sustained. (*Id.*)

9. Where an application for an *extra allowance* of costs under § 309 of the Code, has been made after trial, and *denied*, on the ground that it was not a difficult and extraordinary case; and after a *second trial* a like application is made, the first order denying the application is no *bar* to the second application, where the facts and circumstances on the second trial are *materially different* from those on the first trial. (*Fox* agt. *Fox, ante*, 385.)

10. Where a case has been litigated on the trial on both sides, with unusual pertinacity, by distinguished counsel, and occupying an unusually long period, without appearing to have been unnecessarily protracted—the examination of a large number of witnesses, and difficult questions of law and evidence raised and discussed, and the recovery of a large amount *in favor of the defendant*, it comes within the plain meaning and intent of § 309 of the Code, in being both *difficult and extraordinary*, and an extra allowance will be granted. (*Id.*)

11. Where a claim against *executors or administrators is referred* under the Revised Statutes, and the report of the referees is adverse to the plaintiff, and in favor of the defendants, (executors or administrators,) they are entitled to *costs* against the plaintiff, *as in an action under the Code*. (*Radley* agt. *Fisher, ante*, 404.)

12. The amount of such costs are those given by the Code in an *action* between party and party, prosecuted and defended in accordance with the provisions of the Code. The provision of the Revised Statutes, authorizing the court to adjudge costs as in actions against executors, is in *full force*. (*Id.*)

13. Upon an application for judgment on account of the frivolousness of the

pleading under § 247 of the Code, the weight of authority is against allowing a *trial fee* of $15. Costs of a motion, $10, only can be allowed. (*Bell* agt. *Noah*, *ante*, 478.)

14. By the "act to facilitate the closing up of insolvent and dissolved mutual insurance companies," passed April 21, 1862, it was intended to limit the *costs, besides disbursements, to twenty dollars*, in all cases where actions had been commenced, and *had not proceeded to judgment*, whether they should be referred under the fifth section to a referee, or the issues joined should be tried by the court or a jury. (*Bangs* agt. *Barto*, *ante*, 487.)

15. Reasonable counsel fees incurred in the defence of a suit to restrain the payment of an award, are recoverable upon a bond conditioned for the payment of all costs and damages arising from the obligor's obtaining an injunction or from his contesting the payment. (*Corcoran* agt. *Judson*, 24 *N. Y. R.*, 106.)

16. Where a verdict is set aside as concontrary to evidence, and the charge of the court, the costs of the former trial will be ordered to be costs in the cause and to abide the event. (*Robbins* agt. *Hudson River R. R. Co.*, 7 *Bosw.*, 1.)

17. In a suit against several defendants, where they in good faith and for a sufficient cause appear and defend by different attorneys, and succeed in the action, each attorney is entitled to a full bill of costs. (*Bridgeport Fire and Marine Insurance Company* agt. *Wilson*, 7 *Bosw.*, 699.)

18. The cases in which allowances are provided for in section 308 of the Code are excluded from the operation of section 309 of the Code. (*Hotaling* agt. *Marsh*, 14 *Abb.*, 161.)

19. The power of the court to grant counsel fees out of a common fund belonging to the parties to the action, as a part of the relief which should be given on the final disposition of an equity cause, is not affected by the Code. (*Id.*)

20. The fees of a stenographer, whose services are directed by the court under section 256 of the Code, cannot be taxed as costs in the cause. (*Gilman* agt. *Oliver*, 14 *Abb.*, 174.)

21. In an action to obtain the delivery of personal property where the plaintiff has a verdict for the retu portion of the property, asse $200 in value, and the defend a verdict for the residue, each entitled to costs against the (*Porter* agt. *Wittel*, 14 *Abb.*,

22. Several defendants not uni interest and making separate d by separate answers, who obtai ment in their favor, it is in the tion of the court to restrict the ants to one bill of costs, or to a certain of the defendants costs ing to the circumstances of th (*Harper* agt. *Chamberlain*, 14 408.)

See Attorney, 1. 2. 3. 4. 5.
See New Trial, 9. 11. 12.
See Municipal Corporatio
See Amendment, 1.

COUNTER-CLAIM.

1. The indebtedness of the plain an action against the defendant guaranty for the debt of anoth the defendant's principal, in equal to or greater than the sum ed, cannot be set-off or availed counter-claim by such guaranto principal not alleged to be inso (*East River Bank* agt. *Rog Bosw.*, 493.)

2. Where facts constituting a de not a cause of action, are averred answer as a set-off or counter- the answer cannot be demurred that cause. (*Wait* agt. *Fergus Abb.*, 379.)

See Answer, 2. 3. 4. 5. 6.
See Set-off, 1. 2.

COUNTERFEITING.

1. In order to make counterfeiti offence within the act of congress, *of* 1825, *ch.* 65, *sec.* 20,) it is n cessary for the prosecution to show the prisoner made the base in resemblance of the true coin. (*U States* agt. *Aylward*, *ante*, 142

2. The words "similitude" and semblance," as used in that st must be construed to mean, not a act copy, but such a one as migh ceive an ordinary observer. (*Id.*

3. If the spurious article had not semblance strong enough to de

persons exercising ordinary caution, then the passing was not a public crime. (*Id.*)

COUNTY COURT.

1. The jurisdiction given to the county courts for the custody of habitual drunkards (*Code*, § 30, *sub.* 8) is general, not limited to those having estates less than $250. (*Davis* agt. *Spencer*, 24 *N. Y. R.*, 386.)

2. The reference in subdivision eleven of the same section to the powers of the old courts of common pleas in this matter, does not limit the effect of subdivision eight, but was intended to continue in the county court cases then pending in the common pleas. (*Id.*)

See SUPPLEMENTARY PROCEEDINGS, 1. 2.

See JURISDICTION, 3.

COVENANTS.

1. The acceptance of a *renewal lease*, under an original lease of premises, satisfies only the *covenant to renew*; it does not satisfy any of the other covenants in the original lease. (*Lord* agt. *Vreeland*, *ante*, 316.)

2. Where an *executor* receives property in his own right as a gift, from the testator, it involves the same equitable liability to satisfy the damages arising from the breach of covenants in a lease given by the testator, as when held by the testator. (*Id.*)

See DEED, 9.

CREDITOR'S SUIT.

1. *Each member of a copartnership* has a right to dispose of his interest in the partnership property, in good faith, and for a valid consideration, unless some creditor has acquired a *lien* thereon. And the right of the creditor is subordinate to this power of the partner to dispose of the property *until it is subjected to the creditor's lien*. (*Field* agt. *Hunt*, *ante*, 468.)

2. Where one partner thus transfers his interest in the partnership assets to his copartner, the property so transferred cannot be reached by execution on a judgment recovered against the firm, where *the latter has not been personally served with process*. (*Id.*)

3. The remedy at law has not been exhausted as against the partner not served with process, and of course a *creditor's suit* against the defendants cannot be maintained. (*This affirms the decision S. C. at special term*, 22 *How.*, 329.) (*Id.*)

4. It is *held* in the first judicial district that it is not necessary to wait sixty days—the return day of an execution—before commencing equitable proceedings on a judgment at law, if the execution has actually been returned before the sixty days have expired. (*There are adverse decisions in other districts.*) (*Id.*)

5. A plaintiff cannot maintain an equitable action in his own name against any *debtor* of the defendants in an *attachment suit*, to collect and receive the debts, credits and effects of such defendants alleged to be in the possession of their debtor, without complying with the provisions of § 238 of the Code, which requires an undertaking, &c. to be given by the plaintiff to the sheriff, who has levied the attachment. (*Skinner* agt. *Stuart*, *ante*, 489.)

6. And where there is nothing stated in the complaint to show fraud or collusion, or combination obstructing the ordinary processes of the law, and that the lien of the attachment cannot be enforced without the intervention of the court, in the exercise of its equitable powers, such an action cannot be maintained by the plaintiff, even by the compliance with the provisions of § 238 of the Code. (*Id.*)

7. A creditor in good faith of a manufacturing corporation which was organized, and its business conducted, for the purpose of defrauding the creditors of its president, has no priority of claim to property in the possession of such corporation over a creditor of the president. (*Booth* agt. *Bunce*, 24 *N. Y. R.*, 592.)

8. The purchaser of goods of the corporation under execution against its president, for his private debt, gets a good title as against a subsequent execution against the corporation. (*Id.*)

9. An action by one judgment creditor against another, will not lie for the purpose of determining the question as to the priority of their respective liens upon the equitable property of the judgment debtor in the hands of a receiver. (*Myrick* agt. *Selden*, 36 *Barb.*, 15.)

10. The commencement of an equitable action by the service of a summons and injunction, creates a *lis pendens* and a lien in the nature of an attachment or a statute execution, upon the equitable property of the defendant. But the plaintiff is bound to prosecute his action diligently, if he would retain his lien; or it will cease like that of a dormant execution. A delay of eight years in the prosecution of such an action, after commencement will be deemed a waiver of his right of lien as against a subsequent creditor who has reached a fund of the judgment debtor sufficient to satisfy his claim. (*Id.*)

11. In a creditor's action against a judgment debtor and his debtor, to reach securities held by the latter, the plaintiff is in no better position than the judgment debtor's assignee. A judgment creditor cannot impeach a release by the debtor of a mere contingent obligation. (*McGay* agt. *Keilback*, 14 *Abb.*, 142.)

See Railroad Companies, 23. 24. 25.

See Assignment for the Benefit of Creditors, 12.

CRIMINAL LAW.

1. Where, on an indictment for *misdemeanor*, it appears that the offence consists of a *series of acts*, and a part of the series is a complete misdemeanor, there can be no *merger in a felony*, and the conviction for a misdemeanor will be sustained, although the evidence may show the commission of an act of felony. (*Elkin* agt. *People*, 272.)

2. But where, on such indictment, the act which is the gist of the indictment is a *single act*, and the evidence shows the commission of a *felony*, the misdemeanor may be merged in the felony. (*Id.*)

3. On an indictment for *keeping a disorderly house*, the character of the house cannot be proved by *general reputation*. (*People* agt. *Mauch*, 276.)

4. No one should be convicted of any criminal offence upon *mere reputation* or rumors. (*Id.*)

5. Where an *indictment*, charging *burglary in the first degree*, complies with all the requisites of the statute in describing the offence, except that it omits to state the *mode of entry into the premises*, (by forcibly bursting or breaking the wall or outer door, window, &c.,) it is *fatally defective*, and the defect is *not cured by verdict*. (*People* agt. *Fellinger*, *ante*, 341.)

6. Where the allegations in the indictment charged only *burglary in the second degree*, the jury have no right to find the prisoner guilty of burglary in the *first degree*, because evidence was furnished sufficient for that purpose. (*Id.*)

7. *It seems*, that before the decision of the court of appeals in the *People* agt. *Hartung*, the law was settled, that if a *wrong judgment* be given against a defendant, which is reversed on error, the court of review *can neither give a new judgment against the prisoner, nor send the case back to the court below for the proper judgment. The judgment, being erroneous, must be reversed. A venire de novo can only be awarded where the judgment is* RESERVED ON BILL OF EXCEPTIONS. (*Id.*)

8. An *indictment* for unlawfully, wilfully, maliciously and mischievously driving the horses attached to a freight car, on the Fourth avenue railroad, against another railroad car, then and there being, and then there injuring the last mentioned car, he so intending, &c., does not set up or include the common law offence of *malicious mischief*. The defendant can be considered as guilty of nothing beyond a *hurtful trespass*. (*Williams* agt. *People*, *ante*, 350.)

9. A trespass upon property, although it may be willful and malicious, is not within the offence of *malicious mischief at common law*, unless it was in the *night time, or secretly, without the hope of gain*; or unless it consisted of some act of *cruelty to domestic animals*. (*Id.*)

10. A *law* which makes an act punishable *in a manner in which it was not punishable when committed*, or *which increases the punishment with which the act was punishable when committed*, is *ex post facto* and *void*. (*Shepherd* agt. *The People*, *ante*, 388.)

11. The plaintiff in error was convicted of *arson in the first degree*, committed in 1857, which, under the Revised Statutes, was punishable with death, and was sentenced under the act of 1860, which substituted *imprisonment for life* for the punishment of death, to

imprisonment in the state prison for life. (*Id.*)

12. *Held*, that the provisions of the act of 1860, changing the *punishment* of arson in the first degree, were intended to apply only to offences *thereafter committed*; but if it should be held otherwise, then that those provisions are *ex post facto* and *void*, so far as they were intended to apply to a *crime* of arson in the first degree, committed *before the passage of the act*. In either view of the act and upon either holding, the judgment of the court below must be *reversed*. (*Id.*)

13. Where a judgment against a prisoner is reversed upon the *ground alone that a wrong judgment was given*, upon a lawful and regular trial and conviction, he cannot constitutionally be *tried again*: he must be *discharged*. (*Id.*)

14. (*This law would seem to fully meet and settle Mrs. Hartung's case; for although there was no bill of exceptions in this case, and there was one in her case, yet the judgments in both cases were reversed on the ground alone that there was a wrong judgment given. It is difficult to see how the court can look into a bill of exceptions when there is a wrong judgment brought up by the record, and the error being created by a statutory law.*—Rep.) (*Id.*)

15. In this state there may be a *valid marriage*, though not formally solemnized by a *clergyman*, or *consent declared before a magistrate*. (*Hayes* agt. *The People*, *ante*, 452.)

16. If parties competent to contract, in the presence of witnesses, agree together to be husband and wife, and afterwards cohabit and recognize each other as such, it is a sufficient marriage to sustain an indictment for *bigamy*, in the event of one of the parties having before that time married another, who is still living. (*Id.*)

17. Upon an indictment containing nine counts for embezzlement of different grades, and others for larceny, a verdict "guilty of embezzlement" is equivalent to on acquittal of the larcenies charged, and a bar to any subsequent prosecution. (*Guenther* agt. *People*, 24 *N. Y. Rep.*, 100.)

18. One of the counts for embezzlement being good, the verdict means that he is guity of the offence as charged therein. (*Id.*)

19. An entry by order of the court after the jury was discharged, in amendment of the verdict as first recorded, that "the jury find the prisoner not guilty of the larceny charged," is unwarranted and nugatory. (*Id.*)

20. The word "*may*" in section thirty-three of the "act in relation to police and courts in the city of New York" (*ch.* 508 *of* 1860), is enabling and not mandatory. (*Williams* agt. *The People*, 24 *N. Y. Rep.*, 405.)

21. Whether that section authorizing the infliction of the punishment of grand larceny for the theft from the person of another of less than twenty-five dollars is local within the meaning of article III, section 16 of the constituiont: *Quere*. (*Id.*)

22. Under an indictment charging the larceny of several sums, amounting to more than $25, the prisoner has a right to have the jury instructed to find whether the sum stolen, it being from the person of another in the city of New York, was more or less than twenty-five dollars. (*Id.*)

23. Where there was a defect in the entry of the minutes of the court, in not stating the acknowledgment of indebtedness upon entering into a recognizance, *held*, that the court had no authority *ex parte* to manufacture an undertaking imposing obligations upon the accused and his surety, never assumed by them. (*People* agt. *Felton*, 36 *Barb.*, 429.)

24. A quashing of the indictment which the accused had given bail to appear and answer, was a discharge of the obligation, released the surety, and authorized the prisoner's departure from court without special leave, although another indictment was previously found against him for the same offence. (*Id.*)

See Constitutional Law, 5.

See Contempt, 2. 3. 4. 5.

DAMAGES.

1. No proof of *pecuniary* or *special damage* to the plaintiff or next of kin is necessary to sustain an action brought under the statute by the administrator of the deceased for injuries to the person. (*See to the same effect Oldfield* agt. *N. Y. C. R. R. Co.*, 14 *N. Y. R.*, 310.) (*Keller* agt. *N. Y. Central R. R. Company*, *ante*, 172.)

2. In an action by a father, as administrator of his wife, who was killed by negligence, leaving children, the value of her earnings, and the probability that her children would have received an estate increased by such earnings on the death and intestacy of their father, cannot be considered in estimating damages. (*Tilley* agt. *Hudson River R. R. Co.*, 24 *N. Y. R.*, 471.)

3. But the injury to the children, in the loss of maternal nurture and education, is a pecuniary one within the intent of the statute, and a proper ground of damages. (*Id.*)

4. *It seems*, that in such an action, evidence of the habitual occupation and employment of the deceased is admissible, to show her general capacity and relation to the family. (*Id.*)

5. In an action on a bond given for the purpose of procuring the discharge of a vessel attached, to enforce a lien for repairs, the defendants seek to recoup the damages sustained by them by reason of the plaintiffs' neglect to perform their contract or repairs within a reasonable time, the true measure of damages is not the probable profits of the vessel, but the rent which would have been at that time paid for the charter. (*Rogers* agt. *Beard*, 36 *Barb.*, 31.)

6. Upon the death of a person seized of real estate, all claim for damages done to the estate, and for the rents and profits thereof, down to that time, go to his executor, and belong to the personal estate. A claim for damages done to land occupied adversely by the defendant, cannot be sued for and recovered until the plaintiff has recovered possession. A claim for such injuries cannot be united with a claim to recover the possession of the land. (*Hotchkiss* agt. *Auburn & Rochester R. R. Co.*, 36 *Barb.*, 600.)

7. In an action to recover damages for the destruction by fire, of fruit trees, through the negligence of the defendant, the judge at the trial may properly instruct the jury that the plaintiff is entitled to recover the value of the trees as they stood upon his land at the time of the fire, if he entitled to recover at all; and to refuse a request to charge that the plaintiff can only recover the diminished value of the land, since the destruction of the trees. There is no intrinsic difficulty in estimating the value of a fruit tree, growing upon land, although it has strictly no market or commercial value as a tree, independent of the land which sustains it. Such value can be determined by the opinions of competent witnesses as well as in the case of trees which are usually converted into timber or firewood. (*Witbeck* agt. *N. Y. Central R. R. Co.*, 36 *Barb.*, 644.)

See Railroad Companies.

See Contract, 1. 2. 3. 4. 5. 6. 7.

See Referees and Reports, 3.

See Slander, 1. 2.

See Bonds, 2.

See Trial, 6. 7.

See Breach of Promise, 1. 2.

See Common Carriers, 6. 7. 8.

See Conversion, 1.

DEED

1. Where land is conveyed subject to a usurious mortgage, which the grantee assumes to pay, the mortgagee acquires a right to an appropriation of the land for that purpose, which cannot be divested without his assent. (*Hartley* agt. *Harrison*, 24 *N. Y. R.*, 170.)

2. *Held*, accordingly, that a subsequent arrangement between the parties to the deed, whereby, as between them, it became a mere quitclaim, was inoperative to open the defence of usury to the grantee. (*Id.*)

3. *Quere*, however, whether the personal liability assumed by the grantee is not discharged by the release of his grantor. So held in the supreme court, and the question not passed upon by this court. (*Id.*)

4. An instrument, in the form of a mortgage, but containing the name of no mortgagee, does not become effectual by its delivery to one who advances money upon the agreement that he shall hold the paper as security for his loan. (*Chauncey* agt. *Arnold*, 24 *N. Y. R.*, 330.)

5. Whether it could be made effectual by parol authority from the mortgagor to insert the lender's name as mortgagee: *Quere*. (*Id.*)

6. Where a grantee accepts a deed containing a reservation of lands previously sold and conveyed to another, and enters into the possession of the lands thus reserved, he will be deemed in law to have entered in subserviency

to the title of the owner of the reserved land, unless he can establish the contrary by some clear and unequivocal act or claim of title in himself. (*Rosseell* agt. *Wickham*, 36 *Barb.*, 386.)

7. The statutory provision that every conveyance of land held at the time adversely to the grantor shall be void, has no application to conveyances made by the state as grantor. A patent, issued by the state, conveying its own lands, will be presumed to have been issued regularly; and if it be not void on its face, cannot be avoided collaterally, in a suit between individuals. *Brady* agt. *Begun*, 36 *Barb.*, 533.)

8. Where a decree is made setting aside a deed executed by a judgment debtor, as fraudulent and void against his creditors, the court has no power to direct the premises to be sold, as in case of a sale upon execution, for the purpose of paying the judgment debt. The court in such case acts upon the person and not upon the estate of the debtor, and may appoint a receiver to take a conveyance of the premises from the debtor, which the receiver may then sell, and a title obtained through such sale. (*Walker* agt. *White* 36 *Barb.*, 592.)

9. A deed by executors, as such, with a covenant against their own acts, cannot be construed as containing an implied covenant that their testator was seized of an estate in fee simple; or a covenant on their part to put the purchaser in possession. No covenant can be implied in any conveyance of real estate, whether such conveyance contains special covenants or not. (*Sanford* agt. *Travers*, 7 *Bosw.*, 498.)

See Municipal Corporations, 1. 2. 3.

See Trusts, 1.

See Married Women, 12.

See Lakes, 1.

See Vendor and Vendee, 6.

See Mortgage Foreclosure, 11.

DEFENCE.

1. In a suit by one part owner of a vessel against another part owner, to recover the aliquot part of the premium chargeable to the latter, upon policies effected at his request and covering his interest, it is no defence that the premium was paid by the negotiable promissory notes of the plaintiff, which have matured and are remaining unpaid. (*Hoogland* agt. *Wright*, 7 *Bosw.*, 394.)

2. In a suit against the accommodation payee and indorser of a promissory note, it is *prima facie* a defence, that the plaintiff, at the request of the makers of the note, sold another note made by them, and indorsed likewise by the defendant for their accommodation, for the purpose of paying the first note, and that they realized enough from the latter note to make such payment. (*Burrall* agt. *Jones*, 7 *Bosw.*, 404.)

See Answer.

See Corporations, 2.

DEMURRER.

1. Rule 42 does not require the party *demurring to serve on the opposite party* any copy of the pleadings or other papers when the question to be decided arises on demurrer. (*Gott* agt. *Finch*, *ante*, 193.)

2. A demurrer must reach the *whole* of a *cause of action*. A paragraph cannot be expunged on demurrer, unless it amounts to a *separate cause of action*, and is so stated. (*Lord* agt. *Vreeland*, *ante*, 316.)

3. *Misjoinder* of parties plaintiffs is ground of *demurrer* to the complaint. (*Walrath* agt. *Handy*, *ante*, 353.)

4. In such case the complaint does not state facts sufficient to constitute a cause of action. (*Id.*)

5. Whether matters set up in a complaint, which are intended to constitute a cause of action, do or do not constitute a cause of action, must be *tested by demurrer*. (*Howell* agt. *Knickerbocker Life Ins. Co.*, *ante*, 475.)

See Answer, 2. 3. 4. 5. 6. 8.

See Counter-Claim, 2.

See Slander, 1. 2.

See Receiver, 7.

See Appeal, 25.

See Irrelevant and Redundant Matter, 1. 3.

DISCHARGE.

1. A creditor's uniting with one of two joint debtors in his petition for a discharge under the two-third act, and a discharge of such debtor, releases the

other debtor from liability. (*Alger* agt. *Raymond*, 7 *Bosw.*, 418.)

2. When it presumptively appears that an insolvent's discharge is void for any fraud, the court will deny a motion to set aside an execution issued against such insolvent, and direct issues, triable before a jury, to be framed to test the validity of the discharge. It will not try the validity of the discharge on affidavits. (*Stuart* agt. *Salhinger*, 14 *Abb.*, 291.)

DISCOVERY OF BOOKS AND PAPERS.

1. The right to the *inspection of books and papers*, with a view to the *discovery of evidence*, is distinctly recognised by statute, and is not to be confounded with the production of them as evidence *upon the trial*, or on the *examination of a party as a witness before trial.* (*Lefferts and Borsdorf* agt. *Brampton*, *ante*, 257.)

2. If there is reason to believe, upon the case as laid before the court, that the evidence in reality exists, and is material to the matter in controversy; if the other party admits the possession of the books or documents alleged to contain it; if he also impliedly admits the probability of its existence, *by not denying it*, and no great practical inconvenience will follow from allowing the other party to inspect it, the privilege ought to be *granted*. (*Id.*)

3. Thus, where the plaintiffs brought their action to recover the possession of goods obtained from them by the defendants' assignors, upon *representations alleged to have been fraudulent*, and in their sworn *petition* stated that they were informed and believed that an examination of the books of the assignors, by a competent book-keeper, would enable the plaintiffs to show the assignors were, when they made their representations of solvency referred to in the complaint, hopelessly insolvent, and that they knew that the representations made by them were false. (*Id.*)

4. *Held*, the defendants making no answer to the application, but moved to dismiss it on the ground that the discovery could not be allowed by the practice of the court, that the case appeared to be eminently one in which the court should lend its assistance to enable the plaintiffs to inspect documentary evidence which would show whether the representations made by the defendants' assignors *were true or false*. (*Id.*)

5. The fact that papers sought to be discovered preparatory to trial, may be procured by subpœna *duces tecum*, served upon the adverse party is not a conclusive answer to an application for an order for their discovery. The applicant is not required or expected to give an accurate description of the documents sought. The description need only be sufficiently precise to enable the party who is called on to produce to know what is required. (*Low* agt. *Graydon*, 14 *Abb.*, 443.)

DIVORCE.

1. In the trial of an action for a *limited divorce*, husband and wife are competent witnesses against each other. (*P——* agt. *P——*, *ante*, 197.)

2. In this case, although the wife by living with the husband had condoned the cruelty and inhuman treatment by him towards her, so that she was not entitled to a judgment for a divorce from bed and board, yet as the husband was very penurious, and had declined to provide comfortably for her, the court, under the statute, adjudged that he should pay the wife's costs of the action, and provide for her suitable food and lodging in his own house, and pay her $200 per year, payable quarterly, out of which she could provide herself with clothing and such other articles as she might see fit to purchase. (*Id.*)

3. *It seems*, that although the wife uses language calculated to irritate and provoke the husband, yet, if his treatment of her is *grossly disproportioned* to the provocation, she may nevertheless be entitled to a *divorce*. (*Id.*)

4. *It seems*, also, that selling the husband's property to procure necessaries is *no justification* for *personal violence*. (*Id.*)

5. Parties asking the intervention of the court to annul the marriage contract, must prove a full and complete case. Nothing is to be taken in favor of the applicant by presumption or intendment, as to the facts, even in cases of default in answering, or at the hearing. (*Linden* agt. *Linden*, 36 *Barb.*, 61.)

See Husband and Wife, 1. 2. 3. 4.
See Dower, 1.

DOWER.

1. The court of chancery had no power, in a divorce suit, to require a married woman to accept a gross sum from her husband in lieu of dower. Her acceptance of such sum in the lifetime of her husband, will not defeat her dower; and her formal release of dower to her husband, in pursuance of an order of the court, would be a nullity; she being legally incompetent to execute such an instrument to her husband, except in the single case authorized by the Laws of 1840, viz: upon a sale of real estate under a judgment or decree in partition. (*Crane* agt. *Cavana*, 36 *Barb.*, 410.)

See WILL, 36.

ENLISTMENT.

1. The enlistment of a *recruit, under eighteen years of age*, in the *naval service* of the United States, without the consent of his parents or guardian, is not *binding or obligatory*, although he *took an oath*, when he enlisted, that he was twenty-one years of age. The oath can only be conclusive against the recruit, and not against others claiming a legal right to his services. (*Matter of George B. Webb, ante*, 247.)

EVIDENCE.

1. An *ex parte* written statement of facts, made by a witness, though in their nature they are competent when duly proved, cannot be admitted as evidence. (*Stuart* agt. *Binsse*, 7 *Bosw.*, 195.)

2. Where on the trial of an action by one of several partners who had withdrawn from the firm, against the remaining partners, to recover the value of the plaintiff's interest in the assets, on the 2d of April, 1856, and one of the partners as a witness for the plaintiff testifies to his then estimate of the value of such assets in the latter part of 1855, and that he sold his interest to the defendants in November, 1855, the defendants have a right, on the cross-examination of such witness, to prove by him for what sum he so sold such interest. The rejection of such evidence is error for which the judgment will be reversed. (*Dorrity* agt. *Russell*, 7 *Bosw.*, 539.)

3. The decision of a judge before whom a motion is made, upon conflicting evidence, is conclusive so far as questions of fact are concerned. (*Skinner* agt. *Oettinger*, 14 *Abb.*, 109.)

4. In an action by a tenant against his landlord for damages to the furniture of the former, by negligently setting the leased premises on fire, evidence on behalf of the tenant that the landlord had obtained a policy of insurance on the premises, and received the amount mentioned therein, is properly rejected. In regard to the performance of a lawful act, the presumption always exists that at least ordinary care was used. (*Lansing* agt. *Stone*, 14 *Abb.*, 199.)

See NEGLIGENCE.
See AGREEMENT, 7.
See EXECUTORS AND ADMINISTRATORS, 1. 2.
See CORPORATIONS, 1.
See PARTNERS AND PARTNERSHIPS, 1. 2. 3.
See REFEREES AND REPORTS, 3. 4.
See FRAUDULENT REPRESENTATIONS, 1. 2.
See WITNESSES, 2. 3. 4. 5. 6. 7. 8.
See DISCOVERY OF BOOKS AND PAPERS, 1. 2. 3. 4.
See CRIMINAL LAW, 3. 4.
See LANDLORD AND TENANT, 6.
See PAYMENT, 1. 2.
See NEW TRIAL, 6. 7. 8. 10.
See WILL, 23. 24. 25. 34.
See CONTRACT, 8. 9. 18.
See BREACH OF PROMISE, 1. 2.
See INSURANCE COMPANIES, 1. 2.
See DEED, 4. 5.
See JUDGMENT, 10. 11. 12. 18.
See BANKING CORPORATIONS, 5. 6.
See APPEAL, 13.
See TRIAL, 8. 10.
See SLANDER, 3. 4.
See MANUFACTURING CORPORATIONS, 1.

EXCEPTIONS.

1. If a party asks to have particular items considered in a court of review, and a report set aside for their allowance or disallowance, it is not demanding of him too much to require that he shall, 1st, bring the attention of the referee specifically to them; 2d, make it manifest what disposition the referee has in fact made of them, by obtaining from

him a specific report on that subject. And 3d, except specifically to the report in those particulars. (*Houlahan* agt. *Sackett's Harbor & Saratoga R. R. Co.*, *ante*, 155.)

2. *Exceptions* to findings of *fact* are not required. (*Mayor, &c., of New York* agt. *Erben*, *ante*, 358.)

3. Where exceptions to the *conclusions of law* are not made within *ten days after judgment*, none can be sustained upon an *appeal*, and the case is heard solely upon the exceptions taken at the *trial*. (*Id.*)

4. Section 174 of the Code authorises the court to allow in its discretion exceptions to be served after the time prescribed by section 272 has expired. (*Bortle* agt. *Mellen*, 14 *Abb.*, 228.)

See Appeal, 15. 23.

See Railroad Companies, 51.

EXCISE LAW.

1. The statute (*Laws* 1862, *p.* 476) declares that "it shall not be lawful to sell or furnish any wine, *beer*, strong or spirituous liquors to any person in the auditorium or lobbies of such place of exhibition or performance mentioned in the first section of this act." *Held*, that where the *warrant* charged the defendant with having sold *lager beer*, instead of "beer," it did not charge an *offence* on its face. (*Matter of People* agt. *Hart*, *ante*, 289.)

2. The public keeping of intoxicating liquors on Sunday is not a *misdemeanor* under the police act of 1860. (*People* agt. *Osmer*, *ante*, 451.)

3. Where the facts submitted warrant it, the court may, by virtue of the general power which courts exercise over their officers, order the plaintiff's attorney to show his authority to bring the suit. But such power will not be exercised so far as to dismiss the suit, in an action brought by the commissioners of excise, for a penalty, under the act to suppress intemperance, etc., in behalf of a defendant whose only ground of making the motion is that no complaint was made to the excise commissioners before the commencement of the action; that the defendant had violated the statute, and that the commissioners had not authorised the bringing of the suit. The court in such case will only grant an order to stay the proceedings until the further order of the court. (*Commissioners of Excise* agt. *Purdy*, 36 *Barb.*, 266.)

EXECUTION AND LEVY.

1. It is *held* in the first judicial district that it is not necessary to wait sixty days—the return day of an execution—before commencing equitable proceedings on a judgment at law, if the execution has actually been returned before the sixty days have expired. (*There are adverse decisions in other districts.*) (*Field* agt. *Hunt*, *ante*, 463.)

2. Where an *execution* has been duly issued and duly returned by the sheriff unsatisfied in whole or in part, and the plaintiff has in no wise interfered, he may safely act upon the return of the sheriff, to institute *proceedings supplementary to execution*. And the question whether there was property which the sheriff ought to have taken and sold for the purpose of satisfying the judgment in whole or in part, *cannot be raised*. (*Fenton* agt. *Flagg*, *ante*, 499.)

3. The statute does not give a general right to the vendor of any articles of the class of exempt property, to take any other of that species of property for his debt of purchase money. His right is in the nature of a particular lien on specific property—the precise property sold, and does not extend to any other exempt property. The statute of 1842 was designed to prevent frauds in the purchase of the exempt class of property, by giving the vendor a right to retake the same on execution, notwithstanding the exemption of the statute, precisely as though he had taken a chattel mortgage on the same, which he was seeking to enforce. (*Hickox* agt. *Fay*, 36 *Barb.*, 9.)

4. Hops growing upon the vines, which are produced by the annual cultivation of the owner, are personal chattels, within the meaning of the statute of frauds, and as such are subject to levy and sale like other personal property. (*Frank* agt. *Harrington*, 36 *Barb.*, 415.)

5. An execution cannot be issued upon a judgment which has been satisfied by the filing of a certificate, as prescribed by 2 *R. S.*, 362. The satisfaction, if voidable, must be vacated by the court before execution can be issued. (*Ackerman* agt. *Ackerman*, 14 *Abb.*, 229.)

See ASSIGNMENT FOR BENEFIT OF CREDITORS, 3. 4. 5.

See BAIL, 1.

See SHERIFF, 1.

EXECUTORS AND ADMINISTRATORS.

1. After an executor has filed an *inventory* of property belonging to the estate, he is not precluded from showing that property *not belonging to the estate was inventoried*, and may also show that the property belonging to the estate *was of less value* than the amount at which it was inventoried. (*Hasbrouck* agt. *Hasbrouck*, *ante*, 24.)

2. That is, the inventory is not *conclusive* evidence against the executor, of what the assets consist of, and of their value, although it is *prima facie* evidence against him on the accounting before the surrogate. (*Id.*)

3. Where, in an action for accounting against executors, the trust fund has been deposited in the *Trust Company*, *under the direction of the referee*, to be applied to the payment of any recovery in the action, the executors will not be charged with a higher rate of *interest* than that paid by the Trust Company. (*Young* agt. *Brush*, *ante*, 70.)

4. An *executor*, who has obtained probate and letters testamentary in a *sister state*, where he resides, can dispose (without action) of his testator's *personal property in this state*, without taking out letters ancillary here. (*Middlebrook* agt. *Merchants' Bank*, *ante*, 267.)

5. Where an *executor* receives property in his own right as a gift, from the testator, it involves the same equitable liability to satisfy the damages arising from the breach of covenants in a lease given by the testator, as when held by the testator. (*Lord* agt. *Vreeland*, *ante*, 316.)

6. The person to whom was bequeathed the *personal estate*, or his legal representatives, are proper and necessary *parties*, to conclude any claim hereafter to the estate of the testator, in the hands of his executor. (*Id.*)

7. Where a claim against *executors* or *administrators* is *referred* under the Revised Statutes, and the report of the referees is adverse to the plaintiff, and in favor of the defendants, (executors or administrators,) they are entitled to *costs* against the plaintiff, *as in an action under the Code*. (*Radley* agt. *Fisher*, *ante*, 404.)

8. In such cases it is *irregular* to *enter judgment* upon the report without *an application to the court*. (*Id.*)

9. The amount of such costs are those given by the Code in an *action* between party and party, prosecuted and defended in accordance with the provisions of the Code. The provision of the Revised Statutes, authorizing the court to adjudge costs as in actions against executors, is in *full force*. (*Id.*)

10. An order or decree of the court, entered after trial on a reference, that the plaintiff have judgment for a certain amount against the defendant as administrator, and that he pay said moneys into court, *to await the further order of the court, and to be distributed according to law*, is a *final judgment* against the defendant as between the parties. (*Gray* agt. *Cook*, *ante*, 432.)

11. The defendant may be proceeded against upon such judgment by *execution* to collect such moneys, under §285 of the Code; but a proceeding by an order, as for a *contempt* and *attachment* against him, is *unauthorized*. (*Id.*)

12. An executor who was insolvent and indebted to the estate, having sustained a loss by fire, indorsed on his policy of insurance an assignment of it to himself as executor, and, upon receiving payment, deposited the money in a bank to his credit as executor: *Held*, an appropriation of it in payment of his debt. (*Scrantom* agt. *Farmers' & Mechanics' Bank*, 24 *N.Y. R.*, 424.)

13. It is no defence to the bank, against the claim of the estate, that it paid over the money upon the demand of a receiver of the executor's property, appointed in the suit of another creditor. (*Id.*)

See WILL, 6. 7. 8. 9.

See DAMAGES, 6.

See SURROGATES' COURTS.

See DEED, 9.

See RAILROAD COMPANIES, 47. 48.

EXPRESS COMPANIES.

1. Where an ordinary traveling trunk is delivered to an express company to be

carried by them, and left at a designated place; and the trunk contains valuable jewelry belonging to a third person, which fact was not disclosed to the expressmen, and the trunk, with all its contents except the jewelry, which was lost, without the fault of the express company, was safely delivered, the express company is not liable for the jewelry. (*Richards* agt. *Wescott*, 7 *Bosw.*, 6.)

See COMMON CARRIERS, 1. 2. 3. 4. 5.

FIXTURES.

1. Shelves, drawers and counter-tables, put up by the owner to fit the building for the uses of a retail dry goods and grocery store, and without which the building is not adapted to the business, are, as between vendor (owner) and purchaser, fixtures, and a part of the freehold, and the vender has no right to remove them. For a removal of the fixtures, occurring between the execution of the agreement and the time appointed for the payment of the purchase money and the delivery of the deed and of the possession of the land, the purchaser cannot maintain an action against the vendor. (*Tabor* agt. *Robinson*, 36 *Barb.*, 483.)

FOREIGN CORPORATIONS.

1. The statute of limitations does not apply as a bar to an action in the courts of this state against a foreign corporation. (*Thompson* agt. *Tioga R. R. Co.*, 36 *Barb.*, 79.)

2. Drafts drawn by W., the president of a corporation, and signed by him, with the addition to his name of "Pres't T. N. Co.," for the benefit of the corporation, render the drafts those of the corporation. (*Id.*)

3. The filing of security for costs by a foreign corporation who are entitled to sue in the courts of this state, is not a condition precedent of its right to sue. Their omission to file such security at the commencement of the action is merely an irregularity. (*Persee & Brooks' Paper Works* agt. *Willett*, 14 *Abb.*, 119.)

4. A foreign corporation having an agency and an office for the transaction of its business in one of the counties of this state, is not a resident of such county within the meaning of section 125 of the Code. (*The International Life Assurance Co.* agt. *Sweetland*, 14 *Abb.* 240.)

See FOREIGN INSURANCE COMPANIES.

FOREIGN INSURANCE COMPANIES.

1. A *foreign insurance company* created by the laws of another state, but doing business in this state, under and in compliance with our laws, on being sued by a citizen of this state, cannot remove the cause into the circuit court of the United States, on the ground that it is a *citizen of another state*. (*Stevens* agt. *Phœnix Insurance Co.*, *ante*, 517.)

FRAUDULENT REPRESENTATIONS.

1. Where the plaintiff in his complaint averred that Henriques was insolvent on the 17th Sept., 1857, and that by *fraudulently concealing* that fact from the plaintiff, and by *representing* to him that he was *prosperous* and *successful in business*, he led the plaintiff, on the 4th Sept., 1857, to consign to him $40,000 worth of segars: (*Franchetti* agt. *Henriques*, *ante* 165.)

2. And where the evidence of the plaintiff, among other things corroborative, disclosed that Henriques wrote to the plaintiff on the 17th Sept., 1857, saying that "business is good with me," and that "though money is very scarce, I do not suffer by it," and asking another large shipment of segars; and in *eight days* after such letter he failed, leaving $80,000 of indebtedness, upon his own showing, and $250 worth of effects to meet it, having by one stroke swept away the whole of the segars consigned to him by the plaintiff to pay $51,000 of indebtedness to members of his family, *held*, that upon such a state of facts, the plaintiff was entitled to *go to the jury* upon the question whether Henriques, by concealment and a false representation of his real condition, did not procure the shipment of the 4th of September to be made to him, neither expecting nor intending to pay for the goods, but designing to appropriate them in the way he did. The question was fairly raised, and it was a question of *intent*, which was not for the court, but the jury. (*Id.*)

3. Though the omission of a purchaser of goods for credit to disclose his insolvency is not necessarily fraudulent, yet if the purchase be made with a preconceived design not to pay, it is a fraud. (*Hennequin* agt. *Naylor*, *24 N. Y. R.*, 139.)

4. Such design may be inferred by the jury from the circumstances and conduct of the vendee, not only in respect to the sale in question, but in other contemporaneous transactions. (*Id.*)

5. A party making a representation false in fact, renders himself liable in an action for fraud, although he did not actually know the representations to be false at the time. If a party makes a material representation, without knowing whether it is true or false, and it turns out to be false, an action lies for the fraudulent misrepresentation. (*Craig* agt. *Ward*, *36 Barb.*, 377.)

See Cause of Action, 3. 4. 5.

See Married Women, 12.

GUARANTY.

1. A contract to be "accountable that B. will pay you for glass, paints, &c., which he may require in his business, to the extent of fifty dollars," is a continuing guaranty. The limitation is not of the credit to B, but of the extent of the guarantor s liability. The doctrine of *Gates* agt. *McKee* (*3 Kern.*, 232,) re-affirmed. (*Rindge* agt. *Judson*, *24 N. Y. R.*, 64.)

2. Where a defendant by a valid written guaranty, undertakes unconditionally to pay a sum loaned on the security thereof to a third person, on his failure to pay within a stipulated time from the date of the guaranty, and after thirty days' notice of the principal's default, it is not essential to a right of action that payment was demanded of the principal. It is enough that the principal failed to pay, and that the defendant was notified of the default thirty days before suit brought. (*East River Bank* agt. *Rogers*, *7 Bosw.*, 493.)

GUARDIAN.

1. An *infant plaintiff* cannot commence an action without the appointment of a *guardian*. (*Freyberg* agt. *Pelerin*, *ante*, 202.)

2. Where such an action is commenced without such appointment, the defendant may *move to set aside the summons, and complaint, &c., for irregularity*. He is not confined to his remedy by answer in the nature of a plea in *abatement*. (*Id.*)

See Railroad Companies, 46.

See Infant, 4.

HIGHWAYS.

1. A highway cannot be laid out over grounds acquired by a railroad corporation for the site of an engine-house, &c., necessary for its use at a station. (*Albany Northern R. R. Co.* agt. *Brownell*, *24 N. Y. R.*, 345.)

2. An injunction suit will lie to restrain highway commissioners from taking possession of such a site. (*Id.*)

3. It seems that an injunction suit will not lie in a case where the commissioners would have the right to lay out a highway, but fail to acquire jurisdiction, or where their proceedings were irregular. (*Id.*)

4. The statute, (*ch. 62 of* 1853,) in authorizing the construction of highways across railroad tracks without compensation, does not violate the constitutional provisions against taking private property for public use or impairing the obligation of contracts. (*Id.*)

5. The title which a railroad corporation acquires to its track is qualified as being taken for public use, and is subject to the exercise by the legislature of all the powers to which the franchises of the corporations are subject. (*Id.*)

6. Ground adjoining a saw-mill and used for piling logs, but whose limits are not fixed by fences or other visible marks, nor by definite occupation, is not within the statute (1 *R. S.*, *p.* 514, § 57,) prohibiting the laying out of public roads through mill yards. (*People ex rel. Williams* agt. *Kingman*, *24 N. Y. R.*, 559.)

7. It is the duty of the commissioners, in laying a highway over such ground, to leave a sufficient area for the use of the mill-owner, and their discretion as to the quantum is not reviewable in any other proceeding. (*Id.*)

8. The ditch or canal by which the water is conducted to a mill is not a building, fixture or erection within the meaning of the statute. A highway may be

laid along it, comprehending it in whole or in part within the limits of the road; but if necessary to work the road to its entire width, it must be by so constructing a roadway over the channel as not to obstruct the flow of water. (*Id.*)

9. It is not essential to a highway, at common law or under our statute, that it be a thoroughfare. A road may be laid out by the public authority which has no issue at one extremity, and abuts upon private ground. (*Id.*)

10. Where the grantees and those claiming under them had been in the actual possession of the lands adjoining the public road, for more than seventy years, under a deed which bounded the premises easterly by the road or public highway, without any words indicating a limitation of the eastern boundary to the westerly line of the road, *held*, that the words of the grant included, by fair interpretation, the one-half of the roadbed; and that they were in the constructive, if not the actual possession of the western half of the road bed, sufficiently to enable them to maintain trespass or ejectment. (*Dunham* agt. *Williams*, 36 *Barb.*, 136.)

11. An appeal lies from an order of commissioners of highways, laying out a public highway, to the county judge, by every person who shall conceive himself aggrieved by such determination, provided he be a resident taxpayer of the town, and as such liable to assessment therein for highway labor. The duty of referees appointed by a county judge to hear and determine an appeal from an order of commissioners of highways, stated. (*People ex rel. Ridgeway* agt. *Cortelyou*, 36 *Barb.*, 164.)

12. Where a commissioner of highways institutes proceedings under the statute of 1847, for a re-assessment of the damages of a person, whose land has been taken for a road, or highway, the owner of the land is entitled to notice of the empaneling of the jury, and of all the subsequent proceedings before them. (*People ex rel. Stephens* agt. *Tallman*, 36 *Barb.*, 222.)

13. The fact that a road has been used as a public highway for twenty years or more, will not give the commissioners of highways the right to proceed against an individual, for an encroachment thereon by fences, unless such road has been duly laid out in conformity with the directions of the highway act. (*Doughty* agt. *Brill*, 36 *Barb.*, 488.)

14. A commissioner of highways who enters into a contract with an individual for work, either upon highways or bridges, when no means have been provided by the town, may incur a personal liability, but cannot impose any liability upon his successor in office, or upon the town. The statute does not expressly or impliedly authorise such commissioners to pledge the credit of the town in any manner. (*Mather* agt. *Crawford*, 36 *Barb.*, 564.)

15. Commissioners of highways have the implied power to construct new bridges; especially such bridges as it is the duty of towns to make and keep in repair. But in no case have they any power or authority to construct bridges at the expense of the town, or of the county, unless they are connected with and form a part of an existing highway. (*Id.*)

See Railroad Companies, 39. 40. 41. 42.

HOMESTEAD EXEMPTION.

1. The exemption of property under the act relative to homestead exemptions is a mere personal privilege which the statute secures to the debtor and to his widow and children after his decease, which does not run with the land, and which cannot be transferred to another with the land. The statute does not exempt the property from becoming bound and charged by a judgment, but from a sale on execution, only so long as the exemption shall continue in force. A judgment against the owner of the homestead will have priority over a mortgage subsequently executed by him, as a lien upon the premises. (*Smith* agt. *Brackett*, 36 *Barb.*, 571.)

HUSBAND AND WIFE.

1. Where the *wife*, after her husband's absence for five successive years, and without her having known, during that time, that he was living, (*see* 3 *R. S.*, 227, 5*th ed.*,) married a second husband, (*Griffin* agt. *Banks*, *ante*, 213.)

2. *Held*, that the first marriage was only placed by the law in *abeyance*. It only temporarily suspended the rights of the first husband, unless, by his own neglect or acquiescence, he waived or abandoned them. (*Id.*)

3. The first husband, in this case, having omitted or neglected to resort to the

proper remedy, by filing a bill and proceeding in the manner prescribed by the statute, to annul the voidable (second) marriage, the latter marriage continued in force after the death of the first husband, and had the same force and effect as if, when it was solemnized, the first husband *was not alive*. (*Id.*)

4. A *deed of separation* between husband and wife, which is without consideration, and consequently void, does not affect the husband's rights in the property and business of the wife, or the debts contracted in her name; and such property passes to his assignee, in *an assignment for the benefit of creditors*. (*Id.*)

5. Where the *husband* purchased *lumber* for the building of a house on real estate which he *falsely represented* belonged to him, and on the *credit* of owning such property, when in fact the real estate at that time, and the house afterwards erected upon it with such lumber, belonged to *his wife*, and the house was built with her knowledge and approbation, *held*, in an action in equity by the plaintiff against the *husband and wife* for the price of such lumber, that the facts thus established created an *equitable lien* in favor of the plaintiff *upon the real estate*, and it was thus decreed. (*Mattice* agt. *Lillie*, *ante*, 264.

6. In this state there may be a *valid marriage*, though not formally solemnized by a *clergyman*, or *consent declared before a magistrate*. (*Hayes* agt. *People*, *ante*, 452.)

7. If parties competent to contract, in the presence of witnesses, agree together to be husband and wife, and afterwards cohabit and recognize each other as such, it is a sufficient marriage to sustain an indictment for *bigamy*, in the event of one of the parties having before that time married another, who is still living. (*Id.*)

8. The rights of a wife, as creditor of her husband under the law of France, where the marriage was contracted, continue and attach to the property of the husband where he abandons her and dies domiciled in this state. (*Bonati* agt. *Welsch*, 24 *N. Y. R.*, 157.)

9. Accordingly, where the husband had appropriated the proceeds of real estate inherited by the wife during coverture, and she was, by the French law entitled to priority of payment out of his estate, *held*, that such right to priority exists as against his legatees, though the property bequeathed had all been acquired by him in this state subsequent to his desertion of the wife. (*Id.*)

10. A husband, indebted to his wife in the sum of one thousand five hundred dollars and interest, for property which belonged to her at law, and in the further sum of two thousand dollars, with interest, for which equity would have regarded her as a creditor, transferred to the wife property, real and personal, to the value of sixteen thousand dollars. Such transfer, it seems, is not to be regarded as voluntary. (*Babcock* agt. *Eckler*, 24 *N. Y. R.*, 623.)

11. But, if voluntary, the husband retaining property of the value of ten thousand dollars, and being indebted in only the sum of nine hundred dollars, there is no legal presumption of fraud, but the question is one of fact. (*Id.*)

12. The intent to defraud must be inferable from the circumstances; and, if the facts show that the settlement upon the wife was a proper and reasonable one, in the condition of the husband's estate at the time, it will not be invalidated by his subsequent inability to pay a debt then existing. (*Id.*)

See Married Women, 4. 5.

See Witness, 9.

INFANT.

1. An *infant plaintiff* cannot commence an action without the appointment of a *guardian*. (*Frayberg* agt. *Paleris*, *ante*, 202.)

2. Where such an action is commenced without such appointment, the defendant may *move to set aside the summons, and complaint, &c., for irregularity*. He is not confined to his remedy by answer in the nature of a *plea in abatement*. (*Id.*)

3. The enlistment of a *recruit*, *under eighteen years of age*, in the *naval service* of the United States, without the consent of his parents or guardian, is not *binding or obligatory*, although he *took an oath*, when he enlisted, that he was twenty-one years of age. The oath can only be conclusive against the recruit, and not against others claim-

ing a legal right to his services. (*Matter of George B. Webb, ante*, 247.)

4. It is irregular to institute proceedings in partition on behalf of an infant without first obtaining the authority of the court. And it is erroneous to allow an infant to act in such proceedings by guardian without security. (*Clark* agt. *Clark*, 14 *Abb.*, 299.)

See RAILROAD COMPANIES, 46.

INNKEEPERS.

1. Innkeepers are answerable for the honesty of their guests as well as their servants. In an action against innkeepers by a guest, to recover the value of property lost by the latter, proof of the loss or larceny of the goods from the room occupied by the guest, is alone sufficient proof of carelessness on the part of the innkeepers. What will amount to carelessness on the part of a guest, which will excuse the innkeepers. (*Gile* agt. *Libby*, 36 *N. Y. R.*, 70.)

2. The relation of innkeeper and guest must exist in all cases, or the liability of the former, as such, does not attach. The accepting and keeping of the goods of a guest is accessory to the contract implied by law. Where an innkeeper receives the property of a person who is not in fact his guest, his responsibility is not that of an innkeeper but of an ordinary bailee for hire. (*Ingalsbee* agt. *Wood*, 36 *Barb.*, 452.)

INJUNCTION.

1. Where the defendants in an action in this court, brought by a non-resident plaintiff, obtained judgment against the plaintiff, from which the plaintiff *appealed*, and filed security on appeal; and pending the appeal the defendants commenced an action against the plaintiff and his sureties, on the bond given as *security for costs*, in a district court, where the plaintiff appeared, and the action was tried and resulted in a judgment against the plaintiff, on which judgment the plaintiff moved for a stay of proceedings until his appeal was decided, which was denied, and he then appealed to the common pleas. (*Van Vleeck* agt. *Clark, ante*, 190.)

2. *Held*, that although the defendants should not be allowed to collect on the bond for security for costs, the moneys which they would not be allowed to collect directly on execution, until the appeal was decided, yet the plaintiff's remedy was not by action and an *injunction* to stay the proceedings on the judgment in the district court; but he should have moved this court before a judgment was recovered on the bond, for an order *staying any action* on the same until the *decision of the appeal*. Not having done this, his remedy by action and injunction was too late, as *judgment* had been rendered against him in a court over which this court had no control. (*Id.*)

3. When an *injunction order* has been allowed, and the same has been served, and the parties in the suit have appeared and taken steps in the action, and acquiesced in the injunction, no judge has authority to *modify it ex parte*. (*Peck* agt. *Yorks, ante*, 363.)

4. Section 324 of the Code was designed to allow a judge who had hastily or improvidently granted an order to rectify the error, *if applied to immediately, and before any steps are taken in the action*. It was not intended to give an unlimited right to vacate orders granted *ex parte*. (*Id.*)

5. An injunction can only be granted where it appears by the complaint that the plaintiff is entitled to the relief demanded, and also, that it appears by affidavit that sufficient grounds exist therefor. A defendant may move to vacate it, either upon the complaint and affidavits on which it was granted, or upon affidavits on his part, with or without answer; and the plaintiff may oppose the motion by affidavits in addition to those on which the injunction was granted. (*Fowler* agt. *Burns*, 7 *Bosw.*, 638.)

6. An injunction *pendente lite*, should not be granted on light grounds, nor in doubtful cases. Where the right is not clear, or the danger great, or the apprehended mischief irreparable, the injunction should not be granted until the rights of the parties are ascertained and settled upon full proof, on the final hearing, and the right to it is established. (*Redfield* agt. *Middleton*, 7 *Bosw.*, 649.)

7. An injunction will not be granted before judgment for any purpose where such purpose can be attained by other ordinary processes of the law. It ought not to issue for the purpose of restraining a judicial officer from transcending his jurisdiction—a writ of prohibition

being the proper remedy in such a case. It should not require the performance of any act, but should only forbid performance. (*Ward* agt. *Kelsey*, 14 *Abb.*, 106.)

8. *It seems* that summary proceedings to recover possession of land can be restrained by injunction only when they are used for the purposes of fraud. (*Id.*)

See Trade-Mark, 1. 2. 3. 4.

See Receivers, 7.

See Municipal Corporations, 1. 2. 3. 8.

See Highways, 1. 2. 3. 4. 5.

See Partners and Partnerships, 21.

INQUEST.

See Service, 1. 2.

INSURANCE COMPANIES.

1. A marine policy of insurance "upon the whole tackle," &c. of a vessel, containing a warranty that "the property is free from all liens," parol evidence is admissible that the property insured was the owner's equity of redemption in the vessel which was subject to certain mortgages known to the insurer. (*Bidwell* agt. *North Western Ins. Co.*, 24 *N. Y. R.*, 302.)

2. The existence of such mortgages is no breach of the warranty. (*Id.*)

3. Is a prospectus, distributed by a life insurance company, admissible to vary a provision in a policy issued by it? A disposition indicated to re-examine this question, discussed between the same parties (23 *N. Y.*, 516.) (*Ruse* agt. *Mutual Life Ins. Co.*, 24 *N. Y. R.*, 653.)

4. Premium notes given by the insured each for twenty times the amount of the premium paid in cash, upon contracts of insurance made after the act of June 25, 1853, providing for the incorporation of fire insurance companies, took effect, are illegal and void, and cannot be enforced against the maker. (*Otis* agt. *Harrison*, 36 *Barb.*, 210.)

5. One having an interest in the continuance of the life of another, as his creditor, may insure the life of the debtor, and the contract for such purpose will be valid and binding. The fact that the debt is due to the creditor as a member of a partnership, and from another partnership firm, of which the person whose life is insured is a member, does not affect the rule. (*Rawls* agt. *American Life Ins. Co.*, 36 *Barb.*, 357.)

6. The contract of fire insurance, being a more personal contract, in no way attached to or running with the real property insured, it does not pass with it, without assignment of the policy, either to a grantee or an heir. The executor or administrator is the only one who can make the contract, and enforce it. (*Wyman* agt. *Prosser*, 36 *Barb.*, 368.)

7. A stipulation in a policy of fire insurance, that the insurance shall be void in case the assured, or any other person with his knowledge, shall have existing, during the continuance of the policy, any other insurance on the property not notified to the insurers and mentioned in or indorsed upon the policy, is a material part of the contract between the parties, one which they have a right to make, and the violation of which renders the policy void. (*Gilbert* agt. *Phœnix Ins. Co.*, 36 *Barb.*, 372.)

8. Where the insurers, in pursuance of a provision contained in their policy, have elected to pay the loss by fire, by restoring the building burned, they cannot be required to pay in any other way. No action will lie upon the policy until the neglect of the insurers to comply with their offer to rebuild, within a reasonable time. And no action will lie, upon the policy, after the insured has refused to allow the insurers to enter upon the premises to rebuild, and has himself proceeded to rebuild, without waiting for the expiration of the thirty days within which the insurers were entitled to make their election to rebuild. (*Beals* agt. *Home Ins. Co.*, 36 *Barb.*, 614.)

9. Where a policy of insurance upon a building occupied as an india-rubber factory, and on property and machinery contained therein, with an exception that the company were not to be responsible in case of loss or damage "by explosion of any kind," *held*, the property having been burned up, caused by an explosion of a steam boiler therein, that the company was not liable for the loss, even though a steam engine was necessary, and ordinarily used in the carrying on of an india-rubber factory. (*Hayward* agt. *Liverpool & London Ins. Co.*, 7 *Bosw.*, 385.)

See FOREIGN INSURANCE COMPANIES.

See BILLS OF EXCHANGE AND PROMISSORY NOTES, 2. 3. 4.

See ADMIRALTY, 13. 14.

See COMPLAINT, 12.

IRRELEVANT AND REDUNDANT MATTER.

1. A motion under § 160 of the Code, to strike out irrelevant matters, cannot prevail to strike out a *whole complaint*. (*Howell* agt. *Knickerbocker Life Ins. Co.*, *ante*, 475.)

2. Whether matters set up in a complaint, which are intended to constitute a cause of action, do or do not constitute a cause of action, must be *tested by demurrer*. (*Id.*)

3. Where matters alleged in the complaint, by way of excuse for not paying the premium on a life policy of insurance on the day it fell due, were proposed to be stricken out under section 160, *held*, that if they did not furnish a legal excuse, the plaintiff had no cause of action to recover on the policy; but they were not so *palpably immaterial* in making out a good cause of action as to be disposed of summarily, and to justify the court in pronouncing the complaint bad. The defendants must be put to their *demurrer*. (*Id.*)

See ANSWER, 7.

See MOTION, 4.

JUDGMENT.

1. The right of a defendant to *offer judgment* under section 385 of the Code, in an action regularly commenced against him, is not limited to cases in which he would only confess *a part* of the plaintiff's claim. The offer may be for the *full sum* demanded in the plaintiff s summons and complaint. (*Ross and Burdick* agt. *Bridge*, *ante*, 163.)

2. An order or decree of the court, entered after trial on a reference, that the plaintiff have judgment for a certain amount against the defendant as administrator, and that he pay said moneys into court, *to await the further order of the court, and to be distributed according to law*, is a *final judgment* against the defendant as between the parties. (*Gray* agt. *Cook*, *ante*, 432.)

3. The defendant may be proceeded against upon such judgment by *execution* to collect such moneys, under §285 of the Code; but a proceeding by an order, as for a *contempt* and *attachment* against him, is *unauthorized*. (*Id.*)

4. Where a copy of a decree or judgment, for the payment of money, is served on the defendant without any *demand* for payment being made, he cannot be convicted as of a *contempt* in not paying over the money; there must be a *demand* and *refusal* to authorize proceedings for a contempt. (*Id.*)

5. A judgment by confession entered upon an insufficient statement, but not impeached for actual fraud, is good as between the parties. (*Miller* agt. *Earle*, 24 *N. Y. R.*, 110.)

6. Where the property of the defendant has been sold under an execution upon such a judgment, the purchaser's title cannot be impeached by a creditor having no judgment or lien on the property at the time of the levy. (*Id.*)

7. A judgment by confession is valid as between the parties, though the statement on which it is founded does not conform to the Code in setting forth the origin and particulars of the indebtedness. (*Neusbaum* agt. *Keem*, 24 *N. Y. R.*, 325.)

8. Such a judgment, therefore, upon proof of its *bona fides*, authorizes the creditor to impeach a fraudulent transfer by his debtor. (*Id.*)

9. A statement, it seems, is sufficient under the Code, which, after declaring that the plaintiff had sold and delivered to the debtor large quantities of meat in 1854 and 1855, averred that there was justly due him, upon such sales, a balance of $2,114, with interest from January 18, 1855. (*Id.*)

10. The attestation of a judgment of a state court, in order to make it evidence in another state, under the act of Congress, must be signed by the clerk: the attestation of a deputy clerk is insufficient. (*Morris* agt. *Patchin*, 24 *N. Y. R.*, 394.)

11. Such a defect is not cured by the certificate of the presiding magistrate of the state court that the attestation is in due form, and authorized by the state law. It is immaterial that the attestation conforms to the law of the state: it must conform to the act of Congress. (*Id.*)

12. In order to make the record of a judgment evidence, it must be signed by the officer authorized by law, and must have been filed in the proper office. Where the record itself fails to show these essentials to its validity, *it seems* that it is inadmissible to sustain process founded thereon, even though attested in the manner required by the act of Congress to authenticate a judgment. (*Id.*)

13. A statement is sufficient to authorize the entry of judgment by confession, under section 383 of the Code, which sets forth that "the plaintiff has this day indorsed my notes, payable at bank for $6,000 in all, for my accommodation, and to enable me to negotiate said notes," without any further description of the notes. (*Hopkins* agt. *Nelson*, 24 *N. Y. R.*, 518.)

14. A judgment recovered in a court of record of a sister state, having jurisdiction of the parties and of the action, is conclusive in a suit brought upon it in the courts of this state; and the defendant cannot litigate the question whether the complaint contained in the record of that judgment states facts sufficient to constitute a cause of action; nor whether such cause of action arose in this state, and by the laws thereof no recovery could be had upon it. Nor can such judgment be impeached by proof that it was recovered upon an allegation of misrepresentation and warranty of goods sold by the defendant to the plaintiff, and proof that before the commencement of the action, the defendant sued the plaintiff in a justice's court of the same state, and recovered a judgment therein before the trial of the action against him, for the balance due upon the contract price of such goods. (*Phillips* agt. *Godfrey*, 7 *Barb.*, 150.)

15. The 385th section of the Code does not provide for entering a judgment upon an offer, unless the offer be unconditional, and leaves no facts to be ascertained and determined, to authorise the entry of a judgment. (*Pinckney* agt. *Childs*, 7 *Bosw.*, 660.)

16. Where an action has been tried before the court without a jury, the only authority for entering judgment is the decision of the judge; therefore, a reference to compute the amount of the recovery, if not authorized by the decision, is irregular. (*Chamberlain* agt. *Dempsey*, 14 *Abb.*, 241.)

17. On a trial by the court without a jury, the failure of the judge to specify the relief granted, or the determination of the action, is an irregularity which may be taken advantage of on appeal from the judgment. (*Id.*)

18. A judgment obtained in an action brought to have a deed declared to be a mortgage, which judgment declares it to be a deed and not a mortgage, although it also declares that the grantor is tenant of the grantee, is not evidence on this latter question. A judgment concludes the parties only as to the grounds covered by it and the facts necessary to uphold it. In order to make a judgment record evidence to conclude any matter, it should appear that such matter was in issue. (*People ex rel. Reilly* agt. *Johnson*, 14 *Abb.*, 416.)

See Costs, 1. 2. 13.
See Deed, 8.
See Set-off, 1.
See Amendment, 1.
See Injunction, 1. 2.
See Receivers, 2.
See Execution and Levy, 5.
See Constable's Bond, 1. 2. 3. 4. 5.
See Executors and Administrators, 7. 8. 9.
See Attorney, 1. 2. 3. 4. 5. 12. 13. 14.
See Appeal, 17.
See Married Women, 4. 5.
See Manufacturing Corporations, 1.

JURISDICTION.

1. Where a justice of the peace issues a warrant on a complaint for *bastardy*, and the defendant is arrested and brought before the said justice and *another justice* called to his aid, pursuant to the statute, and the defendant not being ready for examination, applies for an adjournment and executes the proper *bond* for his appearance on the adjourned day, there is no *breach of the bond* by the failure of the defendant to appear on the adjourned day before the said justice and a *different associate justice*, the former associate justice being absent. (*People* agt. *Boardman*, *ante*, 512.)

2. The city court of Brooklyn has jurisdiction of an action brought against the Brooklyn Ferry Company, to recover damages for an injury to the

plaintiff's boat, caused by a collision. (*Crofut* agt. *Brooklyn Ferry Co.*, 36 *Barb.*, 201.)

3. Where A. brought an action in the county court against B., to recover damages for the wrongful detention and conversion of property, and B. demurred on the ground that the court had no jurisdiction of the subject of the action, and the county court rendered a decision sustaining the demurrer. *Held*, that the court had power to enter the judgment of dismissal of the complaint, and awarding costs to the defendant. When a court has the parties in an action before it, it must necessarily obtain jurisdiction, so far as to decide whether it can entertain the suit; that is, to decide whether it has jurisdiction of the action. (*King* agt. *Poole*, 36 *Barb.*, 242.)

4. The superior court of the city of New York has jurisdiction of an action on contract where one or more of several defendants, jointly liable on the contract, reside, or are personally served with the summons within that city. (*Bates* agt. *Reynolds*, 7 *Bosw.*, 685.)

5 Under section 161 of the Code it is necessary in pleading the determination of an officer of special and limited jurisdiction to designate the officer; an averment that such determination was duly made is insufficient. (*Carter* agt. *Koezley*, 14 *Abb.*, 147.)

6. In an action for equitable relief where the matter in dispute does not exceed fifty dollars the action will be dismissed. (*Sarsfield* agt. *Van Vaughner* 14 *Abb.*, 297.)

See CERTIORARI, 1.
See BANKING CORPORATIONS, 8.
See SURROGATES' COURTS, 1. 2. 3.
See JUDGMENT, 14.
See COUNTY COURT, 1. 2.
See ATTACHMENT, 5.

JURY.

See FRAUDULENT REPRESENTATIONS, 1. 2.
See RAILROAD COMPANIES.
See TRIAL, 1. 2. 3. 8. 11.
See NEW TRIAL, 5. 6. 7. 10.
See CONSTITUTIONAL LAW, 6.
See APPEAL, 13.

JUSTICES OF THE PEACE.

1. Where a justice of the peace issues a warrant on a complaint for *bastardy* and the defendant is arrested and brought before the said justice and *another justice* called to his aid, pursuant to the statute, and the defendant not being ready for examination applies for an adjournment and executes the proper *bond* for his appearance on the adjourned day, there is no *breach of the bond* by the failure of the defendant to appear on the adjourned day before the said justice and a *different associate justice*, the former associate justice being absent. (*People* agt. *Boardman*, *ante*, 512.)

2. The return of a justice of the peace to a certiorari, under the Code, must contain all the testimony received by him. (*Orcutt* agt. *Cahill*, 24 *N. Y. R.*, 578.)

3. Where a justice's return sets forth evidence in detail, it is to be considered as stating the whole testimony, unless the contrary distinctly appears. (*Id.*)

See APPEAL, 11. 12.
See ATTACHMENT, 5.

LAKES.

1. An inland lake, five miles long and three-fourths of a mile wide, having no current and no main inlet, is not in any legal or just sense, navigable water. Where the state issued a patent embracing a portion of such a lake within its boundaries, the northern line crossing the lake, but containing no exception of the lake, nor reservation of it, or of the water, *held*, that the grant carried the southern portion of the lake to the grantee absolutely, and the right to land subsequently filled in, where the water was shallow, immediately in front of the grantee's premises. (*Ledyard* agt. *Ten Eyck*, 36 *Barb.*, 102.)

LANDLORD AND TENANT.

1. Where a *monthly tenant* occupies rooms of a landlord, with an agreement to pay *rent in advance*, and leaves the premises the latter part of the month, he is not liable for the rent of the *subsequent month*, which has not become due. (*Fash* agt. *Kavanagh*, *ante*, 347.)

2. Where it appeared that the filth from a privy, either *on* or *adjoining* the premises, flowed over the apartments occupied by the tenant, without any fault on his part, and rendered them unfit to occupy, the tenant was justified in *abandoning* them under the provisions of the "act in relation to the rights and liabilities of owners and lessors, and of lessees and occupants of buildings," passed April 13, 1860. (*Id.*)

3. The injury to the premises contemplated by this act, to authorize a surrender of possession, must be of a physical nature, such as if done by the landlord would amount to an *eviction* of the tenant from the whole or part of the demised premises. (*Id.*)

4. The occupant of *apartments* in a *tenement house* is not bound either to see to the erection of a proper *sink* or *privy* upon the premises, or to cause it to be *emptied* to prevent an overflow. This is a matter which the *landlord* is required to look after and prevent, or else to stand to the consequences. (*Id.*)

5. Where a lease in general terms, whether for life, for years, or for a single year, of land in which an open mine exists, carries the right to the lessee to work the same. And the right of action for quarrying and taking away the stone from an open quarry, is vested in the lessee named in the lease of such quarry, or whoever has his interest in it. (*Freer* agt. *Stolenbur*, 36 *Barb.*, 641.)

6. Where in an action against the defendant to recover rent of premises occupied by a third person, evidence has been given of a conversation, on a specified day between the landlord and defendant, tending to establish a hiring by the defendant, and an agreement that such third person might occupy, and the defendant would pay the rent, it is error to exclude evidence of other cotemporaneous conversations between the landlord and defendant on the same subject. (*Halsey* agt. *Jarvis*, 7 *Bosw.*, 461.)

7. Where a wharf or pier reclaimed from tide-water by embankment, or by raising the bottom with stone, earth or other material, it is a tenement within the meaning of 2d Revised Statutes, 512, which authorizes summary proceedings in favor of a landlord to recover the possession of houses, lands or tenements. An agreement to construct a wharf to be occupied, when finished, by the grantee, at a stipulated rent, accompanied by words of present demise, operates as a lease. (*People ex rel. Ward* agt. *Kelsey*, 14 *Abb.*, 372.)

See Evidence, 4.

See Covenants, 1. 2.

See Specific Performance, 6.

LETTERS OF ADMINISTRATION.

See Executors and Administrators.

See Surrogates' Courts, 5. 6. 7. 8. 9.

LIBEL.

1. The statute (*ch.* 130 *of* 1854) exempting from prosecution for libel the publishers of legislative debates, &c., is prospective only and is no defence for a publication prior to its enactment. (*Sanford* agt. *Bennett*, 24 *N. Y. R.*, 20.)

2. The publication of a slander uttered by a murderer at the time of his execution, is not privileged either under that statute or at the common law. (*Id.*)

3. The statute relates only to statements made in judicial, legislative or administrative bodies in execution of some public duty. (*Id.*)

LIEN.

See Set-off, 1.

See Boarding House Keepers, 1.

See Attorney, 1. 2. 3. 4. 5. 12. 13. 14.

See Creditor's Suit, 1. 2. 3. 4. 9. 10.

See Banking Corporations, 3. 4.

See Execution and Levy, 3.

See Vendor and Vendee, 6.

See Homestead Exemption, 1.

MANDAMUS.

1. Chapter 375 of 1852, required the raising by tax on the town of Genoa of the interest on certain bonds of that town, the money to be received and paid to the bondholders by commissioners appointed for that purpose. The money having been raised, it seems that mandamus to the commissioners is

the proper remedy to enforce payment and not an action against the town. (*People* agt. *Mead*, 24 *N. Y. R.*, 114.)

2. Where there are several issues arising on the return to a writ of alternative mandamus, which are submitted to a jury, a general verdict may properly be directed. And where several special issues are submitted to a jury who, under instructions of the court, render a general verdict, such verdict is equivalent to finding each of the issues in favor of the party in whose behalf the general verdict is formed. (*People ex rel. Hanrahan* agt. *The Board of Police*, 14 *Abb.*, 151.)

3. On motion to quash the return to a writ of alternative mandamus, where the court has sustained the return, it may issue a pre-emptory writ, although the issues raised by the return are found in favor of the defendant. (*Id.*)

4. It is competent for the jury on the trial of issues in mandamus cases to find a general verdict; and if necessary the court will give it effect by applying it to the issues separately. (*People ex rel. Peck* agt. *Board of Police*, 14 *Abb.*, 158.)

See SUPERVISORS, 1. 2. 3. 4.

See CONSTITUTIONAL LAW, 1. 2. 3.

See CHARITABLE AND BENEVOLENT SOCIETIES.

See RAILROAD COMPANIES, 23. 24. 25.

See MUNICIPAL CORPORATIONS, 5.

MANUFACTURING CORPORATIONS.

1. A judgment against a corporation as acceptor of a draft, is *prima facie* evidence against a stockholder, in an action to enforce his individual liability, that the draft was properly drawn, and duly accepted by the corporation. Where the name of an individual appears on the stock book of the company as a stockholder, the burden of proving that he is not a stockholder is cast upon him. (*Hoagland* agt. *Bell*, 36 *Barb.*, 57.)

2. A receiver of a manufacturing corporation will not be appointed in an action brought against it by a creditor at large, who seeks for a dissolution of the corporation and the distribution of its effects, on the ground of its insolvency, and that its trustees, instead of taking proceedings for the dissolution of the company, intend to facilitate the recovery of judgments against it, by certain creditors, with a view to give them a preference, and thus to effect alienations of the property contrary to law. When receivers may be appointed under the statute, of the property of corporations other than moneyed corporations. (*Galway* agt. *U. S. Steam Sugar Refining Co.*, 36 *Barb.*, 256.)

See ASSIGNMENT FOR THE BENEFIT OF CREDITORS, 11.

MARRIED WOMEN.

1. Where a *married woman* carries on the *millinery business* upon her own account, and purchases goods upon credit for such business on her own account, an action may be brought against her the same as if she were unmarried, and a judgment recovered, and the amount collected by execution out of property belonging to her in her own right. (*This agrees with the case of Barton agt. Beer*, 21 *How. Pr. R.*, 309.) (*Klen* agt. *Gibney*, *ante*, 31.)

2. Where, after a trial and verdict for rent due, judgment was entered and execution issued against the defendant, and the defendant moved to set aside the judgment and execution on the ground (disclosed for the first time) that she was a *married woman*, *held*, the evidence showing that her husband had been absent from the state a long time, and tending to show that she kept a boarding-house on her own account, that the motion *be denied, with costs.* (*Collins* agt. *Heather*, *ante*, 132.)

3. Where the *husband* purchased *lumber* for the building of a house on real estate which he *falsely represented* belonged to him, and on the *credit* of owning such property, when in fact the real estate at that time, and the house afterwards erected upon it with such lumber, belonged to *his wife*, and the house was built with her knowledge and approbation, *held*, in an action in equity by the plaintiff against the *husband and wife* for the price of such lumber, that the facts thus established created an *equitable lien* in favor of the plaintiff *upon the real estate*, and it was thus decreed. (*Mattice* agt. *Lillie*, *ante*, 264.)

4. A confession of judgment, without action, by a married woman is void, although the consideration be money

borrowed for and applied to the improvement of her separate estate. (*Watkins* agt. *Abrahams*, 24 *N. Y. R.*, 72.)

5. When husband and wife unite in confessing a judgment, it may be retained as good against the husband, though void as to the wife. (*Id.*)

6. At common law, a husband is entitled to the personal property and choses in action of his wife, and they are vested in him at her death, whether reduced to possession or not, in virtue of his marital right, and not of his right to administration. (*Ryder* agt. *Hulse*, 24 *N. Y. R.*, 372.)

7. The statutes of 1848 and 1849, for the protection of married women, gave no power to the wife to dispose by will of property acquired by her before the passage of the acts, or of the interest accruing after the acts upon money previously given to her, or of the proceeds of her own labor which her husband permitted her to receive, manage and invest in her own name and as if it were her own property. (*Id.*)

8. Evidence of such a course of dealing by the wife with personal property bequeathed to and earned by her, and her husband's declarations that she could give her money to whom she pleased, only establish an omission to exercise his marital rights in her lifetime, and do not imply a relinquishment of his rights in case of survivorship. (*Id.*)

9. A wife, by allowing chattels belonging to her, and which remain *in specie*, to be employed by her husband in the carrying on of a business for their common benefit, does not devote them to her husband so as to render them liable for his debts. (*Sherman* agt. *Elder*, 24 *N. Y. R.*, 381.)

10. Otherwise, *it seems*, as to articles used by the husband as merchandise, whether a part of the goods belonging to the wife before marriage, or purchased out of the earnings and accumulations of the business: *per* ALLEN, J. (*Id.*)

11. An assignment by the wife of the goods and chattels, "as well as all claims and demands for any portion of them," is valid, and caries the right of action for the taking by a creditor of that part of the property which remained *in specie* and was not made merchandise, though used by the husband in his business. (*Id.*)

12. The facts that real estate was conveyed to a married woman, in October, 1849, and that the consideration therefor was paid by the husband; that a judgment was recovered against the husband in May, 1847, and that in October, 1851, another judgment was recovered against the husband for a debt contracted in 1847, do not, of themselves, justify the conclusion that such conveyance is void as against a person becoming a creditor of the husband in February, 1859. No conveyance shall be adjudged fraudulent as against creditors solely on the ground that it was not founded on a valuable consideration. The statutes of 1848 and 1849, in relation to the property of married women, do not affect the question, in such case, whether the deed to the wife was or was not fraudulent. (*Tappan* agt. *Butler*, 7 *Bosw.*, 480.)

13. A married woman, by covenanting to pay a mortgage as part of the purchase money of the mortgaged premises conveyed to her, does not bind herself or any of her separate property other than the land so conveyed, unless such deed and covenant are made in the course of a trade or business carried on by her. (*Brown* agt. *Herman*, 14 *Abb.*, 394.)

See HUSBAND AND WIFE, 8. 9. 10. 11. 12.

See DOWER, 1.

See WITNESS, 9.

MASTER AND SERVANT.

1. A master is responsible to his servant for injuries received by the latter from defects in the building in which the services are rendered, which the master knew, or ought to have known. (*Ryan* agt. *Fowler*, 24 *N. Y. R.*, 410.)

2. *Held*, accordingly, that a girl injured by the fall of a privy attached in an insecure and dangerous manner to the factory in which she was employed, may recover damages from the employer. (*Id.*)

3. The case of *Seymour* agt. *Maddox* (71 *Eng. L. and Eq.*, 326,) questioned. (*Id.*)

4. A master who has not taken sufficient care in employing servants suitable to the work undertaken, or who has failed to direct them properly in its performance, is liable for injuries to others arising from such neglect. (*Carman* agt. *The Mayor, &c., of New York*, 14 *Abb.*, 301.)

See RAILROAD COMPANIES, 34.

METROPOLITAN POLICE.

1. By § 60 of the *rules* of the *commissioners of the Metropolitan police*, of the city of New York, passed under and in pursuance of 27th section of the act of the legislature of April, 1860, it is provided that the superintendent, inspectors, captains and sergeants of police will be deemed to be *always on duty*. (*Hart* agt. *Smith*, *ante*, 425.)

2. By the 34th section of the act of April, 1860, it is declared that "no person holding office under this act shall be liable to military or jury duty, nor to arrest on civil process, or to service of subpœnas from civil courts, *whilst actually on duty*." (*Id.*)

3. *Held*, that the 60th section of the rules of the commissioners must be considered as a mere rule or matter relating to discipline, as between the commissioners and those holding office under them. It cannot be deemed to affect in any manner *the rights of third parties* under the 34th section of the act, when persons holding office under the act *are not actually on duty*. (*Id.*)

4. Though they may be deemed to be on duty, yet if they are not *actually on duty*, these officers are liable to *arrest and to be served with subpœnas*. (*Id.*)

5. The public keeping of intoxicating liquors on Sunday is not a *misdemeanor* under the police act of 1860. (*People* agt. *Osmer*, *ante*, 451.)

6. An order was given to the *relator* as a member of the Metropolitan police by one of its sergeants to proceed to Hamilton avenue, Brooklyn, and either kill a dog which had bitten a child, or bring the dog to the station house. The *relator* did neither, alleging that the order was *illegal*. After a trial before the board of police, he was removed for *disobedience of orders*. (*People ex rel. Dillon* agt. *Metropolitan police*, *ante*, 481.)

7. *Held*, that the order was a *legal and proper* one, which the *relator* was bound to obey. (*Id.*)

8. Such a case is not one in which this court should interfere. The discipline of the police force of a large city to be effectual must be sharp and severe, and vigorously applied. Disobedience of orders is an offence which should not be extenuated. (*Id.*)

9. Where a person is arrested in the day time, in the city of Brooklyn, for violating a city ordinance, it is the duty of the officer to take him before a police justice, or one of the justices elected under the act to establish courts of civil and criminal jurisdiction in that city, passed March 24, 1849. But where the courts are not open when such arrest is made, the person arrested may be detained at the station house, but cannot be imprisoned in a cell at the station house. (*Schneider* agt. *McLane*, 36 *Barb.*, 495.)

See Mandamus, 2.

MORTGAGEE.

1. A mortgagee may maintain a personal action against a grantee of the mortgaged premises who has assumed to pay the incumbrance. (*Burr* agt. *Beers*, 24 *N. Y. R.*, 178.)

2. He may pursue this remedy without foreclosing the mortgage and without joining the mortgagor as defendant. (*Id.*)

3. An instrument, in the form of a mortgage, but containing the name of no mortgagee, does not become effectual by its delivery to one who advances money upon the agreement that he shall hold the paper as security for his loan. (*Chauncey* agt. *Arnold*, 24 *N. Y. R.*, 330.)

4. Whether it could be made effectual by parol authority from the mortgagor to insert the lender's name as mortgagee: *Quere*. (*Id.*)

See Deed, 1. 2. 3.

MORTGAGE FORECLOSURE.

1. The allowance or refusal *of costs* in actions for the *strict foreclosure of mortgages*, is in the *discretion of the court*. (*O'Hara* agt. *Brophy*, *ante*, 379.)

2. Where the *notice* prescribed by § 131 of the Code has not been served, it does not deprive the court of the power in equity cases to *award costs* for unreasonably defending, against defendants upon whom a copy of the *complaint* has been served. (*Id.*)

3. It is not necessary to the *commencement* of any action that a copy of the *complaint* be served upon the defendant; he is brought into court by the *summons alone*. (*Id.*)

4. A *sale of mortgaged premises will be set aside* where the owner of the equity of redemption *appealed in good faith* from the judgment of foreclosure of the county court, but owing to *imperfect justifications of his sureties* in the undertakings given on the appeal, the sale was not stayed, and the plaintiff proceeded and sold the premises, without notice to the owner or return of the undertakings, bidding off the same himself or by his agent for one-third less than their real value, and taking a decree against the owner for the balance. (*Gould* agt. *Libby*, *ante*, 440.)

5. An *assignee of a mortgage* takes it subject to the same *equity* that it was subject to in the hands of the *assignor*, and the rule that it is only an equity residing in the *original debtor*, and not the latent equities of third persons against the assignor that have this effect, does not exclude any one who so far stands in the place of the debtor *as to have acquired his equity*. It does not exclude a judgment creditor of the debtor claiming to redeem. (*Hartley* agt. *Tatham*, *ante*, 505.)

6. Where a defendant in a mortgage foreclosure suit has succeeded to the rights of the mortgagor, by taking a deed of the premises subject to the mortgage, he may insist upon the fact of an *actual partial payment to the mortgagee*, while he owned the mortgage; a fact which ordinary precaution would have brought to the knowledge of the *assignee*, whether he had inquired of the mortgagor or of the grantee. (*Id.*)

7. An assignee in bankruptcy under the act of 1841, who has notice of a suit for the foreclosure of a mortgage pending against the bankrupt, which he could defend in the name of the bankrupt, is bound by the decree, though not made a party nor intervening in the suit. (*Cleveland* agt. *Boerum*, 24 *N. Y. R.*, 613.)

8. *It seems* that the assignee, or his grantees, if not foreclosed, were limited, by the eighth section of the act of 1841, to the period of two years for the commencement of an action to redeem the land mortgaged: *Per* SUTHERLAND, J.; DENIO, GOULD and ALLEN, JS., concurring. (*Id.*)

9. The remedy against a purchaser who refuses to complete his purchase on a sale under a judgment or decree of a court of equity, is by an application to the court to compel him to complete it, or to resell the property and hold him liable for the loss and expenses. A paper signed by an individual on becoming a purchaser of property at a sheriff's sale, is not a contract, either with the sheriff or the plaintiff in the foreclosure suit, upon which an action can be maintained by the latter as the assignee of the sheriff. It seems that the conditions of a sale by a sheriff on execution, imposing upon the purchaser a liability to pay the amount of any deficiency in case of a resale, will not apply to any case except that of a resale made forthwith, upon failure of the purchaser to pay the required percentage of his purchase. (*Miller* agt. *Collyer*, 36 *Barb.*, 250.)

10. A regular foreclosure by advertisement under the statute, of a mortgage which has in fact been paid before foreclosure, but not satisfied of record, and the sale made in pursuance thereof to a *bona fide* purchaser, is equivalent to a sale under a decree in equity; and is an entire bar of all claim of any person having a lien by judgment subsequent to the mortgage, who shall have been duly served with notice of sale. The mortgagor and his assigns may impeach such a sale by showing that the proper statutory proceedings have not been taken to render the foreclosure effectual; but they cannot, after being served with notice of sale, go further and show that the mortgage was fraudulently foreclosed after having been paid, so as to defeat the title of a *bona fide* purchaser of the premises. (*Warner* agt. *Blakeman*, 36 *Barb.*, 501.)

11. In an action to foreclose a mortgage given to secure the purchase money agreed to be paid for the mortgaged premises, where no covenant in the deed has been broken, and no fraud on the part of the grantors, it is no defence that a part of the premises at the time of the conveyance and mortgage was incumbered by an unexpired lease. Where there is a mutual mistake as to a material fact for which a court of equity would relieve, a party desiring relief on that ground must, on discovering the mistake, offer to rescind. The purchaser in such case, there being no fraud, cannot, if he retain the property, avoid paying the full contract price. (*Sandford* agt. *Travers*, 7 *Bosw.*, 498.)

See MORTGAGE, 1. 2.
See USURY, 9.

MORTGAGE OF PERSONAL PROPERTY.

1. No *conveyance* can be sustained on the ground of *good faith*, as against a *prior unrecorded* mortgage or deed for value, unless made for a *valuable consideration*. (*Tiffany* agt. *Warren*, *ante*, 293.)

2. An honest *existing demand* is a valuable consideration; but a conveyance on such consideration is not in *good faith* when coming in conflict with a *prior* conveyance given for value. It is the want of good faith, and not the want of a valuable consideration, which prevents full effect from being given to a subsequent conveyance made on account of an *antecedent debt*. (*Id.*)

3. It was well established on principle and authority, when the statute in relation to filing mortgages of personal property was passed, that subsequent purchasers and mortgagees, on account of *pre-existing indebtedness*, were not holders in *good faith*, when their claims were brought in conflict with a *prior unrecorded* mortgage or conveyance otherwise valid. (*Id.*)

4. A person whose real interest is that of a *mortgagee*, and who has *never taken possession of the vessel*, is not answerable for *supplies*, though he holds a *bill of sale* vesting in him the *legal title*, and though the vessel may be *registered in his name* at the custom house, accompanied by his oath that he is the true and only owner. (*Baxter* agt. *Wallace*, *ante*, 484.)

5. To make a mortgagee responsible for supplies, it must be shown either that he *was in possession of the vessel*, or that they were furnished *at his request*, or by the direction of some person *authorized to contract on his behalf*. (*Id.*)

6. An agreement, upon the mortgage of chattels, that the mortgagor shall keep possession and retail the goods for cash only, paying over the money to the mortgagee, is not fraudulent in law, but presents a question of good faith for the jury. (*Ford* agt. *Williams*, 24 *N. Y. R.*, 359.)

7. The attorney in an execution, who refused to state whether he directed the sale of particular chattels by instruction of his client, and challenged a suit against himself, is estopped from denying that he acted on his individual responsibility. (*Id.*)

8. The owner of such chattels, who states his claim and forbids the sale, may purchase the property without impairing his right of action for the trespass. (*Id.*)

MOTION.

1. An *infant plaintiff* cannot commence an action without the appointment of a *guardian*. (*Freyberg* agt. *Pelerin*, *ante*, 202.)

2. Where such an action is commenced without such an appointment, the defendant may *move to set aside the summons and complaint, &c., for irregularity*. He is not confined to his remedy by answer in the nature of a plea in *abatement*. (*Id.*)

3. A motion to set aside any proceeding on the ground of irregularity must be made at once, and promptly, before the moving party takes any other step in the cause. (*Persse & Brooks' Paper Works* agt. *Willett*, 14 *Abb.*, 119.)

4. In an action upon a negotiable promissory note, an answer that the plaintiff, prior to the commencement of the action, for a good consideration, sold and delivered the notes to *John Doe*, who was the owner and holder of the notes at the commencement of the action, is not frivolous. To warrant the striking out of a pleading as frivolous, it must be clearly bad on inspection merely. (*Smith* agt. *Mead*, 14 *Abb.*, 262.)

5. No application to set aside proceedings for irregularity merely will be allowed unless made within a reasonable time, nor where the party applying has taken a step after knowlege of the irregularity. But the right to put in an answer to an amended complaint is substantial, and a waiver of it should not be implied. (*Low* agt. *Graydon*, 14 *Abb.*, 444.)

See New Trial, 1. 2. 3. 4.
See Attachment, 1.
See Non-Suit, 1.
See Irrelevant and Redundant Matter, 1. 2. 3.

MUNICIPAL CORPORATIONS.

1. Where an act of the legislature vested in the corporation of the city of New York the title to the soil under the water, and the right to fill in and ex-

tend the Battery into the river, not exceeding six hundred feet, with a *limitation on the use of the land*, so to be made out of the water, for any purpose except certain *public purposes* therein expressed, *held*, that any grant or other conveyance of the land to an individual *for the purpose* of widening a pier and to extend it to the permanent or exterior line, or for any such *private use*, would be void, and would justify the state in claiming an *injunction* to prevent such a violation of the conditions imposed upon the corporation. (*People* agt. *Vanderbilt*, *ante*, 301.)

2. The power to compel a *removal* of an obstruction after it has been erected, does not prevent an application to the court to *prohibit the erection* of such obstruction before it is completed. (*Id.*)

3. *Held*, also, that if there was no legal authority for the erection of the pier, it was a *nuisance*, and no *evidence* was admissible to show, that though illegal, it would do no harm. (*Id.*)

4. When the law authorizes the common council of a city to impose the expenses of paving streets, or other improvements, by assessment upon the *owners of property benefited*, the assessment becomes a *lien* upon the lots benefited; and it is an undue assumption of power in the common council to incur the expense and attempt its collection from *tax-payers at large*, even under a prior ordinance which required them thereafter to keep such streets repaved and kept in repair *at the expense of the corporation*. (*Rhinelander* agt. *Mayor, &c. of New York*, *ante*, 304.)

5. Where a sum of money had been raised by the city of New York, in pursuance of an act of the legislature, and appropriated by the common council for the purpose of paying the relator for printing, &c., which sum could not be appropriated to any other purpose, *held*, that it was a clear recognition by the legislature and the common council, to the relator's right to payment, and a direction that he should be paid. And upon the comptroller's refusal to pay, a *mandamus* was the proper remedy, where it appeared no action would lie against the corporation. (*People ex rel. Baker* agt. *Haws*, 36 *Barb.*, 59.)

6. A municipal corporation is not liable in damages to an individual for injuries caused by an opening in a sidewalk, made by an owner of the soil or adjacent land, without proof of notice of the insufficiency or defect, and neglect to cause it to be remedied. (*Hart* agt. *City of Brooklyn*, 36 *Barb.*, 226.)

7. The provision of the act of April 12, 1859, prohibiting the recovery of costs against municipal corporations, unless notice of the claim has been given to the comptroller of the city before suit brought, is applicable to claims for damages on account of negligence of the city authorities, as well as to demands upon contract. (*Id.*)

8. Where a lease, made by a municipal corporation pursuant to a sale for an unpaid assessment, is by law evidence of the regularity of the sale, the court in cases of substantial irregularity will restrain the making of such lease. (*Mathews* agt. *The Mayor, &c. of New York*, 14 *Abb.*, 209.)

See NEGLIGENCE, 1. 2. 3.

NEGLIGENCE.

1. A *corporation ordinance* forbidding a greater rate of speed than that fixed as legal therein, for vehicles in the city of New York, is competent and proper *evidence* in an action for damages caused by being run over by a vehicle in such streets, to show that the plaintiff was free from negligence, though it furnishes no evidence of negligence in fact on the part of the defendants. (*Williams* agt. *O'Keefe*, *ante*, 16.)

2. A citizen of the city of New York is presumed to know of the existence of its ordinances and their provisions, and has a right on the presumption that they will be obeyed. The law of negligence discussed by Monell, J. (*Id.*)

3. Unless proof of negligence on the part of the plaintiff is so strong that the court would set aside a verdict in his favor as against the weight of evidence, it is not proper to take that question from the jury. (*Id.*)

4. Knowingly to allow a child of less than four years of age to go at large in a public street without a protector, is such negligence in his parents or guardians as will, if unexplained, prevent a recovery by him for a personal injury. No matter how gross or evident the negligence of the driver of a vehicle may be, if another, by his own negligence, exposes himself to injury, he has no remedy. (*Mangam* agt. *Brooklyn City R. R. Co.*, 36 *Barb.*, 230.)

5. Where a person employs another to do a piece of work, and the person employed does it by his own workmen, using his own discretion as to the best mode of doing it, and having exclusive control of the matter, and a third person is injured while the work is in progress, by the careless manner in which it was done, the person employed and his servants guilty of the negligence are alone liable for the injury. The liability in such case is confined to the persons guilty of negligence, and to their principal. (*O'Rourke* agt. *Hart*, 7 *Bosw.*, 511.)

See Railroad Companies.
See New Trial, 5.
See Master and Servant, 1. 2. 3. 4.
See Damages, 2. 3. 4.
See Principal and Agent, 2.
See Common Carriers.
See Municipal Corporations, 6. 7.

NEW TRIAL.

1. Where, in an action upon a *promissory note*, the defendant interposes the defence and proves *infancy*, when the note was given, the jury should be *directed* to find a verdict for the defendant, although some facts may have come out on the trial tending to show that the defendant had been doing business for himself, and representing himself as of full age. (*Allgro* agt. *Duncan*, *ante*, 210.)

2. And where, in such case, the judge omitted to give such direction to the jury, but gave them particular instructions as to the law of the case, and they found a verdict for the *plaintiff*, *held* that the verdict should be set aside on a motion made upon the minutes of the judge, under § 264 of the Code, if the awkward phraseology of that section could be applied to the case. (*Id.*)

3. It must be assumed that a motion to set aside a verdict, and for a new trial "upon insufficient evidence," under § 264, means a motion for a new trial on the ground that the *verdict is against evidence*, as was the clear and plain language under the old practice. (*Id.*)

4. A safe rule in such cases is to apply the former practice and interpret the obscurities and deficiencies of the Code by its light. (*Id.*)

5. On a motion for a *new trial* in an action for damages caused by *negligence*, where the plaintiff has been *nonsuited* at the trial, and where he submitted, without objection, to have the question of negligence passed upon by the court instead of the jury, *held* that he is precluded on such motion from insisting that the question of *negligence was one exclusively for the jury*. (*Clark* agt. *Mayor, &c., of New York*, *ante*, 333.)

6. Where the *jury*, on conflicting evidence in a justice's court, found that the defendant (an attorney-at-law) put in an answer for the plaintiff in an action for strict foreclosure, *without authority* from the plaintiff, *held* that there being evidence to sustain the finding of the jury, and the evidence against it not so preponderant as to create the conviction that it must have proceeded from passion, prejudice, corruption or palpable mistake, the verdict must be sustained. (*O'Hara* agt. *Brophy*, *ante*, 379.)

7. Where in an action to recover damages for an injury caused by the alleged negligence of the defendant, the jury find for the plaintiff and assess his damages at six cents; and the uncontradicted evidence in the case is entirely adverse to such a finding, the verdict will be set aside as contrary to evidence. (*Robbins* agt. *Hudson River R. R. Co.*, 7 *Bosw.*, 1.)

8. Where a verdict is contrary to the evidence and the law of the case, as given to the jury by the court, a new trial will be granted, with costs of the former trial to abide the event. (*Jacobsohn* agt. *Belmont*, 7 *Bosw.*, 14.)

9. A motion for a new trial on a case cannot be made as a matter of right, after judgment is perfected. In a case of conflicting testimony, neither party is entitled to an instruction to the jury, founded on the assumption that the testimony of either of the witnesses is to be treated as accurate. A party's right to instructions is limited to undisputed facts, or to a hypothetical statement of facts, which it is left to the jury to determine upon the evidence. (*Gurney* agt. *Smithson*, 7 *Bosw.*, 396.)

10. In granting a new trial where the judge before whom the trial was had committed no error, payment of the costs of the trial and all subsequent proceedings should be imposed as a

condition of granting it; and on granting the order, the costs must be regularly adjusted before the time allowed for their payment, under rule 57, begins to run. (*North* agt. *Sargeant*, 14 *Abb.*, 223.)

11. After a new trial has been granted by the general term on application of the defendant, on payment of costs, plaintiff will not be allowed by the special term to discontinue while the amount of the costs is unpaid. (*Id.*)

See Costs, 5. 6. 16.

See Evidence, 2.

See Undertaking, 1. 2. 3. 4.

See Appeal, 11. 12.

NON-SUIT.

1. It was *held* no error for the judge at the trial to deny a motion to *dismiss the complaint*, where the application was made *during the progress of the examination of a witness*; and where the application appeared in the double character of an *objection to evidence*, and on the ground that there was *no consideration in the agreement* upon which the action was brought. (*Winfield* agt. *Potter*, *ante*, 446.)

See Railroad Companies, 1. 9.

See New Trial, 5. 6. 7.

See Trial, 8.

NOTICE.

1. A judgment creditor having *supplementary proceedings* pending, is not entitled to *eight* days' notice of an application for a receiver by *another creditor*. A less notice is sufficient. (*Leggett* agt. *Sloan*, *ante*, 479.)

See Highways, 12.

See Attorney, 13.

See Bills of Exchange and Promissory Notes, 10.

See Appeal, 23.

NUISANCE.

See Municipal Corporations.

ORDERS.

1. An *order* made out of court, upon notice, must be first *entered with the clerk* before an *appeal* can be taken. (*Code*, § 350.) (*Galit* agt. *Finch*, *ante*, 193.)

2. And when an order is required to be entered with the clerk, and a party is required to give notice of the order, he *cannot give the notice until he has entered the order*. (*Id.*)

3. Therefore, as regards all orders granted on notice, which are required to be entered with the clerk, the party has no right to give the written notice allowed by § 332 of the Code, until *after the order has been entered*. (*Id.*)

4. Where the order was entered May 27th, and the notice of appeal was served on the 27th June, *held*, that the service of the notice of appeal was *in time*. (*Id.*)

5. Rule 42 does not require the party *demurring to serve on the opposite party* any copy of the pleadings or other papers when the question to be decided arises on demurrer. (*Id.*)

6. When an *injunction order* has been allowed, and the same has been served, and the parties in the suit have appeared and taken steps in the action, and acquiesced in the injunction, no judge has authority to *modify it ex parte*. (*Peck* agt. *Yorks*, *ante*, 363.)

7. Section 324 of the Code was designed to allow a judge who had hastily or improvidently granted an order to rectify the error, *if applied to immediately, and before any steps are taken in the action*. It was not intended to give an unlimited right to vacate orders granted *ex parte*. (*Id.*)

See Appeal, 20. 21.

PARTIES.

1. In an action against an *assignee* for the benefit of creditors, brought by a creditor for himself and all other creditors who might come in and avail themselves of the action, claiming an *accounting* by the assignee, and that the assignment be *reformed*, by substituting the proper name of an *indorser* with the plaintiff on a promissory note preferred in the assignment, instead of the name appearing in the assignment, which was alleged to have been mentioned or copied by mistake, *held*, on demurrer to complaint for defect of *parties*, that the *indorser* of the note whose name was sought to be substituted by another, and the *assignees*, together with other *creditors*, standing

in a lower class than that in which such note was stated, were necessary and proper parties, on a re-formation of the assignment. (*Garner* agt. *Wright*, *ante*, 144.)

2. *Misjoinder* of parties plaintiffs is ground of *demurrer* to the complaint. (*Walrath* agt. *Handy*, *ante*, 358.)

3. In such case the complaint does not state facts sufficient to constitute a cause of action. (*Id.*)

4. Actions by public officers, as such, should be brought in their individual names, with the title of their office added. If in an action brought by one as "chamberlain, &c.," no objection is taken on the trial, that the plaintiff is not chamberlain, it will be assumed, on appeal, that the fact of his being the incumbent of the office was taken for granted. (*Paige* agt. *Fazackerly*, 36 *Barb.*, 392.)

See WITNESSES, 2. 3. 4. 5. 6.

See COMMISSIONS, 2. 3. 4.

See SUPPLEMENTARY PROCEEDINGS, 9.

See EXECUTORS AND ADMINISTRATORS, 5. 6.

PARTNERS AND PARTNERSHIPS.

1. Where the defendant denied that the claim in suit was for money received for the benefit of the defendant's *co-partnership firm*, but was money borrowed by his co-partner for his individual benefit, and that it was never appropriated to the use of the firm. (*Best* agt. *Starks*, *ante*, 58.)

2. *Held*, that evidence to show that the money borrowed was not in fact used in the business of the firm, was properly excluded where the evidence was not sufficient to cast any suspicions upon the *bona fides* of the loan being for the firm. Also that evidence to show that on a final settlement of the partnership accounts by arbitration, this debt was not mentioned on either side, was properly excluded. Also, evidence to show that in the formation of the partnership, the partners arranged between themselves to procure what money they should want in their business from a particular source, was properly excluded. Also, evidence to show that no claim was made upon the defendant for the debt for a year and a half after the plaintiff knew of the insolvency of the other partner, was properly excluded. (*Id.*)

3. *Held*, also on the motion for a new trial, that the case belonged to that class of cases of conflicting evidence and doubtful facts, in which the verdict of a jury one way or the other is practically conclusive, and ought not to be disturbed. (*Id.*)

4. The *property of a co-partnership* cannot be seized and sold on an *attachment* issued against *one* of the partners only. It is only the *interest* in the property of the partner in the attachment that can be seized and sold, which is his share in the *surplus* of the property, after payment of the partnership debts. (*Abels* agt. *Westervelt*, *ante*, 284.)

5. The other partner has a right, as against such an attachment, to *retain* the property for the purpose of paying the debts of the partnership. (*Id.*)

6. Where a person under a *private agreement* with a *special partner* in a limited co-partnership furnishes a certain portion of the capital which the special partner puts into the business of the firm in his own name, and is to have a certain portion of the income or profits which the special partner derives from the business, with a privilege of examining from time to time into the business matters of the firm, he and the special partner become thereby *general partners*. (*Buckley* agt. *Bramhall*, *ante*, 455.)

7. They are made so by the operation of the statute, which declares that all persons interested in the partnership shall be liable as general partners, if any *false statement* is made in the *certificate* or *affidavit* by which the limited co-partnership is formed. (*Id.*)

8. A *published notice* of a *limited partnership* does not operate under the statute as an *actual dissolution* until *four weeks* after the publication. (*Id.*)

9. *Each member of a co-partnership* has a right to dispose of his interest in the partnership property, in good faith and for a valid consideration, unless some creditor has acquired a *lien* thereon. And the right of the creditor is subordinate to this power of the partner to dispose of the property *until it is subjected to the creditor's lien*. (*Field* agt. *Hunt*, *ante*, 463.)

10. Where one partner thus transfers his

interest in the partnership assets to his co-partner, the property so transferred cannot be reached by execution on a judgment recovered against the firm, where the *latter has not been personally served with process*. (*Id.*)

11. The remedy at law has not been exhausted as against the partner not served with process, and of course a *creditor's suit* against the defendants cannot be maintained. (*This affirms the decision S. C. at special term*, 22 *How.*, 329.) (*Id.*)

12. Real estate, acquired with partnership effects in collecting debts due the firm, although so conveyed as to make the partners tenants-in-common at law, is, in equity, considered as converted into personalty, for the purpose of subjecting it to the debts of the firm, in preference to those of the individual partners. (*Collumb* agt. *Read*, 24 *N. Y. R.*, 505.)

13. The trustee under an assignment of land which is declared fraudulent at the suit of a creditor, is not bound to account for the rents received and applied to the terms of the trust before the commencement of the suit, or the attaching of any specific lien on the lands. (*Id.*)

14. When notice of change of firm name is relied upon to exonerate a retiring partner, such change must show that he has withdrawn from the business. A change not indicating this, is insufficient to put dealers upon inquiry. (*American Linen Thread Company* agt. *Wortendyke*, 24 *N. Y. R.*, 550.)

15. Accordingly where one of three brothers, under the firm of Wortendyke Brothers, retired, and, being succeeded by H., the firm was changed to Wortendyke Brothers & Co., *held*, that a dealer with the firm was warranted in assuming that all the former partners remained in the business, and, until notice to the contrary, the brother who had retired continued liable. (*Id.*)

16. When there is no agreement to the contrary, each partner, after a dissolution, possesses the same authority to adjust the affairs of the concern, by collecting its debts and disposing of its property, as before the dissolution. (*Robbins* agt. *Fuller*, 24 *N. Y. R.*, 570.)

17. This right is not lost by the fact that the partnership debts are paid; nor, *it seems*, does it depend upon the state of the accounts between the partners, at all events not as against persons, having no notice of the fact. (*Id.*)

18. To enable creditors of a partnership to recover a debt against one as a partner, on the ground that he held himself out as a partner, they must prove affirmatively that he did so represent himself to them, or that they were informed of such representations before the credit was given to the firm. A person not a partner in fact, in a firm, will not make himself liable to creditors, for the debts of the firm, by representing or holding himself out as a partner, unless it appears that the creditors gave credit to the firm after such representations came to their knowledge. (*Irvin* agt. *Conklin*, 36 *Barb.*, 64.)

19. Where a promissory note, made by a partnership firm to one of its members, for money advanced to the firm, is indorsed by the payee to another, after maturity, the holder may maintain an action on the note against the makers. And such a note is subject to any set-off which the partnership has. (*Sherwood* agt. *Barton*, 36 *Barb.*, 284.)

20. In an action for the partition of real property owned by partners in joint tenancy, where it appeared on the trial that the action had been commenced during the pendency of an action brought by the defendant in another court for a dissolution of partnership and an accounting, which involved the real property in question, *held*, that the complaint must be dismissed. (*Danvers* agt. *Dorrity*, 14 *Abb.*, 206.)

21. A covenant in articles of copartnership prohibiting either partner from continuing in any business within one block of the premises occupied by the firm for a limited period after its dissolution, will be enforced by injunction. (*Shearman* agt. *Hart*, 14 *Abb.*, 358.)

See Principal and Agent, 4.

See Jurisdiction, 4.

PAYMENT.

1. Where the complaint averred the payment of a certain sum of money as "an excess of an amount awarded, and not of right due and payable to the defendant; and that said payment was made under a mistake of fact on the part of

the plaintiffs," &c., *held*, that *evidence* as to the validity and correctness of the proceedings of the commissioners of estimate and assessment, and as to the sufficiency of the award made by them to the defendant, was properly allowed under the issue tendered by defendant to such allegations. (*Mayor, &c., of New York* agt. *Erben*, *ante*, 358.)

2. The rule with respect to *voluntary payments* is, that if a party has actually paid what the law would not have compelled him to pay, *but what in equity and good conscience he ought*, he cannot *recover it back* in an action for *money had and received*. (*Id.*)

3. The presumption of payment of the purchase money by one in possession of land under a contract to purchase, arising from lapse of time, cannot be interposed as an affirmative defence to an action to recover the possession of the land. If such presumption is interposed, the fact upon which it proceeds must be affirmatively proved. (*Brady* agt. *Begun*, 36 *Barb.*, 533.)

See GUARANTY, 2.

See ACCOUNT, 1.

See STATUTE OF LIMITATIONS, 4.

See BILLS OF EXCHANGE AND PROMISSORY NOTES, 7.

PERSONAL PROPERTY.

See EXECUTION AND LEVY, 4.

See COSTS, 21.

PLANKROADS.

1. Under the general plankroad act, (*ch.* 210 *of* 1847,) those only who subscribe the articles of association are entitled to stock or compellable to pay for the same. (*Poughkeepsie, &c., Plankroad Co.* agt. *Griffin*, 24 *N. Y. R.*, 150.)

2. The preliminary subscription and other steps prior to the signing of the articles of association are provisional and inchoate, creating no fixed right and imposing no obligation on the parties. (*Id.*)

3. *It seems* that one otherwise liable as a corporator would not be discharged by reason of the legislature's having extended the time for laying plank and permitting the corporation, in the meantime, to act and collect tolls as a turnpike company. *Per* DENIO, J. (*Id.*)

PLEDGE.

1. Goods in warehouse, subject to be withdrawn at pleasure by a factor, on discharging the lien of government for duties, may be regarded as in his possession, so as to support a pledge thereof made by him, independent of the provisions of the act in regard to documentary evidences of title. (*Cartwright* agt. *Wilmerding*, 24 *N. Y. R.*, 521.)

PRINCIPAL AND AGENT.

1. A subscription by the agent of the party to be charged is sufficient under the statute of frauds, though the name or existence of a principal does not appear upon the instrument. (*Dykers* agt. *Townsend*, 24 *N. Y. R.*, 57.)

2. Where creditors receive from their debtor the note of a third person, for collection, the proceeds to be applied on the debt held by them against the debtor, they will be deemed to have assumed the obligation of an attorney or agent of the debtor, for the collection of the demand, and are bound to use ordinary diligence in its collection. Negligence in such a case is a question of fact. (*Buckingham* agt. *Payne*, 36 *Barb.*, 81.)

3. A cause of action for the conversion by the defendant of funds intrusted to him as an agent, for which he has not accounted to his principal, is assignable. Such a cause of action would survive to the personal representatives. Where an agent has duties to perform towards his principal, in the nature of a trust, he falls within the suspected relation, and the law indulges the presumption of fraud, against a release procured by him from his principal, although no fraud is visible to the court. One cannot act for himself as vendor, and as agent for another, as purchaser, in transferring securities. (*Gould* agt. *Gould*, 36 *Barb.*, 270.)

4. An authority given by a partnership firm to its agent, to advance moneys for the purchase of notes or bills to be remitted to the firm, will not, under ordinary circumstances, justify the agent in continuing to make such advances, after being notified of a change in the firm by the admission of new partners. But if the bills purchased, after notice of the change in the firm, have been remitted to the firm, received and receipted by the new mem-

bers, retained by them, and used and applied in their business, this is equivalent to a renewed authorization by the new firm, of the authority given by the old firm. (*Callanan* agt. *Van Vleck*, 36 *Barb.*, 324.)

5. An agent cannot act for his own benefit in relation to the subject matter of the agency, to the injury of his principal. An agent is bound to follow the instructions of his principal; and if he neglects to do so, he will be liable for the loss or damage which his principal sustains. (*Bruce* agt. *Davenport*, 36 *Barb.*, 349.)

6. While an agent, strictly pursuing his authority, commits a wrong, the rule that he thereby binds the principal, does not apply to a case where the agent, departing from his line of duty, is bargaining on his own account, and securing a benefit for his own private advantage exclusively. When an agent does not pretend nor assume to be acting for another, but purely for his own benefit, a subsequent ratification will not bind the principal. (*Fellows* agt. *Commissioners, &c., of Oneida*, 36 *Barb.*, 655.)

7. Where a banker receives a note for collection by a person who is a resident of a foreign country, and transmits it to his agent at the maker's residence for collection, and the owner of the note is fully advised thereof, and of subsequent proceedings for its collection, to which he makes no objection, and the note is finally lost, in pursuing such measures, without any fault of the agent, the owner cannot maintain an action against the agent to recover the loss on the ground of a violation or neglect of duty of the agent. (*Jacobsohn* agt. *Belmont*, 7 *Bosw.*, 14.)

8. A mere agent cannot prosecute a suit in his own name for the benefit of his principal. (*Redfield* agt. *Middleton*, 7 *Bosw.*, 649.)

See Bank Check, 1. 2. 3.
See Negligence, 5.
See Railroad Companies.
See Sale, 2.

PUBLIC OFFICE.

1. In pleading a party's title to public office, an averment that under and in pursuance of the laws of this state, on a specified day, he was duly appointed to fill such office, and duly made and executed his official bond, with sureties, and took the oath of office required by law, and was thereby constituted such officer, and was thenceforth entitled to hold and administer such office, is sufficient on demurrer. (*Platt* agt. *Stout*, 14 *Abb.*, 178.)

2. An action to recover fees of a public office is maintainable against a person who has wrongfully received the fees of such office, which the plaintiff holds or is entitled to hold. A cause of action in favor of a public officer against an intruder for wrongfully receiving the fees of the office, is assignable. (*Id.*)

RAILROAD COMPANIES.

1. A *defendant* may move for a *non-suit* when the plaintiff rests; or he may give testimony and rest, and then move for a non-suit. The refusal of the judge to grant such motion is equally, in either case, a good ground of *exception*. (*Ernst* agt. *Hudson River R. R. Co.*, *ante*, 97, *court of appeals*.)

2. After the testimony has been given by the defendant, and both parties have *rested*, and the defendant moves upon the whole evidence for a *non-suit*, it is *the right and duty* of the circuit judge to direct a non-suit at that stage of the cause, if the plaintiff is not entitled to recover, and a verdict in his favor could not be sustained. (*Id.*)

3. Where there is a *disputed question of fact*—as, whether the engine bell of a railroad train was rung at the proper time before crossing a public highway, and evidence upon both sides is given, which is contradictory—it is especially and appropriately a question for the *jury* to determine the means of knowledge and credibility of the several witnesses, and where the weight of evidence rests upon this issue. (*Id.*)

4. In an action for damages for injuries to the person, caused by *negligence*, the plaintiff must present a case of *unmixed* negligence; a case where the injury is the result *exclusively of the defendant's negligence;* where no negligence or fault of his own contributed in *any degree* to producing such injury. (*Id.*)

5. In no case is it the duty of the circuit judge to submit a case to the jury, unless the evidence is so doubtful or conflicting that a verdict for the plaintiff or defendant could be sustained, and

ought not to be disturbed, upon the principles governing *the review, by the courts, of the verdicts of juries.* (*Id.*)

6. The doctrine that the courts should not *non-suit*, or set aside verdicts, as without or against evidence, in cases of *negligence*, because such verdicts, from the nature of the case, and the character of the facts and circumstances to be investigated, and going to establish negligence, are based so much upon mere opinion, that they cannot possibly be *reviewed*, wholly misconceives the theory upon which justice is administered in this country. (*Id.*)

7. It is not the *jury*, but the *courts* which administer justice. The duty and responsibility of seeing that equal and impartial justice is meted out to all men, devolves, under the constitution, by the common law, upon the *judges of the courts*. Juries are mere *assistants* of the courts, whose province it is to aid them in the decision of disputed questions of fact. If there is no real *dispute* in a case, the court gives judgment. (*Id.*)

8. In the judgment and opinion of a majority of men, *common prudence forbids* the attempt by any person to cross the track of a *railroad* in constant use, without first taking the precaution to *look both ways* upon the track, and see and ascertain that a train is not approaching in either direction; and the omission to do so is, *per se, gross negligence*, in view of the danger to be avoided, and the fatal consequences involved in any accident resulting from such omission. (*Id.*)

9. As upon the whole issue in this case, it was impossible for the jury to find that the plaintiff had made out a clear, affirmative case of negligence on the part of the defendants, *unmixed* with any degree of negligence on the part of the deceased, contributing to the injury sustained, it was not the duty of the circuit judge to have submitted the case to the jury, and the motion for a *non-suit was properly granted*. (*Reversing the decision at general term supreme court*, 19 *How. Pr. R.*, 205.) (*Id.*)

10. No proof of *pecuniary* or *special damage* to the plaintiff or next of kin is necessary to sustain an action brought under the statute by the administrator of the deceased for injuries to the person. (*See to the same effect Oldfield* agt. *N. Y. Central R. R. Co.*, 14 *N. Y. R.*, 310.) (*Keller* agt. *N. Y. Central R. R. Co.*, *ante*, 172.)

11. The question of *negligence* in all cases involves a question of *fact*, and it is only where the question of fact is *free from all doubt* that the court has a right to apply the law without the action of the jury; that is, the facts may be so clear and decided that the inference of negligence is irresistible; and in every such case it is the duty of the court to decide; but when the facts or the inference to be drawn from them are *in any degree doubtful*, the only proper rule is to submit the whole matter to the jury under proper instructions. (*Id.*)

12. The *negligence* of the party, which will *defeat his action* in these cases, is nothing more than a *want of proper care*; and this question is always more or less affected by the conduct of the *opposing party*. (*Id.*)

13. It is not always negligence to cross a railroad track. If the crossing is at a time when no train is due, and cannot be reasonably expected to pass, it is *not negligence*. It is not negligence when a person uses his faculties the best he is capable of under the circumstances. (*Id.*)

14. In this case, the deceased mother and daughter, passengers on a mail train of the defendants' cars going west, left the cars at a station where they desired to stop, while the cars were on a slow move forward, getting off on the south side where there was another railroad track, over seven feet distant; they attempted to cross the latter track, when an express train going east, at the rate of thirty or forty miles an hour, struck and killed them instantly. The two trains should have passed each other two and a half miles west of the station—the mail train being behind time; *held*, that the inference to be drawn from a pretty broad field of facts and circumstances, which legitimately belonged to the jury, rendered it a fit case to be submitted to the jury, and the defendants' motion for a *non-suit* was properly *denied*. (*Id.*)

15. A contract between a railroad corporation and a gratuitous passenger, by which the former is exempted from liability under any circumstances of the negligence of its agents for any injury to the passenger is not against law or public policy, and is valid. (*Wells* agt. *N. Y. Central R. R. Co.*, 24 *N. Y. R.*, 181.)

Digest.

16. It is immaterial whether the negligence of the agents be slight or gross. The supposed distinction between different degrees of negligence, in respect to the liability of common carriers, discarded as illusory and impracticable. (*Id.*)

17. A railroad corporation cannot, by contract, exempt itself from liability to a passenger for damage resulting from its own willful misconduct or recklessness, which is equivalent thereto. (*Perkins* agt. *N. Y. Central R. R. Co.*, 24 *N. Y. R.*, 196.)

18. But in respect to a gratuitous passenger it may contract for exemption from liability for any degree of negligence in its servants, other than the board of directors or managers who represent the corporation itself, for all general purposes. (*Id.*)

19. Whether the corporation is liable to a free passenger, so contracting, for negligence in the construction of the road, as upon an implied guaranty of its security, when the misconduct from which the injury resulted was that of a trackmaster, who knowingly used rotten material in building a bridge, there being no evidence that it was known to the superior managing officers. *Quere.* (*Id.*)

20. *It seems* that the owner of cattle, transported for hire on a railroad, and who goes along in charge of them, under a contract that "the persons riding free to take charge of the stock do so at their own risk of personal injury from whatever cause," is not to be regarded as a gratuitous passenger. *Per* WRIGHT, DENIO and DAVIES, Js. (*Smith* agt. N. Y. *Central R. R. Co.*, 24 *N. Y. R.*, 222.)

21. Whether, as to one who, in the manner stated, gives some consideration for being carried, a contract is valid which aims to exempt the carrier from liability for damages resulting from the negligence of his servants. *Quere.* (*Id.*)

22. The owner of cattle traveling in charge of them, under such a contract, and paying no independent consideration for the conveyance of himself, was injured by the gross negligence of an agent of the carrier in using an unfit and dangerous car. The carrier was held liable by a divided court, four of the judges going on the ground that the contract for exemption from liability was void, as against public policy; and the fifth, that the negligence, as it respected the machinery of transportation, is imputable to the carrier himself. (*Id.*)

23. A railroad corporation which has completed its road between the termini named in its charter or articles, forfeits its franchise by abandoning or ceasing to operate a part of the route. (*People* agt. *Albany and Vermont R. R. Co.*, 24 *N. Y. R.*, 261.)

24. *It seems* that the corporation owes a duty to the public to exercise the franchise granted to it, and that it cannot abandon a portion of its road and incur a forfeiture at its mere pleasure. *Per* DENIO, SUTHERLAND, ALLEN and SMITH, Js. (*Id.*)

25. The remedy, however, is not an action in equity, on behalf of the public, to enforce a specific performance, but by mandamus or indictment, or, by the election of the State, by proceeding to annul the corporation. (*Id.*)

26. The statute (*ch.* 270 *of* 1847) making a company which owns a railroad connecting with one or more other roads, and receives freight to be transported to a place on the line of a road thus connected, liable as common carriers for the delivery thereof, applies as well where one of the connecting roads is wholly beyond this State as where all are within it. (*Burtis* agt. *Buffalo and State Line R. R. Co.*, 24 *N. Y. R.*, 269.)

27. The statute not only imposes the duty, upon the company undertaking it, of delivering the goods at the place of destination, but enables it to make a special contract for their delivery in a limited time. (*Id.*)

28. *Held*, accordingly, that a company whose road terminated at the boundary of this State, where it connected with a chain of roads running through Pennsylvania, Ohio, &c., was liable under its special contract for the delivery of goods, in three days, at a point in Illinois, upon such chain of roads. (*Id.*)

29. *It seems* that such special contract is valid at common law independently of the statute. *Per* DENIO, DAVIES, GOULD and ALLEN, Js. (*Id.*)

30. A party claiming to have been injured by the negligence of another must fail in his action, unless it appear that he was free from any negligence without which the injury would not have happened. The greatest negligence

on the part of the defendant will not cure the defect of the least negligence contributing to the injury on the plaintiff's part. (*Wilds* agt. *Hudson River R. R. Co.*, 24 *N. Y. R.*, 430.)

31. Cases of negligence form no exception to the rule that it is the judge's duty to non-suit where a verdict for the plaintiff would be clearly against the weight of evidence. (*Id.*)

32. One driving in a highway across a railroad is guilty of negligence fatal to an action, if he does so without looking for a train which he would have seen, or listening for signals of its approach which he would have heard, in time to have avoided a collision. (*Id.*)

33. It is also such negligence in one knowing the position of the railroad and the frequent passage of trains, to approach the crossing at such speed as to be unable to stop his horses before actually getting upon the track. It is error to refuse so to charge without the qualification that the defendant must have used proper precautions to notify travelers of the approach of a train. (*Id.*)

34. A contractor for the construction of part of a railroad is not a laborer or servant, within the provision of the general railroad act, making stockholders personally liable for the debts of the corporation. (*Aikin* agt. *Wasson*, 24 *N. Y. R.*, 482.)

35. To corroborate the conductor on a railroad in respect to the time of the arrival of his train at a station, evidence is admissible that he made a contemporaneous memorandum, in compliance with a regulation requiring it; and the time table regulating the running, stoppage, &c., of such train may also be proved. (*Barker* agt. *N. Y. Central R. R. Co.*, 24 *N. Y. R.*, 599.)

36. So, also, evidence is admissible of the regulations of the corporation, and of the custom of its agents, in respect to giving notice to passengers of the necessity of their changing cars in order to reach a given station. (*Id.*)

37. A passenger was pointed by an agent of the carrier to a train then standing in his sight as one which would convey him to Lyons. That train, after running one hundred ad fifty miles, deflected to a branch road not passing through Lyons, but was followed an hour afterwards by another train which passed through Lyons. *Held*, that the passenger was in fault for being miscarried, if, at or before reaching the point of divergence, the carrier used such means as would have conveyed to a traveler of ordinary intelligence, using reasonable care and attention, information of the necessity of his transferring himself to the second train. (*Id.*)

38. If the traveler, without fault on his part, passed the point of divergence, but was apprised of his error and requested to take a return train on which he would have been carried free, in season to have reached a train which would have carried him to Lyons without delay, his refusal to do so, and persisting in remaining upon the wrong train, renders him a trespasser, liable to ejection from the cars. (*Id.*)

39. Ejectment lies by the owner of the fee in land subject to a public easement, against a party appropriating it to private occupation. (*Carpenter* agt. *Oswego and Syracuse R. R. Co.*, 24 *N. Y. R.*, 655.)

40. The laying down in a street by a railroad corporation of its track and rails is such an exclusive occupation as to give an action to the owner of the fee, although the track has not been used, nor connected with other portions of the railroad which were in use. (*Id.*)

41. Where land has been taken for a turnpike, and afterwards transferred, by legislative authority, to a railroad company, without compensation by the latter to the owner of the fee, he may maintain successive actions for damages resulting from such occupation, as a continuing nuisance. (*Mahon* agt. *N. Y. Central R. R. Co.*, 24 *N. Y. R.*, 658.)

42. The use of the land for a railroad is totally different from that public right of passage for which highways were designed. (*Id.*)

43. It is not against public policy, nor unlawful for a railroad company to convey passengers by stage to and from one of its stations and an adjacent village, in connection with and as a part of its business of transporting passengers upon its road; nor is a contract made by it thus to carry passengers *ultra vires*. Such a contract being lawful, the railroad company, in an action for damages for injuries resulting from negligence of the company to

a passenger riding in such stage, is estopped from denying its validity. (*Buffit* agt. *Troy & Boston R. R. Co.*, 36 *Barb.*, 420.)

44. Where there was sufficient proof of an undertaking on the part of a railroad company to transport a passenger and his goods over its road; and that the company's conductors having accepted and treated such passenger's ticket as sufficient, *held* that the law would presume the contract made by the agent of the company on its behalf to transport the passenger and his goods, was valid and binding upon the company until the contrary appeared. (*Glasco* agt. *N. Y. Central R. R. Co.*, 36 *Barb.*, 557.)

45. The obligation of a railroad company is to take whatever is delivered and received as baggage from a passenger, in the baggage car of a passenger train in which the passenger takes his passage, and take it along with and deliver it to the passenger at the place of destination in the usual manner of transporting and delivering baggage. And this obligation applies to all baggage, whether within or beyond the quantity allowed to a passenger included in the price of his passage. (*Id.*)

46. The statute of 1836 and 1838, incorporating the Auburn & Rochester railroad company, was designed to secure the actual attendance of some fit person, before the jury of appraisers, to assess the value of the land required for the construction of its road through a particular county, as guardian or attorney of an infant owner of land, to attend personally to the interest of the infant upon the appraisement; and without such appearance, all the doings of the jury, in the proceeding, are entirely unauthorized and void. (*Hotchkiss* agt. *Auburn & Rochester R. R. Co.*, 36 *Barb.*, 600.)

47. In an action by an administrator, etc., of a person killed by being ejected from the cars of a railroad company, to recover damages for the wrong, the administrator is a competent witness in his own behalf. (*Sanford* agt. *Eighth Avenue R. R. Co.*, 7 *Bosw.*, 122.)

48. In such action, the facts that the intestate entered the car intending not to pay fare, and that he refused to pay fare or leave, and resisted the efforts made to put him off the car, do not of themselves necessarily constitute that concurring negligence or fault which defeats a recovery. If there is no actual negligence of the decedent at the time of his being put off, to which his injury and death may in fact be imputed, the company is liable.* (*Id.*)

49. Where the negligence of two parties using the public highway concurs, and the negligence of each contributes to produce collision and injury, neither can recover damages from the other for the injury so received. If the plaintiff's agent and stage-driver be negligent on his part, in carelessly crossing a railroad track, and receives injury by a collision with a railroad car, it is erroneous to instruct the jury, that if, when the driver of the car saw the driver of the stage attempting to cross the track, the car-driver, by ordinary care, could have slackened the speed of his car, if the brakes had been in good order, so as to have avoided a collision, the defendants are liable. (*Owen* agt. *Hudson River R. R. Co.*, 7 *Bosw.*, 329.)

50. A railroad company is bound to keep its cars in good and safe working order, and is also bound to cause them to be driven in a careful manner; and if in either particular they are negligent, they are liable to any one who, without concurring negligence on his part, is injured thereby, but to no others. (*Id.*)

51. An instruction, that if the jury believed it impossible that the injury to the plaintiff, by the defendants, could have been occasioned in the manner stated by the plaintiff, he could not recover; but that it was not essential to his right to recover, that the injury should have occurred precisely as he alleged, if in fact he was injured by the collision, by the negligence of the company (defendants) without fault on his part, is in substance correct, and a full response to the requested instruction. (*Pollard* agt. *N. Y. & New Haven R. R. Co.*, 7 *Bosw.*, 437.)

See Highways, 1. 2. 3. 4. 5.

See Taxes and Assessments, 3.

See Common Carrier, 9.

See Negligence, 4.

See Bonds, 1.

* This seems to present the question whether, where the decedent was injured by a railroad company while in the commission of a willful trespass against the company, it is equivalent to actual negligence by him when injured by the company.

Digest.

RECEIVERS.

1. The employment of the defendant, by the receiver, in supplementary proceedings, to make collections for him, where it appears no part of the assigned fund has been used for the benefit of the defendant, is not a sufficient ground for a removal of the receiver. (*Ross & Burdick* agt. *Bridge, ante* 163.)

2. A plaintiff at whose solicitation a *receiver* has been appointed, cannot be allowed to prosecute a claim in this court for which a judgment has been already obtained for his benefit and on his behalf by the receiver, in *another court*. (*Tinkham* agt. *Borst, ante,* 246.)

3. The *right of action* to claims for *dividends* improperly declared by an insolvent banking corporation is in the *creditors* and not in the receiver. (*Butterworth* agt. *O'Brien, ante,* 438.)

4. Where the complaint by the receiver averred that the defendant (former president of the bank) used *fictitious notes* in lieu of money of the bank, which he fraudulently used and disposed of, and that such notes were among the assets of the bank. *Held,* that these facts, if proven, would be sufficient to put the defendant on his defence, and showed a cause of action in favor of the receiver. (*Id.*)

5. A judgment creditor having *supplementary proceedings* pending, is not entitled to *eight* days' notice of an application for a receiver by *another creditor*. A less notice is sufficient. (*Leggett* agt. *Sloan, ante,* 479.)

6. The provisions of the statute requiring a receiver to take a prescribed oath and file it, is directory, and the omission to take and file it until after the receiver, as such, has brought a suit, is not sufficient cause for dismissing the suit. (*Dayton* agt. *Borst,* 7 *Bosw.*, 115.)

7. Where a demurrer to the complaint, as not stating facts sufficient to constitute a cause of action has been sustained by the court, it is a conclusive answer to a motion upon the complaint for an injunction and receiver. (*Mowbray* agt. *Lawrence*, 14 *Abb.*, 160.)

8. An order directing the continuance of a receivership during the pendency of any appeal which should be taken from the final decree. *Held,* to continue the receiver's authority, not only during the appeal to the general term but also to an appeal to the court of appeals from an order of the general term granting a new trial. (*McMahon* agt. *Allen,* 14 *Abb.*, 220.)

9. The general term will not interfere with an order at special term appointing a receiver in a case within the discretion of the special term. (*Id.*)

See PARTNERS AND PARTNERSHIPS, 12. 13.

See SUPPLEMENTAY PROCEEDINGS, 5. 8.

See MANUFACTURING CORPORATIONS, 2.

See DEED, 8.

See BANKING CORPORATIONS, 8. 9.

REFEREES AND REPORTS.

1. Where a referee not only decides against the *weight of evidence,* but errs in the application of the *rules of law,* it is error of *fact and of law*. And a wrong result upon *undisputed evidence* is an *error of law*. (*Brown* agt. *Penfield, ante,* 64.)

2. Where the decision of a referee *on a question of fact* is affirmed by the court at general term, it is *conclusive;* that question cannot be reviewed by this court. (*Reformed Protestant Dutch Church* agt. *Brown, ante,* 76.)

3. Where the same *defendants* in several causes, sued by different plaintiffs claiming for labor and team-work done on defendants' railroad for sub-contractors, entered into a written stipulation in all of the causes, providing that all proceedings should be stayed in the above entitled causes, and that they should "abide the result of the final judgment rendered in the case of John Driscoll agt. The Sackett's Harbor & Saratoga Railroad Co., (defendants in these causes,) in which verdict is to be taken on written stipulation as to facts, subject to the opinion of the general term," *held,* that the plaintiff in the John Driscoll case having subsequently obtained final judgment against the defendants, the plaintiffs in each of these cases were, on a reference for that purpose, *simply to prove the amount of their damages,* respectively, allowing the defendants to controvert their proof on that *single point only*. (*Honiahan* agt. *Sackett's Harbor & Saratoga R. R. Co., ante,* 155.)

4. If a party asks to have particular items considered in a court of review, and a report set aside for their allowlowance or disallowance, it is not demanding of him too much to require that he shall, 1st. Bring the attention of the referee specifically to them. 2d. Make it manifest what disposition the referee has in fact made of them, by obtaining from him a specific report on the subject. And 3d. Except specifically to the report in those particulars. (*Id.*)

5. In all these actions where the nature of the *cause of action* is such, that the defendant may be arrested under section 179 of the Code, it must be *stated in the complaint*; otherwise, an *execution* cannot issue against *the person*, unless an order of *arrest* has been served. (*Atocha* agt. *Garcia*, *ante*, 186.)

6. But where the action is one in which the defendant cannot be arrested, without some *extrinsic fact*, forming no part of the *cause of action*, but merely incidental to it, the fact must be stated in an *affidavit*, and an order of arrest must be obtained and served; and the averment of such fact in the complaint will not alone authorize an execution against the person. Hence the averment in the complaint is *immaterial*. (*Id.*)

7. For instance, where the substantive cause of action alleged in the complaint is the *debt* sought to be recovered, and allegations of *fraud* are also averred, the fraud being *incidental*, and only important to the plaintiff as furnishing the ground for obtaining the provisional remedy of arrest; the allegations of fraud in the complaint are *immaterial* and *unnecessary*. The issue to be tried in the action is the *debt*, not the fraudulent contraction of it. The judgment recovered is for the debt, not for the fraud. (*Id.*)

8. Such an action, where it involves the examination of a *long account*, although an order of arrest has been obtained, may be *referred*, under § 271 of the Code, without the consent of the parties. (*Id.*)

9. The "act to facilitate the closing up of insolvent and dissolved mutual insurance companies," passed April 21, 1862, is *not unconstitutional*, as impairing the *right of trial by jury*. A *compulsory reference*, therefore, may be ordered in these cases. (*Sands* agt. *Tillinghast & Griffiths*, *ante*, 435.)

10. The facts found by a referee must sustain his findings upon the law, and the law of the case must be predicated upon such findings of facts. In reviewing a judgment upon a report of a referee, the court acts simply as an appellate tribunal, and must reverse a judgment not warranted by appropriate findings on the questions of fact, where the proper exception is taken. (*Buckingham* agt. *Payne*, 36 *Barb.*, 81.)

11. The report of a referee, like the verdict of a jury, in a case of conflicting evidence, is conclusive as to questions of fact. (*Hoagland* agt. *Wright*, 7 *Bosw.*, 394.)

12. Where the facts formally found by a referee authorize the judgment he directs, it will not be reversed merely because his report does not formally dispose of all the issues, if there is no evidence in the case which would warrant a finding upon the issues not passed upon. (*Alger* agt. *Raymond*, 7 *Bosw.*, 418.)

13. To authorize the ordering of a reference compulsorily, it must appear from the papers on which it is granted, that some or one of the issues will require the examination of a long account. And where there is conflicting evidence before the judge as to that point, his decision will be final, and cannot be reviewed. Where the only evidence is an affidavit that the action is brought to recover the sum of $162, for goods sold and delivered, enough is not shown to confer authority to refer the cause. (*Whitaker* agt. *Defosse*, 7 *Bosw.*, 678.)

See Appeal, 16. 19. 20. 21.

See Executors and Administrators, 7. 8. 9.

RELIGIOUS CORPORATIONS.

1. Where an individual at the formation of a *religious society* promises, by *subscription*, to pay a certain sum towards the erection of a church edifice, and a further yearly sum for the support of the minister, the contract is binding, notwithstanding the society was not legally *incorporated* until some time afterwards, and the church edifice was not then completed. (*Reformed Protestant Dutch Church* agt. *Brown*, *ante*, 76, *Court of Appeals*.)

2. It is not necessary that the promise by the subscription should be to or

with the society in its *corporate capacity*. The society, on becoming incorporated, is, through its trustees, vested under the statute with authority to demand and receive the subscription. (*Id.*)

3. Before persons claiming to be trustees of a religious society, where their right of office is disputed, can maintain an action in the name of the society to restrain individuals in possession and claiming to be the trustees duly elected, from closing the church edifice, and from preventing the pastor from holding religious meetings therein, &c., the plaintiffs must have been peaceably admitted to the office of trustees of the society, or have established their title thereto by a direct proceeding or action, brought for that purpose by the attorney general. The court will not, on motion, decide who are the rightful owners of the society, or determine their right to the office. (*North Baptist Church, Staten Island*, agt. *Parker*, 38 *Barb.*, 171.)

4. Where the subscribers to a paper severally agreed well and truly to pay the several sums set opposite to their respective names, to the treasurer of a board of trustees, to be thereafter elected, said money to be expended in the erection of an institution of learning, to be built of brick, &c., *held* that each subscription should be regarded as a conditional promise or proposition to pay the sum subscribed towards the expense of erecting an institution of learning in the manner and upon the terms and of the description specified in the paper, which promise became binding upon each subscriber when accepted and acted upon by the corporation by proceeding to make contracts, &c., for the erection of the building, &c. (*Wayne and Ontario Collegiate Institute* agt. *Smith*, 36 *Barb.*, 576.)

REMOVAL OF CAUSE TO U. S. COURT.

1. A *foreign insurance company* created by the laws of another state, but doing business in this state, under and in compliance with our laws, on being sued by a citizen of this state, cannot remove the cause into the circuit court of the United States, on the ground that it is a *citizen of another state*. (*Stevens* agt. *Phœnix Insurance Company*, *ante*, 517.)

2. The power of removal of a cause into the U. S. circuit court, where the right of the defendant is expressly doubtful, should not be exercised by the state court. (*Anderson* agt. *Manufacturers' Bank*, 14 *Abb.*, 436.)

RESTITUTION.

See APPEAL, 2. 3.

RIPARIAN PROPRIETOR.

See LAKES, 1.

SALE.

1. A writing in this form, "F. bought of W. one horse, $150. Received payment. W.," given upon the purchase of and payment for the horse, is a mere receipt, and not a contract or bill of sale, so as to exclude parol evidence of a warranty of soundness of the horse by the vendor. (*Filkins* agt. *Whyland*, 24 *N. Y. R.*, 338.)

2. Where goods are sold by a broker without disclosing his principal, the purchaser when sued by the principal for the price, cannot set-off a debt due to him from the broker. Where a sale is made by a factor, the purchaser as a general rule, may set-off a debt due to him from the factor. (*Bliss* agt. *Bliss*, 7 *Bosw.*, 339.)

See MORTGAGE FORECLOSURE, 4. 9. 10.
See JUDGMENT, 5. 6.
See DEED, 8.
See VENDOR and VENDEE.
See SHERIFF, 1.
See HOMESTEAD EXEMPTION, 1.

SECURITY FOR COSTS.

1. There is no enactment either of the Code or otherwise, changing the practice of obtaining and filing *security for costs*. (*Cadwell* agt. *Manning*, *ante*, 38.)

2. A *chamber order*, *ex parte*, containing a *peremptory order* to file security for costs, and in default thereof to show cause why the complaint should not be dismissed, is *irregular*. (*Id.*)

See INJUNCTION, 1. 2.
See FOREIGN CORPORATIONS, 3.

SERVICE.

1. Where a defendant delays until the *second day of the circuit*, to file and serve an *affidavit of merits* in order to prevent an inquest, he is bound at his peril to *serve it* in such a way as, in all reasonable probability, to bring the service to the knowledge of the attorney or counsel of the plaintiff having charge of the cause at the circuit, *before the inquest is taken*. (*Smith* agt. *Aylesworth*, *ante*, 33.)

2. A service made on a *clerk in the office*, *in the absence of the attorney*, must be regarded equivalent to service upon the attorney personally. (*Id.*)

3. Where the *service* of *process* or *papers* upon a person is made by *violently thrusting them upon his person*, the service will be held *void*, although the person or officer making the service may have stated the nature of the papers, and the person upon whom they were intended to be served refused to receive them. In other words, a person or an officer has no right to commit an *assault and battery* upon an individual in trying to serve the papers upon him. (*Davison* agt. *Baker*, *ante*, 39.)

4. Where a person upon whom service of process or papers is desired to be made, *refuses to receive them*, the person or officer making the service should inform him of the nature of the papers and of his purpose to make service of them, and *lay them down at any appropriate place in his presence*. (*Id.*)

5. It is, to say the least, questionable whether *any court can extend the time to appeal*. (*Galit* agt. *Finch*, *ante*, 193.)

See Contempt, 6.

See Exceptions, 4.

SET-OFF.

1. In an action to *set-off judgments*, one against the other, the statute of set-off must control; and the equities of the parties are paramount to the *attorney's lien for costs*. (*Roberts* agt. *Carter*, *ante*, 44.)

2. In cases of counter-indebtedness arising out of mutual dealings, either party is entitled, upon a liquidated debt to him becoming due, to have it set-off against debts which he owes to the other party. (*Schieffelin* agt. *Hawkins*, 14 *Abb.*, 112.)

3. This right may be enforced against an assignee for the benefit of creditors, if the contract creating the debt had been executed, so that the assignor's liability had been fixed before the assignment was executed. (*Id.*)

See Answer, 2. 3. 4. 5. 6.

See Sale, 2.

See Account, 1.

See Counter Claim, 1. 2.

See Partner and Partnerships, 19.

See Judgment, 14.

SHERIFF.

1. Where an under sheriff agreed with the bidders at a sheriff's sale to warrant the title to the property sold, *held* that such an agreement rested upon no consideration of benefit to the sheriff, except as it might tend to increase his fees of office, and that in that respect it was void as against public policy. A sheriff acts officially in selling the property of a stranger to the execution, as the property of the defendant therein. He may take an indemnity from the plaintiff for such an act, when done in good faith, but cannot give an indemnity to the bidders at the sale. (*Ball* agt. *Pratt*, 36 *Barb.*, 402.)

2. After the sheriff had become liable for an escape in taking an insufficient bond from a prisoner in contempt, the prosecutor took an assignment of the bond, after breach of its condition, and also took an order for a further attachment, but failed to issue the latter, and the prisoner was surrendered by his bail. *Held* a waiver of the prosecutor's right of action against the sheriff. (*Weston* agt. *Campbell*, 14 *Abb.*, 410.)

SLANDER.

1. In a complaint for *slander*, where the words charged were, "nothing ails him but the pox; he is rotten with it; he got it," &c., *held* that the words are actionable *per se*. (*Hewit* agt. *Mason*, *ante*, 366.)

2. If the allegations of *special damage* by reason of the words spoken are not sufficiently *specific*, the objection cannot be raised by *demurrer*; the remedy is by motion under the Code (§ 160.) (*Id.*)

3. An action for slander, in charging the plaintiff with having "stolen tea, sugar and calico, and carried it away," cannot be sustained where the proof was that the defendant alleged the plaintiff "*took* tea and coffee from her, and she found them in her things," or that "she had *taken* tea and calico," &c. The words proved not being actionable *per se*, an action can be sustained on them only by proving that they were uttered with intent to impute a felonious taking of the goods, and were so understood by those who heard them. (*Coleman* agt. *Playsted*, 36 *Barb.*, 26.)

4. Where on the trial the variance between the words alleged and those proved are disregarded, and the cause is allowed to go to the jury upon the proofs, upon a charge submitting the actual intent and meaning of the words, it is equivalent to an amendment of the complaint, substituting the words proved for those alleged. (*Id.*)

5. Words charging a person with keeping a whore house are actionable *per se*. In an action for slander the words are to be construed according to their common acceptation; and it is not admissible to inquire of the witnesses how they understood them. (*Wright* agt. *Paige*, 36 *Barb.*, 438.)

See LIBEL, 1. 2. 3.

SPECIFIC PERFORMANCE.

1. In respect to *any agreement*, the nonfulfillment of which will not admit of *pecuniary compensation*, the court will afford relief by a *specific performance*; although it is chiefly with regard to *real property* that the substitution of damages by way of redress is generally insufficient. (*Livingston* agt. *Painter*, *ante*, 231.)

2. Where the plaintiff, as owner of a first mortgage upon leasehold property, claimed that the defendant, who was owner of a second mortgage on the same property, had violated an agreement with him in bidding off the property at the sale thereof on the second mortgage, in the name of another person, who refused to pay certain expenses upon the property and a specified payment on the first mortgage, in pursuance of the agreement to waive the foreclosure of the first mortgage; (*Id.*)

3. *Held*, that if the plaintiff had sustained any injury it was in consequence of the *delay* in not prosecuting a foreclosure of the first mortgage. The damages caused by the delay were capable of being measured and ascertained by a jury; that if the plaintiff was entitled to any redress under the agreement, it was by an *action for damages*. (*Id.*)

4. A decree for *specific performance* to convey real estate by deed will be made after the day fixed in the agreement for its delivery, and the payment or delivery of the consideration therefor, where the *time fixed* appears to have been disregarded by the parties as of the *essence of the contract*. (*Benson* agt. *Tilton*, *ante*, 494.)

5. A *strong evidence* of such disregard by the parties in this case appeared from the fact that the leasehold premises and personal property to be given by the plaintiff as a consideration for the deed of real estate, to be delivered by the defendant, had been for several days, both before and after the day fixed for performance, *in the possession of the defendant by his agents*. (*Id.*)

6. A court of equity can compel the specific performance of a covenant to renew a lease at a rent to be fixed by arbitrators. If the defendant declines to submit to arbitration, the court will fix the rent, or direct a renewal at the former rate. (*Johnson* agt. *Conger*, 14 *Abb.*, 195.)

See TRIAL, 6. 7.

See RAILROAD COMPANIES, 23. 24. 25.

STATUTE OF FRAUDS.

1. H. having made a contract with the defendant to build him a saw-mill on his lands, after part performance, made a sub-contract with the plaintiff to complete the job. The plaintiff commenced work accordingly, but a few days after went to the defendant, informed him he had learned H. was irresponsible, and declined going on with the job. The defendant, to induce the plaintiff to go on and finish the mill, promised that "he would see that the plaintiff did not lose anything by it," and that "he would see that plaintiff got his pay." *Held*, that the promise was a collateral undertaking, and not being in writing was void by the statute of frauds. CAMPBELL, J., dissented. (*Brown* agt. *Weber*, *ante*, 306.)

2. And it appearing further that while the plaintiff was finishing the job, he and his hands boarded with the defendant, under a contract between the parties, and that the defendant furnished some materials to be used in the work, which, under the original contract, H. and plaintiff were to find, *held*, also, that the defendant was entitled to recover the value of such board and materials in this action of the plaintiff. (*Id.*)

3. It was *held*, that the *written agreement* signed by the defendant, on which the action was brought in this case, taken together with an agreement signed at the same time by the plaintiff's assignor, was not void under the statute; construed together, a sufficient *consideration* was expressed; and it could not be treated as an undertaking *to pay the debt of another*. (*Winfield* agt. *Potter*, *ante*, 446.)

See Contract, 8. 9.

STATUTES.

1. Where the defence to a contract is given by a statute founded on grounds of public policy (against stock jobbing), the *repeal* of the statute since the contract was made takes away the *defence of illegality the same as if such statute never existed*. (*Washburn* agt. *Franklin*, *ante*, 515.)

2. The act in relation to the sale of bottles, &c., (*ch.* 117 *of* 1860) imposes no penalty for the secreting of a bottle, though subjecting a dealer in bottles to a search warrant. (*Mullins* agt. *People*, 24 *N. Y. R.*, 399.)

3. A statute which by its terms is to go into effect immediately is operative from the instant of its first passage. The affirmative statute does not take away the common law. (*Fairchild* agt. *Gwynne*, 14 *Abb.*, 121.)

4. On the repeal of a statute which repeals or modifies a previous statute, the latter is revised without formal words. (*Sarsfield* agt. *Van Vaughner*, 14 *Abb.*, 297.)

See Constitutional Law, 7. 8.

STATUTE OF LIMITATIONS.

1. The statute of limitations does not apply as a bar to an action in the courts of this state against a foreign corporation. (*Thompson* agt. *Tioga R. R. Co.*, 36 *Barb.*, 79.)

2. Where on the trial the court found that the defendant passed through this state more than six years before commencement of the action, but was only here temporarily, and that all the defendants had resided in Pennsylvania since the cause of action accrued, *held* that the action was not barred by our statute of limitations. If the debtor comes into this state before process is served on him, and he leaves the state to reside elsewhere, the statute is not a bar, until, after deducting all the time of residing abroad, the debtor has been in this state for six years. (*Gans* agt. *Frank*, 36 *Barb.*, 320.)

3. Whether the absence is repeated, or is one continued absence, is immaterial. There must be full six years spent in this state to make our statute of limitations a bar. (*Id.*)

4. The accepting money upon a contract wherein it was stipulated that there was to be no interest, and the principal payable only at the will of the obligee of the bond, the obligor thereby put it into the power of the latter to postpone the day of payment to such time as suited his convenience and pleasure. But a demand of payment is necessary in such case before the statute of limitations will commence running. (*Sweet* agt. *Irish*, 36 *Barb.*, 467.)

See Bills of Exchange and Promissory Notes, 2. 3. 4.

See Attorney, 10.

STAY OF PROCEEDINGS.

See Injunction, 1. 2.

SUMMONS.

1. It is not necessary to the *commencement* of any action that a copy of the *complaint* be served upon the defendant; he is brought into court by the *summons alone*. (*O'Hara* agt. *Brophy*, *ante*, 379.)

2. The summons requiring one or more joint defendants not originally served with process to show cause why they should not be bound by the judgment (*Code* § 375) should merely require such defendants to show cause within twenty days after its service; but specifying a time and place does not vitiate. (*Townsend* agt. *Newell*, 14 *Abb.*, 340.)

SUNDAY NEWSPAPERS.

1. A contract for the publication of an advertisement in a newspaper to be issued and sold on Sunday is void. (*Smith* agt. *Wilcox*, 24 *N. Y. R.*, 353.)

SUPERVISORS.

1. If a *board of supervisors* disallow an account presented to them to be audited as a county charge, on the ground that *they have no power to allow it*—that the statute does not authorize the allowance; this precludes the *examination* contemplated by the statute under which the board act in the settlement of accounts, and the court can control the action of the board, in reference thereto, by *mandamus*. (*People ex rel. Plumb* agt. *Supervisors of Cortland*, *ante*, 119.)

2. It is otherwise where the board of supervisors enter into an *examination* of such accounts, and reject (or allow) them; they thus exercise their legal *discretion*, and their decision becomes *final*. (*Id.*)

3. The *commissioners of excise* of a county are not, under the statute, limited in their services to *ten days* (at $3 per day.) This limitation is expressly confined to the time they shall spend in their meetings for the purpose of granting license. (*Id.*)

4. It is their duty to *prosecute for penalties incurred*, and the members of the board have the right to charge for the time spent in the performance of that duty; and where they present their accounts to the board of supervisors, properly made out and verified, it is the duty of such board to receive and act upon them. If they refuse to do this, the authority of this court may be invoked to compel them. (*Id.*)

5. The question whether a town has been legally erected may be tested in an action in the nature of quo warranto against one claiming to exercise the office of supervisor of such town. (*People* agt. *Carpenter*, 24 *N. Y. R.*, 86.)

6. The act of a board of supervisors dividing a town and forming a new one from a portion thereof, only described the dividing line, *held* that the uncertainty was cured by the reference in such act to the petition, &c., upon which it was founded, and from which it appeared that the new town was to lie south of the line of division, and by proof *aliunde* that the place named in the act for holding the first town meeting was south of such line. (*Id.*)

7. The statute (*ch.* 194 *of* 1849,) does not, *it seems*, require that the published copy of notice of the application of twelve freeholders for the erection of a new town shall contain the names of such applicants. It is sufficient that the notice posted should be thus subscribed. (*Id.*)

8. An affidavit stating that a notice was left with another person to be posted up, "which was done," construed as a positive averment of the posting. (*Id.*)

9. The act of the supervisors is, it seems, one of a legislative character, in favor of the regularity of which all presumptions are to be indulged. Those who would impeach it, have the burden of disproving a compliance with the conditions imposed by law as requisite to the exercise of the power. (*Id.*)

SUPPLEMENTARY PROCEEDINGS.

1. Where *supplementary proceedings*, having been commenced and continued before a *county judge*, until an order was issued for the defendant to show cause why an attachment for *contempt* should not be issued against him, and failing to show cause, the attachment was issued and put into the hands of an officer for service, and before the service the county judge *went out of office*, having previously transferred these proceedings to his successor in office, *held*, that the proceedings were properly *continued* before the successor in office. An *order* of a *county judge*, dismissing proceedings on an attachment for *contempt* against the defendant in *supplementary proceedings*, is appealable to the general term. (*Holstein* agt. *Rice*, *ante*, 135.)

2. A judgment creditor having *supplementary proceedings* pending, is not entitled to *eight* days' notice of an application for a receiver by *another creditor*. A less notice is sufficient. (*Leggett* agt. *Sloan*, *ante*, 479.)

3. Where an *execution* has been duly issued and duly returned by the sheriff unsatisfied in whole or in part, and the plaintiff has in no wise interfered, he may safely act upon the return of the sheriff, to institute *proceedings supple-*

mentary to execution. And the question whether there was property which the sheriff ought to have taken and sold for the purpose of satisfying the judgment in whole or in part, *cannot be raised*. (*Fenton* agt. *Flagg, ante*, 499.)

4. In these proceedings the court does not appoint more than one person receiver of the judgment debtor's property, however numerous may be the creditors' proceedings against the judgment debtor. One appointment of receiver divests the debtor of his title to all his property. (*Myrick* agt. *Selden*, 36 *Barb*., 15.)

5. Section 292 of the Code, which provides for the examination of a judgment debtor when an execution issued to the sheriff of the county where he resides has been returned unsatisfied, refers to the county where he resides at the time of the issuing of the execution. (*Bingham* agt. *Disbrow*, 14 *Abb*., 251.)

6. Any justice of the supreme court may make an order under section 292 of the Code for the examination of a judgment debtor, without regard to the residence of the justice; but the debtor must be directed to appear in the particular county prescribed in the section. (*Id.*)

7. Where an order for the appointment of a receiver under section 298 of the Code is made, founded on the voluntary appearance and examination of a judgment debtor, it is valid. (*Id.*)

8. A stranger to the action, who has a lien upon a fund sought to be reached by supplementary proceedings, is not entitled to notice of the proceedings, or to be made a party thereto. (*Corning* agt. *The Glenville Woolen Co.*, 14 *Abb*., 339.)

See Receivers, 1.

See Creditor's Suit, 9. 10.

SURETIES.

1. Where the plaintiff has the right to take the *persons of all the defendants* in satisfaction of his judgment, it carries with it the right to proceed against the *bail of one of them*, as to whom there may be a return of *non est inventus*. (*Penn* agt. *Remsen, ante*, 503.)

See Undertaking, 1. 2. 3. 4.

SURROGATES' COURTS.

1. The effect of the repeal in 1837 (*ch*. 460, § 71,) of the restrictive clause in respect to the jurisdiction of surrogates' courts (2 *R. S., p*. 221, § 1,) is to restore to such courts the incidental powers possessed by them previous to the Revised Statutes. (*Sipperly* agt. *Baucus*, 24 *N. Y. R*., 46.)

2. A surrogate has the power to open a decree made by him on the final accounting of an administrator, and to require a further account in respect to a sum received by him with which he had charged himself, as $14.80 instead of $1,480. (*Id.*)

3. There is no positive limitation of the period in which such application may be made, and the lapse of four years does not of itself import laches. (*Id.*)

4. The exemplification of the record of a will, in order to be evidence, under ch. 94 of 1850, must contain the proofs taken before the surrogate. A mere exemplification of the will, recorded as having been proved, is insufficient. (*Hill* agt. *Crockford*, 24 *N. Y. R*., 128.)

5. The statute (*ch*. 460 *of* 1837, § 22,) upon affidavit of the intention to file objections against the granting of letters testamentary to one or several executors, requires the surrogate to suspend the grant of letters as well to any of the executors not objected to as to those who are. (*McGregor* agt. *Buel*, 24 *N. Y. R*., 166.)

6. The issuing of special letters of administration to a collector is discretionary with the surrogate, and though his refusal to appoint such collector be put on the ground of his having (erroneously) issued letters testamentary to an executor, this does not render his discretion the subject of review, on appeal. The remedy, if any, is by mandamus. (*Id.*)

7. The relatives of a decedent are entitled to administer upon his estate under the statute (2 *R. S., p*. 74, § 27,) although not entitled to a distributive share when the letters are granted. (*Lathrop* agt. *Smith*, 24 *N. Y. R*., 417.)

8. *Held*, accordingly, that, where the father of the decedent, who was entitled to his personal estate, had renounced, the brother was entitled to administration before a creditor. (*Id.*)

9. *The Public Administrator* agt. *Peters* (1 *Bradf.*, 100,) overruled. (*Id.*)

TAXES AND ASSESSMENTS.

1. By the system of *taxation* under the provisions of the statutes applicable to the county of Rensselaer and the city of Troy, a *banking corporation* located in that city may be *exempt from taxation* as respects the county tax, under the law of 1853, (*Laws of* 1853, *chap.* 654, § 1, *amending* § 9 *of the former act*,) which entitles a bank to commutation, by paying a sum equal to five per cent. on their net annual income or profits, or to an exemption in case of no net profits or clear income at all; and yet be liable to a *city tax* on their *personal property*, although, by the provisions of the above law, *they have sworn they have none* liable to taxation, by reason of which they are exempt from the county tax. (*Manufacturers' Bank of Troy* agt. *Mayor, &c., of Troy, ante*, 250.)

2. When the law authorizes the common council of a city to impose the expenses of paving streets, or other improvements, by assessment upon the *owners of property benefited*, the assessment becomes a *lien* upon the lots benefited; and it is an undue assumption of power in the common council to incur the expense and attempt its collection from *tax payers at large*, even under a prior ordinance which required them thereafter to keep such streets repaved and kept in repair *at the expense of the corporation*. (*Rhinelander* agt. *Mayor, &c., of New York, ante*, 304.)

3. If the state has the power to levy and collect a tax or assessment to be paid to a railroad company as a compensation for the relinquishment of certain rights, it has the power to direct the transfer of the assessment collectively to the same company, for the same purpose, before its payment. Where commissioners of assessment, appointed under the act of April 19, 1859, for the purpose of compensating the Long Island railroad on their relinquishing certain rights, &c., upon certiorari directed to them, return the proceedings which resulted in their appointment, by which it appears that both the common council of Brooklyn and the supreme court, at special term, determined that a petition by a majority of the persons to be assessed, sufficient in form and character, had been presented to the common council, such determinations will be held conclusive upon that question. (*People ex rel. Crowell* agt. *Lawrence*, 36 *Barb.*, 177.)

See Banking Corporations, 1. 2.

See Towns, 1. 2. 3.

TOWNS.

1. Chapter 375 of 1852, required the raising by tax on the town of Genoa of the interest on certain bonds of that town, the money to be received and paid to the bondholders by commissioners appointed for that purpose. The money having been raised, it seems that mandamus to the commissioners is the proper remedy to enforce payment and not an action against the town. (*People* agt. *Mead*, 24 *N. Y. R.*, 114.)

2. The act directing the commissioners to issue *bonds* "under their official signatures," is satisfied, it seems, by instruments not under seal, and payable to bearer. (*Id.*)

3. The decision in *Starin* agt. *The Town of Genoa* (23 *N. Y.*, 439,) reiterated that a certificate, required by the statute, but not made evidence, that the tax payers had assented to the issue of the bonds, is not proof for a *bona fide* holder of the fact of such assent. (*Id.*)

See Supervisors, 5. 6. 7. 8. 9.

TRADE-MARK.

1. Where it is shown by evidence that the defendant has violated a well known *trade-mark* of the plaintiff, he will be *perpetually enjoined and restrained* by the court from disposing of, selling, or causing to be disposed of or sold, any of the articles bearing the false, simulated or spurious stamp or mark. (*Jurgensen* agt. *Alexander, ante*, 269.)

2. And the defendant will be required to produce, before a *referee* appointed by the court, such spurious articles which at the time of the commencement of the action were in his possession, for the purpose of having the spurious trade-mark *erased* or *liberated* therefrom, by or under the direction of the referee, at the *cost and expense of the defendant*, with the *costs* and *disbursements* of the action. (*Id.*)

3. No dealer in any commodity has a right to be protected by injunction in

the exclusive use simply of a name by which to designate it, which does not express its origin, ownership, or place of manufacture or sale, but merely its quality, kind, texture, composition, utility, destined use or class of consumers, or some other attribute which it has in common with other similar commodities, so *held*, in regard to the designation of gin by the term "Club House," it being established that such name had been long in use as designating a superior kind of gin used in such establishments. (*Corwin* agt. *Daly*, 7 *Bosw.*, 222.)

4. The employment of particular words or insignia as a trade-mark, must be confined to the place where they are used, and its exportation to other places cannot interfere with the right acquired by others previously using them in such places. (*Id.*)

TRIAL.

1. Actions seeking *equitable relief* are to be *tried by the court*; a party is not entitled as a matter of right to have the issues of fact in *such actions* tried by a *jury*. (*McCarty* agt. *Edwards*, *ante*, 236.)

2. After the time to settle the issues in a cause asking *equitable relief*, and for a money demand, to the settlement of which issues the plaintiff has lost his right, on the trial he is not entitled to have the issues settled instanter, or to *amend* his *complaint* instanter, and strike out of the prayer all except the money demand, and to proceed to a jury trial immediately, thus changing essentially the nature of the action and the mode of trial, apparently for the sole purpose of getting the cause before a *jury*; nor to *put the cause over the circuit* to enable him to move to amend the complaint, and settle the issues, without showing a sufficient reason therefor. These matters are addressed to the *discretion* of the judge at the circuit, and cannot be reviewed at general term. (*Id.*)

3. Where the plaintiff in his complaint claims *specific relief* purely equitable, against the defendants, and makes no demand for money or damages, and the facts show that the relation of debtor and creditor exists between the plaintiff and defendants, and that the latter are alone responsible to the plaintiff in an action for a *money demand*, the plaintiff will not be allowed *to change his remedy* by obtaining an order that the issue be tried by a jury as a *money demand*. The complaint must be *dismissed*. (*Craig* agt. *Hyde*, *ante*, 313.)

4. The objection that an *assignment for the benefit of creditors* was not executed by *all the parties*, should be taken at the *trial*; it is too late to raise such an objection, to defeat the assignee's title on *appeal*. (*Colwell* agt. *Lawrence*, *ante*, 324.)

5. It was *held* no error for the judge at the trial to deny a motion to *dismiss the complaint*, where the application was made *during the progress of the examination of a witness*; and where the application appeared in the double character of an *objection to evidence*, and on the ground that there was *no consideration in the agreement* upon which the action was brought. (*Winfield* agt. *Potter*, *ante*, 446.)

6. Where the complaint prays for the specific performance of a contract to convey lands or for damages, but shows that the defendant is incapable of conveying, and the parties go to trial, the court, under the Code, is not to dismiss the complaint, but to retain the case for the purpose of awarding damages. (*Barlow* agt. *Scott*, 24 *N. Y. R.*, 40.)

7. It is no ground for reversing the judgment in such a case, that the trial was by the court without jury, where it does not appear in the case that the objection was taken at the trial. (*Id.*)

8. Where the testimony on the trial is conflicting, it is the duty of the judge to submit the case to the jury. He will not be justified in taking the case from them and directing a verdict for either party. (*Smith* agt. *Tiffany*, 36 *Barb.*, 23.)

9. Where it is obvious that a fact was assumed on the trial, it is as much in the case as if it were expressly proved. (*Paige* agt. *Fazackerly*, 36 *Barb.*, 392.)

10. After evidence has been duly taken bearing upon the issues, on a trial, without objection, the judge at the circuit has no power to strike it out, or to exclude it from the consideration of the jury. (*Hall* agt. *Earnest*, 36 *Barb.*, 585.)

11. Where there is no conflicting evidence upon an issue before a jury, or the weight of evidence in favor of one party is so decided that the court would

be bound to set aside an adverse verdict as against evidence, it is the duty of the judge to direct the jury what verdict to find. A verdict found under the instruction of the court will be deemed correctly rendered in the absence of evidence to the contrary. (*People ex rel. Peck* agt. *Board of Police*, 14 *Abb.*, 158.)

12. In the actions referred to in section 125 of the Code, the place of trial must be laid in a county in which some one of the parties resides, without regard to the convenience of witnesses. (*The International Life Assurance Co.* agt. *Sweetland*, 14 *Abb.*, 240.)

See DAMAGES, 7.

TRUSTS AND TRUSTEES.

1. A trust, in a deed to convey the premises to such person as the wife of the grantor shall by writing appoint is not one of the trusts authorized by law, and is void. And where the trustee is not vested with the right to the possession, rents or profits of the land conveyed, either for himself, or any other person, the deed of trust will be regarded as void under the statute. Where a trust deed is void upon its face, it cannot in a proper and legal sense be considered a cloud upon the title of the premises, so as to authorize the interference of a court of equity to set it aside; powers in trust discussed. (*Hotchkiss* agt. *Elting*, 36 *Barb.*, 38.)

See RELIGIOUS CORPORATIONS, 3.

UNDERTAKING.

1. Where an appeal is taken from the judgment of the special term to the general term, and the proper *undertaking* executed by the appellant and his sureties, under and in pursuance of § 335 of the Code, the *obligation of the sureties* is not fulfilled, and the undertaking satisfied by a reversal of the judgment at the general term, *where the judgment of the general term has also been reversed in the court of appeals*. (*Gardner* agt. *Barney*, *ante*, 467.)

2. That is, the *sureties* are not limited in their liability to the judgment of the *general term*. The *affirmance* mentioned in their undertaking, is an affirmance by the legally constituted tribunal having cognizance *finally* of the litigation. The *reversal* by the court of appeals, when effect is given to it in the court below, is in fact an *affirmance by the general term* of the judgment at the *special term*. (*Id.*)

3. Nor is the liabilities of the sureties at all affected or changed by the fact that when they executed the undertaking there was no law in existence that authorised an appeal to the court of appeals from an order of the general term *granting a new trial*; but before the decision of the general term a law was passed which authorised such an appeal, and under which the appeal in this case was taken. (*Id.*)

4. When an appeal is from a judgment against two defendants, the sureties upon a joint undertaking are liable if the judgment is *affirmed against one*. (*To the same effect is Seacord* agt. *Morgan*, 17 *How. Pr. R.*, 394.) (*Id.*)

See APPEAL, 24.

USURY.

1. Where land is conveyed subject to a usurious mortgage, which the grantee assumes to pay, the mortgagee acquires a right to an appropriation of the land for that purpose, which cannot be divested without his assent. (*Hartley* agt. *Harrison*, 24 *N. Y. R.*, 170.)

2. *Held*, accordingly, that a subsequent arrangement between the parties to the deed, whereby, as between them, it became a mere quitclaim, was inoperative to open the defence of usury to the grantee. (*Id.*)

3. An accommodation note made only for the accommodation of the payee, to enable him to raise money on it, and is sold by him to a third person upon a false representation that it was business paper, and given for value, for a less amount than upon its face purports to be due thereon, so as to secure to the purchaser a greater rate than seven per cent. for the use of his money, the transaction is usurious, and the note is void; whether the purchaser knew at the time he purchased it that it was so made or not. A note not valid in the hands of the payee, cannot, by him be rendered valid by a sale thereof to a *bona fide* purchaser, at a rate of interest exceeding seven per cent. To be the subject of sale it must have a pre-existing validity. Its breath of life cannot be imparted through a usurious transaction. (*Hall* agt. *Earnest*, 36 *Barb.*, 585.)

4. An agreement by a borrower to pay a subsisting debt of his own, in consideration of a new credit, or a further loan, is not usurious, if the promise is to pay only the amount actually due on the old debt, and the amount of the loan with lawful interest. (*Marsh* agt. *Howe*, 36 *Barb.*, 649.)

5. The payment of a bonus by a borrower, to the agent (a commissioner for loaning U. S. money,) through whom the loan is made, without the knowledge or assent of the principal (the State,) does not constitute usury, so as to invalidate the mortgage taken on the loan. (*Fellows* agt. *Commissioners of Oneida*, 36 *Barb.*, 55.)

6. A written contract by which H. agrees to advance to B. $1,500, "on the brig Sophia, * * loading in New York, and bound for San Francisco," and by which B. agrees to pay H. for the use of the money loaned twelve per cent. commission, and seven per cent. interest, and as security to assign to H. policies of insurance on the ship and on the freight, and also to execute a bill of sale of the ship, is usurious. And an action to obtain a re-assignment of the policies and of the ship, commenced more than one year after such assignments, can be sustained notwithstanding the objection as to such time is interposed. (*Braynard* agt. *Hoppock*, 7 *Bosw.*, 157.)

7. A person who takes negotiable paper as security for a loan, from one holding it for collection merely, and without authority to dispose of it, and takes it with knowledge of such circumstances as would excite suspicion and lead a man of ordinary prudence to make inquiry, but makes such inquiries as a man of ordinary prudence would make, and receives information which would naturally be credited; and removes all suspicion, he acts in good faith, and will a title in good faith. Where the loan is made in this state to a corporation, the true owner of the paper cannot impeach the title of the borrower and reclaim the paper, on the mere ground that the loan was at more than 7 per cent., where apart from the force of the fact that the loan was usurious, the lender is a *bona fide* holder for value. (*Belmont Branch Bank* agt. *Hoge*, 7 *Bosw.*, 543.)

8. The contracting party in an action at law upon the contract, or in equity upon securities collateral to the contract, where the defence of usury is interposed, the owner of the property or one having a valid lien upon it by mortgage or execution, is entitled to interpose the defence as a matter of strict right. (*Chamberlain* agt. *Dempsey*, 14 *Abb.*, 241.)

9. In a mortgage foreclosure to which the defence of usury is interposed by a grantee of the mortgagee, an admission that such grantee is the owner of the premises imports that the conveyance by which the grantee acquired title was in hostility to the mortgage. (*Id.*)

See Agreement, 6.

VARIANCE.

See Complaint, 10.

VENDOR AND VENDEE.

1. The vendor in a contract for the sale of land being in default, and the time extended for his convenience, the vendee may insist upon strict performance at the very hour appointed. (*Friess* agt. *Rider*, 24 *N. Y. R.*, 367.)

2. The vendor again making default, but tendering performance after the lapse of three hours, the vendee is not required to assign any reason for his refusal to accept it, and it is, therefore, immaterial that he assigns a reason which is not well founded in fact. (*Id.*)

3. So *held* in an action by the vendor for stipulated damages, where the vendor, on the day for giving his deed, the vendee being then ready with his money, requested a postponement to a fixed hour the next day. At the time appointed the vendee attended, and after waiting three hours, departed. At a subsequent hour of the same day, the vendor tendered a deed, and the vendee stated, as reason for declining, not the lapse of time, but waste of the premises, which was not supported by the facts. (*Id.*)

4. The case of *Gould* agt. *Banks*, (8 Wend., 562), considered and limited, *per* Allen J. (*Id.*)

5. The vendee of goods which had come to his possession, ascertaining his insolvency, deposited them in warehouse subject to the order of the vendor, and notified him thereof by letter: before the vendor had signified his assent, the goods were attached by another creditor. *Held*, that the title of the vendor prevailed. (*Sturtevant* agt. *Orser*, 24 *N. Y. R.*, 538.)

6. Whenever a vendor has manifested an intention not to rely on his lien upon the lands sold for the purchase money thereof, he will be considered as having waived his lien. And so, if a vendor, for a portion of the purchase money, agrees to take a conveyance of other property, and a deed of the latter property is executed by the vendee and delivered in escrow, the lien of the vendor will be gone. If the depositary refuses to deliver the deed, the remedy for such delivery by the vendor is upon the agreement of sale between him and the purchaser. (*Coit* agt. *Fougera*, 36 *Barb.*, 195.)

7. The remedy against a purchaser who refuses to complete his purchase on a sale under a judgment or decree of a court of equity, is by an application to the court to compel him to complete it, or to re-sell the property and hold him liable for the loss and expenses. (*Miller* agt. *Collyer*, 36 *Barb.*, 250.)

8. A vendor who has sold goods and drawn bills upon the purchaser for the price, can rescind the sale, and sue for the value of the goods, if he has good cause for doing so, notwithstanding the bills at the time of the commencement of the action are out of his possession, so that he cannot then surrender them. When he produces the paper at the trial, and there offers to surrender it and cancel the acceptances, it is sufficient. (*Fraschcris* agt. *Henriques*, 36 *Barb.*, 276.)

9. Until the vendee of land has performed the contract on his part, where the payment of the purchase money and the delivery of the deed are concurrent acts to be done at a future time, although he has an equitable interest in the land, and a right to a specific performance of the agreement, he is not vested with the right of property, and cannot assert the legal rights, or claim the legal remedies which belong to those who own the title; and cannot therefore, maintain an action against the vendor for removing fixtures from the premises agreed to be conveyed. (*Tabor* agt. *Robinson*, 36 *Barb.*, 483.)

See Contract, 18.

See Agreement, 6.

See Attachment, 3.

See Mortgage Foreclosure, 9.

See Principal and Agent, 3.

See Fixtures, 1.

See Payment, 3.

VERDICT.

1. *Held*, on the motion for a new trial, that the case belonged to that class of cases of conflicting evidence and doubtful facts, in which the verdict of a jury one way or the other is practically conclusive, and ought not to be disturbed. (*Best* agt. *Starks*, *ante*, 58.)

See New Trial, 1. 2. 3. 4.

See Trial, 11.

VERIFICATION.

1. In the *verification* of an answer *by an agent* of the defendant to an action upon a written instrument, where the allegations of the answer are stated *positively*, and without qualification, it is not necessary that the agent should state his *knowledge* or the *grounds of his belief* in the verification. That part of the verification which refers to matters in the answer, supposed to have been stated upon information and belief, may be treated as surplusage. (*Ross* agt. *Longmuir*, *ante*, 49.)

2. In an action for *divorce for adultery* by an infant plaintiff, the complaint is properly *verified by her guardian*. But the defendant may put in his answer *without verification*. Under the statute, he cannot be compelled to be a witness in any case where he would be exposed to a *penalty or forfeiture*. (*Anable* agt. *Anable*, *ante*, 92.)

3. An attorney having possession of a written instrument for the payment of money only on which action is brought, may verify the complaint whether the plaintiff be within the county or not. The possession of the instrument with information derived from the plaintiff are sufficient grounds of knowledge and source of belief. (*Wheeler* agt. *Chesley*, 14 *Abb.*, 441.)

See Answer, 1.

WARRANTY.

See Insurance Companies, 1. 2.

See Contract, 18.

WILL.

1. *Construction of clauses in a will.*—*Personal property* may be bequeathed *for life*, and then over, either absolutely or contingently. (*Underhill* agt. *Tripp*, *ante*, 51.)

2. A bequest by the testator to his daughter of $1,000, and then declares that this bequest is given to make his daughter equal with his other children who had been advanced; and after a residuary devise of all the residue of his real and personal estate, he says the bequest (of $1,000) which he has given to his said daughter, "she is to have and to hold during the term of her *natural life*, and at her decease is to be equally divided among her children," *held* that this last clause cut down the legacy of the daughter to a *life estate* or *usufructuary interest;* and that her *children* would take as *purchasers* on her death. (*Id.*)

3. An *inconsistent* devise or bequest in the *second* of two testamentary papers (a will and codicil) is a *revocation of the first.* (*Barlow* agt. *Coffin, ante,* 54.)

4. Thus, in case of a devise of the same lands to two persons, while if the devises are in the *same instrument*, the devisees may take jointly or in common; but if they are found in *distinct* testamentary instruments, the *latter* is a complete *revocation* of the former. (*Id.*)

5. Where the *domicil* of the testatrix was in New York—all the *personal estate* was in New York; the will was *proved* and letters testamentary *issued* in New York, *held* that the *legatees* of the personal estate were not chargeable with the expenses of proving and contesting the will in New Jersey, where the deceased had real estate. The decree of the court in New Jersey, directing such expenses to be paid out of the estate, had no force or validity here, and could not make these expenses chargeable to the legatees under the will, in this state. (*Young* agt. *Brush, ante,* 70.)

6. In an action to obtain *construction of a will*, the complaint should state that the testator left property, and also whether real or personal or both. (*Walrath* agt. *Handy, ante,* 353.)

7. If there be no *trust* declared or raised by the will, and the legatees and devisees take absolutely, they must vindicate their rights by an action or actions at law—not by an action in equity for its construction. (*Id.*)

8. A person who is *not executor*, nor in any sense a *trustee*, is not entitled to ask instruction or advice from the court. (*Id.*)

9. In case a *trust* be declared by will, and questions of doubt arise as to its true meaning, any person having an *interest* in the property *held in trust* may apply by action to have the will construed or its validity determined. (*Id.*)

10. *Construction of a will.*—Where the testator, in the second section of his will, directed in these words: "That my executors pay out of the income of my estate to my wife $8,000 per annum, if I shall leave a child or children by her, so long as she shall live and remain my widow;" and then in the third section declared, "if there shall be no child or children, then I direct that my said executors do pay unto my said wife $7,000 per annum so long as she shall live and remain my widow, and pay the residue of the income of my said estate in equal portions unto my brother, John M. Edwards, my sister Frances, wife of William S. Hoyt, and my sister Henrietta, wife of Worthington Hooker;" and in the fourth section directed that in case he left a child or children, his entire estate should remain in trust for their benefit, until such children should arrive at majority, when it should be equally divided among them, "reserving in trust $8,000 per annum for my wife, so long as she lives and remains my widow," and he left no children: (*Pierrepont* agt. *Edwards, ante,* 419.)

11. And it appeared in evidence, that at the time of his death he supposed himself possessed of a clear income sufficient to pay the largest of the annuities bequeathed to his wife, and to have a surplus for the benefit of his brother and sisters, but owing to a depreciation of the estate, the income proved inadequate to pay the widow's annuity of $7,000, *held* that the bequest to the wife, although *demonstrative* as pointing out the fund from which it was to be paid, *was not specific*, so that it failed or abated in consequence of the inadequacy of such fund; but was *general and payable at all events* out of the *corpus* of the estate. (*Id.*)

12. Each case of this nature must depend upon a consideration of the material provisions of the will, and the extrinsic circumstances of the testator's family and estate, which may be fairly brought to bear upon the question of *intent*. (*Id.*)

13. A separate and independent intention to bequeath a sum of money or an annuity at all events, will not be permitted to be overruled merely by a direction in the will, that the money is to be raised in a particular way or out of a particular fund. (*Id.*)

14. The provision for his widow was the primary and most material portion of the testator's intent, while that for his brother and sisters was incidental and subordinate to that. (*Id.*)

15. A trust to receive the rents and profits of real estate and apply them to the use of the issue of the testator's infant children, for a period not exceeding two lives in being, is not void because the beneficiaries are not ascertained. (*Gilman* agt. *Reddington*, 24 *N. Y. R.*, 9.)

16. The statute (1 *R. S.*, *p.* 728, § 55) does not forbid a shifting use for the benefit, in case of the death of the primary beneficiaries, of persons unknown or not in existence at the creation of the trust. (*Id.*)

17. Nor, it seems, does the statute invalidate a trust which may permit the sale of the real estate and the application of the proceeds to the use of such unborn beneficiaries, within the duration of two lives in being. (*Id.*)

18. A provision in a will that trustees in whom real and personal estate was vested, should apply the rents and profits to the use of the testator's infant children and their unborn issue for the lives of the two youngest of three children, though by possibility two or more successive generations might enjoy the benefit for their lives, respectively, does not contravene the statute (1 *R. S.*, *p.* 723, § 18) against the creation of successive life estates, or of a remainder for life upon a term for years, in favor of persons not in being. (*Id.*)

19. The trustees were required to "pay, convey or make over" the real and personal estate upon the death of the two younger children or the expiration of thirty years, to the survivors of such children or the issue then living of such as might be dead, in equal proportions, the issue to take the share of the parent, with a substitutional limitation in favor of other persons: *held*, that the children took a vested fee determinable as to each upon his dying without issue within the prescribed period. (*Id.*)

20. It does not invalidate the trust that it enables the trustees, in their discretion to apply the entire income and profits, or the estate itself, to the use of unborn posterity, to the exclusion of the testator's children. (*Id.*)

21. It creates no illegal suspense of the power of alienation, that the executors after expiration of the trust term, may be required to retain in their possession real and personal property—the ultimate right to which has vested—for the purpose of paying the income to the widow for her life. (*Id.*)

22. The will directed a certain portion of income to be accumulated, without restricting the period to the minority of the children. This provision being void as to the income after the termination of such minority, the surplus goes, *it seems*, to the children as presumptively entitled to the next eventual estate. (*Id.*)

23. The certificate of attestation to a will by a deceased witness is not, it seems, equivalent to his testimony, if he were living, to the contents thereof, but is evidence of an inferior nature. (*Orser* agt. *Orser*, 24 *N. Y. R.*, 51.)

24. Such an attestation, in connection with the other circumstances of the case, may warrant a jury in finding the due execution of the will against the evidence of the other subscribing witness; but would not, it seems, without regard to any intrinsic fact, support such a verdict against the positive testimony of a living witness. (*Id.*)

25. No distinction exists between the force of the certificate, as evidence of what was done and heard by the deceased witness, and of what it states to have been also witnessed by the survivor. (*Id.*)

26. A will gave all the testator's real and personal estate, and declared that the donee was to pay all the testator's debts and a certain annuity. The acceptance of the gift creates a personal liability upon which an action can be maintained at law without any express promise. (*Gridley* agt. *Gridley*, 24 *N. Y. R.*, 130.)

27. Devise of an estate for life to the testator's father, remainder to the heir-at-law and only child of the testator, "after the decease of my father, and when he the said child shall become twenty-one years of age, and become married, and has children, and in case of his the said child's decease be-

fore that period and after my father's decease, then the said real estate" was given over to other persons: *Held*, that (*Roome* agt. *Phillips*, 24 *N. Y. R.*, 463.)

28. The child took a vested remainder, subject to be divested only on his dying under the age of twenty-one. (*Id.*)

29. Upon the death of the life-tenant, the child became entitled to possession on his attaining twenty-one, or, *it seems*, upon his marriage and having children before that age. (*Id.*)

30. The rule reiterated, that *and* is to be taken for *or*, and *or* for *and*, when required by the intent and meaning of the will. (*Id.*)

31. Bequest of personal property to executors in trust to pay an annuity of five hundred dollars, to be increased in their discretion to one thousand dollars, to the testator's son till he attained the age of thirty, and to pay all that should remain of principal and accumulated income to the son upon the condition that he should then, in the opinion of the executors, be solvent. The executors having renounced —*Held*: The provision for the increase of the son's annuity became ineffectual, the discretion being absolute and personal. (*Hull* agt. *Hull*, 24 *N. Y. R.*, 647.)

32. The determination as to solvency of the son at the age of thirty is not a matter of personal discretion; but, as it rests upon a fact judicially ascertainable, effect is to be given to the provision, notwithstanding the renunciation of the trustees. (*Id.*)

33. The provision for the accumulation of income during the interval between the son's majority and the age of thirty years is void, and the income for that period goes as in case of intestacy. (*Id.*)

34. An instrument cannot be proven and established in any form, for any purpose, or between any parties, as a lost or destroyed will, unless its provisions are clearly and distinctly proved by at least two witnesses, or a correct copy or draft as an equivalent or substitute for one of them. The provisions of the statute on this subject are general and unqualified, and are intended as a rule of evidence of universal application to all subsequent cases, are not to be limited to affirmative proceedings taken directly for the purpose of establishing such a will. (*Harris* agt. *Harris*, 36 *Barb.*, 88.)

35. Loose declarations of an intestate that he intended his son should have the farm of the intestate; that it would be all his (the son's); and that he intended to give it to the son; *held* insufficient to authorize the court to infer an *agreement* on the part of the intestate, to devise the farm to the son, as a remuneration for personal services for a number of years, claimed by the son, as done for the intestate and his wife. (*Raynor* agt. *Robinson*, 36 *Barb.*, 128.)

36. Where the testator makes provision in his will that his wife shall receive certain of his personal property, and a certain amount of the net income of his real estate during her life; but does not state it to be in lieu of dower, the widow is not put to her election. (*Tobias* agt. *Ketchum*, 36 *Barb.*, 304.)

37. Religious societies incorporated under the act of 1813, are not expressly or even by implication authorized to take lands by devise, for any purpose whatever, when such devise is made after their incorporation. A gift to a charity, if there is a competent trustee, although there is no ascertained, or ascertainable beneficiary, may still be upheld, provided the charitable use is so clearly and certainly defined as to be capable of being specifically executed and enforced, as intended by the donor, by judicial decree. (*Goddard* agt. *Pomeroy*, 36 *Barb.*, 546.)

38. When by the provisions of the will, after the death of the widow, the executors could make a valid contract for the sale and conveyance of real estate, of which the testator died seized, and the defendants were decreed to specifically perform a contract made by them with said executors, for the purchase of such real estate: (*Hutchings* agt. *Baldwin*, 7 *Bosw.*, 236.)

39. It was *held*, that by the true construction of the will in this case, it could not be determined until after the death of both of the daughters of the testator, and the death of the testator's brother and sister, whose children were in certain contingency named as devisees of the real and personal estate, to whom, under the sixth clause of the will, the property of the testator would pass, and until then there were no persons in being by whom an absolute estate in possession could be

conveyed. (*Du Bois* agt. *Ray*, 7 *Bosw.*, 244.)

See Surrogates' Courts, 4.

See Dower, 1.

WITNESSES.

1. In the trial of an action for a *limited divorce*, husband and wife are competent witnesses against each other. (*P—* agt. *P—*, *ante*, 197.)

2. The examination of a *party* at the instance of the adverse party, under § 391 of the Code, *before trial*, is conducted in all respects in the same manner as a *witness* examined conditionally under art. 2, title 3, chap. 7 of part 3 of the Revised Statutes. (*People ex rel. Valiente* agt. *Dyckman*, *ante*, 222.)

3. That statute provides that if any witnesses attending before any judge, pursuant to any summons, shall, without reasonable cause, refuse to answer any legal and pertinent question, "the officer issuing such summons shall, by warrant, commit such witness to the common jail of the county;" there to remain until he submits to answer, or until he be discharged according to law. (*Id.*)

4. *Held*, that it is the duty of the judge, where the witness refuses to answer a legal and pertinent question, to issue his warrant for the commitment of the witness; that an *order merely adjudging the witness to be in contempt*, is improper, and unauthorized by law. And an *appeal* from such order is for the same reason equally unauthorized. (*Id.*)

5. It is not an open question, that a party examined as a witness, either at or before the trial, may be required, upon a *subpœna duces tecum*, to produce his *books* relating to or containing evidence pertinent to the issues in the action. (*Id.*)

6. And where such party has produced a book of account and proved the same, and has pointed out and explained the charges in it, called for in evidence, he may be compelled to go further, and required *to read out of the book the specific items and charges to which he had referred and pointed*, to the end that the same may be incorporated in his deposition and preserved as evidence. For his refusal to thus read from the book, he may be punished for *contempt*, as before stated. (*Id.*)

7. On the cross-examination of a witness he cannot be asked whether he had been convicted of petit larceny, although he do not object. The party has a right to insist that the fact be proved, if at all, by the record. (*Newcomb* agt. *Griswold*, 24 *N. Y. R.*, 298.)

8. So also the party may object, though the witness do not, to a question whether the latter had made certain statements in an affidavit which was not produced. (*Id.*)

9. Where the wife is admitted as a witness in her own behalf against the objection of the plaintiff that she is an incompetent witness, and is permitted to testify, and evidence of material facts offered to be given by her is excluded on the ground that it is immaterial, a judgment against her will be reversed for that reason. In such a case, the question whether she was a competent witness will not be considered; but, for all the purposes of the appeal, the decision admitting her as competent will be treated as correct. (*Tappan* agt. *Butler*, 7 *Bosw.*, 480.)

See Commissions, 1. 2. 3. 4.

See Evidence, 1. 2.

See Discovery of Books and Papers, 1. 2. 3. 4.

See Constitutional Law, 5.

See Railroad Companies, 47.

See Will, 23. 24. 25.

See Damages, 7.

See Trial, 12.

INDEX.

A.

ACTION.

ADMIRALTY.

AFFIDAVIT OF MERITS.

AGENT.

ANSWER.

APPEAL.

ARREST.

ARSON.

ASSESSMENTS.

ASSIGNEE.

ASSIGNMENT FOR BENEFIT OF CREDITORS.

ATTACHMENT.

Index.

W.

WILL.

WITNESS.

COURT OF APPEALS.

DECISIONS RENDERED DECEMBER, 1862.

Judgment affirmed.

Hadden agt. The People; Moaker agt. The People; Hayes agt. The People.
Dawson agt. The People; Forbes agt. Waller.
Forbes agt. Logan, receiver, &c. (4 *Bosw.*, 475); Glenworth agt. Mount.
Anable agt. Conklin; Clarke, receiver agt. Graham.
Leavitt agt. Pell (27 *Barb.*, 323); Smith, receiver agt. Townsend.
Robinson, receiver agt. Plimpton; Van Alstyne agt. Cook, receiver.
Brainard agt. New York and Harlem R. R. Co.; Pettee agt. Booth et al.
Forrest agt. Forrest (5 *Bosw.*, 672.)
Brendal agt. The Buffalo and State Line R. R. Co. (27 *Barb.*, 534.)
Adams et al. agt. Perkins et al.; Stilson agt. Buel; Hinds agt. Barton.
Remsen agt. Beekman; Kamena agt. Warner (15 *How.*, 5.)
Leonardsville Bank agt. Willard; Kellogg agt. Totten.
Willetts agt. Wait (13 *How.*, 34); Robbins agt. Gorham (26 *Barb.*, 586.)
Cummings agt. Morris; Cooke agt. Beale; Richmond agt. Lockwood.
Thomas agt. Fleary, and 10 per cent. damages; Wiles agt. Peck.
Brown agt. Lewis; Jones and another agt. Sheldon and others.
Bank of Silver Creek agt. Browning; Lilling agt. Candee.
Drew agt. Sixth Av. R. R. Co., and 5 per cent. damages.
Hutchins agt. Camp, and 10 per cent. damages.
Hitchcock agt. Northwestern Ins. Co.
Machin and others agt. Sands, and 10 per cent. damages.
Buffalo and Allegany R. R. Co. agt. Cary.
Timon agt. Howard, and 10 per cent. damages; Phelps agt. McDonald.
Lagier agt. Westcott, and 10 per cent. damages; Ætna Insurance Co. agt. Aldrich.
Dascomb agt. Buffalo and State Line R. R. Co. (27 *Barb.*, 221.)
Sandman agt. Gitsky; Alden agt. New York C. R. R. Co.
Wager agt. Canajoharie Plankroad Co.; Bailey agt. Hollister.
Stryker agt. Mott and others; Wilson agt. Stryker.
Swords and others agt. Stryker and others; Seymour agt. Sturgis.
Tallmadge and others agt. East River Bank; Robinson agt. Wheeler.
White agt. Wheeler; White agt. Madison; Evans agt. Mumford and others.

Judgment reversed.

Shepherd agt. The People (19 *How.*, 44.)
Theological Seminary of Auburn agt. Calhoun.
Bissel agt. The N. Y. Central R. R. Co.; Whalin agt. White; Perry agt. Wheeler.
Wager agt. The Troy Union R. R. Co.; New Paltz Turnpike Co. agt. Dubois.
Kellogg agt. Smith; Forbes and Wife agt. Halsey; Cross and another agt. Beard.
Holdridge agt. Styles; Lamer agt. Meeker and others.
Ladue and another agt. Griffith and others.

Judgment reversed, as to affirmative relief, but affirmed otherwise without costs; order to be settled by Judge Davis.

Dwight agt. St. John.

Judgment affirmed with leave to defendant to have twenty days to answer on payment of costs.

Guynn and another agt. Kettell.

Order of General Term reversed and judgment of Special Term affirmed.

Griswold agt. Havens and others.

Judgment of Supreme Court reversed and judgment of County Court affirmed.

Wilson agt. Miller and another.

Appeal dismissed with costs.

Hill agt. Bond (22 *How.*, 272.)

Order affirmed and judgment absolute.

Tucker agt. Custis; Smith agt. Miller.

Re-argument ordered.

Goulding agt. Davison (28 *Barb.*, 438); Clark agt. The Mayor of New York.
Holbrook agt. Vose (6 *Bosw.*, 76.)
People ex rel. Smith agt. Pease and others (30 *Barb.*, 588.)
Miner agt. Village of Fredonia.
Chenango Bridge Co. agt. Binghamton Bridge Co.

MARCH TERM, 1863.

Judgments affirmed.

Harwood agt. People; People agt. Mason; People agt. Elkin; People agt. Kenyon.

Judgments affirmed with costs.

Butcher et al. agt. Carwin, adm'r; Marsh agt Potter (30 *Barb.*, 506.)
Sands, receiver agt. Boutwell; Hunt agt. Van Wert, adm'r; Porter agt. Havens.
Sill, ex'r agt. O'Keefe; People, &c. agt. Ambrecht (11 *Abb.*, 97.)
People, &c. agt. Vanderbilt; Romaine agt. Allen, receiver.
Commercial Bank of Albany agt. Edwards, receiver.
First Baptist Church, Brooklyn agt. Brooklyn Fire Insurance Company.
Requa et al. agt. Holmes (19 *How.*, 430); Chautauqua Co. Bank agt. Risley.
Ogden, Jr. agt. Andre (4 *Bosw.*, 583); Stevens agt. Commercial Insurance Co.
Shannon agt. Coyelle; Battle agt. Coit et al.; Bank of Auburn agt. Demarest.
Clapp agt. Graves, and Clapp agt. Graves et al. (9 *Abb.*, 20.)
Werely agt. Parsons; Lambert agt. Manin; Ballard agt. Ballard.
Bank of Chenango agt. Brown; Braman agt. Bingham.
Chase agt. New York Central R. R. Co. (24 *Barb.*, 273.)
Looney, supervisor agt. Hughes et al. (30 *Barb.* 605.)
Graves agt. Berdean (29 *Barb.*, 100.)

Judgments reversed—new trial ordered—costs to abide event.

Catlin agt. Tobias; Sands, receiver agt. Sanders, Jr.
Simmons et al. agt. Simmons et al. (26 *Barb.*, 68.)
Clark, ex'r agt. Gilbert (32 *Barb.*, 576); Andrew agt. Artisans' Bank.
Curtis agt. Gano et al.; Same agt. Same.
Hance et al. agt. Cayuga & Susquehanna R. R. Co.
Bank State of New York agt. Farmers' Branch Bank, &c. (36 *Barb.*, 332.)
Merriam agt. Conklin; Cathcart agt. Fire Department of New York.
Exchange Bank agt. Monteith et al. (24 *Barb.*, 371.)
Sloan et al. agt. Van Wyck (36 *Barb.*, 335.)

Judgment of Supreme Court reversed, and that of Sessions affirmed.

People agt. Clements.

Order of General Term reversed, and Special Term affirmed with costs.

Brown et al., ex'rs agt Troy & Boston R. R. Co.; Genesee College agt. Dodge.
Wakely agt. Davidson et al.; Harris agt. Harris (36 *Barb.*, 88, 574.)

Order of General Term affirmed without costs to either party.

Sent, ex'r, &c. agt. McNaughton.

Order of General Term reversed, and judgment for plaintiff on verdict with costs.

Sweetman agt. Prince et al.

Appeal dismissed with costs.

Tanner agt. Tooley, adm'r, et al.

Judgment reversed with costs.

The People, &c. agt. New England Mutual Life Insurance Company.

Judgment reversed, and judgment for defendant with costs.

People *ex rel.* Dunn agt. Board of Police Commissioners (35 *Barb.*, 544.)
People *ex rel.* Titus agt. Same (35 *Barb.*, 535.)
People *ex rel.* Hope agt. Same; People *ex rel.* Gorman agt. Same (35 *Barb.*, 527.)
People *ex rel.* Murphy agt. Same (5 *Abb.*, 241.)
People *ex rel.* McGuire agt. Same;
People *ex rel.* Hanrahan agt. Same (35 *Barb.* 344.)
People *ex rel.* Peck agt. Same (35 *Barb.*, 651.)

Judgment affirmed with damages.

Woodruff agt. Ingersoll—ten per cent.
Black River Bank agt. Permimon et al.—ten per cent.
Hallock agt. Little, sheriff, &c.—five per cent.
McBride agt. Farmers' Bank of Salem—ten per cent. (28 *Barb.*, 476.)
Horton agt. Davies—ten per cent.

Orders of General Term affirmed and judgments absolute for plaintiffs with costs, Supreme Court to assess plaintiffs' damages.

Sheldon et al. agt. Atlantic Fire and Marine Insurance Company.

Order of the General Term affirmed and judgment absolute for defendant with costs.

Ludlam, ex'r &c. agt. Ludlam et al. (31 *Barb.*, 486.)

Special judgment without costs to either party.

Wyman, adm'x agt. Wyman et al. (36 *Barb.*, 368.)

Order of General Term reversed and judgment on report affirmed with costs.

McKinster agt. Babcock et al.

Order appealed from reversed with costs.

Betts agt. Garr, ex'r, &c.

Judgment reversed; and judgment for defendant with costs, with leave to plaintiff to apply to Supreme Court to amend his complaint on proper terms.

Fowler agt. New York Indemnity Insurance Company (23 *Barb.*, 143.)

Cases not decided.

People agt. Duffy; Wright agt. Garlinghouse (27 *Barb.*, 474.)
Caughey et al. agt. Smith et al.; Van Rensselaer agt. Bonesteel (24 *Barb.*, 365.)
Finch agt. Newsam (25 *Barb.*, 175); Emmons agt. American Mineral Company.
Terry et al. agt. Dayton (31 *Barb.*, 519); Hasbrouck agt. Lounsberry.

Ordered that that part of the order of the Supreme Court which avoids an issue, be and the same is hereby reversed, and the residue of said order be and the same is hereby affirmed. It is further adjudged and declared by this Court that Mary Grace Patchin was the wife and is the widow of said deceased, and that she is entitled to letters of administration on his estate, and that the Supreme Court be and is hereby directed to carry this decision into effect, and that neither party recover costs of the other in this Court.

Mary F. Devin agt. Mary Grace Patchin.

Judgment of General Term reversed and order of Special Term affirmed, with costs.

McConochie agt. Sun Mutual Insurance Company.

Judgment affirmed without costs.

People *ex rel.* Commissioners of Emigration agt. Supervisors of Richmond County.

Motion for re-argument denied, with ten dollars costs.

Griswold agt. Haven et al.

[Last two cases argued at present term.]

Applications for copies of opinions should be addressed to E. Peshine Smith, Esq., at Pittsford, Monroe county.

NOTE.

We have given, annexed to these decisions, the *book* and *page* where the cases that are reported in the courts *below* may be found. Undoubtedly others of these cases are reported, but from a change in the titles, or from some other cause, have not been found.

It will be seen at a glance, how few decisions made in the courts below comparatively are *reported;* and it is not probable that over one-half the decisions made in the court of appeals are reported: Thus showing that of the large amount of legal business done in this state, under our present judicial system, and of the decisions made by the courts, but a small portion ever discovers the light of day through the usual sources—the reports. An effort has been lately made, as is well known, by an application to the legislature, to suppress or supersede the reports we have, on the ground that they had become onerous to the profession, &c., and to substitute a series of reports of less number, to be controlled by the state, in their place; but the legislature thought, no doubt, that from the experience the state has already had in managing one set of reports, they had better let alone the business of reporting generally, and leave it where it belongs—in the hands of the judiciary. Now, we do not think this move ever originated with the profession; for what law book is more useful, interesting and instructive, and in general more acceptable to the great mass of practicing lawyers, than a well-conducted, honest series of reports? We admit, that when reports appear upon their face to have been stuffed with much immaterial matter, spread out at much length, for the mere purpose of making a book to sell, they should receive, as they generally do, the silent indignation of the profession. Such works, however, we believe are not common; our present standard reports are doubtless presented to the profession, to a very great extent, free from the objections named; and we think the profession will continue to consider and receive them as containing the law of the land as declared by our courts and judges. If but few cases are reported compared to the great number that are decided, those which do appear should be considered of importance.—Rep.

CPSIA information can be obtained
at www.ICGtesting.com
Printed in the USA
LVHW110823120522
718525LV00006B/8

9 783375 001612